"Windle tells a disturbingly credible story ⟨...⟩ America's war on drugs to weave a plot whe⟨...⟩ ⟨religious extremists mount a⟩ potentially fatal terrorist threat at an unimaginably soft American target. Trained in and financed by South America's infamous refuge for the nefarious, her Islamic terrorists come up against a dedicated American lawman and his fearless best friend. . . . When this gripping story is finished, it will leave you more than a bit worried."

—CLYDE D. TAYLOR
Former U.S. Ambassador to Paraguay

"Jeanette's style . . . is unique and authentic. I must confess I like a happy ending, but Jeanette does a good job of tempering the happy with the truth that life produces both joy and sorrow, happiness and pain, growth and scars . . . life and death. The constant reminder is that God's happy ending is different from ours and, thankfully, very much better. Thus her characters can be deeply hurt, abused, scarred, imperfect—even wrong—and still turn to God."

—CHARLES AVERY
Retired counternarcotics police officer

"Jeanette Windle's descriptive excellence reflects years of experience and personal interaction with people from all backgrounds, especially in the context of Latin America. Her attention to detail builds on extensive research into places and technology. Clearly her best novel yet."

—DON CLEMENTS
Pastor to missionaries, Avant Ministries

"*FireStorm* is a captivating and carefully woven story of intrigue. The author's skill in unveiling her characters, coupled with her vivid descriptions, provides energy and momentum to every page."

—ROBERT B. REEKIE
Cofounder, Media Associates International, Inc.

"It is said that truth is stranger than fiction, but Windle's fiction is so convincing that one hopes desperately that her fiction cannot possibly become the truth. This nail-biting novel is so realistic that one wonders if she has read the minds of potential terrorists. . . . Woven into the drama of frightening and life-threatening circumstances is the portrayal of how Christian faith keeps a person sane and peaceful even when Christ's worst enemies seem likely to succeed. This is a helpful read for those who keep abreast of world events and are concerned with the role that individual Christians can play in combating terrorism."

—WILLARD DICKERSON
Former director of education
American Booksellers Association

"Jeanette Windle knows whereof she speaks. Having grown up and served in two of the most violent countries in the world—Colombia and Bolivia—she knows the territory, the culture, the language, the people, and their customs. With the eagle eye of a reporter who ferrets out the facts, and the skillful pen of a fascinating writer, she has woven together a riveting and sobering story of international intrigue. This book is frightening unless the reader believes in the overruling hand of God in human history—and even then it will give all of us some disturbingly sleepless nights. I heartily recommend this book as fiction so true to life today that we cannot ignore it."

—DAVID M. HOWARD
Well-known author and former director of
LAM, WEF, InterVarsity, and Urbana

"Jeanette Windle always writes an amazingly complex, realistic, and eminently believable story, but it's her mastery of the language that will make you wish the last page would never come. Jeanette is a wordsmith of the first order. . . . Her ability to describe a scene will make it come to life in your mind, and may cause you literally to break a sweat. Pick up any one of her books and she is sure to become one of your very favorite fiction authors by the end of the first chapter."

—CHUCK HOLTON
Former U.S. Army Black Beret and
best-selling author of *A More Elite Soldier*

FireStorm

a novel

JEANETTE WINDLE

Kregel
Publications

FireStorm: A Novel

© 2004 by Jeanette Windle

Published by Kregel Publications, a division of Kregel, Inc., P.O. Box 2607, Grand Rapids, MI 49501.

The persons and events portrayed in this work are the creations of the author, and any resemblance to persons living or dead is purely coincidental.

All views expressed in this work are soley those of the author and do not represent or reflect the position or endorsement of any governmental agency or department, military or otherwise.

Unless otherwise indicated, Scripture quotations are from the *Holy Bible, New International Version*®. NIV®. © 1973, 1978, 1984 by International Bible Society. Used by permission of Zondervan Publishing House. All rights reserved.

The Scripture quotation of Psalm 93:4 is copied from an actual inscription on a plaque at Iguazú Falls and does not match any commonly used English language version.

Cover design: John M. Lucas

ISBN 0-8254-4119-6

Printed in the United States of America

04 05 06 07 08 / 5 4 3 2 1

FireStorm

Prologue

EASTERN AFGHANISTAN

The watcher did not move.

Temperatures had plunged during the night, and the stone floor of the cave, hardly more than a crevice in the rocks, burned through his padded clothing. His breath had built up a crust of ice on the cloth looped across his mouth, beading his eyebrows and lashes with frost.

But the watcher dared not lift a hand to his face or shift his prone position. The first bright fingers of dawn had cleared the jagged peaks across the valley and now probed the cliff face where he hid. Any movement might draw unwelcome attention from the enemy below.

If any remained alive.

Only the watcher's eyes moved to the foot of the cliff where the downed helicopter was coming into focus against the growing light. An American Special Operations MH-47 Chinook knocked from the sky the previous afternoon by a chance-aimed rocket propelled grenade. Flashes of mortar fire still reflected from the snow-packed flanks of the opposite ridge where dawn's creeping edge had not yet banished the night. But no response had come from the Chinook since his comrades' last failed assault, hours earlier.

If the enemy soldiers were dead or even out of ammunition, he could relieve the cramping of his numbed limbs, and perhaps rejoin his comrades in the mountain stronghold—a labyrinth of caves across the valley—to which the remaining forces of the jihad had retreated.

But no.

Even as a finger of light cleared the crumpled rotors of the Chinook, the watcher spotted movement behind it. A prone figure in white mountain combat clothing raised a grenade launcher to his shoulder. Another rose to a crouch beside him, a walkie-talkie to his mouth.

The watcher cursed silently. There had been no more than a dozen of the Americans in all, and at least some of those had been wounded. Their local allies had deserted as soon as it was clear the helicopter would not lift off again. So how was it possible they'd survived the night's constant bombardment, repelling again and again the assault sorties sent out to overrun their position?

And now with the return of daylight, relief was arriving. A wave of F-16 fighters swooped in over the valley, laying down a deadly path of fire right up to the cave mouths dotting the opposite ridge. Behind them droned a second wave of Apache attack helicopters. The mortars went abruptly silent.

Below the watcher, another Chinook settled to the ground. The crew jumped out to help with the wounded and dead as the night's survivors made a dash for the open door. *A foolish Western tradition*, the watcher sneered. His own people were more pragmatic and would not risk valuable combatants to retrieve those already destined to Paradise. His hands itched to teach the Americans their folly. But his AK-47 would do little damage from here and would only serve to draw the retaliatory fire he had avoided until now.

Across the valley, his comrades were resisting valiantly, ducking inside the caves when the enemy aircraft swooped down to drop their bombs, then emerging to taunt the invaders with insolent gestures and shouted insults as they returned fire.

But despite their ferocious resistance, the battle was not going well for the defenders. Their return fire was growing more sporadic, and even as the rescue helicopter lifted off, a missile screamed from the underbelly of an Apache, slamming into the dark outline of an opening in the opposite rock face. When the dust settled, all that remained was the scar of a fresh landslide.

A shudder went through the watcher. His sleeping mat and belongings were in that cave. If he had not been on sentry duty when the attack began, he would have been sealed in there as well.

Disbelief tinged his anger and horror. The watcher had left his birthplace years ago to take up arms for the jihad, beginning with this cold and recalcitrant country called Afghanistan by outsiders. Its own people had proved unwilling to cease their internecine quarrels long enough to become a nation. He had trained and studied and fought here, and over the years he had seen the enemies of Islam pushed back until only the last pockets of resistance remained.

And now, in only a matter of weeks, all that had changed. Instead of their long-awaited establishment of a pure Islamic state, the tattered remnants of the Faithful were being hunted, harried out of their strongholds, and driven to a last stand amid the rocks and caves of the rugged mountains. How was it possible?

It was easy to blame the American weapons. The fighter jets. The attack helicopters. The bombs.

But the watcher could not forget the stubborn handful of enemy soldiers who had hunkered down through the night below his sentry post, doggedly holding off everything the hundreds of freedom fighters in those caves had thrown at them. The holy warriors of the jihad—al Qaeda, Taliban, Hezbollah, Hamas, and the others—were beyond a doubt the most dedicated fighters on the planet, far more experienced in combat than the Americans, and all willing to give their lives for the cause.

Yet time and again since their campaign began, the smallest units of these American soldiers had turned the tide in favor of the same Afghan opposition that had retreated steadily for years.

Special Forces. That was what the Americans called these soldiers. Specially chosen. Specially trained. Specially equipped. The best of the best, their military bragged.

But in this, at least, it would seem their boasting was not without foundation.

By late afternoon, the invaders were winding down their operation. Their Afghan allies had returned to help in the mop-up, sending missiles down tunnels, blowing cave openings shut. Calls to surrender had been ignored, the resistance fighters choosing instead a martyr's death. Bodies littered the mountain slopes, the ice and snow now red with their blood.

Still the watcher did not move. If there was glory in being a martyr, suicide held none. To emerge now was simply to throw his life away without purpose.

So he watched silently, the adrenaline of fury and hate sending some warmth through his numbed limbs, as the last guns went silent and the Americans and their local allies began the task of collecting the dead and whatever evidence was still accessible in the caves.

The watcher stayed where he was until nightfall called a halt to the searches. Then he slid cautiously out of the cave. The narrow ledge was almost as black as the crevice itself, the only illumination now the starlight on snow and the scattered cook fires of the victors' camp. Without rising from his belly, he wriggled around an outcropping of rock. Only then did he rise stiffly to his feet.

The valley was silent except for a murmur of voices carrying through the thin air, the victors having settled down to eat and sleep. Shouldering his AK-47, the watcher wrapped his cloak tightly around himself and turned away into the chill wind whistling through the rocks.

That the jihad had received a serious blow could not be denied. That it was a fatal wound was an American conceit they would someday regret. Cutting the head from an octopus might leave its tentacles helpless. Smashing a wasps' nest simply scattered their stingers until they could regroup. With Allah on their side, the final victory was assured.

And yet perhaps there were lessons to be learned from this setback.

Threading noiselessly through the outcropping of boulders, the watcher returned his deliberations to the downed Special Forces unit. The Americans were infidels. Unlike the warriors of the jihad, they could not possibly know commitment to a cause. Certainly they were not as quick to throw their lives away.

Was it possible that therein lay part of their strength?

Could it be that in its zeal for Islam, the army of Allah had too quickly expended its most fervent members in martyrdom? What if the cost of recruiting and training valuable human resources was not tossed away on a single mission? What if instead these forces were improved upon and honed by experience and superbly equipped, as the Americans did, into a weapon that could strike again and again?

The watcher eased himself through a narrow passage between two rock faces.

The astonishing factor was how little attempt the Americans made to exploit these elite forces of theirs, preferring to utilize them as a deterrent rather than as the powerful offensive weapon they were fashioned to be. If the army of Allah had such a weapon in hand, they would be ruling the world by now.

It was just one more weakness of the infidels, this curious reluctance to shed blood—whether their own or others. But if they were too fainthearted to grasp the possibilities of such a weapon, he was not.

No starlight penetrated the maze of boulders, but the watcher had navigated this route often enough to do it blindfolded. One more left, then a right.

What if the sophisticated equipment and warrior skills the Americans possessed could somehow be melded to the superior will and intellect and fighting spirit of the jihad's finest warriors? Warriors unconstrained by the infidels' weak concerns regarding human rights and civilian casualties.

What could we not accomplish with such a force?

The watcher shook his head as his feet found the goat trail that led down the mountainside. It was not so simple, or it would have been done before. Even if the right men were found, what did he—or others within the jihad—know of the specialized training and knowledge and equipment that gave the invaders their edge? He was not so foolish to think that the Americans would release such knowledge for the asking.

The watcher's misstep sent a shower of pebbles over the side of the path. Unslinging the AK-47, he froze until the rattle of falling stones had died away. But it would seem the victors were too busy celebrating to hear his carelessness. Reshouldering his weapon, he set off with new purpose in his stride. It was true the jihad did not possess the knowledge to do what the Americans had done. But there were others who did. And at least one resided near his birthplace and was known to his family.

As movement drove the stiffness from his limbs, the watcher quickened his pace. It was time to abandon this lost war and begin a new one. He would go home.

By the time morning brought a renewal of the Americans' bombardment, the watcher was two mountain ridges away and approaching the border of Pakistan.

Chapter One

SEPTEMBER 18
VIRU VIRU AIRPORT, SANTA CRUZ, BOLIVIA

The plane door thudded into its socket. Sara's hands clenched in her lap as the flight attendant slammed down the lock.

Come on! Move!

The American Airlines 757 flight had been sitting on the runway for almost an hour, and Sara couldn't help wondering whether she was to blame for the delay. Her muscles ached from steeling herself for a tap on the shoulder that would revoke her hard-won freedom.

The whine of the jets accelerated. She glanced toward the window and caught a flicker of her own tense reflection against the bustling backdrop of the airport. Fine, ash-blonde hair spilling down over the collar of borrowed clothing. Long-lashed amber eyes staring back anxiously amid pale, strained features. Her mouth moving silently in the glass. *Please! Hurry!*

As if her plea were a cue, the plane began to taxi down the runway. The cabin erupted into a cheer. Only then did Sara feel the sting of fingernails cutting into her palms. Forcing her gaze away from the window, she relaxed her hands against her thighs. But she would not feel safe until the wheels were off the ground and the plane was angling away from Bolivian airspace.

Safe.

How long has it been since I felt safe? Not since she'd found out that her new fairy-tale family were not upstanding business entrepreneurs but drug dealers, their mansion built with cocaine profits, and her handsome, young husband a murderer. Not during all the weeks of hiding; or that terrible pursuit through the jungle night.

Not even after her incredible, last-hour rescue—for then had come the questions. Police. Government officials. Her own embassy. Not all of whom wished to concede that Sara Connor de Cortéz, traitor *americano* daughter-in-law of one of Bolivia's most prominent families, was innocent of the charges drummed up against her.

Yesterday had come a brief reprieve when Doug Bradford, the DEA agent who had led the rescue, came to her with an offer of sanctuary and tickets on the evening flight to Miami. The two of them were still clearing customs when the tap came on her shoulder. The local authorities had more questions before Sara could leave the country.

Those questions turned out to be less concerned with the Cortéz drug empire than ensuring that Sara had no plans to file any awkward claims on the assets the Bolivian government had seized from her husband's estate. But it was well past midnight before Sara, her chin stubbornly uptilted against the protests of the one embassy official present, had signed away in triplicate all claims, present or future, to *Industrias* Cortéz or the estate of one Nicolás Cortéz, deceased.

That those signatures left her penniless and homeless mattered little. There was nothing that Sara wanted to take with her from her brief sojourn in this place. No possession. No memory.

The plane was off the ground now. All around the cabin passengers were craning their necks for a last glimpse of loved ones and home. Tension eased from Sara's shoulders, but she did not turn her head. She would not take a final glimpse of tall palms tossing their fronds above grassy fields, of wandering brown rivers sparkling gold under the morning sun and the restless sea of the jungle canopy, of lonely thatched farmhouses and quiet adobe villages.

There was a beauty that Sara had come to know and love down there, beneath the plane's wings. There were many normal, decent human beings. But for Sara, this small Andean country she'd embraced with such joy and hope four short months ago would now forever be overlaid with memories of the terror and pain and grief that had found her there. Memories of the searing image of rage on the face of a man she'd loved. Memories of the ruined, bloody bodies of the two men who had betrayed her.

Her father-in-law, Don Luis Cortéz.

Her husband, Nicolás Cortéz.

If I could just erase it all from my mind . . . I would wipe these last months from my life as if they'd never been!

No, that was not entirely true. There was a peasant family who had offered kindness and refuge when Sara's own countrymen had not. A small shepherd girl whose work-roughened fingers she could still feel sliding into her own.

And a quiet jungle knoll where the Creator of the universe had reached down to touch his strayed child with infinite love.

> Though the fig tree does not bud and there are no grapes on the vines, though the olive crop fails and the fields produce no food, though there are no sheep in the pen and no cattle in the stalls, yet I will rejoice in the Lord, I will be joyful in God my Savior.

Habakkuk 3:17–19. The litany that had carried Sara through the last terrifying weeks settled her churning mind again. *I am leaving this place as empty-handed as the people in those verses. Everything I thought I'd found here is gone. But I am not alone. . . . I was never alone. Don't let me forget again!*

Nor was she entirely without friends.

As a thump signaled the retracting of the landing gear, Sara stole a glance at her traveling companion. Like her, Doug Bradford was not availing himself of a last glance, though he'd lived in Santa Cruz longer than Sara—over five years.

Does he resent his peremptory dismissal from a post he served with such distinction?

If so, he did not show it. He'd already opened his briefcase and was flicking through a sheaf of computer readouts with an abstracted frown. Sara took advantage of his absorption to study him from under lowered eyelashes.

He had none of the careless, almost frightening, aristocratic beauty of a Nicolás Cortéz. His strong features were best characterized as "rugged," and the uncompromising line of his mouth and certain inflexibility of his jaw made him seem older than his thirty years. His unruly brown hair was badly in need of a trim; his medium build appeared deceptively ordinary under the loose, comfortable clothing he wore. Only the narrowed gray gaze—the slow, speculative appraisal that Sara had termed his "cop" look—gave away who he was: Doug Bradford, Special Agent of the U.S. Justice Department's Drug Enforcement Administration.

Once her enemy; now her friend. In fact, he was her only friend besides the Indian peasant family to whose jungle farm he had taken Sara for safekeeping. He had risked life and career to secure her freedom and the downfall of the Cortéz drug empire, and saying good-bye to him had been the hardest blow of leaving the country. Harder even than the prospect of landing in the United States with no money, no job, no place to go.

Then, beyond hope and expectation, he had come to Sara and asked her not to go out of his life. What had softened that cool gray gaze as he'd extended his mother's offer of hospitality? What had been that responding surge in her own heart?

Not the turbulent emotions that had swept her away from her ordered collegiate life in Seattle and under the spell of a charismatic foreigner, Nicolás Cortéz. Sara was still too heartsore, bruised, and shell-shocked for that. But something—though perhaps no more than the first hesitant unfurling of a petal that promises spring will return to the frozen earth.

Sometimes the fig tree does bud.

"So, did I miss a spot?"

Color instantly stained Sara's cheekbones as she realized that Doug's practiced survey of the airline cabin had ended at her face, the suggestion of a twinkle in his eye making it clear she'd been staring too long. An upward quirk at the corner of his mouth softened as his glance dropped to her hands, which once again were clenched tightly in her lap. "Are you okay?"

"Not really. But I will be as soon as we leave Bolivian airspace. I still keep bracing myself for someone to tap me from behind and tell me it's all been a mistake; that I'm under arrest after all." Sara wrinkled her nose ruefully. "Silly, I know. After all, Julio and Diego and Raymundo and the others are all in jail, and everyone knows they're guilty now."

"Well, actually—" The amused curve of Doug's mouth tightened instantly to a straight line as his eyes returned to the computer printout in his hand.

Sara, catching the grim note in his voice, demanded sharply, "What is it? What's happened?"

"Bad news." Doug passed the sheaf of paper to Sara. "An intel briefing from the office. Ramon brought it by the airport when he said good-bye." Ramon had been Doug's partner during the Cortéz investigation. He had managed to keep his name out of the local papers and would be staying on in Bolivia. "Seems the Cortéz still have some clout. This is a judge's order dismissing all charges against your brothers-in-law, Raymundo and Diego."

"But—" Sara skimmed through the printout, outraged. "That's ridiculous! They were part of it all. They helped kill that poor boy!"

"Not by their account. According to their testimony—which changed, of course, once they had to admit that Nicolás was the one that shot Ricardo, not you—they tried to stop Nicolás from killing the boy, but he was so drunk and angry they couldn't get to him in time. As for the cocaine, neither one was at the hacienda when we busted the place, and their names weren't found on any incriminating documents. They're keeping the blame focused squarely on your father-in-law's head of security, Julio Vargas, as the one responsible for any drug dealing at *Industrias* Cortéz. That at least has some element of truth."

"Truth!" Sara cried. "What about *my* testimony? I was there! I told the police what I saw. Raymundo and Diego already admitted they lied about the shooting, so why would a judge believe them over me? As for the drugs, maybe they kept their hands clean while Julio did the dirty work for Don Luis. But they knew well enough where their money was coming from, and they were certainly willing to do anything to keep it coming—even covering up murder. I heard them myself!"

Doug's broad shoulders lifted in a shrug. "It's your word against theirs; and unfortunately, there are too many people here, in and out of the legal system, who prefer to believe the Cortéz are getting a raw deal, no matter what the evidence says, and regardless of the 'hysterical accusations'—that's their description, not mine—of a gringa daughter-in-law."

"So we're declared personas non grata and run out of the country for telling the truth, while criminals like Raymundo and Diego walk away scot-free?" Sara's fingernails were digging into her palms again. "It just isn't fair!"

"No, it isn't fair. But that's the way this business goes. People who should be behind bars get off all the time. Not just here, but back in the States. If they've dealt enough drugs to afford a top-drawer lawyer . . ." Doug snapped his fingers. "It's something you've got to learn to live with in this line of work. You just do your best to nail them the next time around. And there's *always* a next time."

He looked down at Sara's mutinous face, and the grim line of his mouth eased. "What matters is that you're safe now. By tonight you'll be back on American soil, and none of the Cortéz, and not Julio Vargas, or any of their dirty associates will be able to touch you again. You can put this all behind you."

Safe. There's that word again!

Sara forced herself to relax, her head dropping back wearily against the headrest. Doug was right. Jailed or free, the remaining members of the Cortéz clan could not touch her now. She was on an American-owned aircraft approaching the edge of Bolivian airspace, and in a few short hours she'd be back on her own native soil, safely and permanently beyond their reach.

But the euphoric sense of escape that had come with the plane's takeoff had evaporated.

Maybe it'll come back when I'm actually standing on U.S. territory.
But it didn't.

Maybe it was because of the long, jostling lines clearing Immigration, or the babble of what had to be every language on the planet. Or it could have been the view outside Miami International Airport's plate-glass windows with its glimpses of tiled roofs beyond the warehouses and tall palms against a twilight sky that bore more of a resemblance to the country Sara had just left behind than to any other part of the U.S. she'd ever visited. Even after the temporary passport she'd been issued by the American consulate in Santa Cruz had been examined and returned and she was following Doug along the endless corridors and down the escalators to the baggage claim area, there was little to remind Sara that she was back in her own country. It seemed everyone around her was speaking Spanish.

I'm just tired. Last night had held little sleep, and her attempts to nap on the plane had been broken by meals and questions about what she wanted to drink from the flight attendants. A fresh headache throbbed at Sara's temples as she struggled to keep up with Doug's long strides. A feeling of displacement and exhaustion settled over her so that even Doug seemed suddenly like a stranger, frowning and moving briskly along as if he'd forgotten she was at his heels.

But as they located their designated baggage carousel, Doug turned to look at Sara. "You hanging in there?" he asked quietly. "It shouldn't be much longer."

He's got to be exhausted himself, she realized. He'd stayed with Sara at police headquarters until the early hours of the morning. But if he was feeling the effects, it didn't show in his keen gaze or in the confident, lithe carriage of his well-muscled frame. Sara, conscious of her own wilted posture and the bedraggled condition of her borrowed clothing, felt rather like a stray puppy he'd been kind enough to rescue off the street.

Restraining herself from rubbing at her temples, she straightened her shoulders. "I'm fine. Oh, look—there's my suitcase."

Doug leaned forward and hoisted the bag from the carousel in one smooth motion. Neither Sara nor he had much luggage. His precipitous release from duty had not allowed time for any real packing, and the single suitcase now at his feet held the few donated outfits that Laura Histed, the pastor's wife at the International Church in Santa Cruz, had insisted on scavenging for Sara. Ellen Stevens, the Santa Cruz DEA administrative officer, would box up and ship the rest of Doug's belongings to him on a U.S. military transport.

After retrieving his duffel bag, which he swung over one shoulder, Doug grasped the handle of Sara's suitcase in one hand and his briefcase in the other and led the way through Customs and around a long glass wall behind which a waving crowd was waiting to greet emerging passengers. He lowered both pieces of luggage to the floor as he made a swift survey of the waiting area.

"I don't see my mother. I told her yesterday to meet us here if she had time to meet the flight. Otherwise, we'd take the shuttle. Our flight was almost an hour late, and with the time it took to clear Immigration, if she isn't here by now, we'd better just head out."

He had reshouldered the duffel bag and was reaching for the suitcase when a sharp exclamation cut through the babble of the other passengers.

"Doug! There you are! I was beginning to think you'd missed the flight. Of all the—!"

The woman striding toward them, Starbucks cup in hand, was tall and thin and at first glance far too young to have a thirty-year-old son. Only as she approached did Sara see the deep-scored lines around the woman's eyes and mouth and recognize that the auburn waves were the result of a superbly done rinse.

The older woman didn't pause for breath as she glanced at her watch. "I've been pacing back and forth down here for two hours. If I'd known it was going to be this kind of wait, I'd have left you to the shuttle. I finally broke down and decided if I didn't get a shot of caffeine, I'd keel right over. If you weren't here when I got back, I was going to let you make your own way home."

She smelled strongly of cigarettes and was restless enough to have imbibed a half-dozen shots of espresso. Or perhaps with MIA's no-smoking policy, she just needed a fix of nicotine. Her eyes—not gray like Doug's, but green—narrowed as she glanced around. "Well, now that you're here, let's get out of this place. It's raining cats and dogs out there, and the forecast is that it's only going to get worse. Where's your luggage? Surely this can't be all of it! Well then, let me help you get this, and we'll get out of here."

"Just hold it, Mother." Doug firmly removed Sara's suitcase from his mother's grasp. "First things first. I'd like you to meet your house guest, Sara—" He hesitated fractionally before finishing, "—Connor. Sara, this is my mother, Cynthia Bradford."

"Of course. Sara, it's good to meet you."

The uncompromising line of Doug's mouth was back again, Sara noticed, making him even more a stranger. As Cynthia leaned forward for a brief Latino cheek-to-cheek greeting that seemed as much the cultural norm in Miami as in Bolivia, Sara felt a sudden panic. She hadn't really had time since Doug's offer the day before, to wonder about her prospective hostess. Somewhere in the back of her mind she'd expected . . . What *had* she expected? Not an arrogant matriarch, certainly, like her former mother-in-law. But perhaps an older version of the gentle, laughing woman that her own mother was in her faded childhood memories. A kindly mother-hen type, like Laura Histed, the pastor's wife in Santa Cruz.

But not this brittle, restless woman, who was as unlike her son as any two people could be. Had Doug been mistaken about how welcome Sara would be here? Had she herself just made another big mistake?

The throbbing in her temples was growing worse, and Sara had to resist an impulse to turn and flee as Doug picked up the duffel bag and Sara's suitcase, allowing Cynthia to take possession of his briefcase. She trailed after them to the elevator and up two levels to the parking garage. *Oh God, what have I gotten myself into? I don't even know these people—not even Doug really! What am I doing here?*

"Believe it or not, I've been at the airport all day. I didn't call my answering service until I got here this morning to meet last night's flight, so I never got your message about the change. Of course, I'd already canceled a whole day of appointments. Then this rain's had the traffic so backed up it wasn't worth driving home before I'd have to turn around and come back. All I needed was a couple more hours sitting around waiting for an overdue flight to finish off a wasted day. Can't any of these airlines keep to a schedule?"

Cynthia's swift strides stopped at a full-size white van. Ornate letters scrolled *Cynthia's Interior Decorating* across the side. "I brought the van because I was expecting you'd have too much luggage for the car."

She slid open the van's side panel, revealing a stripped-out interior behind the front bench seat. A cardboard box and rolled-up piece of carpet were its only contents. As Doug lifted the luggage inside, Cynthia spun on her heel, her sharp gaze focusing in on Sara for the first time since their brief introduction. "Honey, I just can't believe any woman travels with just one suitcase!"

Hands on her narrow hips, the older woman looked Sara up and down, her shrewd appraisal taking in the purple stains that exhaustion had laid under Sara's amber eyes, the strained pallor of the heart-shaped features, the grief and shock still lingering behind the long lashes. Her narrowed green gaze softened so that there was a sudden, fleeting resemblance to her son.

"Look, honey, don't you pay any mind to my rattling on! Doug's told me what you've been through! Men can be such—" She glanced over at her son and visibly modified her choice of words, "—stinkers, can't they?"

Running a last comprehensive survey over Sara's borrowed shirt and slacks, she added, "We'll go shopping first thing tomorrow. Laying carpet can wait another day."

With that pronouncement she strode around to the driver's side of the van, leaving a stunned Sara blinking back unexpected tears. *Why . . . she really is kind! All that grumbling . . . it's just her way of thinking out loud.*

"Come on, honey, you just climb on up here next to me," Cynthia called over her shoulder as she started the ignition. As Sara moved to obey, Doug's hand shot out to stop her. "Just a minute, Sara."

Slamming the side door shut, he raked his fingers through his hair while letting out a tired sigh. "Look, Sara, you don't have to do this. My mother . . . I tend to forget from one visit to the next just how high-powered she can be. If you'd prefer your own arrangements—well, I'll understand. I just . . . I don't want you feeling you owe me anything if you've got plans of your own."

His mouth crooked into a rueful half-smile. "I know I kind of railroaded you into this. My mother isn't the only pushy member of the Bradford clan."

Despite the wry humor, Sara detected with incredulity an uncharacteristic anxious look in Doug's intent gaze. *He's embarrassed. He's worried I won't like her!*

Oddly, the crack in the DEA agent's normally formidable composure eased Sara's own uncertainty. Maybe she hadn't known this man as long and well as she would like. But she would trust her life—and her future—to the kind of man he had proved himself to be. Decent. Caring. Of uncompromising integrity.

A friend.

"It's okay, Doug," she said gently. "I like your mother. I'm looking forward to getting to know her." A glimmer of a smile lightened her tired face. "And you."

Doug's shoulders relaxed, as if he had just pulled off a difficult mission, and a genuine grin brought sudden youth to his somber expression. "Okay, Sara. You don't know what you're letting yourself in for, but come on."

Chapter Two

Doug's mother was right about the weather. The thunder of rain on the roof drowned out any hope of conversation as the van pulled out of the parking garage. Night had settled in while they were clearing Customs, and a monsoon-force wind sheeted the downpour across the windshield so that visibility was limited to a few feet, and traffic was brought to a crawl.

"Welcome to hurricane season in Miami." Cynthia raised her voice above the thunder. "I hope this doesn't put you off South Florida. I was *thrilled* when Doug called that he was bringing me company. I get so bored on my own, I chatter just to hear the sound of my own voice. It's going to be fun to have someone else in the house. Especially since my son here has declined my hospitality. Surely getting your own apartment at this juncture is a waste of money."

She shot Doug a challenging glance, to which he returned a bland, expressionless look—one with which Sara herself was well-acquainted. Leaning forward, he picked a cigarette butt out of the coin tray. "I thought you quit smoking, Mother."

Cynthia accepted the change of subject with no more than a wry grimace. "I did quit. But this worrying and waiting for you to get out of that awful country . . . well, I slipped a little. Tomorrow it's back to Nicorette. That floor job of mine is a non-smoking residence, and the missus is paranoid about even the smell getting near her carpets."

With an expert twist of the steering wheel, Cynthia swung the van onto the exit ramp leading to the expressway. She glanced over at Sara. "I don't know if Doug told you, but I started my own interior decorating business a couple years ago. Nothing big. Just small remodeling jobs, painting, wallpaper, furniture coordination—that kind of thing. But it keeps me out of the house and the osteoporosis at bay."

They were out on the expressway now, the rain mellowing to a steady downpour and the traffic picking up speed accordingly. Driving in Miami seemed to Sara only slightly less of a free-for-all than the streets of Bolivia, and Cynthia was on edge behind the wheel, maneuvering constantly from one lane to another, one hand ready on the horn. When Cynthia slammed on the brakes to narrowly avoid rear-ending a pickup that had changed lanes in front of them, Sara saw Doug's hand clench and unclench before he asked with commendable evenness, "So . . . did you get the bid for the church bathrooms? Pastor Joe e-mailed that you'd put in to redecorate there. How come you didn't tell me?"

"With all that was going on down your way, it hardly seemed a major issue." A sharp honk warned off a sports car that was trying to cut in front of the van. "I'm still waiting for the deacons to vote. The mills of God may grind slowly, but they've got nothing on a church board."

Resting wearily against the vinyl upholstery, Sara let the conversation flow back and forth above her head. The neighbors' dog chewing up an armchair Cynthia had been upholstering. The wedding of some girl cousin of Doug's. A citrus canker scare necessitating the removal of an orange tree from Cynthia's back yard.

All the small happenings that made up normal family lives.

Ordinary . . . tranquil . . . safe!

Should I be calling any of my own relatives, Sara wondered, *to let them know I'm safely back in the U.S.? Would any of them care?* There were only a few scattered relatives with whom she'd ever had more than a nodding acquaintance. Spending her childhood overseas, where her father had worked the oil fields, was hardly conducive to building strong family relationships.

Just Aunt Jan and her sons.

The proximity to his only remaining immediate family was the reason Alan Connor had chosen Seattle when he'd finally recognized that his thirteen-year-old daughter needed more stability than his nomadic career afforded. It was Aunt Jan who'd initiated Sara into the mysteries of feminine undergarments, makeup, and other areas of education her father had neglected.

But Aunt Jan had three boys of her own, the youngest a year older than Sara, and a full-time career as an accountant with the IRS. While never unkind, she'd had neither the time nor the inclination to play substitute mother to an awkward teenage girl. By Sara's senior year of high school, with her youngest son safely ensconced in a college dorm, Aunt Jan had filed for divorce and accepted a promotion to Washington, D.C. Contact had dwindled to graduation and wedding announcements. Aunt Jan's most recent communication had been a wedding card, forwarded to Bolivia, expressing astonished but detached disapproval of Sara's hasty marriage. *It's your life*—Sara had read between the lines—*If you want to screw it up, that's your choice.*

What would Aunt Jan think now?

And what was the name of that D.C. suburb on the return address? The Cortéz servants have undoubtedly consigned my Rolodex to a bonfire by now.

"I just don't see why you're in such a hurry to look for your own place." The growing acidity in Cynthia's voice drew Sara back to her immediate surroundings. "You don't even know how long you'll be in Miami before you get assigned somewhere else. Is it so hard to be in the same house with your own mother?"

There was pain beneath the tartness, and Sara could feel a silent sigh raising Doug's rib cage beside her. "Mother, we've been through this before. If nothing else, it's safer for you."

"Safer for me, but not for Julie and the babies? Right! Don't humor me, Doug. You sound just like your father!"

"Okay then, maybe we both just need some space." Doug's reply was even, but there was a tightening of muscles along his jaw. Another part of family life—old wounds, old arguments. Straightening up, Sara cast around for a diversion. An incongruity among the office buildings and warehouses caught her attention. A Ferris wheel tall enough to be seen above the verge of the expressway.

"What in the world is that? A circus?"

Doug's swift glance was both comprehending and appreciative. "No, that's the Miami-Dade county fairgrounds. 'The Fair,' as we locals call it. Though, like everything in Miami, it runs a lot more to carnival and glitz than apple pie and 4-H projects."

The carnival rides visible below the overpass had ground to a halt in the rain, but the multi-colored lights still blinked their jeweled outlines against the night. Doug grinned suddenly. "Not that I've ever bothered with the Fair myself. Carnival rides are too dangerous for me. But I've got a fond spot for the place. I did my first deal right down there in the parking lot back when I was a rookie."

"You mean—a *drug* deal? And that isn't more dangerous than a carnival ride?"

"Not this one. It was actually kind of funny . . . though I'll say it didn't seem so at the time."

Sara gave Doug a doubtful look, but it was too dark to see his expression. Was he pulling her leg? "Can you . . . are you allowed to tell us about it?"

"Sure." In the taillight glow of a passing car, Doug's eyebrow arched high.

"If you really want to hear how I made a fool of myself. It's hardly one of the more glamorous moments of my law enforcement career."

"If you've *ever* made a fool of yourself, I'd love to hear about it," Sara answered definitely.

"Well, it was actually kind of a joke, to start with. Part of agent training is coming up with your own undercover persona. Like a stage character, but designed to fool the bad guys—or your training officer. I had strikes against me from the beginning. I was gringo where most of the dealers are Latino, and since I wasn't big into swearing or partying—I'd married Julie by then—the other agents stuck me with a nickname: The Saint. Even started a betting pool that I'd never convince a bad guy I was for real. I just told them that all bad guys weren't low-lives, and for my persona I put together a dirty FAA official. College-educated. Clean-cut. Anglo. And crooked and greedy as they come. Passed with flying colors."

Doug shifted his long legs beside Sara. "Anyway, getting back to the Fair, I was barely out on the street when my GS—group supervisor—gets this call from an informant. A Colombian wants to fly five hundred kilos of cocaine into south Florida and needs to get through our air traffic control net. The GS figures this is a good one for that FAA persona of mine, and he sends back that we've got a corrupt air traffic controller who can talk the plane through the net. Sure enough, the bad guy bites. He agrees to meet us for the payoff in the Fair's parking lot. The partner I'm working with is Latino, so he sets up the meeting with himself as the contact and me as the traffic controller. I don't know who was more nervous—that Colombian or me."

Sara relaxed against the vinyl upholstery, her tension easing. *I love his voice like this.* Deep, even, deliberately humorous, it took her back to another drive, through a jungle twilight, when Doug's stories had also proved a welcome diversion.

He was a good storyteller, and Sara could picture the scene in her mind's eye. A fairground parking lot early in the day, the first thrill-seekers just beginning to straggle through the gates. A dark, unmarked sedan. A young Doug behind the wheel with formal shirt and tie and a Federal Aviation Administration pin on his lapel. A BMW sliding into the next parking slot. Doug surreptitiously wiping damp hands on his slacks as the Colombian, overweight and overdressed, climbed into the passenger seat. His Cuban-born partner, playing the role of Latino underworld contact in the back seat.

"I don't know if he sensed something wrong, or if he just didn't like dealing with a gringo. Colombian dealers especially have this idea that all Anglos are either honest or cops. To nail the guy, we needed him to admit on tape what he wanted from me and hand over the $10,000 we'd arranged for an advance payoff. But he was so nervous we were afraid he was going to blow the deal off."

"How do you get him on tape?" Sara asked, interested. "Bug your car?"

"Not mine, the other agent's. Which is where the funny part comes in. First step in a deal is to sterilize your car. Basically, just go through it to get rid of anything that'll give you away as a cop. Old report forms. Handcuffs. Loose ammo rolling around on the floor. You know, the usual stuff you'll find in any car that's been lived in for a while."

"No, actually I wouldn't know," Sara responded dryly. "I've never found loose ammo rolling around in my car."

Her show of interest was no longer to keep Cynthia's prodding at bay. This was a fascinating glimpse into another world she knew little about. Doug's world. Ahead, the traffic had slowed again to a crawl. Cynthia's fingers tapped impatiently on the steering wheel, whether from the story or the traffic, Sara couldn't tell.

"Yeah, well, anyway, my partner was a real cowboy type. He was always picking up parking tickets on the job, and since it was an undercover car, not registered to him, he'd just stuff the tickets up under the visor and forget about them. I was doing the shakedown, and I was in such a hurry, I didn't even think to check up there.

"So in climbs this Colombian, and he's sweating, and I'm sweating, and I'm sure I'm about to blow my first big one. To make things worse, just as he's giving signals that he's not buying this, I manage to jog my sunglasses and knock them onto the floor. So I go for the sunglasses, and I'm so jumpy I bang my head against the visor. All those tickets come floating down like a snowstorm. There must have been thousands of dollars worth, *years* of them stuffed up there. My partner is frantically giving the signal to call the whole thing off. We know the guy's got to be armed, and we're just crossing our fingers we can get out before he goes loco."

The picture was so vivid that Sara was laughing, and even the impatient line of Cynthia's mouth had relaxed. "So what happened?"

"Believe it or not, the Colombian just started laughing. He said that anyone who'd broken the law that many times couldn't possibly be a cop—and he went ahead and made the deal."

25

"So did you arrest him?" Sara asked curiously.

Doug's arm brushed Sara's as his shoulders rose and fell again. "No, he was just small fry. We took the advance. Set up the deal with the plane. But he never managed to get together the rest of the money for the drugs. He called a couple of times wanting us to front the dope for him until he could sell it. But the GS just blew him off. We'd gotten what we wanted—his connection on the other end. So we turned the ten grand over to evidence and basically ceased to exist. At least the crooked FAA official did. End of story."

"End of story, my eye!" Cynthia threw her son a hard glance as she nipped the van sideways into a gap in the traffic that gained her all of ten feet. "Tell her how it really ended. Tell her what happened to the Colombian."

Doug's tone hardened. "I don't think we need to get into that, Mother."

"Sure we do! She needs to know what she's getting into with this job of yours." Cynthia looked over at Sara, her tone caustic again. "They found him a couple months later in the trunk of a car with a bullet through his head. Apparently, he'd borrowed the money he handed over to the DEA and when he didn't pay it back, the lender decided to take disciplinary action."

Doug made no reply, but even in the darkness of the van's interior, Sara could see the muscles along his jaw bunching up again. A sudden chill raised the hair on her arms. In the relief of her escape, Sara had forgotten her original impression of Doug Bradford.

A dangerous man doing a dangerous job.

Traffic was picking up again. Craning her neck to look over the back of the seat, Sara caught a glimpse through the van's two back windows of the receding lights of the carnival rides still glittering. The wind lashing at the rain made the lights waver against the night so that the rides seemed to be in motion, as if phantom riders were taking turns in the downpour. The whole scene was no longer festive but surreal and oddly disquieting. Doug's story had lost any humor it might have held.

Safe?

Chapter Three

OCTOBER 15
PALMASOLA CORRECTIONAL FACILITY
SANTA CRUZ, BOLIVIA

Julio Vargas picked his way through the alley, stepping gingerly over a heap of discarded vegetable peelings. It had rained again during the night, and the pocked, crumbling concrete was slimy with mud and rotting garbage. At first glance, the former *Industrias* Cortéz security chief appeared unaffected and unchanged by his weeks of incarceration in the notorious Bolivian prison. He wore the same black clothing in which he'd been arrested, his black hair was still slicked back in its trademark ponytail, and his gaze was as cold and flat and unforgiving as ever.

But the signature gold chain and earrings were gone—confiscated by the first prison guard he'd encountered. And a closer look revealed the careful mending and threadbare condition of his shirt and slacks, the stitched sides of his black shoes.

He turned another corner, skirting the limp form of a man sprawled in the muck, a knife hilt protruding between the shoulder blades. One more inmate stabbed in the night for money, revenge, or in a drunken fight. Now that dawn had arrived, the guards would soon stumble over him.

Except for the corpse, the narrow street was indistinguishable from the alley. But a hubbub of clinking and banging, creaking cart wheels, and raised voices confirmed that he'd taken the right turn. Ahead lay the main gates of the prison, where vendors were already setting up their stands for the daily open-air market. Julio quickened his stride at the aroma of frying donuts and *café con leche,* his thin nostrils flaring. Breakfast. If he could remedy the empty state of his pockets.

Squelch! Something repulsively soft flattened under Julio's incautious step. He grimaced with disgust as he grabbed for balance at the nearest wall. It wasn't the first time he had made this mistake, and in Palmasola the canine population was not always to blame.

Then Julio recognized the mashed pulp and blackened skin of rotting bananas. Scraping his shoe against the mucky concrete, he heard a giggle. Ahead of him down the alley, a small boy had turned to watch the show. He was carrying a tray of *salteñas,* a spicy Bolivian turnover, still hot out of the oven, to hawk to the prisoners for breakfast.

Catching Julio's icy glare, the boy lost his smirk and ducked around the corner. Then Julio realized that the dampness of the wall under his hand was not the night's drizzle, but fresh, warm urine. With a furious oath, he caught up to the boy in time to snatch two *salteñas* from the tray.

"I didn't mean it! Please, *señor,* you must pay. My mother will beat me!"

Ignoring the boy's tears, Julio strode on into the open market place around the prison gates. He wasn't at all concerned that the boy might report the theft. The prison guards were more concerned with regulating traffic—and commerce—in and out of Palmasola than in policing the interior. As with the dead man, the only law uniformly applied here was that of the jungle—survival of the fittest.

Housing, living amenities, and even the daily food rations depended entirely on what the prisoner could afford. The alley from which Julio had emerged led back to the Palmasola slums, where a single bare cell with no toilet or water went for as low as twenty dollars a month. The poorest prisoners crammed into these warrens so tightly they had to sleep sitting up.

At the other end of the spectrum was the Palmasola "Beverly Hills," where drug kingpins shelled out thousands of dollars in rent for luxury suites complete with saunas, exercise rooms, satellite TVs, and catered meals.

To complete the disparity, ordinary debtors and detainees still waiting for charges to be filed—a process that could take years—mingled without restriction with the most violent of criminals. Families left destitute by an arrest were allowed to follow prisoners into the jail. So there were children everywhere, working beside their fathers in the carpentry or leather-working shops or dishing up hot meals alongside their mothers in the food stands. They scampered in and out of the prison gates as if the place were their home, fulfilling a vital part of the smuggling operations that allowed this bizarre society to function. The guards paid as blind an eye to the black market operations as they did to the violence and crime that was rampant inside the prison walls.

Drugs. Alcohol. Women. A cell phone for a narco to call his business network. Anything was available to those with money.

Money.

Ducking under a plastic awning, Julio caught the eye of two men who were lolling against a rickety stand. Hair long and unkempt, teeth missing from malnutrition, neither looked like the army officers they had once been. Scrambling to their feet, they fell in behind Julio. Passing back one of the *salteñas,* Julio assuaged his own hunger with the other as the three men headed toward the artisan section of the market. In these weeks of incarceration, Julio had learned the hard lesson of what it meant to have no money.

Or the power that money bestowed.

Locating a wooden table spread with tools and glue for repairing shoes, Julio threaded his way toward it. The first days in Palmasola had been the worst. The corn gruel supplied to prisoners without their own resources was not enough to stave off starvation; the filthy cell, with its dozen other inmates and not so much as a straw pallet, was an outrage. But Julio's bank accounts were among the first things seized with the fall of *Industrias* Cortéz, so there were no funds to improve his living conditions.

As for the remaining members of the Cortéz clan, they hadn't once come down to Palmasola to concern themselves with their faithful employee's well-being or survival. Not that Julio Vargas blamed them. They were doing exactly what he would do in their place . . . denying all association, keeping their own heads down until this all blew over and they could emerge to pick up the pieces.

An acid hatred roiled with the spicy fire of the *salteña* in his stomach. No, it was not his former employers Julio blamed for his present predicament. It was the Americans. The gringo DEA agent, Doug Bradford, who had led the assault that brought down the Cortéz empire. And his employers' turncoat daughter-in-law, Sara, who had betrayed husband and family—for what? Principles? Conscience?

It was something beyond Julio Vargas's comprehension. The girl had money, prestige, a handsome young husband. What more was there to ask of life?

Not that it mattered now. But the single vision that kept Julio going was to find himself free from this hellhole and have those two within his grasp.

The shoe repairman, a petty thief jailed for skimming funds from an artisans' co-op where he'd been treasurer, was already feverishly counting out bills as the three men approached. Julio had been almost—not quite, but almost—desperate enough to soil his hands with street-cleaning or garbage pickup before he encountered his two former military associates, who provided the necessary muscle to launch a "security service" for the prison's entrepreneurial businessmen. A midnight raid of a woodworking shop under the neglectful eye of a guard who pocketed a third of the profits had convinced reluctant inmates of their need for Julio's services.

His "clients" were little better off than Julio himself. But the proceeds of his little enterprise were enough to provide him with better food and a cell of his own, furnished with some purloined pieces from the woodworking shop. In time he was certain he'd climb the ladder into the luxury suites across the way, if not out of Palmasola altogether. But securing his release was a costly proposition considering the notoriety of his arrest.

Again, it boiled down to money.

"Alto!"

Julio finished divvying out his subordinates' breakfast money before turning slowly to face the guard who had called out to him. His mouth thinned. He'd already paid this one off. *If the mongrel thinks he can raise his cut . . . !*

But the sentry hurrying toward him only waved his M-16. "You are wanted, Señor Vargas. You must come with me."

The M-16's ammunition clip was empty, Julio noted ironically, sold no doubt to augment the guard's own meager income. With a shrug, he waved off his two associates and followed the guard. He'd had no visitors since the huge, rusted gates had slammed shut behind him. Most likely, it would prove to be counternarcotics agents again with their endless questions. Yet another reminder that this was a prison and he was at the mercy of others.

Julio soon realized that the guard was not leading him toward the prison administrative block. His thin eyebrows arched in mild surprise as the "Beverly Hills" apartment complex loomed in front of him.

The sentry outside behaved more like a security officer protecting the privacy of his employers than a prison guard. The reason became evident as Julio stepped into a salon many times the size of his own hard-earned cell.

So this is how the other side lives! Carpet on the floor. Leather couches and mahogany tables. A large-screen TV against the far wall. And air conditioning. *While the rest of us pigs are sweltering in the heat!*

"*Coronel* Julio Vargas."

He had not been addressed by his military title in years. He diverted his envious gaze from the TV screen to the two men who were rising from a sofa. *Foreigners,* he summed up immediately. *Middle Eastern.*

The younger of the two was tall and lean, almost gaunt, his beard untrimmed and scraggly, making it difficult to judge his age, though Julio estimated he was under thirty. The other man was plump, middle-aged, and much shorter, but his beak-nosed features, almost identical to the younger man's, marked the two as father and son, or uncle and nephew.

"Yes, I am Colonel Julio Vargas," Julio answered sharply. "Who wants to know?"

Neither visitor responded to his query. The younger man handed the guard an envelope, while the older man swept a meditative gaze over Julio's worn clothing and mended shoes. "Your full name, please?"

Julio's resentment boiled under the heat of the visitor's silent scrutiny. To be dragged here without a bath or change or even a chance to wash the mud spatters from his hands and clothes—even a prisoner had rights!

"And why should I answer? You are not the *militares.* Or the *antinarcóticos.* So what authority do you have to ask such questions?"

The younger visitor twisted his gaunt frame impatiently. "The authority of one sent to remove you from this place," he burst out, "*if* we like the answers to our questions."

The fire in the young man's dark eyes silenced Julio more effectively than the stunning implications of what he had said.

"Fine, then." Julio spread his hands in acquiescence. "If you wish to know so urgently, my full name is Julio Abdul Vargas Haddad."

"Abdul. Haddad. Arabic names." With a graceful hand motion, the older man waved Julio toward a leather chair. "Come. Why should we stand when we can be comfortable? Sit!"

Julio sank warily into the chair. "My mother's father was Lebanese," he admitted. "His family migrated to Bolivia over forty years ago." All at once, the man's hand motions and hint of an accent clicked into place, and Julio added shrewdly, "And you? Your Spanish is excellent, but you speak like one of my mother's people. You too are Lebanese, are you not?"

"We will ask the questions!" the younger man responded harshly. But the older man raised a hand to cut him off.

"Yes, we are Lebanese," he answered peaceably. "From the same community as your grandparents. But you—you were raised by your father's family, were you not? Did your mother teach you her language?"

"My mother taught me the language of her people. But she died when I was still young. I haven't spoken it since I was a child."

"And your father's family belongs to the *militares,* is this correct?"

Julio spread his hands wide. "The Vargas have been loyal servants in defense of this country for generations." As a member of the military police's infamous execution squads, he'd been responsible for the vanishing of thousands of *desaparecidos*—political opposition figures, community leaders, and idealistic university students who'd been made to "disappear" in the years before his country's present experiment with democracy.

The younger man lowered his tall frame to a nearby chair, but reluctantly, as if he hadn't sat on such a piece of furniture in a long time. The taut inflexibility of his posture made Julio wonder if he'd been in the military himself.

"And you—you too served as an officer. Is it true that you were trained by the Americans themselves?"

Julio shrugged. "I was chosen to be part of the counter-insurgency training the Americans offered our military in return for cooperation with their own operations. I graduated first in my class."

"But you have not continued in your family's tradition of military service? Why not?"

The question flicked Julio on the raw, and he rose angrily to his feet. "If you have investigated my past so well, you know the answer to that. Enough! I will not remain here to be humiliated. Tell me the purpose of these questions, or send me back to my cell. How did you find out so much about me? And who is this person you say wishes to remove me from this place?"

The two visitors rose to their feet simultaneously. "We have long known all about you," the older man said calmly. "You have made no effort to avoid notoriety. As to who has sent us, it is your family, and you may be thankful for that."

"Family!" Julio's skeptical glance went from one interrogator to the other. "Now I know you lie! My grandparents are dead. My parents are dead. I have no more family in this country."

"Not in Bolivia. Paraguay. Ciudad del Este."

Ciudad del Este. Another puzzle piece clicked into place. Paraguay was Bolivia's closest neighbor to the south, the one country in Latin America as poor and corrupt as Bolivia itself. Ciudad de Este was Paraguay's second largest city, after the capital of Asunción, and the only reason for its economic development was its strategic location where the borders of Paraguay, Argentina, and Brazil touched. An almost complete lack of border control in the area, known as the Tri-Frontier, made it a haven for the smuggling of anything that had a market. Contraband. Drugs. Arms. Even people.

Julio Vargas had been in Ciudad del Este more than once himself. The wide jungle river arteries connecting Bolivia and Paraguay were a major shipping route for Bolivian exports. Cocaine, hidden in legitimate *Industrias* Cortéz shipments of native handicrafts and other goods, had flowed down the Paraguay and Paraná rivers to Ciudad del Este, then across the border to Brazil and on to Argentina or to oceangoing ships on the Atlantic coast.

Julio was aware that Ciudad del Este had a thriving Arab community, including Lebanese relatives from his mother's family, who had migrated to Paraguay rather than Bolivia. But both his maternal grandparents and his mother had died long before he reached adulthood; until now, his Paraguayan relatives had made no effort to contact him.

"And why should relatives whom I have never even met care what becomes of me? Much less exert themselves to free me from this place?"

"Is not loyalty to one's family reason enough?"

When Julio responded with skeptical silence, the younger visitor swept on, "Besides, there is a job that must be done. And is working with family not better than with a stranger?"

"Ahh!" This was a motive that Julio could understand. "What kind of job?"

"First, one last question." The older man interjected. "It has been a long time since you served the Americans. Are you still loyal to your former masters?"

Fury blazed inside Julio, igniting a fire in his eyes. "*Loyal?*" he spat out. "Yes, I took the training of the Americans. It was advantageous for my career and has proved useful. But they were never my masters. It was the Americans who thrust me into this prison. And why? Because they are interfering imperialists who think they can force their way into our country to dictate what our laws should be and what our people should do. That I should owe them loyalty—never! And if you think to persuade me to be of service to the Americans, the world does not hold enough wealth. I would rot in this cesspool first!"

The two visitors waited without comment until Julio sputtered to a stop. Then the older man's beard waggled in a nod. "Good," he said. "That is the answer we hoped to hear. Then, if you wish, the offer of employment stands. If you will consent to the job, the details will be made clear when the time comes. However, rest assured that it will not compromise your principles. And you will find the remuneration more than acceptable. So! Will you come or stay?"

Julio looked from one bearded face to the other. His head inclined in assent. Though he disliked unanswered questions, he was hardly going to pass up an opportunity to leave Palmasola—and both his visitors knew it.

"Good. Then let us depart."

Julio did not bother stopping by his cell on the way out. He had nothing he cared to retrieve. Nor did he spare a thought to his two subordinates. They were as expendable as Julio had been to the Cortezes. At the gate, the older Lebanese visitor pulled out a sheaf of stamped and sealed documents. They'd clearly paid off the requisite judges and courts, because the guards gave the papers only a cursory glance before waving them through.

The streets around Palmasola were only a little less filthy and ramshackle than the prison itself. But to Julio, the mingling of exhaust fumes and open sewage was the perfume of freedom. While the younger visitor hailed a Toyota Corolla station wagon with a hand-lettered "taxi" sign inside the windshield, the older man handed Julio a manila envelope.

"Your new identification papers. And a passport. Your name is the same— Julio Vargas is common enough—but you are now Paraguayan. There is money, too, and instructions. You will go to Ciudad del Este to the address indicated there. Do not travel by plane. There are too many eyes at the airports. Take the train to Puerto Suarez on the Brazilian border, then find a boat to carry you to Ciudad del Este. Your arrival will be anticipated."

Sliding into the cab after his companion, the older man ordered the driver, "To the airport."

The Toyota Corolla was pulling away before Julio realized he still didn't know his liberators' names. He ripped open the envelope. Its contents were as promised, the sum of money large enough for a sharp "ssst" to issue through his teeth.

A new identity. Cash. With this, he could go anywhere. Make any fresh start he chose.

And do what?

No, his two liberators would not have purchased his freedom and handed him a pile of cash unless there was more—a *lot* more—where that came from. Cupidity alone compelled him to find out what else they had to offer—and no doubt they had taken this into consideration. If nothing else, common sense dictated that he leave the country for a while. And he could make his next move in Ciudad del Este as easily as here.

Julio eyed the altitude of the sun rising above the prison walls. If the shipping schedule *Industrias* Cortéz had used was still in effect, he could make the morning train to Puerto Suarez. The trip would be long, but with no need to hoard the money in his hand, he could splurge on a first class compartment, a good hotel with sauna in Puerto Suarez, and a new wardrobe before taking the next leg south to Paraguay.

Hailing a cab, he ordered the driver brusquely, "To the train station. And quickly!"

Chapter Four

OCTOBER 20
CIUDAD DEL ESTE, PARAGUAY

"He has called. He is on his way from the shipping docks."

Mullah Sheik Mozer Jebai, the spiritual and political leader of Ciudad del Este's Muslim community, muted the sound on the flat-screen TV as the younger of Julio Vargas's two visitors entered the room. Were it not for the gray streaks in the mullah's hair and untrimmed beard, the two men could have been twins, with the same tall, lean frame and smoldering dark eyes.

"Uncle Khalil and I are descending now to the foyer to meet him," the young man said.

"It is well. And Saleh, my son . . ."

"Yes, Father?"

"Has news come yet about the other arrangements?"

"Even now they are being tested and chosen. They will be ready to come as soon as we have made preparations to receive them."

Nodding approval, Sheik Jebai waited for Saleh to leave the office before restoring the sound on the TV. As the angry voice of a speaker rose to a crescendo, the mullah strode to the windows of his top-floor office. Quaint one-story shop fronts with asbestos tile roofs and whitewashed walls stretched out below. Along cobblestone streets bright with the colorful awnings of market stands, the street vendors formed a shifting kaleidoscope with their push carts or wooden trays piled high with merchandise. Tall poles threaded through the bustle, bearing balloons, garishly colored toys, or cotton candy. Rising above the tiled roofs, a scattering of modern buildings glittered with plate glass and chrome.

Only at ground level was the general shabbiness of the city visible, the plastered storefronts peeling and dirty and covered with graffiti. Discarded packaging and other refuse was everywhere underfoot, and the market stands spilled uncontrolled from the sidewalks so that motorized vehicles and horse-drawn wagons had to fight their way through.

None of this disturbed the mullah. After all, his own home city of Beirut had been far more a shambles by the time he fled—and far less profitable. As for the thousands of tourists and visitors who flooded daily into Ciudad del Este, they were not looking for natural beauty. That could be found thirty kilometers upriver, where Brazil and Argentina competed vigorously and some-times acrimoniously for the tourist trade at the fabled Iguazú Falls, the world's largest cascades. Here they came to shop—pure and simple.

A million visitors a year flocked to either the Brazilian or Argentinean sides of Iguazú Falls. A satisfying percentage crossed over to Ciudad del Este, Paraguay's unique, duty-free contribution to the Tri-Frontier economy. As a result, only Hong Kong and Miami boasted larger goods markets than the Ciudad del Este bazaar. Anything could be purchased in the maze of shops and market stands—everything from Rolex watches and Chanel perfume to the latest computer software and brand-name electronic equipment. Little of it was genuine, but that didn't seem to faze the shoppers. If the goods were cheap, the prices were even cheaper.

There were other, less visible, services that Ciudad del Este offered the savvy buyer: drugs; arms; counterfeit IDs, passports, and other documents; the ser-vices of ultra-discreet banks where proceeds of a business deal could be de-posited with no questions asked. All of this made Ciudad del Este an ideal base of operations, if never quite a home.

Sheik Jebai swung around in time to see images on the TV screen of an Israeli missile attack on a Palestinian refugee camp. Terrified people were run-ning away from the smoldering ruins of what had once been a building. A close-up zoomed in on a small boy who stood wailing amid the rubble of his home.

Long-controlled anger burned in the mullah's heart. Saleh was too young to remember the civil war that had torn his birthplace apart and sent the fam-ily into exile. But Mozer Jebai had fought long and hard, battling not only the Christian militia that stubbornly resisted the establishing of Islamic rule within Lebanon, but also the Israelis, who even more stubbornly withstood every at-tempt to annihilate their upstart pretense of an independent state. Jebai had lost family members and comrades before making the decision to seek a better life for his family outside their homeland.

He was not alone. More than thirty thousand of Jebai's compatriots had settled in Ciudad del Este and its counterpart municipality, Foz de Iguazú, across the Paraná River on the Brazilian side of the border. Other Arab communities had found new homes in Uruguay, Ecuador, Bolivia, and across Latin America, where they had prospered. Always among the world's greatest merchants, the Arab immigrants had been among the first to grasp the commercial opportunities offered by the Tri-Frontier's tourist trade and minimal border controls. From the plateglass windows of his office, Sheik Jebai could see the fruit of their industry rising above the squalid sprawl of the bazaar. Department stores. The city's biggest shopping mall. The commercial center beneath his feet. Banks. All Arab owned. Rising above them all, the graceful minaret of the Prophet Mohammed Mosque bore silent testimony to the roots his people had put down in this place.

Even the Paraguayans acknowledged that the Arab community was the economic foundation of the city's present prosperity.

Untouchable . . . so far.

Across the room, the TV screen had shifted to images of a training camp where Islamic jihad warriors with automatic weapons and black scarves hiding their faces were practicing an assault on a mock-up building constructed of canvas and wood. The tape in the VCR was a recruiting video for Al Moqawama, a local cell of Hezbollah, translated "Army of God," a Lebanese militant organization sponsored by Iran.

After the successful strike into the heart of the United States on September 11, 2001, the Americans had come prowling around Ciudad del Este, pressuring the Paraguayans with accusations of terrorist connections within the Arab community, even forcing the arrest of the city's most prominent merchant, Assad Ahmad Barakat, on charges of pirating CDs and funneling the proceeds into Hezbollah war coffers.

Mozer Jebai had led the protest, screaming racial profiling and American interference. A judicious disbursement of funds among certain high-placed local officials had cooled Paraguayan interest in cooperation, forcing the American hunting dogs back into their kennels, for the moment at least.

Of course, the Americans had been right. The prosperity of the last decades had not dulled Mozer Jebai's commitment, and that of others of his community, to the holy war they had left behind. Just as the Irish Republican Army had found a warm welcome and generous pocketbooks within America's Irish immigrant community, so Hezbollah, the Islamic Jihad, and other militant organizations had found support and funding for their cause among the Lebanese Diaspora and others of the Arabic expatriate community, not only in Ciudad del Este but around the world.

In this way, too, Ciudad del Este's unique attributes had been turned to advantage.

From his bird's-eye vantage, Mozer Jebai had a clear view of the most prominent of those attributes: the concrete and steel arch of the Bridge of Friendship that spanned the slow-moving brown waters of the Paraná River, connecting Ciudad del Este with Foz de Iguazú. As always, the bridge was a scene of congested pandemonium. Long lines of tour buses, trucks, cars, and horse-drawn wagons inched through the border crossing. Vendors hawked cold drinks and snacks to impatient passengers. Pedestrians by the thousands streamed across unchecked—not just tourists but peddlers with heavy packs, looking to avoid exorbitant import taxes on their sales goods.

"Intermediación," the Paraguayans euphemistically termed it. The "intermediary trade" of undeclared goods and services, not only across the Bridge of Friendship but also up and down the triple border. Sheik Mozer Jebai and his colleagues had proved as expert at it as in all their business dealings. Not only pirated CDs, but software, black market goods, arms sales, even drug dealing had channeled millions to Hezbollah, Islamic Jihad, and other militant groups. The discreet system of banking made it simple to disburse the funds to where they were needed. Weapons, easily obtained in the arms market and desperately needed for the fighting in the Middle East, were distributed as well across those same porous borders.

Where is he? Surely a taxi ride from the docks cannot take so long.

Mozer Jebai moved closer to the plate glass until he could look straight down to the street. A cab was pulling up in front of the office building. It was too far away to distinguish individual features, but he could see that the passenger who stepped out was male and dressed in black. A second figure stepped out into the open to greet him.

Saleh.

My only son.

Despite his labor on behalf of the cause, despite the fiery speeches he had allowed visiting militants to declaim within the community mosque, he had never expected his son to volunteer. Saleh had been a quiet, devout boy with a brilliant mind and natural athletic skills, graduating with honors from secondary school at sixteen, and already halfway through his engineering degree at eighteen. Paraguay was a world away from the war and devastation into which Saleh had been born, and like any parent, Mozer Jebai had envisioned for him a bright professional future in his adopted country.

Instead, Saleh had chosen to follow a charismatic recruiter to the training camps in Afghanistan, and for the past five years his father had hardly seen or heard from him. His leaders had at least seen the value of allowing Saleh to finish his education, sending him to Germany to complete his engineering degree and a master's in languages. But eighteen months ago, he had again disappeared into Afghanistan, and his father had not known whether he was alive or dead.

Then one day he slipped across the Bridge of Friendship and appeared at his father's door, gaunt, hungry, battle-hardened—and with an idea for a new kind of war.

A tap at the door drew the mullah from the window. Reaching for the remote, he again muted the TV as Saleh strode into the room. His older companion, Khalil, paused in the door to usher in their guest.

Julio Vargas presented a vastly different picture than his two guides had encountered in Palmasola prison. He still wore his trademark black, but the clothing was brand new, the shirt fine silk, and there was again a flash of gold at his throat and earlobes. His hair was combed and sleek, his fingers manicured, and the arrogance had returned to his upright carriage. For whatever reason, these men needed him, and that made his position here one of strength, not subservience. His bronzed Indian features masked a sharp curiosity as he watched his host approach, immediately registering the resemblance to his younger liberator.

Sheik Jebai's greeting confirmed Julio's speculations. "Colonel Julio Vargas. Welcome. I trust my son's arrangements for your trip proved adequate. I am Sheik Mozer Jebai, mullah of our community here in Ciudad del Este. My father's mother was sister of your mother's father. You have met my son, Saleh." Mozer Jebai gave a regal nod toward Julio's older guide. "And the brother of my wife, Khalil Mehri. So we are all family here. Come! Sit!"

At one end of the office, low couches were arranged to form three sides of a square. The flat-screen TV against the wall made the fourth side. As the men settled themselves on the couches, a young woman entered with a tray. Julio hid his impatience behind an impassive expression as the girl served sweet, black coffee and almond-honey pastries. How much more time was to be wasted before he found out why these men had brought him here?

But the mullah waited only until the girl had left the room before putting an end to the small talk. "Colonel Vargas. I am told that you have been trained in special arts as a soldier by the Americans. Tell me of this training."

Julio's mental antenna registered the repeated use of his military title. "It is as I told your son. The Americans offered the training of their elite troops to chosen ones in our own armed forces. I spent a year in their country training in their School of the Americas with other officers from across all of Latin America. I was the best."

The mullah responded with a measured nod. "And yet my son tells me you feel no loyalty to the interests of those who gave you this training. Tell me, when they were attacked, did you feel no obligation to go to their defense?"

Julio now knew the answer they wanted, and he had no qualms about giving it to them. "The training of the Americans was not offered in our interests, but in the interest of their own stupid counternarcotics war," he responded coldly. "They toss their bits of knowledge our way as a rich man tosses bread crumbs to a peasant. As to the attack on their country, I felt they received only what they deserved. Let them taste the fruits of their interference with other nations' affairs."

The mullah nodded again, approvingly. "And to the cause of the attackers? Where do your loyalties lie? Saleh tells me you speak our language."

Switching abruptly from Spanish to Arabic, Mozer Jebai gestured to the TV screen, where the recruiting video was still running, though the sound was muted. "How much did your mother teach you of the true faith and of the duty of the faithful to free the world of the apostate oppression of the Americans and Jews?"

The studied blankness of Julio's narrow features masked his growing incredulity. *Who are these men who claim to be my relatives and yet talk about some kind of holy war as if this country has not been their home for a generation or more?*

Truth was, Julio had seldom even thought of the Lebanese half of his ancestry. Bolivia had been his family's home for as far back as it mattered. As for the never-ceasing conflicts in that distant part of the world from which his mother's family had been so fortunate to escape, he felt nothing. If he were to interest himself in any country beside his own, it would be Argentina. Or Brazil. Or maybe France, if he decided to see Paris. But certainly not the barren landscape of the Middle East, with its wild-eyed, gun-waving inhabitants he could see on the TV screen. From all appearances, it looked even more impoverished and less appealing than his native Bolivia.

Behind his careful lack of expression, he made his decision. Whatever these men had in mind, he wanted no part of it. Nor would he humble himself by responding in his rusty, halting Arabic.

"I am not a religious man," he said curtly in Spanish. "My mother was

Muslim, my father Catholic. Neither practiced their faith in our home. As to the political aspirations of the Arab world—" Julio shrugged "—the only cause I follow is that of myself and my own interest."

"So you are a mercenary then." Saleh leaned forward, his posture taut with anger. "If you do not serve for loyalty or ideology, you will serve for money, am I right? You are for hire to the highest bidder."

"Saleh!" Raising a hand for silence, Sheik Mozer Jebai turned to Julio. "Please, we are not here to pass moral judgment on your former employment. A man must make a living, and we too have found the Americans' greed for stimulation . . . useful."

Julio relaxed fractionally the tightening of his mouth. Then the rumors were true that the *intermediación* of Bolivia's foremost export had reached the highest levels of Ciudad del Este. Perhaps these relatives of his were behind some of the contacts he himself had made on behalf of Luis Cortéz. Was this how they had traced him to Palmasola?

"Forgive my son," the mullah went on smoothly. "He has only recently returned from fighting the Americans in Afghanistan, and he has not yet recovered from the stress."

So that was the emotion he'd seen smoldering behind that brooding gaze. Julio coolly gave the younger man closer scrutiny. The deep scores around his mouth and eyes, despite his youth, told of battle fatigue. The gauntness of inadequate nutrition. The gleam of fanaticism that blazed in his eyes.

Had this boy—for he was little more than that—really left all the wealth this office represented to fight and starve and quite possibly die in the inhospitable wastelands of a country that was not even his own? It was a motivation that held no meaning for Julio, the former colonel. And that his father and uncle would encourage it!

Julio felt a chill that deepened his determination to separate himself from these people as rapidly as possible. Zealots were dangerous.

"The Americans defeated you very efficiently," he commented flatly, not without malice. "They may be greedy imperialists, but the superiority of their soldiers cannot be contested anywhere in the world."

Saleh's fists clenched and unclenched. The boy had much to learn about self-control, Julio noted.

"We were not defeated," Saleh answered just as flatly. "We simply saw the merit of temporary retreat. And it was not the superiority of their soldiers but of their special training and equipment. If we possessed such a force—"

"My son is right," Sheik Jebai cut in. "These American 'Special Forces,' as they call them, are superior in training, not in zeal and will."

He gestured again to the TV screen where recruits with covered faces and AK-47s were now negotiating an obstacle course, leaping low barriers and wriggling under coils of barbed wire. "Could you teach those skills to such warriors as these?"

Julio now saw where this was going, and he was flabbergasted. "You want me to build you a Special Operations Group like the Americans?"

"Yes. And my son Selah would be its leader."

Only long practice kept stunned disbelief from registering on Julio's narrow features. He'd expected a catch in his liberators' offer of employment. Even possibly one that fell outside the boundaries of the law. Otherwise why come to him, and at such cost?

But this was beyond his wildest conjectures.

"It is not so simple," he explained carefully. "It is not simply a matter of duplicating the Americans' training, but of finding men to match the type they choose. The Americans set their requirements high. To become one of their elite soldiers, it takes not just fighting skills but education, intelligence, and many other factors. Even then, many fail. Of the group of top soldiers sent from my country, only three of us completed the course. *These* men—" contempt edged his tone as he gestured toward the TV screen "—could not match even the newest recruits in the Americans' infantry regiments."

Sheik Mozer Jebai's dark eyes smoldered with a fire to match his son's. "I do not need lectures in warfare," he said harshly. "I was killing my first enemies before you were tall enough to lift a gun. We have computers. We have researched and studied the requirements the Americans have set for their troops. We have tens of thousands of candidates around the world eager to serve the cause. Already the process of choosing has begun. All have finished the university with honors. All speak at least two languages. All have combat training. Many have already fought for the jihad. Above all, each is willing to give his life to serve Allah."

"As for me—" Saleh interjected just as harshly. "I too have passed the testing. And I have already proven my valor and dedication. I will not fail the course."

"You do not need to concern yourself for worthy candidates," the mullah added curtly. "The question is—can you do it? Can you replicate the training the Americans gave you? Make our men better warriors than these Special

Forces? Be assured that the remuneration will be commensurate with the task you must perform."

Julio gathered his wits together. If these men were madmen, they were very wealthy madmen. And the idea was not as wild as it had sounded at first. *If* the right men could be found, the right equipment and arms. At the least he'd have better material than the teenage conscripts he'd commanded in Bolivia or the undisciplined rabble he'd forged into a security force for Luis Cortéz.

And not all the Americans' training would need to be duplicated. Certainly not their ridiculous obsession with ethics and human rights. The combat training, yes. Mission planning. Navigation science. And, of course, the expensive technology and weapons the Bolivian military had never been able to afford. If the goal was solely to kill and destroy efficiently and invisibly, not to feed villagers or carry out diplomatic liaisons with local peasants—yes, it was possible.

Personnel would be needed. But he was not the only American-trained military officer in Latin America who had "opted for less restrictive employment." A certain Colombian colleague, for instance, had been one of the elite until human rights fanatics forced him out of the military for his involvement in a certain civilian massacre.

"It would not be cheap," Julio said. "Equipment would have to be acquired. Training sites built. The investment would be substantial."

"Money is no object," Khalil spoke up for the first time. "I will deal with that. You have only to concern yourself with the task."

Julio's mind was racing. Three days ago he had been picking his way through a prison alley without hope of relief. Now? This could go even further than the generous piece he'd had of the Cortéz drug operation. Purchasing arms and equipment. Construction materials. The movement of men and goods in and out of Ciudad del Este. Julio had the necessary contacts, and at every juncture there would be a commission for him. All this on top of the generous salary he had been promised.

What these men chose to do with the training was immaterial. Their success or failure would not be on Julio's shoulders. Best of all, it would be a perfect revenge on the Americans.

"There would have to be a pretext." By Julio's tone the other men knew he'd accepted the job. "The Americans have eyes and ears even this far from their borders. And they have many allies. We cannot openly bring your people here to train."

"We have already thought of that." Khalil tossed a handful of brightly colored brochures onto the couch beside Julio. Picking one up, Julio leafed through the glossy images with growing approbation. "This is brilliant. It will allow for all things, even the movement of equipment and men. And if attention becomes focused on us, it will be easy to deny and even dismantle."

"My son's idea." Mozer Jebai motioned toward Saleh. "Negotiations to buy out the previous owners have just been completed."

Julio looked over at the younger man with new interest. Perhaps the boy did have leadership potential. Julio's eyes narrowed consideringly. If he were to do this, there must be recognition of his authority. He would not be a lackey to these men.

"There is one more thing. An important tool of a Special Operations soldier is invisibility, the ability to blend in to one's surroundings so as not to be noticed."

There was no comprehension in Saleh's cold stare, but Sheik Jebai was already nodding as Julio jerked his head toward the younger man. "The beard goes."

"Done." The mullah rose in a clear dismissal that brought the others to their feet as well. "Khalil, you will take Colonel Vargas to discuss the arrangements that must be made. Saleh—"

He stopped his son with a gesture as the other two men exited the room.

"Father," Saleh burst out angrily as soon as the door was shut. "How can you allow this man to ask me to defile my faith by cutting my beard?"

"Because he is right. We all must do what is necessary to make a success of this mission—whatever it may be. Do not forget that this is your choice." Giving his son a speculative look, Mozer Jebai added quietly, "Tell me, son, what would you have done if he had refused? He knows our plans."

Saleh stared at him. "I would have killed him, of course. Now if you will excuse me, Father, there is much to be done."

Mozer Jebai shook his head slowly as Saleh stormed from the office. No, his son was not the quiet, devout boy who had gone to Afghanistan.

Stepping to the window, the mullah watched until Saleh emerged onto the sidewalk below and strode off down the street. This Julio Vargas had been more positive about the possibilities of his son's plan than Jebai had anticipated. Was it possible this might indeed work? That a true blow might be struck against the enemies of Allah? Would the return be worth the enormous investment of finances and other resources it would take?

Whatever his dreams for his son, Mozer Jebai had not resisted Saleh's decision to join the jihad. Such a decision was deeply personal, between a man and Allah himself, and to choose holy war brought honor not only to himself but to his family. As a spiritual leader, the mullah knew his son's destiny had been sealed before his birth, and if Allah had fated him to be a holy warrior—perhaps even a martyr—then *"insha Allah."* Allah's will be done. One could not fight what was written.

But the mullah was also a father with an only son whom he loved.

A son who had, beyond expectation, been returned to him.

If nothing else, Saleh's extraordinary plan offered the possibility of a future instead of certain martyrdom.

And for that, Sheik Mozer Jebai would happily spend all that he possessed.

Chapter Five

A siren screamed.

Wandering restlessly to the living room window, Sara pushed back the drapes. The street outside was empty, but from somewhere beyond the identical plantation-style houses that made up this Miami gated community, the siren was growing louder, then fading as it raced by.

Police? Ambulance? Fire engine? Never before these last months had Sara seen so much evidence of all three. Especially the police.

One couldn't step outside the community gates without seeing police cars everywhere, cruising the streets, patrolling parking lots, sitting outside schools and grocery stores. And not just one variety. There were green and white Miami-Dade police cruisers. Brown state troopers. White with blue shields of the City of Miami police. Dade County school police. "Rent-a-cop" security vehicles.

As for the sirens, they seemed to be part of every hour, day or night.

Was Miami's overpowering law enforcement presence a good sign or bad?

Speaking of which—

Pushing the drape further aside, Sara leaned forward. *Where are you?*

"You might as well get used to it," Cynthia said from across the room. "You go falling in love with a narcotics agent, you'd better plan on a lot of waiting. And broken promises."

Sara spun from the window, annoyed she'd given away her impatience.

Doug's mother was pedaling furiously on a stationary bike set up in the middle of the living room. The exercise was intended to keep her from smoking. The house still had a faint scent of past relapses, but those were coming further apart now, and Sara had grown used to seeing Cynthia jump onto the bike when the cravings got too strong for her Nicorette.

Dropping into an armchair, Sara picked up a magazine. "We still have time. I—Doug just thought he'd be home early."

After all, he'd already been out most of the night on some sort of raid. When he'd called earlier, it was to say he was cutting his day short and expected to be home by mid-afternoon. Today was Doug's thirty-first birthday as well as the four-month anniversary of their return from Bolivia. Sara's own birthday—number twenty-three—was in just two days. To celebrate all three milestones, Cynthia and Sara had made reservations at one of Miami's more exclusive South Beach restaurants. Reservations that would be wasted if they didn't leave soon.

You go falling in love with a narcotics agent . . .

An image of Doug's strong features superimposed itself over the magazine page. Was Sara falling in love with Doug? Was this the reason for her unease, the nagging of something missing when Doug wasn't with her, the release of tension every time he walked in alive and well? It was all so afield from the breathless, impetuous passion with which Nicolás had exploded into her life. She could not be sure what she was feeling.

Do I want to?

That first night in Miami, Sara had been sure she'd at last left the trauma of the past behind her. But whether it was Doug's story, the eeriness of those carnival rides, or just the inevitable wearing off of adrenaline, the evening had instead been the beginning of an emotional battle that left Sara numb to anything or anyone beyond her own pain and loss.

The sheer momentum of the rescue operation, the frenzy of interrogation, and the media blitz that followed, had not allowed Sara time to assimilate, much less mourn, her altered circumstances. And though reason told her Nicolás had not deserved her love or her grief, Sara found that she did grieve. Not only for the death of her young husband, whom she'd passionately, if misguidedly, adored, but also for the dreams he represented. Dreams of the man she had believed him to be. Of family and home and future.

The activity of the daytime hours made them bearable, though the drone of a helicopter overhead, or a burst of firecrackers from children playing down the street brought flashbacks that left her shaking until she learned to suppress her startled responses. But after Doug went home to his apartment, Cynthia retired to her room, and Sara was curled up alone in Cynthia's guest bed, her carefully erected defenses could no longer stand against the flood of hurt and anger and grief. What followed were storms of weeping, until Sara, lying spent and exhausted in the dark, felt there could not possibly be any tears left in her.

But there always were.

Sleep brought no relief, only nightmares. Horrifying images of broken bodies. An Uzi spitting yellow flames against the night. Scrabbling and crawling endlessly through dank vegetation. The terror of unseen pursuit at her heels. Sara soon grew to dread sleep as much as the hours of tossing and turning.

In all of this, Doug had been wonderful. Taking his accumulated leave and vacation time—a full six weeks—he'd been at Sara's side except to sleep. Almost daily, he had driven Sara out to stroll along the sandy beaches or swim in the lazy, warm surf—sometimes with Cynthia along, but more often not. They'd gotten up early one morning to watch the dawn come up over the Atlantic and then drove over to Florida's west coast to see the sun set in the Gulf of Mexico. Away from his law enforcement responsibilities, Doug was more relaxed than Sara had ever seen him, and he'd tolerantly played tourist with her at the Orlando theme parks and the Kennedy Space Center.

It was something of a shock when Sara realized partway through an Everglades tour that she was enjoying herself. She'd already discovered that Doug was not the taciturn, humorless person she'd once judged him to be. But she hadn't expected him to be as companionable and articulate as he proved. He deliberately drew Sara out whenever she retreated back into introspection, though they both steered clear of any mention of Bolivia or the past few months. But any other subject was fair game. And if USAID's alternative development program was a hotly debated point, similar tastes in spicy foods, science fiction, and a good political-suspense novel were more critical issues. Catching a certain gleam in Doug's eye during a heated political debate, Sara had her suspicions that he was choosing contrary positions, not out of conviction, but for the sheer pleasure of seeing Sara stirred up.

Doug also took Sara to the neighborhood church where he'd married Julie and been introduced to God. And though the members had dearly loved Doug's wife, they welcomed Sara warmly. The pastor had introduced Sara to a trauma counselor, who was one of the church's members. But despite the psychologist's kindness and by-the-book answers, Sara felt he could not understand the world she'd emerged from, and after the first session she did not go back.

Still, as one sunny Miami day slid into another, then into weeks, Sara began to relax and stopped looking over her shoulder. And if grief and pain lingered, it became easier to push them below the surface. Even the nightmares lost their intensity, until one morning Sara woke up refreshed and realized that an entire night had passed without dreams or thoughts of the past.

Another debt of gratitude she owed to Doug Bradford.

Was she in love with Doug, as Cynthia clearly assumed?

Was Doug in love with her?

Certainly he'd done for her, and been to her, far more than any bond between victim and rescuer might obligate. Yet in all these months he had scrupulously adhered to the promise he'd made in Santa Cruz, asking no more of Sara than undemanding friendship, as if he understood only too well her ambivalence, the flinching away from letting anyone close to her bruised heart and soul. There were even times when Sara wondered whether Doug had forgotten that moment in Laura Histed's living room when it seemed the promise of dawn was returning to her heart.

Then would come an instant—in the middle of an animated discussion or stretched out companionably together reading a book—when Sara lifted her eyes unexpectedly to find Doug's eyes on her with a look of such patient, somber *waiting* that a lump rose to her throat.

He hasn't forgotten. He's just waiting for me to get over Nicky like he had to get over Julie.

Sara suddenly realized she'd read the *Newsweek* article through twice without absorbing a single word and slapped the magazine shut. *I want to love him. I should love him. How could I not?*

When had she first even recognized a return of feeling to her numbed heart? She'd missed Doug more than she'd expected when he returned to work. But vacation couldn't last forever, and Sara was neither so selfish nor unrealistic to expect him to remain indefinitely at her side.

His first assignment was a three-week TDY, or "temporary duty assignment," back to Bolivia, during which he'd testified in various closed courtrooms regarding the Cortéz operation and closed out the files of other cases in which he was involved. Doug's official reassignment to the Miami division office had come through with his return from Bolivia, and his hours soon became erratic enough Sara that never knew when she might see him.

Cynthia hadn't allowed Sara time to mope, dragging her into her interior decorating projects. The older woman's frenetic pace proved a welcome distraction, and the money she insisted on paying Sara for her labor allowed her to replenish her wardrobe.

When Doug did have a day—or even hours—off, he was always there. At Christmas, he'd taken off almost a week. It seemed even drug dealers took a breather from their illicit activities during the holiday season. It was Sara's first Christmas within a family unit since her father's death, and she'd reveled in the baking and decorating and shopping, the Christmas programs and cantatas, and the flood of aunts and uncles and cousins on Christmas Day. And one magical moment on Christmas night, after the relatives had gone and Cynthia was in the kitchen, Doug had reached out a long arm, as if his iron control had at last worn thin, and pulled Sara under a sprig of mistletoe.

But that was three weeks ago.

Briiinng!!

Startled into dropping the *Newsweek,* Sara jumped to her feet as Cynthia, without slowing her furious pedaling, snatched up a cordless phone from the coffee table. *At last!*

But Cynthia's tightening lips told Sara it wasn't Doug even before she held out the phone. "For you, Sara. A Jan Thornton."

Jan Thornton? *Aunt Jan!* Sara had dutifully tried to contact her closest relative once she was settled into Cynthia's house. But it had proved more difficult than she'd expected. Jan Thornton was not in the phone directory of the D.C. suburb from which Sara had received the wedding card. Nor had Sara made a real effort to track her down during those first traumatic weeks.

Then it had occurred to her that some of her cousins might still be living in the Seattle area. Calling up the on-line directory, she'd simply started calling all Thorntons named Joseph, John, or Tom in the Pacific Northwest. Seattle had proved a dry well, but she'd hit pay dirt in Richland, where it turned out her oldest cousin, Joe, was now a captain in the Richland fire department.

At least ten years older than Sara, Joe had been long gone from home by the time Sara and her father had moved to Seattle. In the armed forces somewhere, if Sara remembered right. If they'd crossed paths at family gatherings, it hadn't registered. Her cousin had expressed no surprise to find Sara back in the States, and Sara wondered if he even knew she'd been married and out of the country. He'd promised to pass on her new phone number to Aunt Jan.

That was two months ago.

"Hello, Sara." Her aunt's brisk tone was exactly as Sara remembered. "I was glad to get your phone number from Joe. I'd been wondering how you were doing, dear. Forgive me for taking so long to get back to you. End of the year audits, you know. You wouldn't believe what people try to get away with. Now— Joe says you're living in Miami. I must say that was a surprise. And your husband—Nicolás, wasn't it? Is he with you?"

"Nicky's dead, Aunt Jan," Sara answered in a credibly even voice. Had Joe really not told her, or had she just not listened?

"Oh dear! Yes, Joe did say something about him passing away. I'm so sorry. Though of course I had a feeling it wouldn't last. They don't, you know. Green card marriages, I mean."

Sara bit her tongue to keep back a sharp retort.

"At least this way you're left with some good memories instead of having it end in a messy divorce like too many others in your shoes. And with kids caught in some foreign custody battle." Her aunt added sharply, "You aren't pregnant, are you? That isn't why you contacted me?"

"No, Aunt Jan." *Next thing she'll be telling me how lucky I am my husband died! But then, maybe she really thinks so.* Sara tried to dredge up one memory of the man who had been her uncle by marriage for so many years and realized she couldn't. *Uncle Jack? Or was it Jerry?*

"Anyway, I don't know if Joe told you, but I've moved back out to the Seattle area. To be near the grandkids. And now that you're home again, dear, you should come out for a visit. The babies are so sweet, and your cousins' wives are decent girls. You really should get to know them. After all, we are the only family you have. I mean, really, Sara, we've hardly seen you in years."

As if that's my fault! Sara listened impatiently as Aunt Jan chronicled her sons' doings. John, who was teaching high school English in Portland. Tom, recently married and finishing a Ph.D. in accounting at Washington State. Only when she'd finished did Aunt Jan add belatedly, "So what exactly did happen to—what was his name?—Nicky? Joe didn't say."

"He was shot." Sara didn't even try to explain. For one, Doug might be trying to get through. "Aunt Jan, I'm afraid I have to go. I'll get back to you on a visit."

But even as she hung up, Sara knew she wouldn't. She debated whether to laugh or cry. Four months ago, it would have been the latter. But time and the Bradfords had taken much of the sting out of Aunt Jan's tactlessness. Dropping the phone onto the armchair, Sara wandered back over to the window.

Yes, these months with Doug and Cynthia had been good ones and healing ones. Sara had felt protected and cherished and welcomed as never before . . . not even during those first hopeful weeks of married life that had taken her to a strange country and people.

Maybe too protected.

As Sara pushed aside the drapes, her mind flashed to the other memorable event of the Christmas season. Doug kept his personal life firmly separated from his job, and the Miami DO Christmas party was the first time Sara had met any of Doug's associates. She'd been at once impressed with and rather wistful of the camaraderie between the agents, even the female agents who looked as whipcord tough as the men.

Doug was chatting with Peggy Browning, the Miami DO's Public Information Officer, when Sara, momentarily alone and shy about intruding on conversations around her, had drifted over to his side. The two agents were talking over a particularly messy case, and Doug was tossing back Peggy's scathing and pungently colorful observations with a sardonic banter he never used with Sara. He'd broken off the discussion when he caught sight of Sara. "Hey, let's not spoil the evening with blood and gore."

Doug had made the proper introductions and the three conversed cordially for few minutes. At one point, Sara noticed Peggy slanting her an odd look, and when Doug stepped away to greet another agent, Peggy had made a remark that Sara wouldn't soon forget. In a tone that was not unfriendly but cool and uncompromising, she'd said, "Doug's one of the best. Don't you dare clip his wings."

Sara had smiled noncommittally, but the remark made her self-conscious. What did the other agents think of her, the female civilian Doug had brought back from his last assignment? They had to know about Nicolás. It was all in the case files. Did they resent her? Disapprove?

I don't want to clip his wings! I would never want to change who he is!

And yet—

If Sara wasn't sure just when the first warmth of feeling had begun thawing the numbness of her emotions, she knew to the instant when fear had followed. She'd been watching the evening news when a clip shifted to the Miami docks where a young female reporter was announcing Florida's biggest drug seizure of the year. The cameras were positioned to give a clear view of a Coast Guard patrol cutter moored next to a small cargo freighter. The officers leading away a number of handcuffed Hispanics wore Coast Guard uniforms, but Sara spotted several others in black slickers with DEA lettered in white across the back ducking down into the hold of the confiscated freighter. Though the camera shot was from the rear, Sara would have recognized the set of Doug's shoulders and the lean grace of his body movements from any angle.

Sara hadn't been concerned. This was Doug's job, after all, and her initial response was thankfulness that one more bunch of drug dealers would be off the street.

Then the reporter, frustrated in her attempts to thrust a mike at the arresting officers, had broken into an excited description of a gun battle between the patrol cutter and drug runners. Though she hadn't wangled a firsthand account, her cameraman had come up with ample footage of the damage that gunfire had inflicted on both boats.

That was the night Sara's nightmares had returned. Only this time it wasn't Nicolás lying broken and bleeding on the gravel, but Doug. *You're being silly,* Sara told herself repeatedly. *Doug knows how to take care of himself.*

But the fear had only grown, twisting at her stomach when a phone call prompted Doug to slide his Glock into a shoulder holster and head for his car, leaving her restless and unable to concentrate while he was at work, keeping her awake at night when a blocked signal on his cell phone alerted her and Cynthia that he was out on a raid.

Does this mean I'm in love with him—that I am so afraid when he goes out on a case? If it does, I . . . I don't know if I can bear it!

Instinctively, Sara leaned forward to peer further down the street.

"That's why I left his father, you know."

Sara dropped the drape as if it were on fire. Slowly, she swung around to face Doug's mother. Stripping the sweatband from her forehead, Cynthia used it to wipe her face without slowing her pedaling on the exercise bike.

"You said Doug told you about the ranch we used to have down on the Arizona-Mexico border. Did he tell you about the shootout?"

Sara nodded. It had been the pivotal event that turned Doug toward law enforcement and eventually into the DEA—two federal officers shot down in his yard by druggies using the Bradford ranch as a border crossing.

"That was when his father—my ex—got involved with the border patrol. He took courses, became an agent, the whole shebang, just so he could patrol his little piece of the border. When he wasn't working the ranch, he was going out after the smugglers who were coming across. Even apart from the danger to our family, if one of those druggies or wetbacks had decided on revenge, he was never home. We couldn't even count on him to show up for his own birthday party or Christmas. So—"

Old resentment lingered in Cynthia's voice as she pumped savagely on the pedals. "I gave him a choice. The border patrol or us. He wouldn't budge . . . fed me this line about defending his family. So I packed up myself and Doug—Arizona courts were old-fashioned back then about maternal custody rights—and came back here to my family. Sure enough, my ex was dead within a few years. I sold the ranch and never looked back. I never dreamed Doug would follow his father into law enforcement. But Doug is as stubborn as his father."

Sara stifled a sigh at the bitterness of her tone. She had grown to like and respect Doug's mother—and she had assured him of that. Cynthia was intelligent, well-informed, and hardworking, characteristics that were making her foray into home decorating a resounding success. Despite a caustic tongue that gave no quarter to pretension or indolence, she was a soft touch for anyone with a genuine need. She was also strong-willed, supremely confident of her own opinions, and far too independent and easily bored to tolerate being confined behind a desk.

She was, in fact, far more like her son than she liked to admit. But where in Doug, tragedy and grief had led to a bedrock of faith and strength on which Sara herself had leaned these last months, Cynthia had allowed the vicissitudes of life to sour her into bitterness and acidity. For all that she had presently going for her, and her kindness to Sara, Cynthia always seemed vaguely unhappy, as if life were engaged in an ongoing conspiracy to keep her from enjoying it.

Still, in this at least, Sara could sympathize with Doug's mother—though her growing antipathy toward Doug's chosen profession was not the same as Cynthia's. As a Cortéz wife, she'd grown accustomed to long hours and days of waiting on the males of the household. At least Doug's absences involved doing something constructive for society instead of tearing it down.

No, it wasn't the long work hours that Sara minded about Doug's job. *If I could just know he's safe!*

As if Cynthia had the faculty of reading Sara's thoughts—another trait she shared with her son—she spoke up again, this time letting the pedals rest and swinging herself off the exercise bike. "If you really love him," she said sharply, "you'll tell him to quit this crazy job. And if he really loves you, he'll do it."

Sara visualized a certain unyielding jawline and tried to imagine ordering Doug to quit his job—or anything else. "What about Julie?" she asked suddenly. "Did she ask him to quit?"

"Julie!" Cynthia snorted as she reached for a hand towel to wipe herself off. "She egged him on—encouraged every new level he went for. And just look what happened."

But it was Julie, not Doug, who died—in a traffic accident. And his father died of pancreatic cancer, not on the job.

The illogic of her comment struck Cynthia just as it did Sara. Catching herself short, she bit her lip. "I didn't mean to say anything against Julie. She and Bonnie were Doug's life—and mine too." Tossing down the towel, she let out a deep breath that transformed her from an embittered woman to a worried mother. "It's just—Doug's had his share of grief. I don't want anything else to hurt him."

Neither do I! Sara swung around again to look out the window, no longer trying to conceal her concern. A car was turning onto the street. Not Doug's.

"Look, if you're worried, why don't you just give his office a call?" Snatching up the cordless phone, Cynthia tossed it to Sara. "I can assure you they're well used to frantic family members. Try 'one' on the speed dial."

Sara took the phone with some reluctance. It hadn't even occurred to her to use the number Doug had given her for the Miami DO. It seemed so . . . pushy. And if he was busy . . .

Under Cynthia's penetrating eye, she pressed the key for the speed dial. The phone rang repeatedly, and she was about to hang up when a harried female voice came on the line. "Drug Enforcement Administration. How may I direct your call?"

"Hi," Sara said hesitantly. To be asking for a DEA agent on duty because he was late for a date seemed suddenly inexcusably frivolous. "This is Sara Connor. Is . . . is Doug Bradford available?"

The voice on the other end did not seem to find her query out of line. "Oh, hi, Sara. Of course, we met at the Christmas party. This is Karla, remember me? No, I'm sorry, but Doug isn't available. He—uh, isn't on the premises at the moment."

"Uh, okay . . . it's no big deal, but today's Doug's birthday, and he thought he'd be home hours ago. Would it be okay to leave a message?"

"If he calls in, I'll let him know you called." Karla's voice disappeared abruptly off the line, then returned. "Look, Sara, don't worry about Doug. As far as I know, he's perfectly fine. I'll have him call as soon as he makes contact. Now, if you'll excuse me, things are a little hectic around here right now."

Sara stared at the phone in her hand as it went dead. *As soon as he makes contact?* From where? How was it that he was out of contact with his own office? And despite the hurried cordiality, Sara had read tension as well in the voice at the other end of the line.

The dial tone had now been replaced by an insistent beeping. Sara pushed the disconnect button. Apprehension again squeezed at her stomach.

What aren't they telling me? Doug, where are you?

Chapter Six

Doug was in a warehouse parking lot, and things weren't going as planned. Not a new scenario, but an annoying turn.

Shifting his long legs to ease a cramp, Doug spared a glance at his partner behind the wheel of the late-model Lexus. Mike Garcia was younger and slighter than Doug, with good-looking, olive features, and dark hair tied back in a ponytail. His white suit shouted money, as did the three gold knuckle rings, neck chain, and Rolex. The stereotype of a Colombian drug dealer—except that the jewelry, clothing, and car had been requisitioned from Seizures and would have to be returned after the op.

Doug didn't need to check the mirror to know he presented a similar image. Or had. Their contact was almost two hours late, and though they had periodically started the engine to run the air-conditioning, the sun radiating off the parking lot's asphalt had turned the Lexus into a furnace. Under his suit coat, Doug could feel the sweat trickling down his back and only hoped he didn't look as wilted and red-faced as his companion.

Or as nervous.

Doug straightened up as a brown four-door sedan nosed around the corner of the storage facility and proceeded down the street. A Caprice Classic. Not a vehicle he recognized, but Doug didn't need to run a license check to know that this was their contact. He could feel the eyes of its two occupants on the Lexus as the Caprice cruised slowly past.

At the end of the block, the Caprice stopped. Doug made the same swift survey of the parking lot that he knew the sedan's occupants were making. Personally, he didn't like the layout of this place and had proposed a location with less civilian population around. But the CI—confidential informant—who'd set up this meet had, as was too often the case, been more eager to accommodate the bad guys than the law enforcement agency for whom he was supposed to be working.

From the contact's point of view, it was a reasonable choice. The warehouse complex, row after row of huge rectangular units, was a new one. Most of the units were being used for storage, making for little daytime traffic except an occasional cargo truck.

Better yet, the newest row, built in an L-shaped cul-de-sac that formed the end of the complex, wasn't rented out yet. The metal doors of the units behind the Lexus were all shut and locked, and the parking lot was empty.

For the DEA and police units setting up the afternoon's sting operation, the place was less satisfactory. As the bad guys no doubt intended, the empty lot prevented any surveillance units from being stationed close by. Worse, the lot fronted the back side of a strip mall, and the only through-street into the complex ran between a McDonald's on one side and an Exxon station on the other. And though the only business openly operating out of the warehouses was a body shop, whose client vehicles filled the street two buildings down from the Lexus, an enormous sign at the far end announced the presence of Octaviano's Gymnastics, one of Miami's top-ranked gymnastics clubs.

To compensate, Doug had insisted on setting the deal for 1 P.M., allowing time for the McDonald's lunch crowd to thin out and for the entire operation to be long over before children started showing up for gymnastics. But with the two-hour delay, both the McDonald's and the gas station would soon be filling up with after-school customers, and Doug had already seen two minivans turn in to deposit kids at Octaviano's.

Not that any physical confrontation was expected. Still, one always worked under the assumption that Murphy's Law just might come into play. *Anything that can go wrong, will.*

Sliding down into his seat beyond sight of spying eyes, Doug flipped open a cell phone and punched in a set of numbers. The ubiquitous little handheld devices had to a large degree replaced the old Motorola hand radios in stakeouts. They were not only harder to tap into but a whole lot easier to explain if the bad guys noticed.

"It's getting late. Too many civilians. I think we should consider calling it off."

Over the windowsill, Doug could see a red Firebird Trans Am down the street at the body shop. The two mechanics bent over the engine were not the shop's usual employees. They were DEA group supervisor Norm Kublin, and a Miami-Dade PD narcotics unit officer. The Firebird belonged to Doug's present partner, Mike Garcia, who had lovingly restored the classic car as his duty vehicle. A white van parked between the body shop and the Lexus, but not so close as to be conspicuous, held the takedown team.

Two other undercover cars were stationed at the Exxon and McDonald's, ostensibly in line for gas and fast food. Doug was reminded that he was missing his own birthday dinner. If he'd known the waiting would go on this long, he'd have called home. Or had the office call. Maybe even now it wouldn't be too late.

"No, they're moving now," Norm Kublin's clipped tones crackled in Doug's ear. "We've got time."

The Caprice was rolling again, slowly still, but toward the Lexus. Mike had parked well away from the storage unit so that the car sat out in the open with plenty of space all around, a conciliatory maneuver that made it evident they were alone. The Caprice circled around to pull up parallel but several car widths away from the Lexus.

From the end of the L-shaped set of storage units, Doug glimpsed movement. A green and white fender overshooting its stop in the same dirt alley from which the Caprice had emerged. The fender immediately reversed from sight as the driver recognized the mistake, but Doug didn't have to see the vehicle to know what was there. The last piece they'd been waiting for. A Miami-Dade police cruiser.

Norm Kublin's curt tone crackled in Doug's ear. "The cruiser is in position. It's a go! You copy that? It's a go!"

"We copy." Doug dismissed birthday celebration and all other extraneous thoughts from his mind. Time to focus. "Okay, showtime!" He switched the cell phone to vibrate mode. Reaching for the door, he glanced over at his partner. "And for heaven's sake, Mike, relax. You look stiff as road kill in a Montana winter."

Doug kept his hands spread wide as he stepped out into the open space between the two vehicles, though his fingers itched for the Smith and Wesson at the small of his back. Mike followed his lead. So did the occupants of the Caprice—two skinny, dark-complected Latinos, enough alike to be twins.

This was the dangerous part of every deal with an unknown contact. Did you trust the other guy or go for your weapon? And you knew the other guy was asking himself the same question.

Both sides had to trust somewhat in order for drugs or money to change hands. But there was always the chance of a rip-off or a police setup. So both sides kept a suspicious distance and a figurative hand on their weapons until they were not only clear with the goods, but had processed them—either banking the money in their offshore account or selling the drugs without a search warrant showing up at their door.

Only then could a relationship of mutual benefit, if not trust, be established for future deals. And since drug dealing tended to be a short-lived though profitable career choice—odds were high of ending up dead or in prison—negotiating new partners was a continual process.

Doug tried to visualize the scene through his contacts' eyes. Was there anything that would trigger suspicion? The only modification the undercover team had made was a few random piles of packing crates stacked in front of the storage unit behind the vehicles, the only place they'd been able to rig a camera.

Ideally there would be at least one more undercover vehicle at the far end of the storage unit. But it would've been too conspicuous because there was nothing back there but a dirt alley that petered out into an empty area where cement mixers and other heavy equipment had been stationed during the construction project.

The two Latinos—Colombia #1 and #2, Doug dubbed them—made the first move, crossing the distance between the two vehicles. Neither offered a handshake. Building trust didn't extend that far.

"I am Lucas Montero. This is my brother, Eduardo." The musical rise and fall of the young man's Spanish confirmed his Colombian origin. "You are the Miguel Lopez with whom I spoke on the phone? A mutual acquaintance, Juan Padilla, informs us you have merchandise in which we may be interested."

Juan Padilla was the confidential informant who'd set up the deal. The victim of a sting operation himself two years earlier, he'd jumped at his present employment as part of a plea deal to avoid a prison cell. Doug was under no illusion that the man had suffered any genuine change of heart, but Padilla had proven to be a pragmatist with no particular loyalty to his former colleagues. To date, he'd delivered up a number of arrests without his change of allegiance being discovered.

"*Si*, I am Miguel Lopez." Of Colombian parents, Mike was actually Miami-born. He nodded toward Doug. "My pilot, *Señor* Jake Larson, who in the future will be handling my business."

What followed was the standard choreography of virtually any drug deal. Mike and Doug walked around to the rear of the Lexus. The two Colombians followed. Opening the trunk, Mike lifted out a package the size and shape of a kilo bag of powdered sugar. Colombian #1 held it to his nose and sniffed while the other investigated the trunk where nine more identical packages were displayed. Ten kilos of pure Colombian cocaine, also requisitioned from Seizures.

"It is the highest quality," Mike assured the buyers. "We have the resources to move up to one hundred kilos a month."

Is the camera catching all this? Doug restrained himself from looking over his shoulder as he returned the cocaine to the trunk, glancing instead at his partner. Sweat was streaming down the younger agent's face, and Doug could only hope the Colombians would read his rigid expression as resulting from the heat and usual tension of the meet.

Mike Garcia had not been Doug's preferred choice for this op. Unlike Doug, he hadn't come into the DEA through the ranks of either law enforcement or the military, but by the third avenue for applying to the agency—a graduate degree in a field the DEA needed. In Mike's case, a masters in biochemical engineering.

Mike was a bright kid and had of course been through the prerequisite agent training. What he didn't have was street savvy. This was, in fact, his first undercover takedown. But he spoke fluent Spanish and could pass for the Colombian-born drug dealer he was supposed to be.

The next step in the choreography was for the four men to walk over to the Caprice, where they would presumably be shown the cash payment for the ten kilos. Once both sides were satisfied, in a real deal there would then be a quick exchange of trunk contents, and the two cars would speed off in opposite directions, the whole thing having taken no more than a few minutes.

But this was where the deal departed from its usual pattern. Out of the corner of his eye, Doug saw one of the Firebird mechanics straighten up to wipe his forehead. Norm Kublin's tip-off coincided with the scream of a siren. Racing out from the alley, the green and white police cruiser squealed to a broadside in front of the two cars.

The front doors slammed open, and two men in the brown uniforms of the Miami-Dade police leveled handguns over the top of the doors. The one on the driver's side barked, "Police. Get your hands in the air. You're under arrest."

Gotcha! Doug thought with silent satisfaction as his hands shot into the air.

Even as he kept his hands high, Doug memorized the faces of the two patrolmen. The driver was a tall, light-skinned black with a Caribbean lilt to his speech. The other was short, stocky, and Hispanic. Cuban, Doug guessed. Together they represented a reasonable demographic of the Miami-Dade police force.

"Hand over your weapons."

Easing out the Smith and Wesson, Doug laid it on the ground in front of him. Mike did the same with an Uzi machine pistol. The two Colombians added a pair of semiautomatics. While the black patrolman's weapon continued to provide cover, Cuba came forward to kick the guns out of reach and give his captives a pat-down, beginning with Doug and Mike. He removed two ankle pistols with a satisfied smirk before moving on to a perfunctory search of the two Colombians.

"You two. Empty the trunk."

The black patrolman reached inside the police cruiser to pop the trunk as the two Colombians rushed to ferry the cocaine from the Lexus to the patrol car. The real Jake Larson, the ex-con charter pilot whose persona Doug had put together for this operation, would be livid with helpless rage by now, though too macho to let it show. Doug could only hope his own tension would be interpreted as anger. They were almost there. If all went well, there wouldn't even be a confrontation. The two patrolmen would drive off with their haul, tailed by one of the waiting undercover units. The Colombian dealers would do the same.

A day or so later, when these two couldn't scream that they just hadn't gotten around to filing a report, there'd be a knock at their door, the videotape produced as evidence, their bank accounts seized, and two more dirty cops would be spending their retirement behind bars.

The two Colombians placed the last packages of cocaine in the cruiser's trunk. The giveaway to their complicity in the shakedown was that the rogue cops didn't even order them to get the payoff money that should have been in the trunk of the Caprice. But they continued to play the charade, the patrolmen waving their accomplices back to join Mike and Doug.

We've got you! You're going down! Doug exulted even as long practice maintained what he hoped was angry frustration on his face. He spared a glance at his partner. Mike was pale and looked nervous enough to throw up. But that would be expected in the circumstances. The kid had played his part well. In a few more minutes, Doug would tell him so.

That was when Murphy chose to strike.

The Colombians, eager to act their part, were backing up rapidly. Too rapidly. Number 2, Eduardo, came up hard against the stack of crates, his hip slamming into a corner protruding slightly out from the others. The crate wobbled, seemed to steady itself, then tipped slowly outward, carrying with it the crate above.

The crash froze all six men into startled immobility. So did the video camera now starkly exposed to view. On a movie screen it would have been a moment of comic relief. The horrified dismay of the two DEA agents. The bad guys' furious realization.

Then movement returned to the scene. The black patrolman's gun came up. "It's a setup," he screamed out.

Doug and Mike reacted just in time. Bullets slammed into the Lexus as they hit the ground behind the bumper. *Anything that can go wrong will!* Doug groaned inwardly as he grabbed the cell phone from his belt. "Move in! We've got a situation here!"

The information wasn't needed. Down the street, the Firebird was already shooting out of the mechanic's yard, the white van pulling away from the curb. But Doug's shouted order had the effect he intended.

"They've got backup. Let's get out of here." The black patrolman was already clambering into the driver's seat. The Colombians, no longer playing their roles, raced for their own vehicle. Number 1 had the engine gunned even as his brother tumbled into the passenger side. Cuba took time for a final blast at the Lexus before diving into the cruiser.

Doug and Mike waited only long enough to see the door slam before scrambling up and racing to climb into their own car. Tumbling in, Doug scrabbled under his seat for their backup weapons as Mike reached for the ignition. The bullets hadn't struck anything vital, and the engine roared instantly to life. The Lexus shot out after the other vehicles as Doug sat up with a Glock pistol in each hand. The Caprice was several car lengths ahead of the police cruiser, rocketing across the empty lot. Doug spotted the Firebird racing out to intercept it.

Mike did too—and recognized what his boss was planning to do. "He's going to wreck my car, he's going to wreck my car," he moaned even as he stomped on the gas pedal.

The Caprice hardly slowed. Mike let out another moan as the side of the Firebird crumpled under the impact. The heavier sedan didn't even look dented. It swerved a little but kept right on going. However, the Firebird's sacrifice had given the takedown team time to get between the Caprice and the exit to the street. Brakes screeched as Colombia #1 realized his predicament. As the Caprice skidded to a stop, the back of the van burst open. Rifle fire echoed through the warehouse complex as the Caprice shot into reverse.

Doug groaned again. The takedown team was the contribution of the local PD, and this particular precinct had a reputation of being a bunch of cowboys.

But opening fire in civilian territory with families and children around? What had been a routine and carefully orchestrated operation was rapidly degenerating into chaos.

But there was no time to worry about the locals' incompetence. The rogue cops had seen the situation ahead. Their U-turn lifted the police cruiser off two wheels. Doug slammed into the door, then forward against the dashboard as Mike duplicated the maneuver.

Great! We're going to crash, and I don't even have my seat belt on. Wouldn't that be an ironic way to break my neck!

But the Lexus rocked back onto its wheels as both vehicles jolted into the dirt alleyway that circled to the back of the warehouse construction area. As Mike fought the bumpy road, Doug managed to snap his seat belt into place, then reached over to do the same for his partner.

At least there was no exit from the construction road, just the main boulevard across a grassy bank where a sign warned Do Not Enter and three lanes of traffic were flashing by in the wrong direction.

Doug hadn't allowed for their quarry's desperation. Lights and siren went on as the police cruiser gunned its engine up over the bank. Cars began slamming to a stop as the cruiser bumped down onto the shoulder. Doug, holding on grimly as Mike followed hard on the police car's bumper, could only hope no one had been hurt.

The cruiser roared wrong-way up the shoulder a good fifty yards before reaching an intersection. The flashing lights had brought traffic to a halt, giving the cops clear passage as they tore across the intersection. A truck coming in the opposite direction slammed on its brakes as the Lexus swerved in front of it.

At least the kid could drive. Mike was handling the Lexus like an Indy pro, sticking like a leech only a few yards behind the police cruiser's rear bumper. Doug checked the specially modified nineteen-shot ammo clip in his Glock, then flipped open his cell phone. He was relieved to hear his GS on the other end.

"We got the Caprice. A lucky shot took out the windshield." Norm Kublin's dry tone made it clear he shared Doug's opinion of the locals' cowboy tactics. "Where are you?"

Doug read off the street sign that was flashing by.

"We've got backup coming after you," the GS said. "And I'm trying to raise the local boys now. But you're going to have to hang on alone for the next few minutes."

At least. The boulevard down which they were speeding had reached the outer limits of south Miami where u-pick truck gardens alternated with new suburban developments. As traffic dropped off, the police cruiser sped up accordingly, until the speedometer of the Lexus on its heels crept past 100 mph. With relief, Doug heard the scream of sirens behind them. The local boys.

But the rogue cops had ears too. The flashing police cruiser had been slowly pulling away from the Lexus until it had more than a fifty-yard lead. Now it used that advantage to swerve into the first crossroads.

Mike and Doug exchanged grim glances as the Lexus braked to follow. There were at least a dozen gated communities down that road. And any number of schools. All of which had now let out for the day. They could no longer afford to wait for backup. It was time to stop these maniacs before someone got hurt.

The abrupt turn—and Mike's superb driving—had served to close the gap. The Lexus was again at the cruiser's bumper and drawing up alongside when the two agents saw a grassy field to the left of the roadway. They looked at each other again. This was it. Doug braced himself as Mike gave a sharp twist of the wheel.

He'd gauged it perfectly. The impact was not great, though Doug cringed to think what Seizures was going to say when they got the Lexus back. But it was enough to send the cruiser into a swerve. The patrol car went up over the sidewalk and onto the grass. Doug caught a glimpse of Cuba's snarling face glancing back as the cruiser buried its hood in a hedge.

Mike was already slamming on the brakes. Leaving the engine running, the two agents climbed out, both through the passenger door. Keeping the body of the Lexus between themselves and their quarry, they leveled their weapons across the car roof. The two patrolmen were just now stumbling groggily out of the cruiser. Neither one seemed seriously hurt.

Making a hand into a megaphone, Doug called out, "This is the DEA. You are under arrest. Get your hands in the air and step away from the car."

The two rogue cops knew they were cooked. Caught flatfooted in the open with the hedge blocking any dash for escape, they turned around slowly, hands high in the air.

"Okay, careful now. Remove your weapons and toss them this way. You know the drill."

The two patrolmen let their handguns drop to the grass.

"Okay, move away from the vehicle." *Finally something going right!* But Doug had hardly finished the thought when he felt the metal frame of the Lexus lurch under his propped forearms.

65

Florida had few spots that weren't as flat as a pancake, its highest elevation being the landfill covering Miami-Dade's accumulated garbage, which locals had dubbed Mount Trashmore. But apparently the two agents had managed to find one. The residential street sloped downhill at a barely perceptible angle, but it was enough so that, as Doug straightened up, the car lurched again.

Then—no faster than a snail at first, but gathering momentum—the Lexus began to roll.

Mike and Doug exchanged stunned glances before throwing themselves at the side of the car. But the momentum was already too great. A moment later the two agents were standing completely exposed on the verge of the grass. For the second time in an hour, the four men stared at each other in astonished immobility.

Then the two rogue cops dove for their dropped weapons. Doug and Mike sprinted for the only cover in sight—a concrete sign announcing Miraflores Community Park. The two agents managed to get off a shot as they dove behind the sign. Doug winced as a volley of return fire smashed into the concrete.

"Tell me you put it into park!" he hissed, rolling over and back to a crouch. One glance at Mike's miserable face told the answer. But now was not the time for recriminations. Cautiously peering between two ornamental shrubs, he saw that the two rogue cops had taken cover behind the stalled cruiser. They were now at a standoff, neither side able to move without being exposed to the other's line of fire.

But the DEA agents had the advantage. Already, the sirens they had heard in the distance were screaming off the highway and down into the development. A dozen patrol cars swept past the Lexus, which had rolled to a stop against the curb, and screeched to a halt, some bouncing right up onto the grass to form a semicircular perimeter around the scene. As the clatter of assault rifles slamming across car roofs sounded across the open field, Doug tucked the Glock back into the small of his back and rose to his feet.

"DEA," he called out, raising a hand in acknowledgement to two patrol cars directly behind where the two agents had taken cover. "Glad you made it—thanks! Now if you can take these men into custody. . . ."

The circle of assault rifles did not waver, and Doug suddenly noticed that the cold eyes behind the weapons were not focused on the two rogue cops, but on Mike and him. A mega-phone bellowed, "You two behind the sign, throw down your weapons and step out into the open."

Murphy's Law again! This was not their promised backup, but an area unit called in by a roving patrol car or a nervous motorist. With sinking stomach, Doug realized how this must look. A pair of stereotypical scumbag drug dealers in a shootout with two upstanding fellow officers of the law. Cop killers. Glancing around at the grim faces and rifle muzzles, Doug knew he was as close to death as he had ever been.

"You are surrounded. Toss over your weapons and step away from that sign, or we *will* shoot you where you stand!" the officer with the megaphone bellowed.

A dozen bolt-action levers clicked back as Doug reached slowly into the small of his back for the Glock. Behind him, Mike's hands were high in the air, his weapon already tossed to the pavement. Gingerly dangling the handgun at arm's length, Doug let it fall to the grass. From the corner of his eye he saw the two rogue cops grasp their good fortune. Back on their feet, they were sidling away from the cruiser, weapons still in hand. A few more yards and they could make a dash behind the hedge, leaving two *real* armed criminals loose in a civilian neighborhood. Helpless frustration boiled up in Doug. This operation was turning into a disaster! Where was their backup?

"This is a DEA operation," he called out sharply. "Those men are under arrest. Do not let them get away!"

The rifles did not shift an inch. "Yeah, sure, and show us some ID!" a hard-faced patrolman called out from the nearest cruiser.

"I'll get it," Mike took a step forward, his narrow features still tight and apologetic. He was blaming himself for this, Doug knew. Doug's own attention was on the two rogue cops, especially the big, black leader. He didn't like the man's composure . . . he just wasn't worried enough!

Then Mike's comment registered. "No, wait—"

Realization hit Mike at the same instant. He froze, hand still going to his wallet. Doug caught the shift in the black patrolman's expression, and in that heightened sense that danger brings, read his swift appraisal. One, the two agents were carrying no ID except for that of a certain Colombian drug dealer and an ex-con named Jake Larson. Two, a couple of dead "drug dealers" could hardly give witness against a pair of uniformed officers. The "mistake" of their shooting could be written off as a reaction to Mike's "hostile" movement toward his hip pocket.

Mike! The gun came up before the warning could leave Doug's mind. He didn't realize he'd moved until his body slammed into his partner's. The blast came as they hit the ground. The impact of landing was greater than Doug had anticipated, oddly reminiscent of the time a bull calf had kicked him in the shoulder back on the Arizona ranch. Shoving himself free of his partner, Doug struggled to a sitting position.

Incredibly, Mike did not seem badly hurt. Already he was scrambling up, one hand scrabbling for the weapon he'd tossed away. Doug knew he should be doing the same, but the air must have been knocked out of him in the fall, because he was having a hard time drawing in a breath. With helpless inevitability, he watched the black rogue cop raise his gun again.

But a second volley of shots never came, because now at last the cavalry was arriving. With a fresh screaming of sirens, a cavalcade of Miami-Dade police cruisers and unmarked cars raced down the street and up onto the grass.

"DEA!"

Now there was plenty of ID in held-up badges and blazoned across black windbreakers.

"Those men are under arrest." At the harsh shout, the assault rifles at last began to move to cover the two cops.

Then another more urgent voice called, "We've got a man down."

Who? Doug wondered. Mike, after all, was on his feet now, his weapon back in his hand. The black windbreakers sprinting toward them seemed strangely distant, but above Doug, Mike's face was sharply focused, the narrow features white with rage, the grip of his knuckles equally white, and still with that heightened sense Doug knew what he was about to do even as the Glock came up.

"No, don't do it, Mike!" His hand clamped on Mike's wrist, taut as steel under his grip. "He's dropped his gun."

Only then did pain hit him like a sword thrust. Mike looked down as Doug groaned, and the killing rage ebbed from his face. "Doug, you're hit! Get the paramedics over here!" he called frantically. "Man down!"

Dropping the Glock, he grabbed at Doug as Doug's hand slid from his wrist. Through a gathering haze, Doug saw red spread across Mike's hands and white suit as the younger agent eased him backward onto the grass. Only when he saw the worried faces above him did it begin to register that it wasn't Mike's blood but his own.

I've been shot. He narrowed his eyes to focus. Mike's face just above his was tight with misery and anger. Doug opened his mouth to reassure the younger agent, but he couldn't find the breath to speak. Giving up, he closed his eyes, allowing the red haze to carry him away from the pain and down into darkness.

Chapter Seven

Cynthia strolled into the living room, having exchanged her exercise leotard for a hot-pink pant suit and high heels. She glanced at the flaring gypsy skirt and chiffon blouse that Sara had on, then noticed Sara's expression. "Still no word?"

Walking over to the entertainment center, Cynthia turned on the TV. The local news was giving its usual rundown of the day's disasters. A three-car pileup on the Dolphin Expressway. A shooting in Little Havana. Another bank robbery in West Kendall.

"I rescheduled our reservation." A furrow that ran across Cynthia's forehead spoiled the smooth finish of her makeup. "Men can be so inconsiderate! Don't tell me there wasn't a single break when he could've given us a call. Or had that secretary at the DO do it. Oh, my—"

Sara was paying little heed to either Cynthia's grumbling or the litany of Miami crime life, but Cynthia's horrified gasp brought her hurrying over to the TV. A "Breaking News" banner was flashing across the bottom of a chaotic street scene. Sara counted at least a dozen police cruisers, unmarked cars, and fire and rescue vehicles. Uniformed police and the black windbreakers of federal agents swarmed between the vehicles. It was a familiar news scene for any Miami resident, and only the large white *DEA* lettered across the back of the jackets held any interest for Sara.

"A high-speed police chase in Miraflores. The suspects are in custody, but at least one federal officer is down. Identities have not yet been released, pending notification of family members."

Sickness was already gripping Sara's stomach when the camera angle shifted to an ambulance. As a paramedic crew lifted in a stretcher, the camera zoomed in on the pale face and bloodstained white suit of a young man standing nearby.

"Hey," Cynthia stabbed a long, enamel-pink nail at the screen, "isn't . . . isn't that Mike Garcia? The kid who's been working with Doug?"

Sara too had recognized the young agent, one of Doug's colleagues she'd met at the DO Christmas party. Her mouth went dry. *He said he was learning so much working with Doug.*

Brriiingg!

Cynthia did not move, and it was Sara who snatched up the cordless phone.

"Karla here. Are you watching the news?"

The harried voice of the DEA administrative officer was muted by a roaring in Sara's ears. "Yes, we're watching. Was . . . was . . . was Doug out there?"

"Yes, I'm sorry. We'd hoped to reach you before you saw it on the news. First things first. Doug's alive, and he's going to be fine. They've got him stabilized and are moving him right now to South Miami Hospital."

Oddly, now that the worst of Sara's fears had materialized, the sick grip on her stomach eased. She'd had plenty of practice confronting disaster. It was anticipating disaster that was the killer.

By contrast, Cynthia had turned ash white and had sunk down on the sofa. Sara lifted the car keys from her fingers. "I knew this would happen some day," Cynthia moaned as Sara gently steered her out the door and down to the car. "Oh, why didn't he listen to me and quit that horrible job?"

The hospital wing to which Karla had directed them seemed as chaotic as the news scene, with police and DEA agents milling around amid scurrying nurses and orderlies. Sara picked out Doug's GS, Norm Kublin, and Mike Garcia. The young Hispanic agent had traded the bloodstained suit for a T-shirt and jeans. Mike's wife, Debby, whom Sara had also met at that Christmas party, was standing with him. Like Sara, she was Anglo, a petite brunette who at the moment was demonstrably pregnant.

The GS was at the information desk, talking over a chart with the receptionist. Doug's mother made a beeline toward him. Sara could only hope he wasn't going to get the same lecture she'd given Sara in the car. Sara walked over to Mike and Debbie Garcia.

"What happened?" she got out as evenly as she could. "Where's Doug?" Her glance went to Mike's T-shirt, its tight fit showing no sign of bandages underneath. "Are you okay?" she added belatedly. "On the news it looked like you'd been hurt."

Mike dropped his brooding dark gaze from the wall opposite him to look at Sara. "I'm fine. The blood . . . was Doug's." A muscle bunched at his jawline as he nodded down the hall toward double doors marked Surgery. "He's still in there. They think the bullet missed the lung, but his shoulder was torn up pretty bad."

As Sara's face whitened, he added roughly, "Hey, he's going to be okay. They said there's nothing critical."

"But—what happened?" Sara repeated desperately. "Doug said today was going to be an easy one . . . that he'd be home early."

Mike's expression went rigid before he said sharply, "There are no easy ones. There were four bad guys. Everything went to pieces."

His glance went to the other agents, gathered in a knot outside the surgery doors, and he said abruptly, "I'll let Doug fill you in on what he thinks you should know. Now if you'll excuse me . . ."

Sara watched him stride rapidly down the corridor. "He blames himself," Debby said quietly, startling Sara, who had forgotten she was there. "They always do when someone gets hurt. Right now he needs the other guys more than he does me."

Her hands pressed suddenly to her bulging abdomen. "Ooh! I need to get Junior here off my feet. Come on, let's go sit down."

Sara glanced around. Did Cynthia need her support? She spotted Doug's mother still at the information counter. Norm Kublin had detached himself to join his agents, but Cynthia had found a listening ear in the receptionist.

Following Debby to a sitting area, Sara looked back to where Mike had joined the other agents. Despite the differences in height, weight, and appearance, there was something very similar about them. Something in their upright posture, the self-confident lift of their heads, even the restless agility of their pacing. Something in the shoulder-to-shoulder solidarity of their stance, as if they were trying to form a protective huddle against the rest of the world.

Like the Three Musketeers! All for one and one for all, and heaven help the bad guy who hurts one of them.

Sara swallowed against a sudden lump in her throat. Dropping into a seat beside Debby, she demanded tensely, "How can you stand it? How can you live like this, watching them walk out the door every day without ever knowing where they're going or when they might be back? Or if they ever will? How can you stand the waiting?"

"You don't." Debby shifted uncomfortably as Junior chose that moment to protest against his—or her—confinement. "At least not if you want to last in a DEA marriage. It's kind of like marrying someone in the Marines or Special Forces. Except our guys' duty shifts don't last so long, thank goodness. You can't sit around waiting for them to come home to start having a life. You've got to go out and build one of your own."

Debby's smile was tender and serene. But then her Mike was back—and unhurt. "Guys like ours—Mike and Doug and the other agents—they are what they are, and nothing's going to change that. Independent. Aggressive. Okay, make that downright bossy. Always sure they can handle things and always at the front if there's any action. It's what makes them good at what they do."

Another smile, secret and satisfied. "And a whole lot of fun in between. I wouldn't trade Mike for some nine-to-five business type, even if he had a million dollar salary and every weekend off."

Debby's pretty face sobered. "And what the guys want . . . *need* . . . are wives who can be as independent and self-sufficient as they are. What they *don't* need is some country club type who's going to be sitting around the house wringing her hands every time her husband's out on a case, complaining when he's late, and never getting on with life unless hubby's home to take care of things. That's the fastest way to a divorce in this line of work—and let me tell you there's plenty of that! The guys can't concentrate on their jobs if they've got to be worrying their wives are going to hit the roof if they're ten minutes late for dinner. And they need to be able to concentrate—for their own safety as well as the mission."

Sara flinched, though she was almost certain that Debby's words had not been directed at her personally. *Is that what Peggy Brown was hinting at? Do they really think I want to tie Doug down?*

With one hand pressing down on the thin cotton of her maternity dress, Debby shifted to look Sara squarely in the eye, and though she was smiling, her brown eyes were serious. "I like you, Sara. I like Doug too. He's a great guy, and I'd like to see him . . . both of you . . . happy. So I hope you won't mind taking a little advice from someone who's been where you are. You asked how I do it. I have my friends, my social activities, my church. When Mike's home, he comes with me. If he doesn't show up, I get in the car and go alone. Mike appreciates knowing that I'm busy and happy whether he can be there or not. It makes him feel he can do his job without me hanging around his neck. As for what he's doing all day, he doesn't tell me—and I've learned not to ask."

A rise in the noise level drew the two women's attention to the far side of the room. "Look, the surgeon's coming out." Debby said. "He'll let us know when we can see Doug." The sympathy in her eyes removed any sting from her words as she lumbered awkwardly to her feet. "I guess what I'm trying to say is, if you're going to make a go of letting an agent into your life—and your heart—the bottom line is you've got to learn to live without him before you can live *with* him. I know that sounds harsh, but you don't have to go it alone."

Pulling a large square envelope from her purse, Debby handed it to Sara. "Here. I brought this for Doug, but maybe you need it more than he does. I've got this posted on the wall of every room in my house, and I just keep it in mind every time Mike walks out that door."

*　*　*

Sara turned the lamp beside Doug's hospital bed down a notch to its lowest level. She'd finally persuaded Cynthia to go home for a few hours' sleep. Doug's mother had recovered her usual brittle composure once she'd satisfied herself that the surgeon's favorable prognosis was accurate. In Sara's carefully unexpressed opinion, it was just as well that Doug was anesthetized and had fallen into a deep sleep.

The room was semiprivate, but the other bed was empty. Turning the lamp so that even the smallest gleam would not disturb Doug's sleep, Sara watched the still form under the thin hospital blanket. The suit he'd been wearing when shot had been cut off in the emergency room, and the gold jewelry and Rolex taken into custody by Doug's boss, but Doug's hair was still tied back in a queue at the base of his neck. He'd been letting it grow since his return from Bolivia, and though he could still style it ruthlessly into its customary neatness, Sara had been astounded at what a stranger he could become just by catching it back and adding polarized sunglasses and the right clothes.

This chameleon-like ability of Doug's was something Sara had never encountered in Bolivia, where the DEA agents were technically no more than advisors to the host country's counternarcotics forces and were thus prohibited from working undercover. When out in the field, Doug had worn the same camouflage fatigues as the local troops.

Here in Miami, Sara could make a good guess at how Doug was spending his day just by what he was wearing. She hated his "drug dealer costume" most. With the sober suit-and-tie he wore to court, Sara could relax, assured that for a few hours at least no one would be shooting at him.

Sara wasn't the only one to take notice of Doug's shifting appearance. Just last week Doug had dropped by to pick up some forgotten paperwork, wearing the coveralls of a county construction crew. Cynthia's closest neighbor, a nosy old woman as far from the stereotypical cookie-baking granny as could be, had leaned over the fence to make a crude remark about men coming in and out of the house at odd hours. She'd ducked indoors before Sara realized she was referring to Doug in his different guises.

Now, however, in a hospital gown as ill-fitting and ugly as any could be, he looked like none of those men. He looked younger and—with the obdurate line of his jaw relaxed in sleep—more vulnerable. Something painful squeezed at Sara's heart at the volume of bandages wrapping his left shoulder and side, the slackness of his arm with the IV taped to the crook of his elbow.

You've got to learn to live without him before you can live with him. Debby Garcia's words played through Sara's mind. *Nice philosophy, but how do you do it? If you really do care about someone, how can you just let them go?*

Remembering the envelope Debby had given her earlier, Sara pulled it from where she'd tucked it in her purse and slowly opened it. As she had expected, it was a get-well card. The front of the card showed a rocky path with a solitary traveler. Above the traveler was a stylized flight of angels with wings outspread. Inside, the only words beyond Debby's scrawled "We're praying for you, Doug," was a column of poetry that was instantly familiar as Sara began to read.

It was a psalm, one of the many to which Sara herself had clung for answers and comfort during those weeks in the jungle when her only reading material had been the well-thumbed Bible Doug had given her. Psalm 91. In the dim glow of the hospital lamp, Sara read again the majestic, lyrical stanzas.

> He who dwells in the shelter of the Most High
> will rest in the shadow of the Almighty.
> I will say of the Lord, "He is my refuge and my fortress,
> my God, in whom I trust."
>
> Surely he will save you from the fowler's snare
> and from the deadly pestilence.
> He will cover you with his feathers,
> and under his wings you will find refuge;
> his faithfulness will be your shield and rampart.

Then came the litany of terrors:

> You will not fear the terror of night, *[even a jungle night, God?]*
> Nor the arrow that flies by day, *[What about a bullet?]*

> Nor the pestilence that stalks in the darkness,
> nor the plague that destroys at midday.

Sara shivered, but not from the temperature of the hospital room. She'd known what it was to be stalked by enemies who wanted to destroy her.

> A thousand may fall at your side,
> ten thousand at your right hand,
> but it will not come near you.
> You will only observe with your eyes
> and see the punishment of the wicked.

And she had, though she had not expected to live long enough to do so.

> . . . For he will command his angels concerning you
> to guard you in all your ways;
> they will lift you up in their hands,
> so that you will not strike your foot against a stone. . . .
> "Because he loves me," says the Lord, "I will rescue him. . . ."

"Okay, Debby, I get the point," Sara said aloud, then broke off as Doug stirred under the blanket. A grimace of pain twisted his sleeping features. Then his breath grew even again, and the pain smoothed away, twisting at Sara's heart instead.

Do I love him? I know I do. I care more about him than about anyone alive on the earth right now. But am I in love *with him? I'm not so sure that I want to be.*

Pressing her palms to her eyes, Sara was not sure it was exhaustion or tears she was pushing away. "Oh, God," she whispered more quietly. "I know you protected me out there. I felt the shadow of your wings. And yet . . . it isn't always so easy. People do die. They're martyred for their faith. Bad people win out. And if your angels are there, they don't seem to be doing anything. It's . . . it's those other verses instead."

> Though the fig tree does not bud and there are no grapes on
> the vines, though the olive crop fails and the fields produce
> no food, though there are no sheep in the pen and no cattle in
> the stalls, yet I will rejoice in the Lord, I will be joyful in God
> my Savior.

"Oh, God, I thought I'd learned to trust you out there, to rejoice in you even when my whole world is falling apart. And I did—I still do. But that was for me! And to be honest, I didn't really care if I lived or died so long as the mess I'd made was put right. But now . . . every person I've ever loved in my life, you've ended up taking away. And—it's okay; it really is. I know you love me, and I really do believe you know what You're doing with my life. But—I don't think I can bear to love someone again and maybe have you take him away too."

Abruptly shoving back the chair she'd pulled up to Doug's bedside, Sara knelt on the floor, the tiles cold and hard under her knees. Careful not to jar the IV line, she picked up Doug's slack arm and held his hand between her own smaller palms. He did not stir. His flesh was warm, almost feverish, against hers, his breathing so noiseless that Sara watched anxiously until she saw his chest rise and fall under the sheet. Was he really going to be okay, as the surgeon had promised?

Wearily, Sara bent her head until her forehead was resting against the edge of the mattress. Were there really angels encircling this room, this very hospital bed, though she could not see them?

What do I do? What is it you want of me?

Though Sara's senses strained for something beyond sight or sound, there was no answer.

Chapter Eight

Paradoxically, the very fear and worry and sleepless debate of the night before fueled anger when Sara arrived back at Doug's room the next morning to hear cheerful and unruffled male voices in conversation.

"I'll be expecting a complete report as soon as you're out of here," an unidentified voice was saying. "What a screwup—all sides. If nothing else, the marksmanship stunk! I must have counted fifty bullet holes out there and at the warehouse, and the only one that landed was the one that took you out. I'm ordering the bunch of you back to the firing range."

"I wasn't trying to take anyone out. Just keep them from running." Doug's reply sounded as unperturbed as that of his visitor. Pausing in the doorway, a gym bag over her shoulder containing toiletries and clothing she had retrieved from Doug's apartment, Sara saw that the first speaker was Doug's GS, Norm Kublin. Mike Garcia was also there, the two men's tall frames blocking her view of the room.

"Yeah, well . . . we got 'em, anyway," Norm Kublin admitted. "Sanchez and Stirling are locked up, and so are their two little Colombian rat pals. The DA's going for no bail. I guess this is where I should say, 'good job.' At least for the two of you. Can't say much for the local PD. Writing this one up is going to be a doozer. That bit with the car . . ."

Mike glanced at his boss, and Sara caught his discomfited expression before Doug deflected slyly, "You mean, Mike's Firebird? Yeah, that one's going to be hard to explain. Come on, Norm! We've all had our strikes with Murphy's Law. Anyway, the doc says I'm out of here this afternoon. I'll stop by to file a report."

"Well, don't push yourself. And let Mike here do any driving. When that painkiller wears off, you're going to be hurting—don't think I don't know!"

Kublin's angular frame shifted, allowing Sara her first clear view of the hospital bed. Doug was sitting up, the bed adjusted to the upright position, a meal tray across his lap and a cup of coffee in his right hand. Except for the pallor of his complexion, which could be attributed to the bilious green of his hospital gown, he looked little different than his usual self—wide-awake, relaxed, his mouth still curved in a half smile from his derisive retort.

Doug spotted Sara at the same moment. He set down his coffee. "Hi, Sara, brought my stuff?"

As if she had not spent the night worrying whether he was going to live or die. Men! How could these three act as if there had not nearly been a tragedy?

Something in Sara's expression must have communicated their transgression, because Doug's visitors hastily excused themselves.

"See you at the office." Norm Kublin gave Sara a courteous nod as he strode out of the room. Mike lingered to grip Doug's hand. "I owe you one, man. Just give me a buzz when you're ready for wheels."

He shot Sara a tight half-grin before disappearing into the corridor. As Sara crossed the room to drop the gym bag at the foot of the bed, Doug nodded to the chair Sara had left pulled up during the night. "Sit down and talk to me. Oh, and thanks for bringing my things." The twist of his mouth tilted further into a rueful grin as Sara dropped into the chair. "Hey! You look worse than I feel. I thought I was the patient here."

Sara didn't rise to his teasing. Did he have any idea she'd spent most of the night kneeling at his side, holding his hand? If so, he gave no indication. In fact, in her opinion, he was looking far too pleased with himself for the early hour and the circumstances. Lingering irritation edged her tone with dryness. "I'm afraid I didn't have time to catch my beauty sleep last night."

She'd resolved to remain casual, but couldn't keep her voice from wobbling. "Do you know we thought you were dead? When we saw you on that stretcher—"

Doug's grin disappeared abruptly. "Well, I'm not, as you can see. I could wring the necks of those newsies for putting that out before you were contacted. But it wasn't nearly the big deal they made it out to be. In fact, it's not much more than a flesh wound."

Sara steadied her voice again before she could say lightly, "Your mother says if I . . . I cared about you, I'd talk you into quitting."

"I know, I got the same lecture already this morning." Doug's tone did not lose its evenness, but it held a hard note. "And you? What do you say?"

Sara dropped her eyes to her hands, clasped tightly in her lap. "I . . . it isn't my business to be telling you what you should do for a living."

"Isn't it? Sara, look at me! Is that how you feel? About me . . . about us?"

Sara raised her head, her amber eyes huge and dark, her face drawn. "Doug,

I . . . I'm not sure how I feel about you except that I care enough that every time you walk out the door I feel sick. I can't sleep or work or even *think* until I know you are back safe again. I . . . I just can't live like that. Maybe it would be different if I hadn't been out there. If I hadn't seen what you do. Debby Garcia says she doesn't want to know what Mike does, that there's no point worrying about what you can't change. Well, I do know, and I worry. Every time I close my eyes, I see you lying there like—"

"Like Nicolás?" Doug's gray eyes were focused on Sara's face, his mouth no longer slanted with humor. "You're forgetting something," he said sharply. "For all that happened out there in Bolivia, we weren't hurt. Not you. Not me. I'm not saying it wasn't a tight spot. It was—one of the worst I've ever been in. But we came through okay. Just like we came through this time."

"This time . . . but what about tomorrow or the next day?"

"Sara—don't do this to me!" Doug's voice was raw. "I can't do my job if I'm worrying about my own skin. Or is that really what you're asking—that I quit?"

"Of course not! But—maybe an office position?"

Sara hadn't meant to say it, and if she could have, she'd have retracted her words the instant they were out of her mouth. Doug's eyes narrowed further, his mouth tightening. Then, leaning back against the pillow behind him, he let out a tired sigh. "Can you see me behind a desk? Sara, this is what I do—what I am."

It was what Debby had said. What Peggy had meant.

"But . . . it's so dangerous!"

Doug shook his head impatiently. "Not if you're careful. I'm not going to waste time with all the statistics, but whether you believe it or not, a fireman or even a construction worker is more likely to be taken out on the job than a DEA agent. I've never even fired my weapon on the job until yesterday. But even if there is an element of risk, the bottom line is that someone's got to do the job. If not me, than someone else. Maybe someone less prepared and less capable. Do you really think I could ask someone else to stand in the line of fire for me so I can duck down behind a desk out of harm's way? I couldn't live with that. And I don't want to. It isn't just that I like what I do. I'm good at it. There are four less rotten apples out on the street today because of what went down yesterday, and in my book that's what counts."

Doug broke off as he caught Sara's expression. Then he said quietly, "This isn't working, is it? I guess maybe I was wrong to think it could. There are few enough women who can take on the stress of dealing with this job, much less someone who has been through the kind of trauma you have. I had no right to ask it of you."

"No, don't say that! It isn't you. It's me. If I could . . . just stop being so afraid." The twist of Sara's lips did not succeed at humor. "I don't know how you put up with me. I'm such a coward, a wimp. I look at someone like Peggy Browning who can go out there with you without blinking an eye—"

Doug interrupted her with an impatient gesture. "Don't be comparing yourself to Peggy. You don't have her training. And she has never been through what you have. You're not a coward, Sara, believe me. Maybe it sounds cliché, but courage isn't about not being afraid. It's what you choose to do when you're scared to death—and don't forget, I've already seen your choices."

"You're just trying to make me feel better." Sara managed a faint smile as she looked at Doug. Wide-awake and sitting up, he showed none of the vulnerability that had squeezed her heart during the night. Not even the bandages and ludicrous hospital gown were able to diminish his unequivocal masculinity and that air of assured, quiet competence. "What about you, Doug? Aren't you *ever* afraid?"

The angle to which his eyebrows shot was almost comical. "Of course! What do you think I am—Superman?"

This time Sara's smile was real. "Sometimes. Anyone who *likes* having people shoot at him . . ."

"Don't kid yourself," Doug said. "I'm no Clark Kent. But you're right that I don't spend much time worrying about my own skin when I'm out on a job. Too busy, for one. For another—well, I really do believe that God is in charge of my life and that nothing is going to touch me that he doesn't allow. Not that I don't take every sensible precaution—"

Doug broke off with a rueful grin at the look on Sara's face. "Okay, so they don't always work, but I'm still here, aren't I? It's like—well, you remember Pastor Jack's sermon last Sunday? There was something he said that really stuck with me. 'Safety is not the absence of danger, but the presence of God.'"

Doug shifted his long legs, knocking the meal tray so that he had to grab it to steady his coffee. He pushed the wheeled tray table away. "Pastor Jack nailed it right on. If God is really in charge of my life, as I believe without a doubt, then it doesn't matter whether I'm in the middle of the jungle or a shootout or at home watching football. If I'm where he's called me to be, there's no safer place."

"Like Psalm 91."

At Doug's questioning glance, Sara pulled out the get-well card from her purse and leaned forward to hand it to him. "Debby brought this for you, but she figured I needed it more." Doug flipped open the card to glance through it. "All those bits about the terror of night and pestilence and plague and a thousand falling at your side . . ."

"I know the psalm." Doug set the card back on the tray. "I've got a copy posted above my counter at the apartment, which Debby knows. This was meant to be a reminder."

"And the angels—do you really think there are angels out there watching over you on the job? Watching over us right now?"

Doug's eyes didn't leave Sara's face. "Absolutely."

"But they don't always do their job," Sara cried. "Bad things happen. People—good people—still die. You can't just count on not getting hurt."

Doug let out an impatient sigh. "People die crossing the street. Or in bed of a heart attack. The point is, everyone's time comes sooner or later. The Bible says the days of our lives are numbered before we're even born. So are we supposed to spend our lives ducking under the bed, trying to find the safest corner—or live the life God put us here for?"

Doug took a deep breath that made him wince as it strained at his shoulder, then said more calmly, "You remember the rest of Pastor Jack's sermon Sunday?"

"I guess." Sara wrinkled her forehead. "The Old Testament. Book of Daniel. It was one of the first stories I ever learned in Sunday school. Daniel's three friends, Shadrach, Meshach, and Abednego and the fiery furnace. King Nebuchadnezzar threw them in there for refusing to bow down and worship the gold image he built of himself."

"Yes, well, it's what they said to the king when they refused to bow down that really hit home to me. 'If we are thrown into the blazing furnace, the God we serve is able to save us from it, and he will rescue us from your hand. But even if he does not, we will not worship the image of gold.' Talk about guts! They knew God could rescue them, but they had no assurance he would. But that didn't make any difference to doing what they had to do—though, of course, in the end, God did rescue.

"And I guess that's the way I feel. Is God capable of taking care of me out there, no matter how hot things get? You bet! But if the day comes when he tells those angels to stay their hand, that Doug Bradford's done down here and it's time to come on home, then so be it. Until then, I guess I'll just keep on doing what I was put here to do."

When Sara didn't respond, he added on a lighter note, "Hey, don't think that makes me any kind of a superhero! Sure, I don't worry much about God doing his job in my life. If you really want to know what scares me, it's screwing up the job. Making the wrong call. Shooting the wrong person. You can't take back a bullet. Or, hesitating when I should shoot. I've never had to make that decision yet, and I must say I question sometimes whether I can do it—pull that trigger and watch a man go down."

His eyes shifted suddenly from Sara's face to the far wall, his face growing somber as he added grimly, "Or worse, letting down the people I love—again. Not being there when she—they—need me."

He broke off, and Sara finished softly, "You mean Julie?"

Doug did not immediately answer. Muscles bunched along his jaw, and when he finally spoke, his gaze still fixed on the far wall, his voice was raw and low with a pain he had never before allowed Sara to see. "Do you know what it felt like to be on the job—a stakeout for some scumbag drug dealer, for Pete's sake—when the people you care about most in the world are *dying*? I . . . it took a long time to forgive myself for that."

Sara made a swift gesture of protest. "But you couldn't have known! There's no way you can control something like that or be able to prevent every freak accident that could happen."

"No, I'm aware of that," Doug said evenly. This time he turned his head to look at Sara, his eyes unreadable under their long lashes. "Just like neither you—nor I—can guarantee there won't be a stray bullet somewhere, sometime, with my name on it. Odds are, there won't . . . just like odds are against a DUI wiping out your family. But there it is. No guarantees . . . and you seem to want a guarantee. The question is, what do we do about it? I just . . ."

His hand raked through his hair again. "Sara, maybe you don't know how you feel about me. But I do know how I feel about you. I love you. I'm *in* love with you. I want to spend the rest of my life with you. And I'm willing to make some compromises in my job if that's what it takes. Maybe a training position. I've been asked often enough to do some instructing up at Quantico."

But Sara was shaking her head. "No! You were right, Doug. It . . . it isn't going to work. Your mother is wrong . . . and so was I. You were *born* to do what you do. You can't be anything but what you are, and you shouldn't. The world needs people like you. But me—"

Sara took a deep breath before going on resolutely, "I . . . I don't know how to say this. I know you're going to think it's because of yesterday, but it isn't.

I've been thinking about it a long time. I care about you. I could easily fall in love with you. Maybe I'm even lying to myself when I try to think I haven't. And I know that right now you think you're in love with me. But I can't help feeling you're loving something—someone—that isn't really there. Like I did with Nicky. I mean, be honest. If you'd just met me on the street somewhere or at church instead of galloping in and saving my life, would you have given me a second thought?"

Sara hurried on as Doug opened his mouth. "You see, I'm really a very ordinary person who just happened to land for a few months in an extraordinary life where I didn't—don't—belong. I'm not an expert in politics or world events or weapons training or all the other things you know so much about. All I ever planned on being—all I ever studied to be—was a grade school teacher. The kind of person who ends up in some suburban neighborhood with a three-bedroom house, a minivan, the average 2.7 kids, or whatever it is right now, and a teaching position at the local elementary school."

"Plenty of agents live in three-bedroom houses," Doug interrupted. "Sara, don't sell yourself short."

Sara reached out to lay a hand lightly over his mouth. "Please, I have to finish. I've been trying to get up the courage to say this. The truth is, all my life I've been afraid of being alone. First my mother was gone and my grandparents and my brother. Then my father. I guess I just couldn't take having to face the world without a safety net, someone to lean on and protect me. That's why I married Nicky—I can see that now. I had no idea what I was going to do with myself once my senior year was over and I was evicted from my dorm room. I had no family, no place to go, and I was scared. Then along came Nicky and rescued me from those thugs in the alley. I'd been waiting for my knight in shining armor, and there he was. And I jumped at it—at him—without taking any time to see what was behind it or listening to any of my friends' warnings.

"Then when he let me down, along came another shining knight—you. You saved my life and brought me here, and all these months you've protected me and shielded me from having to face up to reality. I'll bet you'd never even have told me of today's shootout if you hadn't been hurt, would you?"

"Is there anything wrong with wanting to protect the person you care about?"

If it hadn't been Doug, Sara might have thought the stiffness of his reply was indicative of hurt feelings. "No, of course not. And please don't think I don't appreciate all you've done. But I can't stay wrapped up in cotton balls and leaning on someone else forever. It isn't fair to you, or good for me. I don't know what I'd have done without you and Cynthia these last months. But at some point I have to learn to stand on my own two feet. To stand alone—not leaning on someone else. And I won't really be alone. You gave me that."

Though the fig tree does not bud . . . I will rejoice!

"And me? Us? You appreciate all I've done—is that all there ever was between us?"

Sara had to swallow to keep the lump in her chest from rising into her throat. "You deserve better than me, Doug. That's the honest truth. Someone independent and strong and competent at life—like Peggy Browning. Someone who can stand by your side and be a partner instead of being a burden. Who . . . who isn't pulled down by memories. Can't you see that?"

"I can see that *you* believe it." Doug leaned back against the uptilted mattress and closed his eyes. Sara noted anxiously the white lines pinching around the base of his nostrils and corners of his mouth. Maybe he was hurting worse than he admitted. But a moment later he opened his eyes and gave Sara a long, even look. "So—what are you planning?"

"What I should have done in the first place last summer when I graduated. I was going to tell you last night at dinner. Not all this, but that I've been offered a job. Someone at church put my name in for it. Second grade teacher in the ESL program here in Miami-Dade, starting Monday. The teacher they had last semester is taking maternity leave. One of the other single teachers told me she was looking for someone to share an apartment. I wasn't planning on taking her up on it, but now—well, I'll be moved out by the time you're released. Your . . . your mother has been wonderful, but I can't impose on her forever, and I know she will understand."

"So . . . just like that, you're going to walk out of my life—and my mother's. She at least deserves better."

"Oh, Doug." This time Sara could not keep the lump out of her throat. "I'm not going anywhere . . . not even out of the neighborhood. And I love your mother. She's a friend. So are the people at church. I'll be around."

"And me?" Doug's face was wiped free of emotion now, his expression the inscrutable one Sara had once known well, and it twisted at her heart even more than the pain she'd glimpsed earlier.

"I—" Sara steeled her heart against an impulse to throw herself into his arms, bandages and all, and wipe that impersonal look from his face and eyes. *No, I have to do this . . . because Doug won't, even if he comes to recognize I'm right. He's too kind . . . too chivalrous. And he deserves to be free from me hanging around his neck—as much as I need to learn to walk on my own.* "I think it's better we not see each other . . . at least for a while."

"Until I've gotten over you, you mean." Doug's even tone was as expressionless as his face.

"Maybe until we both can see more clearly." There was no more to be said. Or rather, there was a lot, but it would only further hurt both of them. Rising to her feet, Sara nodded toward the gym bag. "I think everything you need is there. Good-bye, Doug."

It wasn't easy to make a dignified exit with tears misting her vision. Sara raised a casual hand to brush it over her lashes as she walked toward the door, though she had little hope she was fooling Doug. She had reached the door when she checked suddenly and swung around. As she'd expected, Doug's eyes were still on her, cool and unreadable.

"I forgot." Pulling out a small gift-wrapped box from her handbag, Sara walked quickly over to set it beside Debby's get-well card on the meal tray. "I got this before . . . well, before. Happy birthday."

Chapter Nine

JANUARY 21
IGUAZÚ RAIN FOREST

"Thirty seconds."

Zip-lines tumbled out the open doors of the helicopter.

"Twenty."

On either side of the helicopter, two black figures slid after the ropes, backs to the night, until their combat boots encountered the skids.

"Ten."

Julio Vargas slowed the helicopter to a hover one hundred meters above the jungle clearing.

"*Vaya! Vaya!*"

At the go signal, the four crouching figures kicked away from the skids. Four more slid out after them, kicking off before the first group had hit the ground. One stumbled and went down hard, but the other seven were already up and disconnecting the zip-lines from their safety harnesses. Unslinging their automatic rifles, they loped across the clearing toward the square shape of a building at the far end, their night-vision goggles adding an odd snout-like shape to the running silhouettes in the green phosphorescence of Julio Vargas's NVG helmet.

As the team approached the building, they disappeared from view. A few brief muzzle flashes signaled the onset of the assault. Then darkness, followed by a crackle in Julio's earpiece. "Mission accomplished. All targets neutralized."

Julio grunted grudging approval. This was the night's third insertion exercise, and this team had outpaced the others by at least thirty seconds. Not surprisingly, young Saleh Jebai was the team leader. Arrogant fanatic that he was, he'd proved as formidable a soldier as he'd claimed to be.

Julio dropped the helicopter down to hover just above the ground while the assault team clambered back aboard, their injured member supported between two of his teammates. Banking above the jungle canopy, Julio headed back toward the base camp. He'd have to make another trip to retrieve the ground personnel who had been setting up targets and serving as observers to the training exercise. Dawn was still an hour away, but even if he were spotted by a passing Cessna, the red and white search-and-rescue markings on the UH-1 Huey wouldn't raise any eyebrows.Regardless of one's views on anthropology and empire-building, the Jesuit missions had protected the Guarani Indians, the region's predominant population group, from both Spanish and Portuguese slave traders. This protection had allowed for the development of a rich culture in arts and music, woodworking, artisan crafts, and agriculture. Still remembered by locals as a golden age, the mission era came to an abrupt end when the Portuguese and Spanish monarchs signed an agreement to drive out the Jesuit missionaries, freeing the Guarani territory and its inhabitants for exploitation by traders and colonists. The Guarani fled back into the rain forest, where they resumed a Stone Age lifestyle for another century or more. The adobe mission complexes were left to crumble into ruins. Though a few had been restored for the tourists in recent decades, the jungle had swallowed up the smaller outposts so that even their locations were forgotten.

This particular mission was buried deep inside the Iguazú World Heritage Site, a rain forest preserve encompassing several hundred thousand acres on the Brazilian and Argentine sides of Iguazú Falls, a crescent-shaped curve almost three kilometers wide where the waters of the Iguazú River tumbled over the steep edge of the continental plateau to form the world's most extensive cataracts. Julio couldn't imagine how anyone had made it past the falls to this inhospitable location before the days of helicopters and motorized rivercraft. The Jesuits must have been as dedicated and determined as some of his present charges.

The site had been deserted for almost two centuries when a relative of Sheik Mozer Jebai had stumbled over the ruins while hunting jaguar in the reserve, an illegal but highly profitable pursuit. For a time, Hezbollah recruiters had used the site as a training camp for local Muslim youth. Saleh had been one of them.

The mission's only surviving structure was the church itself, and that only because the burnt-clay tiles of the roof had kept decades of monsoon rains from washing away the thick adobe walls. The tiles must have been manufactured on-site, as there was no way the heavy material could have been ferried upriver from another settlement. The rain forest had closed in on the ruins, led by tangles of liana vines that had crawled through windows and up walls,

and a hardwood giant more than two hundred feet tall that had fallen across the sanctuary so that much of the roof was caved in.

A section of the building that had been a dormitory wing was still solid, and the square, low-ceilinged rooms had been stripped of vines, the rotting door and window frames replaced. The stockade walls and thatched huts of the Guarani converts were long rotted away, but a clearing back of growth around the church had exposed the wild offshoots of their crops. Banana plants and plantains. Citrus and mango trees. Patches of cassava, the jungle staple.

A wide stream around the edge of the clearing made a defensible perimeter, part of a maze of waterways interconnecting the rain forest, from shallow creeks, invisible through the thick jungle canopy, to rivers more than a kilometer wide, like the Iguazú and the Paraná, which formed the border between Brazil and Paraguay. The waterways proved to be the key to supplying the training camp.

While Mozer Jebai and his network were screening candidates for training, Julio Vargas set himself the task of building a team of instructors and acquiring the necessary equipment. He lost no time in contacting a Colombian colleague whose role in a civilian massacre had ended his military career. The Colombian, in turn, recruited a Venezuelan acquaintance, a former officer of GAC FAC, Venezuela's crack commando unit, who had mastered every aspect of his Special Forces training at Fort Bragg except the course on ethics. After a decade spent organizing security for a Colombian drug lord, he'd been left unemployed when a competitor arranged the narco's assassination.

With Julio's expertise as a pilot, the three men qualified to teach all the necessary bases of training except engineering and explosives. For those, Mozer Jebai had supplied a Palestinian demolitions expert, whose wealth of experience included fashioning car bombs and explosive belts for suicide bombers. For communications and medical skills, there were graduate degrees among the recruits themselves.

On the supply side, Julio had been astonished to discover that anything he could possibly need—short of military-grade weapons—was freely available for purchase over the Internet. Better yet, much of it had been adapted for civilian use. Tactical gear. Combat vests. Global positioning systems and radio equipment finer than the armed forces themselves possessed. Laptop computers rugged enough to stand up to wilderness conditions. Night-vision goggles and tracking devices of every sort. Even thermal imaging equipment. There was so much available that Julio, who had spent much of his military career trying to train conscripts with insufficient and defective equipment, had to restrain himself from overbuying. It was necessary, after all, to maintain the appearance of a legitimate "jungle trek" business.

This cover story, Julio had grudgingly admitted, was one more indication of Saleh Jebai's leadership potential. His plan had been as simple as it was brilliant. One of the fastest growing segments of Iguazú's tourist industry was jungle trekking. There had long been boat trips out into the spray of the cataracts, helicopter rides above the falls, as well as the usual boardwalk and nature trails that did not venture far from the falls. As more adventurous tourists began to discover the Iguazú region, longer nature trips were added upriver from the falls and into a few carefully charted waterways around the perimeter of the rain forest preserve. A more recent addition was the so-called survival treks, where qualified individuals could learn skills similar to what Julio was now teaching his recruits. Rappelling and rock climbing. Jungle and riverine navigation. Foraging for food, water, and shelter.

An outfit called Jungle Tours had been running a variety of tours into Iguazú for more than a decade when Khalil Mehri negotiated a buyout. Soon, rain forest survival treks were added to the excursion options on Jungle Tours' Web site. Though these particular adventures were routinely "sold out," Jungle Tours was happy to recommend other available tour companies to disappointed clients, and the appearance of a thriving outfitting business provided a legitimate rationale for Julio Vargas's equipment purchases, including the acquisition of a riverboat and the red-and-white Search and Rescue helicopter. The flat bottom of the boat allowed for navigation of all but the shallowest streams, and with GPS technology it had only been a matter of time and patience before a route was traced from more heavily trafficked rivers into the intricate network of waterways that meandered under the cover of the jungle canopy to the old mission.

The camp was well beyond the beaten path, deep inside the rain forest reserve on the Brazilian side. But even if a stray adventurer had stumbled across the training grounds, he would have found nothing unusual in the Rain Forest Survival Treks logo stenciled boldly across T-shirts, inflatable boats, and backpacks.

The sophisticated rope-climbing course strung among the branches of several large mangos on the edge of camp might have drawn some attention, but it was nothing that wouldn't be found in other survival courses closer to civilization. Other artificial structures were not necessary. The jungle terrain itself was a training ground that would put any artificial facility to shame.

All military gear and other suspicious equipment was stored well out of sight when not in use, in case a park ranger happened across the camp. But the entire Iguazú World Heritage Site, thousands of square miles of jungle, was patrolled by only a few dozen rangers, and these seldom ventured off the few cleared roads around the tourist center of Iguazú Falls. And if some nosy visitor did make it past the posted sentries—well, the jungle was vast and there were always those careless tourists who never returned.

* * *

Julio stooped to enter the doorway of his quarters, one of the small square rooms in the old dormitory wing, which he shared with his Colombian and Venezuelan colleagues. The Palestinian instructor preferred to room with his fellow Muslims, crowded into the three remaining rooms of the dorm. The adobe walls had been scraped down, replastered and whitewashed, and the mahogany beams holding up the ceiling were in surprisingly good shape. But the floor was only tamped earth, and the room smelled strongly of centuries of mildew and decay. Sleeping hammocks, a few crude shelves, and a table were the only furnishings.

The entire camp was similarly austere. Despite the funds available for setting up the camp, not a single *centavo* had been spent on personal comforts, not even a TV and VCR. Alcohol, playing cards, and gambling were forbidden, as well, which left reading as the only leisure entertainment. Light was provided by Coleman lanterns at night, but the library consisted mainly of Special Forces training manuals, books on military and guerrilla warfare, survival techniques, Spanish and English language courses, and engineering textbooks—all purchased off the Internet. Several copies of the Qur'an and other religious writings in Arabic were also available.

Bathroom facilities consisted of an outhouse and a bucket rigged from a tree branch for showering. Still, Julio and his colleagues weren't complaining. In return for a few months of deprivation, they'd been promised a large enough deposit in numbered Panamanian bank accounts to ensure their creature comforts for the rest of their lives if they weren't too spendthrifty. For Julio, the accommodations were far superior to the Palmasola prison.

Julio couldn't complain, either, about the quality of training candidates he'd received. There were thirty young men in this first batch, all in their twenties. All spoke at least two languages, some four or five. All had a Western university education, mostly in Europe, but others in the United States. All had been through other training camps, either in Afghanistan, Sudan, or Malaysia. All had also seen combat, some years of it, either in Afghanistan, Lebanon, the Palestinian territories, Chechnya, or Bosnia.

Sometime during the months between Julio's release from Palmasola and the inauguration of this camp, all had undergone an equivalent of the Special Forces Assessment and Selection Course, or SFAS, a brutal program of long marches with heavy packs, limited rations, obstacle courses, sleep deprivation, and other challenges designed to make any but the most determined candidates drop out. Ironically, for those who'd spent years of jihad scrambling around the deserts and mountains of the Middle East's rugged terrain, the physical challenge of the course had proved minimal. But then, raw physical prowess had never been the downfall of the jihad's recruits.

Julio also was pleased with the variety of the candidates. Over half were Arabic, but not all had obvious Middle Eastern features. Others from Malaysia and Indonesia could pass as Native American, Mexican, or Andean Indian. Six were black, including two American Muslims, two from Sudan, and two from southern Egypt. There were three other Americans as well, two of Yemeni descent, the other Jordanian.

The Persian and Pashtun recruits, from the Caucasian nations of Iran and Afghanistan, could pass for any variety of European, as could the Chechens. The medic was a Palestinian doctor whose internship in a West Bank emergency room, patching up the results of Israeli raids, had fueled his quest for revenge. A third of the candidates spoke Spanish, and all spoke English to some extent.

Despite Saleh's aspirations, however, they would never be able to compete with the Americans, although Julio would not tell them so. Not even Julio, first among his country's candidates, could fully measure up. The American recruits came in with years of regular army experience and discipline, and their training was far more intensive than Julio's camp could provide.

Still, they did not need to compete, because their planned target was also less formidable—an unsophisticated and unsuspecting civilian population, rather than the armed opponents that American Special Ops soldiers were trained to combat. Neither were Julio's trainees hindered by the American obsession with human lives, an incalculable edge in itself.

These thirty recruits were smart and determined. They had attacked every aspect of the training with a single-minded ferocity that awed and chilled even Julio Vargas, who had taken more than his share of human lives. But then, he only killed people who got in his way. These men didn't seem to care who they killed.

Storing his flight gear on a shelf, Julio emerged from his quarters. The thirty candidates, still doing push-ups on the open green between the ruined church and the river, could have been any group of young men involved in athletic training.

Though it would never be possible to conceal from an expert eye what these men were about, the first aspect of training Julio had tackled was the all-too-easily profiled stereotype of the Islamic fundamentalist. Beards and long hair had been replaced by neat contemporary hair styles. Clothing had undergone a similar routine; even the camouflage fatigues used for training exercises were a civilian version purchased from an outdoor sports outfitter.

No Arabic was permitted; the official camp languages were Spanish or English. Each man carried new identification, produced by one of Ciudad del Este's best counterfeiters, and it was with this new identity that each candidate was introduced into the training program. Saleh Jebai, for instance, was now Sebastian Garcia. Those who could not speak Spanish were given American or European identities, depending on the proficiency of their English and their ethnic appearance. None carried identification from a Muslim-majority nation, and part of their training course work was developing a cover story to go with their new identity. Learning to blend in to a civilian population was a major priority: to ameliorate the arrogance and aggression that was part cultural and part the result of their militant training, to be always courteous and friendly and helpful to the locals with whom they came in contact, and to obey the local laws.

Open expressions of their faith had also been forbidden, even at the camp. There would be no breaking off in the middle of a training exercise to bow to the ground in prayer. Fortunately, the mullah, Sheik Mozer Jebai, had concurred that the successful exercise of the jihad superseded the requirements of ablutions and corporate prayers in the scales of Allah.

There were other classroom studies: working with explosives, communications and GPS systems, warfare tactics and mission planning, and less lethal training in battlefield medic skills from the Palestinian doctor. But the bulk of the training covered the skills these men had come to learn—what the American military called "unconventional warfare." Land navigation and survival skills were taught by the simple method of dropping units into the jungle at ever-increasing distances with no more technology than a compass and pen and paper. A GPS tracker allowed Julio and the other instructors to monitor the teams' progress, but every unit had spent at least one night up in trees out of reach of jungle predators before learning how to reliably track their way back to camp.

Julio had chosen to import all technical gear from the United States, not only because the population size and widespread Internet shopping made his purchases less noticeable there, but because past and present business connections made it simple to organize a regular pipeline for shipping goods south. Weapons were purchased locally from Ciudad del Este's impressive black market.

Though the candidates' physical conditioning was excellent and their soldiering skills adequate, Julio had soon discovered that these warriors of the jihad had a propensity for indiscriminately firing their automatic weapons, as if ammunition were a limitless resource. Hours every day were spent in target practice and breaking down and cleaning a variety of weapons, as well as training in hand-to-hand combat.

All the candidates had made swift progress in these skills, but teamwork had proved harder to master. After the first three weeks, Julio had divided the recruits into three teams, a variant on the U.S. Special Forces' twelve-man ODA—Operation Detachment Alpha—units popularized by Hollywood as the A-Team. In these units, they'd moved on to simulated missions—ambushes, reconnaissance, and practice raids. The building they attacked had been built by the recruits from plywood floated in on the riverboat. Its walls were movable to enable practice in a variety of assault scenarios. Here too, the shortfalls of their militant training became quickly evident. It was one thing to be willing to fight—and die—ferociously. But patience and discipline, the willingness to spend hours creeping up on a target, planning and rehearsing a mission until every detail was perfected, going to what sometimes seemed absurd lengths to ensure that mission success was a certainty, not a probability—these were the characteristics that gave the Americans their edge and which Julio had tried in vain to carry back to the Bolivian armed forces.

At least this bunch was willing to work at it, fueled enough by their hatred of the Americans to want to beat them at their own game. And they'd come a long way in the past several weeks, as demonstrated by last night's successful exercise.

Their morning Physical Training or PT now completed, the recruits walked over to the big clay pots that kept boiled water cool for drinking. The tang of strong coffee mingled with the scent of baking bread wafted deliciously from a thatched shelter where two Guarani women were preparing breakfast over an open fire. Julio wondered sometimes what they thought of the activity they observed in the camp. Not that it mattered. They would not be leaving this place. Meanwhile, they kept the camp tidy and were excellent cooks, their black braids hanging down perilously close to the flames as they cracked eggs into a clear consommé that would accompany the coffee and flatbread.

But first the "after-action review," the AAR from last night's excursion. Turning from the dormitory wing toward the old church, Julio paused to tug on a large brass bell hanging from a tree branch. As effective as any public address system, the clanging drew the recruits immediately toward the huge, carved wooden doors of the church sanctuary.

Though the fallen hardwood tree had caved in the far end of the room where the altar had been, the sanctuary was still the largest roofed space in the camp, and the recruits had erected a wooden partition to wall off the debris. A layer of kiln-baked clay bricks made a floor underneath, and the recruits had built rough tables and chairs to fill the area, which served as classroom, community hall, and communications center. The stripping down and cleaning of weapons, and more dangerous class exercises such as practicing with explosives, were carried out in a scattering of thatched shelters built at some distance from the main buildings.

The teams were clearly pleased with last night's performance as they settled into their seats. Julio proceeded to puncture their self-congratulation.

"Do not consider that because you managed to destroy your target you have done well. Team One, you lost two men. Team Two, three men. How was it you did not consider that the enemy would have a guard posted?"

"We did consider it," the Team One leader protested. "And we were careful in our approach. But we did not think they could see us in the dark."

"And you did not consider that perhaps they too had the foresight to obtain night vision capability?"

"It was a civilian target. An industrial complex."

"A civilian target with security set up by a company that includes former Special Forces personnel, as you would have known if you had studied the intelligence briefings. Do not ever again underestimate the security of even private American companies. They can afford to hire the best. Saleh . . . Sebastian." Julio cursed himself for the slip as he noticed swiftly hidden grins. "How did your team anticipate the sniper?"

The Team Three leader shrugged. "It seemed only logical to assume any capacity we had, they could have too. The sniper was placed where I would have chosen. I saw the movement of his weapon in the window. Though if there had been more than one with night vision, we might not have been so fortunate. It would have been wiser to land further away so that they were not alerted by the noise of the helicopter."

"As would have been the case if this were not a simulation," Julio said sharply. The Colombian instructor, who had played the role of security guard, was looking discomfited. Brilliant as the Team Three leader might be, he was a pain in any portion of the anatomy you cared to name.

"And you too were not entirely successful in your mission. They were able to begin destroying important computer files before you neutralized the last target." Julio looked around at the recruits. Some looked crestfallen, others angry, a few with a practiced lack of expression. Saleh was one of these. "Tonight when we have finished the day's exercise, we will run the simulation again," Julio said.

"No."

Julio stared at Saleh incredulously. Here was another sharp difference from the Americans. Julio could not conceive of one of the men with whom he'd trained speaking contrary to a superior officer. But then Julio was not a superior officer here, only a hireling, and this young man was among those who held the purse strings, as he was only too well aware. Still, this breach of discipline could not be ignored, or the recruits would get the idea it was Saleh who was in command here rather than Julio.

"No?" he answered flatly. In the black ice of Julio's glare, Saleh dropped his gaze.

"What I meant," Saleh said, with a conciliatory note in his voice, "is that I—we—grow tired of these simulations."

A murmur of assent swept the room.

"All of us have fought before. We have seen the blood of our enemies, seen our brothers drop at our side. These games we play, useful though they may be for training, are not the same. You cannot truly judge whether we would have succeeded or failed by the points allotted by your instructors. We understand the need to practice, to be perfect so no bodies are left behind to give us away. But we are tired of the games. We feel it is time to train for a real mission with a real objective."

The Colombian and Venezuelan instructors looked furious, but the others were nodding. A wrong move here could spark all-out rebellion.

"You wish to fight like the Americans," Julio answered coldly, "yet you question their training methods?"

And yet—

Julio broke off his rebuke as his mind began to work furiously. Part of Special Forces training was learning to think outside the box. Yet he himself had confined his thinking to the box of the American training he'd received.

Why not a real mission? The Americans used simulations because they had no true mission except for training. *And because of their ridiculous moralistic restrictions on unleashing their strength against their enemies.*

But Julio and the men he was training were not under those restrictions. Saleh was right. How much more effective it would be to train with a real target and real opponents. But where—and who? It would have to be kept simple. At least to begin with. And far enough from here so as not to compromise the ongoing operation.

Wait—

Of course.

Why not?

"Sebastian, you are correct," Julio said aloud. "To make use of the American skills does not mean we should be trapped into the weakness of their thinking. Still, we cannot move too fast or too far lest we risk exposing all we have accomplished so far. I have a target in mind that will fit those requirements nicely. And you, Sebastian, will be leader of the team that carries out this mission."

Chapter Ten

"I did it!"

Sara caught the astonished eye of a neighbor setting out garbage as she took the last three steps from her second-floor apartment to the sidewalk with a skip and jump. But this afternoon she couldn't concern herself with the public image of the neighborhood's newest elementary school teacher. She had to restrain herself from grabbing on as the two deliverymen wrestled her purchase up two flights of stairs into the apartment and through the narrow door of her bedroom.

I really did it!

Her first paycheck was in the bank. She had paid her share of the month's rent and utilities, made her first payment on a secondhand Dodge Neon, set aside her tithe for Sunday, and budgeted enough of the remainder for the sofa bed the two men were carefully lowering to the carpet. One month past her twenty-third birthday, she'd proved—to her own satisfaction at least—that Sara Connor was more than capable of surviving without family, husband, or well-meaning friends.

And quite nicely, thank you!

The accomplishment was a heady feeling, and Sara's smile reflected her elation as she tipped the two men and hurried back to admire her newest acquisition. The sofa bed was not new, but it was in good condition, and its replacement of the borrowed mattress she'd been using transformed an overcrowded bedroom to a gracious, if small, sitting-room.

Using what she'd learned from Cynthia over the last few months, Sara had stripped away peeling wallpaper and tightened the beige carpet, painting the walls a soft green and finishing the single window with white sheers and forest-green drapes. Pushed against a wall, the sofa bed, with its matching green-and-beige pattern, now opened up the scanty floor space. A desk with computer setup—a refurbished HP the school had been selling off—was tucked into one corner. A pair of overstuffed armchairs, two bookshelves, and a coffee table, all from the Salvation Army, completed the furnishings.

A walk-in closet kept the rest of Sara's belongings neatly out of sight. It wasn't the Cortéz mansion, but it was hers—a place to which she could retreat if she chose. As much as she liked her new housemate, Melanie, the girl had a taste for late nights and parties, that Sara didn't share.

The front door slammed, and a babble of voices erupted into the apartment. *Speaking of whom—*

A moment later, Melanie poked her head around Sara's open door, then came in when she saw the new decor. "Cool, I like what you've done with the place! Ready to hit mine next?"

Melanie Gomez, the elementary school's art teacher, was a statuesque redhead, with flaming curls inherited from an Irish mother, and a deep tan complexion from her Cuban father. "Come on out. Larry and Kim are here."

But her two guests were already crowding into Sara's room to inspect the interior decorating project. Kim Rocha, a third-grade teacher and native Miamian of Philippine descent, lived with another single teacher in the unit directly below Sara and Melanie. Larry Thomas shared an apartment several units down with one of the P.E. teachers. The two-level apartment complex was less than a ten-minute walk from Juan Rivera Elementary School and so had become a popular housing option for single teachers, as well as lower-income families.

Larry was the elementary school counselor—and looked the part. Tall and lanky, with a slight stoop as if downplaying his height, he was already showing signs of a receding hairline, though he was not yet thirty. Not that he wasn't a good-looking man. His features were still somewhat boyish, and his mild, inquiring gaze and diffident smile gave the impression he was always a bit amused by his surroundings.

Melanie certainly gave every sign of finding him attractive, though Larry never seemed to notice.

Sara stifled a sigh as she noticed Larry's hopeful brown eyes fixed on her. She'd first met him at the neighborhood church that Doug and Cynthia attended. In fact, he'd been the one to inform Sara of the job opportunity, and once she'd taken the position, he'd gone out of his way to introduce her to the other teachers and make her feel welcome.

If Sara could only rid herself of the suspicion that his interest in her had grown beyond welcoming a new neighbor to the block.

"We're heading over to the skating rink," Melanie said cheerily as her companions made the appropriate murmurs of approval. "Got to blow the cobwebs out after the bad art I've seen today! Then Kim and I at least were thinking of cruising down to South Beach. Maybe take in a night show. There's a new Brazilian samba band. Want to come along? You too, Larry, and your roommate if he wants."

"No, thanks. I've got my self-defense class in a half-hour." Sara indicated the leotard she was wearing under her shorts and sports top. "And a ton of homework to correct tonight. Unlike you, Melanie," she added teasingly, "I've got to *read* mine. Thirty essays on 'What I Did During Christmas Vacation.'"

"Self-defense class?" Kim stopped checking the titles on the bookshelves to stare at Sara. "You're kidding! What is it with people moving here that they all worry they're going to get mugged or something? I've lived here my whole life, and I can tell you it isn't nearly as bad as people say."

"I'm not worried about getting mugged." Sara didn't even try to explain how irrelevant Miami's crime statistics had been to her decision. "It's really just a straightforward martial arts program. And a bit of target practice too. If nothing else, it's better exercise than the gym," Sara shrugged. "And it never hurts to be prepared."

"Target practice, too?" Kim's thin eyebrows shot up. "You mean, guns? Well, if that isn't totally un-P.C. for J. R. Elementary. Just don't tell anyone in Admin you're one of those weapons freaks. Around here they figure you're either practicing to use it on someone, or you're one of those redneck wackos who put dead animals up on their walls."

"Don't worry. I have no plans to do either," Sara said wryly. "Now if you guys will excuse me, I've got to run. The instructor does not take rush hour traffic as an excuse for being tardy. Feel free to try out the couch," she called over her shoulder as she snatched up her handbag and headed out the door.

And wouldn't I love to see Doug's face when Kim gets going on political correctness, Sara grimaced humorously, clattering down the stairs. *Or Kim's if she caught sight of the bearskin rug or jaguar pelt in Doug's apartment.* That both animal furs were the result of self-defense would matter zilch to Kim.

Sara caught herself up short. Now how had that thought slipped through her defenses?

Difficult though it had been, Sara had kept her resolve in the weeks since she'd walked out of Doug's hospital room. Though she had visited Cynthia twice, she had neither seen nor spoken to Doug. Starting classes had left her too busy to brood over her decision, and once she'd heard from Cynthia that Doug was out of the hospital and back at work, she'd had no reason for further anxiety over his personal well-being.

I know I did the right thing. Certainly, she had proved she could make it without Doug Bradford or anyone else. Still—

I miss him! The sudden poignant longing was so strong that it stopped Sara on the steps. She missed glancing across the room at Doug's stoic expression when someone like Kim uttered an absurdity that would set the corners of his tight lips twitching. She missed talking to someone who knew a world bigger than this safe suburban neighborhood. Missed his dry humor and shrewd observations, the twinkle that could light those cool gray eyes to warmth. Missed the protective feel of his lean, muscular frame beside her.

No! It was time to put the past behind. And Doug was part of that past. Sara started again down the stairwell. It would be best just to erase that whole period from her life. To go back to the point in time before a tall, handsome stranger had strolled into a dark Seattle alley—and into her heart. Back before the four short months of her marriage. Before these past several months with the Bradfords.

Sara stopped abruptly again on the bottom step. But what *was* "back"? What had she been in those days before Nicolás Cortéz? What had her life held?

Nothing! The realization shook Sara with a sudden panic. Oh, yes, there'd been classes. Exams. The daily routine of an orderly, disciplined life. Despite her inner rebellions, she had always been a compliant daughter, an honor-roll student, a "good girl."

My friends always thought I was so self-contained, responsible, and . . . and serene. Calm, cool and collected Sara—until Nicky. But I wasn't really! I was just—waiting. Putting in time while I did everything expected of me.

Not that there hadn't been fun times. But Sara could not remember a time when she'd felt pure, unadulterated contentment—at least not since the day when most of her family had been killed on that Bogotá expressway, and her father had checked out emotionally, leaving a small, lonely girl to cope for herself. She'd learned to put off the present in favor of some future "happily ever after" that would somehow magically restore the happiness she'd lost.

With Nicky, I thought I had found it. But even then, it was more about the future—the family and children and home I'd dreamed of—than what or who he really was.

And with Doug . . . I . . . I wanted a guarantee there'd be a future—growing old together, kids, grandkids, retirement, the whole works—before I was willing to risk a "now." All these years I've hidden from my loneliness . . . from losing everyone I loved . . . by dreaming that tomorrow things would be different. And in the meantime, I've never gotten around to really living today—the good or the bad!

So what does the present hold?

Sara's car keys were in her hand, but she made no move toward the Neon at the curb. *Oh, God, if there's anything I've learned in all this, it's that no amount of waiting is going to bring happiness, because it isn't the circumstances in my life—not even people to love—that makes me happy. It's . . . it's something inside me. Something from you. A joy no matter how bad the storm outside is raging, like Doug found after Julie died. I felt it once on that hillside. Can I know it now? Here? Without ever knowing what the future holds. Or if it holds anything?*

And if I do live in the "now," what am I living for? Doug has so much purpose in his life. What purpose is there in anything I do?

Her ESL students, maybe. Thirty precious little souls. All of them facing as great a challenge as Sara ever had in her own nomadic childhood. Only yesterday, her patient probing had uncovered the fact that a certain uncooperative small boy was not the sullen troublemaker she'd assumed, but he was deathly afraid of the beating his Haitian stepfather had promised if the school had to call his home.

These kids had so little. Sara could make a difference in their lives at least. And there were friends. Maybe not like Doug, but people worth knowing.

"Sara?"

Sara whirled around, a startled hand going to her throat. "Larry!"

He hurried down the stairs until he was below Sara on the sidewalk. From her vantage on the second step, they were just about eye-to-eye. "I was hoping I'd catch you before you drove off. I didn't want to say anything up there in front of everyone but . . . I know you've got homework, but there's a classical jazz concert at the American Airlines Arena tonight. Nothing too wild. I was hoping if you weren't on with Melanie for South Beach, you might like to go."

Larry hesitated before adding, "I didn't want to say anything up there either, and I hope you won't think I'm intruding on your personal life, but—well, you know how small churches are. I know you had it pretty rough down there in South America, so I do understand about the self-defense class, even if Kim doesn't. And if you ever want to talk about it—"

Sara looked into his sympathetic brown eyes. Larry was such a *nice* person!

Kind. Considerate. Great with the kids. Sara had seen the wonders he'd worked with some of the more difficult students in her class.

He was even cute, as much as any guy she'd met in Miami.

And safe—as Special Agent Doug Bradford would never be.

Larry was part of her "now." Would he be part of her future too?

Or would Sara always be longing for what she couldn't have, like the adolescent addict of fairy tales she'd once been, who wouldn't settle for less than the knight on a white charger and so missed the possibilities of happiness that real life offered.

The warmth of her smile brought eager light to Larry's earnest features. "Sure, I'd love to go to the concert. What time do I need to be ready?"

Chapter Eleven

FEBRUARY 19
SANTA CRUZ PROVINCE, BOLIVIA

Julio adjusted his night vision goggles. A phosphorescent blur sharpened into the outline of a tin roofed structure whose screened-in walls revealed a row of army cots. Under a canvas awning the nylon hammocks used for draining processed cocaine sagged with the day's production. Camouflage netting, draped from tree to tree, hid the site from aerial surveillance.

As Julio had hoped, the Brazilian drug lord, whose payload Julio had hijacked for the Cortezes last summer, had not shifted his production site. Had he even guessed where those missing five tons had ended up?

Julio cautiously turned his head to survey the rest of the camp. The maceration pit, where coca leaves were trampled into pasty base, was empty. But despite the late hour, a pair of Coleman lanterns revealed the stooped shapes of a dozen peasant laborers busily shoveling the hammocks' contents into one-kilo plastic bags. An open thatched shelter held barrels and five-gallon plastic containers of the chemicals used in processing cocaine. Sulfuric acid. Kerosene. Hydrochloric acid. Ether. All highly flammable.

Perfect!

The glare of the lanterns flared brightly in Julio's NVGs. He removed them with noiseless stealth. Not that he was worried about being heard—or seen. From atop a fuel drum, a transistor radio blared a popular samba. The workers swayed to the music as they measured and stuffed.

Three armed guards kept a casual eye on the proceedings. One was propped up against the fuel drum with an AK-47 across his knees, while the other two prowled the perimeter of the camp. All three men had their eyes on the workers rather than on the jungle around them, which meant their night vision would be practically nil.

It was almost too easy.

Returning the NVGs to his eyes, Julio shifted his survey from the camp to the blackness of the jungle night. Even knowing the position of each assault team member, he could not detect so much as a black shape or flicker of movement. His students had learned their lessons well.

Then the sharp point of a twig or thorn dug through his fatigues into his inner thigh, and his approval gave way to irritation. *So what are we waiting for? Conditions won't get any better.*

But the order was not his to give. He was only an observer here, not in command. He was ready to grab at the offending barb, combat discipline or not, when an explosive *crack* drowned out the samba. A second *crack* followed. Both of the patrolling sentries jerked hard, their hands flying from their weapons. As they went down, a burst of automatic weapons fire opened up, raking through the camp in a fireworks display of tracers. The remaining guard didn't even get his AK-47 up before he slumped against the fuel drum, the Coleman lanterns illuminating the astonished shock on his face.

Screams rose above the gunfire and radio as the peasant workers scattered frantically from the drying hammocks. None made it far. Those few who managed to duck into the trees ran into another barrage of fire. Two men stumbling sleepily from the bunkhouse were dropped where they stood.

Just as quickly, it was over. A month of planning and hours of stealthy approach for an adrenaline rush lasting less than sixty seconds. But then, that was the way a successful mission was supposed to work.

The gunfire tapered off, leaving only the frenzied beat of the samba until a single impatient gunshot blew the radio from the fuel drum. A brief silence was broken by Saleh's "all-clear" in Julio's earpiece. With a grunt of relief, Julio rolled over to pluck the thorn from his thigh.

By the time he rose to his feet, black shapes were drifting into the camp. Walking out into the open, Julio noted with approval the neat hole between the eyes of one of the sentries. Saleh strode over to join him. The team leader was recognizable only by his height and the authority of his body language, his face a blur of shadows under the green and black camouflage paint.

Saleh broke his stride upon hearing a groan from the ground. Drawing a pistol from his belt, he leveled it downward and squeezed off a single shot.

"It was all so easy," he said to Julio as the two men surveyed the carnage. "So fast!"

"Do not be overconfident!" Julio answered sharply. "These were but peasants. Stay focused until you have completed the mission."

The other team members were checking bodies. Another single shot rang out. The team's two demolition sergeants were already rigging charges to the thatched shelter. They moved on to the bunkhouse and the drying hammocks as the other men heaped the dead bodies in the center of the camp.

Less than fifteen minutes after the first sniper's shot, the assault team was on its way back to the river. The inflatable rafts that had brought them downriver were pushing off from the shore when the explosive charges detonated. The kerosene, sulfuric acid, and other chemicals created a fireball that rose high above the jungle canopy. If not for a soaking rain that had fallen earlier in the day, the entire forest might have gone up in flames.

The team maintained combat discipline all the way back to the riverboat. Saleh had been right on all accounts, Julio grudgingly conceded as the men climbed aboard the boat. Not only had the mission been successful, it had gone more easily than he'd expected in every respect. The precision with which the team—and its leader—had carried out the plan had been a thing of beauty and exhilaration. So much better than the "war games" the Americans played.

So why not do it again? There were plenty such targets to be found. Added supplies would be needed, and a forward operating base established to minimize moving gear back and forth. But the supply pipeline from the north was now well-established, and Julio still had friends—or at least contacts—who owed him favors.

The adrenaline rush of the mission spurred Julio's thinking as he began to make his plans.

Chapter Twelve

FEBRUARY 24
MIAMI, FLORIDA

Doug yawned. He wasn't tired. He'd had more consecutive nights' sleep in the past several weeks than in years. He was bored.

Rotating his left shoulder to ease a lingering cramp, he surveyed his desktop with a jaundiced eye. It was the cleanest he'd ever known it, another sign of boredom. Every contact report had been typed into the computer, the case notes filed away. Even the loose ammo, pens, paperclips and other paraphernalia rolling around in his desk drawers had been sorted and returned to the little cups and bins supplied for them.

He grimaced. The place looked like Mike's cubicle now, not his own. Six weeks of busywork were too many for any injury short of permanent incapacitation. It wasn't even as if his gun hand had been affected. But Norm Kublin had flatly refused to let him back on the street until Doug received written clearance from his physician.

With any luck, that would be tomorrow.

Doug rotated his left shoulder again, clenching and unclenching his fist as he did so. The shoulder was still a little stiff but no longer painful. Doug had already scheduled some target practice following tomorrow's all-clear.

Meanwhile . . .

Doug picked up the last item on his blotter, a stack of computer printouts about two inches high, a listing of cargo manifests that had come into the Port of Miami over the past week. With all his paperwork caught up, he was justifying what the taxpayers shelled out for his salary by "trolling for bait," surfing through databases for anything suspicious that might catch his eye. In recent months, illegal narcotics had turned up in shipments of soap, aluminum ingots, roofing tiles, and asphalt, and a variety of other trade goods.

Scanning through a manifest of German pharmaceuticals, Doug slipped it under the bottom of the stack, followed by a manifest about a shipment of electronics from Hong Kong. It wasn't that none of those items would hold cocaine or other drugs, but out of millions of items entering the Port of Miami each week, where would a handful of DEA and Customs agents start to look?

Doug scanned down the next sheet, automatically started to slide it under the stack, then sat up suddenly, his boots sliding from his desk to hit the floor with a thump. *Wait a minute!*

Doug read through the manifest more slowly. A cargo of concrete tubing shipped from Barranquilla, Colombia, to Miami. With cement as cheap as it was and surely no shortage of concrete tubing in the U.S., why would *anyone* bother manufacturing them in Colombia, then pay the freight costs to ship that enormous weight to Miami for resale?

Unless . . .

Unless those posts were worth more than the concrete.

Doug reached for the phone. Whom did he know down in Customs? Tim McAdams. No, he'd retired while Doug was in Bolivia. Maybe Hector Morales, unless his transfer had come through.

Civilians had the idea—abetted by Hollywood—that an operation like this started with a bunch of super sleuths up at headquarters piecing together secret intelligence and organizing their vast array of resources into a well-coordinated campaign to take the bad guys out. In reality, *everything* was personal. Every major investigation started out with a local agent like Doug noticing some person or piece of intelligence that just didn't smell right, like these concrete tubes, then picking at it and piecing together data until there was enough information to take further up the totem pole.

Even then the agents didn't cool their heels waiting for headquarters to follow up on the data. They'd be waiting until Armageddon. Instead, they typically called in a fellow agent or a narcotics officer at the local precinct, talked to the group supervisor, or pulled in some favors over at Customs or the Coast Guard.

It might seem an inefficient and roundabout way to run a law enforcement agency, but only to those who'd never tripped over the miles of red tape the higher levels of bureaucracy liked to throw in the path of any agent actually trying to get something done. Only when the legwork was done and every report filed in triplicate would headquarters jump on board to share in the credit.

Or so it seemed to the agent at street level.

Institutional rivalry between law enforcement agencies didn't help. The

Federal Drug Identification Number assigned to every case or seizure was given to the agency that pulled off a deal. Whoever claimed the FDIN not only received credit for the bust—and credit was what counted on the annual report to the Congressional budget appropriations committee—but also any assets seized during the arrest. In this case, it could possibly be an entire freighter.

A bad guy could slip away while the desk jockeys were arguing over jurisdiction. That was why field agents preferred to cultivate their own contacts that they could call when a deal came up. They would throw each other an occasional case in return for cooperation, and leave the interagency politics—and the budget—to the headquarter pukes.

Again, everything was personal.

Doug spun the Rolodex, then paused as he spotted Mike Garcia threading his way through the maze of cubicles that Doug shared with the rest of his enforcement group. "Hey, Mike, you were down at Customs last week. Is Hector Morales still there?"

"No, he left last month." Mike let out a low whistle as he glanced over Doug's shoulder. "Looks fishy, all right. Try Louie Rodriguez. Mention my name and the Jamaican rum bust last month. He owes me for that."

"Thanks. I owe you one. Want to pop down there with me?"

"Sorry." Mike dangled a pair of car keys. "The Bird's finally coming out of the shop. I'm heading over to pick it up."

"They fixed the Firebird?" Doug said incredulously. "I didn't know there was enough left to bother with. How did you talk them into that?"

"I had to track down the parts myself. And do the math that it would be cheaper than trashing it and issuing a new vehicle. I'm taking Debby and Junior out for a spin just as soon as I sign off on it. Anyway, gotta go. You shouldn't have any problem with Louie. He's a good guy." Jangling the keys in farewell, Mike walked away. "Just don't forget—last month, Jamaican rum bust."

Doug grinned as he went back to his Rolodex. Being a father had certainly given Mike more assurance.

It does that to you!

His eye flickered to a framed photograph no longer buried in the usual mess of his desk. A young woman holding a toddler against a backdrop of Miami beachfront, the tiny girl's mischievous smile and dark curls a younger version of her mother's. Julie's pregnancy was not yet visible in the photograph.

No, he wouldn't go down that path of memory. He was happy for Mike, and that was that.

His mouth twisted as he reached past the photograph to pick up the latest addition to his desk, a pewter replica of a famous World War II sculpture. He turned the figurine over in his hand, a soldier in infantry gear standing on a rise, head lifted, eyes narrowed and watchful, automatic rifle steady in his hands.

Even Doug could see the resemblance. The inscription read "Standing in the Gap." It was the birthday gift Sara had left with him when she walked out of the hospital room.

She does get it!

But whether Sara understood or not was irrelevant to the present—or the future. *I thought she was for me, God. I guess I heard you wrong.*

Doug knew that his mother still saw Sara and spoke to her regularly by phone. But he'd respected Sara's wishes and had not tried to contact her since she'd walked out of the hospital room and out of his life—although it hadn't stopped him from cruising through her new neighborhood to satisfy himself about the security arrangements.

He also knew who Sara's new neighbor was and couldn't even resent it. Larry was a good man, the kind of solid, decent, *safe* man Sara probably needed and that he himself would never be. And it was, of course, a relief to know that Sara had someone nearby she could depend on if she ran into any difficulties. He wished them both well.

A pang wrenched at Doug's chest, but he pushed it away with the discipline that came from long years of practice. Plenty of the guys were single. It was a career hazard in this job. Maybe it was for the best. Either way, a job remained to be done.

Replacing Sara's birthday gift, Doug reached again for the Rolodex. *Louie Rodriguez.* Had he filed that under *R* for Rodriguez or *C* for Customs?

He had just located the number under *C* when the phone rang. Doug snatched up the receiver. "Yep?"

"Ramon here." The voice on the line didn't sound as if it was coming from the other side of the equator, thanks to Uncle Sam's satellite communications network.

"What's up?" Doug replied, skipping the usual pleasantries. Ramon Gutierrez had been the closest Doug had had to a partner during his last hectic months in Bolivia. That something was up was a given. Ramon did not do social calls.

"A lot. You remember David Stout?"

"Sure. Blond, short, and fat. Supposedly works for some international aid agency. Bought a mansion in Las Palmas just before I left."

"That's the guy."

"And . . . ?" Doug prodded impatiently.

"We got him. As you might have guessed, all those trips stateside weren't to attend some international aid conference." Doug could almost see Ramon's wolfish grin. "That's why I'm calling. He just boarded the American Airlines flight to Miami—four inches too tall."

"Coke in his shoes," Doug filled in the blank. "What an idiot! Does he think we don't know that one?"

"Well, he's obviously been getting away with it for a while," Ramon answered reasonably. "And now we know why. We had our guys watching the whole thing. He never cleared Customs—just walked around through the back door with their pilots, laughing and joking the whole time. He's got high connections at Viru Viru, that's for sure. We're making the busts at this end right now."

"And you want me to pick him up at this end?"

"No, the opposite. I need you to get ahold of Customs up there to make sure he gets through to his final destination—which happens to be Chattanooga, Tennessee, if you can believe it. I'm already talking to the SAC there. They're setting up a team to take him down—and with any luck, his contact too. Better yet, Tennessee gives twenty-to-life for mules instead of a slap on the wrist like Miami."

It's all personal.

"I'll get on it and call you back," Doug agreed.

"One more thing. Uh—" Something ominous in Ramon's pause sent Doug's mental antenna shooting high. "There's something else you should know. Your friend Julio Vargas? He's gone."

"What do you mean *gone*? Where? When? I thought he was in Palmasola."

"So did we. And according to the system, he still is. We'd never have known he'd gone AWOL if a judge for one of the hacienda cases hadn't insisted on hearing Julio's testimony in person. He was nowhere to be found. No one even knows how long he's been gone. The paperwork must have been paid for with cash, and of course none of the guards remember anything about his release."

"And he hasn't shown up anywhere else? Surely there must be *some* trace of the guy!"

"You know better than that, Doug. It isn't like life down here runs on a computer data network. Unless something happens to get his name entered into some Interpol file somewhere, we're not likely to stumble over him. Especially if he was smart enough to get out of the country. There must be thousands of guys named Julio Vargas out there. And that's if he kept his own name."

You win some, you lose some! Doug thought savagely. And it sure seemed at times he did more losing than winning. "Well, keep your eyes open."

"We will; don't you worry. Oh, and speaking of Interpol, we've had another interesting incident. Remember that Brazilian last summer, the one whose pilot we picked up who'd had his plane forced down and was scared to death the Brazilians were going to take it out of his hide?"

"Sure, one of those hauls Vargas hijacked with that Huey of his. We never did get the Brazilian, if I recall. He kept on his own side of the border. And we never found his production lab either."

"Yeah, well, we have now." This time there was satisfaction in Ramon's narrative. "Not that we can claim any credit. The place must have got hit by a bomb or something. We picked it up on satellite surveillance . . . looked like a fireball boiling out of the jungle. We sent a couple agents along with the *antinarcoticos* to check it out—including yours truly. I've got to say it was one professional job. I couldn't have taken it down better myself—except all the dead bodies. Of which there were plenty, though the explosion didn't leave much in the way of forensic evidence. The explosive, by the way, was C-4. Same stuff we use."

"Stuff we've donated in bulk to the local counternarcotics units," Doug retorted. "Who knows how much has been sold off on the black market."

"Maybe," Ramon admitted. "But you can guess what the local media is saying."

"Let me see . . . that the DEA took the place out—and murdered a bunch of helpless peasants?" Doug said dryly. "So what else is new? What do *you* think?"

"Who knows. If there wasn't *lots* of coke residue left behind, I'd figure the Brazilian's got a competitor who hired himself some mercenaries. But whoever hit the place didn't bother taking the coke with them, and there had to be a few million worth of dope there."

"Well, keep an ear to the ground." Doug was not particularly interested in the woes of a certain Brazilian lowlife. "I guess it's too much to hope our Brazilian friend was on site when it blew."

"I wouldn't know. That at least will come screaming up the grapevine sooner or later. Hey, did you hear Kyle has a girlfriend? That cute little Bolivian secretary from Chemical Seizures. She comes about up to his belly button."

"Most girls do." The office gossip continued for a few moments before Ramon rang off.

Doug set down the receiver but immediately snatched it up again and began to dial. It wasn't the number for Customs that he found himself punching out, but one that he shouldn't even have had memorized. What would Sara say when she found out that her erstwhile prison warden was out and on the loose?

Like she needs to know right this minute? For what? It's just going to upset her, and it isn't like she can do anything about it.

Admit it, Bradford. You've just been looking for an excuse to get in contact.

In any case, Sara would be teaching at this hour. Without completing the ten digits, Doug slapped down on the disconnect button and began dialing the number for Customs.

Chapter Thirteen

MARCH 13
PUERTO SUAREZ, BOLIVIA-BRAZIL BORDER

A third cocaine lab in the Guarayos Forestry Reserve was destroyed in an explosion yesterday. Along with the deaths of a dozen laborers, this latest blast instigated a forest fire that has spread to hundreds of hectares, destroying several Indian settlements and threatening a fishing village on the Pirai river. The American embassy denies that the attacks mark a new offensive by their counternarcotics personnel. However, leaders of the Association of Coca Growers are denouncing the violence as a direct and illegal American assault on their livelihood as well as the sovereignty of the nation of Bolivia. Thousands of coca growers are threatening further disturbances and roadblocks if the perpetrators of these attacks are not found and punished.

Saleh Jebai folded the newspaper and dropped it on the deck of the riverboat. "Interesting how these *cocaleros* can be found in the middle of committing a crime and yet protest that they are victims."

"We have certainly stirred up a hornets' nest." Julio took a long draught of cold beer purchased from the same riverbank vendor as the newspaper. "From now on every production site will be on alert and heavily armed. It is time we changed tactics."

"And left this country. It is too small to avoid notice forever." Saleh cast a glance down the line of moored boats. In Puerto Suarez, a busy river town on the Bolivia-Brazil border, they were just one more cargo boat in town for supplies. But by the law of averages, sooner or later someone was bound to get nosy . . . or some border patrol agent would to want to poke through the boat before taking their bribe.

"Yes, I concur." That the Americans would be blamed for his training missions was a side benefit Julio hadn't foreseen. If nothing else, it proved that even his countrymen's inexpert eyes recognized a professional job of the sort carried out by the Americans. The danger lay in arousing too many questions among the Americans themselves, who knew good and well they weren't responsible. Better to quit while their assaults could still be dismissed as infighting among the *pez grande,* the "big fish" of the drug cartels.

Still, one last slap at the Americans couldn't hurt.

"We will give them some breathing space." Julio dropped the empty beer can on top of the newspaper. "I have leased a DC-3 and am making arrangement for a delivery of parachutes and other gear to begin jump training. When it comes, we will move north to the Chaco for drop exercises and desert training too. Meantime, we begin planning for a new class of mission."

Chapter Fourteen

MIAMI, FLORIDA

Pow! Punch! Lunge! Kick!

Dropping her gym bag just inside the apartment door, Sara kickboxed her way across the open living room–kitchen area.

Crash!

A dining table chair tipped over under the same sideswipe that had put Sara's self-defense instructor flat on his back an hour earlier. She'd been the first in the class to manage such a feat, but then few others had her motivation. *I will never be helpless again!*

Mid-lunge, Sara caught sight of herself in the mirrored sideboard beyond the dining table. She wrinkled her nose at the tousled hair and sweat-reddened face above the spandex leotard and running shorts.

You look like a cross between a psychiatric ward escapee and Wonder Woman!

Smiling triumphantly, Sara walked over to the kitchen counter. Seven new messages were blinking on the answering machine. Sara pushed the play button before heading into the bathroom to grab her robe. "This is Sara de Cortéz, no? Rosedalia Gasser here from Santa Cruz, Bolivia. I am president of the Miami chapter of the NFWO. I was given your name as a former member in Santa Cruz and would like to invite you to participate in our meetings the second Thursday of each month. If you will call me at this number . . ."

Sara listened incredulously as she stripped off the leotard and dropped it into a laundry hamper. She'd been less than excited to find out that Miami was home to a sizable Bolivian expatriate community, as it was for ex-pats from every country in Latin America. The economic chaos resulting from the inroads Doug and his fellow DEA agents had made against Bolivia's most profitable export was driving more and more of the moneyed class to liquidate their remaining assets and relocate to a more comfortable life in Miami.

But that enough of the upper crust had relocated to form a local chapter of the exclusive National Federation of Women's Organizations, a euphemism for the social club of Bolivian bluebloods her mother-in-law had chaired back in Santa Cruz, drove home a reality that Sara been doing her best to ignore. Who had given this local chairperson her name and phone number? Sara had counted herself fortunate not to have encountered any of her in-laws' past associates from Santa Cruz. Could it have been the one Bolivian teacher Sara had met in the ESL program? Or the airline stewardess from La Paz in her self-defense class? Sara had made no secret that she'd moved to Miami from Santa Cruz. She hadn't thought it necessary.

She punched the delete button. Sitting around while a bunch of wealthy aristocrats bragged about mansions, maids, and social position had bored her stiff when her mother-in-law had dragged her to the club meetings. Voluntarily attending one here in Miami was the last way she'd waste her time.

The next three messages were for Melanie. Then a male voice that did not bother identifying itself. "Sara, I'm shopping for Kim's wedding present this evening. I thought maybe we could go together on it. Melanie too, if she'd like, of course. Call me when you get in."

Kim Rocha had astonished her friends when she suddenly announced her engagement to a marine lieutenant stationed in Miami with Southern Command. The wedding would be in just two weeks, because her fiancé, Ray, was being transferred to the Philippines. Kim would spend her honeymoon visiting her parents' birthplace for the first time.

Sara's thumb hesitated on the delete button. Larry had been increasingly attentive lately—always there, without ever crossing the line into pushy, handy when her car broke down last week, and certainly a godsend with advice during some of Sara's more difficult classroom situations.

But shopping together for a wedding present was too much of a "couple" thing—especially since Larry knew as well as Sara did that tonight was Melanie's monthly artists' association meeting. As much as Sara appreciated his help, she did not like the assumption both he and others seemed to be making that there was an automatic place for him at her side and in her activities.

Her thumb completed the deletion. She still needed to pick out a gift for the bridal shower, but she'd hit the mall this evening on her own. Turning on the shower to warm up, Sara listened to the last two messages as she grabbed a one-piece coral jumpsuit and sandals from her closet.

The first was from Aunt Jan. "Call me, Sara, please. I've got a new cell number."

Sara programmed the number into her own cell phone before listening to the final message. This one was from Mrs. Fougere, mother of her troubled little Haitian student. Sara had finally wrangled a parent-teacher conference. To her relief, she'd found that Mr. and Mrs. Fougere were not the abusive, uncaring parents she'd feared but bewildered immigrants lost in a way of life and culture of child-rearing that was totally alien to their own. Despite her lack of experience, Sara had found herself giving more parental than educational advice. She'd even scraped up a battered copy of James Dobson's *Dare to Discipline* to send home with Jean Pierre.

Mrs. Fougere's emotion was audible as she thanked Sara, ending the message with an invitation to a Haitian "jerk" feast Saturday to meet the rest of the family. And that, Sara decided as she showered, was one invitation she'd accept. Score one small victory for the embattled public school system—at least her own minute role in it.

Sara waited until she was headed toward the mall before dialing up Aunt Jan's new number. A hands-free phone setup for the Neon had been her latest indulgence, a great time-saver with the number of calls she had to return from parents.

"Hello, Sara, dear. I was hoping you'd call before I left the office." Sara could hear her aunt's fingers clicking on a keyboard. "I'm on DSL right now looking at some ads for teaching positions. Did you know we have quite a shortage out here? I've been doing some checking. Even for the summer sessions you could have your pick if you put in an application fairly soon."

Sara murmured something noncommittal. To her surprise, Aunt Jan had called several times over the past few months, each time urging Sara to come out for a visit. More recently she'd turned her energy to persuading Sara to move back permanently.

"I know you kind of fell into a job situation out there. But this is your home territory. This is where you have family. You're welcome to stay with me until you get established."

Sara had a strong suspicion her aunt's recently empty nest was at least partially responsible for this sudden urge to reestablish contact with her only niece. Still, she found herself warming to her aunt's persistence.

After all, Aunt Jan is right. They are my family . . . my only family. Her choice was a simple one. She could hold a grudge—and really, Sara hadn't been Aunt Jan's responsibility, ten years ago or ever. Or she could let the past go and open herself up to a relationship with her closest remaining blood relations.

Aunt Jan misinterpreted Sara's silence. "If it's financial, dear, please don't let that hold you back. I have an excess of air miles built up. I'd be only too happy to send you the ticket. I've been checking the public school schedule out in Miami. You have spring break coming up in a few weeks. If nothing else, take a couple of weeks and come out and get to know us again."

"I'll check it out and let you know." And this time Sara found she meant it.

Strange how things work out, Sara thought as she left a message on the Fougere answering machine. She'd finally surrendered the years of longing for family and belonging, and now without any doing of her own, family had stepped back into her life.

God is good. Not was. Not will be. He is good!

The lines were not original with Sara. They'd been part of last week's sermon at a new church she was visiting. But she embraced them as much as the pastor had. Rolling down her window to breathe in the crisp, clear air of a South Florida spring, Sara felt an unexpected contentment bubble up inside her. It was as if she'd emerged from a long illness. The cloudless arch of sky seemed somehow a deeper blue, the grass a more emerald green, the caws and squawks and twitters of Miami's abundant feathered population more melodious than she'd ever known them to be.

That exhilaration lasted as Sara wandered through the mall, poking her head into specialty shops. What did a teacher who'd been on her own for years still need to set up housekeeping?

Sara was debating a black lace confection in the window of Victoria's Secret when she overheard a supercilious female voice raised in angry Spanish from inside the boutique. The speaker either did not care she was being heard or assumed the other shoppers around did not understand, but the Spanish obscenities punctuating her tirade were not what made Sara stiffen.

"What do you mean, you cannot accept my application? Does it not say right there on the wall behind you that you are seeking help? How can you say you must have a different visa paper? All of my acquaintances are working without this visa. You are simply . . ."

Sara listened in stunned amazement to the continuing outburst of invective. It wasn't just the regional accent to the Spanish, but the very arrogance and inflection of the tone. Could it be . . . no, that was impossible!

Sara moved to the doorway of the boutique in time to see the speaker storming away from the sales counter. Tall. Voluptuous. The swinging shoulder-length dark hair and striking olive features of an Italian model, a figure Sara would have once given at least a molar or two to possess.

Sara blinked. It couldn't be!

And yet it was. Reina.

Nicky's cousin, whom everyone in Bolivian high society, including Reina herself, had assumed would marry the Cortéz heir until he brought home a plebian *gringa* as his wife. What could Reina possibly be doing in Miami? And looking for work? The most onerous work Reina had ever done was buffing her nails between manicures.

Reina's stormy glance landed on Sara at the same instant. Her long, angry steps stopped in mid-stride, the expression on her beautiful, furious features was as stunned as Sara knew her own must be. Reina unfroze first.

"You!" Reina's hand went up as she covered the last few strides. She was several inches taller than Sara and far angrier, and Sara was totally unprepared. The force of the slap sent Sara staggering back so only the doorjamb slamming into her back kept her from falling.

Behind Reina, Sara saw the shop clerk reach under the counter, and by the time Sara recovered her balance, a security guard was approaching.

"What is going on here?" Taking in the imprint of a hand on Sara's cheek, the guard grabbed Reina by the upper arm. He was Jamaican by accent and very large, and after an initial angry glare, Reina did not try to resist his grip. A hand to her cheek, Sara blinked away tears of pain and shock. That had really hurt! *So much for self-defense. I can't even see a slap coming!*

Then she straightened her back and turned to the guard. "Thank you for your help, but it's nothing. Just a personal disagreement that got out of hand."

The security guard did not look convinced. "You can press charges against her if you like, miss. We caught the whole thing on tape."

Sara shook her head. "That won't be necessary. She isn't going to touch me again, are you, Reina?"

Under Sara's hard gaze, Reina shook her head grudgingly. After asking Reina to kindly remove herself from the store, the security guard released her and walked away. But not too far. Sara saw him watching them and was pleased to see that Reina too had noted his continued surveillance as she spun around and stalked out into the mall.

"What was that for, Reina?" Sara said as she hurried to catch up. "This isn't Bolivia where you can slap around your maid or anyone else you choose. What are you doing here, anyway?"

"That?" Reina spat out. "That was for everything! You have destroyed my life. And were it not for the arrogance of your police, you would receive far more than a slap. Thanks to you, I have lost my home, my money—and the man I loved," she added, rather belatedly. "Even the demeaning labor of selling underclothing is denied me."

"But—" Sara cut into her ranting, bewildered. "What are you talking about? You aren't even a Cortéz, just a cousin. You didn't lose your home or anything I know of when they seized the estate . . . including anything that was supposed to be mine," she added heatedly. "It seems to me I'm the one who should be complaining here, not you!"

"And how do you think we lived?" The hiss of Reina's voice was as soft and deadly as one of her country's poisonous reptiles. "Where did you think our money came from? Everything we had—for all of us in the family—came from *Industrias* Cortéz. How did you expect us to live when that was gone? Where were we to get more when you destroyed everything we had built up?"

"If 'everything' was drug dealing," Sara retorted, "I can't exactly feel sorry for you. But that doesn't explain what you're doing in Miami. And where are Nicky's sisters—Delores and Janeth? And Diego and Raymundo? I heard they're not in Santa Cruz anymore. Do you know where they went?"

"Of course! Right here in Miami with me," Reina spat out triumphantly. "And why not? We are not criminals! Do you think you are the only one who can come here to this place? Miami is for the Latinos, not you gringos. There are many of our friends and relatives here already. Though if we had known you were here as well—" Her eyes narrowed with speculation. "If I were you, I would go northward with all speed to your own country before Raymundo and Diego learn where you may be found. Do not think you can expect not to pay for what you have done to us."

The sheer intensity of hatred and triumph glittering in Reina's dark eyes was daunting, and Sara explored the pit of her stomach for the quiver that should have been there. But instead of fear, she felt only anger. This was *her* country! The land of her citizenship. And here, at least, whatever they might think they could do back in their own country, the Cortezes did not hold sway as kings.

"Go ahead and tell them!" Sara replied through gritted teeth. "I'm not leaving. This time you're in *my* home, *my* country—not yours. To anyone here, the Cortezes are just a bunch of sleazy drug dealers. And if you step out of line, I'll have the police down on you so fast you won't be able to move!"

It was as much a slap as Reina had given Sara, and if hatred were actual fire, Sara would have been a piece of blackened carbon lying on the mall floor.

Reina drew herself up to her magnificent full height, then caught the eye of the security guard and took a step back from Sara.

"We shall see," she hissed. But the impotency of her threat was evident even to her, because she was the first to look away. Spinning around on impossibly high heels, she stormed away.

Sara was breathing hard as she watched Reina disappear into the crowd. The adrenaline was still pumping through her body, and when she glanced down, she was dismayed to see that her hands were shaking. Not from fear, but from sheer, unadulterated fury.

Despite Sara's brave words, it wasn't that she didn't take Reina's threat seriously. Whatever excuses Diego and Raymundo had pawned off on the Bolivian authorities, Sara knew that her former brothers-in-law were capable of violence—and revenge. She'd been there when Ricardo died; she'd seen them holding down the poor boy and had seen the looks on their faces as Nicky's gun came up.

But, as she'd told Reina, she was no longer a helpless prisoner in the Cortéz stronghold. This was her country. And here there were resources to stop sleazes like Diego and Raymundo.

The question was how her former in-laws had made it to Miami? What kind of immigration officials would give visas to the family members of a major drug cartel? Or were they in the country illegally?

If so, Sara could do something about that, at least.

On impulse, she hurried back into the boutique. Reina had been empty-handed when she came storming out. Maybe—

"Excuse me, miss, but would you still have the application that woman who was just in here filled out for your job opening?"

The sales clerk showed both doubt and curiosity in her expression. "Well, I don't know. . . . We're not supposed to give out information on our employees."

"But she isn't an employee," Sara wheedled persuasively. "Look, you saw what she did to me. Her name's Reina. You can check on the application. And she was my former husband's girlfriend. She made some threats. All I want is to find out where she lives so I can let the police know if she tries something else. I just thought—well, if she happened to step out and leave her application lying around, that isn't really your responsibility, is it?"

"No, it sure isn't!" Reaching down behind the counter, the clerk set a wastebasket down with a thump. "Hey, I know about ex-girlfriends. They can be some scary!"

The application lay in a crumpled wad on top of the trash. "Thanks!" Sara gave the clerk a grateful smile. As she left the boutique, she smoothed out the sheet of paper. The address Reina had scribbled was in Coral Gables, one of Miami's more exclusive neighborhoods. So much for Reina's whining about money.

So to whom does one report something like this? Not to the police, unless Sara planned to press assault charges. Immigration? Sara wouldn't know where to start. No, there was only one person she could call on this. Besides, he needed to know. This might conceivably make a difference to his case.

This time Sara wasn't sure whether it was apprehension or anticipation that gripped her stomach as she dug in her purse for her cell phone. It had been so long.

It was a letdown when the DO administrative officer broke the news that Doug was out of town. "Fishing, I think, down in the Keys with some of the guys. The roster says they're planning to be back Saturday night. I can get a message through if it's urgent."

Karla's tone held a note of surprise that Sara would be calling. What had Doug told his colleagues?

"No, it isn't urgent," Sara assured Karla hastily.

Besides, this wasn't something to be done over the phone. If Doug was due back Saturday evening—tomorrow—then there was another option. He was not the only reason she had started visiting another church. It was just too hard to refute Larry's logic that there was no point in driving two vehicles from the apartment complex to the church each Sunday. *And I am not going to walk in there on Larry's arm like he's—*

But if Sara wanted to see Doug, she'd just have to grit her teeth and accept Larry's carpool offer. Doug would be at church if he was in town, and Sara could either catch him there or make a major issue of tracking him down. Besides, it would be good to see the people who had befriended her in those early months, especially Cynthia, whom she hadn't seen or spoken to in weeks.

Chapter Fifteen

MARCH 15

Neither Doug nor Cynthia was there when Larry and Sara walked into the church foyer. Sara's response to the warm greetings and hugs was distracted by keeping an eye and ear out for the Bradfords' arrival.

As the first worship song was ending, Sara was relieved to see Doug and his mother making their way down the central aisle. Though Cynthia showed no sign of noticing Sara, Doug looked her way immediately—but he did not make eye contact or look her way again as he ushered his mother into a pew a few rows in front of Sara. Nor, as she had hoped, did he make his way toward her once the service had ended. Was he still so angry over her decision? Or was he simply abiding by her request—dismissing Sara from his thoughts and his life?

Threading out into the crowded foyer, Sara marked where Doug was standing beside his mother, waiting with commendable patience as Cynthia's hands waved in animated conversation with a friend. Looking straight across the crowd, Sara deliberately caught his eye. Still, Doug made no move to detach himself from his mother's side, the corner of his mouth sloping down in a familiar twist as he glanced from Sara to Larry at her side. His expression was so discouraging that Sara almost turned on her heel and headed for the door.

Larry noticed the interchange and turned to look at Sara. His Adam's apple moved up and down as he laid a hand on Sara's arm. "Uh, Sara . . . maybe I got the wrong idea here. If you are still—well, if there is still something between you and Doug Bradford, I don't want to intrude. You just have to tell me if you want me to back off."

Any sympathy Sara felt at the anxious look in his brown eyes was superseded by impatience. Why did friendships between men and women have to get so complicated?

Gently, she removed Larry's hand from her arm. "I am not involved with anyone, Larry," she said firmly. "But I do need to talk to Doug . . . so if you'll excuse me."

Doug glanced away as Sara started toward him. Most of the throng was taller than Sara, so she had to keep stopping to take her bearings. By the time she squeezed through a final knot of chattering teens, Cynthia was nowhere in sight, but Doug was still where she'd pinpointed him, his head bent courteously toward an adolescent girl who had stopped to talk to him. Her round young face was lit up with animation and pleasure.

Sara understood. Doug was wearing the suit and tie that only Sundays or a court date could get him into, the form-fitting jacket and slacks accenting his superb fitness, unlike the looser clothes he usually wore. And the self-confident lift of the head and air of competence would always make him stand out in a crowd.

It was a self-confidence in total contrast to the arrogance bred into a Luis or Nicolás Cortéz, or even the polished facade of the oil executives Sara had grown up around, whose complacency seemed rooted more in outward appearance and connections than in any personal inner qualities.

A lack of self-consciousness was as close as Sara could describe the assurance that was so much a part of Doug's character and that of the other agents she had met. An outward focus, as if there were simply too many more important things to do than worry about the impression they were making on others. In the agents' sharply defined world, it was simply irrelevant what anyone thought of their appearance or actions, except as it affected an agent's ability to get the job done.

Which in itself was an attractive trait, Sara admitted. Especially after the posturing and ladder-climbing that was such a part of Bolivian high society and the international business scene Sara had known.

All in all, Special Agent Doug Bradford was a very attractive man, Sara decided as she saw him flash a rare grin. Strange how little thought she'd given to that before. A friend, yes. A person on whom she could rely implicitly. A comforter and bulwark against danger.

But now, after the weeks apart, it was as if she was seeing him for the first time. Or at least with a fresh perspective. But she was no longer a victim, the damsel in distress, so Doug was no longer her rescuer, her savior. Instead, he was—if not a stranger, then at least a man on whom Sara had no more claim than . . . than that blushing teenager.

Yes, an enormously attractive man, Sara said to herself as Doug turned lazily to face her, as if he'd known full well she'd been waiting to speak to him.

And I?

That the thought crossed her mind at all was a further indication of how far she herself had traveled in recent months. For so long, the impact her appearance might have on others had been a matter of total indifference, as long as she was neatly and decently attired. The not caring had been curiously freeing, and even now it was with detached appraisal that Sara glanced at her reflection in the glass of a large plaque on the foyer wall.

Why did I always find myself so . . . nothing? Was it because I had no one to tell me I was the most beautiful little girl in the world, at least to them? Because I was no one's little princess? Even with Nicky, I always felt somehow that he only thought I was beautiful because I was blonde, and Bolivian men liked blondes.

The dark wood under the glass offered back a wavery image, but it showed well enough the flaxen shine of her long hair spilling down over the simple black dress she'd chosen for church. The subtle application of makeup emphasized the contrasting amber of her eyes with their impossibly long lashes. And though her heart-shaped features and average height would never grace a fashion show runway, she was healthy, fit and—thanks to those self-defense classes—in the best physical condition she'd ever been in her life.

As for the rest, she was above average in intelligence, college-educated, hardworking, capable, even in possession of a reasonable sense of humor.

I have nothing I was not given, nothing of which to be proud. But neither is there anything of which to be ashamed.

The whole thought process had taken less time than it took for Sara to walk past the plaque, and with the winking out of her reflection, Sara pushed all thoughts of herself out as well.

As she crossed the remaining distance that separated her from Doug, his cool, appraising gaze narrowed on her face, even as his posture became more relaxed. He leaned against the wall in a comfortable slouch more suitable to his weekday attire than to the suit he was wearing.

It was part of his agent training, the ability to narrow his concentration on one focal point—or one person. Or maybe that ability was what made him a good agent. Either way, it could be an attractive quality—or extremely irritating if you didn't feel like being the bug under a microscope.

Gathering herself up to her full modest height, Sara lifted her chin to meet the challenge of those steady gray eyes. "Doug, I need to talk to you."

Doug detached himself from the wall, his mouth sloping downward derisively. "Hello, Sara. It's good to see you, Sara. You're looking well. How are you doing? It's been a long time."

Sara laughed. "Sorry! I didn't think you were into pleasantries. Let me start again. Hello, Doug. Long time no see. How are you doing?"

Doug's scrutiny narrowed further on her laughing face, and his mocking expression disappeared. "You really are looking well, Sara," he said quietly. "Different."

He swiftly scanned from the merriment in her eyes to the touch of pearls at her throat and earlobes that only an expert would recognize as costume jewelry, down to the simple black dress, and back up to the tilt of her chin and the smile playing around her lips. "You look—whole again," he added slowly.

Sara's smile grew serious as she met his gaze. "Yes, I think you're right, Doug. I *am* whole again. I guess . . . it just needed time." With a lighter note, she added, tilting her head to run a quick survey over Doug, "You're not looking bad yourself. New suit?"

Doug's lips twitched. "Mom's idea of birthday shopping." Taking a stride away from the wall, he got down to business. "You said you needed to talk to me. Somehow I don't think a mutual admiration session was what you had in mind. What's up?"

His gaze cleared the top of Sara's head, and the line of his mouth grew suddenly straight. "Is it Thomas? Do you have news, and I'm the last to know?"

Glancing backward, Sara spotted Larry hovering not far away, conspicuous now that the crowd in the foyer was thinning out.

"Of course not!" she retorted indignantly. "He just gave me a ride! Come on."

With impatient strides, she headed for an open door across the foyer. The "brides' room," as it was called, was fitted out with mirrors and flower arrangements, and was usually empty, unless there was a wedding or a worshipper in need of solitude. Spinning around as Doug kicked the door shut behind them, Sara demanded, "What is it with you men that everything has to be about relationships—romantic relationships, at that?"

"Because it usually is," Doug replied dryly, but the hard line of his mouth relaxed. "So, if this isn't an announcement, what could we possibly have to talk about after, let's see, almost three months?"

"Reina. Did you know she is in Miami?"

Sara saw the answer in Doug's face. She told him about the encounter in the mall, leaving out only Reina's slap. She might have known nothing would escape the DEA agent's observant ear.

"So you're telling me the security guard just showed up. Give me some credit, Sara." Taking Sara's chin in his strong fingers, Doug tilted her face so that her cheek was in the light of a window. His voice hardened to a dangerous note. "She hit you, didn't she?"

"Ow! Not so hard." Brushing away Doug's hand, Sara said ruefully, "I thought I had the makeup right. Anyway, that's irrelevant. She was angry . . . and I can see her point of view, even if I don't appreciate being the target. What matters is that they're here in Miami. Not just Reina, but Diego and Raymundo. Janeth and Delores too, I suppose."

Pulling Reina's application from her purse, Sara handed it to Doug. "Here's the address she put down. I hope it's enough to find them."

Taking the paper, Doug glanced down at the scrawl of handwriting. "So . . . what exactly is it you're hoping I can do here, Sara? Are you concerned about the threats—that Diego and Raymundo might really come after you? Are you asking for police protection to be assigned?"

"No, of course not," Sara answered impatiently. "Reina doesn't know where I live, for one, and I don't know how she'd ever find out. I'm not in the phone book. The apartment's in Melanie's name. It was sheer accident we ran into each other. Though—"

Sara told Doug about the call from the NFWO chairperson. "I suppose it's conceivable, if they get together with other ex-pat Bolivians, that they could get my number the same way she did. I never thought to keep it some big secret. But I'm not afraid of Diego and Raymundo, not here in my own country. Even in Santa Cruz they were always talkers, not doers. They never stuck their own heads out to take any risks for their dirty money. Don Luis would go for revenge in a minute. But Diego and Raymundo—they wouldn't come after me unless there's something in it for them. But that doesn't mean I want to live in the same city—*my* city—with them. Can't you just call Immigration and have them deported or something? I mean, they can't be in the country legally, can they?"

A gleam had appeared in Doug's eye at the phrase "my city." But he shook his head. "I wish I felt as confident. I don't suppose I can talk you into moving away from that apartment—and phone number."

He lifted his wide shoulders at Sara's expression. "I didn't think so. At least don't be handing out your biographical data or any other personal information to anyone else. And I don't want you going anywhere alone, do you understand? Oh, and you might want to have Larry or someone check your locks and security system."

Sara was torn between irritation and amusement. "Yes, sir!"

Doug did not respond to her mock salute. His unsmiling expression evaporated Sara's amusement. "As for getting them deported," he continued, "I'm afraid that may not be so easy. Don't forget, your in-laws were cleared of any wrongdoing by the Bolivian courts."

He raised a hand as Sara opened her mouth to protest. "Whatever you saw or heard. As for Reina, legally at least, she and her family aren't connected to this case at all, except by blood."

"*And* blood money!"

Doug ignored Sara's comment. "You said they couldn't be in the country legally. I hate to disillusion you, but if having a family member on the Interpol lists as being under investigation for corruption, bribery, human rights abuses, illegal enrichment *or* drug dealing disqualified you for a visa, a good portion of Latin America's ruling class would be sealed inside their borders."

Doug shoved Reina's application into a pants pocket. "I'll check this out. But I've got to tell you that if they had the application fees, there's every likelihood they're in the country legally. As for anything else, however things are done in Bolivia, here we have something called 'due process of law.' A guy is innocent until proven guilty. You of all people know how important that little piece of American law is. And by that law, these guys are innocent. Unless they're implicated in a crime here on American soil—and convicted— they have every right to make a new life for themselves here—same as you and I do."

That Sara knew he was right didn't make it any easier to hear.

"Do you really think they're here as good citizens, just trying to make a new life for themselves?" she said. "Where did they get the money, for one thing? You know they were broke when things settled down in Santa Cruz. That address is Coral Gables. How are they living? And why, of all the places they could go, would they come right here where we just happen to be living? Are you telling me none of that matters? That Reina is right, and they can get away with it here, just like they did in Bolivia?"

She turned away blindly toward the door, groping for the knob. "I guess I was pretty dumb running over here thinking I had some important intel you should have for your job. Well, I won't bother you anymore."

Doug didn't appear to move swiftly, but he was suddenly between Sara and the door, his hand covering hers on the doorknob. "No, you were right coming to me. Don't *ever* hesitate to come to me for anything. I mean that."

He took a step back from the door and went on more evenly, "As for your information, no, I don't think the Cortéz are here to be good citizens. And they won't be getting away with anything, trust me. I don't know what they're doing here. I can *guess*—and it's got nothing to do with us. They came for the same reason they all come. Why exile themselves in Europe or somewhere else when in Miami they can be with their own people and have all the benefits of living in Latin America without any of the drawbacks of a Third World country? They may even be legit this time. But that doesn't mean they aren't scumbags. They deserve to be behind bars, whatever their legal status, and I can promise you this: If there's so much as a grain of dirt under a rock somewhere that can build a case against them, I'll find it."

There was something dangerous in his smile as Doug added grimly. "This time the Cortéz are on *my* turf, and they're going to find out what that means."

Sara's breath went out of her in a rush. "That's all I wanted to know. Thank you." Her hand went again to the doorknob, but she did not immediately turn it. "Well . . . I'd better go. My ride is probably getting impatient."

Under lowered lashes, she glanced back at Doug, who had perched himself on the arm of a sofa, his long legs stretched comfortably in front of him. For a few moments there'd been the familiar, easy communication between them. But now Doug was wearing the bland, inscrutable expression he reserved for strangers, suspects, and people for whom he did not particularly care.

Sara gathered courage with a deep breath. "I . . . well, before I go, I've been wanting to ask how you've been. Is everything going okay? At work, I mean." Sara's glance went to the smooth material of his suit coat. "Is your shoulder okay?"

There was the smallest twitch of Doug's mouth, a slight thawing of his remoteness. "My shoulder's fine. I'm fine. I've been back out on the street a couple weeks now. We had a big bust last week—you might have caught it on the news. Otherwise, same-ol', same-ol'."

He finished with a shrug and upraised eyebrows, and the ensuing silence quickly began to stretch into awkwardness. At least for Sara.

He's never been one to fill in any empty gaps with words, she reminded herself ruefully.

"Well, I'm glad. I . . . I've been worried about you." This time Sara did turn the knob. "I guess this is good-bye then."

Doug did not move from his lounging position. "Yes, I imagine Larry-boy out there is chewing his nails by this time," he said dryly. "Pass on my regards, and do have him check your security. Oh, and call me if anything else comes up. Or even if it doesn't. I—my mother has missed you. I know she would be tickled pink if you dropped by."

That last bit at least wasn't an exaggeration. Both Cynthia and Larry were in the foyer as the door swung open. Larry had an uncharacteristic impatience on his boyish features that made Sara grit her teeth at Doug's shrewd assessment.

"Oh, there you are!" Cynthia cried out. "Doug, I was about to hotwire the car and leave without you. Sara, I thought I saw you. You're looking great."

"It's good to see you too, Cynthia." Sara glanced back over her shoulder at Doug, who was wearing his bland look again, one corner of his mouth tilted downward in a satirical twist. "Could you . . . would you mind letting me know what you find out, Doug?"

His gray eyes bored into Sara's with an intensity that made them appear almost black. "Do you want me to?"

"Yes," Sara said simply.

"Then I will." As both Cynthia and Larry closed in on Sara, Doug got to his feet, exited the room, and strolled away.

Chapter Sixteen

MARCH 16

"So what should we do?" Janeth wailed.

In the two days since Reina had stormed in with the news, the younger of Sara's former sisters-in-law had shifted from disbelief to shock and anger—and fear.

The disbelief came from long acquaintance with her beautiful cousin. This was just the sort of bombshell Reina might invent, in a bid for attention, if not out of malice or even boredom. The phone book revealed no Sara Connor or Cortéz, nor a Doug Bradford.

But Reina's fury was too convincing for a lie, and it had soon occurred to Delores, Janeth's older sister, to call the social power broker in the ex-pat Bolivian community, Rosedalia Gasser of the NFWO. Miami might be a city of millions, but there was still only a certain segment that mattered, and among them the grapevine of gossip still moved quickly. Not only did the chairwoman have a phone number, but the name of the Bolivian flight attendant who'd given her the number. The young woman was flattered by a call from one of her country's foremost families. If she had no address, she knew the name of the art teacher who often accompanied Sara to the gym. And a Melanie Gomez was listed in the phone book.

"Are you sure it was my son's *americana* wife and not some other *gringa*? There are many with such blonde hair in America, and they look much alike." Perched rigidly on the edge of an armchair, Sara's former mother-in-law, Mimi, sat with a straight-backed elegance that belied her age, her patrician features as cold and unyielding as the marble floor under her feet. Only the whitening of her fingers on the arms of the chair betrayed her fury.

"No, it was Sara," said Raymundo from across the room. "She has not changed. The gold of her hair, the eyes, the slimness of her figure—" he broke off hastily at a glare from Janeth. "I sat across the street for more than two hours this morning before I could be sure. When a woman emerged, tall with red hair, I too thought perhaps it was an error. But then Nicky's woman arrived in a car with a man. There was no mistaking her. She was dressed for a party, but it was early in the day for a party. The man was very solicitous. But it was not the agent Bradford; of that I am certain."

"So, already she has another man then?" Reina spat out from a recliner. "I always said the *gringa* was a tramp."

"Perhaps," Raymundo shrugged. "Though he did not kiss her, and he went into another nearby apartment. Perhaps he is only a neighbor."

"Then where is the American agent Bradford?" Diego demanded. "We know she left Santa Cruz in his company. You should have questioned this neighbor."

"And alert them that we are making inquiries?" Raymundo snapped back. "Don't be stupid."

"But what do we do?" Janeth wailed again. She glanced around the spacious Coral Gables home with its oriental rugs, soft leather sofas and armchairs, the tasseled lamps and gilt-framed paintings. It was not the Cortéz mansion, but it had been an adequate sanctuary. The laughter of children came from a nearby recreation room.

"Must we run again? We have only begun to accustom ourselves to this place. Our children are happy enough. There is everything we need, if not enough servants. I do not wish to move again to another country—one that may be less convenient than this."

"But if she calls her American friends—this Bradford—and tells him we are here, then it will begin all over again." Delores was crying quietly. Her children were older, already in grade school, and they had been the most traumatized by the upheaval of their pampered and tranquil lives. "If we have so easily found where she is living, how should she not be able to find us? We have not tried to hide. We will be shamed here as we were in Bolivia. And after we stooped to allow this *gringa* with no pedigree to be part of our family. It is not to be borne."

"So get rid of her!" Lounging carelessly against the soft upholstery, Reina glanced around at the startled faces with a malicious twist of her lips. "Come, let us not pretend the Cortéz cannot be ruthless, if it is necessary. She killed Nicolás and Don Luis, did she not?" No one contradicted this version of events. "Are we then to let her walk away without avenging their deaths? Have the Cortéz grown so soft?"

There were swift side glances, but no response. Reina was coming close to putting into words things that propriety demanded should not be stated, and the disapproval on the faces around her made that clear.

"Reina, you are a foolish girl!" Mimi was the first to speak, her icy distaste enough to make Reina sit up sulkily. "Do not ever speak such wicked thoughts aloud."

"Foolish! She's just plain stupid." Janeth glared at Reina. "It is your doing. What possessed you to go to this mall to demand a job? Do we not have enough that you would stoop to work behind a store counter like some *empleada?*"

"It is the way things are done here in America," Reina said sullenly. "The allowance Raymundo and Diego have made is not enough to purchase the things I must have. And in this country, even those of good family work. There is no shame."

"Enough!" Mimi raised an imperious hand. "What is done is done. The question is, where do we go from here? Raymundo . . . Diego. Luis is not here to make these decisions anymore, so you must do so. Must we leave—or take other measures?"

Raymundo and Diego exchanged glances. In their early thirties, both showed evidence of a stocky, powerful build, softened by too much food and alcohol and too little exercise. Marrying a Cortéz had been a windfall for both men. Since their wives came with a secure income, the decision to propose marriage had been the last mental exertion either man had been required to make.

With the collapse of *Industrias* Cortéz, that decision had turned out to be less advantageous than anticipated, but it was too late now to change the path of history. What would their formidable father-in-law have done? In one thing, Reina was right. He would not have allowed either the woman or the American agent to walk away unscathed. But Raymundo and Diego were less interested in Cortéz honor than in survival. What they needed—what both men craved—was a stronger will to take the decision out of their hands.

The answer came to both simultaneously. "We must contact Julio Vargas," Raymundo voiced aloud. Diego nodded. "He will know what to do."

The two Cortéz sons-in-law had asked few questions when their former security chief contacted them with a proposal to establish a procurement and shipping business in Miami. They had not even wondered why Julio should bother with the expense of locating his former employers instead of dealing with a local firm. Vargas had long served the Cortéz family. It only seemed natural he should continue to prove of service to them now.

Though there was nothing deferential in Julio's response when Raymundo dialed the emergency number he'd left them. This turned out to be an extension of the Paraguayan travel agency listed on the manifest of every consignment of goods Julio had asked them to put together. Naturally enough on a Sunday afternoon, the call to Rain Forest Survival Treks reached only an answering machine. Vargas had warned them the number was only a holding place for messages, and it might be days before he could return a call. But in fact, it was less than five minutes before the phone rang. "Yes? I was in the office when your call arrived. This better be urgent."

Julio was coldly furious at the story Raymundo had to tell, but not for the reasons the Cortéz men expected. "You idiots! Why are you so shocked? The girl is an American. The agent Doug Bradford came to Bolivia from Miami. Did you not even bother to read my reports? It is unfortunate, but not a surprise that they should choose to locate themselves in Miami, nor is it odd that your paths might cross. If your cousin, the beautiful but stupid Reina, had refrained from uttering threats, that would have been an end to it. Now there is no doubt you are right. The girl will call her friends—the agent Bradford and others. Your cousin should have stayed in Bolivia!"

Raymundo couldn't agree more. "So what do we do? We have spied out her living quarters. Should we hire someone to put a full surveillance on her? Or—?"

"You will do nothing!" Julio's harsh command both startled and offended Raymundo. "After all the trouble I have gone through to establish you respectably in Miami? Have you so little brain that I must do all the thinking for you?"

Raymundo didn't attempt to answer that one.

"Or is it that you still do not understand how such matters work in America. You have done nothing wrong. You have not entered the country illegally. You have no charges filed against you. This agent Bradford may sniff around as he did in Santa Cruz, but he will find nothing he can use against you. And that being so, he cannot touch you. Their own laws work in our favor this time, but only so long as you stay away from the *americana*. If you raise one finger to bother her, go near her once or make a single threat, you will give reason for the American authorities to come down on you as they please. Of more importance—" Julio's tone grew icy "—your employment will be at an end, with the handsome remuneration you have been receiving. You are not the only ones I can find to do the job you do, only the most convenient. Do I make myself clear?"

What he'd made clear was that the relationship between the Cortezes and their former security chief was not what Raymundo had assumed. Raymundo answered sullenly, "Yes, we understand. But what if there is trouble? If this Bradford and the girl continue to cause difficulties?"

"If there is trouble, we will deal with it then. Meanwhile, it is not all a loss. At least we know now where Bradford and the girl are. It is always useful to know where one's enemies are to be found."

This time the implacable chill of Julio's tone was more to Raymundo's liking. "Meanwhile," Julio went on with a more conciliating tone, "I came into town to speak with you, so your call is not as inconvenient as it might have been. I have another list of purchases I wish for you to make."

Chapter Seventeen

APRIL 3

Using a pair of tweezers, Doug picked up a clothing boutique sales tag and shook off a banana peel. The price on the tag was enough to elicit a soundless whistle. Pushing aside scrapings of *paella,* he peeled back a plastic bag. The paper underneath turned out to be only a wadded Kleenex.

Doug stifled a yawn under the surgical mask that, however effective against infection, did nothing to filter unpleasant odors. A midnight raid of a South Beach club had brought him back to the office after 4 A.M., and he was scheduled to meet Norm Kublin and a Customs inspector on the docks at eight. A smarter man would be spending the intervening hours catching a few winks. But a drive-by of the Cortéz place on the way to the raid had finally netted the three Hefty sacks spread out on a drop cloth in front of him.

What Doug had hoped to find were some credit card receipts, an incriminating phone number—*how about a list of clients or drug shipments?* So far all he'd learned was that the Cortéz clan didn't bother with generic brands, their women were clearly not on a fixed budget, and the children seemed to live on Spaghetti-Os, macaroni and cheese, and frozen pizza. Ugh! And at least one of them was still in diapers.

Giving the decomposing mass a final prod, Doug stepped back from the table. Theoretically, all agents in a DEA enforcement group were created equal. In practice, one privilege of attaining a GS-13 status was passing the messier chores off to newer recruits. Peeling off latex gloves and the mask, Doug gave a nod to the neophyte, two months out of Quantico, who'd been foolish enough to volunteer his services after the raid.

"Okay, Rick, looks like that's all we're going to find. Go ahead and clear this up. I've got a couple address checks to make before heading down to the docks."

Doug didn't linger to see the young man's expression before heading for the sink to scrub his hands, then outdoors to his tan Ford Taurus. Unlike Mike, he preferred to remain anonymous during a stakeout. Doug sniffed discretely as he crossed the parking lot. Was that the scent of garbage lingering on his clothes? Well, they'd just have to air out. He didn't have time to drop by the apartment if he wanted to swing by both the Echevarrias and Cortezes before sunrise.

Gustavo Echevarria was the recipient of the concrete tubing that had roused Doug's interest last month. Unfortunately, the shipment had passed through Customs and was long gone by the time Doug made it through the red tape. But the weeks since then had not been wasted. Surveillance of Echevarria's home and business had turned up some interesting associates, along with a rather large gap between earnings and assets. All of which was due to hit the fan this morning when Echevarria's latest shipment of tubing reached Customs.

Doug cruised slowly past Echevarria's colonial-style home. Between 4 and 6 A.M. was the best time for a drive-by, because even the most swinging of bad guys crawled into bed for a few hours. Yes, there were Echevarria's Hummer and BMW. If he showed up for that Customs inspection in a few hours, they had their man.

The Cortéz residence was less than ten minutes' drive from the Echevarrias, not as much a coincidence as it might seem since Coral Gables was a popular district for upscale expatriate Latinos. Doug pulled up under a mango tree, one of several stakeout spots he'd used in the last three weeks. Sliding back the driver's seat to stretch his legs, he reached for a thermos of coffee. It was still dark enough that the Taurus was only a shadow under the low-hanging branches, but a street lamp offered a well-lit view of the Cortéz driveway.

Tracking down the Cortéz clan had so far proved as easy as for any local resident—and as unincriminating. Doug had made his first drive-by the same Sunday Sara gave him Reina's address. The Cortéz home was as opulent as its address suggested, one more colonial-style mansion, its burnt-red tiles clashing with that garish pink that Miami residents preferred to call "coral."

On that hot Sunday afternoon, Doug had seen no sign of movement from the house, but with the support of a thermos and a sack of Dunkin' Donuts, he'd lingered until dark. His patience had been rewarded when the front door finally opened and seven adults emerged. One had to be the nanny, judging by the screaming preschooler she was trying to restrain. The others Doug recognized as Sara's sisters-in-law, Delores and Janeth, and their husbands, along with their cousin Reina, looking as beautiful and venomous as ever. Doug sat up straight as he caught sight of the last person. Doña Mimi Velasquez de Cortéz. So the Cortéz matriarch had chosen to accompany her children and grandchildren into exile.

All but Mimi and the nanny had piled into a spanking-new minivan that Raymundo backed out of the garage. Doug noted down the license plate number and that of the BMW parked beside it. He spent the rest of the evening trailing the group, netting a meal at the Hard Rock Cafe, two South Beach night clubs—and nothing of professional interest.

Zilch was also the net return on Terry O'Brien's computer search when Doug turned address and license plate numbers over to him on Monday morning. Running the names through NADIS, the Narcotics and Drugs Identification System, had resulted in an immediate *ping*. But that was a no-brainer. The counternarcotics database indexed every human being anywhere in the world who'd ever come in contact with American law enforcement. Brother-in-law, cousin, employee of a dealer—if their name had been so much as mentioned in a DEA-6 or any other counternarcotics report, it would be in NADIS. As for the Cortéz clan, Doug himself was responsible for their presence in the database, and he was already well acquainted with the useless tidbits on file.

An INS search revealed how the Cortezes had disappeared from Bolivia and into Miami without a red flag going up. Their visas were issued properly in their own names, to Doug's disappointment, and with no attempt to falsify their country of origin. But they'd been issued from Madrid, Spain, rather than La Paz. With the flood of Latin American passport holders traveling through Miami International Airport on any given day, a Diego Martinez or Raymundo Pinzón arriving with their families from Madrid would arouse as much interest as a Bill Smith or Tom Jones.

A motor vehicles check revealed that only two of the clan—Diego and Raymundo—had been issued driver's licenses. So far no tickets. The minivan and BMW turned out to be registered in the name of a local business, Tropical Imports & Exports. The house was registered in the same name, and the business was listed on Diego and Raymundo's resident visa applications as local sponsor and guarantor of gainful employment for the two men.

Gainful employment! Doug snorted derisively as he poured another cup of coffee. A gray haze above the red-tiled roofs signaled dawn's approach, and any number of cars had already pulled out of driveways to beat Miami's infamous rush hour traffic. But from inside the Cortéz residence there was no hint of movement . . . no surprise.

O'Brien's discreet hacking into TI&E's employment records had indeed found Diego and Raymundo listed as employees at a salary that drew another whistle. Clearly he was in the wrong profession. But unless the two men worked from inside the Coral Gables mansion, it was difficult to see what they were doing to earn their exorbitant salaries.

Drive-bys after work, during lunch breaks, and other odd hours netted only that the Cortezes were as big on partying as they had been back in Santa Cruz, their driveway and sidewalks crowded with vehicles at least three times a week. Doug dutifully noted down the license plates, but these turned out to be members of Bolivia's wealthy ex-pat community, most of them connected to each other in a tangle of marriage and blood relationships.

And if I hassle the whole bunch, I'm profiling!

On other nights, it was the two couples and Reina who went out, cruising home in the early morning hours with their car stereo blaring loud enough to rouse the local cemetery. They certainly didn't act like people trying to avoid attention.

And however late Doug hung around in the morning, the only movement he'd ever caught was the nanny getting the older children off to the school van that picked them up. It seemed Diego and Raymundo's employers were generous enough not to expect them to check in to an office anywhere. That was no different than when they held vice-presidential positions with *Industrias* Cortéz back in Santa Cruz.

The TI&E records did offer one explanation for the luxurious standard of living the family was maintaining. If they'd laundered a sizable chunk of family assets into foreign businesses like Tropical Imports & Exports, those assets at least would have gone untouched in the seizures of Cortéz properties. *Industrias* Cortéz had done enough legitimate business in Miami over the years to make it possible.

The street lamps switched off as the dawn brightened. Doug poured a last lukewarm cup of coffee and began thinking of bathroom sites. He'd have to move soon, not only because of the growing light, but because of the time. His GS would not take kindly to a late arrival for mission planning, and if he wanted to swing by his own apartment for a shower and shave before moving into the day stretch of what had become a double shift, he needed to hurry.

Giving up on the coffee, Doug dumped it out the window and reached for the ignition. But he hadn't yet turned the key when a grinding sound down the street had him hastily straightening up. Finally some action!

The garage door of the Cortéz home finished its upward slide, and the BMW backed into the street. It turned to head toward Doug, and as the driver floored the accelerator to race down the empty street, two dim figures behind the windshield took focus. Diego and Raymundo.

Doug waited until they turned the corner before easing out after the BMW. The early departure was at least a change from the usual schedule. Doug thought regretfully of bathroom and shower before dismissing both from his mind to concentrate on keeping the BMW in sight. This was made easier by the usual morning slowdown already taking effect. Hitting the Dolphin Expressway that connected Miami International Airport to the east coastline reduced the BMW's pace to a crawl. Doug, a discreet dozen vehicles behind, checked his watch. At least they were headed the same general direction as where he was to meet Norm Kublin and the rest of the mission team.

Indeed the driver of the BMW might well have been reading Doug's mind, easing off I-75 at the same exit Doug had planned to take and turning into the port area where cargo ships berthed at the long row of piers. This was no rare appearance at the office. His interest now well roused, Doug followed the BMW as it turned down a street bordering the piers.

Ships ranging in size from fishing trawlers and small freighters to huge cargo ships and oil tankers were docked as far as the eye could see, their hulls high enough to block any view of the bay beyond. One was the Colombian-registered freighter whose shipment of concrete tubing Doug was scheduled to inspect in less than two hours. Turning in the opposite direction, Doug tailed the BMW, growing more cautious with each block, occasionally even stopping to ensure that a casual glance back would not spot the Taurus.

But the occupants of the BMW drove straight to a pier where one of the smaller freighters was docked. Not that any of these ships were what Doug would term small. Perhaps three hundred feet long and thirty wide at the beam, the freighter carried a crane derrick on deck for unloading and loading cargo. And from the movement of the crane, it was presently in use.

Pulling up a block away, Doug rummaged out a pair of binoculars. This was more like it! *Industrias* Cortéz had used just such shipments of goods to bring cocaine into Miami and other ports. Was this the answer? If Diego and Raymundo were up to the old family tricks, it would be a pleasure to nail them.

But it took only a few minutes to determine that freighter was loading, not unloading, cargo. Two container trucks were parked near the gangplank, and a team of stevedores was maneuvering a quantity of crates and boxes to where the crane could swing them aboard. Diego and Raymundo disappeared up the ramp, only to reappear shortly with a burly seaman wearing the cap of a commercial sea captain. The foreman who had been directing the stevedores joined them. Diego carried a clipboard and was to all appearances tallying the merchandise against the foreman's paperwork.

Without lowering the binoculars, Doug reached for his cell phone and punched in the DO number. As he'd expected, O'Brien was already at his computer banks. "Terry, I need you to check out a ship for me. Name's *Buena Vista*." Doug read off the identification numbers painted on the hull and added his own description and size estimations.

"A three-hundred-foot freighter? I thought you were checking out a cargo ship. Doug, just where are you?" the intelligence analyst demanded. "Kublin called here not five minutes ago screaming that you're supposed to be down at the docks."

"I *am* down at the docks." Doug didn't go into further explanations. "Just get me what you can on those numbers. Owner, country of registration, etc. I'll stay on the line."

Doug could hear O'Brien's overweight wheezing, the clatter of a keyboard, and the grunts and hmms with which the intel analyst punctuated his thought processes. Raymundo and Diego had disappeared on board again by the time O'Brien was back on the line.

"It's registered. Belongs to a local company. Tropical Imports and Exports. The company is incorporated here in Miami, but they maintain offices in Panama, Ecuador, and Paraguay. Pretty standard for an import/export company dealing goods south. They own just one ship, the *Buena Vista,* and a warehouse in town. I can dig up the cargo manifests if you need them, but that'll take some time."

"Sure, do that, but no rush. I've got what I needed. Thanks!"

"Yeah, well, it isn't the ship you're scheduled to take down this morning," O'Brien retorted. "I've got the specs on that right here—just faxed the latest arrival data over to Kublin at Customs. You wanting that too, or have you caught up to Kublin?"

"Just print me out the cargo manifests." Doug broke the connection. The problem with having a good intel weenie on tap was that they never stopped digging for data—even when it was none of their business.

But O'Brien was right. Doug was out of time. And the intel was clear enough on the surface, if disappointing. As employees and possibly shareholders of Tropical Imports and Exports, the Cortéz duo had every reason to be down at the docks, supervising the latest loading of cargo destined for points south. If they'd been muscling barrels and plastic containers on board, Doug might have suspected they were smuggling chemical precursors for producing cocaine. But whatever was in those crates and boxes, they didn't hold corrosive liquids.

Doug shifted the gear stick into reverse. Maybe they really were just trying to start over like so many of the Bolivian ex-pat community. In any case, there was little more Doug could do. For all Reina's bluster, Sara had heard nothing more from her erstwhile in-laws. Unless something criminal turned up, or a definite threat against Sara herself, Doug had too many other cases pending to continue investing hours in surveillance that had proved unproductive. And speaking of pending cases—

Doug's cell phone shrilled at his belt.

"I'm on my way," he cut into Norm Kublin's impatient query.

"It's about time! We've already started final mission prep. It's a go for 10 A.M. Get your butt down here."

"I'll be there in five minutes."

No longer concerned with concealment, Doug swung the Taurus around and sped the opposite direction along the docks. All that remained was to contact Sara and let her know the results of his investigation, little as it was. Though she was probably on her way to school by now. Besides, a face-to-face report was more courteous than the terseness of a telephone conversation.

Doug swung into the parking lot of the Port of Miami Customs office, nipping neatly into a space next to Norm Kublin's Toyota Camry. That South Beach Italian restaurant Sara liked so well would be an appropriate environment to convey information of this significance.

Strictly business, of course.

Chapter Eighteen

Sara's thoughts were not on the Cortéz investigation or Special Agent Doug Bradford. To be sure, for the first few evenings after her encounter with Reina, she'd braced herself with every shrilling of the phone. But as three weeks slid by without further contact, her initial panic and anger had faded to embarrassed discomfiture. Had Doug even taken her seriously? She'd studiously avoided calling to find out, and when she'd heard no more from him than from her former in-laws, she'd deliberately pushed both below the surface of more pressing preoccupations.

Writing "good work" across the last vocabulary quiz, Sara reached for a stack of math worksheets. With no further complications from her encounter with Reina, she'd given in to Aunt Jan's urgings to fly out for spring break. By adding a few unused sick days, Sara was extending the visit to two weeks—less than her aunt had pressed for, but about as long as Sara cared to impose herself. She still wasn't entirely convinced how welcome she would be. Her plane left before dawn tomorrow, which meant that all grades for this quarter had to be in before she left the classroom today.

As she scribbled a grade on the first worksheet, Sara glanced over at her single detention student. Tears were still streaming down the little girl's olive cheeks as she bent over her homework. Sara sighed.

Something was going on with little Elisa that she didn't understand. The girl was bright, eager to learn, and cooperative. Her English was excellent for having spent her first eight years in the highlands of Ecuador. Yet she consistently failed to complete homework, and her test scores, in math especially, were wildly erratic, as if what she committed to memory one day simply slipped away the next.

I wonder what her home situation is like? Once she was done here, she'd give the mother a call.

That reminded Sara she had yet to check her day's messages. While she scanned the next set of multiplication problems, she rooted around for her cell phone and keyed in the answering service.

Two telemarketers. *Like I'm going to call them back!*

Then the red grading pen went still as Sara heard Doug's deep voice.

"Sara, I've got some info for you. Can you meet me at Romano's, South Beach, 7 P.M.? Leave me a message at the office if you can't. Otherwise I'll plan on seeing you there."

She glanced at her watch and groaned. Barely enough time to get home, changed, and to the restaurant. The time of the message was recorded as 1:30 P.M., when Doug had to know Sara's cell phone would be turned off for class. So he'd chosen not to talk over the phone. Hurrying through her final grade totals, Sara cut short Elisa's detention and hurried the several blocks to her apartment, arriving to find Doug's same terse message on her home answering machine.

It's only a status report on the Cortéz. But that didn't keep Sara from making a careful selection of dress and makeup. Only when she was dressed did Sara realize she was wearing the outfit she'd purchased for Doug's ill-fated birthday celebration and which he'd never had the opportunity to see. The bold colors of the gypsy skirt swirled around her calves as she grabbed up her purse to dash down the stairs.

Sara remembered her intended call to Elisa's mother as she drove. At the next stoplight she rummaged for the number and dialed the call.

Traffic was worse than she'd allowed for, and Doug was already seated when Sara walked in, still on the phone with Elisa's mother. He'd showered and shaved and taken the time to change into a sport coat and tie, his hair slicked back into unusual neatness and still a bit damp. He looked—good, Sara admitted. He also looked tired and remote, the long fingers on one hand drumming impatiently on the tablecloth.

Then his impatient gaze landed on Sara, and as he rose quickly to his feet, Sara saw something flare in his eyes that banished his fatigue and detachment. By the time she reached the table, though, his expression was unreadable. Doug waited until the waiter had taken their order before detailing tersely and precisely what he'd uncovered to date about the Cortezes.

"I wish I could say we'd found evidence of criminal behavior. It would have been a pleasure to bring them in. But at this point, everything looks aboveboard. Even their paperwork is legit, which is where we nail a lot of these guys. That being the case, I'm afraid there isn't much more we can do. Sure, they don't deserve to live in our country—not to mention the circumstances surrounding their financial situation are suspicious at best. Unfortunately, you can say that—and worse—about plenty of others who've been given legal residence here."

Sara lost her appetite for the basket of fresh-baked rolls the waiter had deposited on the table. "Are you still going to keep a watch on them, then?"

Doug hesitated ever so slightly before responding. "Time and manpower's the problem. The bottom line is, we've got no grounds for the expenditure of resources a continued surveillance would entail. Even if I did it on my own time . . . well, the reality is, I can't keep it up forever. There's too much else on my plate—and the DEA's."

His eyes narrowed on Sara's face. "Does that bother you?"

Sara suddenly realized she was crumbling her roll. Hastily, she dropped it on her plate. "Not as much as it would have a few weeks ago," she admitted honestly. "But—well, I guess they haven't done anything to hurt me. Maybe you're right. Maybe they really are just trying to make a fresh start—like I am. I don't like it. I know what they are . . . what they've done. But if that's the way it's got to be, then as long as they stay out of my life, I think I can let it go."

Sara raised her long lashes to look Doug squarely in the eye across the table. "I . . . I want to thank you for everything you did. I know the long hours you've been working. Your mother told me. And I know how much time it had to take to find out all this. I'm sorry to have put you to all the bother—but, thank you anyway."

Doug did not look especially pleased at her gratitude. "I was just doing my job," he answered with what to Sara seemed unnecessary curtness. "They're criminals involved in a former case. Regardless of what they're doing here, they needed checking out."

Sara blushed painfully. Did he think she was implying he'd done it just for her?

Unexpectedly, Doug reached across the table and covered the fingers that had been playing with the bread roll. His hand was somewhat rough and his grip firm. His serious, intent eyes held hers. Her breath caught slightly, but she didn't pull her hand away.

"Don't ever hesitate to come to me with anything that concerns you—or anything at all," he said forcefully. "Promise me that, Sara. You'll never be a bother."

They were interrupted by the arrival of the main course, and Sara took the opportunity to snatch her hand away. Doug leaned back in his chair, an ironical gleam replacing the intent look, as the waiter refilled their glasses and offered grated parmesan. Doug did not try to continue the conversation until the waiter had gone and he'd cut into his filet mignon. When he did, his tone was light and he surveyed Sara's flushed cheeks thoughtfully. "So—how's everything else? You looked preoccupied when you came in. An irate parent?"

"No, just a parent." Between bites of shrimp scampi, Sara told Doug about Elisa. "It's funny how you jump to conclusions. She's such a nice kid and her English vocabulary is so good, I just assumed it was the usual gifted ESL child with lack of encouragement at home. Turns out it's the other way around. Her parents are American medical doctors who adopted her while they were with an aid organization in Ecuador. From what I heard, they love her very much and have been working very hard with her. That's why her English is so good. But she was adopted out of conditions of severe malnutrition, resulting in some learning difficulties that are becoming more evident as she gets older. We're going to start some testing. At least she'll have the comfort that she isn't being 'bad' when she can't keep up."

Doug listened without interrupting, thoughtfully eating his steak, and Sara could not tell if she was boring him. But each time she would have ended her story, he asked her a question that kept her going. When she noticed he was almost done with his meal and she had barely touched hers, she lapsed to silence.

"You're really good at this, aren't you?" he said slowly with a slight smile tugging at one corner of his mouth. "And braver than I'll ever be. I'd rather face an Uzi any day than a class of rowdy kids." He put down his knife and fork and reached for his napkin in his lap. "So . . . are you happy? Have you been making—do you have future plans yet?"

Am I happy? Sara had to stop and think about that one. It was a question she hadn't considered in a long time. And yet—

I am happy! she realized somewhat incredulously. *I'm busier than I ever thought I'd be, and the challenges are harder than I ever expected. But I'm doing work I love . . . and work that matters and that's helping people. I have no idea what next month holds or next year. But today, right now—yes, I really am happy!*

"Yes, I'm happy," she said aloud, giving him a straight look as she added meaningfully, "And, no—I have no future plans. If by plans, you mean Larry Thomas."

Doug didn't confirm or deny her implication, but the upward curve of his mouth acknowledged the hit.

"And you? Have they made you GS yet? Are you still working with Mike?

How's the baby?" Sara eyed the tired lines around Doug's eyes and mouth. "You look like you haven't slept in a week. They keeping you out again all night?"

Sara knew Doug too well to expect he'd comment on a case in progress, and he didn't. But he told her about Mike and Debby's baby. "He looks like any other baby, if you ask me. Mike, of course, is practically jumping out of his Kevlar vest. Fortunately, Debby's sensible enough to keep his feet out of the clouds."

The empty plates disappeared, replaced by coffee and cheesecake. Doug's name had come up for Group Supervisor, but the appointment would not take effect for another month. Ramon had sent Sara greetings from Santa Cruz along with news that Ellen, the DEA administrative officer, had organized a team of volunteers to take over Sara's work at the orphanage. Cynthia's interior-decorating business had grown so that she'd had to hire two assistants.

Sara in turn told Doug about Aunt Jan's surprising reentry into her life. "I think she must be lonely with Tom married now. Or maybe she feels sorry for me with Nicky gone. Though after two weeks of my company, she may decide she doesn't want an oddball niece moving back into the family fold," she added impishly.

Doug didn't smile in return. "You aren't really thinking of moving out there."

Sara's eyebrows went up at the sharpness of his tone. "I hadn't even thought about it."

She changed the subject to talk about the latest publication by an author she knew Doug liked, and he followed her lead. The surrounding tables emptied and filled again. The waiter poured a third round of refills on the coffee. It all seemed so . . . right, so natural, that it wasn't until the waiter placed the check with a suggestive cough in front of Doug that Sara realized how late it was. Suddenly, passionately, she wished she didn't have to walk out to her car and drive home alone, not to see Doug again until some other emergency arose, if ever.

She was shocked at the intensity of her wish. As Doug reached for the check, Sara straightened up hastily. "I'll . . . I . . . need to make a stop."

Before she could stand up, Doug abandoned the check and reached across the table to capture her hand again. Sara could not move without drawing all eyes to their table. Per usual, she could not quite read his expression, but it held something that was making her heart race and her breath come more quickly. As if Doug too were feeling the spell of the last hour, he said urgently,

"Sara, this evening has been . . . I don't want it to end. I've missed you. I've missed . . . *this*."

His gesture wasn't referring to the atmosphere of the restaurant or the exquisite meal they'd finished. "I know we need to go. You have a plane to catch, and I—well, you guessed it right: I've been up thirty-six hours straight, and if I don't get some sleep, I'm going to make a fool of myself by falling asleep in my water glass. But . . . I don't want you to just walk out of here. I want to see you again."

"About the Cortéz?" Sara asked breathlessly. She did not try to withdraw her hand this time. It would have been futile. "Or just to see each other . . . to be friends—like before?"

The jerk of Doug's body was impatient enough that it would have knocked over his water glass if he hadn't grabbed for it in time. "No, not to be friends!" he said between clenched teeth. Sara would have thought he was angry were she not drowning in the blaze of his eyes.

"Not to be friends," he repeated, this time more evenly. "Let's get one thing straight right now. I have no intention of being a big brother or buddy to you. I want something more, and I think—I *hope*—you do too. Okay, you needed some time and space. I respected that. I've been patient. But you're not 'little girl lost' anymore. You're a woman—and a strong one. I've missed seeing you and being with you. And I'll serve you warning right now: I intend to do everything in my power to convince you that we belong together. To *woo* you, if that isn't too outdated a term."

Sara's breath was no longer coming fast. She could not breathe at all. She felt at once the impulse to throw herself into his arms and the lingering instinct to flee. The tempest of emotions threatened to sweep away her hard-earned equilibrium.

Taking a deep breath, she forced her whirling thoughts to settle themselves. "Would it—would it be too cliché if I asked . . . if . . . if I could pray about this? At least—at least until I get back from Aunt Jan's?"

Doug withdrew his hand abruptly. Sara's fingers felt cold and vulnerable. "Not at all," he said stiffly.

Pushing back his chair, he rose swiftly to his feet and tossed several bills onto the tray with the check. The corners of his mouth slanted upward as he stepped away from the table, but the determination in the line of his jaw caught Sara's breath again. "Just don't take too long, and don't even *think* about staying out there. I'm not Larry Thomas. I'll come after you."

Chapter Nineteen

APRIL 3
SANTA CRUZ PROVINCE, BOLIVIA

The red glow of the sentry's cigarette flared and subsided in a casual rhythm. Even without the distraction, he would not have spotted the prone shapes scattered among the ornamental shrubs that dotted the dark lawn. Two other guards, also smoking, paced the veranda that ran around the two-story hacienda.

The estate was one of many luxury ranches that had sprung up in recent years along the highway that U.S. aid had built from Santa Cruz through the coca-growing Chapare region to the highland cities of Cochabamba and the capital of La Paz. Thoroughbred Arabians were the official source of the owner's sudden millions, though had anyone cared to do the math, it wouldn't add up.

A close former associate of Luis Cortéz, the owner had been a thorn in the side of the DEA for years, openly flaunting cash and his political connections. But because unexplained income was not a crime in Bolivia—only actual possession of cocaine—the Americans had yet to convince a court to take him into custody. That old standby, *ley de posesión,* or "law of possession," still protected Bolivia's wealthiest citizens. The *americanos* simply gritted their teeth and waited.

Tonight, the wait would end, courtesy of Julio Vargas.

A rustle in the bushes drew one of the sentries down from the veranda. Strolling out onto the lawn, he stopped for a deep drag on his cigarette. Two silenced rounds from an MP-10 submachine gun zeroed in on the red glow. The sentry slumped to the grass, one more black shape against the night.

"Clear!"

"Clear!"

The muted crackle in the earpiece of the team leader's headset told him the other two guards had been neutralized. He paused to listen. The shrill chorus of cicadas and frogs had not missed a beat. No sound or light came from the main hacienda house or the outbuildings that housed the *campesino* laborers. If anyone had awakened, he was even more stealthy than the strike force.

Impossible.

"Go! Go!" The leader's soft but urgent command activated the prone shapes among the bushes. Rising silently to their feet, half the ten-man team fanned out around the perimeter. The others drifted like shadows across the lawn and onto the veranda. The phosphorescent green of their night vision goggles marked their objective, a side door the guards had been using.

The door led into an untidy room crowded with army cots and a card table cluttered with playing cards, empty beer bottles, and cigarette butts. A small TV and radio were perched on a shelf. A door across the way opened onto an unlit corridor. To the left, an archway marked the entrance to a well-equipped kitchen facility. Two strike force members glided silently in that direction, but only for a quick appraisal. Earlier reconnaissance by a telephone repairman, actually one of the team's communications specialists, had supplied a map of the hacienda's interior. These were the servants' quarters. The target lay down the hall to their right.

The five-member unit paused outside a door leading to the maids' sleeping quarters. This was to be a selective operation: containment of nontargeted personnel, and a surgical strike at the mission's objective. Leaving one operative outside the door in case anyone awoke, the team leader led his remaining force through a spacious foyer and up a wide, curving staircase to the second floor.

Outside an ornately carved mahogany door, the leader slid out a small, flat pack of tools, once a burglar's trade secret but now available commercially to anyone wanting to learn the art of lock-picking. They weren't necessary. The doorknob turned without resistance, and the heavy door eased open noiselessly.

Reconnaissance had confirmed the absence of any guests or family members in the house, and the middle-aged owner's wife knew better than to remove herself from the Santa Cruz mansion her husband generously provided her. The young woman sprawled on the king-size canopy bed was a model who'd found that playing mistress to the overweight and balding "entrepreneur" snoring beside her was a far better financial proposition than the occasional role in local TV commercials.

Two MP-10s came up. A pair of double-tap silenced rounds flared in the green glow of the NVGs. Around the stilled and silent shapes, a black stain began to spread across the sheets.

The team leader and his companions slipped downstairs and back out onto the veranda as noiselessly and unnoticed as they had entered. He whispered a command into his mouthpiece, and Team One began melting back into the ornamental bushes and trees that in daytime made a tropical paradise of the hacienda grounds.

An hour later, they were back under the canvas cover of a three-ton farm truck, to all appearances one more load of vegetables or dry goods rumbling down the highway to Santa Cruz for the morning's open-air markets.

* * *

Team Two's mission also came off without a hitch. The warehouse of black-market chemicals had been easy to locate, because Julio Vargas had himself traded with this trafficker on more than one occasion. A side effect of Bolivia's cocaine production was that it was now possible to amass as great a fortune smuggling chemicals *into* Bolivia as smuggling cocaine out. Kerosene. Ether. Sulfuric acid. Pure cane alcohol. All strictly controlled substances, and therefore highly profitable on the black market.

And all highly flammable.

The second strike force had not even bothered with stealth. Driving up to the gate in an army jeep and camouflage fatigues, they informed the two night guards that they were a counternarcotics unit conducting a surprise inspection. The frightened guards offered no resistance, dropping their service revolvers as soon as they saw the automatic rifles. A few sticks of C-4 did the trick. The team even took the guards with them, though more for PR than humanitarian reasons. They dropped the two men off a few blocks away before detonating the plastic explosive by remote control.

The destructive force of exploding untold barrels and five-gallon jerry cans exceeded all calculations. Screaming neighbors scrambled out from under burning roofs as the army jeep roared out of the neighborhood. The fallout from the explosion dropped flaming debris on housetops for blocks around.

* * *

At target three, Julio Vargas raised a pair of night-vision binoculars to his eyes. The house on the other side of an unpainted brick wall was no mansion. Though sprawling in size, the residence itself was simple, whitewashed brick.

The surrounding grounds consisted of a dusty patio cluttered with vehicles and work projects. The security was that of any middle-class home: broken glass cemented along the top of the wall, strands of barbed wire, a pair of barking dogs. Nothing about the exterior hinted at the luxurious furnishings and modern American appliances inside the whitewashed walls, the computers and satellite phone. No one would have guessed that the owner, Eduardo Quispe, a self-styled leader of the *cocaleros* union who claimed to be a man of the peasant masses, defending his nation's sovereignty and the sacred coca leaf of his Inca ancestors from the oppression of the Americans and their counternarcotics war, had actually amassed considerable real estate holdings, or that his children attended an elite private school.

The DEA knew all about him, however. About all the gifts given to him by his grateful followers; and the campaign finances, of which he seemed to have an endless reserve, that had secured him a seat in the legislature. How the head of an organization dedicated to producing an illegal product could run for public office on a campaign of expanding that illegal product—and win—was something that baffled and infuriated American law enforcement.

Quispe's congressional seat also gave him diplomatic immunity, another quirk of Bolivian politics, which preserved his freedom even when he'd been caught red-handed during a raid on a jungle cocaine lab. In the ensuing newscasts, he'd looked smug and pleased with himself, unlike the young soldiers injured in a dynamite blast he'd set off. Which hadn't kept Quispe from claiming that the DEA had tortured him and threatened his family during his brief detention. All of this made Eduardo Quispe one of the human beings most loathed by the American counternarcotics agency, and the perfect nail in the scaffolding Julio was now deliberately erecting on which to hang his old adversaries.

Pfft! Pfft! Two silenced shots ended the dogs' barking. For the team's forward operating base, team leader Saleh Jebai had chosen a three-story building under construction next door to Quispe's property. The caretaker, who slept in a shack at the rear of the lot, had already been immobilized with duct tape. The strike force quickly scaled the wall between the two properties, thick rubber mats protecting them from the barbed strands and glass. That there was no *sereno* on duty, the night watchman many neighborhoods hired to patrol their streets, indicated that Quispe had no serious worries about his safety at the hands of the Americans.

From the concrete slab that would one day be the third floor of the new building, Julio watched as a burst from a silenced Uzi blew the lock off Quispe's front door. A few startled screams were swiftly stifled as team members fanned out into the sleeping quarters. In his earpiece, Julio heard Saleh's cold warning that he'd blow the head off the next person who made a noise. A babble in the background quieted immediately to the muffled sobbing of one small child.

Lights went on in the house. Lowering his binoculars, Julio hurried down an unfinished staircase and ran over to the entrance to the Quispe compound. A farm truck, with a canvas tarp forming a roof over the top of the slatted wood sides, was already backing in the gate. There was no reason for Julio to be here on this mission—Saleh was carrying out the operational plan with his usual precision and skill—but he wouldn't have missed the expression on Eduardo Quispe's face as he stumbled down the steps, two submachine guns at his back prodding him up into the back of the truck.

Inside the house, Julio found Saleh and other team members herding Quispe's extended family into an interior room. Bars protecting the windows and a solid wood door would make it an adequate prison until the team completed its withdrawal. The adults and older children were too cowed to resist the prodding of the rifle barrels. But one small girl, no more than five or six, pulled free from an older sibling's grip to swing around. Tears streaming down her cheeks, she stared uncomprehendingly up at the black alien shapes towering over her.

"Who are you?" she wailed. "What are you doing with my grandfather?"

Saleh slung his weapon over one shoulder and squatted down to the child's level. "We're *americanos*," he said in deliberately accented Spanish. "And we're here to take your grandfather for a ride."

Chapter Twenty

MIAMI, FLORIDA

"Look who finally crawled out of bed." Mike glanced over from the TV screen as Doug walked into the conference room. "Hey, Doug, take a look. You made the news."

The conference room had the usual table and chairs, but Mike and several other agents were at the far end, where a TV/VCR combination and a pair of old sofas allowed agents to study surveillance tapes or catch a World Cup play-off game during office hours. With Miami the unofficial capital of the Latin American world, soccer was a departmental passion.

The tape in the VCR was last night's local news coverage of the raid at the docks. The team had gathered to watch the recap. Norm Kublin was not among them, Doug noted, strolling over as Mike rewound the segment. It was well into the morning. Doug had managed a full eight hours of sleep for once. By all rights he should have the day off after his thirty-six hour shift. But he'd caught the short end of the stick and had to do the write-up on yesterday's raid. It was Kublin's not-so-subtle punishment for Doug's late arrival at the docks.

Doug leaned over the back of a sofa as the news clip began to play. For all Kublin's screaming, yesterday's operation had been textbook perfect. The cocaine had been there all right, taped inside the tubing, and they'd arrested both the ship's crew and Echevarria. On the TV screen, the young, good-looking Colombian was keeping his head down in a vain attempt to hide his face from the camera, his hands cuffed behind his back. Grasping an arm on either side were Norm Kublin's immediate superior, Associate Special Agent in Charge Kurt Hauser, along with the Public Information Officer Peggy Browning. Behind them—

Doug frowned as the procession advanced down the gangplank. He'd thought he'd ducked in time when he saw the TV crew, but the camera had caught him emerging from the hold, his face turned away but the DEA lettering highlighted on the back of his jacket.

No agent liked to see his face on camera, recognizable or not. That was the reason a "perp walk," as agents termed the parading of a suspect for the news cameras, was carried out by administrative personnel whose job it was to be visible to the public. When you had to go back on the streets, the last thing you wanted was to have your next contact recognizing your mug off the evening news.

Too much of this, and Doug would find himself behind a desk, like Peggy Browning and Kurt Hauser. A promotion, sure. But who wanted their only action to be parading some scumbag for the TV cameras?

Doug headed for his cubicle without watching the rest of the coverage. If the raid had already made the news—something he seldom bothered to watch—there was no reason he couldn't have answered Sara's questions last night, except habit. You didn't talk about a mission until it hit the news, and even then you said no more than was doled out to the news crews. The DEA, like the FBI, bred a tight-lipped bunch, and those who liked to hear themselves talk didn't last long.

Doug pulled up the DEA-6 form on his computer screen but didn't begin typing. It was not the report in front of him Doug was seeing, but the sweet young face that had been across the table from him last night. He'd meant what he'd told Sara. He had learned to walk alone in a hard school after Julie and the babies were gone. He'd even rediscovered a degree of contentment, his job providing long periods when he was simply too busy to think about it. After five years, he'd come to accept that he might always be alone. He'd walked away at Sara's request, steeled himself to pick up the burden of solitude again, and even wished Larry Thomas well.

But no longer. He'd seen the look in Sara's eyes when she walked into the restaurant, a look he'd despaired of ever seeing. He'd read the easy sense of familiarity that ran warm between them as they talked, the reluctance when she'd pulled away to walk out. Sara could fool herself that they were not meant for each other. But not Doug. And this time he would not sit passively back and give up without a fight. If Larry Thomas or anyone else wanted her, he would have a challenge on his hands.

Doug was a pro at facing up to challenges.

He picked up the pewter soldier that Sara had given him and rubbed a thumb over the smooth metal. What was it about her that had gotten so completely under his skin? No other woman had in these five years—and more than one had tried. None had wrapped herself around his heart, becoming a part of his life until, try as he had, he could not rip it away. She was very different from Julie, who'd been so much his heart and life that Doug had believed no one could fill the hole her death had left. Sara was slight and blonde; Julie had been tall with an athletic stride and the dark coloring of her Italian mother. Julie had come from a loving home with parents who still held hands after forty years and siblings who enjoyed being together and took pride in each others' accomplishments. Sara, like Doug himself, had come to adulthood battle-scarred by loss and pain and loneliness. Neither would ever know what it was like to be undamaged, though both had learned to compensate.

In other ways, Sara was very much like Julie. They felt deep compassion for the small and helpless and hurting. Integrity made their decisions very black-and-white. They lacked self-interest or guile. Both had courage, though Sara didn't even recognize in it herself. It was courage that had led Sara to stand up to Luis and Nicolás Cortéz when it would have been so easy to keep silent. And it had taken courage to walk away from the Bradfords.

Doug set down the pewter statue. It had taken him a long time to admit that Sara was right. His instincts, honed by his job, had been to protect her, to shield her from any further unpleasantness in her life. In so doing he'd denied Sara the space, the growing time that had strengthened him after Julie's death.

Yet she had grown!

A grin played at the corners of Doug's mouth. Yes, the Sara who'd walked into church and later into that restaurant with her chin up and a challenge in her eyes was a far cry from the listless, traumatized girl he'd accompanied to Miami. It was like watching a butterfly spreading wings that had been there all along.

Julie would have liked Sara, would have approved of her as a person. It was odd to think that the two women might have become good friends. His memory of Julie was cheering him on right now. Her generous personality and deep love for Doug would not have wanted to see him alone.

Sara will make the kind of mother that Julie was. A pain twisted in Doug's chest as he reached out to touch the laughing faces with their tossed dark curls in the framed photo across the desk. *Good-bye, sweethearts. I miss you so.*

Setting his jaw in a line that both Sara and Julie would have recognized, Doug made a decision. He'd give Sara until she came back from Washington. Then they were going to have it out.

"Doug, long-distance on line three. Bolivia."

Rick Acevedo thrust his head over the partition of Doug's cubicle. He was the new agent who'd stayed behind to sort the Cortezes trash three nights ago. Rick reached over the partition to drop a stapled printout onto Doug's desk. "This came in over the fax. He said you should take a look at it right away."

"Who?"

But Rick was gone. Doug picked up the fax as he reached for the phone. A call from Bolivia would likely be Ramon getting back on the Tennessee bust. That had worked out as planned, with Ramon's team scooping up the mule as he cleared airport security in Nashville—though, as expected, they'd had to forfeit the FDIN to Customs.

"Doug Bradford here."

"Bradford? This is Jim Weeks, La Paz."

Jim Weeks was Resident Agent in Charge or RAC of the DEA field office in Bolivia's capital, which was housed in the American embassy. That made him the senior agent in Bolivia, though Grant Major, the Santa Cruz RAC, might dispute that.

"Bradford? I'm going to have to ask you to keep this conversation confidential. Do you understand?"

Doug's eyebrows shot up even as he answered, "Sure, I understand."

"Good. I'm told you worked closely with Ramon Gutierrez down in Santa Cruz your last year in Bolivia. Off the record, what is your opinion of him? I'd appreciate complete honesty."

As if anything was really off the record! This was beginning to shape up like a performance review. But why would the La Paz RAC be calling up Doug for an assessment of one of Grant Major's agents? "I'm not sure exactly what you're looking for," Doug said cautiously. "He's good. One of the most competent agents I've ever worked with. Certainly the bad guys he's put behind bars have found him so."

"And what about the ones he hasn't? Would you consider Gutierrez capable of resorting to vigilante tactics if he considered justice wasn't being served under present conditions?"

Doug was stunned by the question only for the instant it took to begin putting puzzle pieces together. "You're asking if he's capable of planning and carrying out some of the incidents that have been all over the Bolivian press lately, is that it?"

Doug gripped the phone to speak coldly and deliberately. "I'd have to see it with my own eyes before I'd believe Ramon Gutierrez capable of directing *or* participating in such actions—and even then I'd wait for him to give me an explanation. Ramon is not only one of the finest agents but one of the finest men I've been privileged to work with."

"That may be," Week's tone was dry, "but someone is out there running around the countryside like some vigilante superhero dispensing justice at the end of an M-16. Have you seen the fax I sent you?"

Doug scanned through the two stapled sheets quickly and incredulously. Week's concern was understandable enough. A well-known Santa Cruz businessman, whom Doug himself had spent numerous fruitless hours trying to nail for drug dealing, murdered with his mistress in bed. An explosion of black market chemicals that had burned down a whole city block. And the final item.

Doug let out a low whistle. "Someone kidnapped Quispe? Well, you won't be getting tears from any of the team. But why blame us? These guys make enough enemies among themselves."

"Eduardo Quispe's family insists it was American soldiers who kidnapped him. They say the kidnappers even admitted it. And the folks who pulled off last night's little incidents were no band of feuding traffickers; they were trained commandos. We have too many eyewitnesses, including the guards from the warehouse and a caretaker who lives next door to Quispe. Like you said, Ramon Gutierrez is one of the best, and one of the few agents here with Special Forces training. And he doesn't exactly have a pussy-cat résumé."

Was it possible? Sure, Ramon, like all the agents, had done his share of grumbling over the scumbags they were forced to let go, time after time, when they knew they were guilty as sin. Worse yet was having to hobnob with the sleazes at embassy functions if they had high enough political and social connections.

But, no! Despite Ramon's urban gang roots, he'd come too far and was too proud of the discipline and education he'd received along the way to break every tenet of his army training indulging in vigilante actions. More significantly, there were too many individuals involved. Dozens by the description of last night's triple raids. With the level of corruption permeating Bolivia's counternarcotics forces, it was hard enough to keep the DEA's own operations from leaking out to the bad guys. There was no way an agent could keep this kind of extracurricular operation a secret. Not unless the entire DEA force on the ground there was implicated. As for witnesses, they were notoriously unreliable. They saw what they wanted or expected to see.

"Maybe," the RAC conceded when Doug explained his reasoning. "But there are Bolivians who are saying we are all involved. They're calling for a complete investigation of our activities and relationship with their military, even demanding our expulsion from the country."

"It'll blow over," Doug said. "It always does. If anyone really believed we were guilty of all the accusations the Bolivian media has happily repeated over the years, we'd have been out of the country long ago. Remember the stunt Quispe pulled last year when he had those *cocalero* women bawling on television that the DEA was abusing them during the eradication program? When the American embassy demanded that a doctor be allowed to examine the alleged victims, Quispe said he couldn't subject the women to public humiliation by identifying them to the medical authorities. This is *after* they'd been happily showing their faces all over the news. As for who these guys really are, has anyone checked out former Bolivian military who've had any specialized training? Maybe one of the cartels has put together an army like they've done with the paramilitaries in Colombia and is picking off the competition."

"That's an idea," Weeks admitted. "We'll look into it. And we'll take under consideration the rest of what you've had to say. If anything else comes to mind, give me a call."

What a mess! For once Doug was glad he was out of Bolivia. He just hoped none of this mud would stick to Ramon. He was a good friend as well as a fine agent, and if it weren't for Weeks' order of confidentiality, he'd pick up the phone and give Ramon a heads-up.

Doug read though the fax again, noting details he'd skimmed over before. Three separate teams at three separate locations. Soldiers in combat gear claiming to be American. Too many witnesses had heard that to brush it off.

No one in any counternarcotics agency was going to work up too much outrage over a bunch of narcotraffickers getting picked off—except for the recoil on the DEA itself. Were there players in the drug underworld who hated each other and the DEA enough to deliberately stage something like this, hitting two birds with one stone?

Sure!

But which would have the resources and know-how to do it?

"Doug?" Rick's head appeared over the partition again.

"Yes?" Doug demanded with some asperity.

The new agent dropped another stapled document onto Doug's desk. "Sorry, I didn't mean to interrupt. I forgot this."

Doug's lips twitched at the expression on Rick's face. Had he really looked like he was about to bite the kid's head off? Another college recruitment like

Mike—the kid could speak four languages—he'd be a more effective agent when he was less impressed by Doug's years in the field.

"What is it?" he said more mildly.

"The report on that Cortéz trash run you asked me to wrap up. I finished it yesterday. Doesn't look like much that I could see, but it's all there listed by categories. Oh, I did find one other scrap of paper wadded in with the diapers. Looked like a sheet from a notepad. You know, the kind you keep by the phone. Some sort of shopping list for a client, from what I could make out. The original was too—messy."

Doug grinned again at the distaste on the younger man's face. So he'd learned why new agents got tapped with this kind of job.

"But I've attached a photocopy there at the back. Maybe it means something to you if it doesn't to me."

Doug was already flipping through the report. Rick had gone the extra mile, neatly listing every bit of trash down to the last eggshell along with every piece of writing or printing, however small, the originals photocopied in a neat stack and stapled to the back. Such zealousness would wear off once the kid had been in government service a year or two.

Doug nodded his appreciation. "Nice job. Thanks."

His eye landed on the last photocopy Rick had attached. The scrap of paper, crumpled as it appeared in the photocopy, did look like the kind of note a person taking a phone call from a client might have jotted down—the name of the person calling and beneath that a list of the items requested. Despite the blotches, whose origins Doug preferred not to know, he could make out that the list was for some sort of wilderness outfitters. It included an assortment of climbing and skydiving gear—parachutes, goggles, rappelling harnesses, heavy-duty gloves, outdoor clothing items, along with some specified communication and GPS systems.

Nothing inconsistent with an outdoor trekking agency such as Doug had seen listed on a dozen other manifests in his investigation of Tropical Imports and Exports.

But if the name scribbled at the top meant nothing to Rick, it meant everything to Doug.

Julio Vargas.

Chapter Twenty-one

APRIL 4
SANTA CRUZ PROVINCE, BOLIVIA

The body slid over the gunwale with a limpness denoting that rigor mortis had come and gone. Naked and pale, the body bobbed just below the surface, only too visible if any watercraft were to come any closer.

Then the muddy water began to churn. Julio Vargas watched until the husk that had once held the spirit of Eduardo Quispe disintegrated into a maelstrom of roiling scaled backs, teeth, and bits of bloodied flesh.

Tales of piranhas devouring unwary swimmers were grossly exaggerated. The toothy aquatic species, like its feathered counterpart, the vulture, was a scavenger, avoiding live, healthy prey. But given a whiff of blood in the water—an ingredient Julio had handily provided by a gunshot to the base of the skull—and a school of piranha could dispose of organic evidence with an efficiency and speed that any Mafia don would give a sizeable chunk of change to possess.

Julio nodded toward the churning water as Saleh strode up to the side of the boat. "This was a good choice. Better than allowing the body to be found. Now his disappearance will forever remain a mystery. The rumors will be that the *americanos* have taken him to their prisons. His followers will be rioting for months."

Then one of them would step into Quispe's slot as *cocalero* leader, and all would return to normal. In his time, Eduardo Quispe had been as useful to Julio as to anyone dealing in Bolivia's chief export. Men like Quispe played an essential role in maintaining a plentiful flow of raw materials to the production labs. Not to mention funneling "political contributions" to the peasant unions, who could be counted on to disrupt any serious counternarcotics effort.

Despite his utility, Quispe's death elicited no more than a shrug from Vargas as the bloodied water grew quiet again. There were always plenty more where he came from, people willing to sell out their countrymen and any moral scruples in exchange for a lifestyle of luxury.

"And what if they go from suspecting the gringos to wondering if it is someone with a grudge against the Americans? Or a quarrel among the narcos themselves? Or even something else?"

As Julio stepped back from the gunwale, Saleh handed him a newspaper folded to the front page. They'd picked up several Santa Cruz dailies before cutting the boat loose from the banks of the Pirai River that morning.

"DEA or Cartel?" screamed the headline.

"The newspapers are still blaming the Americans, but some are raising questions as journalists are in the habit of doing." Saleh's tone was tight with disapproval as he fixed Julio with a hard look. "I do not like it. Last night was too much. We have stayed too long . . . drawn too much attention to ourselves. We did not come here to fight your war of vengeance against the Americans, but our own. Too many questions and we will jeopardize our own mission."

Julio glowered at the rebuke. Saleh was again losing sight of the teacher-student relationship. And yet he knew the young man had a point.

Grudgingly, he admitted aloud, "You are right. The game here is played out."

"Then let us turn to the mission for which we have trained. To target these criminal elements has been an effective training device, as I anticipated, if strategically pointless. But my father and those who have poured out funds for this experiment grow restive. They did not invest so much that you might take your revenge on those who mistreated you in this country. They demand to know when the weapon for which they have paid so highly will be unleashed."

"Do they?" Julio's thin-bridged nostrils flared. "Are they questioning my training? Are you? Do not let arrogance deceive you, Sebastian." The emphasis on Saleh's pseudonym held subtle condescension. "Your idea for training exercises was a good one. But so far you have gone against peasants and drug dealers, not trained fighters. It will not be so easy in America, however unsuspecting they may be. Nor has my choice of targets been a mistake—or 'strategically pointless,' as you say. If we have drawn attention to one area, it will not drift elsewhere."

Julio's narrow shoulders lifted. "Still, as I have said, you are right. It is time to move forward."

Julio glanced around the boat at the other men, five or six members of Team Three, who were posing as the crew of the riverboat. The rest of the assault teams had broken up to filter back into Paraguay by twos and threes, some by boat, others by train or bus. They'd of course avoided the airlines, a guarantee of scrutiny in the present global climate. The men were lounging under the awnings, out of the burning jungle sun, except for one at the prow and another on top of the cabin roof, who remained on sentry duty, though they carried no visible weapons. Their watchful eyes scanned the water traffic and riverbanks.

Julio's eyes lingered on the rooftop sentry for a moment before he turned to address Saleh. His narrow mouth spread into a slit of a smile. "We will do one more mission—the most difficult. One which will suit both our purposes. It will be your graduation exercise. And it will confirm to everyone that this is all a matter of drugs—and Bolivia. When we leave and do not return, they will not look for us elsewhere."

Saleh listened as Julio outlined his plan, his look of disapproval gradually fading. "It is a well-conceived plan," he said when Julio had finished. "But when it is done, there will be no more delay. We will turn to a mission worthy of the purpose for which this force was created."

Chapter Twenty-two

APRIL 4
MIAMI, FLORIDA

Tilting his desk chair back on its wheels, Doug again read through his Cortéz file, finishing with the shipping records of TI&E exports, which Terry O'Brien, with his usual expediency, had waiting for Doug when he arrived at the office this morning. At least a dozen shipments had gone south on the *Buena Vista* to a company called Jungle Tours in Ciudad del Este, Paraguay. And the most recent manifest included the precise list of items requested by a Julio Vargas and found in the Cortéz trash. Judging by the date, Doug had watched the cargo being loaded yesterday on the pier.

I knew it! A leopard doesn't change its spots—or a jaguar his stripes would be more appropriate in this context. It was only a matter of waiting for the latest camouflage to slip.

For a brief interlude, Doug entertained the possibility of coincidence. Julio Vargas was, after all, one of the more common Hispanic names, and this had been Paraguay, not Bolivia.

But, no. Diego and Raymundo running an export business shipping into the Tri-Frontier. That was a coincidence. Julio Vargas gone missing from Palmasola prison? Another coincidence, maybe. But together? Doug simply didn't buy coincidences of that magnitude. A map of South America told too much of the story, to start with. Ciudad del Este had been a major transshipment port for *Industrias* Cortéz products. How many of those shipments had carried Cortéz cocaine would never be known. Now the remaining clan members just happened to be working for an import/export company with clients in Ciudad del Este. And where would Julio Vargas be more likely to head when he slipped out of prison? Across the Bolivia-Paraguay border to a familiar business locale with a thriving black market.

No, this was no coincidence. And if Julio Vargas was at the other end of

Diego and Raymundo's shipping pipeline, there had to be a drug connection. The last three weeks of searching just hadn't rooted it out yet.

Doug reached for the phone. Customs had made a haul yesterday with the FDIN for that concrete tubing to their credit. Three hundred keys of cocaine in that single shipment. The debt would be on their side for some time.

"Louie Rodriguez? I need a ship stopped from leaving port. If it hasn't sailed already."

He should have taken dogs on the ship yesterday. But he'd focused on the fact that they were loading instead of unloading cargo. Had he waited long enough, would he have seen Diego and Raymundo leave with something more than their clipboards? Or had the drugs been off-loaded earlier? Even if they had, the K-9 units did wonders at sniffing out the smallest residue where drugs had once been stored.

But then yesterday he'd had neither time nor probable cause to board that ship. That was the way it always went—too many leads and too many suspicious characters. You had to pick and choose your battles. And yesterday's battle had been Mr. Concrete Tubing. A victorious one at that.

Well, if the ship hadn't left port, they'd have a second chance.

Doug picked up the shipping manifests again. Jungle Tours was far from TI&E's only client. The *Buena Vista*'s cargo included a variety of American-made technical equipment, along with food and clothing items sold down south to the rich and the ex-pat communities. Jif peanut butter. Karo syrup. Nestlé chocolate chips. Purina Dog Chow. Brand-name children's clothing. Destinations included ports in Panama, Ecuador, Peru, Chile, Argentina, and of course, Paraguay.

The Jungle Tours orders all fell into the same category as the shopping list Rick had recovered. Every kind of equipment a well-funded jungle safari might require was there. Motorized inflatable boats. Water-carrying vest packs. Field rations and a wide assortment of communications and GPS systems. The climbing and skydiving gear Doug had already noted. High-powered hunting rifles.

But no chemicals or anything else that could be used in drug production. Doug ran through the return cargos. From Ciudad del Este were listed shipments of hand-woven hammocks, *yerba mate,* the traditional Guaraní tea now becoming popular in health stores and specialty shops, Indian handicrafts. Even a shipment of Paraguayan harps.

Any or all of them could hold drugs. Or they could all be clean.

Doug reached for the phone again as the red button for his line lit up. "Bradford here."

It was Louie Rodriguez. "I'm afraid your ship has already sailed. Would you like us to put out an APB to the Coast Guard? It's only twelve hours out of port. If it stays on its filed sailing plan, we can find it easily enough."

"No." There was no point wasting Doug's present favor over at Customs on what was undoubtedly a clean ship. But according to O'Brien's intel, the *Buena Vista* was due back in U.S. waters in about ten days. "Just get it entered into EPIC, will you, Rodriguez? Thanks! I owe you one."

EPIC was the classified government computer system that tracked everything from ship registrations to corporations, banking, or international commerce. The Coast Guard maintained an EPIC watch list, and if they were doing their job right, every ship they came across in the course of their patrols went into their computer. If a ship they encountered turned up on the watch list, they would notify the appropriate authorities immediately. And follow up any instructions entered with the EPIC listing—whether to stop and search, follow, or just report. Much, in fact, like a police APB on land.

"I don't want them spooked. Just have the Coast Guard keep an eye out for them and let us know when they approach our waters again. We'll take it from there when the time comes."

And that was about as far as Doug could go until the *Buena Vista* was headed back to Miami. It was these periods of waiting that necessitated agents working on half-a-dozen cases at once—to alleviate the boredom, if nothing else. You fitted a puzzle piece into this case and another in that. Then every so often, like yesterday, you got to place the last piece in one of the puzzles.

Letting his chair crash back down on its wheels, Doug glanced around. He caught Rick Acevedo's eye and waved a hand. Sifting through every bit of data in TI&E's past, present, and future was another good exercise for the DO's newest recruit. At worst it would be less unpleasant than rooting through the Cortéz household garbage.

Chapter Twenty-three

Doug Bradford was not the only one with connections at Customs. Like the majority of his fellow Miamians, the administrative assistant assigned to Louie Rodriguez was a foreign-born resident. Rashid Al Fayed's family had escaped the civil war of Lebanon when he was ten.

His cousin's family had been more fortunate. They had left Lebanon two generations earlier and were as American as Rashid would never be, with his lingering accent and memories of a war-torn childhood. Continuing a centuries-old family tradition of trade, they had built a thriving import/export business over the decades. It was they who had it made possible for any number of extended family to follow them to the land of opportunity, including Rashid and his parents and siblings.

Despite the scandals of corruption, drug dealing, and money laundering that were as much a part of Miami as the beaches and night clubs, Tropical Imports & Exports had never attracted so much as a sniff from any law enforcement agency. So why was the DEA all of a sudden requesting an APB on TI&E's freighter, the *Buena Vista*?

Rashid liked his present job and had every intention of parlaying it into a successful career in civil service, as one could do in America through education and hard work. But his commitment to the job did not supersede family loyalty. He knew, even if these stupid DEA agents did not, that his family's honor would never permit stooping to traffic in drugs. So what harm could there be in giving his cousins a heads-up as to what was coming their way?

"Al?" he said when his cousin came on the line. "There's something you should know."

* * *

The unrelenting jangle of the phone conveyed anger even before Raymundo managed to stagger out of bed and lift the receiver. He winced at the blast of fury bellowing across the line. Late as it was into the morning, last night's party had been even later. Perhaps it was the headache pounding at his temples that made so little sense of what he was hearing.

"I do not understand," Raymundo broke in carefully. "Has a problem arisen concerning the *Buena Vista* and our cargo?"

"Forty years in Miami, and we've never had a problem with the authorities. And now this! What have you been doing to unleash the DEA on us? If you've been messing with drugs on our ship and in our cargos, I don't care what your arrangements are with our family connections down in Paraguay, you're out! And so is your cushy little arrangement for collecting a salary you don't earn. We've done what was requested of us, no questions asked. But that wasn't supposed to include drugs. Whatever you're up to, you're not dragging this family down into it. My father may feel loyalty to his family, but my loyalty is to this business and the future of this family."

"No, no, no! There are no drugs, I swear! It must be a random check. Or—"

Adrenaline proved better than Tylenol for snapping Raymundo out of his hangover.

"Look, if it is the DEA, then it is nothing. There is an agent here in Miami with a vendetta against our family. But he has nothing, and he will find nothing, I swear to you. Do you think we are foolish to risk your goodwill in this country? For what? We are being paid well enough."

"Fine. Just fix it. And if there's any problem out of this, every cent's coming out of your hide—and your next paycheck."

By the time Raymundo replaced the receiver into its cradle, Diego had staggered into the room. He swore viciously as Raymundo relayed the phone call.

"It must be Bradford. Vargas said that if we left him alone, he would give up and go away. Clearly he was wrong."

"So what do we do now?" Raymundo's headache was interfering with his efforts to think. "Should we call Vargas again?"

"No!" Diego shook his head, then wished he hadn't. "He was very angry last time that we did not handle the matter ourselves. If we trouble him again over this *americano* agent, he may do as he threatened and discontinue our arrangement. Then where would we be? No, this time we must think how to deal with this ourselves."

Both men lapsed into the silence of mental labor. After all, they did possess brains, though Luis Cortéz had never allowed them to be involved in the decision-making process. Surely there was a way to resolve this situation. What would their formidable father-in-law do if he were faced with such a problem?

"Of course!" Diego snapped his fingers. "The warehouse raid, remember?"

"Don Luis made a fool of Bradford when no drugs were found." Raymundo's spreading smile held pleasurable reminiscence. "Do you remember how much trouble he found himself in, even with his own American bosses? And the stories on the television and in the newspapers of his brutality and destruction?"

"We will draw him again to attack us," Diego said. "And once again, when nothing is found, he will be discredited and left to look like a fool. Then he will not dare touch us again."

"After all," Raymundo agreed, "as Vargas has said, we are doing nothing illegal. The *Buena Vista* will reach Paraguay in a few more days. I will book the tickets. We will fly down and board the freighter there for its return."

Diego nodded, a process that left him clutching at his own temples. "And when we have finished discrediting the *americano* Bradford, only then will we inform Julio Vargas of our success."

Chapter Twenty-four

APRIL 4
SEATTLE, WASHINGTON

Even blindfolded, Sara would have known she was back in the Pacific North-west the moment she stepped from the plane. Not even the oily fumes of avia-tion fuel and other airport odors could mask the crisp, clear fragrance of Puget Sound whistling through an open door in the corridor just outside the plane hatch. The scent of evergreen and roses and the salty tang of the water itself. A rich, damp perfume of natural abundance.

Brrrr! And cold!

Late March in Miami meant blue skies and eighty degrees. Sara shivered as she passed the draft of the open door, beyond which she could see baggage personnel already unloading the cargo hold. Pausing to open her carry-on, she dug out the jacket she'd had the forethought to throw in at the last minute.

Sara paused again as she emerged inside the terminal. Aunt Jan had said her cousin Joe would be picking her up. Would Sara even recognize him? Joe had left Seattle years before Aunt Jan moved east, and Sara wasn't even sure she remembered what he looked like.

But even without his hearty wave, it proved easy enough to pick her cousin out of the crowd. Slim and wiry, he had the same flaxen shade of hair as Sara, though his was cropped short, and the same long-lashed amber eyes. In fact, he looked startlingly like pictures Sara had of her father when he was a young man.

"Sara Connor," Joe said as he stepped forward to take possession of her travel bag, "I'd have recognized you anywhere. It's easy to see we crawled out of the same end of the gene pool. Welcome home."

Welcome home. It was good to be back in the Pacific Northwest.

Joe chatted amiably as they walked through the airport and out to the park-ing garage. When they reached the freeway and merged into traffic, Sara rolled her window down a crack and drew in a deep draft of air. The refreshing breeze caught at the back of her nose and throat. Though she'd been gone less than a year, she'd forgotten just how fresh and green it could be here. Not that tropical Miami and Santa Cruz weren't green. But this was the deeper, richer green of pines and cedars and fir trees instead of palms.

"Nice tan there, Sara," Joe threw Sara an appraising glance. "You must catch a little more sun down there in Miami than we do around here."

Sara grinned back. "Yeah, well, what is it they say about Puget Sounders? 'They don't tan—they rust'?"

"Seattle Rain Festival: January 1 to December 31," Joe tossed back.

"Don't forget summer. August 1, isn't it?"

The two cousins grinned at each other, and Sara felt a weight slide from her shoulders as she settled back into her seat. *I was right to come. I needed to come.*

"It really is good to have you here," Joe added. "Mom and Denise—my wife—have really been looking forward to you coming. And our boys. I don't think you ever met any of them, but they're excited to meet our only cousin. And I can promise you won't be seeing much rain once we get home. Mom did tell you we don't live in Seattle anymore, right? Richland is about a three-hour drive from here, on the dry side of the hill. So if you've had a long flight and would like to take a nap, feel free to stretch out." Joe nodded toward the back seats. "There's plenty of room without the tribe."

Joe followed up the offer with a huge yawn. When Sara looked at him with surprise, he grinned ruefully. "Sorry! I got off a twenty-four-hour shift this morning. We had a warehouse fire in the night that turned pretty nasty."

Sara had totally forgotten her cousin's profession. Now for the first time she noticed what looked like a fresh burn across his right ear and down his cheek. "And you had to drive all the way up here to pick me up? I'm terribly sorry! There was no reason I couldn't have caught a bus."

"It was no trouble, really." But Joe yawned again.

Sara laughed. "It looks to me like you're the one who needs the nap. I slept a good part of the flight here. Why don't you let me drive? If you'll trust me with your car, that is. I promise I drive a lot better than the last time you saw me."

"Hey, I've been to Miami. Anyone who can drive down there can handle this. But I don't know what Denise would say about putting a guest to work."

"I'm not a guest," Sara said firmly. "I'm family."

"Yes, you are." Pulling over to the shoulder of the highway, Joe turned off the ignition and handed Sara the keys. "I think I'll take you up on that, mainly, because I think you're a safer driver than I am at the moment. You're going to catch I-90 up ahead here, and then hook south on 82 at Ellensburg. Other than that, just keep it on the road and wake me up when you start seeing signs for Richland."

After climbing into the back seat, Joe didn't stir for the next three hours. Sara found the open countryside a real treat after Miami's urban congestion, and she was actually grateful for the solitude. She blinked back tears at the familiar beauty of the snow-packed peaks and evergreen forests as she crossed over Snoqualmie Pass.

Joe had been right about "the dry side of the hill." As soon as I-90 dropped out of the mountain pass and into the flat plateau of southeastern Washington, the white and green of snow and fir changed abruptly to beige, brown, and gray.

Sagebrush intermingled with tinder-dry prairie grass seemed to be the main vegetation where irrigation had not produced farm crops. The only touch of green was an occasional willow or juniper tree stunted by the strong winds that whipped across the prairie. The farther south she drove, the more desolate the terrain became, stretching flat and barren in all directions except for the occasional bluffs and hills that were as bleak and lacking in foliage as the open plains. There was little snow cover, only a few drifts blowing up against fences along with a profusion of huge tumbleweeds.

And yet, there was a beauty in the very openness, desolation, and wildness of the scene. *Wouldn't want to be out there in it, though.*

Occasionally, Sara spotted a herd of deer grazing behind a range fence or a hawk swooping down in pursuit of its prey. A coyote loped across the road, barely avoiding the tires of Joe's SUV.

Then all signs of life abruptly disappeared. For as far as Sara could see, both sides of the highway were charred black. Stretches of ground still held enough heat to generate vapor where the chill air made contact. Vultures circled above charred lumps that Sara realized with horror were animals that had been caught in the inferno.

Joe woke up and slid over the seat into the passenger's side as Sara reduced speed to survey the devastation. Running a hand over his face and hair, Joe grinned at Sara. "That was a lifesaver. Thanks. Want to pull over? We're almost there, and the directions get a little more complicated from here on in."

Sara had barely registered the sign they'd just passed, announcing that

Richland was thirty miles ahead. "What happened here?" she asked as she pulled over to let Joe take the wheel. "It looks like a war zone."

"Wildfire," Joe answered laconically. "This one was just last week. Probably cost—" he surveyed the scene with a judicious glance "—oh, a few thousand acres. Took maybe five hundred firefighters four days to get under control. What we call a Type II incident. See there? They're just rolling up the incident base now."

They were beyond the charred territory now. Joe nodded to an open field they were passing. It held a mixture of trailers, heavy equipment, and a lone helicopter. Whatever crop had been planted was now thoroughly churned up by crisscrossing vehicle tracks.

"I don't see any fire trucks," Sara commented.

"We use more aircraft and people on the ground with shovels and rakes than fire engines for a wildfire. But the gear that was here has already moved out to a new incident up near Spokane. They're hoping to get it under control before it moves past Type III. If it reaches Type II, they'll have to activate a new base, and most of this equipment will move up there."

Sara looked at her cousin with respect. "I never realized firefighting got so complicated." She wrinkled her nose. "To be honest, I never thought about it at all."

"You wouldn't, living in Seattle, or Miami. Anywhere wet. But out on this side of the mountains, wildfires are on everyone's mind. In a bad year we lose a million acres." Joe shook his head. "It's a bad sign to have fires this early in the spring. It's been a dry winter—not nearly enough snow on the ground. It's going to be a bad fire season."

There was cultivated land again on both sides of the highway, mile after mile of long trellises. Joe nodded toward them. "At least the fire didn't get this far. There'd be a lot of unhappy people if this all burned—and not just locals."

"What are they?" To Sara, the dry mass of vegetation hanging from the frames looked like gnarled, dead twigs.

"Hops and grapes. Mainly hops. They call this area the hop capital of the world. Beer companies from around the world get hops here."

Straight ahead now, in the flat valley that ran to the brown flanks of a long, low ridge, Sara could see a grid of streets and buildings that had to be Richland. But Joe turned the Expedition off the main highway onto a secondary road.

"We don't live in town," her cousin explained. "We have a couple acres in a new development on the Columbia River."

This road too was bordered by trellises. Beyond the fields, Sara caught a glimpse of the wide, high-banked river that provided water for irrigation. Sara nodded toward the hops and grape vines. "Is this your main industry, then? I wondered what would support an entire city clear out here in the middle of the desert."

Joe threw Sara a quizzical glance. "You don't know? I thought everyone knew about Richland. What did you study in school?"

The highway was crossing a rise now. Off to the left rose a bleak razor-backed ridge. Straight ahead was a vast plateau covered with more sagebrush and tall prairie grasses and wind-stunted bushes. Joe nodded to a sign beside the highway. "The agriculture's something that's come in these last few years with modern irrigation. *That* over there is our major industry around and our biggest employer. The only reason this isn't still desert and a few wandering Indian clans."

Sara read the words on the sign aloud. "'U.S. Department of Energy, Hanford Site.' Energy production? It does ring a bell. At least Hanford does."

"Not just *any* energy. Nuclear energy. That sign is Uncle Sam's euphemistic title for the Hanford nuclear reserve. The biggest collection of nuclear reactors and waste on the planet. Five hundred eighty-six square miles of it. You've heard of the Manhattan Project, I'm sure, that built the first atomic bomb? This was a major part of that program. As well as all our nuclear weapons development since. And energy too," Joe conceded. "Hence the 'Department of Energy.' This area still depends heavily on nuclear energy for electricity. The Hanford site employs a few thousand people and, one way or another, pays the salary of the biggest part of this area's population. Including the fire department, so I'm not complaining."

Joe abruptly dropped the subject as he made another turn. "Well, here we are. Home."

The road became a residential street, the homes widely spaced with ample yards. Irrigation had made possible plenty of shade trees and ornamental shrubbery, so that to all appearances they might have been back in Seattle. To the right, a deep gully had prevented further building, and a glimpse of rolling hills beyond the houses gave the illusion of being out in the country. Joe turned into one of the driveways, in front of a two-story ranch-style home.

"Mom's house is just a few blocks down the hill, but she won't be off work for a couple hours. She'll be here for supper, though. Then you can talk sleeping arrangements. You're welcome to stay with us. I know Denise would be happy to have you."

Sara glanced with surprise at her watch. After a seven-hour flight and the drive down, her body clock said it was evening. Then she remembered the three-hour time change. She climbed stiffly down from the Expedition and gazed off in the distance as she stretched her legs. Joe's driveway was three houses from the end of the street where the pavement ended in a cul-de-sac. A few yards beyond, the artificial barrier of irrigated trees and plants gave way to the barren plateau that Joe had identified as the nuclear reserve. Far out on the plateau, beyond a long chain-link fence, Sara spotted what looked like a huge, concrete chimney thrusting up over the horizon. A nuclear reactor?

But she had no more opportunity to wonder because the front door of the house slammed open, and two small boys came tumbling down the steps, followed more sedately by their mother.

Denise Thornton was taller than Joe, big-boned without being overweight, with a mane of flaming-red curls. Sara liked her from the moment she bestowed an exuberant hug on her husband, and then on Sara.

"So good to meet you," she said as she ushered Sara indoors. She turned again to Joe, who was carrying in Sara's luggage. "How are you doing, honey? You must be ready to drop. Why don't you head to bed while I take care of Sara."

"No need. I slept while Sara drove all the way down. I'm going to head into town to pick up the stuff for the barbecue tonight. John and Alyssa should be in from Portland by the time I get back. Maybe Tom and Diane too. They're off for spring break too," he explained to Sara, "so they're driving in to spend a few days. You've given us an excuse for a family get-together. The first time since Tom's wedding."

Setting the suitcases down in the front hall, Joe kissed Denise and raised a hand to Sara. "See you in a bit, Sara. Make yourself at home."

"I am so sorry!" Sara apologized to Denise as Joe left. "I feel terrible that he had to take that drive after being up all night."

"Oh, please don't apologize," Denise assured her, leading Sara into the kitchen. "He's gotten by on a lot less. It was sweet of you to let him sleep. And it isn't as bad as it sounds. He gets two days off now. Then it's twenty-four hours on, four days off. And they can catnap at the station if there're no fire calls. It's worked out really nice for him to have a few days off while you're here. Now—"

Denise lifted the younger of her two sons, a toddler around two years old, into a high chair. The older boy, about four or five, scrambled into a chair on his own. "Why don't you pull up a chair and rest. I'm about to make Josh here and Jonathan a sandwich before they go down for a nap. Can I make you one? Or some microwave pizza? You must be hungry after that drive."

Sara was hungry. What passed for an in-flight meal had been barely more than a snack. "Whatever you're having sounds great."

Denise was already bustling around, setting the table with sandwich fixings and popping a pair of individual deep pan pizzas into a toaster oven.

"Do you know how much you look like Joe?" she commented over her shoulder. "I'd know the Connor look anywhere." Denise nodded toward her sons, both as towheaded as their father and Sara. "It does carry through the genetic line."

Setting a mug of coffee in front of Sara, Denise pushed a creamer and sugar bowl her direction. "Joe told me you were in the area when we moved out here two years back, and I really did plan on calling you once we settled in. But somehow, with Joe's job and the kids, the months went by before we knew it."

"Please, don't even think about it." Adding cream and sugar, Sara savored the hot drink. "I could've made contact as easily as you. I don't know why I never did."

"That's different," Denise set a peanut butter and jelly sandwich in front of each boy. "Who ever heard of a college student calling her relatives, especially someone she hardly knows."

"Well, I'm really glad we've met now," Sara answered with sincerity. She looked around the kitchen as Denise jumped up to remove the pizzas from the oven. Her eyes fell on a large photograph framed above the table. It showed a sleek, long combat helicopter settled in front of a hangar. Only at second glance did Sara notice the two human figures posed in front of the helicopter, both in uniform. "Is that you with Joe? Were you in the army too?"

"Yes, that's how we met," Denise said, sliding a hot cheese pizza onto a plate in front of Sara. "Joe flew choppers, and I was his mechanic, if you can believe it. I put in for electronics training, but that's the army for you. That's Joe's Apache. He was training to go to the Persian Gulf—Desert Storm, you know. But it was over before he deployed. By the time Afghanistan came along, he was out, so he never did fly combat."

Sara studied the picture of Joe and Denise in front of the Apache. She'd learned more about her cousin in the last two minutes than in her entire life. "So what made him leave flying to become a fire fighter?"

"Job competition." Denise answered succinctly. "After the Gulf War, so many chopper pilots demobilized, and most of them were older and more experienced than Joe. As to why fire fighting, I guess Joe's the type of guy who can't sit behind a desk. If he couldn't fly, he was going to do something that would keep him outdoors. As a fireman, he gets the adrenaline rush, but he also knows he's making a difference." Pouring herself a mug of coffee, Denise slid into a chair across from Sara. "Don't feel sorry for him. He's in the Army Reserves. A weekend every month he's out at Fort Lewis flying his Apaches and Blackhawks. And when wildfire season gets started, he's on call for the Forest Service too."

* * *

After the late lunch, Sara took Denise's suggestion to lie down for a nap at the same time as the boys. By the time she awoke, John and Alyssa had arrived from Portland. Sara's youngest cousin, Tom, and his new bride, Diane, pulled in just as Sara emerged to greet them, and Aunt Jan arrived shortly thereafter.

Aunt Jan's petite frame was not reflective of her force of personality. She'd run her children, household, and career with the efficiency of a drill sergeant. She breezed into the kitchen, already talking.

"Denise, I see you've cut back the lilacs," Aunt Jan said by way of greeting. "Maybe a shade less pruning next time, dear. I think you're going to lose that one on the left. Oh, Sara, there you are. Boys, come give Grammy a hug. Did you have a good flight, Sara? Forgive me for not meeting you, but at least you've had a nice chance to visit with your cousins. My, you haven't changed a bit."

If you only knew, Sara thought as she submitted to her aunt's tiptoed hug. Aunt Jan had changed more obviously in the last three years. The full graying hairstyle was now clipped finger-length and restored to the same flaxen-blond as Sara and her cousins. And she'd taken off at least twenty pounds since the divorce.

In Sara's memories of Aunt Jan, she was always bustling around, making sure everything was under control, while trying to placate Uncle Jack, who was usually into his second six-pack by dinner time. Her tension had typically dampened everyone else's enjoyment.

Now she looked relaxed and even happy as she sat down to play with her grandsons. Why was Sara only now recognizing that Aunt Jan hadn't had such an easy life either?

"What happened to Uncle Jack after the divorce?" she discreetly asked Denise when they had a moment alone.

"He's in some alcohol rehab center near Spokane," Denise answered under her breath. "Joe goes up there sometimes, but he's never asked me or the boys to go along. Too unpleasant, he says. The rest of the family won't go near him. Even Joe can't take it for long. Can you imagine being such a jerk your own family can't stand being around you?"

It explained a lot of what had hurt and bewildered Sara as a lonely teenage girl who'd felt firmly shut out of a family bond that did not include her. Perhaps instead of shutting her out, it had been their own problems they'd been shutting in.

But Aunt Jan hadn't changed in every way. As soon as the barbecue was cleaned up, she hustled Sara out the door, having firmly told Denise that Sara would be more comfortable at the duplex. As Sara wrestled her luggage in from the car, Aunt Jan looked her over critically. "No, you haven't changed at all, dear. You still look about sixteen. It's the hair, honey. We'll fit in a trip to the salon while you're here. Now that you're a career woman, you want to be taken seriously."

Without giving Sara a chance to answer, Aunt Jan led the way through a sliding glass door onto the balcony. The wind whistling across the open plateau chilled Sara's Miami-thinned blood so that she pulled her jacket tight around her shoulders. The height of the balcony gave an unimpeded view of the enormous span of desert sky. The twinkle of human habitation down the hillside and across the valley was no match for the sharp-edged glitter of the constellations overhead. Though it was cold, the air was crisp and clean with the pungent scent of sagebrush and a hint of snow and pine.

"Don't you love that country smell?" Aunt Jan said as Sara drew a deep breath. "I've been a lot of places, dear, but I have yet to find anything that beats the Pacific Northwest. I'm still counting my blessings at being back. Washington D.C. was interesting, but crazy."

She reached up to give Sara a pat on the shoulder. "And now you're home too, dear, and I do hope you'll stay."

Sara made a noncommittal sound, but for the first time since the flight from Santa Cruz had landed at Miami International Airport, she felt she was indeed back in her own country and on her own native soil. Of any place in her nomadic life, this corner of the globe had been the most home.

Sara lifted her eyes to the jeweled splendor of the night sky. A move back west would be a prudent course of action, even more so than Aunt Jan could know. For one thing, it would remove Sara far enough from Nicky's relatives that she'd never have to worry about the Cortezes again. A month ago, it would have been an easy decision to accept Aunt Jan's invitation. Especially now that she had met Joe and Denise and their two small boys, who'd already captured her heart. But a month ago, Sara had not sat across a restaurant table from Doug Bradford and seen the fire in his eyes. Would he really come after her if she did not return to Miami? She knew better than to underestimate his resolve.

Did she really think that Special Agent Doug Bradford would back off any course of action to which he'd made up his mind?

Chapter Twenty-five

APRIL 13
IGUAZÚ FALLS, BRAZIL

Julio Vargas watched the last rappeller touch down safely at the base of the cliff and scramble into an inflatable raft. They'd had to bring the teams here to the basalt rock faces of the Iguazú River gorge to train, because there were no such facilities near their jungle base. The good part was that the rappelling skills they'd need for their next mission would seem like a cakewalk after these wet, slippery cliffs.

Into his radio mouthpiece, Julio ordered, "That will do for today. Let's get everything up and on board."

As the team began scaling back up the cliff, the drone of an engine rose above the roar of the river. An excursion helicopter, cruising up the gorge for an air tour of the Iguazú Falls, came into view, flying low along the riverbed, almost level with Julio and his climbing party atop the bluff.

Julio waved casually to the tourists peering out the window. He had no objection to being noticed. "Rain Forest Survival Treks" was clearly lettered on the backs of the shirts the athletic young men climbing the cliff face were wearing. It only added to their cover story to be spotted doing "survival trek" activities.

At the top of the bluff, the team members folded the rafts down into the smallest dimensions possible and lifted their gear into the Huey helicopter waiting on the flat outcropping of rock. When the last rappeller was aboard, Julio lifted off, but instead of turning back toward their jungle base , he flew low over the rain forest canopy toward the Paraguayan border and Ciudad del Este beyond. He'd just received a radio message from the trekking office that Diego and Raymundo's latest shipment was in. Besides, there were other matters to which he needed to attend, and the men had all earned a decent hotel bed for the night.

It said much about the laxness of border control along the Tri-Frontier that

Julio had yet to be challenged as he skimmed across the Paraná River, which divided Brazil from Paraguay. When the Huey touched down on the gravel landing pad in the Jungle Tours parking lot, the men loaded into a tour shuttle for the drive to the hotel. The sunburned young men with packs of climbing gear would be one more group of tourists entering the lobby.

Leaving the team to make their own evening plans, Julio caught a taxi across town to Mozer Jebai's office. It was time to check in with Saleh. Julio was not happy with the tight scheduling of their next mission, only two weeks after the last, but it was essential that this final exercise be linked firmly with the others in the minds of the authorities. Once the mission was completed, the mysterious strike force would disappear, leaving all those questions permanently unanswered.

Then there would be time to take Diego and Raymundo's latest shipment of skydiving gear and fly the newly leased DC-3 up north to the Gran Chaco to begin preparations for the strike team's jump training. A virtually waterless and uninhabited plateau covering the northern third of Paraguay, the Chaco was ideal for training paratroopers for desert fighting. By the time they were finished cycling the teams through this final phase of training, the "drug cartel infighting" in Bolivia would be long off the front page, and the strike force could safely turn to its real targets.

Assuming the success of their present mission. The biggest drawback was the lack of detailed blueprints of the facility. But they'd have the element of surprise and numbers, and everything else was largely in place from past missions. Julio wouldn't have proposed the target if he didn't think the mission could be accomplished.

And if it satisfied his own personal objective as well as his employers, so much the better.

A thin smile split Julio's narrow lips as he tossed a bill to the taxi driver and entered the tall office complex owned by Mozer Jebai. If he'd believed at all in the faith that burned in the hearts of his strike team members, he might have considered that fate—or Allah himself—had placed him in this position of revenge.

* * *

Saleh had no doubt at all that Allah had appointed him to this place and time in history. Like many other revolutionaries, he'd come to the conviction that only by smashing the old order could a new and decent society be established. A rule of law instead of anarchy and self-will. Allah's law, whose strict *sharia* code would not allow the individualistic liberty and accompanying debauchery that characterized Western civilization and contributed to the present world chaos. Only simple, unquestioning obedience. And with it, restored order.

Saleh glanced up from the computer monitor as his father's secretary ushered Julio Vargas into the office. "The men did well today," Julio informed him. "They are as ready as they will be. We leave in three days. The mission is scheduled for a week from today. You will, of course, lead the assault."

"Of course." In practice, if not by official designation, Saleh had emerged as leader of the special operations group, not just his own team.

Julio strolled around the desk to glance at what Saleh had up on the screen He recognized only an occasional English word on the display. "I will admit, you have all come farther than I expected when you first proposed the idea. And now you will at last have the opportunity to strike an American target."

Saleh's fingers didn't slow on the computer's keyboard. "The target is a fitting conclusion to our training program. But the goal is not to inconvenience American holdings overseas; it is to strike at the underbelly of the infidels themselves. I am researching the possibilities for our next target right now. When I am finished, perhaps we can discuss the Bolivia travel arrangements."

Another subtle reminder that in this room Julio was only an employee. With a shrug, Julio sank into a leather armchair and pulled up another for his feet. The air conditioning was refreshing after the heat and humidity outside, and he was curious to observe his pupil's chain of reasoning. He still held a veto if Saleh's choice was impracticable.

Saleh dismissed Julio from his thoughts as he returned to his prior concentration. The question was how to fulfill the original mission objective—to inflict serious injury to the enemy, then slip away to strike again and again. What was the infidel nation's soft underbelly that they could exploit?

He pulled up the day's AP-Reuters headlines for the United States. A landslide had trapped a party of skiers in the Rockies. The western states were already battling their first wildfires of the year, blamed on unseasonably dry weather. Environmental activists were protesting a fire's close sweep to a nuclear research lab in Idaho. Another activist group was marching on a hydroelectric dam in the Midwest, protesting local government corruption in the dam's upkeep.

The collapse of a subsidized-housing apartment complex in Chicago was being blamed on shoddy construction. On the Arizona-Mexico border, an ATF raid had netted a cache of weapons from sniper rifles to bazookas and RPGs.

Saleh paused on that one. Could it be one of the sleeper cells that he would be counting on for his own operation's support? But, no, these were white American militia. Too bad their grievances against their homeland were too far afield from his own to make useful allies.

Saleh narrowed the field to specific search words. *Nuclear facilities.* These were the sites every militant group dreamed of hitting. Consequently, they were as protected and impregnable as a fortress. *Water plants.* To poison an entire city's water source would be an exploit unmatched even by the destruction of the World Trade Center. But further research soon made it clear these purification plants were almost as well protected as the nuclear facilities, surprisingly so.

Saleh called up another Web page and studied a layout map of Washington, D.C. Random bombings on American soil would terrorize the nation, but the payoff was limited and suicide missions were not part of Saleh's plan. He pulled up a new file with growing impatience. What he wanted was to inflict critical injury to the enemy, whether or not he got credit. In fact, it was preferable *not* to receive credit. The training missions in Bolivia had taught him how much more could be accomplished through misdirection and laying of blame on others—if one's purpose was actually to win a war and not merely self-promotion. Despite the bombings and shootings carried out by his comrades in al Qaeda, Islamic Jihad, Hezbollah, and other militant groups, a single natural disaster caused more devastation. For that matter, the one forest fire his team had accidentally set had done far more damage than all the C-4 they'd used.

Invisible. Unattributable. Accidental. How much damage did such "accidental" natural disasters cause to America every year? Saleh returned suddenly to the first news clips he'd read. He pulled up a file he'd previously dismissed. Then another and another.

He straightened up so abruptly that Julio was roused from his armchair slumber. "I know how we can do it," Saleh said, excitement tinging his voice. "We will be the worst disaster to hit the Americans in all their history. Even better, it will all be the result of their own shortsighted and iniquitous folly."

This time it was the student who outlined the plan to the instructor, diagramming swiftly across sheet after sheet of paper, printing off file after file. Julio, searching incredulously and wordlessly for a flaw, recognized with a jolt that his student had already passed his graduation exam.

Chapter Twenty-six

APRIL 13
RICHLAND, WASHINGTON

Sara enjoyed herself more than she'd ever expected. Early spring in eastern Washington was far too cold for any of the leisure activities she might have suggested, but her cousins possessed a boundless inventiveness—and a restlessness that kept the household hopping. They organized bowling and ice-skating outings, and rock climbing at an indoor facility that left Sara dangling—and laughing breathlessly—thirty feet above the ground. When they weren't planning activities, they were outside kicking around a soccer ball or on the trampoline with Joe's two boys. It came as no surprise to Sara when she discovered that her cousin John coached track as well as taught English. Had she ever really known her cousins?

The wives kept pace with a tranquility that showed they were used to it. Occasionally, they would escape with Sara to the mall or a movie for "girl time," as they put it. Aunt Jan had her own hectic work schedule with tax season nearing its climax, but she joined them at Joe's home for supper each evening.

After the first two days, Joe went back for his forty-eight-hour shift. When he returned, yawning and smelling of smoke, he insisted he was ready to leave immediately for the drive up to Seattle. Everyone spent the next two days camping out at Tom and Diane's student apartment and visiting the familiar Seattle tourist attractions. The Space Needle. Ye Olde Curiosity Shop. Pike Place Market. And, inevitably, the Fireman's Museum down on the Seattle wharf. Jonathan and Josh had as much fun feeding the seagulls and watching the ferries dock as Sara remembered from her own stateside childhood visits.

They returned to Richland with only one day left before Joe had to return to the fire station and Tom and John had to head back to their respective campuses. Richland was a quiet town with the meticulous layout of well-controlled urban planning. With neighboring Pasco and Kennewick, it was part of the

Tri-Cities, encompassing about 100,000 total population, most of which had grown up to service the thousands of government workers employed by the Hanford nuclear reserve. What surprised Sara was how little emphasis was given to the area's major industry. Signs referred to the Department of Energy, not Hanford's controversial power source. Sara saw no military presence or any overt security beyond the occasional chain-link fence out on the plateau. Much of the Hanford facility could have been office buildings or manufacturing complexes anywhere.

As they were enjoying a leisurely breakfast around the dining room table, Sara finally got around to voicing her curiosity.

"Joe, when we got here, you mentioned this whole area grew up around the nuclear weapons program, that it was the biggest nuclear waste dump on the planet. I guess I was expecting . . . well, I'm not sure what I was expecting. Nuclear waste raises images of horror movies and Greenpeace activists. But so far all I've seen is one of the nicest, cleanest towns I've ever been in."

"You weren't just pulling my leg, were you?" Sara added suspiciously. After a week of her cousins' brand of humor, she couldn't be certain.

"Pulling your leg?" Joe repeated with an injured tone. "Would we do that?" He cocked an eyebrow toward his two brothers across the breakfast table. "Guys, I think we need to take Sara on a boat ride."

"A boat ride?" Now Sara was sure they were pulling her leg. "In this weather?" Sara looked doubtfully at Denise, but her cousin's wife was shaking her head and laughing. "Not me! We've all been out there. Besides, the boat won't take more than four. But it's worth going, Sara. I can lend you a thicker jacket."

"Go where?" Sara demanded.

"The Hanford Reach," John told her with a grin, adding, like the school teacher he was, "It's educational. Every American citizen should get out there once in their lives. They used to run tours, but since 9/11 those have been suspended. The only way to get a good look now is by boat up the Columbia River."

Sara was grateful for the heavy down jacket Denise pressed on her as her cousins maneuvered Joe's speedboat from its trailer down the launching ramp into the Columbia River a short drive from the house. The sun was bright despite a cold wind, and her cousins weren't even wearing jackets.

Joe slanted Sara a teasing grin as he gunned the speedboat away from shore. "Miami's turned you into a tropical bunny. This is well into spring around here. Tom's even talking about waterskiing."

The high banks of the Columbia River rose to sheer cliffs as the speedboat left the buildings of Richland behind. Within fifteen minutes of leaving the dock, the gracious luxury homes that occupied much of the riverfront near town had given way to empty terrain. In place of human habitation, there was wildlife everywhere. Sara had never seen so many birds—or so much variety. Herons and geese and hawks and any number of species that Sara couldn't identify. Herds of mule deer wandered along the edge of the bluffs. Joe nodded to the wide, empty spaces above both sides of the river. "This is the Hanford Reach. A stretch of about fifty miles of river that runs through the Hanford site. Everything you see on both sides now is part of the nuclear reserve."

"It's so beautiful," Sara commented. "And peaceful."

Joe shrugged as he steered the boat through a channel between two islands. "A lot of the reserve has been given over to wildlife refuges and ecology reserves. Good PR for the DOE and doesn't cost Uncle Sam anything, since no one is allowed to live on the Hanford site anyway. But don't let that pretty scenery out there fool you. There's plenty of reason why a lot of people call this place the dirtiest spot on the planet. Take a look over there. Tom, give her a turn at the binoculars."

Sara's youngest cousin handed her a pair of binoculars. Sara followed his instructions on focusing the glasses, and what had been a gray blur well up ahead on the left bank became a collection of rectangular concrete buildings, tall metallic towers, and more of the chimney stacks Sara had seen her first day out on the plateau.

"It looks like some kind of industrial complex."

"It's a nuclear reactor." Joe eased the throttle to an idle that made it easier to keep the binoculars on target. "Oh, don't worry, it's been shut down," he added as the binoculars dropped involuntarily from Sara's eyes. "There's a dozen of those complexes along the Hanford Reach, built along the riverbanks to use the water of the Columbia as coolant. All but one back over by Richland which produces electricity for this region, has been shut down. No, it's not the nuclear reactors that give people the occasional nightmare out here. It's what they've left behind."

Joe was steering the speedboat onto the opposite bank now. He and his brothers had clearly done this before. They pulled the boat up to a rocky beach and moored it to a wind-stunted willow, then waved for Sara to follow their quick strides up a steep trail to the top of the bluff. Appropriating the binoculars, Joe searched the horizon before handing them back to Sara. "Take a look right over there. Way out on the prairie. You can only see it from this height."

Sara's search revealed an odd landscape. In the middle of the sagebrush and prairie grass was an enormous rectangular stretch of pavement dotted with clusters of lighter-colored ovals and circles, along with concrete box shapes, antennas, and poles. A collection of American flags fluttered from one long line of poles.

"That's a tank farm. Doesn't look like much, but under each one of those round clusters is a steel tank filled with radioactive waste from the reactors. One hundred seventy-seven of them altogether, full of more than fifty-five million gallons of the most lethal stew that exists on this planet. The bad part is that most of those tanks were built fifty years ago in the early days of the nuclear weapons program, just kind of assuming that later scientists would figure out how to clean it all up before the tanks got beyond their design life. Now a lot of the tanks are leaking. The DOE admits at least a million gallons have leaked out into the ground table. Parts of that plateau are so hot with radioactivity you can't go out there without air tanks and radiation suits.

"I was on the fire marshals' team assigned to assess Hanford's fire codes. They let us take a peek inside one of those tanks down there—by remote camera, of course. The stuff was boiling up inside there like a big vat of bubbling molasses with the air bubbles popping up. Except those air bubbles are hydrogen, which will explode like a bomb if it gets too hot. Uncle Sam spends a fortune keeping the stuff stirred so it doesn't reach critical mass and blow the tank. If it ever did or a single spark was ever introduced into that mess, you could kiss Richland good-bye, along with who knows how much of the Northwest that would be contaminated for a few thousand years."

Joe reached over to shift the focus of Sara's binoculars. "Then you take those mounds over there. See, right there, just too regular to be natural? There are tunnels with railroad lines underneath those. When they've got a piece of nuclear waste too large and radioactive to be handled, they load it onto a flat car, drive it into one of those tunnels, shovel dirt over it , and forget about it. That pretty countryside out there—people have no idea how much deadly poison is buried underneath. In trenches and barrels, as well as all those tanks and pools. Even parts of nuclear submarines. All in all, two-thirds of all the radioactive waste in this country."

"Then there's the K-basins further upriver from here. Basically, they're just a couple of Olympic-sized pools holding eighty percent of our nation's spent nuclear fuel, mainly uranium rods from reactors. The pools are decades past their life expectancy. I was part of that inspection team, too, and even a fireman knows rusting steel and crumbling concrete when he sees it. The stuff is inert as long as oxygen in the air doesn't come in contact with it. But if one of those basins ever loses its water cover, it would set off a chain reaction that . . . well, put it this way: The U.S. wouldn't need to worry about some rogue terrorist group getting their hands on a nuclear bomb."

Sara lowered the glasses, appalled. "But that's horrible! If there's that much danger out there, why isn't someone doing something about it?"

"Oh, they are," Joe answered matter-of-factly. "Hanford is on the agenda of every Congress. They've allocated billions of dollars to clean it up. At best, though, they figure in twenty years they'll have ten percent of the waste contained."

"And if something happens before then?" Sara asked. "What if a fire did get into those tanks? Or an earthquake cracked those basins?"

"Actually, we did get a fire out here," Joe admitted. "June 2000. It started with just a crash of two vehicles on the highway across the river over there. A few sparks got into that dry sagebrush and grass we've got out there, and with the kind of winds we get, in three days half the nuclear reserve was up in flames. It didn't get anywhere near the K-basins, but it did make it within two miles of those tank farms before it burned out."

Joe gazed across the landscape and shrugged. "I will say I do have the occasional nightmare of what might have happened if that fire had raised the temperature in those tanks enough to set off that hydrogen."

"Then why do you live here?" Sara demanded. "Why does anyone live here when they knew they're sitting on . . . on a time bomb? How can you take it so calmly?"

Joe smiled at Sara's intensity. "I guess we don't spend much time thinking about it. The people who live here are a patriotic bunch, and they're proud of working for Uncle Sam, especially during the Cold War when the missiles produced here were what was standing between us and the Soviet Union. And Richland's a nice place to live. Like you said—quiet, clean, one of the best education and medical systems in the country. It's a good life for kids. Beats Seattle, any day. Right, guys?"

"Hey, don't look at me," John protested, putting up his hands. "Why do you think I'm sticking to Portland? I've heard the stories about glow-in-the-dark squirrels out here."

"Just stories," Joe said. "At least as far as I've been able to check out. I guess it's like California. Everyone knows the Big One's going to hit someday, but you don't see people fleeing L.A. It's been fifty years, and nothing's ever happened, and I guess those of us who live out here are taking the chance nothing ever will."

Sara raised the glasses again to the landscape across the river. The flat prairie, with its low, dense vegetation, looked peacefully still and serene, not at all deadly. Even the DOE complexes with their neat chain-link fences looked innocuous. The herd of deer feeding along the perimeter of the tank farm clearly sensed no peril in what lay beneath their grazing heads.

"And if there was another fire? Would you be involved in fighting it?"

"Sure! I was in on the last one." Joe took the binoculars back from Sara. "I'm wildfire qualified. I may work in town, but when fire season gets bad enough, they bring in firefighters from anywhere they can pull them. I'm in the Reserves and chopper-qualified, which means I've got two strikes for me if they're calling up extra personnel."

"Two strikes *for* you?" Sara repeated incredulously. "You sound like it's a big plus being called up to risk your neck fighting a fire on a nuclear waste dump."

"It is." Joe grinned at her. "Hey, don't let anyone kid you. It's not like any firefighter *wants* to see a fire break out. But you don't spend all that time training without wanting to put those skills to good use. And it sure beats sitting behind a desk."

He's just like Doug!

In fact, there was much about her cousin that reminded her of Doug. A likeness she'd have recognized earlier, except that she'd been doing her best not to think about him. Was there something about these high-risk service professions like fire-fighting and law enforcement that bred physical and mental toughness, the calm, almost laid-back competence, a restlessness that would not be confined behind a desk harnessed to strong sense of civic responsibility, that Sara had come to recognize in men like Doug and Joe?

Or were these types of men simply drawn to such occupations?

Joe gave Sara a brotherly pat on the shoulder. "Hey, we brought you out here because it's a tourist must-see, not to scare you. Believe me, I wouldn't be living here if I didn't think it was safe for my family." He cocked an eyebrow at his brothers. "Tom, are you still crazy enough to try waterskiing in this wind? If you are, we should break out the gear."

"Sure, why not! The sun's shining. You did put in the wetsuit."

Sara lingered on the top of the bluff, savoring the momentary solitude, as her cousins scrambled down the steep trail and huddled in discussion over a pile of ski gear on the rocky beach. As much as she'd enjoyed renewing family ties, she'd been surrounded by people every moment of every day since she'd arrived. She had promised Doug that she'd think and pray about what he had said about their relationship. But except for that fleeting moment on Aunt Jan's balcony, she had not done so. Not just because she'd never been left alone with her thoughts, but because she had not wanted the confusion of her own emotions to spoil her enjoyment of what had turned out to be an unexpectedly delightful vacation.

And it is just a vacation. As much fun as she'd had getting to know her cousins and revisiting childhood memories, it wasn't home here. Not anymore.

You can't go back, she had come to recognize. She'd felt more regret leaving Cynthia Bradford's untidy townhouse than she would Aunt Jan's pin-neat apartment. Still, it had been a worthwhile trip in every respect. Whatever the future held, she now knew she had family. And from now on she'd make it her own responsibility to keep in touch.

She raised her eyes and surveyed the wide expanse of open land across the Columbia. *So if this isn't home, Sara, where is home? Miami?*

Incredibly, as the days had passed, Sara had found herself actually missing the chaotic, unruly metropolis of Miami. Not the maniac driving or urban congestion or seemingly constant sirens. But the people. Her students and fellow teachers. The colorful mix of languages and cultures that at first had seemed so alien. Now it seemed strange to walk through a checkout line without speaking Spanish. And the church she had gone to with her cousins, though friendly, lacked the vivid ethnic mix of her new Miami church. Apart from the nine years she'd spent in Seattle, Sara's childhood experience had been more like the polyglot mosaic of peoples and cultures she found in South Florida. Only now was she realizing how well it fit her.

And warm weather. Sara pulled her jacket collar up around her neck as a chilly gust wreaked further havoc on her hair. Her blood had definitely thinned in the last year.

And yet—home isn't a place, not for me. For all the fledgling roots Sara was putting down in Miami, as she had in so many places and countries over the years, was there anything she would not be able to walk away from if she had to rip up those roots, as she'd also done countless times over the years?

Only Doug.

The realization hit her with some force, as if the subconscious energy she had expended to keep thoughts of Doug away had served to give them greater weight.

Home isn't a place. Home is Doug. Miami would be *home because Doug's there. But I could go anywhere, move to any country—even back to Bolivia—and it would still be home if Doug was there.*

Sara's hands tightened in her jacket pockets. *Debby told me I had to learn to live without him. I think I've learned to do that. But I want to live* with *him . . . wherever he goes for whatever time God gives us together.*

"Sara!" At a shrill whistle from her cousins, Sara rose stiffly to her feet, brushing the dirt from her jeans before starting down the trail.

Is it time? Oh, God, I don't want to make another mistake. Please, make it clear enough for even someone as thick-headed as me to get it right!

Chapter Twenty-seven

APRIL 16
MIAMI, FLORIDA

Doug grabbed his cell phone out of the coin tray as his Ford Taurus turned into the DO parking lot. With all the new regulations, he really should get one of those hands-free units, but he hadn't gotten around to it. *Just one more piece of high tech to keep track of out in the field.*

"Yep." Anyone who didn't know who Doug was without identifying himself had no business on this line.

"Hey! Louie Rodriguez here. I'm down at the port. You know that ship you asked me to put on the EPIC watch list?"

"The *Buena Vista.*" Sliding out of the Taurus and beginning to stroll toward the building, Doug stretched his neck wearily while holding the phone to his ear. "What's up?"

"Your ship. We just got a call. A Coast Guard cutter spotted her—oh, not more than two hours ago. Right on course heading back into U.S. territorial waters. You want a SAS, or what?"

The Customs inspector couldn't possibly make a personal call to every agent whose listing popped up on the EPIC watch list. Doug was still cashing in points for that concrete tubing. "How far out are they?"

"Twenty-four hours, more or less. At their present speed and according to their shipping schedule, they should be crossing into our waters a little after dawn tomorrow."

Doug stifled a yawn before responding. It had been a long, frustrating night and was shaping up to be an equally long day.

"No, if we're going to stop and search, I want to be there." Doug raised a hand in greeting to Mike Garcia and the new agent, Rick Acevedo, as they passed him in the corridor. "Besides, if I'm not mistaken, TI&E has the *Buena Vista* registered as a Panamanian flag ship, not U.S. Let's keep it simple. Can we wait until they enter our waters and hit them from this end?"

"Should be no problem. Let me do some checking." Doug could hear the screech of chair wheels on tile, then the Customs inspector came back on the line.

"The Coast Guard has a patrol boat, the *Whidbey*, on the roster to head out at dawn tomorrow. I know the captain, Craig Bjorge, well. Our wives work out at the same gym. He could swing up to intercept the *Buena Vista*. Only thing is—" Louie paused, "—he isn't much on having outsiders aboard."

Stop-and-Search was a Coast Guard operation, and though the DEA technically held jurisdiction over any counternarcotics operation, the commander of the *Whidbey* didn't appreciate a landlubber coming on board and telling him how to run his outfit.

"I understand perfectly," Doug replied dryly. "You can assure your friend I have full confidence in the professional competence of the Coast Guard. I will happily stay in the background and keep my mouth shut. But this one I've got to see through myself. I know this bunch. They've gotten away with way too much already, and if I can help it, they're not going to slide out of this one."

"Let me give you a call back."

Slapping his cell phone shut, Doug stopped at the kitchen for a mug of coffee before heading to his desk. The inky color and "cooked" smell indicated it had been sitting in the pot for much of the night. He dumped a pile of creamer on top of the steaming surface and pocketed a couple of sugar packets for later application. Caffeine was the goal here, not taste, but he'd learned his lesson about "all night" coffee. When he reached his cube, he set the mug on the desk, wriggled out of his windbreaker and Kevlar vest, and slumped into his chair. His proposed SAS operation wasn't as unequivocal as he'd told Louie. He still had to get authorization from Norm Kublin for this new move, and Norm would have to go up the line to his own immediate superior, the Assistant Resident Agent in Charge of their field division. Which meant beginning the tedious task of writing up the necessary cables.

A cable, or *twix*—slang for the old teletype abbreviation TWX from the precomputer age—was to the planning of a mission what the DEA-6 was to its aftermath. Every piece of the operation plan, short of going to the bathroom, had to be written up in excruciating detail and sent up the chain of command to be ripped apart and picked to pieces before grudging approval for the mission trickled back down. Only too often, the cables would come back down with demands for explanations of things that anyone who'd been out of their padded desk chair in twenty years would know. Or insisting on changes or postponement. Or even nixing the operation altogether.

Meantime, if an agent waited for the stamp of approval before making plans, no mission would ever get off the ground. So while cables went up and down the line, the real work got done the old-fashioned way. On the phone. Calling in contacts and a favor or two. With any luck, authorization came through before the op team was scheduled to walk out the door.

On this one, though, Doug had no hesitation about enlisting Kublin's support. Not after last night's bust of a rave party where Doug's team had netted the largest haul yet of so-called club drugs. Thousands of doses, all sitting pretty in the back offices of a South Beach disco. And not just butterfly-stamped Ecstasy pills. There was also a bagful or two of clover-green Rohypnol capsules and bottles filled with a clear liquid that Doug knew without even waiting for the test results were Ketamine and GHB.

Giving up on the mug of coffee—you could never add quite enough creamer and sugar to make it palatable—Doug stretched out in his chair and closed his eyes. He was bone tired. And not just because he'd spent the night rounding up lowlifes instead of stretched out on his Sealy Posturepedic. He was tired of seeing people—kids—screwing up their lives and futures for a few hours of mindless indulgence.

Where were the adults who should be watching out for the best interests of these kids? Or were they off somewhere indulging in their own self-destructive pleasures while their children danced and drank and drugged their lives away?

Well, any number of those partygoers would be spending the day in either juvenile or adult court, depending on which ID they'd produced. And maybe some of them would take it as a wake-up call that would turn them onto a different course.

Doug sat up with a jolt as his cell phone beeped.

"You're on," Louie Rodriguez informed him succinctly. "The *Whidbey* leaves port at 6 A.M. If you're there, Bjorge says you're welcome to ride along. Just don't be late. He wouldn't wait for the president."

* * *

At the Port of Miami Customs Office, Louie Rodriguez replaced the phone in its cradle. From a nearby work station, one of his assistants got to his feet and headed briskly toward the restroom. He waited only until the door to a stall swung shut behind him before he pulled a cell phone from his pocket.

* * *

ATLANTIC OCEAN

"You want me to turn this ship and run from the American Coast Guard?" the captain of the *Buena Vista* demanded incredulously.

Captain Pedro Ramirez was just about fed up with his two passengers. They were arrogant and abusive, critical of the food and the accommodations, and they considered it their right to wander onto his bridge at any time, asking questions, disrupting his routine, and distracting the crew with demands for cold drinks or Jamaican rum.

But he did not raise his protests too loudly. The captain of even a cargo freighter was king on his bridge, but the vessel under his feet did not belong to him. Like his deck hands, the Panamanian captain was only an employee of the corporation holding the *Buena Vista's* title papers. And these two men were senior executives in that corporation. The CEO, Al Fayed, had introduced them to Captain Ramirez himself. Even so, an American captain might have argued further. But here Diego and Raymundo's arrogance stood them in good stead. It never crossed either one's mind that this hireling pilot would dispute their orders, and their colossal self-assurance was such that it never occurred to Captain Ramirez to question their presence or their authority to use his ship as they were doing.

Still, Ramirez was a captain, and his first responsibility was to the well-being of his ship and crew, not the corporation. "We cannot outrun the Americans. It would be *loco* even to try. If you have brought on board cargo which you do not wish them to find, then I would advise you to get rid of it now before we cross into American waters. You do not know the American Coast Guard as I do, if you consider that your recent construction efforts in my cargo hold will fool them for a moment. I at least have no wish to spend the next years rotting in an American prison."

Raymundo and Diego exchanged amused glances. They had just gotten off the radio-phone to their employer, from whom they'd learned of the *americano* Bradford's latest move. It couldn't have worked out better! They'd expected to have to do some discreet maneuvering to attract the attention of the Coast Guard. Now they just had to make sure they rendezvoused with the *Whidbey*, and the rest of their preparations would be ready to go.

The two Cortéz sons-in-law had not bothered to inform Al Fayed that they were calling from the bridge of the *Buena Vista* rather than from their own home. Time enough when they were successful to let their Miami employer and Julio Vargas know what a brilliant stratagem they had employed.

"We are not fools," Raymundo snapped. "If we were smuggling drugs, it would be with complete discretion, and the Americans would never know it was under their noses. No, you need not be concerned for your ship. You will be in port tomorrow as planned. This is just a little game we are playing with the Americans."

Chapter Twenty-eight

How do they do it? Forcing acid back down his esophagus, Doug cast an envious eye at Captain Craig Bjorge and Boatswain's Mate First Class Matt Lawson as they moved easily from instrument panel to radar plot to chart table, their bodies swaying in automatic compensation for the up-and-down bounce and side-to-side roll of the patrol boat as it plowed through white-crested waves.

Doug wasn't sure he could manage a single step from the rail against which he'd lodged himself. He hadn't felt like such a greenhorn since his first cattle muster at age twelve. Five years in landlocked Bolivia seemed to have wiped out any sea legs he'd acquired during his earlier Miami stints. Outside the wheelhouse windows, dawn should have been above the eastern horizon by now, but a gray drizzle made little distinction between the low-lying rain clouds and the sea below, cutting visibility to under two hundred yards.

"The *Whidbey* is a 110-foot Island class patrol boat, named after Whidbey Island on Puget Sound. It's twenty-one feet across the beam, displacement about 160 tons. She isn't big, but she's fast, top speed about thirty knots. More than enough to outrun any druggies."

Captain Bjorge's practiced patter made it clear that Doug wasn't the first civilian invader too VIP to be banned from his bridge. A red giant of a man who must have had more than one Viking ancestor, the captain didn't smile, but Doug caught the glint of pure enjoyment in his sharp gaze as he broke off to ask solicitously, "Sea too rough for you, Agent Bradford?"

"It's a little bouncy," Doug said with his own practiced casualness, though offered through gritted teeth. *And I'd like to see you on a bronc!*

"Lawson, some Dramamine for our guest." Captain Bjorge actually held the military rank of lieutenant, but the commanding officer of any ship was still a captain, even if that ship was little more than thirty yards long with a crew of only sixteen. "We don't like to take a chance of losing passengers over the side," he added as Lawson stepped nimbly across the cabin. "Especially DEA. Too much paperwork."

In contrast to his commanding officer, Boatswain Lawson was a thin and wiry twenty-something, whose crew-cut head barely reached Captain Bjorge's massive shoulder. Handing Doug a pill and plastic cup of water, he commented laconically. "Yeah, the last agent we had aboard spent the whole trip puking over the side. We had to strap him up to one of our SAR safety harnesses."

"Search and Rescue," Captain Bjorge translated. Pouring hot water into a narrow-topped, wide-bottomed travel mug, he added a tea bag before passing it to Doug. "Chamomile. We keep it on board for our civilian passengers."

Doug ignored the jibes, but he took the Dramamine and washed it down with the tea. Battered pride was no reason to jeopardize his mission performance.

By the time the drizzle abated, with a corresponding improvement in visibility if not smoothness of ride, the Dramamine had done its work and Doug had even managed to edge away from the railing, feet braced wide apart to meet the oncoming swells, as he'd observed the crewmen doing. A thin ribbon of blue sky now stretched between the swollen rain clouds and the gray heave of the waves.

"The *Buena Vista* will be visible over the horizon in about two minutes," Captain Bjorge said with a sideways glance at Doug. The time for jibes was past. Now it was time to get to work. "You're sure she's carrying?"

Left unspoken was the understanding—shared by both men—that an SAS operation was a considerable expenditure of both manpower and operational budget that would need to be justified in the next budget report.

"Nothing's sure, you know that," Doug responded dryly. "But they're dirty— I'd bet my next paycheck on that."

"Here she comes," Lawson called from the radar plot.

Despite his announcement, the surrounding circle of ocean and sky remained empty. Then Doug saw the top-heavy superstructure of the *Buena Vista* rise above the curve of the horizon, followed by the wide-beamed hull thrusting upward in the heavy swells. The clarity of its dark outline against the pink-blue band of the eastern horizon was deceptive. The freighter was actually still a mile or more distant.

The smaller profile and white paint of the Coast Guard patrol boat would be far less visible against the gray waves. The freighter plowed on toward the *Whidbey* for another full sixty seconds.

"They're well inside our waters now, sir, straight on course. No, there they go!" A tinge of excitement crept into Lawson's unruffled announcement. "He's heading out to open water, sir. They must have seen us."

The movement on the radar screen took dimension outside the tough Plexiglas of the wheelhouse window as the freighter made a hard turn to the left, wallowing in the swells as the bow began to come about.

"They're dirty, all right," Captain Bjorge pronounced with satisfaction. "Good call, Bradford. But they can't possibly be stupid enough to think they can out-run the Coast Guard. Talk about a dumb move. They'd have been smarter to stay on course and hope to bluff their way through. Foreigners! They might as well have waved a red flag in our faces."

He reached for the radio mike. "*Buena Vista,* this is the U.S. Coast Guard. Heave to and prepare to be boarded."

To no one's surprise, there was no response. Unlike a pleasure craft, a commercial ship was required to keep a constant radio monitor, making the only legitimate excuse for being off the air a broken communications system—not a likely possibility in this case.

"Okay, we'll do it the hard way. Lawson, I want you to take charge of the boarding party." Captain Bjorge shot a sharp glance toward Doug. "You feel up to joining them, Bradford?"

"I'm in." Doug steadied himself and followed Lawson down a ladder to the deck, where a crew member was removing the cover from a 25-millimeter cannon. A sharp increase in the *Whidbey's* speed didn't seem to bother the young petty officer, but Doug grasped for the railing as he emerged on deck.

You've got nothing to prove, he reminded himself grimly, taking note of the amused glances from the crew. All he needed was a broken leg before even boarding the *Buena Vista.*

The six-man boarding party were breaking out weapons, two with shotguns, the others with 9-millimeter Berettas. Flak jackets went on under orange life vests. Doug adjusted his Kevlar vest under a borrowed life jacket and checked his Glock.

The *Whidbey* had twice the knot capacity of the freighter, but Captain Bjorge kept his speed down, so that it took a full half-hour to close the distance, ample time for the crew to settle in at their battle stations. By now it would also be abundantly clear to the crew of the *Buena Vista* that the Coast Guard patrol boat was on their tail. Doug knew that Captain Bjorge would continue to try to make radio contact with the freighter, so there would be no room for excuses that their quarry hadn't understood they were being chased down.

Borrowing a pair of binoculars from one of the seamen, Doug used the intervening time to study the activity on board the *Buena Vista.* He could see movement on deck, but if they were dumping cargo overboard—a favorite maneuver of druggies cornered at sea—he didn't see any evidence floating in the ship's wake. After the Stop and Search, the patrol boat would take a more leisurely survey of the surrounding water.

As the *Whidbey* closed to within a few hundred yards, a siren blared from somewhere above Doug's head, followed by the same curt order that had gone out over the radio. The volume of the loud-hailer was piercing enough that no one within a radius of a mile who wasn't stone deaf could claim not to have heard.

"*Buena Vista*, this is the United States Coast Guard. Heave to and prepare to be boarded. We will not ask again."

The warning was repeated in Spanish. On the bow and stern decks, the crew members behind the deck guns tensed. But a warning shot—the next step in the Coast Guard manual—proved unnecessary. The *Buena Vista* was already powering down its engines. The *Whidbey* cut its own engines to an idle. The deck guns remained trained on the *Buena Vista* as the boarding party launched the rigid hull inflatable boat the Whidbey carried for such missions.

As the RHIB bounced across the swells toward the freighter, Doug realized that he should have borrowed a rain slicker as well as the life vest. But as always when an op was underway, he ignored the physical discomfort as he concentrated on the mission at hand.

The bellow of the loud-hailer ordered the *Buena Vista* to lower a ladder. From Doug's vantage point, the mass of the freighter was evident. Though small by cargo shipping standards, it was at least three times the length of the *Whidbey* and twenty times its deadweight tonnage, giving the patrol boat the look of a brook trout challenging an ocean tuna. But with the *Whidbey*'s deck guns visibly trained on the *Buena Vista,* there was only a slight delay before a head appeared at the rail and a Jacob's ladder tumbled down the side of the hull.

The two shotgun toting members of the boarding party remained on the RHIB, covering their companions as Boatswain Lawson clambered up the wooden rungs of the rope ladder, followed by the other two crew members and Doug. Once the advance crew was over the rail, the last two tied up the RHIB so it wouldn't drift off and climbed up to join them.

This was the point of greatest danger to the boarding party if the freighter's crew did have hostile intentions. Notwithstanding the threat of the deck guns, the Coast Guard's rules of engagement stated that the patrol boat could not fire unless the *Buena Vista* fired first. But the boarding came off without a hitch.

According to Terry O'Brien's intel reports, the crew size for a freighter of this tonnage was about a dozen. At least half of them had already gathered on deck by the time the boarding party was aboard. A tall, dark-skinned Hispanic was easily identifiable as the freighter's captain, though the resplendence of his dress whites and cap was more often seen at the captain's table of a cruise ship than on the rust and grease-streaked deck of a shoestring-budget cargo vessel. Outrage quivered in his voice and every inch of his frame as he demanded, "I am Captain Pedro Ramirez. What is the meaning of this?"

"We have reason to believe this ship is carrying illegal cargo," said Boatswain Lawson in fluent Spanish. If you will give your crew the required instructions, we will be conducting a search of this ship."

The captain drew himself up to his full height and responded with unmitigated fury. "You dare insinuate that we carry drugs on this vessel? There is nothing illegal on this ship. And if there is, you can be certain I know nothing about it."

It was the opening gambit of every runner caught with his hand in the cookie jar. Doug, remaining unobtrusively in the background as protocol demanded, let his gaze sweep over the blustering captain in a swift scan of the crew and deck.

The ethnic mix of blacks, Hispanics, and East Indians was standard for a Caribbean ship crew. None gave evidence of concealing arms or undue wariness. Unlike their commanding officer, they hadn't taken time to change, but were dressed in well-worn and soiled work clothes. All but—

Doug's cool survey narrowed speculatively as he took in the two expensive gray suits advancing purposefully across the deck.

It can't be! No one could be that stupid. The business end of a drug network did not dirty its hands by personal contact with the poison that paid for their mansions and filled their offshore accounts. But he'd spent too many hours surveilling those stocky, soft-bellied figures and smug, self-satisfied faces to mistake the Cortéz sons-in-law at any distance.

"Then why did you turn to run when you spotted us?" Lawson was asking politely and reasonably.

"We did not notice you. We had a difficulty with our port engines. We were simply turning to test the adjustments that had been made."

"And that's why you didn't answer your radio either?"

"We have been having problems with our communications system," the Panamanian captain said smoothly. "As you can see, we are not in the position of the Americans to have always the newest and best of equipment."

Barring dress uniforms! A momentary silence prevailed as Diego Martinez and Raymundo Pinzón strode up to the boarding party. Their furious glances toward Doug signaled immediate recognition.

Doug's speculative gaze narrowed further. Was that triumph he detected?

Diego erupted first. "So this is the meaning of our delay. What has this agent of the DEA—" He gave the acronym its Spanish pronunciation of *day-ah* "—been telling you to occasion this outrage?"

His self-assurance and complete lack of guilty concern was enough for Lawson to throw a swift and questioning glance at Doug. Only Lawson and Captain Bjorge knew that Doug was DEA, though most of the *Whidbey*'s crew undoubtedly had their suspicions.

"You know this man?" Lawson demanded.

Raymundo drew himself up like a puffer pigeon. "Certainly we know this agent. He has been carrying out a personal vendetta against our family for years. In our country he was reprimanded for harassing our family and our business. Like too many of the *americano* agents, he cannot see a Latino experiencing success without accusing us of dealing in drugs. Now that we have moved our business to Miami, he has again taken advantage of his position to harass us. Is this permitted in America—the hounding of innocent people because of a personal grudge? It was he who set you upon us, was it not? We are not criminals! Verify for yourself instead of listening to the lies of this troublemaker. You will find soon enough that we have many friends in Miami who can vouch for us."

As if that means diddly!

But there was something eminently respectable about those sober gray suits and power ties, and the captain's spotless whites. Lawson shot Doug a second questioning glance while the boarding party members who understood Spanish looked uncomfortable. The DEA was not universally popular with its fellow government agencies, but it rankled Doug to see one of the boarding team—a Hispanic-looking seaman—nodding his head when Raymundo spoke of the harassment of Latino businessmen. But Doug had long experience in hiding his anger behind impassiveness, and he returned Lawson's glance with a signature bland look.

Unfortunately, there was truth in Raymundo's ranting. Doug had no concrete evidence except his long acquaintance with *Industrias* Cortéz. The Coast Guard had agreed to this mission on little more than his good word. If they came up empty—

This time, the air of triumph was unmistakable as Diego spread his hands expansively. "But search if you wish. You will find nothing, and we will be calling our lawyers as soon as we set food on shore."

The Coast Guard boarding party began the search procedure, but much of the enthusiasm had gone out of the morning's venture. Doug did no more than tag along, even when a freshly painted bulkhead aroused some excitement.

A certain amount of material damage was an inevitable side effect of any drug search, because smugglers were rarely considerate enough to leave their merchandise in the open. The bulkhead sported a large and jagged hole by the time the Coast Guard searchers were satisfied that nothing was concealed inside. Crate lids were pried up, packages of *yerba mate* sliced open. An elegant mahogany armoire worth several months of Doug's salary became a casualty when one of the *Buena Vista* crewmen dropped his end as it was being moved.

Doug was lending a hand with a freezer compartment filled with Ecuadorean shrimp when Lawson came down to the hold to look for him.

"It's looking like you called it right after all," he said with some return of his earlier enthusiasm. "Come take a look. You too, Gonzalez . . . Bremer. Just leave all this. If we haven't struck it this time, we're not going to find it."

Captain Ramirez, Diego, and Raymundo were on hand when Lawson led Doug and the other two boarding party members into the freighter's crew quarters. The rest of the boarding party was already present, the two with shotguns had them unslung and ready. If there was going to be action, it would be now.

"Take a look at this," Lawson pointed out to Doug triumphantly. "Fresh varnish. And if this room isn't two feet short of what it should be, I'll eat my measuring tape."

"This" was the far wall of the mess hall. The crew used it as a recreation center as well, and the boarding crew had already ripped away a large entertainment center, leaving gaping scars in the fake wood paneling behind it. Sure enough, this was of recent construction, the paneling a lighter shade than the other three walls, varnish along the border trim gleaming with recent application. Lawson's tap-tap reverberated with the hollow resonance of empty space rather than the dull thud of solid matter.

Doug understood Lawson's enthusiasm. It was the classic "look for" in the

Stop and Search section of the Coast Guard manual. A freshly constructed wall with an attempt at concealment. Though Doug couldn't judge with his unaided eye, he had no doubt Lawson had made accurate use of his measuring tape.

But he'd seen Diego and Raymundo exchange glances when Lawson ordered two of the boarding crew forward with fire axes. He gave a mental shrug. It was too late to raise an objection now. This charade would have to play itself out.

It was another hour before Lawson called it quits. Diego called the parting shot as a glum boarding team dropped back down the Jacob's ladder. "You'll be hearing from our lawyers!"

Doug didn't miss the less-than-friendly glances from the boarding crew as the RHIB skittered back over the swells to the *Whidbey.* His silent scrutiny of the ocean was neither embarrassment nor apology. He'd known the instant he caught the self-satisfaction on Diego and Raymundo's overfed faces that this mission was shot, however little choice there had been to go through the motions. It was reminiscent of the blown warehouse raid at *Industrias* Cortéz in Bolivia, though Diego and Raymundo lacked Luis Cortéz's sheer dramatic flair and aristocratic presence.

And brains.

Don Luis had lured Doug into that warehouse, planting the bait, bribing the soldiers to cause more destruction than necessary, and of course ensuring that Doug had come up empty-handed. As result, a discredited Doug had been yanked off the investigation, leaving Don Luis with a free hand to continue expanding his cocaine empire under the facade of his legitimate business conglomerate.

But Diego and Raymundo seemed to have forgotten that in the end Doug had been vindicated—and the public record showed it. And this was America, not Bolivia. And Diego and Raymundo were two sleazy lowlifes, not the country's leading entrepreneurs. If they thought to discredit Doug by a clumsy simulation of Don Luis's ruthless tactics, they had a surprise coming. Yes, today's operation could hardly be classified as a success. Yes, he'd used up a lot of brownie points and would have to come up with a lot more probable cause the next time he asked the Coast Guard for a Stop and Search. But if these two thought that one dry run was enough to discredit Doug on his own turf, it showed how little they knew. This was hardly the first dry run a Stop and Search had netted the Coast Guard—or the last. As for Doug, he had too many positive hits to his credit for one cold shot to tarnish his reputation as an agent. And if Diego and Raymundo thought they could scare Doug off with tactics like these, they'd find out they had just the opposite effect.

What was clear was that he'd have to find another tree to bark up if he wanted to continue this investigation. Which brought up a more important issue. The Cortéz sons-in-law had known Doug was coming. This had been a carefully orchestrated campaign from their presence in Armani suits and that ridiculous captain's uniform, to the oh-so-casually disguised fake wall.

So who had tipped them off? At the very least, Doug was going to make it his business to find out.

Chapter Twenty-nine

Diego and Raymundo were strutting like a pair of roosters as they strode into the Coral Gables house that evening. Don Luis had treated them as little more than errand boys during their years in the family. He'd put more faith in his security chief than in his own sons-in-law. But now they'd shown what they were capable of, and their only regret was that their father-in-law was not around to witness their triumph.

So instead, they bragged to Delores and Janeth, who as well-trained Cortéz wives murmured appropriate admiration even while their minds remained on their children's activities and tomorrow's NFWO tea.

Before the two men went upstairs to bed after a sumptuous meal and plenty of wine, they called to leave an animated, if garbled, message on the answering machine at Rain Forest Survival Treks. They were still deep in slumber the next morning when a shrill ringing penetrated their fogged brains. It took another long, sleep-sodden moment for Diego to identify the acid tone on the other end.

"Diego . . . Raymundo . . . what kind of sloths have not yet risen at this hour? Listen carefully. I do not have time to waste. I have a new list for you to acquire. This time the shipping instructions are different. Now read back to me what I have dictated."

Diego, wishing he'd drunk less Argentinean wine the night before, read the list back dutifully. "But how are we possibly to acquire these things?"

"They are all for purchase in America," Julio responded coldly. "You do have the Internet service, do you not? Then get on it and begin searching. You have all the money you need, so that will not be an issue. Now, what is all this babble about the American agent Bradford?"

Diego had switched the phone to speaker mode when Raymundo had come into the room, and the two men's bragging accounts tumbled over each other as they related the last week's adventures to the smallest detail.

"Our contact in the Customs Office will alert us if Bradford makes any further moves against our shipping ventures," Raymundo finished proudly. "And he is certain to receive a reprimand from his superiors once our lawyers present our complaints. I do not think we need anticipate any further trouble from the American."

The silence was deafening as Julio gathered up a full measure of cold fury.

"*Idiotas!*" he shouted, the crackled spatter from the speakerphone reverberating off the tile floor and stucco walls of the room. "Did I not warn you about this before? That you should dare to do such a thing without consulting with me—have you lost what little wits you possess?"

"But . . . you told us not to bother you further with the American."

Julio cut off Diego's apologetic defense. "I did not think you would be foolish enough to take matters into your own hands. Have you not learned by now the folly of poking at a hornet's nest? You should have left the Americans to do their search unimpeded. They would have gone away when they found nothing of interest. But now—the more you have meddled, the more Bradford will be wondering what you are trying to hide."

"But . . . we did not mean. . . . We had no idea he—"

"Enough! If there was time, I would replace you with someone whose brains fill more than a thimble. Now I have no choice but to use a pair of *idiotas.* We will have to hope there are no further repercussions from your little adventure. As long as he does not know of your connection to me—he does not know, does he?" Julio broke off to inquire sharply.

"Of course not . . . how could he? . . . There is nothing written down, only the phone calls from a legitimate business."

The truth was, Diego and Raymundo had no idea what Julio's connections were—to them or to this Rain Forest Survival Treks. That it involved something legally questionable, they took for granted simply because of the quantities of money involved. How any of it related to past Cortéz transactions, however, baffled them.

"We will take care of this order immediately."

"And do nothing else at all without consulting me! Or you can be sure it will be more than your new life in Miami you will find yourself losing."

* * *

CIUDAD DEL ESTE, PARAGUAY

Incompetent fools! Julio slammed down the receiver so hard that the young Lebanese secretary who served as receptionist for RST knocked discreetly on the office door. "Sir, is everything all right?"

"Yes, of course everything is all right. Return to your work."

Rashima's official job description was little more than window dressing—greeting walk-ins and directing their inquiries to other adventure tour operators. But as far as Julio was concerned, her real job was that of spy for Mozer Jebai and his brother-in-law, Khalil. He was certain she eavesdropped on his phone conversations and no doubt listened to any messages when he was out.

Julio swore viciously in gutter Spanish. The Cortéz blunders had at least located the American woman and the agent Bradford for him, and under other circumstances it would have been a pleasure to deal with them as they deserved. But Julio never put pleasure before business—or profit. And he'd dealt too many times with Special Agent Doug Bradford to be sanguine about his intrusion into the equation. For two *centavos,* a sum of far less value than an American cent, he'd replace his Miami suppliers. But there was no time now. Not just because the riverboat was floating at the docks, loaded and ready for their final venture into Bolivia. Barely two months remained before the "Weapon of Allah," as Saleh and his father so dramatically dubbed their strike force, was scheduled to be unleashed on an unsuspecting American public. There was little enough time to procure every item he'd been commissioned to deliver. He could not afford to be searching for more competent partners.

Of course, he had no doubt that Mozer Jebai could come up with an alternative, as the mullah had offered when Julio pleaded for more time in planning the American mission. His Lebanese relatives seemed to have an entire network of contacts around the world. But too much of this operation had already slipped from Julio's control. Diego and Raymundo were at least his own men, and he knew that they would act under his orders, however ineptly. And there was his commission to think about on every item the Cortezes shipped south, modest enough to avoid Rashima's scrutiny but a steady addition nonetheless to his numbered bank account. Julio did not need the attractive, snooping Lebanese receptionist adding an audit of his supply line to her other duties.

Striding out through the reception area, Julio favored Rashima with a cold, flat glance that dropped her eyes instantly to her desk. His mood did not improve as he emerged from the tour agency and walked through the Jungle Tours parking lot to the riverbank, where the team members who'd be accompanying the riverboat over the border were already on deck.

The novelty of this job was wearing off. Julio had signed on to train Mozer Jebai's Special Forces recruits. He had not bargained for being pulled into this new American venture of Saleh's. Worse, because they needed his expertise as a pilot, he had been trapped into an active role.

The added commission they offered was worth the risk, but this American mission would be the end. Julio would obtain the equipment Saleh wanted, do his part of the operation, and with it consider his contract sufficiently fulfilled. Already he'd begun training Saleh to fly the Huey. Once that was done, they wouldn't need Julio anymore.

The riverboat was moving slowly upriver when another niggling consideration arose to disturb Julio's thoughts. Would it be so easy to leave these fanatics behind? Would they just let him walk away with the knowledge he now possessed? Julio had disposed of too many potential "problems" himself over the years to be trusting.

No matter. When the time came, he'd simply apply the lessons he'd been teaching and vanish. That was, after all, the point of a numbered account. Rio had women, beaches, and an infrastructure designed for a fugitive. Buenos Aires would be nice—or Santiago. Perhaps even Costa Rica.

Definitely not Bolivia or Paraguay.

As to what Diego and Raymundo would do when their employment dissolved into thin air—well, maybe for the first time in their spoiled, indolent lives, they'd have to find real employment.

Julio began to relax into the hammock he'd slung under a deck awning. Once this was over he'd have earned time for some pleasure.

Like a visit to old enemies.

Chapter Thirty

MIAMI, FLORIDA

Doug slapped a file down on Norm Kublin's desk. "There it is! Right in front of our noses all the time. Just look at the name of that clerk in Rodriguez's department. Fayed is hardly a common name. I don't think it's any coincidence that it's also the name of Tropical Imports & Exports' CEO."

Setting down his coffee mug, Norm Kublin picked up the file, his sharp gaze zeroing instantly on the Customs personnel list Doug had marked. "So you're saying . . . ?"

"We were blown! One of those flukes. Rodriguez is pulling Fayed in now for questioning, but I'm betting he's some relative who tipped off his family that we had them on the EPIC list and were nosing around. That's why we came up empty. The whole *Buena Vista* op was a charade—from running away to that obvious fake wall. They wanted us to come after them."

"Maybe. But you still came up empty. We aren't going to get the green light to go after the *Buena Vista* again any time soon." Kublin laid down the file. "Have you thought that maybe you haven't come up with anything because they really aren't dealing anymore? They panicked when they found out you were nosing around and pulled this stunt to get you off their backs?"

"No!" Doug said sharply. "Not with Julio Vargas in the picture. He hasn't done an honest day's work in decades. Besides, if the Cortéz are clean, they'd be stupid to pull a stunt like this when all they'd have to do is sit tight, scream for their lawyers, and wait for us to go away—"

As Doug's voice trailed off, Norm Kublin picked up the conversation. "You're sure they wouldn't be that stupid? Most of these guys need only a whiff that the DEA is on their tail to wet their pants, even if it's just their own guilty conscience."

Doug conjured up an image of two smug, fat faces. Guilty conscience or panicked stupidity? He shrugged. "Either way, you're right about one thing. The *Buena Vista* lead's a bust for now. But there's the other end. I figured I'd give Paraguay a call and see if they've got anything on record. We know Vargas was buying a tour agency running excursions out to Iguazú Falls. Plenty of rivers for moving drugs in that area. Maybe Asunción has a lead on either this Jungle Tours or on Vargas himself."

Norm Kublin took a long sip of coffee before answering. "Fine, give 'em a call. Meanwhile I need you to take a look at the Echevarria file. His lawyers have thrown in some new wrinkles."

It was afternoon when Doug got through to Ciudad del Este. During most of his years in Bolivia, the DEA had maintained only a modest office in Asunción, the Paraguayan capital, and Ciudad del Este was just a temporary duty posting. However, Doug had known most of the handful of agents working the other side of the border from joint counternarcotics operations.

Since the World Trade Center attacks, both DEA and FBI presence in the Tri-Frontier region had been significantly increased, and Ciudad del Este now had a full field office, albeit with only two full-time DEA personnel working with the local Paraguayan counternarcotics forces. Of the two names the Asunción office supplied Doug, the intelligence analyst's, Andy Williams, was unfamiliar. But Chris Patterson was Special Agent in Charge, if a two-man office deserved such a fancy title.

It must be siesta hour, Doug surmised by the yawning disinterest he met when he finally got past the Paraguayan secretary to an American voice. "Williams!"

The intel analyst sounded incredulous when Doug explained the information he was seeking. "Julio Vargas? You kidding, man? That's like asking for John Smith. Sure, we can rustle you up a Julio Vargas—or a hundred of them. I've got one on my own informant list. What makes you think this is even the same guy you're after?"

"Look, his mug shot's in your files. Just take a look at it and show it around. See if anyone's seen him around town. More to the point, around this tour agency, Jungle Tours. And if you could dig me up anything on the owners, I'll owe you a big one."

"Can't promise anything, but we'll get back to you."

Even a look took time, so Doug was neither surprised nor disappointed when he hadn't heard back by the time he left the office late in the evening. His lateness was due to a renewed search through O'Brien's extensive files on Tropical Imports & Exports. Al Fayed, the CEO, was of Lebanese descent, Doug learned, a refugee who'd been in the country at least four decades and held

American citizenship. Though Cousin Rashid over in Customs would likely lose his position over the *Buena Vista* incident, or at least be removed from access to sensitive information, TI&E itself would not receive so much as a reprimand. There being no law against receiving a tip from a family member that a government agency was nosing around in their business.

Still, if TI&E had ever shipped goods for *Industrias* Cortéz, it must have been through an intermediary, because there was no record of any cargo originating in Bolivia. Which meant nothing. What Doug needed was to impound the *Buena Vista* and have the lab guys go over it with a fine-toothed comb. If there'd been cocaine anywhere on board in the past few months, there was bound to be some residue.

But that was a request Doug knew better than to make.

The next morning, when Doug returned from a court hearing on the Echevarria case, he found a message waiting from Ciudad del Este. Andy Williams picked up his return call.

"You've got something for me?" Doug asked. "Let me guess—you've IDed Vargas."

"We sure have," the agent answered dryly. "Any number of them. I've got your mug shot and the stats in front of me now. Medium height, black hair, black eyes, bronze complexion, high cheekbones. Matches half the male population down here. So far every informant we've got is sure he knows at least one Julio Vargas who matches that mug shot. And of course they all want to be paid for the intel."

It was a wrinkle Doug had already considered. It was tough to make a good ID on someone from a two-by-two inch Bolivian police photo.

"What about Jungle Tours? Were you able to find out who owned it?"

"We certainly did." Doug was not encouraged by the note in the intel analyst's voice. "Jungle Tours, along with any number of other businesses and properties here in Ciudad del Este, just happens to belong to one of this city's most prominent citizens, Sheik Mozer Jebai, who also happens to be the leader of the Arab community here."

Now that *was* interesting. "He wouldn't happen to be Lebanese?"

"As a matter of fact, the bigger part of the Arab community here is Lebanese Muslim. Jebai too, likely as not. That would be easy enough to check out."

So there was a possible connection between Jungle Tours and TI&E, if not the Cortezes. "Any rumbles the guy's been involved in drug dealing?"

"There's always rumbles if a family's got enough money down here, you know that. But they aren't part of any present investigation, if that's what you mean."

"Then what will it take to start one? Can you have your guys nose around for some kind of three-way tie between this Jebai, a Bolivian corporation called *Industrias* Cortéz, and a Tropical Imports & Exports agency in Miami? The Miami agency does a lot of shipping to this Jungle Tours, and I doubt it's coincidence that they are also owned by a Lebanese family. And if you could get one of your locals to narrow down that mug shot to a Julio Vargas directly connected to this Jungle Tours, you'd be doing me a great favor."

It was a simple enough request, the kind made from one DEA field office to another on a regular basis, part of the "you scratch my back, I'll scratch yours" network that made the whole unwieldy bureaucracy work. So Doug was not prepared for the sudden silence on the other end, a silence so prolonged he'd begun to think he'd been cut off when a new voice came on the line.

"Bradford? Chris Patterson here. We met in that Avianca Airlines case a few years back."

Avianca Airlines. That was why the name was familiar. Doug had been one of the Miami agents involved in "Operation Orchids," which had uncovered a network of cargo personnel shipping heroin through the Colombian national airline's shipments of exotic flowers. The agents had been given a wink to take a few flowers home to their wives. Chris Patterson, a desk jockey down from D.C., had raised a stink about misappropriation of evidence—even though the flowers had been summarily hauled out anyway and dumped on a garbage heap somewhere. Only the RAC's intervention had averted a reprimand on the local agents' records.

Well, that was then, this was now.

"May I ask just what your interest is in Sheik Mozer Jebai?" the SAC went on without further small talk, not unfriendly, but definitely cool.

"Just a fishing expedition, really," Doug said. "The name cropped up with a case I'm working on."

"And do you have anything more concrete than a fishing expedition that connects Jebai to any illicit activity?"

"Not concrete, no. That's what I was hoping you might turn up . . ."

"Look, Bradford," Chris Patterson cut in. "I don't know how much you're aware of the situation here in Ciudad del Este. But the Arab community is considered a financial pillar of this city."

Doug *was* aware. He made it his business to read up on every political situation or location pertinent to his job—and that included Ciudad del Este. It was an odd piece of the Latin American puzzle that the immigrant communities were invariably the most prosperous part of the economic scene. Arab. Korean. Chinese. Mennonite. Even the occasional North American expatriate. They'd all done well for themselves in their adopted countries, and often wielded more political clout than the citizens of those countries themselves.

In Ciudad del Este the Arab community was only a few decades old, the greater part of them Lebanese who'd left their country's bloody civil war by the thousands, but there were also Syrians, Iraqis, Jordanians, and Egyptians. If they'd escaped with little from their own countries, they had very quickly parlayed that little into financial prosperity. In Ciudad del Este, no one argued that they were largely responsible for building that rustic riverbank town into the international goods market it was today. If there were the usual rumors that copyright piracy, drug dealing, and the general traffic in black-market trading was responsible for more than one Arab merchant's rapid rise to fortune, it made them no different from other prominent members of Paraguayan society.

"And in the Arab community here," Patterson was saying, "Sheik Mozer Jebai is *the* financial pillar, one of the wealthiest men in this city. He is also the spiritual leader of the local mosque."

Doug didn't like where this was going. "Since when did we start letting a man's bank account and social position determine whether we check him out?" he interjected with a mildness that reflected his need for the SAC's cooperation.

"That's not the point," Patterson answered sharply. "And you at least should recognize the situation we've got going down here. You were in Bolivia when 9/11 went down. You can't be unaware of the investigations we've had going down here."

Yes, Doug was aware. Before September 11, 2001, the American public had been generally ignorant of and even less interested in the activities of Arab expatriate communities scattered around the Third World and inside the U.S. But the DEA and U.S. intelligence agencies had been keeping an eye on these groups for years.

A common misconception among Westerners was that *Arab* and *Muslim* were interchangeable terms. In actuality, a large proportion of the Arab expatriate population were Christian or even secular. Some communities dated back more than eighty years to emigration from the Turkish-ruled Ottoman empire, where non-Muslims ranked as second-class citizens. But a growing number of Islamic fundamentalist migrants had begun feeding into these communities in recent decades.

The Lebanese Muslim *diaspora* especially, coming as so many had from the Muslim-Christian civil war and its accompanying crusade to annihilate Israel, had strong ties to Hezbollah, the Iranian-backed "Army of God." Much of their involvement was simply funneling funds to Hezbollah efforts in Lebanon and Palestine, as well as to the Islamic Jihad, al Qaeda, and other extremist Muslim organizations. Hundreds of millions of dollars were estimated to have been channeled through Ciudad del Este, including the proceeds of smuggling operations and drug trafficking. Hence, the DEA's interest.

But it wasn't just money. Known Hezbollah operatives had also been spotted by intelligence agencies moving through the Tri-Frontier area, as well as listed members of Islamic Jihad, al Qaeda, and other Muslim extremist groups. A Hezbollah cell in Ciudad del Este had been linked to the bombings in Argentina of the Israeli embassy in 1992 and a Jewish community center in 1994. A number of indictments had been made detailing the selling of false documents to Arab nationals, including the arrest of the Paraguayan consul in Miami shortly after 9/11 for selling hundreds of false Paraguayan passports, including those issued to sixteen identified terror suspects from Egypt, Syria, and Lebanon—all on their way to Ciudad del Este.

None of this had been any secret to international intelligence agents. But what the Arab exile community was up to from the sleazy safety of a Third World country had not been an American intelligence priority. The DEA's own investigations had been related only to the trafficking of drugs, not the destination of their profits.

Until the U.S. became a direct target. Within days of the World Trade Center attacks, joint task forces of FBI, CIA, and DEA agents had been swarming through Ciudad del Este and other Arab colonies throughout Latin America.

"We had a couple guys from our office go down your way after 9/11," Doug conceded. "I wasn't involved, but I read the reports."

"Well, I was involved. And if you've read the reports, you know what we found. Al Qaeda and Hezbollah recruiting tapes in the local mosques. Phone accounts under false names networking numbers in Pakistan, Egypt, Sudan, Saudi Arabia, and the U.S. Black-market CDs and weapons mixed in with Islamic militant propaganda in some of the warehouses we raided. And, of course, any number of financial documents showing transfer of funds to questionable accounts in the Middle East. We even managed to pressure the Paraguayans into arresting some of the more prominent suspects. A major victory in the war on terrorism."

"A victory." Doug echoed the other agent's ironic tone. "I was heading off to Miami about then, but I've kept current."

"Then you know how it turned out. The Arab community started screaming racial profiling from here to the Middle East. You know the routine. American persecution of Muslims. U.S. invasion of local sovereignty. Before we could blink, most of our suspects were out free again. Lack of evidence, the Paraguayans said. According to local authorities, everything we found was legitimate business dealings or just your garden-variety crime syndicate. Their pretty little country couldn't possibly hold terrorists."

"And this Sheik Mozer Jebai?"

"Oh, he led the screaming. We know Jebai's as radical as they come. He fought with the Hezbollah back in Lebanon before he immigrated here. As leader of the local mosque, he's brought any number of extremist mullahs over the years to preach jihad to the new generation. We have his name on financial documents transferring funds to known Hezbollah fronts. Of course Jebai says the donations were all for humanitarian causes, and there's nothing illegal with wanting freedom for your homeland. We found out the hard way who holds the real clout around here. And how many local politicians Jebai has in his pocket." There was a bitter note in the SAC's voice.

Doug stifled a sigh. The review of current events was interesting, but it hardly seemed relevant enough for the cost of long-distance from Paraguay to Miami, even if it would be on the taxpayers' bill and not Doug's. "Look, Patterson, all I'm interested in is tracking down a two-bit drug dealer who just might be working for this Jungle Tours. So what's the bottom line here? Are you telling me anything that belongs to this Mozer Jebai is untouchable?"

"What I am saying is that this guy has managed to stir up plenty of sympathy for himself down here. If we're seen going after him again without ironclad probable cause, it's going to backfire in our faces. They'll be saying that, since the Americans couldn't get him for terrorism, they're trying to frame him for drug dealing. And if you think we can send out any of the locals we're working with to investigate without it getting back to Mozer Jebai, you've been stateside too long. No, I'm sorry, but it is the opinion of our superiors all the way up to the White House that the war on terrorism takes precedence over the war on drugs. And it's going to take a lot more than a generic name that might or might not be a Bolivian drug dealer you once knew to get authorization for messing around the Jebai applecart again. You do understand."

Oh, Doug understood all right. It was only too familiar, he thought savagely as he hung up. Luis Cortéz, too, had been supremely confident that his family's money, social standing, and political clout placed them above the law. And he'd been right for too many years.

But this Sheik Mozer Jebai and his pals weren't even citizens of the country they'd bought off. Not that *that* mattered. In South America, only Bolivia could match Paraguay for sheer corruption and opportunistic politicians. The entire history of Paraguay told of a string of despotic dictators, culminating in thirty-five years under General Alfredo Stroessner, whose use of murder, torture, and political purges was at a level with that of Stalin or Saddam Hussein. And of course he'd been siphoning off of the poverty-stricken country's scant resources into his own pockets and those of his cronies

A coup in 1989 had returned Paraguay to civilian rule, but not much had changed. Stroessner's Colorado party was still in the driver's seat, and various former Stroessner cronies merely took turns in the presidential palace.

Virtually every political leader had come under indictment for corruption and graft so manifest that it could not pass unnoticed even in a country that expected such behavior of its leaders. The most recent president remained in office only because the legislature had not quite come up with the two-thirds majority needed to impeach him for driving stolen luxury vehicles and piling up unaccounted-for millions in his overseas bank accounts.

Meanwhile, eighty percent of the population subsisted in a level of poverty that again was exceeded only by neighboring Bolivia. Small wonder, in a government so strapped for cash, that drug trafficking had been allowed to flourish openly, not to mention crime syndicates looking for safe haven from as far afield as Russia, China, and Africa, as well as the usual Colombian and Brazilian mafias.

So whatever political expediency demanded that the State Department and U.S. government personnel bleat about mutual aid and teamwork with the Paraguayans, no DEA agent had any illusions about the level of serious cooperation they could expect on either terrorism or counternarcotics.

But if Doug could understand and even sympathize with Chris Patterson's position, it still left the question of his own next move. Tilting back his chair, Doug stared at the ceiling long enough for Rick Acevedo to tiptoe by, clearly under the impression that his colleague was napping. Doug's chair came down with a crash loud enough to spin the younger agent around.

Norm Kublin was still at his desk when Doug strode into his office.

"I need authorization for travel to Asunción and Ciudad del Este," Doug told the GS without any preamble, "and up to a week to nose around."

Kublin slapped down his coffee mug and stared at Doug in disbelief. "You can't be serious. What brought this on?"

Doug shrugged. "I can't go any further into the Cortéz case without going to Paraguay and doing some digging around."

For the next twenty minutes, Doug laid out his reasons and his plan. Norm Kublin's espresso grew cold while Doug talked.

"You see why I've got to go myself," Doug finally concluded. "No one else can identify Vargas. And the local office is too afraid of its own shadow when it comes to upsetting the Arab business community, to dig out the intel I need."

The GS was already shaking his head before Doug finished. "Doug, I'm surprised at you, I really am. I've backed you up on a lot of things—mainly because you have a knack for being right. But you know I can't authorize a trip to Paraguay out of this office's budget on what you've got. And you know as well as I do that if I bump your request up the chain, you're going to get the same response you got from Patterson."

His sharp eyes narrowed shrewdly as he added, "Look, Doug, take some friendly advice. You're a good agent . . . one of the best I've ever worked with. But face it, on this one you're not being objective. Okay, so it's personal. These guys got away from you. I've read the files. But maybe you just need to back off and let this one sit awhile. Give them time to get careless. They always do. As for Paraguay, let the agents down there do their job. If something comes up, they'll let you know soon enough. We've got a lot of cases with a lot more to go on heating up right here to be wasting all your energy on past history."

Kublin had a point, Doug admitted to himself. After all, it had taken three years of patient digging and biting his tongue to bring down *Industrias* Cortéz. Diego and Raymundo didn't have it in them to match the cleverness and care of Don Luis. Sooner or later, whatever they were up to, they would make a mistake. And with its long record of institutional perseverance, the DEA would be there to nail them when they did. The logical thing to do—the professional thing—would be to walk away.

If it weren't for Sara.

And Julio Vargas.

Norm Kublin had never looked Julio Vargas in his cold, flat killer eyes as Doug had. Doug would never forget the sick knot in his stomach when he'd found out that Vargas had kidnapped Sara. And Vargas would have killed her with no more compunction than swatting a butterfly, if not for the fact that Doug had gotten there in time to save her.

That the Cortéz clan had invaded his territory and Sara's had been cause enough for concern. The addition of Julio Vargas to the equation was far more disturbing. So much so that Doug had, for the first time, been relieved that Sara was far away on the West Coast.

But Sara would be returning soon. And if there was no love lost between Julio Vargas and Doug, Vargas's antipathy for Sara was far more virulent. To his way of thinking, she had betrayed him and his employers and had been responsible for his incarceration. The interrogations after his arrest had made that clear.

I wonder if it would be possible to talk Sara into prolonging her vacation out west?

Logical or not, Doug could not just let this one go and wait for developments. Not without pushing as far as he could to find out just what Vargas's interest was in Miami and Tropical Imports & Exports. Doug didn't buy it for an instant that the former Cortéz security chief had settled down to be some kind of tour guide. Nor did he suppose that Diego and Raymundo hadn't passed on to Julio any information they'd acquired about Sara's whereabouts.

None of which Doug tried to explain to Norm Kublin. The GS would be the first to tell Doug that his personal life and emotions had no place in a DEA investigation. And he would promptly remove Doug from any further involvement in the case. Doug rose to his feet.

"You're right. The Cortéz and Julio Vargas are old history. I withdraw my request."

Norm Kublin looked up at Doug suspiciously. He clearly wasn't buying the kind of easy acquiescence he'd just received, especially after a glance at Doug's determined jawline.

"Blame it on stress," Doug said charmingly, clapping his hand to his left shoulder. "I guess I just went back to work too soon after that shooting, wouldn't you say? I really should have taken that sick leave the doctor recommended. He warned me I might strain things during the healing process if I overdid it, and I guess he was right. Nothing a couple weeks total rest without any job worries won't cure. So I'm sure you won't mind if I change that request to a couple weeks of sick leave."

Norm Kublin was silent, his sharp gaze boring into Doug. Then he said slowly, "This isn't about the girl, is it? Are you seeing her again? Because if this is some personal vendetta . . ."

Doug's tone hardened as he cut in. "I've seen Sara only twice in the last four months, both times on business. But—" he shrugged again— "okay, yes. To some extent you're right. Sara almost lost her life at the hands of those guys. And I was responsible. I wasn't careful enough. I just want to make sure it won't happen again."

His firm mouth curved into a grim smile. "Be assured, I have no intention of upsetting our war on terrorism. And I couldn't care less if the entire country of Paraguay gets away with drug dealing or murder. I just want to make sure there aren't any loose ends down there that will come back to bite us."

Norm Kublin was the first to shift his gaze. Throwing up his hands in a gesture of surrender, he said, "Okay, I can't stop you. You've got the sick leave coming. But just keep in mind that any vacation travel you do will be strictly as a civilian—and at your own expense."

"I don't have anything else to spend my salary on," Doug answered dismissively. "I do need a good, long vacation—to rest the shoulder. I've always heard Iguazú Falls is one of the 'must-sees' of the world. Never got time to see them while I was in Bolivia. Maybe I'll check them out."

Norm Kublin pushed back his office chair with a screech. "Get out of here before I change my mind."

Chapter Thirty-one

APRIL 17

Passport civilian, rather than diplomatic. For this trip, the anonymity of being a tourist was an advantage.

Three changes of clothing. Toiletries. His Bible and the latest Tom Clancy novel. A pair of hiking boots and a lightweight waterproof jacket—it was, after all, well into fall south of the equator. That still left room in the backpack for his laptop and other odds and ends. Doug had learned the hard way not to pack anything he couldn't swing over a shoulder and carry off the plane. He weighed his Glock pistol in his hand before tossing it aside. The downside of traveling as a civilian was no weapons. But then, he had no plans to engage in any activity that might require the use of a weapon. For all his fuming, Doug understood only too well Chris Patterson's perspective. It wouldn't be the first time the Feds had put a damper on a DEA investigation in the name of national security or intelligence gathering of their own. And Doug had no intention of interfering with whatever game his side was playing with this Sheik Mozer Jebai or anyone else in the Arab community of Ciudad del Este. All he had in mind was simple reconnaissance. Locate a certain Julio Vargas and find out what his present connection happened to be with some recently arrived Coral Gables immigrants.

What he really needed was to draw Vargas out of the safe haven of Paraguay and onto U.S. soil, assuming the Julio who'd called in the shopping order to Diego and Raymundo really was the former Cortéz security chief. Doug couldn't know that for sure until he made a positive ID with his own eyes.

Once that was done, there'd be time to think of the next step. Vargas might have bribed his way out of Palmasola, and he might be sitting pretty in the criminals' paradise of Ciudad del Este. But unlike the Cortéz menagerie presently living the good life in Coral Gables, the U.S. Department of Justice still had plenty of outstanding indictments against the right-hand man of the Cortéz cocaine syndicate. They hadn't bothered to serve the indictments only because the guy had been rotting in a Bolivian jail that made Alcatraz look like a country club. If Doug could nab Julio on U.S. soil, he and Sara both could stop looking over their shoulders for at least the next twenty years to life.

Zipping the duffel bag shut, Doug dropped it at the door. He'd never told Sara about Julio Vargas's vanishing act from Palmasola. They hadn't been in communication at the time, and there'd been little point in worrying her with the knowledge that a sleazeball who'd tried to murder her was now on the loose somewhere in South America.

By the time Julio's connection to the Cortezes in Miami had surfaced, Sara was already on the plane to Seattle, and though Doug had found himself reaching for the phone any number of times in the last two weeks, he hadn't dialed the cell phone number engraved on his mental data banks. It wasn't just that there was little reason to ruin Sara's vacation with something she could do nothing about. Doug had agreed to give Sara space and time to think and pray about their future, and he couldn't deceive himself that calling her up to talk about Vargas was anything but a selfish excuse to break that resolution.

But now her two weeks were up, and tomorrow she would be flying home. Doug's initial impulse had been to surprise her at the airport, perhaps even springing for flowers and chocolates. But putting her on the spot in public hadn't seemed quite fair, and Doug had reluctantly modified that mission plan to a dinner invitation on her answering machine.

But now when Sara flew in, Doug wouldn't be there. And though breaking appointments at a moment's notice had been a part of his life to which he hadn't given a thought in years, it suddenly seemed intolerable that Sara should return to find him gone without a word.

Abandoning the duffel at the door, Doug strode back across the apartment.

Chapter Thirty-two

RICHLAND, WASHINGTON

Denise heard the Expedition first, her ear long tuned to that particular engine signature. Josh and Jonathan were tumbling down the front steps by the time the car door slammed outside. Denise greeted her husband with a hug as Joe entered, a small boy wrapped around each leg.

"Are you okay?" she demanded, rubbing a smudge of soot on one jawbone to satisfy herself it wasn't a burn.

"I'm fine—just really tired. It was quite a fire." Joe's normal return to duty had been disrupted by a wildfire in central Washington that spread so swiftly toward the apple and cherry orchards that made up much of the region's economy that every available firefighter within two hundred miles was called in to throw up a firebreak.

"Did you get to fly, Dad?" Jonathan demanded.

"I sure did, a great big Huey with a bucket full of water underneath." Releasing Denise, Joe wearily peeled off the fire-resistant yellow coat of his firefighting outfit. "Hi, Sara!"

Sara emerged from the kitchen door where she'd lingered, unwilling to interrupt the family reunion. She sniffed delicately at the smoky odor still clinging to Joe's flannel shirt and jeans. "Don't like my cologne eh?" Joe grinned.

Sara wrinkled her nose at him, well accustomed by now to her cousin's dry humor. "I wouldn't pay good money for it, that's for sure. No, I just thought it was interesting how different the smoke smells from that other fire last week. More like a campfire—or marshmallow roast."

"It's the real wood smoke instead of a bunch of burning chemicals. Denise has gotten so she can tell you exactly what kind of fire I've been at just by the smell of my clothes." Joe ruffled his wife's red curls, ran a hand over his unshaved jaw and yawned. "Well, I'd better go wash this off."

He grinned again at Sara as he reached down to peel his sons off his legs.

"I'm just glad I made it back before you flew out. I was afraid I was going to miss it. You're sure we can't change your mind about heading back east?"

Sara shook her head with a smile of her own. "No, I've got to go. I've used up every sick day from here to Christmas, and I'm sure my substitute is beginning to think I've been struck by lightning or kidnapped."

"And there's someone waiting for you, isn't there?" Joe added quietly as Sara broke off. "I understand. Just remember, you've always got family here if things don't work out—or if they do."

Beside him, Denise smiled her agreement. Sara swallowed at a lump in her throat, her eyes opened wide to keep back the sudden sheen of tears as she answered shakily, "Don't worry, you won't be getting rid of me so easily this time around."

A jingle in her purse allowed Sara to turn away to unearth her cell phone. It had to be Aunt Jan making arrangements to take her to the airport tomorrow. No one else around here had this number.

But it was not a brisk, female voice that demanded, "Sara?"

"Doug?" Sara saw Joe and Denise exchange an understanding glance at her pleased surprise. By the time she escaped out of earshot into a guest bedroom, concern had replaced the pleasure. Sara would be back in Miami in twenty-four hours. Doug wouldn't break his agreement not to call her unless something had happened.

"What is it? Are you okay? Is it Cynthia?"

"Mom's fine. So am I. Really, Sara, do I only call with bad news?" Sara relaxed as she heard the smile in Doug's deep tone. Then he grew serious. "No, I—just wanted to let you know I'm going out of town, out of the country."

Sara was unprepared for the bitterness of the disappointment that swept over her. She groped for the edge of the bed and sat down. Here she was, finally ready to step off that plane and give him the answer he wanted, and he wouldn't even be there.

No, she wouldn't dwell on the irony.

You accepted how it would be. Deal with it!

"I . . . I understand."

"No, you don't." Doug's response was urgent, sharp. "Do you think I don't want to be here when you get home? That I didn't plan to be here? You *are* coming home, aren't you?"

Home. "Yes, I'm coming home tomorrow. I—you said you're leaving the country? Another TDY?" She was proud of the evenness of her question.

"Yes. I wouldn't go if it weren't urgent, believe me. But—something's come up, and it concerns you as well as me." Swiftly, Doug explained the developments of the last two weeks. "I can't just drop it. You know what Julio's capable of. If we're not going to be looking over our shoulders for the rest of our lives, this guy's got to be put somewhere he can't touch you—anyone involved—again."

"Doug, I understand." This time Sara's response carried more conviction. "And I understand, too, why you didn't tell me. You were trying to protect me again. Hey, it's okay. I'm glad I didn't know he was out there. But—why did you decide to tell me now?"

"Maybe so you'd understand why I have to go now before you get home." His deep voice roughened in a way that interfered with Sara's breathing. "I've been waiting for you to come home, Sara. I couldn't just leave without letting you know. I shouldn't be long . . . just a few days."

"Doug," Sara interrupted again, vehemently. "You don't have to explain. If you feel it's important to go, then you do it. Just . . . let me know what happens, okay?"

"Sure, I'll call you as soon as I know anything."

There was so much more Sara wanted to say. *I'm ready now, and I want to tell you so. I don't care anymore if we have to be apart, so long as we can be together too.* But now wasn't the time. Not when Doug was going into action, when he needed to be focused on the mission ahead. There'd be time later. "Please, I'd appreciate that. And you watch your back with Julio. I'll . . . I'll be praying for those angels of yours to watch you too. Just don't give them too much to do."

"Psalm 91," Doug said. "Hey, no worries. This is just a scouting trip. I'll be back before anyone misses me. Oh, and if you do need to get a hold of me, you've got my cell phone number, but if it's offline, here are some others." Doug gave Sara the phone numbers of the Asunción and Ciudad del Este field offices. "Someone there will know where to get a hold of me."

Now it was Doug who lingered on the line. "Sara, I've got a plane to catch right now, but I—"

"But what?" Sara asked as he broke off.

"Nothing." Sara heard a sigh. "At least not that I want to talk about over the phone. Take care of yourself, Sara."

With a click, he was gone.

Chapter Thirty-three

SANTA CRUZ, BOLIVIA

From an unframed window in the raw brick, Julio Vargas trained his binoculars downward on the neighboring property, the pounding and chiseling and shouting of the construction workers around him providing a stark contrast to the quiet courtyard ten stories below.

It had been two days since the riverboat slid across the Paraguay-Bolivia border. The river patrol monitoring that particular tributary of the Paraguay River was familiar enough now with their coming and going that they hadn't even bothered setting foot on deck before the customary *propina*—a tip or bribe, depending on how one chose to translate it—passed from one bow to the other.

The rest of the strike force had filtered in to their Forward Operating Base or FOB in Santa Cruz by the time Saleh and the boat crew transferred the crated gear from the docks to a truck for transport into the city. The FOB was a typical middle-class house, surrounded by high walls, whose owner had been happy to receive his rental fee in cash. If their on-site appraisal confirmed the advance team's reconnaissance, the raid would be tomorrow night.

Julio's reaction to the plan was mixed. It was the first time he'd played no role in operation planning, other than his original choice of target. But as far as he'd seen, every move the advance team had made was flawless, the mission planning seamless. A reminder that despite the skills they'd had to learn, these men had been hunting down enemies long before they came under Julio's tutelage.

Keeping his profile in the shadows, Julio shifted the binoculars to study every corner of the neighboring property. A modest three-story building surrounded by a high, white perimeter wall topped with inward-curving black spikes. There was no American flag or other insignia to identify its occupants. The only anomaly to distinguish it from any other business along one of the city's main thoroughfares was a huge satellite dish, which was invisible from the street, if only too conspicuous from Julio's tenth-story vantage point. The *americano* DEA did not care to advertise its base in the city. But there wasn't a player in the drug trafficking industry who did not know what lay behind that nondescript blank wall.

A startled shout from the scaffolding above Julio's window alerted him to a rusty spear of rebar that plummeted past him before being intercepted by a heavy netting stretched between the construction wall and the building next door. A grim smile stretched across Julio's narrow mouth. This was what had given him the idea for their present mission. It had to be galling for the Americans, with their vaunted yen for secrecy and clandestine activities, to have a twenty-story office building going up right where scores of windows offered a ringside view of their every movement, every shift of the parabolic antenna thrusting upward at the center of the satellite dish.

It would be interesting to know who had acquired the necessary building permits for this invasion—and how much money had changed hands. Just marking which informants were slinking in and out of the interrogation rooms on the outer veranda would be useful to more than one prominent citizen.

But it was enough that the present development was perfect for Julio's own designs. His one concern had been that in the months since he'd last passed by, the construction might have progressed past the point of easy access guaranteed by the construction crews. But the pace of construction had been true to the excruciatingly slow pace of every other building project Julio had seen across the city. With workmen everywhere, pouring concrete forms, laying bricks, or taking a siesta in a corner, even the Americans' efficient surveillance would not notice a few extra laborers. The two Malaysians chipping away at the concrete floor behind Julio were part of the advance team, their ethnic features allowing them to blend in as the Indian laborers they purported to be. They would alert Julio if a supervisor poked his head into the room.

Outside the perimeter wall next door, two guards with M-16s slung carelessly over their shoulders, sprang to attention as a Landrover turned off the boulevard. When the wide, black gate slid open, the Landrover cruised around to the back of the building. However frustrating the Americans must find the present situation, they weren't stupid. A long section of roofing covered the parking area behind their headquarters so that Julio could not see the Landrover's driver exit the vehicle and enter the building. Any other outside activities similarly took place under the cover of the roof, beyond the reach of any spying eyes from the construction site. In the courtyard, Julio had glimpsed only an occasional visitor being led from a pedestrian gate to the front entrance of the headquarters building.

Julio took note of a surveillance camera swiveling on top of the entrance. The construction safety net had been strung high enough above the paving stones of the courtyard to allow for unseen passage beneath it as well.

Though the courtyard was now quiet, there'd been plenty of activity during the time Julio had been watching. SUVs moved in and out of the gate. An army truck disappeared under the back roofing filled with troops in field fatigues. Some narco would be unlucky tonight.

Tomorrow it would be the *americanos'* turn at bad luck, assuming the rest of the team's planning went as well as this afternoon's reconnaissance. The activity next door had been tapering off over the last hour, with far more vehicles pulling out through the black gate than turning in. The American agents were packing it in for the day.

Night was falling fast, and it would soon be too dark to work on the construction site. Already, the clamor had dropped considerably, as laborers began picking up their tools and heading out. Soon the watchmen would be around to make sure the building was cleared out before setting their own sentries for the night. By then Julio and Saleh, who was studying the same scene from a different vantage point, had to be gone, along with the two "laborers."

Julio lingered long enough to watch the Landrover drive back out the gate. The DEA headquarters must be almost empty now of personnel, except for the newly arrived guard contingent. However satisfying it would be to make a direct attack on the American agents, Julio was not so foolish as to pit his graduating recruits against such well-armed and capable opponents. This attack was simply to prove a point. A symbolic gesture, perhaps, but powerful nonetheless. To hit the Americans in their own lair. To prove the impotency of their security arrangements. It would also confirm that the earlier attacks were not the work of the Americans, but that was a small matter.

As far as Julio Vargas was concerned, once this operation was completed he was willing to let his own desire for revenge rest.

Chapter Thirty-four

APRIL 18
ASUNCIÓN, PARAGUAY

The American Airlines 737 banked over Asunción just as the sun was clearing the rolling, jungle-cloaked hills and cultivated farmland surrounding the Paraguayan capital, giving Doug a superlative view of the wide, lazy Paraguay River, one of the country's major transportation arteries.

Asunción itself was a surprisingly modest city for a Latin American capital. The others tended to be sprawling, congested metropolises, including some of the largest urban concentrations in the world. A handful of modern high-rises rose above the traditional clay tile roofs and whitewashed Spanish architecture of the city center, with its narrow streets designed more for ox carts than motorized vehicles. The taxi driver, pegging his gringo fare as a tourist, made an unnecessary detour to show Doug the Plaza of Heroes with its shaded walks and stately legislative buildings, followed by a spectacular view of the presidential palace, perched high on a bluff.

The American embassy wasn't far from the presidential palace, its stately sweep of lawn and fortified walls intended not for aesthetics, but to keep a wide and easily monitored buffer zone between the American diplomatic community and any hostile intent beyond the high perimeter fence.

The taxi driver followed instructions to turn in at the well-guarded gate, but then Doug changed his mind. Checking in with the country RAC might be the political thing to do, but it would set Doug back half a day and wasn't likely to add anything to the intel Chris Patterson had given him. Nor did Doug need the lecture he was bound to receive about respecting his tourist visa and not overstepping the bounds of his civilian status.

Tapping the taxi driver's shoulder, Doug directed him instead to the bus terminal. With buses leaving on the hour, traveling overland would be faster than waiting for the rare local flight. If at some point he needed anything from his colleagues here, he could always call them from Ciudad del Este.

The driver obediently turned the cab around. Fifteen minutes later, they had left behind the wide, tree-lined avenues and stately homes of the capital's elite neighborhoods and were jolting through narrow, potholed streets with graffiti-splashed adobe buildings and tin-roofed shacks. In the dirt courtyards, women scrubbed clothes in washbasins or cooked over open fires. Packs of undernourished children playing soccer with a knot of rags abandoned their game to chase after the taxi as it lumbered by.

This is the real Paraguay, Doug thought grimly, *to which the owners of those luxury estates around the embassy deliberately turn a blind eye.* That poverty bred corruption was a favorite axiom of American sociologists and academicians, conveniently ignoring the millions of destitute refugees who had arrived on U.S. shores to find the American dream through sheer hard work and honest endeavor.

From Doug's experience, it was the other way around. Corruption bred poverty. What might these countries have become if the greedy ruling class hadn't stripped every asset to fill their own rapacious pockets all these years?

Not that Europe had been any different during the Dark Ages, when the Continent's resources had been locked up in castles and cathedrals while the peasants labored and starved and died in their own thatched shacks. It just went to show that human nature never changed. But for the grace of God—and Doug meant that literally—and the social experiment of a small group of men grounded in godly values, the United States might have turned out this way. More than most Americans, Doug had seen enough to wonder what might happen to that American experiment in liberty if traditional values ceased to prevail in public policy.

The bus terminal was in one of the more rundown parts of the city, crowded with Guarani Indians and Indian-Spanish *mestizo,* lining up for tickets or loading bundles onto cargo racks. Doug's medium build and sandy hair stood out a head above the black-haired, dark-skinned sea of humanity. Sidestepping a food vendor, he absently swatted away a pickpocket's groping hand as he used his superior vantage point to locate a ticket window and wade toward it.

Paraguayan buses were among the worst Doug had encountered anywhere, with wooden benches for seats and rusting undercarriages, not to mention livestock both inside and lashed to the roof. But there were bus lines that catered to tourists and businessmen, and Doug squeezed into a line behind a young French couple and a cluster of local Korean immigrants. Despite the misspelled "Paraguay Toors" emblazoned across the side, the bus proved worth the extra fare, with reclining seats, air-conditioning, and a Jet Li movie for entertainment.

Tilting his seat back as the bus pulled out, Doug closed his eyes. The night's flight with its refueling stops in Panama and Manaus had hardly been conducive to sleep. Ciudad del Este lay six hours away, and Doug had already run through every shred of intel at least a dozen times. The most profitable way to spend the intervening hours would be to catch up on much-needed rest. With the discipline of long experience, Doug tuned out the yowling and shrieks of a kung-fu fight scene, the rock station the driver was playing in the background, and the excited whispers of the French couple behind him, and was asleep before the bus left the city limits.

* * *

Doug woke up feeling much more alert but ferociously hungry, a reminder that his last meal had been a pre-dawn roll and fruit cup, which the airline passed off as breakfast. Glancing at his watch, Doug saw that he'd slept for five-and-a-half hours. The bus would soon be arriving on the outskirts of Ciudad del Este. The highway ran straight as an arrow across a flat plain that had once been cloaked with dense rain forest but was now stripped away for farming and grazing. Charred stumps of slash-and-burn clearing still dotted the corn patches and banana plantations along the road.

What little prosperity the country possessed was in the cities, where trickle-down economics from the luxury neighborhoods had spawned a meager middle class. Except for the occasional hacienda belonging to the elite class, the rural landscape was still characterized by the thatched adobe or bamboo shacks that were home to much of the population.

Any passengers who were still sleeping awoke with a jolt as the bus driver slammed on the brakes to avoid a mob of Brahmin cattle. On the edges of the herd, a party of gauchos with wide-brimmed sombreros tipped against the sun, cracked their whips as they urged their unruly charges across the highway.

There was a timelessness in the snap of the whips and unruffled shouts, the powerful crush of animal bodies, and the superb horsemanship of the Paraguayan cowboys, that might easily have been found in the American Southwest—were it not for the tasteless billboard rising up behind them, a bikinied model offering American cigarettes at a price that definitely did not include import duties.

The billboards became more frequent as the bus approached the city. Other advertisements were painted on buildings and vehicles and any other rentable surface, garish colors screaming offers for every name brand conceivable: Rolex watches. Sony TVs. Dell computers. Nike High-riders.

As Doug disembarked, the street vendors descended on him before he could even push his way out of the bus terminal, thrusting trays of cheap souvenirs and knock-off watches in his face. Balancing his backpack across his chest where a sharp knife couldn't slit the strap, Doug fended off the sales hawks long enough to reach a sidewalk food stand where wooden skewers of meat sizzled on a charcoal grill. Walking on with two of the shish kebabs in hand, Doug suppressed an audible groan of pleasure at the combination of spices and grease. Whatever mystery meat this was, it beat hands-down the New York sirloin he'd eaten before leaving Miami.

A young woman in a miniskirt and low-cut blouse called to Doug from a doorway as he dropped the empty skewers on the ground, there being no garbage receptacle nearby. In other surroundings, her insistent greeting might be suspect. But here, she and her counterparts in other doorways were simply saleswomen hired to coax tourists off the street into indoor boutiques that offered a reputedly higher grade of knock-offs, pirated goods, and even a reasonable selection of genuine articles.

Doug thought Ciudad del Este was one of the ugliest cities he'd ever known, despite a respectable skyline of modern high-rises that testified to the capital pouring into the region. It wasn't just the crass commercialism, the garbage-littered streets, and in-your-face salespeople, or the crowds of credulous tourists that fueled the market for cheap fakes. It was a feeling every DEA agent developed if they stayed in the business long enough. A sense of too much wealth on display, too much money being tossed around, too much new construction—far more than the visible business infrastructure could account for. It was a feeling Doug had known in Santa Cruz, with its juxtaposition of millionaire neighborhoods and children starving in the streets. He felt it even in Miami, more than he cared to admit.

As if to underscore the point, an advertisement plastered in the window of an electronics shop caught Doug's eye. The poster offered the latest in sat-phone technology, illustrated against a background of lush rain forest. The tagline read, "Even in the deepest jungle, never be out of touch with your business partners."

Yeah, right! The target demographic for the ad was so blatant that Doug could only laugh. *Which local industries require business communications from the middle of the jungle? Not to mention, which industries can afford that five-figure asking price?*

Shaking off a persistent vendor, Doug hailed a cab. He'd brought with him the address and phone number of the local DEA field office, and touching base there was the first order of business, civilian status or not. Not because he was legally bound to check in. But this was their territory, and professional courtesy dictated letting them know that an off-duty agent was roaming around in it.

Besides, there was Murphy's Law. This might be a simple reconnaissance trip for Doug, but he never counted on things going as planned. If events at home had constrained him to go this one alone—a situation he would recommend to no one—checking in with the locals at least meant there'd be someone to come looking for him if he dropped down a black hole. You *always* planned for someone at your back.

Doug glanced at his watch again. If Ciudad del Este was anything like Santa Cruz, the office would be closed by now. The secretaries would work regular hours, if not the agents. Instead, Doug leaned over the seat and asked the driver for a hotel recommendation. This was given with such alacrity that it made Doug suspect the guy had an arrangement with the hotel. But when it proved to be four-star property with a spectacular view of the Bridge of Friendship—and reasonably priced by American standards—Doug nodded his approval, adding a generous tip to whatever commission the cab driver was getting from the hotel.

Once the bellhop had shown him to his room and excused himself, Doug unearthed his cell phone from the bottom of his backpack, another precaution against pickpockets, and called the field office. As expected, he got the after-hours answering machine.

"Patterson, Doug Bradford here. I'm in the city for a few days and would like to touch base. I'll drop by the office as soon as possible tomorrow morning."

Next, Doug set up his laptop and opened the files he had saved to the hard drive before leaving Miami. He scrolled through an attractive selection of postcard views culled from the Jungle Tours Web site—a sign of legitimacy that knowledgeable tourists learned to look for—and reviewed a listing of tours and other services offered by the company. He jotted down the Ciudad del Este address. His best start might be to act like a tourist and check out Jungle Tours—and Iguazú Falls—for himself.

Two listings in the material grabbed Doug's attention. The first was a helicopter tour of Iguazú Falls. Vargas was a helicopter pilot. Was it possible his connection to Jungle Tours was as simple as an available job opening?

The second listing, for Rain Forest Survival Treks, apparently a subsidiary firm, roused Doug's interest chiefly because that type of venture was more suited to the equipment the Cortezes had shipped south—GPS systems, hunting attire, walkie-talkies. From the sales blurb, it looked like one of those eco-nature survivalist tours Doug had seen advertised on other Iguazú Web sites. The kind that taught tourists how to find their way out of the jungle, eat off the land, and cook over a campfire, without ever stretching their discomfort level too far.

Of even more interest was a parenthetical note that Rain Forest Survival Treks currently was booked to capacity. Were the tours really so popular? Or could Vargas be using backwoods excursions like these to hook up with his old drug connections? Maybe even smuggling out the drugs somehow through the participants? It was the kind of scheme that made sense of the whole Vargas-Cortéz connection.

Doug jotted down the info. Judging by the address, the Rain Forest Survival Treks office was right next door to Jungle Tours. It too would be worth closer scrutiny in the morning. Right now, however, it was time to find some dinner. Two skewers of mystery meat, however tasty, didn't stick long to the ribs.

What was the name of that mixed-grill place Ramon and I tried during our last operation over here?

234

Chapter Thirty-five

APRIL 18
SANTA CRUZ, BOLIVIA

At three in the morning, the construction site was a very different place than during the day. A silent black hulk reared above the glow of the street lights, its pylons and webs of scaffolding thrusting skyward, creating a stark, jagged silhouette more reminiscent of a bombed-out shell than the high-rise it would be.

Standing at an unframed window overlooking the DEA compound, Julio Vargas focused a pair of night-vision goggles. The early stages of the operation were similar, though on a much bigger scale, to the kidnapping of the *cocalero* leader Eduardo Quispe. Last night, Saleh and Julio had confirmed the advance team's night security report with the simplest of ploys. Strolling down the street in uniform, two MPs heading home, they'd stopped to knock at the tin-roofed shack that housed the caretakers during the months of building.

The two *sirenos* who had clambered out of their hammocks to answer the door were not really guards but elderly watchmen, whose primary task was to keep petty thieves from carrying off construction materials. Their army-issue revolvers were probably not even loaded, Julio had noted with disgust. They'd groveled appropriately when Julio demanded why neither was on duty, clearly hoping the two MPs would not ask about an open case of locally brewed *Ducal*. The counternarcotics troops posted at the compound next door hadn't even stepped away from their guard hut when Julio finished his scathing lecture and he and Saleh ambled on down the street.

Ironically, the *sirenos* had taken Julio's chastisement to heart. Tonight, only one was dozing in his hammock while the other completed a sleepy round with a scrawny mongrel traipsing along at his heels. But his attention was focused on the well-lit boulevard, where street punks and addicts prowled between the spotlights, rather than on the darkness of the construction site, where black shadows were even now swarming over the back property wall.

Julio might have let the *sirenos* live. The team carried tranquilizer darts, and these were only harmless peasants. But Saleh followed the training manual to the letter, and that precluded leaving an unneutralized enemy at their backs. Two well-placed shots from a silenced submachine gun with night vision scope tore out the patrolling sentry's throat and dropped the small dog in its tracks. The second *sireno* didn't even stir in his hammock as a third shot ended his employment.

The next part required more caution. Unlike the construction site or Eduardo Quispe's dwelling, the DEA headquarters had security systems and surveillance cameras and guards who were both awake and armed.

Through the dim, green light of his NVGs, Julio counted the human shapes moving around below. Only three, fewer than expected from the advance team's earlier surveillance. So much the better. One was pacing a regular route inside the perimeter wall, disappearing at intervals around the far side of the building, eventually circling around through the roofed garage area and emerging from under the netting. The other two were at the usual post inside and outside the guard hut in front of the pedestrian gate.

The advance team had scouted out the surveillance cameras, as well. There were at least four visible around the property. Here the advantage of the construction site as a launch pad came into play. Although the cameras panned around to cover every square foot of the courtyard, they couldn't swivel upward to cover twenty stories of unfinished construction. The floodlights illuminating the property only cast into deeper shadow the black bulk of the emerging high-rise.

As soon as the perimeter-patrolling guard disappeared again around the corner of the building, Julio heard "Go! Go!" in his earpiece. The first wave of black shapes zip-lining down the side of the apartment building was hardly visible, even through NVGs. The moment of greatest exposure and danger came as the team members dropped into a pool of light cast by the floodlights across the netting stretched between the two buildings. But it was only for a moment. The first team member down drew his combat knife to slash a wide cut in the netting and dropped into the slit. The others slid through behind him. The hole in the netting was visible only from a bird's-eye vantage.

There'd been a question as to whether the netting was rigged with a motion sensor. But with regular debris slamming into it, Saleh had taken a calculated risk that the constant alarms would be too annoying to bother. The netting worked both ways, not only offering protection from falling objects but effectively shielding from view anyone underneath. The black shapes vanished, and the courtyard was as silent and still as before.

A pause followed, during which the inside guard should have rounded the back of the building and emerged from under the netting. He didn't. Then the pedestrian gate in the outer wall opened, and the other two guards stepped inside, swinging the gate shut behind them. Though Julio could not see or hear anything from where he stood, he knew the mission plan: A few Spanish phrases on the patrolling guard's Motorola indicating he'd found something of interest and requesting backup from his companions. From a window somewhere above Julio's head, two snipers took aim, the silenced shots hardly more than a *pop*, and the two guards went down. To any street bum wandering along the boulevard, the guards had simply stepped inside the gate.

As soon as the guards dropped, a second wave of black forms zip-lined down the side of the building, Julio and Saleh among them. More silenced sniper shots took out surveillance cameras as the second team dropped through the netting. As Julio's feet touched down at the bottom of the line, his NVGs allowed him to sidestep the patrolling guard, who was now a slumped, dark bundle on the ground with a puddle of black spreading around him.

At Saleh's swift order, the black figures dispersed to their assignments, invisible beneath the netting and garage roofing even to the sniper team still providing cover from above. The Palestinian bombmaker and his demolition specialists began taping their payloads to the base of the satellite dish, and along the sides of the building to a gas main in back. Others ran Det-Cord from one charge to another.

Saleh, the mission planner, was not so foolish as to assume there weren't other layers of security the advance team had missed. Perhaps alarms were already sounding at an American official's personal residence or the barracks of the local counternarcotics division. With more prep time, the team might have ferreted out and disabled such security precautions. But that would have vastly complicated their mission. If all went as planned, it would also not be necessary. In three minutes they'd all be gone. Taking out the surveillance cameras had not been to disguise their visit so much as to keep the team's masked faces from being uploaded to an orbiting satellite, as Saleh's research had shown was possible. The attack itself would be announced soon enough.

A burst from Saleh's Uzi SMG blew in the building's rear door. No immediate response issued from inside, but at Saleh's orders a dozen team members fanned out to search the building. Saleh and two others took the main corridor. He had reached only the third door when he waved his companions to a halt and swung around to Julio, who was coming up behind him. "There's something wrong here."

Julio had already seen it. The doors along the corridor were not locked, as would be expected at this hour, but were standing wide open. Not only that, but the rooms were empty—no computers or communication equipment, combat gear, file cabinets, bookshelves, desks, or any other signs of a law enforcement agency at work. Julio's eyes narrowed at the rectangles of dirt and too-clean patches of paint that showed where furniture and wall pictures had recently been. Striding to a kitchen area at the end of the hall, Julio spotted a stove and refrigerator still in their cubicles. The refrigerator was empty, though it had not been cleaned.

Ducking quickly into two other rooms, Saleh found only a battered wooden table in one, and a blackboard and shelving still nailed to walls in the other. Julio shrugged as Saleh spun around to demand furiously, "What is this? Where are the Americans?"

But figuring out what had gone wrong would have to come later. Their three allotted minutes were ticking away. At Saleh's furious command, the Palestinian demolition team began setting charges inside the building. "Clear, clear, clear," sounded in Julio's headset as the search teams confirmed that the building was indeed empty.

As the disappointed assault team faded back outside into the dark, the Palestinian stooped to set a timer before joining the others at the bottom of the zip-lines. This time they did not bother climbing farther than the second floor before sliding noiselessly through a window. The snipers caught up with the strike force as they sped down the stairwell to the ground floor. The perimeter patrol that Saleh had set around the block joined the others at the farm truck parked in a nearby alley. Right on schedule, the truck pulled out of the alley, with two advance team members in civilian clothing up front, and the assault team and their gear under cover in the back. The entire operation had lasted less than ten minutes, from throwing the first grappling hook over the back wall to motoring away through the deserted streets of the city. If nothing else, they could take pride in a flawless execution of the mission plan.

The truck was lumbering into a quiet side street when two Landrovers raced by out on the main boulevard. The truck had traveled two more blocks before they heard the blast. Screams and running feet erupted into the streets. Debris began raining down. The driver floored the accelerator as a chunk of satellite dish bounced off the truck's hood. Julio, peering back through the side slats to watch the fireball boiling up into the sky, could only hope that the American DEA agents in the Landrovers had reached their headquarters before the charges detonated.

Chapter Thirty-six

APRIL 19
CIUDAD DEL ESTE, PARAGUAY

Ciudad del Este's DEA field office was a smaller version of the Santa Cruz compound—a rented property in an upscale neighborhood with high enough walls and a deep enough perimeter of open courtyard around the house to satisfy the embassy's security requirements.

But to anyone in the know, the two soldiers out front with M-16s and donated American Motorola hand radios were a dead giveaway. So was the late-model Landrover with tinted windows and double panes of bulletproof glass that was pulling away as Doug strode up from where the cab had dropped him at the corner. Low-profile or not, there probably wasn't a dealer in Ciudad del Este who didn't have this address on his Rolodex.

Along with his Glock, Doug had left his DEA badge and business cards in Miami. But he didn't have to argue his way past the guards. After a look at his passport and one expert glance over Doug's well-muscled frame, the first guard murmured into his Motorola that an *americano* agent wanted to talk to the *jefe*. The other kept his M-16 at least casually directed in Doug's direction until the inside guard emerged to escort Doug indoors.

"*El jefe no está*," the guard told Doug as they followed a short path up to the front door. "*Pero el otro americano, sí.*"

So the RAC, Chris Patterson, wasn't here. The American who was must be the intel analyst, Andy Williams.

The downstairs living area of what had been a wealthy home was now crowded with desks and tables, computer equipment and file cabinets. The walls were covered with maps and whiteboards for mission planning. The place was boiling with activity for this early hour of the morning, and there were far more locals than in the Santa Cruz office, all wearing army fatigues.

The guard stopped outside an open door. "Señor Williams."

Through the door Doug could see an array of computer and radio equipment. He stopped in mid-entry as his eye landed on the man sitting in front of the intel gear. He was black, mid-thirties, well-muscled—and sitting in a wheelchair.

The wheelchair was already rotating around. "Doug Bradford?" Doug recognized the voice from his phone call two days before. The man's handshake was strong despite his immobility from the waist down. "Andy Williams. Just got your message." He nodded toward a phone setup. "Welcome to Paraguay."

"Thank you." Doug gave the intel analyst a quizzical look as he released the handshake. "I know you! At least I know who you are. I'm sorry, I wasn't thinking on the phone."

"Yeah, that's me," Andy Williams gave a rueful grin as he shoved a folding chair toward Doug. "Advanced Ranger training in Panama. I'm the agent who fell."

Doug straddled the chair. "You were in Miami for rehab. I'd heard—"

The intel analyst glanced down. "Yep, paralyzed from the waist down. Stupidest thing you ever saw. Twelve years in the field—not a scratch. Go in for a refresher course and a freak fall on the obstacle course puts me in a wheelchair. They offered disability, but I'd go crazy. So I decided to retrain. My brain at least wasn't paralyzed."

He caught Doug's swift questioning glance around. "Surprised to see me down here? It's actually easier than stateside. The cheap labor. Here I've got a maid, gardener, my inside guard helps with the lifting. There's some good clinics if you've got medical insurance. And you can't beat the standard of living with hazard and hardship pay."

Williams wheeled his chair over to a counter where an electric kettle was steaming. Picking up a hollowed-out gourd that fit into his palm, he filled it with hot water and added what looked like a silver straw "You drink *mate*?"

Mate, the national drink of the Guaraní as well as much of southern South America, was actually the broken-up leaves and twigs of the *yerba mate* bush. This was stuffed inside a *poro*—the gourd Andy Williams was using—sugar added to taste, then hot water poured in to steep. The silver "straw," or *bombilla,* had a bulbous end studded with pinpoint holes, allowing the drinker to suck up the liquid without the fiber.

To Doug, the stuff tasted like the silage it was. But learning to drink *mate* was a requirement for working in these parts. More importantly, it had the caffeine kick of Cuban espresso. When Doug nodded, the intel analyst prepared another *poro* and handed it to him, along with a gourd being used as a sugar bowl.

"So what can we do for you? If it's intel, there's nothing new since we talked. If you're looking for Patterson, you must have just missed him going out the gate."

Doug nodded.

"To be honest," Williams continued, "we weren't expecting a personal follow-up on this."

And don't particularly welcome it! Doug set down the *poro* on the closest empty counter space. "Look, Williams—Andy. I'm not here to make any waves in your pond. I'm on vacation . . . just taking a look at the local sites. In fact, I'm heading out to a travel agency right now, okay? But if I'm taking a look around and just happen to ID an escaped convict here on false documents, it seems a win-win for everyone if the locals could scoop the guy up and ship him back across the border. The guy's here illegally. And whatever the feds have cooking, my man, Julio Vargas, is neither Arab nor Muslim. All I'm asking is that if I can make a positive ID, some effort be made on this end to send Vargas back where he belongs. Or are we supposed to just quit doing our jobs down here until the war on terror is over—whatever year that may be?"

The sarcasm Doug couldn't quite keep out of his last question drew a sharp glance from Williams. But there was a sardonic note in the intel analyst's response that matched Doug's.

"Hey, I've got no problem, though I can't speak for Patterson. Document fraud's serious stuff. And frankly, we don't take too well here to other government agencies telling us how to do our jobs—or not do them. So any agent wants to come through here on vacation, he's welcome—so long as he doesn't overstep his bounds. And if that agent happens to spot someone off a wanted poster somewhere, it's any good citizen's responsibility to let the local authorities know."

As Doug rose to leave, Williams wheeled his chair out to accompany him to the gate. "If there's anything else we can do, let us know," he added as the guard held the gate open. "And please do forgive us if our hospitality hasn't been quite up to snuff. That bomb blast at the Santa Cruz office last night has everyone scrambling."

"What?" Doug spun on his heel with an abruptness that had the guards wheeling around and leveling their automatic rifles. "What did you say about a bomb blast?"

Andy Williams's eyebrows rose sharply. "You didn't know? I guessed I assumed since you'd served up there, you were in contact. Yeah, there was some kind of attack on the DEA compound in Santa Cruz during the night. Not a lot of details yet, but terrorism hasn't been ruled out."

His features tight, Doug excused himself as quickly as courtesy allowed and grabbed the first cab back to his hotel. Iguazú would have to wait. He delayed only until he'd kicked his door shut before punching out the familiar number of the Santa Cruz field office. To his relief, pickup was immediate. Doug relaxed as he recognized the laconic "Yep!"

"Hey, Ramon. Andy Williams down here in Ciudad del Este just told me someone had blown you guys up. Guess they missed the phone lines. Or is it the usual media hype?"

"Oh, no, they blew us up all right," Ramon answered cheerfully. "The compound's gone along with half that apartment building going up next door. Shouldn't have put a dent in the place, but it looks like their foundations weren't up to specs. You'd think a bomb hit them instead of us. Just as well it came down before anyone was living there. Whoever did the inspections over there is going to be in for some major payoffs to weasel out of this one."

"Ramon!" Doug cut in sharply. "I'm not interested in who paid off what where. Did any of our guys get hurt? Who was in the building when it blew? And how did it happen anyway? Where was security?"

"Oh, nobody was in the building. Nor much of anything else for that matter. Don't tell me you thought—yeah, guess I did forget to tell you last time we talked that we were moving. We finished clearing the place just two nights ago. A little too close for comfort, can you believe it? Just think if we'd been running a night raid down there when the place blew."

Doug sat down hard on the bed as Ramon went on with a cheerful narrative that made Doug want to wring his friend's neck.

"You do remember the apartment building that was going up next door when you left? Well, you should've been here these last few months. Tools falling on people's heads, workmen and who knows who else watching every move we made. Major's been pushing for a bigger place ever since we doubled the number of agents. But you know the bean counters upstairs.

"Anyway, when a bunch of Congressmen came through right after that guard got brained and saw the net we'd rigged just so we could walk around our own back yard, all of a sudden there were funds coming out our ears. Chalk one up for Grant Major. We've got a great new place right out on the edge of town— belonged to one of the ex-pat oil companies. No neighbors for a hundred meters around. To keep our old neighbors guessing, we've been moving out bit by bit after dark. All they got last night was the satellite dish, which SouthCom was supposed to upgrade anyway. The building's gone, of course, which has upstairs screaming already. Selling the place was supposed to help cover the cost of this one."

"I just can't believe no one was hurt," Doug cut in again. "There's got to be guardian angels up there with singed wings! So who do they think is responsible?"

"Well, actually, a few locals were killed. Not in the blast. They'd been taken out beforehand." Ramon wasn't unfeeling, but his reaction to casualties did reflect his Special Forces training and street upbringing. "Three guards and the two watchmen next door. We're taking a collection for the families. As to who did it—that's anyone's guess. But from the professionalism, my money's on the same bunch that's been taking down the druggies."

"Well, put me down for the collection. I'll send a money-order soon as I'm back in Miami. At least it gets you guys off the hook," Doug said. "Not even the most anti-American narco-lover is going to be accusing you of blowing yourselves up."

"Ha! You'd think! Would you believe there's already been local commentators suggesting we moved out because we *knew* this was going to happen? We just can't win—not unless we catch these guys. So what are you doing down in Paraguay?" Ramon changed the subject abruptly. "I thought you were working out of Miami these days."

"Still trying to track down Julio Vargas." Doug explained his pseudo-vacation, but ID-ing an escaped felon was tame compared to the excitement on Ramon's end, and the conversation went immediately back to there.

"Yeah, well, you spot him, let us know. We can put some pressure on the locals at this end anyway. Meanwhile, have fun. Wish I was there. We got off light, but the cleanup's going to be messy. Just wish I could have seen the look on the faces of whoever it was when they walked in there and found the place empty. Only bit of humor in the whole mess."

Now that he'd squeezed out of Ramon that at least no one he knew was hurt, Doug could return to his own schedule. Locking his laptop in the room safe, Doug placed his passport, a digital camera, and other odds and ends he'd need during the day in a camera bag he'd thrown in for the purpose. Anything left in the room was expendable. Not that he expected pilfering in this price range of hotel. It was just habit from years of bedding down in less savory surroundings.

The address for Jungle Tours turned out to be an entire street of tour agencies, every business a clone of the next with signs offering the cheapest tours to Iguazú or Itaipú Dam or the duty-free markets of Ciudad del Este.

Across the street was a huge parking lot, perhaps the reason the tour agencies all chose to cluster together. Along with Jungle Tours were signs advertising Iguazú Tours, Tri-Frontier Tours, Tropical Tours, and every other possible variation offering precisely the same services. Beyond the parking lot, Doug could see the Paraná River and the Bridge of Friendship, across which every tour bus had to pass to reach either the Brazilian or Argentine sides of the world's greatest cascades.

Digging a palm-size pair of binoculars from his camera case, Doug walked over to the cover of a Tropical Tours shuttle for a swift survey of the parking area. No, he hadn't been mistaken. On the far side of the buses, where a patch of gravel served as a landing pad, were two helicopters. One of these was a large civilian adaptation of a Vietnam-era Huey, with the markings of a Search and Rescue unit. Doug had seen several like this in Bolivia, most of them donations from U.S. military surplus.

The other was a smaller machine. Doug took in the bright red paint and lettering on the side with a grunt of satisfaction. Jungle Tours. And an adjustment to the focus revealed an occupant in the pilot's seat. Was his search ended already?

But even in the flight helmet, Doug could see the pilot was too light-skinned, his features too Caucasian to be Julio Vargas. Dropping the binoculars back into his camera bag, Doug headed across the street to a door beneath a bright red Jungle Tours sign on the third storefront down. A welcome blast of air-conditioning greeted him as he pushed open the door. So did two young, attractive receptionists, their low-cut blouses and miniskirts as bright red as the Jungle Tours lettering. One of the receptionists was behind a desk, buffing her long nails. The other was settled into the comfortable leather seats of a waiting area, leafing through a Spanish version of *Vogue* magazine. Both jumped to their feet when Doug walked in.

Doug's smile had proved an effective investigative tool long before he'd been in law enforcement. "Good morning. I'm wondering if you could help me. I'd like to take one of your tours today. But I'm trying to find someone as well. An acquaintance of mine I'm told is working for Jungle Tours. Now that I'm here for a few days of vacation, I'm hoping to make contact with him."

And if that wasn't as skillful a prevarication as you could get without telling a lie! Pulling out a copy of Julio's Interpol ID photo, Doug showed it to the two women. "His name is Julio Vargas. Do you know where I might find him?"

He caught the doubtful looks even before they shook their heads.

"No, I am sure he does not work in any of our tours." The nail buffer leaned forward from six-inch spikes to study the photo again. "Are you sure you have the right agency? There are many here. Or—" She exchanged a glance with Ms. *Vogue*. "Maybe your friend is with Rain Forest Survival Treks? Their employees do not come through this office."

Bingo!

"Of course. Rain Forest Survival Treks. I've been reading about them on your Web site." Doug beamed at the receptionists. "That's the tour I was hoping to sign up for. Can I do that here? Or do you know where I can contact them personally? And maybe my friend as well."

"Oh, no, I am sorry, *señor*." This time it was the desk receptionist who spoke up. Their office is next door, but they are not open at this time. See? It is still locked."

Following the sharp tap of her high heels to the door, Doug stepped out onto the sidewalk. Sure enough, the metal shutters next door were still rolled down over the display window and door. Unlike the other agencies along this street, Rain Forest Survival Treks saw little need to advertise their tours because only a discreet "RST" above the shutters identified them.

Doug stepped back into the air-conditioned office of Jungle Tours. "So when will they be open? I've come a long ways for one of their treks. I'll be very disappointed if I can't get a reservation while I'm here. And touch base with my friend."

Both heads were shaking. "That is impossible," the desk receptionist told Doug. "Not if you are here only for a few days. Those tours are always full. They must be booked well in advance. And because the tours go out and stay for a long time—not every day like ours—they have no need to be open on weekends."

Of course. Doug grimaced to himself. He'd flown out Friday night, spent Saturday on the road. That made today Sunday. Somewhere in the commercial bustle that made no separation between workdays and the weekend, he'd lost track.

"There is a woman who comes in during the week," Ms. *Vogue* offered. "But she never stays long. Only when there are people coming and going."

"And how often is that?" Doug asked.

"Sometimes not for a week or two. They come in on the big helicopter for supplies. Other times they are here more often."

"The last couple weeks, there was a group coming in and out almost every day. We kept seeing the helicopter land," added the desk receptionist. "But then they left."

"The last time was only a few days ago," Ms. *Vogue* chimed in. "I saw people next door then."

"And you don't recognize my friend here as one of them?" Doug asked, showing the photo again.

Both heads moved from left to right. "We are too busy to be looking out windows," the desk receptionist said. "And they do not often come up here. We only see the helicopter land—and sometimes vehicles. If someone comes, they move quickly in and out. The only one I know for certain is the woman who works there."

Doug took the "too busy" with a grain of salt. From their avid interest, he guessed they spent plenty of time observing and speculating about any activity next door. Which could mean that Julio Vargas had indeed never been here. Or that they weren't telling the truth. Or that Julio Vargas was well aware of curious eyes and made it his business to "move quickly in and out." Something as simple as a hat made great camouflage.

"In any case, if they have only recently left, they will not be back for some time. But please do not let this disturb your vacation plans in our city. We have many excellent tours." The desk receptionist offered a handful of brochures.

"And of far greater comfort and beauty than these survival treks of theirs," Ms. *Vogue* added. "The morning buses have already left. But they will return to make a second trip at noon. It will be too late to see both sides today, but perhaps another tour tomorrow?"

Doug shuffled through the brochures while he gathered his thoughts. The main tours were, of course, for Iguazú Falls. He'd never been to the falls, despite their proximity to his last DEA post. He'd just never been able to spring the days loose from work. Or perhaps it would be more honest to admit that going alone had just never appealed to him. But he'd flipped through plenty of photo albums, the falls being a favorite R&R trip for agents with families.

The Iguazú River itself was one of the continent's principal waterways, more than a mile wide and meandering for more than eight hundred miles west before merging with the Paraná right at the point where Paraguay, Brazil, and Argentina intersected to create the boundaries of the Tri-Frontier area. The

Iguazú divided Brazil and Argentina, while the Paraná separated Paraguay and Brazil. The last part of the Iguazú's westward passage ran through some of the planet's last virgin rain forest, a half-million acres on the Brazil side and another hundred thousand across the river in Argentina, protected from developers as part of a Natural World Heritage site.

But what a million tourists a year came to see was not lush, unspoiled jungle but the falls themselves. At some distant point in history, a rift in the continental plateau had created a crescent-shaped cliff face two-and-a-half miles long and hundreds of feet high, over which spilled the entire monumental flow of the Iguazú River in a series of cascades higher than Niagara Falls and far more spectacular. The falls straddled the border between Brazil and Argentina, with the lion's share of the falls stretching more than a mile on the Argentine side. However, Brazil's more modest half-mile stretch offered the best views, so that both countries had built a thriving tourism industry on their share of this natural wonder, and most tours recommended a visit to each side.

With no access to the falls, Paraguay had lagged behind in tourist revenue until civic leaders with an eye for opportunity revamped the modest town of Ciudad del Este into a duty-free shopping bazaar offering every genuine, fake, or just plain illegal product available on the planet.

Then in the 1980s, Paraguay had invented its own tourist attraction when strongman president Alfredo Stroessner decided it was time to exploit the country's most plentiful resource—water. He and his cronies raked in fortunes from the resulting international loans and investments, and in the process they created the world's largest dam, Itaipú, to match the world's largest falls. Just a few miles upstream from Ciudad del Este on the Paraná River, Itaipú Dam was five times the size of the former world record holder, Egypt's Aswan Dam, backing up the Paraná River to form a lake of more than five hundred square miles. Itself more than four miles wide, the dam also had the highest output of electricity of any power plant on the planet, which it sold to neighboring Brazil and Argentina. Though the concrete monstrosity could not be described as pretty, it was definitely impressive.

With the Itaipú Dam straddling the Paraguay-Brazil border a few miles north of Ciudad del Este, Iguazú Falls straddling the Brazil-Argentina border a few miles west, and the world's third-largest goods market in Ciudad del Este itself, the combined attractions offered a neat vacation package whose colossal profits for all three sides of the Tri-Frontier explained why there was little enthusiasm for any international law enforcement efforts that might upset the applecart.

Or the golden goose. One of those metaphors.

Doug glanced up from the brochures to meet two pairs of hopeful eyes. *If these two ladies have really never seen Julio Vargas, is it worth wasting the rest of the day taking a tour? On the other hand, with RST firmly locked down next door, what leads are left to follow?*

"Okay, I'll take the Iguazú tour," Doug gave in with a wry grin. "The Brazil side if there isn't time for both." If perhaps one of the tour guides recognized Vargas, the trip wouldn't be a total bust.

"When did you say the next tour is running? Or—" Doug had a brainstorm. "What about that helicopter I saw out there? That's one of yours, isn't it? Any chance he can fly me out to the falls? Maybe I could catch up to the rest of the tour and make both sides of the Falls today after all."

"Well—" The two pretty faces looked at each other doubtfully. "The pilot does not ferry passengers," they said in unison. Something about proper border clearance. The helicopter was one of two that flew out every morning to Iguazú to give short charter hops over the falls. This one was still in town only because of an engine difficulty that had just been resolved.

"But it is possible something can be arranged for an additional fee, perhaps," suggested Ms. *Vogue*. "We will need to speak with the pilot. It would require cash, as it is not official, of course."

"Of course," Doug agreed with a knowing tilt of the head. Cash. The international lubricant. It was a game he'd played often enough in the last five years. He dug out his wallet. "How much?"

"Perhaps twice the regular tour fee—since the trip will be much quicker. And an additional tip for the pilot?" The desk receptionist spoke into a handheld radio. "The helicopter is ready to leave, but the pilot will wait five minutes if you wish to accompany him."

"Oh, and you will want a rain poncho. It is very wet at the falls." Ms. Vogue offered a square plastic package that was the same bright red as everything else at Jungle Tours. "The price is much better if you purchase it here than at the falls."

Doug counted out the bills in American dollars and handed them to the two women. He repeated the process outside with the helicopter pilot. Stuffing the bills into a pocket of his flight coveralls, the pilot handed Doug a helmet and shouted above the roar of the engine, "Have you ever flown in one of these before?"

Doug, with a mental image of the seatless and comfortless Hueys he'd endured on numberless counternarcotics raids, nodded. Taking his place in the copilot seat, he showed the pilot Julio's Interpol photo and shouted back, "Have you ever seen this man before?"

The pilot gave the photo no more than a cursory glance before shrugging. The helicopter sprayed gravel over nearby tour buses as it rose. It was too loud inside the chopper for conversation. Doug's flight helmet was unequipped with a microphone and the pilot showed no inclination to use his own. So Doug replaced the photo in his wallet and turned his attention to the view outside the windshield. Might as well take a look at what a million tourists a year paid good money to see.

Chapter Thirty-seven

As the helicopter flew across the Paraná River, the congestion of tour buses and other vehicles on the Bridge of Friendship below made Doug doubly glad he'd chosen air travel. Then they were in Brazil.

So a helicopter can move back and forth across the borders without being challenged, Doug jotted down mentally. *At least one with local registration.*

The development below ended abruptly as they reached the outer boundary of the World Heritage site. The rain forest here was taller and denser than what Doug had slogged through during his years in Bolivia. Even with binoculars, he could see only the largest tributaries through the heavy jungle canopy.

It must be a smuggler's paradise down there. If you can avoid getting lost yourself.

With the noise of the engine and rotors, it only gradually dawned on Doug that the growing thunder in his ears was not from the helicopter. Then suddenly the jungle canopy broke away in front of them, and for the first time in weeks the whereabouts of Julio Vargas was not preeminent in Doug's mind.

What looked like a crescent-shaped bite out of the jungle below was not a single waterfall, as the brochure had made it appear, but hundreds of separate cascades all pouring with enormous power over the densely forested lip of the plateau. Some plummeted higher than Niagara in a single drop to the gorge below. Others spilled over ledges and between thickly green islets.

And the sound.

"The Lord thunders over the mighty waters." Doug had never quite understood that description of the voice of God in Psalm 29 or the triumphant shout of the redeemed before God's throne in Revelation. He did now. The roar of the falls was so loud he could no longer hear the rotor blades or engine. The incalculable force of the water crashing down into the river below sent spray shooting up into the air to bead even the windshield of the helicopter. In that tossed up mist were rainbows—not one, but dozens.

As hard to impress as Doug considered himself to be, and not one to be distracted by scenery, he nevertheless found himself swallowing at the sheer beauty. The only word that came to mind was: *Wow!*

I'm going to have to bring Sara here someday.

Something in Doug's expression triggered the pilot into tour guide mode, because for the first time he used the mike on his flight helmet.

"Beautiful, no?" he shouted. "Over on this side you will have the best view. You can walk right out over the falls. Over there in Argentina—see? That is the biggest falls. *La Garganta del Diablo,* it is called. And surely it is like entering the throat of the devil to go in there. But the *loco* tourists, they go in and out in the little boats. And that island below the Devil's Throat—that is San Martin, where the movie *The Mission* was filmed. Robert DeNiro, eh? He made our falls famous."

Come on, you've got a job to do. Doug tore himself away from the magnificence of the scenery. Even from here he could see swarms of people everywhere below, crowding boardwalks, perched with their cameras along the cliff tops opposite the falls, bouncing through the edge of the cascades in rubber Zodiacs. But up above the falls—

For all the breathtaking power of the Iguazú's big show—billions of gallons spilling over the cliff face into the gorge below—the section of river Doug could see upstream was astonishingly placid, moving with seeming laziness between its mile-wide banks with no indication that the entire enormous mass was about crash over the edge of the world. Even a small motorized boat could maneuver easily. Into the Iguazú River ran countless tributaries and smaller streams that made the entire ecosystem one vast transportation network. And within the national park there were neither towns nor rural dwellers unless a few nomadic Indians remained. The tourists themselves did not move more than a mile or so from the falls, other than the occasional "jungle trek," and even those would not risk their valuable clientele by straying too far off the beaten path.

If I were Julio, that's where I'd head. And what better way to move around unnoticed than through a conveniently overbooked survival trek agency.

The helicopter was dropping now for a landing, Another helicopter, this one with Iguazú Tropical Tours painted on its door panel, buzzed by close enough to make the Jungle Tours pilot swear into his mike. The asphalt helipad sat opposite and almost level with the falls. Behind the landing area, a pink-and-white crenellated complex rose from the plateau. The pilot gestured toward it as he shouted, "Hotel Das Cataratas, if you should wish to stay in the park. It has an excellent restaurant, too."

"Thanks for the ride." Doug unobtrusively dropped another bill onto his seat as he removed his flight helmet and climbed out. "Any chance you'll be here at the end of the day if I want to get a ride back to Ciudad del Este?"

Removing his helmet, the pilot grinned and spread his hands wide. Younger than Doug, he looked to be of pure German descent—not surprising given the sizable ethnic minority in Paraguay, including Alfredo Stroessner, their late unlamented ruler. Still, the Aryan appearance mixed with native Spanish and Latino body language struck Doug as oddly incongruent, even though he knew it shouldn't.

"For you, any time," the pilot said with an ingratiating smile.

And your money. Doug filled in the unspoken truth as the bill disappeared discreetly from the copilot's seat and into the pilot's pocket. "By the way," he added as the pilot turned away to greet an approaching group of tourists. "The Jungle Tours boat rides? Where would I find those?"

"Oh, Jungle Tours does not keep its own boats here. We cannot transport them back and forth each day, and the local guides will not allow us to interfere with their own business. We simply make connections for our tour groups to take the boat rides either here or on the Argentinean side."

So the inflatable boats Vargas ordered were definitely not for Jungle Tours, despite what the shipping manifest said. Doug walked away swiftly as the pilot began boarding his new clients.

The Hotel Das Cataratas sat at a serene distance from the noise of helicopter liftoffs and the bustle of tourists. Aside from the pink-and-white color scheme, the hotel looked much like the Jesuit mission its design had duplicated, with colonial Spanish architecture, towers, parapets, and wrought-iron balconies. The main transportation hub of the park, Cataratas Station, lay in the opposite direction, with green shuttle buses, taxis, and a miniature train that was just pulling out as Doug approached. There was no sign of a Jungle Tours bus.

"The tour buses stop at the entrance of the park," a ticket seller told Doug. "In here only our own transportation is allowed."

"Except the helicopters." Doug cocked his head toward the helipad.

The ticket seller lifted her shoulders. "Perhaps because the park does not have its own helicopters. If you wish to find your tour bus, you must take one of those green shuttles out to the main gate."

Great! Still, now that he was inside the park, he might as well take advantage of his vacation days. When the ticket seller informed him that the train would not return from its three-mile eco-tour for another forty-five minutes, Doug opted for a quarter-mile walking tour that skirted the precipice opposite the falls and led down to a lookout area and the boat tours. He decided to make constructive use of the time by flashing Julio's photo at any tour guides he came across, before heading out to the park entrance to talk to the Jungle Tours bus drivers.

Doug began the trail with his usual swift stride. But by the time he was out of sight and sound of the station's bustle, the tautness began to ease from his shoulders and he eased off the pace. However urgent his mission, it was hard to remain uptight when swarms of butterflies more colorful than he'd ever seen swirled around him with every step, each small cloud with its own color design. Yellows with red bandings. Navy blue and white. Peacock turquoise and purples.

Unfortunately, the butterflies weren't the only insect life. Doug grimaced as a large spider scuttled across the walkway. They too were everywhere, their webs beaded with mist so that they might be mistaken for Ciudad del Este's famed spider lace.

"Hey!" Doug stopped short as a diminutive hand grabbed at his pant leg. The hand belonged to a creature Doug recognized from the brochure as a coatimundi, a long-tailed raccoon-like animal with the face and snout of a rodent. Scrambling up Doug's pants and shirt onto his shoulder, the coatimundi chittered aggressively. Doug placed it firmly back on the path. "Sorry, I don't have anything to eat."

A chatter of voices drew the coatimundi off like a rocket. Swinging around, Doug spotted a party of tourists coming along the path behind him, eating as they strolled. A heavyset woman tossed the animal a potato chip. *Mistake!* A half-dozen more of the animals scampered out into the path. The first coatimundi swarmed up the woman's bare leg onto her shoulder, one paw grabbing a handful of hair, the other snatching the chip bag.

Grinning, Doug lengthened his stride to leave the shrieking, shooing party behind, noting as he did so a sign that read in three languages: Don't Feed the Monkeys. Nothing about thieving raccoon-rodents.

The rain forest closed in above the path, and a pair of monkeys chattered anxiously overhead. A flock of brilliant blue-and-green-and-red macaws rose with a flutter and wheeled out over the precipice. He couldn't see the falls yet through the vegetation, but a deafening thunder left no doubt they were somewhere nearby. It was very hot, with a tropical humidity that had to be approaching one hundred percent and seemed to increase with every step. But heat was a discomfort to which Doug had become accustomed in recent years. He paused to read a stone plaque someone had set up beside the path. Its inscription was in English:

> Mightier than the thunders of many waters, mightier than the waves of the sea, the Lord on High is mighty. (Ps. 93:4)

So I'm not the only one who's thought of that "mighty waters" image. Below the scripture verse, the anonymous sponsor had engraved into the rock: "God is always greater than all our troubles." *Ain't that the truth!*

Ahead, a mushroom cloud of mist boiled up above the vegetation. As a turn brought the trail out into the open, Doug discovered why he'd been pressured to purchase the red rain poncho.

This was what he'd seen from the helicopter, but down here at close range, the impact was immeasurably greater. Straight across from where Doug stood was the greatest flow of the falls—*la Garganta del Diablo*. The Devil's Throat. It was a horseshoe-shaped gorge hundreds of meters across within the greater crescent-shaped canyon, over which the Iguazú River plunged without ledge or islet to break its fall for two hundred feet. The mist thrown up by its force was so heavy that Doug couldn't make out where the water was landing.

The spray brought welcome cooling, enough that Doug waited until his shirt was wet through before shaking out the rain poncho. Ahead, a knot of unprepared tourists ran screaming back down the trail, camcorders tucked futilely under their clothing.

A metal catwalk led onto an observation platform out over the water so that Doug could actually look down at the falls. Though rainy season had officially ended several weeks before, the water was still running close to peak, in places only feet below the catwalk. In contrast to the pristine white cascades one saw from a distance, here Doug could see that the water was actually the same muddy red as every other river in the region, the result of the high iron content that turned the soil red as well. The same red, Doug suddenly realized with a grin, as the poncho he was wearing. So there was a point to Jungle Tours' color scheme.

Doug rested his elbows cautiously over the rail, pushing back the hood of the poncho to cool his head as well as his face. The ceaseless roaring flow of the water was hypnotic, and for one instant of vertigo, Doug had the rushing sensation that he was about to be swept over the edge like those medieval maps of a flat world where the ocean rushed endlessly over the rim.

Straightening up hastily, Doug focused instead on one of the rubber boats battling the current below. He wasn't even tempted. Like many whose daily job held regular hazard, Doug felt little attraction to risking his neck unnecessarily in the name of entertainment. Not even the life jackets would keep those boaters safe if they bobbed much closer to those tons of water crashing down.

Safe.

Doug's mouth twisted wryly as the rubber boat gunned its engine into reverse, backing to a safer distance from the cascade. And since when had *safe* ever been an operating word in his own life?

Was he wrong in not quitting the lifestyle he'd chosen? In not retreating to a safer distance as that boat had done? As his mother had pleaded with him to do? As Sara wanted? Doug knew well enough it was love and concern, not selfishness, that prompted the two women in his life to want him safe—or as safe as one could be in an uncertain world.

Would Julie have come to feel that way too in time? With the passing years, would she have come to hate his job and the hazards that went with it as much as Sara and his mother did? Certainly the divorce rate among his friends had made Doug see just how hard it was to expect a family to live with the constant uncertainty. And yet there were those who made a success of it, too.

So was he wrong in putting his job above their need for security? Should he instead, as his mother told him often enough, be considering his own safety for the sake of his family? Until Sara came into his life, the question had been a moot point, though like any single agent he'd had plenty of lures cast in his direction.

But now things had changed. He realized that he wanted to spend the rest of his life with Sara. And he wanted it to work. He'd caught a quiver in her voice—one she'd tried hard to control—when she'd made that quip about not giving his angels too much to do. And he'd meant it when he'd offered months ago to apply for a teaching position.

What would he have done if she'd said yes?

Probably keel over with a heart attack from sheer boredom. Wouldn't that be a joke!

But the restless drive for action had never been what this was about. As Doug had told Sara, he believed in what he was doing, believed in his calling to this service as much as if he'd been called to a mission field somewhere. And missionaries knew what it meant to leave security behind to go to places where he wouldn't dream of being caught. Not without plenty of backup!

If everyone's first concern was to watch their own back, where would this world be?

"Mightier than the thunders of many waters."

"Safety isn't the absence of danger, but the presence of God." The phrase from Pastor Jack's sermon echoed through the roar of the falls.

God isn't about safety first, Doug reminded himself, his lean body braced against the spray and the roar and the rush of the water that crashed against the pilings of the observation platform and shook the metal deck. His gray eyes narrowed to keep the mist from blurring the fantastic panorama of the torrent above and below him. *That's God out there. Mighty. Awesome. Powerful. Wild even. Like the thunder and lightning of a storm. But not safe.*

And nowhere in all his reading of Scripture had Doug ever seen a call for God's children to consider their own personal safety—or even their families'—as an end in life. The Lord Almighty had sent his followers to battle giants, marauding armies, evil tyrants, and the forces of hell and darkness itself. Never had the God of storms and torrents called his followers to crawl into a hole and set a watch on their own backs.

I can't do it! I wish I could for Sara's sake—and Mom's. But I can't quit. Not until God tells me as loud and clear as that waterfall out there it's time to quit.

And if that meant losing Sara, if the answer she gave to the question he hadn't been able to ask over the phone was a resounding "no," then no matter how great the pain, Doug had to believe that God carried that part of his life as much in the palm of his mighty hand as all the rest.

You've got me in the storm, God, because someone's got to be out there nailing down the loose roof shingles and pulling people from the floods. Why me, I've got no business asking. But I believe—and I will always believe, no matter what happens—that the eye of my storm will always be smack in the middle of your hand. And there's no place I'd rather be.

A shudder went over Doug that was only partly due to an extra-heavy gust of spray. He just hoped that piece of profound thought hadn't been prophetic.

Chapter Thirty-eight

In the end, it was hunger that drove Doug back up the trail.

Hotel Das Cataratas had a five-star restaurant, and Doug had spotted any number of more modest eating establishments back at the park's transport station. But he'd lost too much time wool-gathering down at the overlook. Stopping at one of the kiosks along the trail, Doug bought a bottle of Guaraná, Brazil's local soda, a bag of salted plantain chips and two locally produced nougat bars.

The nougat proved cloyingly sweet, but it was packed with peanuts for protein. Doug washed it down, along with half the plantain chips, as he rode a glass-sided elevator down to the base of the cliff. Though the panoramic view of the falls was spectacular, Doug was too absorbed in his thoughts to notice. At the bottom, a trail offered access to the boat rides. Doug showed Julio Vargas's ID photo to each of the boat operators, but was met with the same response—hunched shoulders and outspread hands—at every turn.

On his way back up, Doug peeled off the poncho and used the front of his shirt to dry off the ID photo, which was wet with mist. By the time he made an unproductive round of concession stands and ticket vendors, the photo was as crumpled as his clothing. Deciding to change the location of his fishing expedition, he took a green park shuttle out to the main entrance. There he found the tour buses he'd been looking for earlier, their drivers stretched out for *siesta* while awaiting their passengers' return. The brilliant red paint of the Jungle Tours buses made them easy enough to pick out, but Doug had no better luck with their drivers than he'd had inside the park.

It wasn't the quality of the photo. To any local who'd actually crossed Julio Vargas's path, the high cheekbones and narrow, almost gaunt features, thin slit of a mouth, and especially the cold, flat gaze were recognizable enough.

Doug's lack of success was not particularly disappointing. On the contrary, it was more telling that he'd found no one to identify his quarry than if he had. Canvassing the service personnel in the park had been a long shot, but Jungle Tours itself couldn't have more than a few dozen employees. That a man with enough access to company funds to make costly purchases in the agency's name was completely unknown to the receptionists and the drivers was instructive. Whatever Julio Vargas was doing in Ciudad del Este or with Jungle Tours, it wasn't building a new and respectable career in the tourism industry.

In truth, now that he'd seen the layout with his own eyes, Doug had no doubt where he would find Julio Vargas. Next door at this Rain Forest Survival Treks outfit. Setting up an illicit operation inside a legit business. Operating in plain sight of anyone nosy enough to check him out. Conveniently "booked full" to prevent authentic tourists from seeing whatever was really happening on these "survival tours." The whole setup stank of a classic Vargas—or Cortéz—operation. Like he'd said before, leopards like Julio Vargas didn't change their spots.

So what was Julio doing out there with GPS equipment, rubber boats, and whatever else Diego and Raymundo had ordered in for him? Another cocaine lab? Or just a new export route through jungle too remote and untamed to be troubled with law enforcement?

Those answers would only come if he could locate Julio Vargas, a prospect that seemed less and less likely here in these beautiful surroundings. Still, with nothing else to fill this Sunday afternoon, Doug would finish going through the motions at least.

The Argentine side of the falls was close enough to swim across, were it not for the turbulence of the water. Practically, getting there involved taking a taxi back down the main highway a number of miles, then across the Tancredo Neves Bridge that spanned the lower Iguazú River between Brazil and Argentina. Another entry fee at the Argentine national park entrance put Doug back only a few hundred yards from where he'd started, this time with an even more spectacular frontal view of the Devil's Throat maelstrom. But Doug didn't bother with sightseeing here. *Maybe someday with Sara, if miracles still happen.* He restricted himself to a round of the Jungle Tours buses parked at this entrance, then entered the park to make a similar round of park personnel, boat operators, and two Jungle Tours guides he happened upon who were herding charter tours in their brilliant-red rain ponchos.

At the helipad, he thought he'd struck oil when a pilot who was between tours took the photo and brought it close to his face. But then he gave the photo back with a shake of his head. "I had an idea I might have seen him. Perhaps on a helicopter tour. Have you asked on the Brazilian side?"

By the time Doug decided he'd done his duty for one day, the ID photo was damp and crumpled enough that even Doug himself wasn't sure he'd recognize the creased visage. He'd have to stop by the Internet facility he'd noticed off the lobby of the hotel and print off another from his laptop JPEG files.

By the time Doug had reversed his trip back to the Brazilian side of the Iguazú River, sunset was staining the sky above the falls. This spectacular vista was predictably a popular helicopter tour, and Doug had to wait until orange and red and pink had faded to artificial flood-lights before he could track down the helicopter pilot who had brought him.

"Yes, I am leaving soon. It grows too dark for further tours," the pilot told Doug. "For the same fee, you are welcome to ride with me."

The trip back followed the red flow of taillights along the highway, the twinkling spires and neon lights of Foz de Iguazú, on the Brazilian side of the river, giving visual orientation before the arch of the Bridge of Friendship came into view above the dark ribbon of the Paraná River. Beyond, Doug could see the night glitter of Ciudad del Este.

The noise of the helicopter again made conversation next to impossible. Doug, deep in thought, didn't even try, but simply handed the pilot the agreed fee as they touched down in the Jungle Tours parking lot. He was climbing out of the copilot's seat when the pilot asked suddenly, "Did you find the friend you were looking for?"

Doug shook his head. "No, no luck. I guess he doesn't work with Jungle Tours after all."

The pilot stuffed the bill Doug had given him into his breast pocket. "I have been thinking since you showed me that picture that perhaps I have seen that man before. May I see it again?"

"Sure, why not." Unearthing the crumpled photo, Doug waited impatiently as the pilot carried it to a spotlight, smoothing out the creases to study it. The pilot glanced up. "Yes, I am sure I have seen this man. Is there a reward for information to find him?"

Like he hadn't shelled out enough into this guy's pocket. "For information, no. If I find him, perhaps."

"Then—" The pilot tilted his head toward the Search and Rescue helicopter that was still sitting on the gravel helipad. "I have seen a man who looks like this picture flying that helicopter. It only comes into the city rarely, and I am at Iguazú during the day. But I saw it land a week or so ago when I was delayed again with difficulty with my engine. The pilot must have gone elsewhere, because the helicopter has been sitting here since then."

Bingo! Doug's impatience evaporated instantly. This was a lead—not the least because Doug hadn't told the pilot that his "friend" was a helicopter pilot. That Julio would be flying that SAR machine fit in well with all the other pieces. Except for its civilian markings and lack of gun mounts, there was little fundamental difference between the red-and-white chopper and the hijacked Huey Vargas had flown in Bolivia.

Doug walked over to the pilot. "Tell me, what is your name?"

"Alberto. Alberto Stroessner." *It figured!* The pilot's teeth flashed white in the spotlights as if he was used to Doug's response. "No relationship to *el presidente,* though—except perhaps very distantly. Too distant to be of benefit to my family."

"Well, Alberto." Doug pulled out another twenty-dollar bill from his wallet, searched around further, then remembered he hadn't brought his business cards. Rummaging for a Jungle Tours brochure instead, he scribbled his cell phone number on it. "If you see this man again, call me at this number, and there will be something more. Just please don't tell him I'm looking for him. I'd like my visit here to be a surprise."

"Why not?" With a shrug, the pilot took the money and phone number, adding slyly. "He is not truly a friend, is he? Does he owe you money?"

Doug spread his hands and shrugged. "Maybe. And maybe he's a business contact I need to find. To you, what does it matter?"

The pilot's white teeth flashed again. "Nothing at all. Be sure I will call if I see him. And if I should return to find the helicopter gone, you would wish me to call as well, eh?"

"You do that."

* * *

The next morning, Doug flagged down a taxi and again gave the Jungle Tours address. As he rode through the streets of Ciudad del Este, he turned over in his mind the events of the previous day.

Will Alberto call me, or would he run straight to Vargas if he saw him?

If Doug had read the pilot's mercenary streak right, he wouldn't go to Vargas unless he figured he could squeeze more "oil" out of Julio than he might expect from Doug. This was one time when being American worked to Doug's advantage. He had learned from experience that Americans were widely assumed to be the best paymasters in these parts, topped only by the drug mafias.

And with the narcos, you never knew if you'd get a payoff or a knife across the throat.

As for the pilot, sometimes you just had to make the call and keep your fingers crossed.

Paying off the taxi, Doug selected a sidewalk café across the street and down the block from Jungle Tours and its neighbor. Both businesses were still closed, the metal shutters down over the windows and heavy wrought-iron grates locked over the doors, but the café was busy with breakfast customers sipping their morning *mate*. Doug ordered a *poro* and *sopa paraguaya*, a custard-like cornbread with cheese, and settled in to watch the other side of the street, tipping the floppy-brimmed hat he was wearing further down over his face. Like he'd said, a hat was a great impromptu disguise, and he had no wish to be noticed by any of the Jungle Tours personnel he'd met yesterday.

His breakfast had just arrived when the two receptionists showed up. The grate came off the door, the metal shutters slid up, and tour guides and bus drivers began filtering in.

Doug was nursing a second *poro,* and the first tour groups were being shepherded across the street to the waiting buses before he saw any activity at Jungle Tours' neighbor. He almost missed it in the growing bustle of shoppers and sightseers signing up for tours—a young woman on foot threading her way down the sidewalk. Doug set down the *poro* as she stopped under the RST sign, now the only business along the street with its shutters still down, and pulled out a key ring. Tossing a bill on the table to cover his tab, Doug strode swiftly through the crowds.

The young woman had unlocked the grate over the door and was lifting it down when Doug reached the RST office. She didn't bother to roll up the metal shutters, but proceeded to unlock the door, then pushed it open, maneuvering the heavy grate indoors with the ease of long practice. Catching at the door as it began to swing shut, Doug entered behind her.

The inside layout of the trekking agency was a duplicate of next door with a large reception area in the front and a pair of doors at the back, both closed. Doug caught at the grate as the young woman rested its weight on the floor.

"Here, let me help you with that." Lifting the grate from her, Doug asked, "Where would you like me to set this?"

The young woman looked startled, not only to find herself with a client, but at his offer of help. She nodded toward the nearest corner, where Doug was quite sure the grate did not belong and from which she'd undoubtedly move it as soon as her visitor left. But Doug propped it up against the wall she'd indicated. By the time he was finished and turned again to address the woman, she had recovered her composure and was settling herself behind a desk.

"May I help you?" she asked with a raised eyebrow.

"I hope so." Doug unleashed his most engaging smile. "I'm here for the survival trek, but I was told by your associates next door that my party left without me. If there is some way I could join up with them . . . I've traveled a long distance for this."

"You were to be on the survival trek?" The young woman's dark eyes measured Doug's lean, muscled frame, the khaki slacks and shirt, the sandy hair from which he'd removed his floppy hat. "You speak Arabic?"

Now Doug was startled. What an odd question. The young woman herself looked as if she might speak Arabic. Though her Spanish was flawless, her features were strongly Mediterranean with the large, dark eyes and slightly beaked Roman nose common to the Middle East. Given that Jungle Tours was owned by a Lebanese family, it was not out of the question that one of Ciudad del Este's Arabic immigrants would work in the business. Perhaps even a family member. But what possible connection could speaking Arabic have to a survival trek?

Doug didn't allow his surprise to show as he grinned and responded with the only two words he knew, *"Insha Allah."*

His accent was not convincing, because she immediately frowned and said coldly, "I'm sorry. There must be some confusion. Our survival treks are fully booked and will not have any openings for some time. If you have a reservation, then perhaps it is with another agency. There are several who operate such tours in this area."

"No, I'm sure it was Rain Forest Survival Treks. See, it's posted on the Web." Doug pulled out of his camera-bag a printout of the Jungle Tours Web site data that he'd run off that morning in the hotel's Internet facility. "I'd really like to catch up with the rest of the group, if it's at all possible. I'm told they occasionally return for supplies. Would it be possible to speak to the guide, at least, see if there's any way to still join up with them?"

"No, I'm sorry," the receptionist said flatly. "They will not be returning for some days, and I do not know when that will be. As for your information—" She took the printout from Doug's hand. "Here is your error." She pointed out the last line of the Rain Forest Survival Trek information. "As you can see, it says we are presently booked full. If you will call this number, perhaps in the future an opening will arise. Or if you wish such a tour for your present vacation, then as I stated, there are other agencies that provide such services."

She handed back the printout along with another sheet of paper. On it was a list of tour agencies. "Now, if you will excuse me. We are not open for customers, and I have much work to do."

It couldn't have been a clearer dismissal, and Doug didn't bother arguing. Neither did he dig out Julio Vargas's photo. Not because he didn't think she'd recognize it, but because he was convinced she would. One way or another, this young woman was part of whatever Vargas had going—if only to chase away importunate tourists.

Which brought up another point. If Rain Forest Survival Treks was no such thing, but Julio Vargas's new drug venture, who was bankrolling the operation? *Presumed* operation, Doug reminded himself. Vargas had walked out of Palmasola without a centavo to his name. Doug had made sure of that. Yet he had ample funds to import high-priced equipment clear from the U.S. Not to mention, the Cortéz clan's opulent lifestyle in Miami. Someone was bankrolling that.

The most obvious suspect was, of course, the respected community leader Sheik Mozer Jebai, who owned Jungle Tours. Vargas, after all, had never been his own boss. He'd always worked as someone else's henchman. If Jebai held the purse strings, it would be just like Vargas's "MO." He liked to do the dirty work for someone who needed to preserve an aura of respectability. Doug was a big believer that criminals follow predictable paths, what police called the *Modus Operandi* or MO. Like the leopard's spots, bad guys tended not to depart from a familiar way of doing business.

Now, an Arabic receptionist and her odd question were two new straws in the haystack. Small ones, to be sure, but Doug had started with less. If he could prove a connection, it might even be the drugs-for-terror-funds pipeline that the FBI, CIA, and DEA had been digging around for down here. If so, Doug could count on a little more cooperation than he'd received to date.

But not yet. Chris Patterson was a by-the-book bureaucrat who liked things in well-defined black-and-white, not nebulous suspicions. Doug could well imagine what Patterson would say if he went back to him now. *"You're telling me this Julio Vargas is running a drug op for a respected Arabic community leader through his tour agency. And your entire reasoning is that no one there has ever seen the guy and their survival treks are booked full? Oh, yes—and the Arabic secretary asked if you spoke Arabic."*

Unfortunately, gut instincts never sounded very plausible when translated into black-and-white. But that was par for the course. The rule of thumb was that you followed your gut until you turned up something so concrete that the higher-ups could no longer ignore it.

On this one, "something concrete" meant eyeballing Vargas firsthand. Uncooperative as she'd been, the RST receptionist had let slip one piece of information that might be useful. She was expecting these trekkers, whoever they really were, back in days, not weeks. And when they showed, Doug was betting Julio Vargas would be with them. All he had to do was keep an eye on Rain Forest Survival Treks until they showed up.

Which would be easier if I could talk Patterson into just one team of operatives to stake out Jungle Tours, RST, and that SAR helicopter. But that was where the whole vicious cycle came around again, because until Doug had proof that there was a wanted fugitive, he couldn't get the surveillance, and once he had the proof, he would no longer need it.

So it came down to doing it the old-fashioned way—by himself.

The biggest disadvantage for good surveillance was that Doug was only one person and an obvious foreigner. More than that, he was an American. It wasn't just his coloring. The pilot Stroessner was as sandy blond as Doug. It was something less definable in the way that Americans walked and carried themselves that even Doug could pick out on the streets of a foreign city. The freedom walk, someone had termed it. That head-high, self-confident, careless stride of a people who had lived free for so long they considered freedom from fear itself a given right. Doug had heard the joke more than once down here. The British walked as if they ruled the world. The Germans walked as if they wanted to rule the world. The Americans walked as if they couldn't care less *who* ruled the world.

Like all jokes, its humor came from the element of truth it contained, and regardless of actual physical appearance, Doug had never met a Third World native who couldn't pick out a gringo within a few strides.

On the plus side, the streets of Ciudad del Este thronged with tourists, American and otherwise. Jungle Tours itself was set in a tourist hub, where street vendors took full advantage of the consumer market that tour groups represented, and any number of eating places and bars offered entertainment for sightseers who became bored with nature.

So Doug would be a tourist—a very obvious one.

Strolling through the crowds, Doug kept RST in his peripheral vision even as he stopped to do some shopping. A wide sombrero. A beige, unmarked baseball cap. A sunshade of translucent green plastic. Three different pairs of sunglasses. Two pairs of sandals. Boots. And an assortment of cheap printed shirts and Bermuda shorts. If Americans stood out in the crowd, they were also said to all look alike.

Doug was making his last purchase when a particular movement down the street caught his eye. For all her claims of work to do, the RST receptionist was already emerging. Doug drifted back toward the agency as she replaced the grate and started up the sidewalk the way she'd come. A beach hat now replaced his former headgear, and a wildly patterned Hawaiian shirt flapped untucked over his khaki slacks. Polarized sunglasses and the shopping bags completed Doug's new ensemble, but his quick disguise proved unnecessary. The receptionist didn't glance back once.

After several blocks, the young woman turned a corner that brought her out of the pedestrian crowds and onto a principal boulevard. Stopping at the corner, she looked up and down the street. Doug turned his back to study a case of fake Rolexes. But she was not checking for pursuit. A moment later, a city bus pulled up to the curb, and she climbed on. Doug hurried out to the street to hail a cab. The driver's face showed no reaction to Doug's request to follow the bus.

The bus stopped and started again several times picking up passengers and letting them off, before Doug saw the woman step down. The bus stop was outside one of the newer high-rises in the city center, and as the bus moved off, the young woman walked straight to the building. Noting a security guard just inside the glass doors, Doug didn't bother to get out. Instead, he palmed the digital camera from his case and managed to focus in the telephoto in time for a close-up before the woman disappeared inside. Jotting down the name and address of the building, Doug directed the cab back to his hotel.

At the hotel, Doug cranked the air-conditioning to full blast while he typed up a report on his laptop. There was no point in returning to his post until after the *siesta* hour. Even Ciudad del Este's more commercially minded citizens followed the Paraguayan custom. Shutters would come down over display windows, and streetstand owners would stretch out under the shade of their awnings, while tourists with any sense retreated into the air-conditioning of their hotels until the peak of the day's heat passed.

In the late afternoon, Doug sauntered back through the same streets near the row of tour agencies. This time a sombrero topped off a gaucho getup, complete with a bandanna around his neck. The cowboy boots needed breaking in, Doug discovered by the end of the first block. At least a limp added to the dissimilarity from that morning's costume. Strolling through the crowds, Doug leisurely picked through cheap electronics, Guarani handicrafts, and perfumes, the corner of his eye behind the polarized sunglasses on the tour agency. From the RST receptionist's statements, Doug had little expectation of results that first afternoon. Sure enough, the place remained silent and closed-up for the rest of the day.

Jungle Tours, by contrast, had plenty of activity. Sunburned tourists with knapsacks moved in and out in a steady flow. Only one visitor attracted Doug's notice, a tall, imposing older man in an expensive business suit and full beard, who stepped out of a black Mercedes. Because of the usual knot of tour buses, shoppers, and pedestrians, few cars bothered turning down this street. The locals had long learned to make a detour, and most cab drivers insisted on dropping passengers a block or more away. So when the Mercedes muscled its way through the crowd and stopped in front of Jungle Tours, Doug abandoned the Sony digital camera he was pretending to examine and turned his full attention to the scene down the street. The man's features, visible through the telephoto lens of Doug's own digital camera, were even more Mediterranean than the receptionist's. *Could this be the owner? Jebai?*

The man didn't linger long at the tour agency. When the Mercedes slid away from the curb, Doug flagged another cab. The driver's expression when Doug asked him to follow the black car was even more bland than the last driver's had been. Doug smothered a grin. It was no laughing matter, of course, but not even in Santa Cruz had he ever experienced such blatant, shoulder-shrugging acceptance of apparent skullduggery. Who were those three Chinese monkeys? Hear no evil. See no evil. Speak no evil. Only this was surely not what that Chinese philosopher had in mind.

The Mercedes' destination turned out to be the same high-rise to which Doug had followed the RST receptionist. The bearded older man appeared from the back seat, and the Mercedes moved away. Doug's eyes narrowed speculatively as the man walked into the building.

Doug made a mental note to ask Andy Williams for access to his photo files. It would be instructive to make an ID on those two. And to check out some business data, such as who owned the high-rise, and when exactly this Mozer Jebai had acquired Jungle Tours?

Doug instructed the cab driver to circle back and drop him where he'd started. He strolled around as night fell. The restaurants and bars filled up, spilling raucous Latin-pop music out into the streets. Doug stayed long enough to see the Jungle Tours helicopters fly in for the night. But though he passed within yards of yesterday's pilot, Stroessner's indifferent glance carried no glimmer of recognition. So far, Doug's simple camouflage was proving effective.

Chapter Thirty-nine

APRIL 24
CIUDAD DEL ESTE, PARAGUAY

On the fourth morning of his surveillance, Doug examined his reflection in the bathroom mirror with less confidence. The brilliance of the polarized sunglasses was a little much with the sickly green cast of the plastic sunshade.

Replacing the glasses with a more subdued pair, Doug glanced over the mustard-yellow and green shirt hanging loosely over beige shorts, the tire-soled sandals on his feet, and newly acquired fake Rolex on one wrist. *Heartland America dresses for the tropics!*

The trouble was, no matter how he varied his dress and activities, there was only so long he could play the wandering tourist before some vendor or café waiter noticed that he looked familiar. If they hadn't already. And though Doug now knew every Jungle Tours employee by face if not by name, he had nothing more to show for the long hours of charade. The RST receptionist had shown up briefly every morning, sometimes for fewer than fifteen minutes. Checking for phone messages, Doug guessed. Otherwise the place remained closed up.

Doug had also heard nothing from Alberto Stroessner, though he'd positioned himself to watch both Jungle Tours helicopters lift off each morning and return each evening. The man in the Mercedes hadn't appeared again, and though Doug had spent a number of hours loitering around the high-rise into which the Mercedes passenger and the receptionist had disappeared, he had not caught sight of either one there again.

And now he was heading into another weekend.

If this were back in Miami, he could keep up a drive-by like this indefinitely between other cases, as he had with the Cortéz surveillance, waiting patiently for something to break. But his sick leave time was dwindling rapidly. Last night, Norm Kublin had called, demanding to know if Doug had booked his return flight. The club drugs case was falling apart, and they needed Doug on the witness stand.

Two more days max. If Doug had nothing by the end of the weekend, like it or not, he'd have to concede defeat. At least he had a few names and faces that could be followed up, though he didn't feel at all inclined to ask Chris Patterson for any assistance.

You win some, you lose some. But on this one, Doug did not feel at all philosophical about losing. With a last adjustment of the green sun visor, he grabbed up his camera bag and headed for the door. He was in the elevator when his cell phone rang. Doug grimaced as he flipped it open, prepared to once again deflect an angry Norm Kublin.

"He's here! I'm sure it is him."

"What?" The elevator doors opened and shut again on the hotel lobby before Doug placed the excited Spanish accent. "Stroessner?"

"Yes, you do remember our arrangement?" The upward swing on the last word made it a question instead of a statement. "You said you would pay if I saw him."

"You're saying you've seen Vargas? That he's there at Jungle Tours?"

"The man in the picture—I do not remember his name. Yes, he is here. He is walking around the helicopter. No, now he is going back to the office."

Doug's hand tightened exultantly on the cell phone. *You lose some, you win some!* "I'll be right there. Just wait for me."

"I cannot wait. The office is already asking why I have not lifted off." *Translated: Why lose one fee while waiting for another?* "But I will be back this evening. You will pay as you have promised?"

"I always keep my promises. Call this number tonight. If I don't answer, leave a message where I can find you, and I will make sure your effort is compensated. That is, assuming this man is the one I am seeking," Doug warned.

"If not, I will continue to watch," the pilot said unconcernedly. "But something is happening. The man who is here—he is the one I have seen before piloting that helicopter. And now they are preparing to fuel it. That means it will lift off soon. *Bien,* I must go, but I will call tonight."

It could be the local SAR unit fueling up to search for a lost tourist. Still, Doug shelled out the extra amount to hire one of the hotel cabs instead of walking out to the street as he usually did. Fifteen minutes later, he stepped down at the corner of the Jungle Tours parking lot.

Stroessner was right about the activity, Doug saw as he threaded his way through the buses and shuttles. *Something's going on.*

Next door to Jungle Tours, the grate had been removed from the RST door, and for the first time the shutters had been rolled up. Outside, a farm truck was pulled up to the curb, and workers on the back were unloading burlap sacks. Rice, from the heft of some of the bags. And beans, or possibly lentils. Stalks of plantains, the tropical cooking banana. Other stalks of regular eating bananas. All green.

From behind the tail end of a tour bus, Doug discreetly trained his binoculars on the SAR helicopter across the lot. Yes, there was a hose snaked to it from a fuel tank. There were also a number of people around the helicopter, dashing Doug's plans for a closer inspection. A mechanic in coveralls was handling the hose. Dropping his focus under the belly of the helicopter, Doug counted at least two pairs of boots walking around on the other side. On this side was a slim, dark-haired figure in a flight coverall.

Doug's fingers tightened on the binoculars, then slackened with disappointment as the figure turned around. This pilot was definitely not Julio Vargas. He was much younger, and something about the close-cropped dark curls and olive features brought to mind yesterday's Mercedes passenger, if it weren't for the lack of a beard. *Another family member?*

On the other hand, it would have been impossible for Stroessner to mistake this man for the photo Doug had showed him. *And Stroessner did say he saw the other man walking toward the office. It would be premature to give up just yet.*

Trading the binoculars for the digital camera, Doug snapped a shot, then chose one of the few remaining cafés from which he hadn't yet mounted surveillance and settled in for his usual breakfast watch. This time he opted for thick, syrupy coffee, the only alternative to *mate.* He was getting tired of drinking silage.

The farm truck pulled away just as Doug was pouring a second cup. Almost immediately, another vehicle pulled into its place: a white Volvo pickup. Doug's interest sharpened as several men climbed out of the cab and began loading the stack of supplies into the pickup bed. Catching the glance of a hovering waiter, Doug restrained himself from reaching for his binoculars. But even at this distance he could see that the newcomers were all young and fit. Julio Vargas was not among them. Unlike the cheap work clothes of the farm truck laborers, they were all dressed alike in khaki T-shirts and shorts. RST was lettered across the back. So these were the trekkers Doug had begun to doubt existed.

Doug was not the only one interested in the pickup's arrival. The man in the flight suit had swung away from the helicopter when the pickup pulled up and was now walking rapidly toward it. Dropping a bill on the café table, Doug sauntered out into the shopping throng, extracting the digital camera as he went. As he wandered abreast of the RST office, he began shooting, seemingly aimless tourist shots of a fruit stand, a shoeshine boy, a balheron vendor, but including in the sweep quick close-ups that caught the faces of the new pilot and the young men loading the pickup. Doug increased the telephoto to maximum magnification. *Click. Click.*

Click. The digital camera was still framing the pickup when the RST office door swung open. A human figure stepped into the frame past one of the loaders, and Doug found himself looking through the lens straight into the cold, black eyes of Julio Vargas.

Chapter Forty

As Doug might have expected, Vargas was head-to-toe dressed in black. A gaucho-style hat tipped down to cast a shadow over his face, but the black clothing and gold jewelry was signature Vargas, and the camera's telephoto magnification compensated for the shadow of the hat so that Doug could make out even the deep lines scoring both sides of the narrow mouth, the chill gaze seeming to bore directly into Doug's eyes so that he found himself taking an automatic step backward, only by reflex snapping the shot before breaking contact.

But Vargas showed no interest in the tourists thronging the street as he walked around the pickup, eyed its contents, then climbed into the cab. The young man in the flight uniform slid into the cab with Julio, and the other men vaulted themselves into the pickup bed on top of the load—except for one who walked around to the driver's seat.

The driver leaned on the horn to open a passage as the pickup moved away from the curb. By now Doug had his tailing down to a routine. He threaded through the crowd after the slow-moving vehicle, keeping an eye out for a cab as he did so.

But this time his pursuit hit a snag right away. He had just marked a taxi coming down the street on the far side of the parking lot when the pickup made a left at the same corner. As it broke free of the pedestrian throng, it immediately increased speed so that Doug had to break into a lope to keep it in sight.

Rounding the corner, Doug wished he'd chosen a less colorful costume for the day, especially as he saw heads turn in the back of the pickup. To make matters worse, he saw another tourist flagging down the same cab he'd marked. Doug slowed his stride to blend into a wandering knot of sightseers, frustration tightening his jaw as the pickup disappeared around another corner.

Now what? There really wasn't much Doug could do except return to his stakeout and hope Julio Vargas would return. Ciudad del Este was a congested city of almost a quarter-million people, not the kind of place you could cruise for a single vehicle.

Pure stubbornness kept Doug walking as far as the next corner, and as he paused under a billboard promoting Sabrosa cooking oil, the frustrated line of his mouth curved upward in pure enjoyment. *God does have a sense of humor!*

Just beyond the tour-bus parking lot, a dock area edged the lazy, brown flow of the Paraná River. With its proximity to the Bridge of Friendship and the zone's tourism infrastructure, this stretch of riverbank was crowded with warehouses, boatyards, and piers. And at the piers, boats. Lots of them. Riverboats. Fishing boats. Outboards. Even dugout canoes, and a single sailing yacht docked for repairs some distance upriver.

Closer at hand, not more than fifty yards from where Doug stood, the white pickup he'd been pursuing was bumping down the first rutted dirt alley leading to the river's edge. If that wasn't the way it went in this business! Dead end after dead end until you were ready to give up. Then, bam! Something totally unexpected would break the case wide open.

Doug drifted casually to the cover of a fishy-smelling stack of crates before raising the binoculars. The pickup had pulled up at a wooden pier. Floating at the end of the dock was a large, flat-bottomed riverboat.

Doug trained the binoculars on the pier. The men who'd loaded the pickup were now unloading it, carrying the heavy sacks and stalks of fruit down to the boat. On the boat itself, others received the goods, hefting them over the gunwale. Three of the men onboard were dressed in RST safari outfits; several others wore the cheap cotton fabric of peasant laborers.

Doug spotted Vargas's black-clothed figure on deck, amid the swirl of activity, the young man in flight coveralls at his side. Doug zoomed in on the two men. The younger man was doing the talking while Julio nodded assent. Despite his apparent youth, he was clearly not a hireling of the former Cortéz security chief. There was too much authority in his hand gestures and the calm deliberation with which he spoke. Again, Doug was struck by the resemblance to the older man in the Mercedes.

Doug's eyes narrowed speculatively behind the binoculars. Except for Vargas himself, the men in the group—including the boat crew—bore some striking similarities. They were all male, to start with, not surprising for the work they were doing. But they were also uniformly young and fit, not a paunch in the bunch. Even those in laborer's clothing looked healthy and well-fed, which was unusual among the dirt-poor river dwellers. Where the group varied was in ethnicity. Several could be Hispanic from any number of countries. Others were black—Brazilians, maybe, from across the river. There were Caucasians and Asians, and at least two had the same strong Mediterranean features as Julio's companion. Even the boat crew was not the typical Guarani-mestizo mix of the Paraguayan lower classes.

The truth is, Doug admitted grudgingly, *these guys are precisely the mix of young and athletic adventurers who could be expected to sign up for a rain forest survival trek like I saw on the Jungle Tours Web site. Is it possible my two plus two equals twenty-two instead of four?*

Unless *all* these respectable-looking young men of clearly differing nationalities were accomplices of Julio Vargas, an improbable scenario, it seemed likely that this was a legitimate tourist enterprise.

Is it more likely that Julio could be running his operation—whatever that might be—under the noses of a legitimate group of tourists? That might be difficult, but not impossible, especially if even a couple of those young men are working for him. In which case, Julio's young companion, with his air of authority and striking resemblance to the older man in the Mercedes, might be just the liaison Doug would expect to find between his quarry and whoever was bankrolling Vargas's present occupation.

Unfortunately, Doug couldn't begin to make that kind of judgment without more intel than he had now. Unfortunately, judging by the supplies being hefted aboard the boat, not to mention the helicopter being refueled, it would seem Vargas's appearance in Ciudad del Este was intended to be brief. Once again, Doug itched for the photo files Andy William was bound to have on the local Arab community, including the owners of Jungle Tours.

Doug's mind raced through options as the rest of the pickup load disappeared into the riverboat. One thing was sure. He couldn't go this alone anymore. And now that Doug had something to give the local field office, he should finally get some action there.

Julio Vargas and his companion broke off talks as the last bag was hefted over the gunwale. At a curt hand gesture from the younger man, Doug noted with interest, the loading crew started back to the pickup. Julio and the man in the flight uniform followed them up the pier.

Doug ducked out of sight until the pickup rumbled past, waiting until the sound of its engine blended into traffic before emerging with a cautious eye on the group still aboard the riverboat. At least it looked like Vargas wasn't casting off in the next five minutes. Doug would just have to cross his fingers it wouldn't be in the next thirty either.

In the busy commercial zone, Doug had no problem flagging a cab. With an

275

added tip, he was at the DEA field office in ten minutes. One of the two guards had been on duty at Doug's prior visit, and if his expression lost some of its impassivity as he took in the green sunshade and Hawaiian shirt, he immediately raised his Motorola.

"*El agento americano* Bradford is here."

An electronic buzz signaled the unlocking of the gate. Doug strode inside after the guard. With any luck, he'd get Williams again and avoid having to explain the whole thing from the beginning.

But it wasn't the intel analyst who met Doug inside the front door of the former residence. Instead, it was Chris Patterson. Doug saw that even though it had been six years, Patterson hadn't changed much. A few years older than Doug, he was shorter, with a softness of frame that spoke of more time behind a desk than in the field. The flaxen-straight hair, pale blue eyes, and borderline albino complexion reminded Doug of his first impression of the man: *Must be a bummer for undercover!*

"Doug Bradford, right? Williams said you'd been through." The tone of the agent's voice was every bit as annoying in person as it had been over the phone. "I figured you were long gone by now."

"As you can see, I'm still in town," Doug answered with a civility he wasn't feeling. "Fact is, I'm in a bit of a hurry, and I'm going to need your help."

Doug tamped down his impatience to explain as quickly as he could what he'd found out in the last days and his own analysis of it. As Doug talked, Patterson led the way through the living area, with its swarm of local counternarcotics personnel, into a private office. He didn't sit down at the desk or offer Doug a chair.

"You can see the urgency here," Doug finished. "I'll have a full report as soon as I've got a minute to write it up. Problem is, it looks to me like they're about to weigh anchor and ship out again at any moment. I need a surveillance team. And at least two tracking devices, maybe three or four if you have them handy. And a GPS unit, of course, to track them. If we can get that scrambled before the target disappears on us, that'll give us a breather to call Asunción and your local colleagues in our fellow agencies and see where they'd like to take it from here."

Chris Patterson stopped fiddling with a file on his desk to give Doug a cold stare. "You *are* kidding. First you go against my specific request not to poke around the Arab community, especially Mozer Jebai's business. Now you come in here asking for a surveillance team? And a GPS unit? Are you *loco*, Bradford?

Didn't we already discuss this on the phone? The answer was no, if I remember correctly. And I have a photographic memory," he added superciliously.

Which might explain how you made it into the DEA. It certainly wasn't for your law enforcement skills or deductive reasoning.

Aloud, Doug answered patiently, "That was before we confirmed this really is the guy we've been tracking. Now I'm telling you, I've IDed Vargas personally. He's right here on file."

Doug held up the digital camera. "What more do you want? He's an escaped fugitive with outstanding indictments against him in both American and Bolivian courts. He has to be here on phony documents. So what's the problem with having your local team scoop him up? I'd think you'd be anxious to find out just what kind of illegal op he's running in your territory now. Especially if there really is a connection to this fanatic the FBI and CIA have been dying to nail."

"You've offered no proof the guy's running an illegal op. As for tracking devices, you can't just go around bugging someone on a whim. You seem to forget we're in this country to advise and train nationals to conduct their own war against narcotics and corruption, not to infringe on the sovereignty of an independent nation by running our own operations on their soil."

Right—and how do you think we've brought down every cartel that's been taken out in the last twenty years? Sure, "training nationals" was a noble goal, if you could count on those trainees not to rack in their own cut from the druggies, which happened often enough to make the whole project discouraging. But whatever the official rationale, every field agent knew good and well that the ultimate purpose of maintaining a presence in these places was to take out the criminal organizations that threatened the good ol' USA—with local cooperation or without it! Where *had* this idiot come from? *Washington, D.C. City of policy wonks and politicians.*

Chris Patterson leaned forward to tap the computer screen on his desk. "I've been reading your record, Bradford," he said with patronizing affability. "You were quite a cowboy up there in Santa Cruz."

It wasn't the first such comment that had come Doug's way. Being a "cowboy," with its implication of reckless behavior, was an accusation leveled only too often at field agents, usually by State Department weenies who'd never lifted their own padded rears out of a desk chair. A cartoon Doug had seen in the in-house embassy news publication not long before leaving Santa Cruz was typical of their humor. The cartoon showed a black-tie embassy event with all the usual penguin tuxedos milling around a reception hall. In a corner stood a pair of cowboys with Stetson hats and six-shooters, one asking the other, "How'd they guess we were DEA?"

Maybe that's how you get to be a SAC—by crossing over to the other side so all those rules and regulations in the handbook become more important than getting the job done.

But Doug gave the SAC a pleasant smile that did not show his gritted teeth. "Guilty as charged, actually. I was born and raised on an Arizona ranch . . . learned to ride a bronc before I ever rode a bike."

"Yeah, well, maybe Grant Major let you guys run on a long leash up there. But in my jurisdiction we do it by the book. I'm sure you understand our situation here. Maintaining diplomacy among the community we serve is of an utmost priority. But I will pass this intelligence to our national colleagues and see what can be done to initiate an extradition process. Now, I hope you won't mind seeing yourself out. I am rather busy at the moment."

Doug gave up on the effort not to dislike Patterson. "What I understand," he said, "is that you should have signed on at State, not the DEA." Pivoting sharply on his heel, Doug stalked out, making only a minimal effort to paste on a civil expression as he passed through the Paraguayan counternarcotics personnel. *Of all the narrow-minded, hidebound, bureaucratic idiots who thrive on parking their rears behind a desk and making life hard for the real agents who do all the work, this guy sets the standard.*

The worst of it was that it was snakes like Chris Patterson, with their smooth-tongued inability to act and boot marks on their lips, who ended up back in D.C. at some fabulous GS level, telling agents like Doug how to sneeze.

The guy deserved a slap-down. Still, Doug's crack had been stupid, even if it felt good. Now he had another enemy he didn't need.

Doug broke off his mental fuming as he passed the open door of the communication center and spotted Andy Williams inside. The intel analyst was bent forward in his wheelchair, his fingers flying over a computer keyboard. On impulse, Doug stepped inside. Glancing up from the computer screen, Williams gave Doug an abstracted stare. Then his focus sharpened, and he grinned. "Hey, Bradford! So you're still in town. Did you find the perp you were looking for? Oh, yeah—and did you ever get a hard copy of the intel on that business you were researching . . . Jungle Tours, right? I ran one off somewhere around here."

The intel analyst had clearly paid no attention to his SAC's exchange with

Doug. With a glance over his shoulder, Doug came further into the room and eased the door shut behind him.

"Actually, yes, I did find the guy just today. At the tour agency, just where our intel put him. That's why I came by. To set up the surveillance. Speaking of which, you got a tracker and GPS unit I can use? The sooner the better, if you do. This guy's giving off vibes he might skip town any minute."

"Going to follow him out of town, eh?" the former agent commented knowledgeably. "Sure, I can do that. As you can see, we don't rate a tech agent here, so I double on equipment. At least I understand a user manual, which is more than you can say for Patterson. Matter of fact, we just got in a great new unit— got a range you wouldn't believe. Can even track an aircraft in this jungle. If you can keep the air drag from ripping off the tracker. That's been the biggest complaint so far. It isn't so easy to slap one on the *inside* of the plane."

"I'll take that hard copy too, if it's handy," Doug added as intel analyst wheeled over to an equipment locker across the room. "In fact, maybe you can answer one question for me. Just when did this Mozer Jebai acquire this Jungle Tours agency?"

Williams rustled through a stapled sheaf of paper before handing it to Doug. "Hmm, that's interesting. The papers were signed just a week after your man Vargas skipped from Palmasola."

Chapter Forty-one

Doug was not consciously smiling when he left Andy Williams's office, but his expression must have been pleasant enough that a female Paraguayan agent sidled his direction with a demure smile. Doug nodded a courteous acknowledgement and kept walking. The culture down here was far more pragmatic about love and marriage than in North America, and a U.S. passport meant green cards and an escape from poverty. Doug could be hunchbacked, bald, and sixty—or married, for that matter—and it would make no difference. It had become a cliché in the ex-pat community—the DEA, embassy, or oil company male stationed down here with his pretty, young *latina* wife and an ex- and family back in the States.

After hailing a taxi and climbing in back, Doug took time to strip himself of the flamboyant tourist persona, stuffing the Hawaiian shirt under the seat in favor of a plain beige T-shirt that matched his shorts. Depositing the green sunshade with the shirt—an extra tip the cab driver would sell if he couldn't use—Doug pulled his floppy-brimmed hat from the camera bag. The driver took in the transformation in his rearview mirror, but didn't say anything.

The clothing exchange left him just enough time to glance through the hard copy Andy Williams had given him. Bypassing the text, Doug flipped through the photos. There were a number of the Jebai clan, including a shot of the local mullah Sheik Mozer Jebai, a bearded man in robe and turban gesturing emphatically in what appeared to be some kind of speaking engagement. Probably the mosque. He wouldn't be wearing that outfit to his office. But even with the difference in attire, Doug could see it was the man from the Mercedes, the owner of Jungle Tours.

There were no photos of Jebai women except a few large-group pictures too indistinct in these photocopies to make out faces. Any number of the submissively bent covered heads could have been the RST receptionist—or none of them. But Doug paused at another photo. A boy wearing cap and gown. High school graduation. Saleh Jebai, according to the caption. The mullah's only son.

Doug studied the picture more closely. Yes, take away the sober interest and openness of that young face, add a few years and pounds, and it was the young man in the flight uniform who had been talking so authoritatively to Julio Vargas.

Folding the file as the cab reached the waterfront, Doug stuffed it into his carry bag. The pickup truck was back, he saw as he stepped behind a stack of lumber to focus his binoculars down the bank. Whether this was a second load or there'd been several since he left, Doug had no way of estimating. But what the young men in khaki were loading onto the riverboat now was not food supplies.

Doug zoomed his binoculars to maximum on a crate two men were carrying up the gangplank. His jaw tightened to grim satisfaction as he read the letters stenciled on the side. Tropical Imports & Exports. *Well, wouldn't you know.*

Trading the binoculars for the camera, Doug began shooting pictures. He now had the last link in the chain. Tropical Imports & Exports to the Cortezes. The Cortezes to Julio Vargas. Julio Vargas to Rain Forest Survival Treks. RST to a certain Muslim community leader suspected of funneling funds to militant Islamic groups overseas. And whose only son was, if not acting as Vargas's superior, certainly not his subordinate.

What remained to be discovered was what and where this chain led. Doug had revised his first speculation that Vargas was running another jungle lab, such as he'd managed for Don Luis. That would be unfeasible unless every one of these young trekkers was an accomplice. But a chance rendezvous with another boat on a back waterway. A rice sack or two stuffed with Bolivia's finest dropped over the side. Or a trekking camp that was also a drop site. What could be easier for Julio and this Saleh to arrange?

And perhaps others as well. There were two in that crew who looked strongly Middle Eastern. Was that the reason for the RST receptionist's odd question? Had she mistaken Doug for one of Julio's associates?

If so, she'd recovered quickly. Doug would have to hope she hadn't mentioned her insistent gringo visitor to Julio, assuming she was involved.

Who all was involved could be determined later. *What* and *where* were all that mattered now. If Doug could find out where this bunch was heading, or pinpoint the jungle base camp that Vargas was using for his "treks"—better still, find some incontrovertible evidence of Vargas's drug conduit, enough that even a desk jockey like Chris Patterson couldn't ignore it.

Logic still pointed toward the *Buena Vista*—at least when they weren't expecting a visit from the DEA. But how did it get on—and off? If Doug could track a cargo on board from this end, he'd have probable cause for another SAS, Chris Patterson or no Chris Patterson. Still, it wouldn't be as easy as Doug would have liked.

He switched back to his binoculars to study the situation. The tracking unit that Andy Williams had signed out to him was a beautifully scaled-down version of an older-model tracker that law enforcement agencies had been using for years. The old-style unit was a black metal box the size of a deck of playing cards, and the units were magnetized so a casual slap against a car bumper could attach one to the underside. This new one was also magnetic, but closer in size to a credit card. Slapped on anything metallic or tucked into a bag or box, it could be tailed at leisure from a considerable distance on the GPS unit Williams had included.

But far too many members of Julio's party were milling around for Doug to consider stealing closer to the riverboat. Some were unloading the crates; others were strolling the deck or standing at the prow or stern, watching the river.

Doug started walking back toward the Jungle Tours office instead, threading through the labyrinth of buses and shuttles rather than following the street. He halted briefly to survey the SAR helicopter. The fuel line had been detached, and the mechanic was gone. Despite Andy Williams's warning, Doug was tempted to saunter over and slap the tracking unit onto the chopper's underbelly and hope for the best. But from this angle he could now see two pairs of boots on the far side of the aircraft. It would be risky to step close enough without being noticed.

The white pickup was forcing its way back up the crowded street as Doug reached the far side of the parking lot. This time, both Julio and the young man Doug had now identified as Saleh Jebai disappeared inside the agency.

Doug kept watch as two more crates appeared from inside the building. These were big enough that it took four of the young men to lift them. The pickup moved away immediately, its bed only half-filled. They were turning the corner when Julio and Saleh emerged from the agency. This time Julio was wearing a flight coverall over his black clothing. His flight helmet was already in place, though the front piece was hanging loose.

Doug suppressed a frustrated groan as the two men crossed the street toward the helicopter. If he didn't make a move, he was going to lose both the chopper and the riverboat. But what move could he possibly make that wouldn't be spotted before he got within ten feet?

The blare of a truck horn diverted Doug's attention. A farm truck was pushing its way down the street. Doug watched with interest as it pulled up in front of the RST agency. *Isn't that the same market truck that had delivered food supplies earlier? Maybe that wasn't the white pickup's last load.*

His conjecture was confirmed when the back of the truck swung down to form a ramp, and the same ill-dressed laborers he'd seen earlier began lifting down market goods. Dry goods this time. Twenty-kilo flour sacks. Sugar. Mate. Sabrosa cooking oil in large, square five-gallon containers.

Metal containers.

Letting the tracker drop into his palm, Doug slipped forward into the crowd, wishing he didn't have the distraction of the GPS unit's heavy carrying case or his own camera bag. But circumstances were never optimum, and it was now or not at all. He drifted through the throng of pedestrians crowding past the unloading zone, his peripheral vision fixed on a laborer coming down the ramp, an oil can in each hand. Doug adjusted his gait. Took a half step forward. Then a step sideways.

The laborer jerked his head around to glare at the clumsy foreigner who'd just bumped into him. "Oh, *lo siento*," Doug apologized in terrible Spanish. "Please, let me help here."

"It isn't necessary." The laborer snatched his load away as if Doug had planned to steal it—maybe not such an uncommon scenario around here— but not before Doug felt the satisfactory *thwack* of the magnet attaching itself.

And none too soon. Even as Doug melted back into the crowd, the agency door opened and the Arabic receptionist appeared.

"Why are you dumping this on the sidewalk?" she demanded angrily. "It will be stolen here. Were you not told we lost a sack of rice and a bag of lentils from the last load? Leave it on the truck until the other vehicle arrives. We will not purchase from you again if we lose any more supplies."

Doug faded back across the street as the laborers reluctantly began reloading the dry goods. The metal oil cans were manufactured locally, the welding creating a half-inch ridge around the bottom so that unless the cans were turned on their side, a risky proposition as the spouts had a tendency to leak, it was unlikely anyone would spot the flat black magnet on the bottom.

In any case, it was the best a surveillance team of one could come up with. His decision was confirmed by the throp-throp-throp of rotor blades slowly picking up speed behind him. Angling his head around, Doug saw the SAR helicopter lifting slowly above the parked vehicles. The side panel was open, and a number of the RST trekkers were crouched in the back. Doug watched the helicopter bank out over the water toward the Brazilian side of the Paraná River. Now his only option was the riverboat—and that oil can.

Doug released his breath as a warning honk signaled the pickup's return, but he didn't relax until the market laborers had moved the truck's contents to the pickup bed. Judging by the amount of food he'd seen loaded, the group must be preparing for siege instead of a single trek.

The RST receptionist emerged once again to pay off the market truck as the pickup pulled away. When the truck had driven off as well, the receptionist pulled down the metal shutters and disappeared back inside. She reemerged almost immediately, locking the grate back into place over the door, and walked swiftly down the street.

As she disappeared, Doug turned and made his way back to the docks where the rest of the food supplies were rapidly disappearing into the bowels of the boat. He kept a close watch for any goods coming off the boat instead of on, but if there had been drugs aboard, they'd been removed before Doug's arrival.

This time he needed a more long-term surveillance post than the lumber pile. He found one inside an abandoned cardboard appliance container, with a stoved-in corner that allowed him to keep watch on the riverboat. He remained vigilant as the unloading finished and the driver moved off to park the pickup among the Jungle Tours buses. The driver returned on foot and joined the boat crew on deck. They were swarming about, some covering supplies and boxes with tarps and tying them down, others using a hose from shore to fill a water tank. They were definitely an efficient bunch.

The sun was high, and Doug found it increasingly difficult to blank out the heat and humidity, not to mention the smell in his crouching spot, which must have been home to some sort of animal before Doug came along. The bottle of water he'd tucked into his camera case was long gone, but the sweat was still tricking down the back of his neck. At last the noisy rumble of the riverboat's engine came to life. Two of the trekkers loitering on the pier vaulted aboard, while another cast off the mooring lines. The riverboat moved slowly away from the bank, its prow turning to face the center of the wide river.

As the boat picked up enough speed to create a wake, Doug lifted the GPS unit from its carrying case. The screen glowed green-gray as he turned the unit on. He grunted his approval as a tiny blip-blip moved across the screen in the same trajectory as the riverboat churning lazily upriver. His oil can was definitely on board and doing its job.

Now Doug needed to find his own transportation. If he stayed where he was and the riverboat kept moving, it would be out of range of the handheld GPS unit in an hour or two. Andy Williams's powerful equipment could get a satellite fix on the tracking unit anywhere on the globe, but Doug was not about to place himself back within Chris Patterson's reach until he'd finished with his borrowed equipment.

The biggest problem was the riverboat's head start. Any boat that Doug could hire would not be able to overtake it. And there weren't any roads to speak of out in the rain forest.

Which left air travel.

At the moment, Doug only knew one local pilot.

Returning to the hotel, Doug treated himself to a leisurely filet mignon, then retired to his room. He plugged in the GPS unit for recharging, retrieved his laptop from the room safe, and brought his DEA-6 report up to date. He kept an eye on the riverboat's trajectory until it reached the top of the screen and blinked out.

To that point, the riverboat kept to the main channel of the Paraná River, as Doug expected. But at some point he knew the boat would head into the back country, and he would have to do some guesswork to chart their progress from there. The map he had spread out on the bed was the best he'd been able to find, with an expanded scale of Iguazú Falls and Itaipú Dam, along with the road systems connecting the tourist attractions and the cities of Ciudad del Este and Foz del Iguazú. But only the major waterways were shown. There was no indication at all of how many smaller rivers and streams might lie under the rain forest canopy.

Once the DEA-6 was up to date, Doug locked away the computer and lay down for a nap. With time on his hands, he might as well make good use of it.

It was growing dark when Doug emerged from the hotel again and made his way back to the tour-bus parking lot. No longer bothering with stealth or disguise, he waited for the Jungle Tours helicopters to come in for the night. Alberto Stroessner's face lit up when he spotted Doug waiting for him.

"*Amigo,* it is so good to see you!"

Or my wallet, Doug groused to himself as he handed the pilot an envelope.

After a discreet glance inside, Stroessner tucked it into his flight coverall. "Then you found the man you were looking for?" he demanded shrewdly.

Doug answered with a noncommittal shrug and a question of his own. "Alberto, would you be interested in earning another commission? I'm looking for a pilot and an aircraft. Cessna or helicopter, I'm not picky. But I'll need the aircraft for several hours—maybe all day. Do you know where I could find either one—or both?"

The pilot's blue eyes contracted with avarice. "You understand it would be expensive," he said. "The pilot would have to give up all other tours for the day. There would have to be compensation for that. And the cost of taking up an aircraft for only one person."

"I'll pay it," Doug interjected firmly. This was going to be one expensive mission, unless he came up with something big enough that Norm Kublin could be talked into approving his expense account retroactively. If not—

Doug gave a mental shrug. He wasn't married and had found little enough on which to spend those five years of hazard pay in Bolivia. This wasn't going to break his bank account. "If the pilot will take a money order."

"American dollars?" At Doug's nod, Stroessner spread his hands. "In that case, *señor,* I will fly you myself." He gave a wink and a nod toward the Jungle Tours agency. "Just between you and me, of course."

Doug was already shaking his head. "I'm sorry, but not in that." He jerked a thumb toward Stroessner's helicopter. "It's too—" Doug groped for a tactful adjective, "—colorful."

He might as well have saved the effort. Far from downcast, Stroessner nodded knowingly. "Ah! You wish to be more discreet. It will be a little more expensive—"

What a surprise!

"—but I have a cousin who flies a helicopter for a foreign company. For a fee it can be arranged to acquire the helicopter for a day. And my cousin will replace me here for the day if you wish me as a pilot."

Doug didn't bother asking if this cousin had the authority to rent out the company chopper. He didn't want to know. He simply negotiated a big enough commission that he could count on Stroessner to stay up all night, if need be, to make arrangements. Before they went their separate ways, they agreed on a departure time for the morning.

Chapter Forty-two

APRIL 25

Liftoff was only an hour later than agreed on. The helicopter that settled into Julio Vargas's empty spot carried the acronym of an international mineral survey company, presently under contract by the Paraguayan government to assess exploitable resources. Stroessner could not have made a better choice if he'd tried. No one would question a survey chopper hovering over the jungle. So long as some company executive didn't come looking for the corporate aircraft.

The pilot made no comment when Doug brought out the GPS unit, and Doug offered no explanation. With the riverboat long gone, Doug was forced to develop a search grid to begin the hunt. He figured that any base Julio Vargas would use for his survival treks was not going to be in a populated area, which cut out ninety percent of southeast Paraguay with its cleared forests and farmlands. He also ruled out the Paraguay River watershed, to the west of the Paraná, leading north into the vast plain of the Gran Chaco, which comprised the entire northwest region of the country. It was largely uninhabited, but it was also a wasteland with brutal weather conditions, rivers that dried up one day and flooded the next, and wide-open exposure to aerial surveillance. In other words, the last territory Vargas would choose.

Which left the obvious choice of any *rain forest* survival trek—the jungle, most of which in this region was locked up within the Iguazú World Heritage Site. Once again, Vargas's old MO.

Doug first directed the helicopter north as far as Itaipú Dam, only twelve miles north of Ciudad del Este. The massive concrete wall of the dam came into sight long before they reached it.

It was definitely impressive. The four-mile curve of the wall was so long that Doug couldn't see both ends at the same time as they drew close. The seventy-five story dam was high enough that it loomed above the helicopter as Stroessner approached from downriver and powered upward to fly over the top. Above the dam, in what had once been farming country, the lake was too extensive to measure by eye, though Doug had read somewhere that it spanned 520 square miles.

Doug dragged his attention away from the dam to look at the GPS and an Iguazú area map. He was assuming the riverboat would have come this far north at least before turning off into the maze of tributaries that fed into the flooded river. It seemed a logical place to lose oneself in undeveloped territory.

Doug directed Stroessner to fly north a third of the lake's length, then turn west to begin a search grid heading back south to Ciudad del Este. Next, they turned east into the Argentine boundary of the Iguazú rain forest, then west again, and north, repeating the pattern in a back-and-forth sweep. Again, Doug was astounded at how easy it was here to skim across from one side of a national border to another.

He didn't even attempt to locate the riverboat from the air. The jungle below formed an impenetrable canopy, except where the major rivers wound their brown snake tracks through the green. Outside the rain forest preserve, where the jungle had been largely cleared for cropland, ferries, motorboats, canoes could be seen plying the watery thoroughfares. Inside the park, traffic dropped off to an occasional canoe.

They were into their second hour of flight, and Stroessner's glances toward the GPS unit on Doug's lap were growing more inquisitive when a blip popped suddenly onto the edge of the screen. Gesturing for a course correction, Doug leaned toward the window to peer down as the blip on the screen began to center with the direction of the helicopter. They were upriver of Iguazú Falls, over some of the densest rain forest anywhere on the planet. Except for the Iguazú River itself when they passed over it, Doug could see nothing but the jungle canopy below, even when the GPS unit indicated they were flying directly above their quarry.

Doug marked the coordinates on the tourist map, though they were already stored in the GPS unit's memory. A backup never hurt, and pen and paper didn't break down or blow a fuse. Though Doug couldn't see through the tree cover, the GPS showed the blip still moving. The riverboat's slow pace and the meandering route it had to take through the jungle, had made this intercept exercise possible. But now that he'd acquired the signal, Doug could only hope the boat would reach its destination soon before the helicopter had to head back for refueling.

Stroessner was looking antsy as he studied the fuel gauge. "Thirty minutes," he announced tersely a short time later. "Then we must turn back. Unless you wish to walk out of the jungle rather than fly."

Twenty-five minutes later, the blip abruptly stopped. Doug stared at it for a full minute before he was convinced it really wasn't moving anymore. Training his binoculars on the jungle below, he searched for any break in the canopy that would indicate why Vargas had chosen this particular set of coordinates. But there was nothing to see below except tall hardwoods with their webs of lianas and parasitical creepers looping from one tree crown to another in an unending tangle that made up a single vast highway system for monkeys and sloths and other creatures that lived a lifetime in these treetops without ever touching the ground.

Doug didn't allow the helicopter to hover too close to the spot where the GPS unit indicated his quarry to be, not even to check more closely for a break in the jungle canopy. Instead, they spent their last five minutes tracing a lazy loop around the area to satisfy Doug that the blip on the screen wasn't going to pick up and move again.

Programming the final coordinates into the GPS, Doug jotted them down as well on his map, then signaled an impatient Stroessner to head the helicopter back toward Ciudad del Este.

Packing away the GPS unit, Doug thought furiously. Up until now it had been possible, if inconvenient, to work solo. He'd accomplished what he hoped to by this trip—tracking Vargas and presumably locating his base of operations. He even had a reasonably solid hypothesis of what his adversary was up to.

But to complete any mission objective—in this case, to take Vargas out, along with whatever network he'd set up, and get him back behind bars—at some point surveillance had to shift to an actual offensive operation. And that Doug could not do alone. He had to have mission support.

And cooperation from the local authorities.

Which didn't leave a lot of options.

Stroessner insisted on shaking Doug's hand once he'd checked over the money order Doug handed him. "Any time, anywhere you need to go," he said extravagantly, tucking the money order into his flight uniform. "You have only to call me for service. And, please, if you have any friends who need transportation, I will be happy to offer them the same services I have given you."

No doubt. The guy's earned a month's salary off me in the last few days!

Detaching himself as tactfully as possible, Doug caught a cab back to his hotel. After a mental debate, he decided a phone call to Chris Patterson would be more prudent than a face-to-face confrontation. Not that Patterson was any less angry over the phone.

"Bradford, I know what you pulled, and I can assure you I have every intention of filing a formal complaint. Now you get down here immediately and turn over that equipment."

With a grimace, Doug held the cell phone further from his ear as the other agent continued to rage. "Now hold on, Patterson," he broke in at the first opportunity. "Just listen a minute, okay? I found Vargas. I tracked him to his camp. I have the coordinates, and I have every reason to believe he's running a drug operation there."

In a few sentences, Doug outlined what he'd done that day. "Now, you want apologies, I'll be happy to give them. But if we're going to do anything about this guy, I need your cooperation. I can't do this myself."

"And what do you want me to do about it?" the SAC demanded nastily. "Just who do you think I am that you can come down here, expropriate—no, *steal*—my equipment, run an op in my jurisdiction, and then tell me what I need or don't need to do?"

"I thought you were a DEA agent," Doug responded sharply. Then he modified his tone. "Patterson, look—I'm sorry if I've offended you, but we don't have time here for personalities. There's no way to guarantee how long Vargas is going to remain at these coordinates—or that someone isn't going to stumble over that tracker. Now, if you aren't interested in cooperation, just say so, and I'll make some other calls. Asunción, for one. And be sure I'll let them know why I'm not dealing with the local office."

There was a short silence on the other end. Doug knew the calculations that were going on in Patterson's mind. It was one thing to brush Doug off when he'd had no proof Vargas was even in-country, to demand he come up with more than speculation. Okay, Doug had done that . . . and now he'd narrowed it down even more. For Patterson to flat-out continue to refuse to investigate a lead that was not only of interest to the DEA but potentially other federal agencies as well could backfire badly, and Patterson knew it.

Doug recognized the rustle of area satellite maps being unrolled. If he could get a set of those instead of this tourist map, it would make his own job easier, but somehow he didn't think Patterson would respond well to a request at the moment. Then the SAC came back on the line. "You do realize these coordinates are in Brazil."

"Of course I realize," Doug answered. "They're in the Iguazú reserve north of the falls. I already told you that."

"Then I guess that settles it." There was no mistaking the note of both satisfaction and triumph in Patterson's voice. "That isn't our jurisdiction. You'll have to deal with the Brazil field office."

"But—they're a thousand miles away over in Brasília. You're right next door! Don't tell me you don't have a working arrangement with the authorities on the other side of the border."

"Hey, we don't have a big, fancy office like you do in Miami and Santa Cruz— or a big staff of agents either," Patterson said coldly. "We've got two guys, a wide-open border, and a lot of drugs. And all we've got to work with here are a handful of locals on either side of the border, who may or may not be compromised themselves. Don't tell me how to do my job, Bradford. You're just going to have to work with our timetable down here. *Mañana*, okay? Oh—and if you're thinking you'll get more speed from the Brazilians, think again. Just look how long it took to talk them into picking up Barakat—and he was operating right out in the open."

Assad Ahmad Barakat was a wealthy local Lebanese merchant, a self-confessed Hezbollah militant who'd fled across the Bridge of Friendship from Ciudad del Este to Foz de Iguazú after 9/11 when the U.S. authorities applied pressure on Paraguay to have him picked up. Only after months of additional pressure had the Brazilian authorities reluctantly taken Barakat into custody. Unpleasant little worm that he was, Patterson had a point. If it was difficult in Bolivia to get the authorities to move against prominent citizens, here it was nearly impossible. With a far smaller DEA presence and at least as much local corruption, Doug could understand why Patterson and Williams had chosen to throw up their hands and focus on their overt mission of training the locals in counternarcotics techniques.

Still, if Patterson couldn't see the difference here, he didn't belong in a field office. Vargas wasn't a prominent citizen—or a local. He was a fugitive who was conducting operations in an international rain forest preserve where he had no legal right to be, even if he was doing no more than his advertised survival treks. And if Patterson didn't have contacts with local authorities on both sides of the border, he wasn't doing his job. At the least he could grab an insertion team of those Paraguayan agents, as Doug had done so often in Bolivia, and take them upriver on a training mission. If tourists could move freely back and forth across the borders, no one was going to tell Doug that the local DEA and their trainees couldn't do the same.

It's all personal. Unfortunately, that cut both ways. Doug had made an enemy, and now he was paying for it. It infuriated him that a personal grudge could jeopardize an entire operation. He'd grown spoiled during these past months in the U.S. where the DEA had absolute jurisdiction across any county or state line, and Doug had only to pick up the phone to demand immediate cooperation from any local police force. Now he was back to the frustration of trying to do his job in a Third World country. But if five years of such frustration had hammered anything into Doug, it was how to keep an iron rein on his temper.

So he refrained from smashing his fist against the wall—he might need that hand, after all—and counted silently to five before answering with commendable evenness, "I'm afraid I'll be needing to get back to Miami before Brazil can make a move. But I will be following up on this. And I'll be sending a copy of my six report over to the office. At least take a look at what I've got."

"Sure—just make sure you return our equipment while you're at it." With a sharp click, the line went dead.

* * *

So where do I go from here? Sliding open the glass door that led from his hotel room onto a small balcony, Doug leaned his elbows on the concrete barrier separating him from a fourteen-story drop and gazed broodingly out over the red-tiled roofs and high-rises toward the brown stretch of water dividing the city from neighboring Brazil.

The easiest choice would be to throw in the towel—call the airport and book the next flight home. It wouldn't really be a defeat, regardless how much it felt like it. He'd done his best. He now had the positive ID and corroborating intel he'd come to Paraguay to find. Whether from Miami or here, he had every intention of doing just as he'd told Chris Patterson. The Brazil country office. Asunción. FBI. CIA. Norm Kublin. Whatever pushing and screaming it took up and down the chain of command, he'd rattle cages until he got a response.

Problem was, Chris Patterson was right about that too. All that took time. And what guarantee did Doug have that his quarry would give him time to rattle those cages and get a response mobilized on the ground?

On the other hand . . .

No, you can't do that! Are you nuts?

And yet why not?

The thought gathered force in Doug's mind. He still had forty-eight hours before Norm Kublin expected him back and ready to step onto the witness stand. He knew where Vargas was. And if he wasn't foolhardy enough to think he could take Vargas down on his own, it wasn't true he'd gone as far as he could solo down here. If Patterson was unable—or unwilling—to seize the bull by the horns, what was to keep Doug from doing it himself?

Well, for one thing, it would break one of Doug's cardinal rules: *You don't walk into a situation without backup. You know that! How many recruits have you pounded that into?*

Except sometimes there wasn't a choice. If he could, he'd call Ramon in Santa Cruz and ask him to drop over for some jungle R&R. But forty-eight hours didn't leave any margin for waiting. Besides, Ramon was in the middle of that bomb mop-up.

Doug watched a motorboat idle its way under the Bridge of Friendship. *This is doable. I've got the GPS unit. I can rent a boat or dugout canoe with an outboard motor at Lake Itaipú or any riverside village. The biggest snag will be tracing that maze of rivers and streams to where we picked up the riverboat's position. But anywhere a riverboat can go, an outboard can make it easily. And once I rendezvous with that first set of coordinates, every twist and turn after that is programmed into the GPS unit.*

It could work. If I can get in close enough to take some pictures—and, with any luck, catch some kind of illicit activity—a follow-up team would have some solid intel to go on. And at least I'll know what Vargas is up to out there.

The motorboat cleared the bridge and puttered on downstream as Doug weighed the pros and cons. Despite Chris Patterson's accusations, Doug was no cowboy. On the contrary, he had every intention of collecting his pension someday, God willing, and he believed strongly in taking every possible precaution and planning for any foreseeable contingency.

But here—other than the inherent risks of going it alone—he wasn't greatly concerned for operational safety. He had trekked back country alone on leave, both in North American wildernesses and in the jungle. His own survival skills were excellent. As for any security forces employed by Julio Vargas, he'd dealt with them before, as well. Those that Vargas had trained for the Cortezes were little more than armed thugs. And if Vargas was using outbacking tourists as a cover, getting close enough for surveillance would be a cinch. Even if Doug found an actual drug operation, it wouldn't present much more of a challenge.

After all, all he was looking to do was get close enough to eyeball the situation, take some pictures, and get out.

He knew he was going to do it even before he consciously made the decision. The only other option was to walk out of here onto an airplane home without seeing this thing through. That he could not abide, especially if anything happened down the road because of his lack of action.

Straightening up, Doug brushed whitewash from his forearms. Now that the decision was made, he had a lot to do. This expedition might be pushing the envelope more than he liked. But it wouldn't be without his usual careful preparation and every possible precaution in place.

A call to the airport came first. The best flight back turned out not to be through Asunción but Ciudad del Este–Buenos Aires–Miami, leaving Monday evening.

This was Saturday afternoon, which left just over forty-eight hours. At least half of that would have to be allocated for river travel. Though the riverboat had a considerable head start, Doug knew it was traveling slowly and that once twilight fell, they'd have to tie up somewhere for the night. Traveling in the pitch-black jungle night with no way to see snags and mud bars would be a suicidal proposition. By the time the riverboat made it across Lake Itaipú and started up one of the tributaries, they wouldn't have more than three to four hours travel time before nightfall. They might go another three to four in the morning before Doug could lock on to their signal. So, a maximum of eight hours for him to make up.

A lightly loaded canoe or small boat with a good outboard motor could travel half again the speed of the riverboat. Even allowing for navigating cross-country in unfamiliar territory, Doug estimated he could make up the time. If he acquired his boat, readied everything tonight, and started upriver at first light tomorrow morning, he'd reach the programmed coordinates with several hours of daylight left for scouting. If all went well, he would start back downriver before nightfall. Even camping out for the night, he would be back in Ciudad del Este with ample time to catch his flight.

Next came supplies. He would procure the necessary fuel along with the boat. He'd pick up food and other items at the bazaars on the way to the dock. The only thing left was to put a backup plan in motion—which was not quite the same as having actual backup along but a prudent precaution nonetheless. He wasn't expecting any serious situations on this expedition, he had no intention of allowing himself close enough to another human being for hostilities, and he knew the jungle and its rivers too well to be concerned about the travel itself, but having a healthy respect for the unexpected had helped him survive his profession thus far.

There might be guys who were cowboy enough to insert themselves into hostile territory, trusting their own wits and abilities to bring them back out. But Doug wasn't one of them. If circumstances compelled him to go this alone, at least he intended to ensure plenty of backup to come after him if anything went wrong.

Hauling out the laptop, Doug opened his unfinished DEA-6 report and brought it up to date, including all of today's activities, both sets of coordinates he'd marked on the map, and a detailed explanation of his present mission plan. He added the reservation number and flight number for his trip home and phone numbers for Norm Kublin, his mother, and Sara. The GPS unit contained its own global positioning signal, with which Andy Williams could track down its whereabouts, if necessary (something that obviously hadn't yet occurred to Chris Patterson, or the SAC would be knocking down his door by now). If Murphy's Law struck and Doug didn't return on schedule, at least they'd know where to come looking for him.

After finishing the report, Doug hauled the laptop down to the guest Internet facility off the hotel lobby. He had uploaded the file for three e-mail addresses—the local field office, the Miami DO, and Ramon Gutierrez in Santa Cruz—when the next snag caught him, an all-too-common occurrence in a Third World country like this: The local Internet server was off-line.

Instead, Doug asked the attendant to hook the laptop to a printer and ran off three copies of the report. As he slid them into a manila envelope, he flipped open his cell phone.

"Hey, Doug. About time we heard from you. I was beginning to think you'd gone missing on us and I was going to have to call out the troops. Or gone back to Miami without letting me know. So did you turn up Vargas?"

"Hey, good to talk to you too," Doug responded caustically, but his shoulders eased at Ramon's cheerful tone. Only now at the sound of his friend's voice did it hit home just how isolated and on guard he'd been feeling since he'd arrived in Paraguay. "Yes, I found him. And I lost him. That's why I'm calling."

Doug repeated the same basic report he'd given Patterson. Ramon was silent for a moment when he finished. "You're sure about this, man?"

"That he's out there—one hundred percent. That this is the best move to go after him—maybe eighty. You give me another option and tell me you'd do any different, and I'll listen."

"Hey, the moves stack up the same for me, only I'd take Patterson out into a dark alley and have a serious discussion first. You always were more law-abiding than me." Doug could picture the wolfish grin on Ramon's dark features. "I just wish you'd hold off until I could get some leave and join you."

"No can do. I've got forty-eight hours and Norm Kublin screaming down my back," Doug said briefly. "I just wanted you to know what's up before I take off. Oh, and I'm sending you a copy of my six report via the local office. I should be back long before you get it, but just in case—"

"I know. Murphy's Law. Just call as soon as you get back into town so I can cancel the cavalry."

"Will do."

Doug flipped the cell phone shut, addressed the envelope and added a CD of JPEG files with the digital photos he'd taken. Restoring the laptop to the room safe, Doug sorted what he'd take with him and called the front desk to inform them of his Monday afternoon checkout. Retrieving the cell phone charger from a plug-in, Doug wrapped it around his phone. Unlike the sat-phones Doug carried on official missions, his cell-phone service wouldn't reach outside the city, so there was no point in adding it to the load.

But even as he was thrusting the bundle in with the laptop, Doug retrieved the cell phone. Little time as he had, there was one more phone call he had to make before disappearing into the jungle.

Chapter Forty-three

MIAMI, FLORIDA

Stretching luxuriously out on her sofa bed, Sara tucked a cushion under her head and kicked off her shoes with a groan of relief. Although it was Saturday, she'd been at school all day monitoring makeup testing, and she'd swear she hadn't stopped moving for three seconds at a stretch since rolling out of the bed in the morning.

Reaching a lazy arm for the remote control, she switched the TV on to cable news—then wished she hadn't. The news report was about more rebel fighting in Colombia, rioting by coca growers in Bolivia and Peru, and another counternarcotics plane shot down in guerrilla-controlled jungle.

"Where is he?" Sara found herself saying aloud as the news camera skimmed across a canopy of broad green leaves and vines that looked disturbingly familiar. "Is Doug down there in any of that?"

Switching off the TV, she jumped to her feet and reached for a stack of homework. In the week since her return from Seattle, she'd done her best to follow Debby Garcia's advice.

Until you learn to live without him, you can't live with him.

Get on with your life.

This was Sara's test. If she couldn't handle one week of Doug doing his job in a foreign country without some measure of control over the knot in her stomach, even thinking of a life together wouldn't be fair to Doug—or to herself.

So far, it hadn't been as difficult as she'd anticipated. Thirty-two rambunctious nine-year-olds left little time for brooding. One evening, she'd driven over to visit Debby and the baby; on another, she'd chaperoned an elementary dance. Melanie and other friends kept the apartment noisy at night when they weren't dragging Sara to some social function. The only opportunities she'd really had for worry—and prayer—were once she'd unfolded the sofa at night to sleep.

Father God, You know where he is right now if I don't. I know your angels are watching him. Just keep him safe, and bring him home.

She was checking the first test on a stack when the front door slammed open. She recognized the rushed footsteps. *Melanie, back from jogging.* With no more than a perfunctory knock, her bedroom door burst open.

"Hey, Sara, guess what!" Melanie was in a sports leotard, her red mop of hair damp with exertion. "You're not going to believe who's back in town. Come talk to me while I change."

By the time Sara set down her work and followed her roommate into the living area, Melanie was in the bathroom, a rush of water signaling the turning on of the shower.

"Okay, tell me—who's back in town?" Sara called through the door.

"Kim and Ray."

Sara had to wait until Melanie came out, toweling her thick hair dry, to elicit any further information. "Ray got some leave, so they flew in from Manila—got in last night. They're staying at Kim's parents for a week or so."

The sound of a blow dryer drowned out Melanie's voice again. Disappearing into her bedroom, she emerged in a hot-pink jumpsuit with a slash of matching pink lipstick that should have clashed badly with her coloring, but was instead strikingly attractive, if original.

Guess that's why she's the art teacher.

"You want to tell me how you found out all that jogging?" Sara asked aloud.

Melanie's eyebrows went up. "What do you think cell phones are for? Hey, I get a lot done jogging."

Melanie started for the door as the bell rang. "That'll be Larry, right on time. The guy is so punctual it kills me." She threw a grin over her shoulder. "A bunch of us are going to crash Kim and Ray—hear about the honeymoon and all. You're in, aren't you?"

"You arranged all that while running three miles?" Sara demanded incredulously.

"Sure! You gotta learn multitasking, girl, if you want to get anywhere." Melanie opened the door for Larry Thomas and his roommate, Bill, the P.E. teacher at the school. Larry's eyes went directly to Sara as he came in. She hid an inward sigh as she returned his smile. Larry was no longer making any attempt to conceal how he felt about her.

He's such a nice guy. He's just—not Doug. If he'd only turn his attention to some other fortunate female. He didn't even seem to notice that Melanie's smile was warmer for him than for Bill.

"Sure, I'll go with you guys. Just give me a minute to change out of my school clothes." An electronic bar of music interrupted Sara. All four people in the apartment groped for their cell phones before Melanie said, "That's yours, Sara."

She was already digging into the purse she'd left on the counter. "You guys go on," she said hurriedly as she located her phone and hauled it out. "I'll drive over myself when I've changed." Melanie and Bill started for the door. Larry lingered as Sara put the phone to her ear. "You want me to wait and give you a ride?"

Sara waved abstractedly toward him as she started toward her room. "Hello?"

"Sara?"

"Doug!"

Larry took one look at Sara's face lit up with pleasure, and turned away. She didn't watch him follow the others from the apartment. Kicking her door shut, she turned the lock. This time she wasn't going to be interrupted. "Doug, where are you? Are you back in Miami?"

"Why is that the first question everyone always asks?" There was humor in Doug's deep tone. "No, I'm still in Ciudad del Este."

"Then—" Sara heard the front door close. She sank down on the sofa, keeping disappointment from her voice. He was alive and well, that was all that mattered. "I'm glad you called. How is everything going?" *When are you coming home?*

"Not as well as I'd hoped," Doug admitted. "Though probably as well as I had any right to expect. I located Julio Vargas. He's here all right. Looks like he's up to his usual. The main thing now is to get him back behind bars."

Doug went on without elaborating, "Sara, I don't have much time, but—well, I'm going to be out of town for a bit. I wanted to let you know before I got out of phone range—in case you happened to try to call. It'll just be for a day or so. I've got a flight booked back to Miami arriving Tuesday. You *are* back in Miami."

The last statement was actually a question, and Sara smiled to herself at its sharpness. "Yes, I'm back in Miami."

"Good. Then I'll hope to be seeing you Tuesday. Meantime, if anything comes up while I'm out of contact—with the Cortéz or anything else—call Norm Kublin or Ramon in Santa Cruz. Let me give you their personal cell phone numbers."

Sara scrambled for a pen and wrote down the numbers as Doug dictated them. Someone who didn't know Doug might assume by his tone that he was talking to his secretary. But the mere fact that he had taken time in the middle of a mission to call said far more to Sara than any words. "Do you want me to pick you up at the airport?"

"No, I'll be getting in early in the morning, and you have school. I'll just take a shuttle. But—well, if you don't have dinner plans, would you mind holding them for me? I—there's a lot more going on here than I can give over the phone. You did say you wanted an update."

"Of course," Sara said quickly. "I don't have anything scheduled, and—I do want to hear everything."

"We'll plan on that, then."

There was a pause, long enough for Sara to think she'd been cut off. Then Doug said slowly, in a very different tone, "Sara, last time we were together, I asked a question. You said you needed time to think and pray. I'm not the real patient type, so just tell me flat out—has this been enough time?"

A hint of uncertainty, which Sara seldom heard in Doug's firm, assured voice, tightened her throat. She swallowed before she got out, "Yes."

"Then—that dinner Tuesday—any chance we might have a heart-to-heart?"

Sara could no longer keep the love and longing from her voice. "Oh, Doug, yes! Just—come home safe."

Sara heard Doug release his breath. "Thank you for letting me take that with me," he said quietly. "I'll see you Tuesday, then. And I'll call when I get back into town Monday. You'll probably be in school, but I'll leave a message."

"No!" Sara interrupted sharply. "No, please call, even if I'm teaching. I'll have my cell phone on. I . . . I just want to know you're back."

"I'll do that."

"And Doug!" Sara gripped the cell phone hard, not willing to have the call end. "I . . . your mother has the prayer group at church praying while you're down there. Is there anything specific you'd like us to remember?"

"Just every step I take and everything I do. Until Tuesday, Sara."

I love you, Doug Bradford. Sara sat for a long time with the phone in her hand before she remembered her evening plans and got stiffly to her feet.

Chapter Forty-four

CIUDAD DEL ESTE, PARAGUAY

Doug didn't bother praying over every next step. It was something more than one church member who knew what he did for a living had asked. *Do you pray over what to do next?* To Doug's way of thinking, therein lay fatal indecision. Agonizing over whether to turn left or right, whether this jungle trail or that was God's will, or whether to draw a weapon or not, could cause dangerous hesitation at a time when there might only be a split second to make up his mind. Maybe even get someone killed—including himself.

For Doug, God was in control of every part of his life, including the training and experience he'd allowed Doug to acquire. So long as Doug's decisions, split-second or not, were made as best he could in accordance with his training, experience, and the situation at hand, then he figured that whatever came next was also in God's plan, whether or not he'd had time to stop and pray on the spot.

Still, this was one time when the right decision didn't seem so cut and dried. *God, am I taking the right step here? If you're trying to tell me something, you know I've got a head like a rock. You're going to have to be loud and clear.*

Doug paused in his packing to flip through the small travel Bible that went with him everywhere. The ribbon was inserted at Psalm 91, the words Sara had set on his tray before walking out of his life. He'd read them so many times that he no longer needed to look.

"He who dwells in the shelter of the Most High will rest in the shadow of the Almighty. . . . He will cover you with his feathers, and under his wings you will find refuge. . . . You will not fear the terror of night nor the arrow that flies by day, nor the pestilence that stalks in the darkness. . . . He will command His angels concerning you to guard you in all your ways."

Okay, God, I know the words, but it doesn't leave this any clearer. I guess I'd call Vargas a terror and pestilence, all right, and it's my job to stop him. But whether I've made the right decision here sure isn't jumping out at me. What I do see is that you know what's out there, if I don't, and I sure do appreciate those angels posting guard. So I guess I'll just have to make the call based on what I've got on hand and trust you to sort the rest out.

Doug dropped the Bible into the backpack, adding only a single change of clothing, the GPS unit, and the contents of his camera case. Changing into a khaki shirt and slacks and his hiking boots, Doug clapped the gaucho sombrero to his head and hoisted the backpack. A decent two-way radio or satphone and some MREs, not to mention a dozen local troops with M-16s, would have been nice. But you worked with what you had.

With no desire to run into Patterson or Andy Williams, Doug dropped the manila envelope off at the guardhouse in front of the DEA field office. Using the guards as a mail drop was routine in the diplomatic community. Doug had even received party invitations that way in Santa Cruz. The guard simply nodded when Doug handed him the envelope. *"Para el jefe americano?"*

"That's right, for the American boss," Doug affirmed. He glanced at his watch as the guard set the envelope on a shelf inside the guard shack. It had been early afternoon when Stroessner turned the helicopter back toward Paraguay. Now the afternoon was advancing quickly.

Climbing back into the cab, Doug negotiated for the driver to chauffeur him the rest of the afternoon, then directed him to the bazaar. Bottled water—lots of it. Canned Spam, bananas, a sack of crusty rolls, and more of the peanut-packed nougat bars would have to do instead of MREs. Two heavy-duty flashlights and plenty of spare batteries. A machete, well-honed.

The next stop was a sporting goods store. Though he was traveling solo, it would not be without a weapon. Humans were not the only predators to be found in the jungle and its rivers. The variety of available arms was astounding, all of which would require a background check and waiting period back home. Here they even took Visa. Doug paused over a Heckler-Koch MSG-90 sniper rifle, a beautiful set-up that would have set him back a month's wages. But it was heavy and of little practical use in the jungle. He settled instead for a Colt .45 pistol, whose punch was enough to knock out even a twenty-foot caiman at close range, and added a Kimber Model 84M .308 Winchester rifle that would be lightweight enough not to slow him down.

The Itaipú dam was a twelve-kilometer drive north of Ciudad del Este, and Doug had the cab driver cross over the Bridge of Friendship to put him on the Brazilian side. On Doug's tourist map, a large inlet of the lake just north of the dam connected to a winding blue line that disappeared westward into the dark-green hatched section identified on the map as the Brazilian portion of the Iguazú rain forest. This was the launch point Doug had chosen. But locating the tributary wasn't easy, because the map didn't show that the whole area had grown to one endless metropolitan sprawl from lakefront luxury homes to riverbank slums.

The cab driver was looking glum by the time Doug found himself perusing a waterway whose general orientation corresponded to the one on the map. If not the exact tributary, it was bound to connect to others that would take him in the right direction.

The river here was several hundred meters wide and deep enough to have plenty of traffic from riverboats and larger cargo vessels. The riverside buildings were ramshackle—one- and two-room hovels with roofs of corrugated tin or cheap asbestos tile—and the street was an unpaved alley that petered out into the red clay of the riverbank. Thatched shelters with cooking grills and a few cobbled tables and benches offered ethnic meals and bottled drinks to locals and the odd tourist who wanted to experience the "real" Tri-Frontier. Rusting three-wheelers were available to rent by the half-hour for racing up and down the mudflats.

Boats too.

The cab driver looked distinctly unhappy when Doug asked him to drive out onto the mudflats, but his commission had been a generous one so he obeyed. The surface cracked under his tires as he pulled up near a number of canoes hauled up on the banks. Two had outboard motors, the others long poles laid across their hulls. The owners squatted at the water's edge, cleaning the day's catch of fish for sale to the open-air restaurants up on the bank.

The men's Spanish was worse than Doug's Portuguese, but Doug succeeded in discovering who owned the bigger of the outboard motors, a Guarani Indian too shriveled with age to look as if he could still be earning a living. Age hadn't dulled his business sense, however. Doug might as well have bought the craft outright by the time he counted out the American dollars the old fisherman demanded for two days' use of his boat along with a further deposit to ensure this foreigner returned his property.

At least the exorbitant price included the old man's fishing gear, several jerry cans of fuel, and a patched canvas to keep out the rain, along with two paddles and a pole that indicated maybe the outboard motor wasn't as reliable as the owner insisted. Doug was no longer keeping track of expenses. As one recent U.S. president had said when there were bad guys to face, "Whatever is necessary for however long it takes."

Unloading his belongings, Doug paid off the cab. The driver gave him an odd look when Doug told him he'd be remaining in this neighborhood. "You are sure you wish to stay in this neighborhood? It is not safe here for gringos."

Doug lifted out the Kimber and slid the pump back with a click that got the attention of the watching fishermen. "I'll be fine."

His timing had worked out well. The sky was fading above the brown stretch of river as a smattering of macaws and parrots wheeled down to roost among the trees and thatched eating shelters. A breeze blew the aroma of frying fish and grilled meat across the mudflat, a reminder to Doug that he had yet to eat a cooked meal that day.

But as the cab crunched across the mudflat, Doug noticed the eyes of the men shifting measuringly from the wallet he was putting away to the Kimber. Maybe hot food was a luxury he could forgo after all. Clambering into the canoe, Doug yanked the starter cord on the outboard motor, listened until it was running evenly, then waved a cheerful farewell to his audience on the bank. As the canoe putt-putted out from shore, Doug reached with resignation for one of the nougat bars. To think there'd been a time when he liked these things.

* * *

The landing where the riverboat was tied up was across an open green from the crumbling mission walls of the old Jesuit outpost. Moored to a pair of thick hardwood posts thrust deep into the mud of the bank, the riverboat bobbed gently under the tramping of boots. The removal of supplies should have been accomplished hours earlier, but the boat crew had been expected to turn out for afternoon PT along with the rest of the teams. Now the sky above the ruined bell tower was fading from pink to green, and an aroma of lentil stew was drifting across the clearing from the huge cooking pots.

Part of the mission force was already eating, their spoons clattering hungrily on the enamel plates. But the boat crew had been tersely ordered back to finish off-loading the supplies before darkness rendered the ancient stepping-stones invisible. From a stack of rice sacks hauled up from the boat's hold, Mehri Assad hoisted a bag to his shoulder. Grabbing a container of cooking oil with his free hand, he stepped out onto the gangplank, two boards laid from gunwale to bank. His impassive face did not show his anger.

Yemen by birth, and scion of a prominent merchant family, Mehri had been recruited into the jihad from the engineering program of an elite German university. To be chosen from among thousands of candidates for this training had been a great honor, and he'd minded none of the difficult training, the sweat and thirst, the jungle marches and combat simulations.

But this chore—and too many others to which the infidel Julio Vargas had assigned Mehri and his comrades—was menial labor, fit for peasants or women, not warriors. But the task force leader, known to the others as Sebastian Garcia, had echoed sharply Vargas's judgment that the task was too much for the Indian women. And because objections led only to such assignments as twenty-four-hour guard duty or the greater humiliation of latrine detail, Mehri had learned to keep his anger to himself.

While the dry season had technically arrived some weeks ago, it never really stopped raining in the jungle. The drizzle that had chased the supper crowd under the thatched shelters was turning the riverbank into a muddy quagmire. Tightening his grip on the bag of rice, Mehri stepped off the wooden boards onto the slippery footing of the bank. As he did so, he spotted another Yemeni team member squatted down under the nearest shelter, calmly eating his supper.

"Hey, what do you think you're doing, Ahmed—Alejandro?" It was bad enough that his compatriot was shirking, but the man was also of the peasant class. That he should be relaxing while Mehri performed this menial labor was beyond the pale. "You get over here to work."

Mehri took another hasty step as a crewmate stepping off the gangplank jostled him. The double distraction and awkward heft of the rice bag was enough that Mehri did not notice the stepping-stone until his boot caught against it.

Stumbling, he grabbed at the burlap sack as it slid from his shoulder. But to do so, he had to release the oil container. Slamming against the stepping-stone, the container tipped over, its lid popping off so that the cooking oil gurgled out into the mud. Cursing angrily, Mehri thrust the bag of rice at a crew member and grab at the overturned container. He was setting it upright when he caught sight of the small, black rectangle attached to the metal bottom.

Ignoring the oil pouring out on the ground, Mehri turned the container upside-down. An electrical engineering major in Germany, Mehri had been trained as Team Two's communications specialist, and unlike the Guarani peasant women who should have been handling the oil container, he knew exactly what he was looking at.

Chapter Forty-five

CIUDAD DEL ESTE, PARAGUAY

"Get those reports off to Asunción tonight if you can. And don't forget we've got those congressmen flying in to poke around next month. We'll have to book housing."

Chris Patterson didn't slow his rapid stride across the front work area of the field office as he spoke. The local personnel were already packing up to leave, and he was running late to shower and change before he was scheduled to meet the chief of police and mayor of Ciudad del Este for dinner. Even if the locals didn't seem to heed their wristwatches, he considered it his duty to set a proper example.

"Sure, I've got nothing going tonight," Andy Williams murmured dryly, keeping up easily in his wheelchair. Tom White, the country RAC over in Asunción wasn't going read these reports before Monday morning. *He* had a weekend life! But in this office, things ran more smoothly if you saved your arguments for battles that mattered.

"*Señor.*" The SAC had just yanked the front door open when a guard sprang to attention on the doorstep—one of the outside guards, Patterson noted with a frown, with no right to be wandering inside the compound. Then his eyes fell on the manila envelope the guard was holding out.

"Mail for you, señor. From the *americano* agent Bradford."

"Bradford!" Chris Patterson's mouth tightened with annoyance. He could guess why Bradford had dropped his mail off with the guard. The so-and-so wasn't willing to face him. For two cents, he'd send a squad out and haul him in. Misappropriation of government property would sound good on his next report.

"When did he bring this by?" he demanded sharply.

The guard's shoulders rose and fell under his fatigues. "Some hours ago."

"And you're only now bringing it to my attention? You know any mail is to be delivered immediately!"

"I forgot," the guard said simply.

Patterson snatched the envelope from the guard. "Well, don't forget again. You might want to remind yourself of the waiting list in your commander's office of soldiers who would jump at the chance to make your salary."

As the crestfallen guard shouldered his M-16 and hurried back to his post, the SAC strode back across the work area. He knew well enough what was inside the envelope. The report Bradford had said he was sending over. And he had zero interest in whatever else Special Agent Doug Bradford had to say.

A table at the back of the room was piled high with computer readouts and other files awaiting attention. With a Frisbee toss, Chris Patterson added the manila envelope to the heap.

"That's it. I'm out of here."

Chapter Forty-six

IGUAZÚ RAIN FOREST

Collecting his debriefing notes, Saleh Jebai glanced over at Julio Vargas, who was bent eagerly over a plate of lentils and rice. Saleh's own plate was waiting, but he was still too flushed with triumph to feel hunger. It was for operations such as he'd just detailed on the blackboard, not piddling drug raids, that he'd envisioned this force. Still, even those had helped him refine his tactics. How long had the jihad set its sights on huge, visible targets, only to fail miserably? Now with thirty men Saleh had accomplished—what? At the least, the disruption of an entire country's drug traffic. He would bet that every narco in Bolivia would sleep tonight with a weapon under his pillow and an uneasy bodyguard at his door.

The disruption wouldn't last long, of course. But if so little effort could put an entire nation on edge, how much more exhilarating it would be to turn such tactics on his true enemy. And it was so easy. One had only to read the news to see how much more of America's strength and finances were sapped by false alarms than in real attacks. Now, even the threat of a bomb did as much to disrupt their airports and roadways and government systems as a bomb itself.

Not that his force had worked so hard to become mere "threats."

His force. This latest mission had made it clear who was in charge here. The lackey Vargas and his cronies had done the job for which they'd been paid. But now this was Saleh's force, just as it had been his dream, his vision.

He swung abruptly to address Vargas, who was still bent over his plate. "So . . . your suppliers in America. When will we know if they have obtained the equipment I requested? We must have it on schedule."

Vargas flushed with annoyance. Saleh had grown increasingly insolent since he'd moved beyond Julio's training. But he answered the young man evenly, "It takes time to gather such merchandise. It is not available in their supermarkets. It will be there when needed. So long as you have the purchase price.

You are aware that this will be very costly," he warned. "More than all we have spent to date."

"My father will authorize what is needed," Saleh said sharply. "You need not concern yourself for that, only carrying out your orders."

Julio wiped a stray lentil from his mouth, only the darkening of his high cheekbones betraying his anger. It was definitely time to leave these fanatics before his position deteriorated to errand boy.

"So long as what I am owed is deposited into my bank account, do you think I care what you choose to spend? It will be worth it, in any case, to see the Americans humbled again. They will learn not to interfere in the lives of others."

"We will do more than humiliate the Americans," Saleh responded flatly. "We will bring them to their knees." Saleh did not bother hiding his own contempt. His former instructor was a fool. No, not a fool—an infidel, as much as the Americans he despised. To him, this was all a game. A game of revenge, but still a game. He could not begin to understand that this was a holy war—and America was only one battlefront.

Allah's will, as expressed through *sharia* law, would prevail over these so-called human rights and freedoms and personal choices that proliferated in "Christian" countries—along with the degradation and moral perversion to which such freedoms inevitably led. Ironically, it was the Christian missionaries, who had wormed their way into the holy lands of Allah with their hospitals and famine relief and aid projects, who understood this war for what it was, daring to encourage good Muslims to convert to their God, as if the penalty were not death under *sharia* law. But unlike the followers of Allah, these missionaries chose to offer their message and their God with meekness and bribes of kindness. Their concept of martyrdom was to turn their cheek and be slaughtered instead of striking out to destroy the infidel.

Which is why they will lose.

Saleh was reaching at last for his congealing meal when the sanctuary doors burst open.

"Sebastian . . . sir!"

Saleh recognize the communications specialist of Team Two, Mehri Assad. Saleh alone was aware of the team members' actual identities.

"Sir." Mehri dropped a small object onto the nearest table. "I felt this should be brought to your attention immediately. We just uncovered it among the supplies."

As Julio stared at the small black strip of metal, Saleh reached to pick it up, noting the oily feel. He turned it over, then handed it to Vargas. "It appears to be some kind of magnet."

Julio turned it over. "Is this a piece from some of the new equipment? Or something mistakenly mixed into the shipment?"

"No, it is not ours—and it is not a mistake," Mehri said grimly. "It is a GPS tracking device of the latest American design. I found it attached to the bottom of an oil can."

A GPS tracker! It looked like no tracking device Julio had seen, but he didn't doubt the communications specialist's assessment. His eyes narrowed with stunned fury. *How is this possible? We have been so careful! Is there a traitor in Mozer Jebai's camp? Unless—*

Julio's eyes narrowed further. Could it be that this device was directed at him rather than the training operation? Diego and Raymundo had sworn they'd given Bradford no reason to connect them with him or Paraguay. Perhaps they were telling the truth, perhaps not. But there was no denying they'd focused the American's attention again on themselves, and he at least would never underestimate the intelligence or tenacity of his old adversary. Was there any thread at all that Bradford could follow here?

There was Tropical Imports & Exports and their shipping client, Jungle Tours. The Americans were uncannily skillful at obtaining information in their computer networks. That the American agent would bother tracking such a tenuous connection halfway across the hemisphere seemed doubtful, but if Bradford hated Julio as much as Julio hated him, who knew to what lengths he might go?

Dropping the tracker, Julio wiped his hands with a handkerchief and stalked over to the communications center. The RST office would be empty until Monday, but they had a backup number for emergencies. Dialing the number, he handed the sat-phone to Saleh. Saleh needed no explanation.

"Father, we must speak to Rashima, your secretary. Yes, I am aware she will have gone home by now, but this is urgent. Send the Mercedes, if necessary."

In less than an hour later, the jungle sat-phone rang. "We have her here."

Julio took the receiver. "Has an American come in to the office lately? Muscular, with light hair and gray eyes. He may have asked for me."

"There are always tourists." For once the female spy sounded apologetic. "But there was one like you describe, almost a week ago. He did not ask for you, but he said he was to have been in your party. He wanted to know when you would return and if there was a way for him to join you. I thought at first he was perhaps Chechen, but it became clear he was an infidel. So he must have confused our office with another agency. I told him nothing, of course, and I did not see him again."

"Bradford. It had to be him." Julio let out a curse. If Diego and Raymundo's fat necks were between his hands right now—he'd warned them against arousing a man like Bradford. As always, they were both arrogant and stupid.

"Bradford?" Saleh demanded sharply as Julio replaced the sat-phone.

"The American agent who put me in Palmasola." Julio was thinking furiously. If it really was Bradford, at least this operation would not be compromised. Bradford was after him, not this place. Somehow he'd tracked Julio to Ciudad del Este and spotted him when those food supplies were being loaded up. Julio knew what Bradford would be looking for. Drugs. A production lab in the jungle such as he'd found in Bolivia.

He would find something else.

Still, to pass this place off as a trekking base to a lost tourist was one thing. To a trained agent like Bradford would be another matter. And if he came with an entire assault team like before?

No. Bradford couldn't possibly know what he would find here. The tracker proved he was just fishing. And Julio knew better than any American the red tape and transnational bickering it would take to mobilize Brazilian or Paraguayan authorities to mount an incursion into a conservation site under international protection. It was less than a week since Bradford had starting poking around down here, and no more than twenty-four hours since he could have spotted Julio. This was a reconnaissance expedition. And if Bradford knew Julio's operating procedures, Julio was as well acquainted with Bradford's. The American would be snooping around for confirmation, possibly with a few other DEA agents, maybe even alone if the *Buena Vista* fiasco had really discredited his investigation.

"And why would this American agent be here?" Saleh demanded. "How could he know of our affairs? And what are we to do if he has tracked us here?"

"This has nothing to do with our mission," Julio assured him. "This is a private matter. However, we cannot allow him to find this place and get out alive."

The narrow line of Julio's mouth stretched into a grim smile. Why should he complain if Bradford were to make his way here? Hadn't he prayed to whatever dark force controlled this farce of a universe to bring his enemy into his grasp? Now his prayer had been answered. And unlike his last disastrous encounter with the DEA agent, this time Julio would be waiting with a force every bit as skilled and well prepared as Bradford himself.

"Sale—Sebastian, there are still some lessons you have not yet had opportunity to practice."

Once again, the young leader anticipated the next step. "We have a welcome to prepare, I assume. Mehri, sound the bell and tell the men to assemble."

Chapter Forty-seven

APRIL 26
IGUAZÚ RAIN FOREST

As evening fell, Doug opted for a night on the river instead of going onshore. He was only too aware that the river district was one of the most lawless areas in a region that was itself among the more lawless on the planet. At least the river held only caimans and anacondas—and the occasional passing boat that might see easy pickings in a lone traveler. He tethered the canoe to a post marking a mud bar several kilometers upriver from the last riverbank village he'd seen. Even so, he dozed with a hand on the Kimber, and gave up trying to sleep altogether once the graying of dawn lightened the muddy waters enough to see a canoe length ahead.

Stretching to loosen his muscles, Doug waved a greeting to an early fisherman who eyed him curiously from another canoe. He started the outboard motor at set an upriver course. With the khaki clothing, the gaucho sombrero tipped over his tanned features, and the tarp covering the rifle and other supplies, he should pass from any reasonable distance as just another local fisherman.

As the canoe began putt-putting upstream, Doug used the machete to hack open a can of Spam. The rolls he'd picked up fresh the day before were already hard enough, he discovered, to break under his teeth. But it was food. What he really wanted was his morning coffee, black and strong. But with no Starbucks in sight, he turned his attention to the GPS unit instead.

Several hours later, Doug was beyond boat traffic and settled areas. He'd turned off the main tributary an hour into the morning, working his way east toward the area hatched as rain forest on his map. There was no way to be sure he was duplicating the riverboat's exact course, but by keeping to channels deep enough for the bigger boat and heading in the same direction, he could make a logical approximation of their route.

The cleanly marked boundary of the Iguazú World Heritage Site on the map was not duplicated in real life. A number of villages and slash-and-burn clearings had encroached on the edges of the nature reserve. But the further Doug penetrated into the maze of waterways, the more scattered these became, and the rain forest became taller and denser. This was triple-canopy jungle here, some of the densest on earth, the biggest of the hardwoods stretching their branches over an acre or more.

At one point, Doug heard the throp-throp-throp of rotor blades. But the helicopter didn't pass close enough for Doug see it through the trees before the sound dwindled.

As Doug turned into a swift, narrow channel, he realized that the sky had disappeared altogether, towering hardwoods on the banks overlapping their crowns in the middle, a tangle of lianas looping from limb to limb to form a single net overhead.

At the next fishing village, he pulled up to shore. Asking directions went against his grain, but sometimes pragmatism superseded masculine dignity. The village was no more than a dozen thatched houses perched on stilts high enough to show what kind of floods ran through here in rainy season.

The Guarani fishermen of the village were already out on the river, and the women and children scampered up bamboo ladders into their huts at the sight of the stranger. But an old man chewing a stalk of sugar cane on the bank proved willing to take a look at Doug's map. A life of gnawing the hard stalks had rotted away the old man's front teeth, making his scant Portuguese even harder to understand. But he seemed to understand well enough the significance of the map and the two dots Doug had marked there. After close scrutiny, he took Doug's pen and drew in a maze of winding lines.

"These will take me from here to this point?" Doug repeated carefully.

"*Sim! Sim!*" was all Doug understood through the sugar cane pulp. "Yes, yes!"

Giving up, Doug left his remaining nougat bars as payment. American currency had no value out here. From the look of delight on the old Guarani's face as he spat out the pulp and tried a taste, the sweets were more than adequate remuneration.

Surprisingly, the improvised directions proved accurate enough. One turn led Doug into a swamp too full of drowned snags and reeds for the riverboat to have made it through. But a check of the map showed the error to be his, not the old fisherman's.

Still, it was a jolt when he took his bearings one more time and realized that at some point in the last hour, his position had begun to overlap the coordinates he'd programmed into the GPS unit. Doug was on a fast-flowing river now about a hundred yards wide, with only the enormous height and spread of the canopy overhead shielding the river from aerial view.

Slapping at a mosquito, Doug unearthed the army-issue repellant that had been in the camera case. It was scentless—perfume could give away a soldier's position—but perhaps for that reason the bug life out here didn't seem to take it too seriously. Slapping again, Doug added another layer to his face and hands, his head turning from side to side to scan the banks. His final coordinates for the riverboat were still at least an hour ahead, with several further turns in the maze of waterways, but he could already feel the muscle tension, the heightened alertness that went with impending action.

He tensed further as the bird calls and chattering of monkeys was broken again by the drone of an engine. Doug reached to kill the engine as the throp-throp-throp of rotors grew louder. This time it passed directly overhead, flying low enough for Doug to catch a glimpse of the chopper's underbelly and runners through the branches before it disappeared on the same heading marked on the GPS map.

Vargas?

Soberly, Doug started up the outboard again, but his vigilance was even more determined as he motored up the river, and he stayed close to shore where the underbrush growing out over the river offered additional cover—and animal life.

Doug grimaced as a scrape against a low branch knocked a coiled, sleeping boa constrictor into the canoe. Grabbing the nonvenomous snake by the tail, he tossed it back up on the bank. Uncoiling as it landed, the snake made a beeline under a wide frond and disappeared.

He saw no sign of human life, and the normal jungle orchestra of monkey chatter, screaming parrots, and bellowing tree frogs carried on undisturbed. But the tension grew the farther Doug advanced along the route mapped out on the GPS screen. When the canoe made yet another turn into a much smaller stream, Doug abruptly cut the outboard and reached for a paddle.

Perhaps it was only the steam-bath temperatures, melded with the acrid, musty primeval odor unique to a tropical rain forest and the closing-in of vegetation that made the air seem so oppressive. But after twenty minutes of paddling, Doug let the canoe drift and picked up the binoculars. He saw no reason for anxiety, but after completing his slow scan of the shoreline, he picked up the paddle again and steered the canoe into shore. The closer he got to the final coordinates, the greater the possibility of running into a sentinel or a pack of trekkers out doing whatever they did in this inhospitable place.

Hauling the canoe up onto the bank, Doug pushed it deep under a patch of elephant ears, the palm-shaped fronds drooping over the hull so that no further camouflage was needed. Doug left half the water and food along with the fuel under the tarp. The rest went into the backpack. Hoisting the pack to his back, Doug picked up the Kimber and faded noiselessly into the jungle.

His tension eased once he was no longer sitting like a trapped duck on the open river. Under cover of the rain forest, he slid forward silently from one patch of vegetation to another, every sense focused for a movement, sound, or smell that didn't belong, anything that was not of nature. This was what he was trained for, and Doug knew without any false humility that experience had made him one of the best. Only a jungle Indian or someone with training equal to his own might possibly pick out his invisible progress.

He wasn't far into his trek before he conceded that he wasn't going to make it back downriver before nightfall. He'd be fortunate to make it back to the canoe. With the GPS unit, it was possible to strike out cross-country to his final coordinates. But with no idea of what was out there, Doug had chosen the more prudent and longer route following the twists and turns of the riverboat's passage.

The wide river channel also allowed for a proliferation of plant growth along the banks. The challenge of working through patches of elephant ears, towering ferns, and masses of vines, without snapping a twig, kept Doug to an excruciatingly slow pace, not to mention the ground under his boots, which was squelchy with dampness.

He kept a sharp lookout now for outlying sentries. Not that he'd ever seen a drug op yet where the guards bothered leaving their base beyond the range of their transistor radio. And if Julio were really using legitimate tourists, they'd be doing their thing on drier ground away from the river where the height and thick canopy of the hardwoods, towering 150 feet or more above the ground, kept the forest floor too gloomy for undergrowth.

Doug's biggest concern was that Vargas would stumble onto the tracking device. But the signal was still broadcasting, and it hadn't moved from the location to which he'd tracked it by air. If Doug could slip in and out before the cooks got to that particular container of oil—maybe even retrieve the tracker, if circumstances permitted—they'd never even know he'd been there.

His riverbank course made one final turn upstream from the canoe. The channel here proved far shallower, with mud bars emerging here and there from algae-choked water, and only the flat bottom and minimal draft of a riverboat would have allowed a boat that size to pass this way. But the GPS coordinates were clear. When he was within a half-click of his target, Doug dropped to a belly crawl, storing the GPS unit in his backpack before inching forward on his elbows and belly.

It was a tedious process with a pause every few meters to watch and listen. Doug could see little but broad fronds and leafy ferns above and around, and he was considering pulling out the GPS unit again when he finally heard the low murmur of human voices. A few body lengths further, and he caught a glimmer of open sunlight ahead. Then the vegetation broke away so suddenly that had Doug been walking, he couldn't have avoided an involuntary step into the open.

Doug lay still, not even reaching for his binoculars as he assimilated the scene before him. Whatever makeshift jungle camp he'd been expecting, it was not this. The crumbling adobe church was ancient, and Doug knew enough of Paraguay's history to recognize that it was one of the Jesuit missions abandoned centuries ago in this region.

But the chopped back vegetation, the whitewashed adobe walls and new tiles patching the roof, the thatched shelters scattered around the open clearing—these were all recent additions. To Doug's right, a widening of the stream bed, whether natural or artificial, had created a docking area, and there Doug spotted the riverboat. Its deck appeared deserted.

This place was in the deepest heart of the Iguazú rain forest. The towering hardwoods spreading their acre-wide embrace above the old mission explained how the ruins had remained hidden all this time. Only one space was open to the sunlight, and that was a recent clearing in front of the old church. Lowered onto it, as if dropped down a deep green well, was the SAR helicopter.

But it wasn't the facilities, as incredible as they were in this wilderness, that narrowed Doug's gaze. It was the inhabitants, at least two dozen fit, young men—more than Doug had seen in Ciudad del Este—scattered about the clearing. And they were no longer wearing safari shorts and T-shirts, or cheap peasant clothing, but the civilian version of army fatigues that had become popular among big game hunters and back-country militia in the U.S.

Under the thatched roof of an outdoor kitchen, two Guarani women dangled their long braids over cooking pots. Catching a metallic glint behind them, Doug cautiously raised his binoculars. Several of the five-gallon oil cans, along with other rainproof containers, were stacked beyond the cooking fire, one presumably with the GPS tracker attached to its metallic bottom. The kitchen shelter backed onto untrimmed jungle. That would make it easier for Doug to retrieve the tracking device.

But Doug's apprehension intensified as he moved the binoculars back to the other shelters. In one thatched roof a number of trekkers in fatigues were gathered around rough plank tables, working on . . .

Doug zoomed in with stunned disbelief. *Those are weapons they're cleaning! And not for hunting, either.*

He catalogued the weapons he could see. Uzis and M-16s. MAC-10s. There was even one of those Heckler-Koch sniper rifles with the NVG scope he had seen in the sporting goods store in Ciudad del Este. Under another thatch— *Are those bars of C-4 on the table?*

Beyond the thatched shelters, down near the river, he saw a group of men engaged in martial arts training.

Doug's disbelief grew as he angled the binoculars upward and noticed a maze of ropes stretched among the branches of a mango grove. Except for the unorthodox anchors, it looked just like the ropes course at the Quantico, Virginia, training ground. A slight movement drew Doug's eye to a platform of planks suspended between two of the limbs. A man in fatigues lay there, aiming a pair of high-powered binoculars in Doug's general direction. If Doug hadn't known he'd been too careful to be spotted, he'd have thought the man was staring directly at him. The man raised a handheld radio to his mouth. Below, two other men strolled out from behind the ruins, automatic rifles cradled easily in their hands. One of them held a German shepherd to a tight leash.

Doug's stomach tightened. Somehow, somewhere, he'd miscalculated. This was no safari camp—and neither was it a drug operation.

Letting the binoculars drop on their strap, Doug reached around to his pack for the digital camera. The armed men working out from under the trees and patrolling the perimeter were nothing like the armed thugs Doug had seen working for Vargas and countless other narcos. They were obviously professionals—like Doug himself. Maybe even better. They were like the elite troops he had been privileged to train with during his Ranger days.

Where does Vargas fit into all this? And why?

Doug's every instinct was screaming that it was time to pull out. But first he had to complete the job for which he'd come. Easing the digital camera from his back-pack, Doug began snapping shots. This looked like an op for the Feds or CIA, not counternarcotics. Whatever it was, at least it would be recorded on film.

Doug was zooming in on the helicopter when the old ruined sanctuary's massive wooden doors swung open. Doug's hands froze on the camera. *At last, Julio Vargas.*

Striding down the church steps came the imperious former security chief from *Industrias* Cortéz. Beside him was the young pilot now IDed as Saleh Jebai. Both had shed their flight coveralls in favor of civilian fatigues. Saleh had an Uzi submachine gun hanging casually over one shoulder. Doug snapped shot after shot as the two men rounded the helicopter.

Then a close-up zoomed in on what Vargas was carrying, and Doug stiffened, the camera almost dropping from his hands. He knew what he was seeing, and an icy chill roiled down his spine. Nothing in his long counternarcotics experience would have led him to anticipate such a device in the hands of a drug trafficker in a Third World wilderness.

The piece of equipment was a portable sensor designed to identify a human body heat signature through vegetation or concrete or even metal. Until only a few years ago, this gear was still classified by the Department of Defense. Now, like so much else, the technology had been made available for a high enough price for civilian applications, such as finding survivors of avalanches, earthquakes, or landslides.

Doug tensed as the two men advanced in his direction. This couldn't be coincidence! He had to get out of here—and fast. But he hadn't moved the first muscle when a sound locked him into place. A metallic click from somewhere behind and above his head.

The knot in Doug's stomach didn't diminish the lightning speed with which he rolled to a crouch, the Colt .45 coming up in his hands. But he lowered the weapon immediately, recognizing the futility. Two men in hunting fatigues were standing above him, their weapons bearing down directly at his head. Doug threw a glance at the vegetation around him. If there was the smallest chance, he'd make a break for it.

But there wasn't. Another man stepped out of the underbrush to his left, and from the corner of his eye, Doug saw Julio Vargas and Saleh Jebai closing the gap across the clearing.

"Oh, God!" burst softly through Doug's teeth.

When one of his captors spoke, it was a line right out of every Grade B action movie Doug had ever seen.

"Buenos dias, Señor Bradford. We have been expecting you."

Chapter Forty-eight

"Down on your face! Hands behind your back!"

An M-16 butt between the shoulder blades propelled Doug out into the open and down on the ground. One of the force members kicked the Kimber .308 out of reach while another snatched up the fallen pistol and ripped the pack from Doug's back. When Julio Vargas reached the fallen prisoner, he knocked away the gaucho sombrero.

"So, it is you!"

Not that there'd been any doubt. Julio and Saleh had flown into Ciudad del Este that morning to interview the RST receptionist personally. Saleh had pulled from the Internet a back issue of *El Deber*, the Santa Cruz newspaper, with a photo of Doug glowering in the shambles of an abortive warehouse raid. Rashima had made an instant ID.

Upon their return, Saleh had established a wide perimeter around the Jesuit ruins. The tightness of his expression showed his anger that none of the sentries had detected the American's approach. Without the body heat sensor, they'd not have spotted their prey. On the other hand, the DEA agent had obviously not discovered Saleh's hidden force members either, or he wouldn't be this close.

Julio tossed the black magnetic rectangle of the GPS tracker onto the ground in front of Doug, who had been forced to his knees, his hands already bound behind his back. "Is this what you are looking for, Señor Bradford?"

Julio nodded toward another force member, who was stepping out of the underbrush with a heat sensor unit identical to the one in Julio's hands. "We have known where you were for the past hour," he added with a sneer.

"I didn't allow for one of those. My mistake." A trickle of blood ran down from one of Doug's cheekbones, but his expression was unreadable. Lifting his head, he glanced around the clearing. "So—you've moved up in the world since I saw you last, Vargas. What is this place—some kind of terrorist training camp?"

His swift gaze swept the clearing again, taking in the weapons-cleaning detail, the martial arts practice, the dozen or so men in fatigues who had gathered at a distance to watch the unfolding drama at the edge of the clearing. His eyes narrowed. "Now wait—those raids over in Bolivia. That was you, wasn't it!"

Julio's reaction was swift and instinctive. Dropping the sensor unit, he whipped an M-16 from one of the guards and slammed the butt viciously across the side of the Doug's head. The explosion of blood only fueled his rage. How many times on the filthy floor of that Palmasola cell had he dreamed of having this man in front of him, of seeing that gringo face dissolve into fear and horror and then death? Grabbing Doug by the hair, he yanked his head back viciously and ground the barrel tip of the assault rifle into his blood-drenched jawbone.

Julio Vargas was a killer by nature. But killing was business for him, perhaps occasionally even for pleasure. Rarely had he allowed rage to interfere with his cold calculation. He knew only too well that mistakes followed losing control. The last such time had been with a military commander who had betrayed Julio's trivial pilfering to cover his own grand larceny. And though it had proved satisfying to see the man's life bubble away from a slash across his throat, it had also left Julio on the run until Luis Cortéz found a use for his services. That lesson had instilled caution in Julio.

But now that burning desire to kill, and to kill painfully, possessed him again. The pressure in his brain tinged his eyesight with red, and his hand shook as his forefinger tightened on the trigger.

"No, what are you doing?" Saleh slapped the barrel upward, sending a spray of gunfire into the branches of an avocado tree. "Do you want to kill him here and now? Before we've had a chance to interrogate him? You said there were lessons to learn here. Then let us see what he knows."

Under Saleh's firm grip, the infusion of blood ebbed from Julio's suffused features, and he lowered the assault rifle. "Yes, you are right. This man is an American agent with a wealth of information. It would be foolish to waste it."

A cruel smile replaced Julio's rage. "It will give opportunity for another area of instruction we have not yet covered. Instruction the Americans are too weak to teach their soldiers, but at which my own countrymen have long been expert."

Saleh needed no explanation. He had no qualms about torturing prisoners. "Then let us remove him from here."

Releasing Doug's hair, Julio let him slump to the ground. He relieved his frustration with a kick to the ribs instead. At least the American's indifference had been wiped away, masked by blood. In fact, he looked dead, curled unmoving on the ground.

Saleh bent to feel for a pulse at the base of the neck. "He is still alive. Call the medic."

The Palestinian doctor was already heading across the clearing, black bag in hand. Julio dumped out Doug's backpack, lifting the GPS unit from the pile. "Ah! So this is what he used to follow us here. I have never seen one like this."

"So what do we do now?" Saleh pressed. "If the Americans have sent this man, will not others be on his heels? What if there are others now whom we have not yet detected? If we must evacuate this place, should we not begin preparations?"

"Don't be in such a hurry." Julio smirked to himself at the anxious note he caught in Saleh's questions. "Look at these things. Do you see a radio? Or any communications equipment at all? No, I know this man. He is what the Americans call a 'cowboy,' one who prefers to go his own way. He is known to work alone and even against his superiors' commands when he is not in agreement. No, if there were others with him today, then he would have a means of communication with them. And our detection units would have also found them."

Julio tossed the empty backpack onto the heap. "He does not even carry a means to communicate with his base. The American forces do not work that way. No, he came here after me, alone and unsanctioned by his government. Of that I am sure. It is not the first time. Still, it is urgent we find out what he has uncovered in his prying."

Julio turned to where the Palestinian doctor was now pulling medical supplies from his bag. "When will it be possible to interrogate the prisoner?"

The doctor glanced up from a roll of bandaging. "He is unconscious, of course. But the wound, here above his left ear, is not serious, a superficial gash, no more." With much of the blood wiped away, Julio and Saleh could see the long, wicked slash, and naked bone visible between the gaping edges. A nasty laceration, despite the doctor's reassurance. "It will take some stitches, but the man will recover. I expect him to regain consciousness soon."

"And drugs? How soon can they be administered?"

The Palestinian considered the question. "As soon as the prisoner regains consciousness. Though in his condition it may prove dangerous for his recovery."

"Do it."

Chapter Forty-nine

MIAMI, FLORIDA

Letting herself hurriedly into the apartment, Sara headed straight for the answering machine. Had Doug called yet?

Her first impulse had been to stay home today, in case Doug got back early from wherever he'd gone. But she'd reminded herself firmly of Debby's advice and had accepted Melanie's invitation to join in the social events surrounding Kim and Ray's visit. After all, Doug was quite capable of leaving a message or calling. After church that morning, Sara and Melanie had picked up the newlyweds and headed to the beach, along with Larry and Bill. Then Kim, ever the music teacher, had insisted on dragging everyone to an outdoor jazz fest.

Only when the group had decided to move from the concert to check out the South Beach night life did Sara excuse herself. She at least had to be awake for school in the morning.

The answering machine was blinking 0 for messages. And her cell phone hadn't rung at all. Paraguay was in the same time zone as Miami, and it was almost midnight. If Doug had made it back into cell-phone range, he'd have called by now.

Unfolding the sofa, Sara crawled into bed and turned off the lamp. But not to sleep. Where was Doug sleeping right now? Bedded down somewhere in the jungle? Was anyone watching his back for anacondas and jaguars—or human predators?

Sitting up suddenly to switch on the light, Sara reached for the Bible on the end table beside the lamp. It was the same well-thumbed Bible that Doug had given her that terrible night in Santa Cruz when she'd been fleeing in despair from the murderers who were hunting her through the dark. The ribbon guided her to the right page.

He who dwells in the shelter of the Most High will rest in the shadow of the Almighty. . . . You will not fear the terror of night . . . nor the pestilence that stalks in the darkness. . . . He will command his angels concerning you to guard you in all your ways.

The terror of night.

Sara thrust away her own too-vivid memories of a jungle night. Better to think of Doug's mission. Had he found Julio Vargas by now? It would be a relief to know that horrible man was back behind bars.

A shiver went through her at a sudden image of those flat, cruel, *dead* eyes boring into hers. She fought back the uneasiness that was chilling her stomach. Premonition? Or had she still not learned what it would take to love a DEA agent?

The terror of night.

Father God, I keep forgetting that if I don't know where he is, you do. You're with him out there as much as you're here with me. Wherever he's camped tonight, please ask those angels to put their wings around him and keep him safe.

Carefully replacing the ribbon at Psalm 91, Sara set the Bible back on the table, shut off the light, and settled down at last to sleep.

Chapter Fifty

APRIL 27
IGUAZÚ RAIN FOREST

"It is truly amazing the punishment a human body can absorb and still continue to function."

Julio shook his head over the sprawled, limp form on the mud floor. The cell to which they'd just returned their prisoner was one of the unrestored rooms in the crumbling wings that led off either side of the old church sanctuary. It afforded Julio no small pleasure to see that conditions were even worse than the Palmasola cell to which Bradford's interference had condemned him. The clay tiles of the roof were broken through in one corner, vines weaving down through the opening to cover the dank walls with sickly pale tendrils. Mildew left a green sheen where there were no vines, and the perennial rains trickling in kept the floor a mud pit.

Stepping through the rectangular opening where the door had rotted away, Saleh coughed as the mildew caught at his nostrils. "Who can breathe in here? Are you sure he's still alive?"

Inside the cell, the Palestinian doctor straightened up from his cursory examination of the prisoner. "He is still alive, barely. I warned you about the drugs. But he should recover if he does not catch pneumonia."

His tone held only minimally less indifference than Saleh's shrug. "At least we know now he came alone," Saleh said. "Still, he is an American government agent. If he disappears here, questions will be asked. And they will know from his reports where to begin their search. Perhaps, as he has come without official authorization, a few days will pass before they ask questions. But sooner or later, the trail will lead them to this part of the jungle. Is there any option but to abandon this place? Invisibility has been one of our greatest weapons. We cannot risk our existence becoming known—especially at this time."

"Then we must ensure that the trail does not lead the search here."

Saleh smothered another cough as he glanced over at Julio. "You think to dispose of him elsewhere?"

"No." Julio nudged the limp form on the floor with his boot. A groan signaled the return of some level of consciousness in the prisoner. Julio eyed the bruised features, the shallow breathing, with gratification. Now that his initial rage had subsided, he could see that Saleh had been right. Dying was too easy a way out. "Bradford still holds useful information. And there are other ways to make a man disappear. Can you not see what I am thinking?"

Saleh studied the unconscious American—the strong features, the tangled filthy hair that had been the color of beach sand. Abruptly, he snapped his fingers. "Of course. He will disappear. But as you say, he will disappear far from here. Back in his own home. So that when the search is made, it will never be associated with this place. Or anyone named Julio Vargas."

"It sounds as if you have a plan?" Julio said.

"You know the Chechen from Team Three."

"Yes." Julio grasped the significance of Saleh's choice even before the younger man began explaining. It was actually a far more sophisticated plan than he himself had thought of, but he did not let that show in his expression as he nodded with condescending approval. "Very good. Precisely what I was thinking of myself."

* * *

Hamzan Kasumov—or Heinrich Koch, according to his present German passport—had been born in Grozny, the capital of the former Soviet republic of Chechnya, though his tall, broad-shouldered frame and blond hair would allow him to pass as a native of any number of Western nations. Among the six languages he spoke, his English had been honed through months of practice with the Yemeni-American force members. And he possessed another useful gift—a photographic memory.

It was Monday afternoon when the SAR helicopter deposited Kasumov at the Jungle Tours helipad. All he carried off the helicopter was Doug's backpack. If the clothing he'd found inside fit him a bit snugly, it was not noticeable. The gaucho sombrero tilted well forward over his tanned Caucasian features completed the disguise.

Catching a cab to the prisoner's hotel, Kasumov strolled into the lobby and buzzed the elevator. The desk clerk glanced up briefly but found nothing remarkable to hold his attention. He returned to sorting through paperwork as the Chechen disappeared into the elevator.

Arriving at the fourteenth floor, Kasumov found the right room number and inserted a card into the electronic lock. The door clicked open. Bolting the door behind him, he went immediately to the room safe. The key to the safe, along with the card key for the room, had been among the possessions in the prisoner's pockets. Opening the safe, he removed the computer and cell phone he found there. Powering up the computer, he called up recently accessed files, noting among them the Jungle Tours Web pages.

Ignoring these, he pulled up the most recent file, the report Bradford had filed before his trip, and deleted it. The report had already gone to the local American counternarcotics agents, but that couldn't be helped. But if they remained as unhelpful as the prisoner had indicated under interrogation, perhaps the Chechen's next actions could ensure the report remained buried there.

Returning the laptop to its carrying case, the Chechen packed up the remaining possessions the American had left in the room. Setting the backpack by the door, he added the GPS unit in its carrying case, then punched one of a series of numbers he'd memorized into the cell phone. The gringo who answered was presumably one of the local American agents.

The Chechen sneezed into a handkerchief he'd found among the American's belongings, then said in well-rehearsed, if muffled English, "Bradford here. Just wanted to let you know things haven't worked out, and I'm heading back to Miami." He sneezed again and added a cough. "Sorry, but I seem to have come down with a rotten cold. Anyway, I'll be sending your equipment over before I fly out, so tell the guards to keep an eye out for it. I'll send a follow-up report from Miami."

"Don't bother." The American on the other end sounded distinctly annoyed. "Just get our stuff back in the same condition you took it. And don't think because you've turned it in, I won't be filing a formal complaint."

A receiver slammed down on the other end before the Chechen had a chance to dismiss himself. Swinging the backpack onto his shoulder, he picked up the GPS unit and made his way down to the lobby. The counter was busy with a tour group checking in, and the clerk hardly glanced up as the Chechen shoved Doug's passport and room key across the counter.

"Room bill, please?"

Kasumov paid with some of the American dollars the prisoner had carried, adding a tip generous enough to catch the clerk's attention. "I hope you enjoyed your stay in our country," he said formally, shoving the receipt across the counter before turning hurriedly to another guest.

Flagging down a cab, Kasumov recited the next address he'd memorized. Ordering the cab to pull up short of the guard shack, he passed the GPS unit to the driver. "Give this to the guards. Tell them it is for the American boss."

The guards accepted the carrying case with a disinterest that indicated they'd been forewarned. One walked over toward the cab, but after a glance into the back seat where the Chechen sat with the sombrero tilted to shade his face, he walked back to the guard shack.

The procedure at the airport was even easier. The ticket agent barely glanced from the Chechen's face to the ID photo before handing the passport back. "Yes, Señor Bradford, we have your reservation. How would you like to pay for this? We do accept American credit cards."

The ticket price exceeded the remaining cash lifted from the prisoner's pocket, and forging Bradford's signature to a credit card receipt was more than the Chechen felt competent to do. But his mission planning covered this. Pulling out the American's battered wallet, he counted out the hundred-dollar bills his task force leader had provided. The ticket agent examined the bills, but only to ensure they were genuine, then handed over the ticket.

The flight was tedious, but uneventful. The Hispanic immigration officer in Miami gave the blond passport photo only a cursory glance before slamming down his stamp. "Welcome back to the United States."

This was Kasumov's first trip to the U.S., but his Yemeni-American tutors had coached him well. The airport shuttle was right where they'd told him to expect it. By the time the driver delivered him to the requested address, it was midmorning. Though Kasumov assumed that most Americans would be at work at this hour, the shuttle's arrival produced a twitching of curtains at several nearby apartment windows. Down the block, an elderly black woman hobbled out onto the sidewalk to check out the excitement.

"So you are back, Mr. Bradford," she called out with a Caribbean accent. "Where did you go this time? You look like Indiana Jones. You know, the movies? Harrison Ford?"

The Chechen didn't turn his head, but he gave a casual wave as he checked for the right apartment. Yes, the number on the second-story apartment straight ahead matched the one tagged on the house key he'd been given. And there in the parking slot was the Ford Taurus he'd been told to expect. Striding confidently up the stairs, he removed the gaucho sombrero as he bent over the lock to give a good glimpse of sandy hair to any watching eyes.

Once inside the apartment, he dropped the backpack on a table and removed a pair of thin work gloves—one piece of clothing that hadn't been among the prisoner's possessions. Moving swiftly through the apartment, he took note of the scattered possessions in the living/kitchen area, the unmade bed, the bathroom, and another door leading into a utility room. There he found a washer and dryer—and a basket full of dirty clothes. Dumping out the backpack, he added the clothing to the hamper, keeping out only the shirt the prisoner had been wearing when found. He deposited the toiletries onto the bathroom counter, not bothering to put them away. Tidiness did not seem to be a characteristic of the apartment's tenant.

Finished unpacking, the Chechen made a careful survey of his surroundings. What would an American do when he returned home from a trip? The Yemenis had made a list. Kasumov headed first for the phone. Seeing a number of messages blinking on the answering machine, he pushed the button and let them play. The majority were from a woman who seemed to be the prisoner's mother. One curt message, from "Kublin"—whom the Chechen's briefing had identified as the American agent's superior—demanded that Bradford call the office immediately upon his return. Deleting the messages, the Chechen picked up the phone and dialed the number from memory.

"Drug Enforcement Administration," a female voice said. The Chechen cleared his throat hoarsely. His orders were to remain brief. Unlike the agent in Paraguay, this woman worked with Bradford and might know his voice intimately. "Doug Bradford here."

"Oh, hi, Doug, you're back, then. Good! Norm has been screaming for you to get down here. You'd better report in ASAP."

The Chechen sneezed and coughed, then mumbled hoarsely into his borrowed handkerchief, "That's why I am calling. I picked up a bad flu in Paraguay so I won't be in for a day or two. I wouldn't want to contaminate the whole office."

"Well, you do sound pretty bad. I'll tell Norm. But he won't be happy."

Kasumov broke the connection before he had to speak again. Then he unplugged the phone and strung a modem line from the phone jack to Bradford's laptop. Calling up the Internet server, he entered the password for e-mail access. How his leader had obtained the password, he didn't bother speculating. The agent's backlog of office e-mail was a long one, and the Chechen didn't waste time reading it, just clicking through quickly to open each file. But he did pause on an e-mail from Norm Kublin, the American's supervisor. Its contents were much the same as the message on the answering machine—get in here immediately.

Sitting down at the table, Kasumov typed in the reply his force leader and the Yemenis had crafted, and which he'd practiced writing until it was etched in his memory.

"Got back in town this morning, but I picked up a rotten flu or something while I was down there, so don't expect me for a day or two. No point having the whole office come down with it. I'm going to make one call before crawling into bed. One of the Colombian informants has been in touch. He says he has what we want—you know the case. It shouldn't take more than an hour or two. If he comes down with pneumonia, no sweat off my back."

The last sentence made no sense at all, but the Yemenis had insisted it would be understood, so he typed the words exactly as they'd written them down.

After sending the e-mail, Kasumov powered down the computer. The last item on his list was the postal service delivery. The Chechen didn't like exposing himself to public view again, but his orders were clear. Selecting the next key marked on the prisoner's key ring, he thrust his head outside. The old woman had vanished indoors.

Tilting the gaucho sombrero back over his face, he walked swiftly to the corner mailboxes. The box matching his key was overflowing. Bringing the pile back to the apartment, he unearthed a knife from a kitchen drawer and sliced open the envelopes. Finished, he left the stack of mail on the table beside the computer and glanced around the apartment. Was he missing anything?

If so, it wasn't included on his list. Dropping Doug's passport on the table, he picked up the American's wallet and cell phone. These would go with him. He added them, along with the shirt he'd kept aside, to a smaller knapsack he'd thrust to the bottom of the backpack. No luggage at all on his return flight would arouse attention he didn't need.

The Chechen was leaving the apartment when the phone rang. He lingered to listen as the answering machine kicked in.

"Bradford, if you're there, pick up." Kasumov recognized Norm Kublin's irritated voice from the earlier message. "Don't you tell me you'll be down in a day or two. If you're well enough to track down the Colombians, you're well enough to talk to me!" There was a pause, then an exasperated, "You get this, you call me! I don't care how late it is; I don't care how sick you say you are. Call my cell if I'm not in the office."

Click.

The message was the last perfect touch. Throwing a final glance around the apartment, the Chechen locked the door behind him. This time his objective was the Ford Taurus out front, the last phase in his mission. Sombrero still over his face, he walked leisurely to the vehicle, using a third marked key to unlock it. Starting the engine, he gunned it noisily and backed slowly from the parking slot.

The difficulty was abandoning the vehicle where it wouldn't be immediately found. Getting back to the airport afterward was secondary. He had used most of the fuel in the Taurus' tank when he made his decision—a big orange storefront called Home Depot, close enough to the airport that he could see the planes swooping in to land.

The parking lot was full of vehicles, but he drove around to the back. This area bustled with trucks moving in and out, and workers unloading building supplies. But the Chechen's initial reconnaissance had noted a scattering of smaller vehicles, presumably owned by store employees. Nobody seemed to notice as he positioned the Taurus between a company van and a small moving crane. With any luck, in a business this size, it would be days before its ownership was questioned.

Walking through the unloading zone into the back of the store, he emerged through the front entrance and began the long, hot hike to the airport. Halfway there, he removed the American's wallet, keys, and cell phone, wrapped now in the shirt he'd retained, and dropped them into a dumpster.

At the airport, he took time to wash up before presenting himself to the ticket counter. He counted out most of his remaining cash for a flight to Brazil, this time using his German passport. He was in Manaus before he called the final number engraved in his memory. The call consisted of only five words.

"The American no longer exists."

Chapter Fifty-one

APRIL 28
MIAMI, FLORIDA

Sara stretched stiffly. She'd fallen asleep sitting up, with her legs tucked under her in the corner of her unfolded sofa bed. Through the wall, she could hear Melanie's choice of radio stations, the source of the heavy rap beat that had jolted Sara back to consciousness.

He still hasn't called.

She looked at her alarm clock. Past midnight. If Doug's flight hadn't taken off yet, he'd be clearing Customs and boarding. No, if he hadn't called by now, he wasn't going to.

But he promised!

Sara stifled the mental lament. "Sure, and he could have run late and had to dash for his plane," she said aloud. Or his cell phone could have been stolen or run out of battery.

Don't make this personal. He'll call when he gets in.

Still, Sara slept fitfully and was awake when the radio in the next room went suddenly and blessedly silent. As she walked out the door on her way to work, she told herself not to expect a call before midmorning. By then, Doug should have easily cleared Customs. But she couldn't keep her ears from straining for her cell phone throughout the day, and her students had to call her attention back to their schoolwork on more than one occasion.

By the time she was driving home, annoyance began to vie with her blunted anticipation. Okay, so something had prevented Doug from keeping his promise to call when he arrived back in Ciudad del Este. But his flight to Miami would have arrived hours ago. How long did it take to pick up a phone and make a local call? He'd asked her to reserve dinner for him. Or was she supposed to sit home ready for whenever he might show? She had planned to skip her self-defense class to meet Doug for dinner. But now—

I am not going to fall into the trap of sitting around waiting for his life to intersect mine.

When Sara returned from the gym, there was still no word from Doug. She sat fingering her cell phone. The restaurants would be filling up. Did she dress, hoping he'd come or assume by now her evening plans were canceled?

So call and ask! Phone service did run both ways. *You aren't a teenager anymore! And Doug isn't some guy standing you up for a date. He's the man you hope to spend the rest of your life with.*

Before second thoughts could make her hesitate, she snatched up the cell phone and pushed #1 on her speed dial. It rang. And rang.

On the fourth ring, Doug's message service clicked in. "Doug this is Sara." *Be as poised and self-assured as Melanie calling a guy.* "Uh, maybe I misunderstood, but I had the idea your flight was due in today and we were on for dinner tonight. Give me a call when you can."

Sara followed up with #2 on the speed dial, Doug's home phone number. Her heart made a momentary leap at the deep-toned "Bradford residence." But Doug's voice went on to say, "No one is available now to take your call. Please leave a message after the beep."

Infusing self-assurance into her message was harder this time. Breaking off, Sara dialed again.

"Sara!" Cynthia sounded pleased to hear from her, if rushed as ever. "Have I heard from Doug? Not since he left on vacation—or sick leave, or whatever he was calling it. Why he should want to fly clear down to South America to rest up when there are so many places—and *clean,* at least—right here in Florida. Anyway, I've given up keeping track of his trips. He'll call when he gets back."

"Well, that's just it. I thought he was supposed to be back this morning. We had plans for dinner."

"Really!" Cynthia's voice sharpened to alertness. "That's . . . wonderful! I hadn't realized—"

"It was just dinner," Sara put in hastily. "To talk some things over. Business—to do with the Cortéz case. Doug was checking a few things out while he was in Paraguay. Maybe . . . maybe I got his flight wrong."

"Maybe," Cynthia said dryly. "And maybe some interesting new case came up, and he changed his plans. Like I said, I expect him when he walks in the door. Not that he's got much excuse this time. He's supposed to be on R and R, not a case. But they never do leave their jobs behind. If he was visiting one of his buddies down there and they invited him out on some mission, you can bet he'd jump at it and never give a thought to dinner plans."

Cynthia paused, then added with a diffidence that was uncommon for her, "I'm glad you're seeing Doug again, Sara. I was afraid. . . . Anyway, I'm glad."

"Thank you, Cynthia."

Sara was smiling as she snapped the cell phone shut. But she sat for some time in silent thought after she'd hung up. Maybe Cynthia was right. There'd been a change of plans and Doug would call her sooner or later. But she couldn't be as sanguine about it as Doug's mother was. This was not about a missed phone call. Sara hoped she was not so immature as to get her feelings hurt over that. She'd never forgotten Debby's gibe back when Doug was in the hospital about agents' wives who got their noses out of joint because their husbands didn't call in when they were going to be late for dinner.

But Sara knew something that Cynthia evidently did not. Maybe Doug would extend his leave to give Ramon or one of his other agent friends a hand on a takedown. But Doug wasn't visiting friends on R and R, and his scheduled return had nothing to do with dinner plans. It was because his boss was screaming down his back. The only thing that would have kept Doug off that flight would have been the reason he was there—Julio Vargas. And if he hadn't kept his promise to call, it was because he was still out of phone range.

Or something's gone wrong. Maybe he lost his way in the jungle. Or maybe—

No, Sara would not allow herself to imagine worse. Whatever had changed Doug's plans, he'd call when he could. Meanwhile, she might as well settle herself to wait. *Don't be getting your gut in a knot when you can't do anything about it.* That was one of Doug's sayings, a product of his Arizona ranch upbringing, which he liked to trot out when Sara was fretting over the injustice of the world—or the Bolivian justice system.

Still, when there *was* something you could do, Doug would be the first one out doing it. What had he told her? If anything went wrong, call the office. Or call Ramon. He'd been talking about Sara, not himself. Still—

I don't want to embarrass him if he just got bumped to a later flight. I'll give it twenty-four hours. If I haven't heard anything by then, something's wrong.

* * *

APRIL 30

Sara waited thirty-six hours, only because by the time twenty-four rolled around, it was after business hours at the DO. Cynthia called after work Wednesday. "Have you heard anything?"

When Sara responded in the negative, Doug's mother demanded, "There isn't anything you're not telling me, Sara."

"Just—" Sara hesitated. The last thing she wanted was to get Cynthia worked up, most probably for nothing. "If I hadn't called you, would you have expected to hear from Doug by now?"

"No. But I'm just his mother. He never told me he'd call. Or made dinner plans. You sure you got the right date?"

"Yes, I'm sure," Sara admitted reluctantly.

"Well," Cynthia's voice brightened. "If there was any problem, the office would let us know. In this business, no news really is good news."

If Doug was on official business—which he wasn't!

By recess the next day, Sara gave up all attempts to concentrate on her class. She called in an aide to take over for an hour and shut herself into the staff bathroom to be alone. She started to call Doug's office, then thought better of it.

I need to call Ramon.

Special agent Ramon Gutierrez, the second contact number Doug had left with her, was on the ground down there. And he was Doug's friend. She'd had little opportunity to further her acquaintance with him before she left Bolivia, but the thin, wiry Hispanic who'd been Doug's closest working partner in Santa Cruz, was a hard person to forget. And despite the dangerously aggressive aura he projected, Sara hadn't forgotten his part in her rescue and how courteous he'd shown himself to be once the shooting was all over. If anyone knew what was going on with Doug, it would be Ramon. *I just hope he's in town and not out on an op somewhere.*

Sara was relieved when Ramon answered her call, but his first response when he found out who was calling banished her good feelings. "Sara, where's Doug?"

"I was hoping you'd know," Sara faltered. "He called me on Saturday, and said he'd talked to you. He told me he'd found Julio Vargas and was tracking him down somewhere. He said he'd be back in Ciudad del Este on Monday at the latest. He had a flight to Miami on Monday night. He was going to call before he left. But he never did. I . . . I was hoping maybe he was delayed, that you two were on something together. Are you saying you haven't heard from him either?"

"Not a word," Ramon said grimly. "And he told me the same thing—that he'd call to let me know he was back. I've been sitting on my hands here, just waiting to see if he needed me to pull some strings—rustle up a local posse or something. But nothing. He isn't answering his phone either. I've been leaving messages for two days."

"I know," Sara said. "I . . . I didn't want to say anything to his mother, but I'm getting a little worried."

"Yeah, well, so am I. Tell you what. I'll call down to our guys in Ciudad del Este—see what they've heard. Meanwhile, you call the local office there and see if he's checked in with them. I'll call back when I get something. I'll tell you one thing. If he just decided to head home without filling me in, he'd better have a real good excuse, or I'll wring his neck."

"I just might join you," Sara said. "Oh—do you need my cell number?"

"No need. Doug made sure I had it before he did his disappearing act. . . . Wanted to make sure you were covered in case of emergency."

"Now that sounds like Doug," Sara said.

"Yeah, it does," Ramon agreed soberly. "Which is why I don't like this one bit. Doug isn't the sort to just drop out like this. Not just because he's a stand-up guy, but because you don't just leave your backup hanging. Not if you're Doug Bradford anyway."

For once Sara could wish she didn't agree so wholeheartedly with Ramon. But there were still of plenty of less alarming explanations. Sara had spent enough time in South America to know the possibilities as well as Ramon. If a vehicle or boat motor broke down, you didn't call AAA. You hiked out. At least with Ramon on the case, she could be sure he wouldn't let it go until Doug was accounted for. Sara knew him well enough to be sure of that.

Now for the call she'd been putting off. Sara's reception at the local division office had hardly been cordial since she'd exited Doug's life those months ago. Reluctantly, Sara punched out the number. Her reluctance increased when the agent who picked up turned out to be Peggy Browning.

"Sara?" the female agent said coolly. "What a surprise! Looking for Doug?"

"Yes, actually." Sara gritted her teeth. She was not going to allow the female agent to make her feel inadequate again. "I'm really sorry to bother you, but I was just on the phone with Agent Ramon Gutierrez in Santa Cruz. He suggested I give you a call. Doug's plane was due in from Paraguay two days ago, and when he didn't get in—well, when we never got word of a schedule change, I have to say I've been a little concerned. Have you had any word on his plans?"

Sara could well imagine Peggy's plucked-thin eyebrows going up. "Sara, what are you talking about?" the female agent said impatiently. "Doug got in on Tuesday morning."

It was as if one of those rough Florida west coast breakers had hit Sara smack in the chest. "That's impossible! He would have called."

"Yes, well, maybe he's been busy." Implications dripped from every syllable. *Maybe he just didn't want to call you.* The insinuation that she was a jilted girlfriend chasing after Doug stiffened Sara's back and her voice.

"You don't understand," she said evenly. "His mother hasn't heard from him either. She thinks he's still in Paraguay."

"Trust me," Peggy retorted dryly. "Men don't always keep in touch with their mothers."

Sara was in no mood to argue the point. The revelation that Doug was back in Miami was still such a stunning blow that she could hardly breathe. "May I at least speak to him?"

"He's not available right now. He's been out sick the last couple of days. I'd suggest you try his home before calling here next time."

"I did—"

The line was dead for a long moment before Sara lowered the phone. She felt dazed and nauseous. That some accident might have befallen Doug had been a growing anxiety. But this! This was a kick in the stomach. *Doug, how could you?* She had already reconciled herself to the long absences, being set aside for the urgency of the job. So long as Doug came back to her, it didn't matter. But how could he be in town for two days without bothering to let her know, after promising to call, knowing as he did how sick with worry she would be? She had grown accustomed to broken promises and lies from Nicolás Cortéz. To think that Doug was cut from the same cloth hurt unbearably.

Was it something I did? Had Sara misread the blaze in Doug's eyes that night at the restaurant, or the implication of those phone calls? Or had his time in the jungle given him leisure to change his mind? Was Peggy Browning right? Was he trying to avoid, if not a jilted girlfriend, at least someone to whom he felt he owed—what?

An explanation, for one. Tears stung Sara's eyes. Then anger began to kindle, burning out the pain. *You could at least have the courage to tell me to my face!*

But with that thought, her anger immediately snuffed out. Sara rubbed a hand across her eyelids. The problem was, Doug *had* courage. More than any man she'd ever known. And integrity. No matter how hard she tried, whatever facts stared her in the face, she could not reconcile what she knew about Doug Bradford with a man who would choose a coward's way out to dodge a broken promise.

Besides, what about Julio Vargas? Doug had told her he was on Julio's tail. That he would abandon an investigation that he had flown to Paraguay at his own expense to pursue was even less conceivable than his apparent discourtesy to her.

Even if I were a total stranger, if Doug had promised to find out something for me and knew I was waiting and worrying to hear, he wouldn't let me down.

And if that were true, then . . . then . . . the implications of that were even worse than Doug's betrayal. Sara's stomach twisted again as she opened her phone and dialed the DO again.

"Yes?" Peggy Browning's crisp response sounded distinctly annoyed when she found out it was Sara.

"Agent Browning, please don't hang up. Look, I know you think I'm just chasing Doug and that he's trying to avoid me or something. But it's not like that. Doug called me from Paraguay, told me he'd be in Tuesday morning, asked me to meet him for dinner. It wasn't personal, believe me." *Not all, at least.*

"He had some important business to discuss with me. Official business. Now if you tell me that the Doug you know would just come into town and not bother to follow up an appointment—or call to change plans if he couldn't make it—then I'll hang up and not bother you anymore. Just tell me first, you said Doug's been out on sick leave. Have you actually seen him yourself or talked to him since he's been back?"

The ensuing pause was long enough that Sara took the phone from her ear and looked to make sure the call hadn't ended. Finally, Peggy said, in a voice that for once was not sarcastic or cynical, "Actually, come to think of it, I haven't seen him. He called in sick when he got home. I think Karla took the message."

"Is that someone asking for Doug?" Sara recognized Norm Kublin's gruff voice interrupting in the background. "Sara Connor? Let me talk to her."

The GS came on the line and got right to the point. "Sara, if you see Doug, tell him to get his butt in here or at least give me a call. That is, if he plans to continue working for this office. He isn't in Bolivia anymore. He can't just take off whenever he wants and not keep in touch."

"But—that's why I'm calling," Sara said. "I haven't heard from him either. Mr. Kublin, I know something's wrong! This trip to Paraguay—I don't know what all he told you, but it was related to me, not just Doug. The narco he was hunting down, this Julio Vargas—"

"Yes, I know the connection," Norm Kublin interrupted. "But there was nothing there. It turned out to be a dead end."

"A dead end?" Sara repeated blankly. "But—when Doug called me . . ." Sara broke off. "How do you know if you haven't seen him?"

"Because he called to say so when he got back. *Before* he went AWOL. It was the last we've heard from him, as a matter of fact."

"Then you talked to him yourself?" Sara said slowly.

"Not exactly. Karla talked to him. He'd caught some kind of cold down there and was coughing and sneezing so bad she could hardly get anything out of him except that he was in town and headed to bed. Which is where we've assumed he's been the last two days."

"So no one's actually seen him. Then how do you even know it was him? Anyone could call in coughing and sneezing and say they were Doug."

"Because," the GS said decidedly, "he followed up with an e-mail to let me know what went down in Paraguay. And that would have to come from him."

"What did it say?" Sara demanded. When the GS didn't answer, she added, "Please, Mr. Kublin, this isn't about one of your operations. It's about Doug!"

"Well—okay. It didn't say much except the whole thing was a dead end, and he'd given up and was going to bed. That was it except that he'd arranged a meet first with some Colombian informant. Said it wouldn't take more than an hour or so. He had no business going out on his own," the GS added force-fully. "I called him back and told him so, ordered him to report immediately, no matter how sick he was. He'd already left. I haven't heard a word from him since."

"Maybe . . . maybe because it wasn't him." Dread was growing in Sara. "What if someone got his laptop? Anyone could have written that e-mail. Please, Mr. Kublin, this isn't like Doug. When he says he's going to do something, he does it. And he called me all the way from Paraguay to say he was checking a lead on Julio Vargas, that he'd call me before he flew home. I know he would have if he could. And his mother, too. She thinks he's still in Paraguay—but he always leaves a message when he gets in, even if it's the middle of the night, to let her know he's home safe."

"You may have a point," the GS admitted slowly. "But that e-mail came in on our own agency server, from Doug's own address. The server's encoded with a password. An outsider can't just get in and type a message, even if he had Doug's laptop, which is very unlikely. I don't see how it can be anyone but Doug."

"So maybe someone got the password from him! Maybe . . . maybe he was forced to write it. Come on, a cold on the phone? It's classic! At least check out to see if it was really Doug who called in. Please, I *know* something is wrong, and not just because he didn't call me. Because he didn't call you. Or Ramon Gutierrez in Santa Cruz. Doug lives his job. And he has a thing about covering his back by letting people know where he is—just in case of trouble. He wouldn't just go off like this."

"Well, he's certainly been a stand-up guy as long as I've been working with him." Sara waited as the GS thought silently on the line. Then he said, "I guess it wouldn't hurt to check out his home residence. Maybe he was sicker than he let on."

A new thought. *Could that be the answer? Did Doug come home with one of those weird tropical diseases that seem to abound in the South American jungle? Has he been so sick he didn't even remember his plans? Maybe he's been lying in bed for the last two days without anyone even bothering to check up on him!*

But what about this deal with a Colombian informant?

Sara glanced at her watch and realized that the hour for which she'd requisitioned the aide was up. But she couldn't go back to class now while waiting for a return call from the DEA—if they would even bother.

"Maria, you've going to have to take over the rest of the day," she told the aide as she hastily collected her personal effects from her desk. "Please let the office know I've been called out on urgent family business."

"But what do I do with them? I don't have a lesson plan." The aide was already speaking to Sara's back.

"Whatever," Sara tossed over her shoulder. "Read them a book, watch Barney, you decide."

Would racing to meet a DEA agent be considered an acceptable excuse if a traffic cop pulled her over? Sara pushed the outer limits of the traffic flow all the way to Doug's apartment, squealing into a parking slot just as Norm Kublin and Mike Garcia were jogging up the stairs. The GS was ringing the doorbell as Sara hurried up behind them. His mouth curved down into a frown when he saw Sara, but he offered no objection. Mike's alert gaze was scanning the street. "His car isn't here."

"I noticed." Doug's superior slanted a sharp glance down at Sara. "Doug isn't going to thank you for this if he's out buying groceries. You do realize that, without a warrant, this is breaking and entering."

"No, it isn't." Reaching under the metal railing of the stairs, Sara removed a key, attached there by the magnet on its head. She'd learned its whereabouts when Cynthia sent her from the hospital to pick up Doug's stuff. Neither agent made any comment, but they stepped back willingly to let Sara unlock the door. Covering their rears? *You're getting as cynical as Doug.*

A pressing thought banished her nascent smile. *Where is he? God, please let him be all right. Let him just be out shopping like they said.*

The apartment looked tidier than the last time she'd seen it. Her eyes were drawn directly to the empty backpack and the laptop on the table. Mike Garcia's long legs carried him to the table before Sara could move.

"That's all Doug's. He's been here, all right." Mike shuffled through a handful of mail from a pile beside the computer. "He's picked up the mail. And here's his passport." Picking up the passport, Mike flipped it open. "That settles it. Here's the re-entry stamp. Tuesday."

Sara's heart felt chilled as she checked the stamp for herself. So she'd been wrong and Peggy Browning was right. Doug *had* come home. She walked through the apartment. The bed was unmade and crumpled. That meant nothing. It had been like that the last time she was here. In the utility room there were dirty clothes in the hamper. Sara picked up one of the shirts, patterned garishly in mustard yellows and brilliant green. It was not a style Sara had ever seen Doug wear. *So how much have you seen him in the past few months?*

In the bathroom, toiletries spilled out over the counter. They were Doug's, all right. Sara recognized the well-used toothbrush and a shaving case she herself had packed up to take to the hospital. Sara picked up the toothbrush, then put it down again and opened the medicine cabinet.

Slamming the mirrored cabinet shut, Sara stared blankly at her pale features. Then she walked back out into the main living area. Norm Kublin was playing the messages on the answering machine. Cynthia's voice was there as well as Ramon's and Norm Kublin's, all more than once. Then Sara's own voice caught her ear.

Sara stood stock-still in the middle of the room until the recording wound to the end. Her appeal for Doug to call her sounded more hesitant than she'd hoped. It was the last message. Norm Kublin didn't look her way as he cleared his throat.

"Mike's right, Sara. This does settle it. He's home. Guess he just doesn't feel like talking to anyone until he's back up to snuff. Only question is, where is he now and how long does he think he can get away with this before I get him canned?"

Sara didn't move. Something was not fitting in here, and it wasn't the humiliation of having her phone appeal aired in public. She stood motionless long enough that the two agents fell silent and turned to stare at her. Then a mental switch clicked, and Sara hurried over to the refrigerator. The two men watched her suspiciously as she opened the refrigerator and bent inside to study its contents. Slamming it shut, she feverishly opened the cupboards over the sink, pulling a kitchen garbage can out before swinging around to face the two agents.

"Mike," she said tensely, "Is there any way to get into Doug's laptop there and see when he last checked his e-mail?"

Norm Kublin straightened up his big frame from the counter where he'd been watching her and said slowly, "Why do you ask that, Sara? What are you seeing that we don't?"

"What I'm seeing is that if he was ever here—" her voice grew tighter "—he didn't stay long, and he hasn't been back. Not for at least two days."

"What are you saying, Sara?" Mike broke in. "We know he was here. Just look around."

"Oh—men!" Sara was caught between a laugh and a scream. "I did look. You didn't. Don't you ever clean your own house? You said Doug called in sick with the flu, so sick he couldn't come in long enough to make a report. Now, how sick would he have to be, Mike? He wasn't even home from the hospital last time before he was insisting on going in to the office. But there's no sign of medicine anywhere in the apartment. No Nyquil. No Tylenol. No used glasses beside the bed. There isn't even any cold medicine in the bathroom. And Doug's toothbrush is dry . . . he certainly hasn't used it today. And look at the kitchen."

She swung back around to open the refrigerator door, giving the two agents a clear view of the bottles and jars inside. As the two men exchanged a baffled glance, Sara exclaimed impatiently, "Don't you see? The only thing in here is ketchup and mayonnaise and pickles and all the other kind of stuff you leave when you go on a trip because it doesn't spoil. Okay, so Doug's not feeling well, so he hasn't stocked up on groceries. But after two days, wouldn't he at least buy some 7-Up, or some juice, or bread—or *something*?"

Sara yanked the kitchen garbage can out from under the sink. "It's empty. No blister packs of Immodium or envelopes of cold medicine, no cans or juice cartons, not even fast food wrappers. It's like someone emptied the trash to go on a trip and never came back."

Moving across the room to the table, Sara picked up a handful of the mail. "And all this! Look at it. It's been brought in and the ends of all these envelopes slit open. But look how neat they are—like no one bothered pulling the letters out of the envelopes. Look at this. A couple of bills. Wouldn't he at least pull the invoice out to see how much he owed? And I wonder if the mail has been picked up out at the box the last two days.

"And the phone messages. That first one from you Mr. Kublin was date-stamped Tuesday afternoon. Which means someone checked—and deleted—all the messages that came in while Doug was in Paraguay. But no one has checked the answering machine since then. Which means—"

Sara faltered. She had both agents' full attention now, but that was no comfort. She could only wish desperately that her trail of logic was wrong.

"—which means that if Doug came in Tuesday morning from Paraguay, he left without reading his mail or buying groceries. And he's not been back since."

The two agents exchanged a long, measured glance. Then, without any verbal communication, Mike bounded over to the table while Norm Kublin headed for the door. Sara watched as Mike ran a modem line from the laptop to the phone jack. He'd brought the Internet server on line by the time the GS strode back in and dumped a fresh pile of mail on the table.

"That's a couple days' worth," he added tersely to Mike's questioning glance, "I picked the lock. I don't think Doug will be filing a complaint."

Mike Garcia opened Doug's e-mail inbox. His handsome, young face turned sober as he looked over at Norm Kublin. "She's right. The last transaction shows the file was opened just before 10 A.M. on Tuesday. I don't have the password to see what he's got for new mail."

"I do." Brushing the other agent aside, Norm Kublin bent over the keyboard and typed in a series of characters. "It's an agency server," he explained as he did so. "I have the passwords of all my group. So if you're going to cheat on your wife," he added with a half-grin toward Mike, "don't do it on your office e-mail."

The smile disappeared as he accessed the account. "There's the e-mail I shot back at Bradford when he didn't pick up the phone, telling him to forget the

Colombian and get his butt down to the office. That was about 10:30 Tuesday. It's never been opened."

He looked grimly at Sara. "Okay, you've convinced me. This is now an investigation." He shut down the laptop and closed the lid. "You've got the makings of a good agent, Ms. Connor."

Chapter Fifty-two

How is someone supposed to feel when the center of their universe is ripped away?

It was an odd question for Sara to ask herself. After all, she'd seen her world rocked on its foundations before. But it had been different, if not easier, to live with terror threatening her own life than with this growing fear and dread for someone she now loved. At least when she'd been waiting at the hospital after Doug got shot, she'd known what was happening. Had he felt this helpless when she vanished into the Bolivian jungle with Julio Vargas?

But at least he'd been able to do something about it, to channel his adrenaline and worry and rage into mission plans and jungle treks and assault operations.

All Sara could do was wait.

She sat, numb, on the outside steps of Doug's apartment house, where she'd been banished when a swarm of DEA agents arrived to dust for prints, search through cupboards, huddle over the laptop, and whatever else a Crime Scene Investigation unit did.

She was resting her head wearily on her knees as she waited for someone to tell her what to do next when she heard her name. Raising her head, Sara recognized the lithe figure of Peggy Browning hurrying up the walk. The agent took the stairs two at a time, stopping several steps below Sara, which left her at eye level. As Sara lifted her chin to look, Peggy's appraising eyes swept over her.

"Kublin says you deserve credit for putting the pieces together. Good work. I guess you were right, and we were wrong."

"I don't want to be right," Sara answered tiredly. "I just want Doug found."

To Sara's surprise, Peggy came up two more steps, enough to drop a hand on her shoulder. "I know. We all do." Peggy paused to clear her throat, and her voice was gruff when she added, "We're sending an agent over to talk to Doug's mother. I thought you might be willing to go with him. Cynthia's going to need some support."

Sara scrambled to her feet. Here at least was something to *do* instead of watch. Mike Garcia was one of the two agents detailed to contact Doug's mother.

If Sara needed any further assurance that she was now being taken seriously, it was the whitening of Mike's knuckles against the steering wheel.

Cynthia had been a DEA mother too long to miss the significance of the two agents on her doorstep. Her face draining of color, she turned to Sara and spoke through stiff lips. "They don't know where he is either, do they?"

Sara shook her head mutely as Mike Garcia stepped forward. "Look, Mrs. Bradford, may we step inside to talk? Yes, it's true we haven't been able to ascertain where Doug is at the moment, but there may well be an explanation."

Mike's companion was a stocky Anglo in his forties, with an abrupt manner and butch haircut reminiscent of a Marine drill sergeant. It became clear to Sara within the first few minutes that he was no friend of Doug's. Her irritation grew to anger as the tenor of his questions became evident.

"When was your last contact with your son? Has he been under any unusual stress? Has he expressed financial difficulties? Has your son ever abused alcohol or drugs? Has he demonstrated any sudden increase of income? Does your son have a significant other to whom he might have turned if he were in trouble?"

Cynthia was growing more agitated with each question. "What are you trying to say?" she burst out finally. "That my son disappeared on purpose? That he took a drug payoff or something and ran off with it?"

Cynthia's voice rose higher, her tone stiletto sharp. "Look, my son has given his life to work for you people. He puts in terrible hours, risks getting shot every day, and he won't quit because he feels it's his duty, no matter what I say. And you're going to sit there and insinuate he's doing something illegal?"

She was on her feet now, tears running down her face. "Get out of my house—now!"

Jumping up, Sara put her arms around Doug's mother. She glared from the stocky interrogator to Mike Garcia. "Mike, you at least know Doug. You're his friend. You know better than this."

The young agent looked even more uncomfortable as he hauled his lanky frame off the sofa. "I'm sorry, Sara, but we have to do this. It's procedure, and I can't let personal acquaintance get in the way. You know that."

"Fine!" Sara snapped back. "If you need to grill someone, grill me. I've been interrogated by experts. I'll answer any questions you have."

"Oh, we'll be talking to you," the stocky interrogator said smoothly. "What exactly is your connection to the missing agent, Ms. . . . Connor or Cortéz?"

It was a return to those final days in Bolivia: the suspicious, hard faces;

answering the same questions over and over; the skepticism and deadpan expressions that never told Sara if she was believed or not. Sara soon lost count of the number of agents, police investigators, and others who had questions about what she knew of Doug's trip to Paraguay, what he'd said to her about Julio Vargas, and what her relationship was to Doug's investigation. She left out only those glimmers of a more personal relationship that had surfaced in those last encounters. At least they'd soon lost interest in questioning Cynthia.

When the questions finally wound down and Sara stood up to stretch, Cynthia's hand had shot out to detain her. "Please, Sara. Don't go. I . . . I hate to ask it of you, but I need someone who . . . who cares about Doug as much as I do."

Sara put her arms around Doug's mother again. "Of course, I'll stay. Just let me pick up my car and a change of clothes."

Sara didn't leave Cynthia's side for the rest of the weekend, calling in sick for her Friday classes. Cynthia canceled her own projects, as well, spending her time pacing or furiously pedaling the stationary bike when no one was there asking questions. On the second day, Cynthia lit up her first cigarette in months, and though Sara detested the smell, she bit back any comments.

That night, Ramon finally called.

"No, I don't have anything." He immediately punctured Sara's first rush of hope. "I'm sorry I haven't called before now. It's taken some time to track things down here. To be honest, your ASAC up there, Kublin, didn't want me talking to you at all. But I figure you've got a right to know what's going down if anyone does."

Sara's hand was damp on the receiver as she listened. "I finally tracked down Ciudad del Este. The SAC there confirms that Doug came back through town on Monday. He told them he'd hit a dead end and was leaving town. He even went by the office to return some equipment. They sent someone out to check the hotels. They found where he'd stayed and confirmed that he checked out Monday afternoon. American Airlines confirmed that he picked up a reserved ticket and boarded the flight. I'm sorry, Sara. I still don't know why he didn't call . . . maybe he was just running late. But that's the end of the trail down here. And from what Kublin tells me, it's pretty clear he made it as far as Miami at least."

Ramon's voice turned somber. "Sara, I've never been much of a praying man—not the way Doug is. But I'm doing some praying now."

Sara swallowed. "Yes, so am I."

"Hey, he'll turn up." Sara tried to take comfort in the confidence Ramon infused into his voice. "He always does. That dude's one tough hombre."

He'll turn up. He had an accident. He's in a hospital somewhere, unconscious, and his ID was lost so they couldn't contact his next of kin. He got mugged and left in the Everglades to walk out. He had to go undercover with the Colombians and it's been too dangerous to try to call.

He'll turn up.

Sara's assurances to herself—and Cynthia—grew less convincing with each passing day. She had to badger the DO to get any information about the progress of their investigation. After a third callback in one afternoon, Peggy Browning finally came on the line to give Sara a brusque summary.

The neighbors had confirmed seeing Doug return from his trip on Tuesday morning. One woman confirmed seeing him drive away in his car. The apartment had yielded only three sets of fingerprints besides Mike's and Norm Kublin's—Doug's, Cynthia's, and Sara's. Which at least ended any further insinuations of a "significant other."

As to the Colombian informant Doug had set out to meet, the GS hadn't yet narrowed down which case Doug had been referring to. And though Mike and the other agents shook down every informant they knew Doug had dealt with, none admitted to an appointment with Doug or so much as a whisper anywhere in Miami's underworld of a gringo agent gone missing.

On Monday, Sara had no choice but to return to class. Even if she were willing to jeopardize her job by further absence, it wasn't fair at this late date to pass the students off to yet another new teacher. Besides, there was something comforting in the small, eager bodies and bright faces crowding around her. Here, at least, Sara was in control, and her young students still believed that Teacher could make any problem go away.

Sara was dismissing class for the day when her cell phone rang. "They're coming over, Sara." Cynthia's tone was brittle with tension. "They say they have news. Please, come as quickly as you can."

If it was good news, they'd have said so, just as they'd been quick to reassure Cynthia and Sara on the horrible day of the shooting. That they insisted on delivering the news in person tightened Sara's chest and stomach so that she had to force air in and out of her lungs as she drove. A glance in the mirror as she pulled up in front of Cynthia's showed a face so pale that her lips were bloodless and dry.

A number of cars were in Cynthia's driveway and on the lawn. Two green-

and-white Miami-Dade police cruisers, Mike Garcia's red Firebird, and Norm Kublin's Chrysler. All hope that she'd misread Cynthia's call faded when she saw Norm Kublin's and Mike Garcia's grim faces among the daunting male horde crowded into Cynthia's living room.

"Sara!" The pain in Cynthia's tone drew Sara straight across the room. She threw an arm around Doug's mother and guided her to the nearest sofa. All the while a roaring sound filled Sara's ears as she looked from the tears spilling down Cynthia's face to the somber group of agents and uniformed police officers.

"Sara, I've just been informing Cynthia of some new developments," Norm Kublin said. Sara had never heard his gruff voice so gentle, and it tightened her chest even more. *No, don't say it. I don't want to hear it. If it isn't said, it hasn't happened.*

Then, because she could keep it in no longer, Sara burst out, "You found him, didn't you?"

The GS shook his head. "No, but we found his car . . . at a Home Depot up near the airport. After seeing it there for several days without ever moving, the security guard finally reported it as suspicious. When the license plate turned up on our missing persons watch, the local precinct called us. The security guard says he first saw the car there last Tuesday."

"How can he be so sure?" Sara got out shakily.

"When all you do is watch cars all day, you get to know them like—well, like a teacher knows her students. If the security guard says it was there Tuesday, I'm betting my pension he's right. And there's more."

This time it was Kublin's broad chest that rose and fell in a tight breath. "We found Doug's cell phone along with his wallet and keys. They turned up at the landfill. We've continued to call his number, and when one of the sanitation workers heard it ringing in the garbage, he dug it out. The reason we found the items all together was because they'd been wrapped up in a shirt. One of Doug's shirts."

The GS hesitated before going on, and when he continued, Sara heard genuine pain in his voice. "Cynthia . . . Sara, I'm sorry to have to tell you this, but the shirt had considerable bloodstains on it. We've got further testing to do, but a preliminary analysis indicates the blood was Doug's."

"No . . . no!" As Cynthia's voice rose, Sara placed her hand on the older woman's. It was as icy as her own. When Cynthia subsided, sobbing, against Sara's shoulder, Sara said as steadily as she could manage, "Just . . . just tell us straight out what you're saying."

"There's no easy way to say this." The other faces whirling around Sara's line of vision showed the practiced stolidity of men accustomed to delivering bad news, but Mike's face reflected the pain in Norm Kublin's gruff tones. This was no easier for these friends and colleagues of Doug's than for the women who loved him. "Something has gone badly wrong, of that we have no doubt. A meet gone sour. A setup. We don't know. Maybe he got too close to something big. We will not stop this investigation until we've found out what happened. But we have to face the strong possibility that Doug may be—gone. The only other possibility is that he junked everything, dumped his own ID in the garbage, and skipped town."

"You don't believe that!" Sara cut in sharply.

"No, I don't," Norm Kublin answered soberly. "And not just because of the other evidence. Doug Bradford was a good man, one of the best."

Sara flinched at the past tense. Norm Kublin caught her reaction. "Hey, there's always hope. Don't give up yet."

He avoided the two women's eyes as he stood up to leave. Sara, searching his granite expression, saw no evidence he believed what he'd just said.

Numbness carried Sara through the next weeks of school, a smile pasted to her lips that evaporated the instant she shut her car door every afternoon. She called the DO daily for developments on the investigation, but the news was never good. The DNA analysis confirmed that the bloodstains were Doug's. They'd gone over his car with a fine-toothed comb, lifting dozens of prints. Some matched informants on record as having been in the car. Others could not be traced. They interviewed a Colombian trafficker who'd been among the identified prints. There was hope he might have information, though early interviews had not been promising.

When she couldn't stand it any longer, she drove down to the DEA offices and asked to speak to Norm Kublin. She was ushered, if somewhat grudgingly, into his office.

"Isn't it possible this Colombian just kidnapped him?" Sara cried after the GS had closed the door and perched on the corner of his desk. "Maybe . . . maybe he's just lying tied up somewhere, waiting for you to come and rescue him."

"I wish I could believe that," Norm Kublin answered. "But you kidnap for ransom or information—or political advantage. And there has been no attempt at ransom or political demands. As for information, it is calling down the wrath of God to nab a DEA agent on his own turf. We would—*will*—hunt the perps to the ends of the earth, and the narcos know that. They couldn't hope to keep it a secret forever in this town—someone somewhere always talks, and we have the underworld hotline thoroughly penetrated. There is simply no info that Doug would've had that would be worth the risk to a trafficker. And if they'd kidnapped a federal agent, they wouldn't keep him alive once they had what they wanted. After all, they couldn't ever turn him loose. No, this smells like a setup or a meet gone bad, a trafficker panicking and trying to hide the evidence—that fits the pieces we have here. But I cannot in good conscience hold out any hope that he has been kidnapped."

As if he suddenly realized he was talking to a grieving family member, not another agent, Kublin rose abruptly to his feet and excused himself. Sara kept her eyes wide open to keep the tears from spilling out until he was gone. *I will not think!* she told herself fiercely. She would not allow the terrible images conjured up by the ASAC's blunt admissions invade her mind. So long as they were still searching, as long as she was still in contact with Doug's coworkers, she could convince herself that Doug was only on TDY, overdue on a mission. He'd be back—somehow.

Ramon called once. "I heard about the results of the investigation, Sara. I can't tell you how sorry I am . . . and sick and angry. Doug was the best—and my friend." His voice then turned so cold Sara that had a sudden, chilling glimpse of what it would be like to be a lawbreaker staring down that icy resolution. "Whatever happens, Sara, I want you to know they won't get away with it. No one takes out an agent and walks away—not if it takes years to track them down."

Unlike Norm Kublin and Mike Garcia, Ramon made no attempt to offer hope. As days, then weeks passed, there were fewer developments to report. Finally, one afternoon, Peggy Browning told Sara curtly that if anything further developed, they'd be the ones to call her.

Sara was still staying with Cynthia. Doug's mother had begged her not to leave her alone, and Sara's assent had come easily enough. She couldn't bear to be in her own apartment right now anyway, parrying the questions and sympathies of her roommate and friends. It was bad enough that she ran into them at school every day. Larry Thomas, most of all.

He met Sara on the front steps when she arrived in the morning, squeezing her hand sympathetically, asking what new information she had on Doug. If his kindness and the concern in his brown eyes were less genuine, it would have been easier to shrug him away. She was aware of his silent sympathy—

and his stronger feelings—every time she saw him. Finally, she began avoiding the teacher's lounge and using a side entrance in the morning. Handling one more person's emotions was more than she could deal with right now.

One day, when all her resolve couldn't keep the pain and worry battened down any longer, Larry found her sitting behind her desk in her empty classroom, her body rigid with the effort to hold back tears.

As he threw a sympathetic arm around her shoulder, she let herself be drawn back against him. It did feel good to rest against a solid chest, to feel strong arms holding her, to know someone cared and that for this moment at least she didn't have to smile and be strong. Relaxing, Sara let the tears spill over and down her face.

"Sara, I'm so sorry," Larry said huskily into her hair. "Doug was a man I respected, and I know how much you cared for him." As her tears came harder, his voice grew rougher, his arms tighter. "He had no business doing this to you. You take a job like that, you take a risk of this happening. But you have no business leaving people behind to break their hearts over you."

At that Sara sat up and disengaged herself. "I'm sorry, Larry, but I can't agree with you. Doug did what he had to, what he was called to do. And I—I knew what he was before I . . . I ever cared for him."

Larry let her go, but there was pain in his brown eyes as he looked down at her. "I know. I didn't mean . . ."

He stopped, his Adam's apple bobbing convulsively. "Just remember I'll always be here if you need me." His mouth twisted ruefully. "Since I'm not the type to ever put myself in harm's way."

Sara forced a smile. "You've been a good friend, Larry. And I won't forget you're there if I need you."

"A friend." Straightening abruptly, Larry walked out of her classroom.

At home, Cynthia made no attempt to downplay her bitterness and rage, and there were times when Sara felt she couldn't stand another hour of the furious pedaling and chain-smoking.

"They know he's dead," Cynthia told Sara passionately. "Why don't they just say it so we can start picking up the pieces and get on with this rotten life? Oh, sure, they've got to cover their rears before they come out in the open, but they gave up a long time ago."

Her fury broke down into bitter tears. "I've known this was going to happen for years. I've braced myself for it. I did all I could to get my son away from these people. And now—what do I have left?"

It was a heart cry that Sara knew all too well. If she could only give Cynthia the comfort she herself had found.

"Though the fig tree does not bud, and there are no grapes on the vines, though the olive crop fails and the fields produce not food . . . yet I will rejoice in the Lord, I will be joyful in God my Savior."

But when Sara haltingly tried to share her own experience with Cynthia, the older woman rounded on her angrily. "Don't give me that rubbish. Don't I get enough of that at church? Where was God when someone hurt my son and cut him and spilled his blood? I'm not interested in rejoicing in the middle of a war zone. I just want my son alive and breathing, with arms I can feel around me and a voice I can hear saying, 'I love you, Mom,' even when I've been mean and nasty and unreasonable. . . . Oh, you don't have to say anything, Sara. I know what I can be!"

Sara had no reply. How could she when all she wanted were the same things? Doug's strong arms holding her close. His deep voice with that intimate note that was only for her. Those gray eyes blazing.

No, I won't think! Oh, God, where are you? I can't bear it!

It had now been seven weeks since Doug's disappearance, ten since the restaurant dinner that had provided the last precious memories for Sara to play over and over again in her mind. It was now the last week of school. She had an end-of-the-year party on Wednesday, followed by packing up her classroom on Thursday and Friday.

Sara didn't want to think about how she was going to occupy her hands and mind when school was finished. The rainy season was overdue in South Florida, and to Sara it was only fitting to walk outside and see parched lawns, shriveled flower beds, and drooping, brown fronds on the palms. The thirsty, desiccated landscape mirrored her own heart.

Chapter Fifty-three

JUNE 12

After loading the last box of her classroom supplies into the trunk of the Neon, Sara drove over to Cynthia's. Her sensors went on alert when she found Doug's mother sitting at the kitchen table, looking composed but drawn, with a cigarette burning between her fingers.

"Cynthia, hi. Is everything okay?" She was totally taken off guard by what came next.

"Sara, I've been talking to Doug's office," Cynthia started right in, her voice brittle with control. "They . . . *we* feel it's time we planned a memorial service for Doug."

Sara's carefully erected defenses finally crashed in on her. It was as if a wound still numb from impact had suddenly been laid open to the air, and the pain of it lanced through her like a knife. She dropped her purse and car keys on the table as the emotion boiled over the top.

"No! No, you can't do that!" Her own vehemence took her by surprise.

Cynthia leapt to her feet and enveloped Sara in a fierce hug, the cigarette crumbling to ash behind her back. "I know, Sara. I know how you feel. I loved him too. But we can't keep our lives on hold forever. We have to go on. And Doug deserves to be remembered and honored."

"But they haven't even found him yet," Sara cried.

"They may never find anything." Cynthia's control cracked for a moment, and Sara saw the older woman's anguish before her proud carriage stiffened. "It's been seven weeks. If they haven't found anything by now, it's because there's nothing to find. We—"

Her voice broke, then steadied. "I want his body, if I can't have my son. I want a real funeral. I want to know what happened to him, how he died, who was responsible. But I've been around long enough to learn that life doesn't always give you what you want. And I'm not letting my son slip forgotten out of everyone's mind while they all go on with their lives. At least he deserves a memorial service in his own church with his friends and family and to be honored for his service to his country."

Sara found she couldn't breathe. "Cynthia, I—I'm sorry, but I have to get out of here." She snatched up her purse and keys and headed blindly out the door.

"Sara, wait!" Cynthia called from the doorway as Sara fumbled her way into her car. Ignoring the plea, Sara gunned the Neon down the street.

Where do you go to be alone and cry to heaven in this vast city where every park holds staring eyes and every beach is cramped with humanity?

Sara turned south. There was one place she knew would be empty on a mid-June day like today. She pushed all thoughts to the margins and kept her mind focus on the flow of rush hour traffic until she saw the sign announcing "You are now entering Everglades National Park" and turned off the road.

Slowing impatiently at the entrance for a park pass and tourist map, Sara drove only a short distance into the park before turning off onto one of the less-traveled scenic trails. Except for the Neon, the parking lot was empty. Sara started down the boardwalk, slapping at mosquitoes as she went. The mosquitoes were the reason that tourists avoided the Everglades during this season, and if it hadn't been for the unusually dry weather, they'd have been unbearable. As it was, they were enough of a nuisance that by the time she reached the observation platform at the end of the boardwalk, she was wishing she'd thought of repellent in her hasty departure.

Posted signs warned of possible flooding, and though the drought had kept the water table too low for that, the swamp still spread out below the observation platform, its surface rife with algae and choked with mangroves whose exposed roots formed a tangled web through which the murky water glinted gold in the fading evening light.

The last time Sara had come here, it was with Doug. Then, as now, the dank, warm humidity, the whine of mosquitoes, and the impenetrable swampy tangle of vegetation reminded her starkly of the South American jungle. The green canopy of mangroves, stretching as far as she could see, took her back to a jungle hilltop where she'd fallen flat in the dust and faced the loss of all she'd counted dear in life. With Nicolás Cortéz, she had grieved for the loss of her illusions and her faith in a man who had never really existed; for the loss of her dream of a future and a family.

This was different—and far worse. Doug was no illusion, not like the pasteboard Prince Charming she'd once imagined Nicky to be. Along with his integrity and gentleness and the deep faith that had roused Sara to respect and then longing, Doug could be brusque and impatient and brutally caustic, not to mention altogether too bossy and overly protective.

He was real. So real that as Sara closed her eyes against the deepening twilight, it seemed that if she only wished hard enough, she'd hear his quick step behind her, smell the muted cologne he wore when he wasn't heading for a stakeout, feel his arms around her, his hands in her hair, her head against his chest.

Oh, Doug!

The longing opened Sara's eyes—to an empty platform. She'd stood there long enough that the sun had dropped below the tossing sea of mangroves, the last streaks of pink above the Everglades fading to green, the swamp water below now black. A mosquito settled on her arm, and when she didn't move, it dipped its nose until Sara finally swatted it away. Soon the park rangers would be coming around, making sure that day visitors like Sara were headed out of the park. But Sara couldn't bring herself to leave.

Here in this simulation of the jungle where she had first come to know Special Agent Doug Bradford, she could still push away the reality that his coworkers and friends had accepted weeks ago, the sorry truth to which even Doug's mother had now been willing to face up.

He's gone. Doug is dead. I will never see him again. He will never tell me that he loves me, never ask me to be his wife.

"No! No!"

The answering scream of a heron startled Sara into silence, and she let her head drop forward until it rested on the wooden rail of the platform. It was very dark now, far away from any reflection of urban lights. From somewhere nearby Sara heard the flapping of a large bird, perhaps the heron winging down to roost for the night.

> He will cover you with his feathers and under his wings you will find refuge. . . . He shall give his angels concerning you to guard you in all your ways; they will lift you up in their hands so that you will not strike your foot against a stone.

"Where were your wings, God?" Sara demanded of the empty swamp. "Where were your angels when someone spilled Doug's blood on that shirt? How could you stand by and watch them hurt a man who loved you and followed you with all his heart?"

The pain was overwhelming, and sobs shook Sara's body until she could not tell whether the cries of anguish were the startled screams of the heron or coming from her own raw throat. *Oh, God, where were you when the man I loved died in pain without so much as a friend at his side?*

The heron rose angrily and flapped away for a quieter roosting spot. Then as sheer exhaustion began to overcome her, in her anguish Sara felt a touch she'd known before on a jungle hilltop half a world away. Not a physical touch, but a still, quiet Presence pouring over her soul with such love that she could only cry out again.

Where was I? How could I? I let my own Son walk out of the wilderness to pain and suffering and betrayal and death. My angels stood by in their legions at the cross, helpless to intervene, while I watched my Son die—for you. And when they lifted him in their hands, it was to bring him home—to me. My ways are not your ways, nor my understanding yours, but know that I have loved you and I have loved Doug with an everlasting love, and neither of you will ever be alone.

The tears came again, hard and fast, but this time they were the beginning of healing. *Oh, God, I know if Doug's gone, he's with you. And whatever terrible things happened out there, you never left him alone. You were with him as you've been with me. I know your ways aren't mine, and maybe someday I'll understand what purpose you had in letting this happen.*

But, oh God, right now I just miss him so much!

And yet, though allowing herself to love someone had once again brought intolerable pain and loss, Sara could not regret having known—and loved—Special Agent Douglas Bradford, DEA. His perspective, his steadying influence, had brought a richness into her life, made her a better, more complete person. In the beginning, had Sara known how it would all end, she might have walked away from those first tentative stirrings of emotion. But now she would not trade a moment of Doug's presence in her life, however brief it had turned out to be.

> He who dwells in the shelter of the Most High will rest in the shadow of the Almighty. I will say of the Lord, "He is my refuge and my fortress, my God in whom I trust."

The words of the Psalm shifted to the refrain that had sustained Sara all these months, and she recited the familiar words aloud to the dank mangrove swamp and the black sky above with its emerging stars and the Presence whose shadowing wings spread wide above it all.

> Though the fig tree does not bud, and there are no grapes on the vines, though the olive crop fails and the fields produce not food, though there are no sheep in the pen and no cattle in the stalls, yet I will rejoice in the Lord, I will be joyful in God my Savior.

This time Sara went on to the end.

> The sovereign Lord is my strength; He makes my feet like the feet of a deer, He enables me to go on the heights.

The strength and resilience of a deer. Already, Sara could sense a change, a peace that began to infuse her heart, working the pain and the loss—not out to the corners where she might have pushed it, but into the fabric, where it would always be a part of who she was. Eventually, her tears would dry and she would go back to the world, chin lifted high, and be strong, as everyone expected. And if she now felt that her heart would never mend, she knew by experience, it wouldn't always feel this way. A day would inevitably come when she'd find life worth a smile again. Maybe life would even hold love again. But if not, it didn't matter; because, however brief, she'd known love as deeply as any woman had.

I will not forget again, Father God. I have been loved. I am loved now. And if I am still hurting inside, I choose to believe you hold my future in the palm of your hands.

And yet, even as Sara bowed her head in surrender, she was still reluctant to accept the reality of Doug's death. Even as her heart quieted to peace, her mind stubbornly rejected the idea that Doug's indomitable personality had been erased from the earth, that she'd never again in this lifetime see his lithe, broad-shouldered frame striding toward her, the quick lift of his head and narrowed alertness of his eyes. *Why can't I just let him go?*

Sara straightened up from the rail so suddenly that the heron, from whatever new resting place it had chosen, flapped and fluttered and screamed again.

"Because he isn't dead!"

The statement was so stunning that Sara couldn't believe she'd voiced it aloud. *Are you crazy?* Certainly the law enforcement agencies investigating Doug's disappearance would say so. They'd gone over the case with a fine-toothed comb, piling up brick after brick of evidence into an incontrovertible wall of conclusion.

And yet, they haven't found a witness—or a body. Sara flinched at the image, then forced her mind to consider the facts as they were known. If no trace of Doug's whereabouts had surfaced in all these weeks of searching and shaking down every underworld contact, neither had a single rumor of the disappearance and death of a federal counternarcotics agent. Not even a whisper.

Yes, there was the seemingly indisputable evidence of Doug's return to his apartment, the abandoned car, the bloodstained belongings. *But is there any other possible way that those same puzzle pieces would fit?*

One by one, Sara examined the strands of evidence by which the case for Doug's death had been woven together. All of them rested on one assumption—that Doug had boarded a plane in Ciudad del Este and arrived Tuesday morning at his apartment.

All the evidence certainly pointed that way. But just as certain, in Sara's mind, was a piece of evidence that no one else seemed to care about: *Doug had promised to call.* She remained unshakably convinced that he'd have kept that promise if at all possible—if not, by some unavoidable circumstance, before he left Paraguay, then certainly before he would leave the apartment to chase down an informant whose message he'd just received.

And the "dead end" that Doug had supposedly come to—which both the Miami and Paraguay field offices had mentioned—how was that possible? He had tracked Julio Vargas to Ciudad del Este. He'd called Sara to say he was hot on the fugitive's trail. Even if he'd returned to town empty-handed, his trip to Paraguay was anything but a dead end. If one tip didn't pay out, Doug would not throw up his hands and quit. He'd simply shift to a different approach and keep on digging.

That was what had nagged at Sara all these weeks, had kept her numb and disbelieving when everyone else seemed perfectly willing to accept the fact of Doug's death. *I don't believe it was Doug who told the office it was a dead end or who wrote that note or who sneezed and coughed on the phone.*

But if not Doug, then who? And where was Doug? What terrible things had been done to him to result in that bloodstained shirt?

More urgently, if someone had tried to make it look as if Doug had returned to Miami, that was seven weeks ago.

What reason or hope do I have that he'd be kept alive until now?

No, she would not allow herself to dwell on what she could do nothing about. But for the rest—

If he's alive, I will not rest until I find him. If I have to go to the ends of the earth myself, I'll do it. If he's dead, I won't stop until I find out what happened to him—and God help those who've hurt him, because I won't rest until they pay for it. Either way, I'm done waiting. It's time for some action. And Cynthia can just forget about a memorial service, at least if she wants me there, because until I see his body in front of me with my own eyes, I will not believe he's dead.

Newfound purpose banished her exhaustion and her grief. Straightening her slim frame, she left the observation platform and threaded her way back down the boardwalk, a hand on the railing to guide her through the black night. Her feet had just adapted to the asphalt of the parking lot when a beam of light stabbed at her night-adjusted vision.

"Lady, what in tarnation are you doing out here at this time of night?"

The beam bobbed on Sara's face, and what the park ranger saw there, Sara couldn't be sure, but the beam dropped and the interrogation gentled.

"You okay, lady?"

Sara nodded, then remembered to speak aloud. "I'm fine. I . . . I'm sorry. I just lost track of time."

"Well, we'll let it go this time, but you need to head out of the park. There's no camping in here after dark. If you'll get into your car, I'll follow just to be sure you're on the right road."

How's that for diplomacy!

Obediently, Sara climbed into her car and drove back out to the main road. In her rearview mirror, she could see the ranger's flashing signal a discreet distance behind her. She found the intermittent flashes somehow comforting, like a night-light accompanying her through the darkness. Driving steadily toward the park entrance, she began mentally formulating her first plan in weeks.

The flashing light blinked out behind Sara as the ranger, satisfied that she was obeying orders, turned off onto another road. A sudden pang of doubt struck Sara as she found herself alone again on the long, black ribbon of road.

Am I just deceiving myself to think that Doug could still be alive? Is it arrogance, or some other elaborate form of denial, to insist that I could be right and everyone else is wrong?

As the lights of Miami's sprawling skyline illumined the night sky ahead with a yellow haze, Sara shook off her misgivings. *I don't care. Whether he's dead or alive, I have to know. And I won't stop looking until I do.*

Chapter Fifty-four

JUNE 12
IGUAZÚ RAIN FOREST

The prisoner wasn't sure whether he was dead or alive until the blackness into which he'd retreated began to lift and the aches and pains that racked his battered body resurfaced. This last session had been particularly brutal, and a sharp pain in his left side warned of at least one more broken rib.

As the shadows of oblivion continued to lift until he could no longer escape into them, Doug rolled over with a groan. The effort landed him in an icy patch of mud. Beyond his view, he could hear the steady dripping of rainwater through the broken tiles of the roof. Shivering as the dampness seeped through his clothing, he managed to slide a muddy hand under his shirt to probe his rib cage, now thrust sharply enough against the skin for him to trace the bones underneath. Though painful, there were no jagged edges he could feel. With any luck, this one was just cracked, not broken.

With his hand pressed to his side, Doug inched backward from the mud puddle until he felt the solid bulk of an adobe wall behind him. Inch by agonizing inch, he used the support of the wall to push himself to a sitting position. Across the cell, the guard had been alerted by the movement, and as Doug wearily lifted his head, he found the man's eyes on him, glittering black in the blue-white glow of the Coleman lamp hanging from the door frame.

The cell was the same small, dank room in which Doug had been imprisoned since the first protracted interrogation session. The guard might have been the same one too. In the beginning, through the haze of exhaustion and pain, all these young men with their fit, lean bodies and fanatic eyes had looked the same, crouched down on their haunches just inside the door, an M-16 resting across their thighs, narrowed gaze never leaving Doug for an instant. But over the weeks, he had learned to distinguish their features and even measure time by their shift changes. When he was conscious, anyway. He had to concede there might be some gaps. The rotation had also given Doug a good estimate of how many men were in the camp. Several dozen, at least.

This time, Doug had been unconscious longer than usual, because his last memory was of the dappled, green luminosity of morning sunlight filtering through the jungle canopy and into the open door of his cell. That opening was black with night now. He shifted his position, trying to find a place of relative comfort—or less discomfort. The adobe bricks of the wall were cold against his back, their chill permeating the muddy rainwater soaking through his clothes so that he began to shake in earnest. The deep breath he drew to control his tremors served only to place further strain on the cracked rib under his palm.

At least they hadn't bothered to tie his hands and feet this time while he was unconscious. During his first weeks of captivity, they hadn't been so careless, twisting his hands brutally behind him and lashing them to his bound ankles so tightly that were it not for the occasional reprieve for meals and using the latrine, Doug would have lost the use of his extremities.

He had no idea what Julio Vargas had told his young accomplices, but he must have convinced them that Doug was a very dangerous man, because even when he was bound hand and foot, they kept a safe distance. One guard always hunkered down just inside the rotted door frame, and another sat outside for backup.

But after the last three sessions, Doug had regained consciousness to find himself blessedly free of bonds. Even without a mirror, it wasn't difficult to understand why. The gauntness of his frame, the stark thrust of cheek and jaw bones under the skin, which even the overgrown beard and hair couldn't hide, the fever-dulled eyes, and the painful slowness of every movement, hardly projected a menacing image.

Whether this relative freedom resulted from indolence or latent compassion on the part of his captors, Doug didn't care. It was enough that he could move himself out of the quagmire. He slumped forward, pressing a wadded cloth against his mouth, as another deep, rattling breath brought on a paroxysm of coughing that not even the stabbing pain of his cracked ribs could stop. He wrenched and writhed until he was sprawled again in a daze of exhaustion. His "handkerchief," a length of gauze left behind from one of his injuries, was as filthy and bloodstained as his clothing.

It could be worse, Doug realized, even through the pain. The ribs they had broken in that first interrogation, whose calcified joining Doug could still feel under his fingers, had taken more than a month to heal. This pain would be gone within a week, assuming the cracked rib was allowed to heal without further stress.

Doug had become intimately acquainted with his body's rate of healing. Cigarette burns scabbed over within days. The bruises never left long enough for him to determine whether they were fresh or healing, but lacerations would knit together in a week or so if they were not broken open again. The electric cattle prod, however, was another story. Though it left few outward signs, it was excruciatingly painful, especially given that Vargas was expert at finding those nerve endings that delivered the most pain signals to the brain.

Vargas's personal favorite, forcing fizzy mineral water laced with hot pepper oil up the nasal cavities, was actually losing its effectiveness. It had been done so often that Doug could just close his eyes and visualize biting into a *jalapeño*—a food he planned to boycott permanently if he ever made it out of here.

The worst of it was that these petty, stupid tortures were totally unnecessary. Doug was not some World War II intelligence agent with plans for the Normandy invasion in his head. Unlike Special Ops trainees, DEA agents were not given SERE training—the Survival, Evasion, Resistance, and Escape course designed to prepare Special Forces for the risk of becoming prisoners of war—because DEA agents didn't expect to be dropped behind enemy lines with vital information. The rule of thumb in a situation like this was simple—spill your guts! The agency did not ask the impossible of its operatives. They knew that anyone could be made to talk with enough time, brutality, and drugs. If an agent was captured, they assumed the knowledge he possessed was compromised. They would immediately pull out their assets and go on to a new case. There were always plenty of sleazeballs to nab.

Doug had done precisely what was expected of him. He'd spilled his guts with no illusion of exceptional courage. The information he divulged—investigative techniques, details of training, use of informants, mission planning—might be of use to a drug dealer. But it was also out there in the public domain, as writers from Tom Clancy on down had found easily enough. Julio had spent a number of sessions demanding details of the Cortéz op. Doug had kept nothing back. There'd been no big secret, just standard police investigation. The reports were sitting in triplicate in any number of Bolivian government offices, which again meant they were in the public domain for anyone willing to pay for them.

But Julio Vargas didn't care. Whether he really thought Doug was holding something back, or he simply delighted in causing pain, he would escalate the brutality of his interrogation techniques until Doug finally lost consciousness.

The same went for Julio's torture trainees, no matter what answer Doug gave. The young man that Julio called Sebastian, but whom Doug had identified as Saleh Jebai, was the worst. While his subordinates worked Doug over, he would watch, arms folded across his chest, with the clinical interest of a doctor observing medical interns.

It was this clinical, almost classroom, detachment that baffled Doug when he wasn't too wracked with pain to think about it. Just who were these people, and what was going on here?

Though Vargas had refused to confirm it, Doug was convinced that this bunch was responsible for those Bolivian raids. The selected targets. The simultaneous precision strikes, suggesting a fair-sized company of elite soldiers. The sophisticated battle gear Doug had seen before his capture. The pieces fit together too well for coincidence.

The more pressing question was why? What was in this for Julio Vargas? Just settling old accounts? Blowing up the DEA office would fall into that category. But Vargas was not just a hothead. He was a mercenary whose first priority was monetary, regardless of his lust for revenge. The sheer cost of training and supplying such an assault force just to wipe out a few old rivals and discredit the DEA—it just didn't compute. Besides, where would the guy get that kind of money? When Vargas was shipped off to Palmasola, Doug had made it top priority to strip him of every asset he owned.

If this were a novel or a movie, someone would conveniently let slip what they were up to. Then Doug would use his superior training and some overlooked high-tech gadgetry to escape and tip off the authorities. Real life was not so simple. In real life, it wasn't that hard to hold someone prisoner, especially when one had a considerable numerical advantage. That was why countless prisoners of war and other hostages were held captive—often for years—without ever escaping. Like it or not, even a trained and experienced agent like Doug was not likely to outwit his captors.

The reality was that these guys were far more experienced at capturing and breaking prisoners, in the infliction of pain and sheer brutality, than any Westerner from a democratic society could begin to fathom. Just ask the thousands of *desaparecidos,* or "disappeared" citizens, who had vanished into Latin American interrogation cells.

Doug's living conditions were as much a part of the breaking process as the torture itself, and Doug had no doubt that every discomfort was deliberate. There was nothing in the room but the dirt floor, crumbling mud-brick walls, leaky roof, and occasional animal life. Cockroaches. Spiders. Geckos crawling down the walls and scampering along the rafters. Nothing from which even MacGyver could fashion a means of escape.

Of more consequence, Doug hadn't been given a blanket, much less a sleeping mat or hammock. Though the abandoned mission was nestled in the middle of a tropical rain forest, it was well south of the equator. And though April had been relatively warm, as the weeks passed into May and June, the *sur,* or south wind, began blowing off the winter snow pack of the southern Andes. It never quite froze, but temperatures could drop thirty degrees Fahrenheit in twenty-four hours. Even when the sun broke through the jungle canopy, the thick adobe walls held the chill for days.

With his clothes now tattered and filthy with dried blood and mud, Doug was never warm. The problem was compounded when rainwater ran down the walls and flooded the floor. The perpetual dampness accelerated the growth of mildew until even Doug's clothing and boots were covered with a moldering green dust.

At first, hunger had been as much a torment as the cold and mildew. The camp ate well, judging by the tantalizing odors that drifted through the doorway. But Doug's rations, morning and night, were always the same—a miniscule blob of boiled cornmeal with a nauseating hint of meat gone bad and an occasional scrap of bone. From his years in Bolivia, Doug had a strong suspicion he was receiving the leftovers of what was cooked up for the German shepherd he'd seen when he arrived.

The water he was given to wash down the swill was just as meager, and Doug had to restrain the impulse to bury his face in the dirty rainwater trickling down the walls. All he needed on top of everything else was dysentery.

The craving for water never abated, but the weeks of physical abuse and poor diet had dulled his appetite until only by strength of his will was he able to force the scant nutrition down.

As for the dropped clues that any self-respecting action hero would have gathered by now, Doug had come up empty. Whoever these people were, they maintained a tight, professional discipline. Other than during the relentless interrogations, they never spoke to Doug except to bark out an order. These came in either Spanish or English, sometimes with the fluency of a native, at other times with a variety of accents.

More impressively, they didn't speak to each other in his presence, even during the long hours on guard duty at the open door. Only once, during a shift change, had a guard spoken in a language Doug could not identify. The other guard had immediately silenced him. Clearly, there were foreigners among the group, and Arabic was a logical guess, given that Jungle Tours was owned by an Arabic family—and there was no reason to assume that Saleh was the only one of his countrymen here. But in this remote jungle outpost, why should it matter what language they spoke?

Unless they're trying to hide their Arabic ties. If Doug's suspicions were correct, and this was a drug smuggling operation tied to Mozer Jebai with his well-known Hezbollah sympathies, maybe the mullah preferred to keep even the *narco* underworld from speculating as to where his drug proceeds were being funneled.

A lot of ifs.

And that still did not explain this camp. A serious training facility, if Doug had ever seen one. With the allegations of Hezbollah and Hamas activity in the Tri-Frontier, it was easy to think of an Islamic conspiracy—except for those raids on drug targets. None of that was related in any way to the war on terror.

Or maybe this was a concerted effort by the Arabic drug connections to take over the market, reminiscent of the wars in the 1980s between Colombian drug cartels, whose private armies were better equipped than Colombia's national armed forces.

As a theory, it had some support. Though the adobe walls were too thick for Doug to make out the words, the cadence of barked orders and responding shouts were just like PT back at Quantico. Doug also heard the rapid fire of automatic weapons, further evidence that his guards knew how to use the weapons they cradled so casually across their thighs.

Doug was never allowed beyond the gloomy shadows of his cell, except for interrogation and to use the hole in the ground that was his latrine. The latter was not to spare Doug any humiliation, but because Julio and Saleh—and presumably his guards—didn't want to deal with the smell inside the cell. The rankness of Doug's unwashed body must be bad enough by now, though he had grown so accustomed to it that he no longer noticed.

Those brief outings had at least allowed Doug to identify where he was being held—the farthest room of one of the abandoned wings of the compound. The interrogations themselves were conducted inside the mission's sanctuary. Even through the pain, Doug had taken note of the communications equipment and the classroom setup, the tables filled with onlookers as if the torture of an American government agent was some kind of graduate course they were taking.

But if Doug even briefly considered using those rare occasions when his bonds were loosened to make a dash for freedom, he didn't hold on to that hope for long. Any time he was outdoors, his hands were lashed behind his back and he was escorted by at least four guards. At no time was he allowed to pass anywhere near the thatched shelters where he might snatch up a weapon, even a kitchen knife. His latrine had been dug in full view of the camp, with no screening vegetation anywhere nearby.

Even if he could get away, he harbored no illusions that he'd get far. Maybe in the early days, when he'd still possessed a reasonable amount of strength. His muscled frame was healthy and inured to hardship enough to absorb considerable punishment—for a while. But the compounding effects of poor nutrition, physical discomfort, and lack of exercise were as debilitating as the physical abuse. In recent weeks, it had been all Doug could do to hold himself upright for the walk to the latrine or interrogation sessions.

The physical deprivation had lowered Doug's immune defenses until the chills that shook him were not just from the cold and dampness. Whether the tightness in his chest was just a bad flu or the result of exposure to the mildew, didn't make it easier to breathe. His cough rattled in his chest until even the guards looked uncomfortable, whether out of concern for their prisoner's well-being or their own health.

The only benefit of Doug's ill health was that it had taken the zest from the interrogation sessions. It was difficult to beat answers out of a prisoner who only coughed and wheezed in response. His trips to the old sanctuary grew further apart, and at some point, which he hadn't been conscious enough to remember, his ankles were no longer lashed to his arms, and his hands were retied in front of him so that the guards didn't have to undo them for meals. The pleasure of being able to double over when he coughed, or to curl up against the cold, were almost worth the weakness that had triggered the change.

Once, Doug had resurfaced to consciousness to find the medic bending over him. While Julio and Saleh watched, the man had given him an injection, that Doug hoped was an antibiotic, and counted out some capsules. From the medic's terse comments to Julio and Saleh, Doug had gleaned the information that the troubled, feverish delirium from which he had emerged had lasted an entire week. That was when the bonds had come off altogether, and for a few days Doug had even received some real food—hot beef broth and thick rice-and-potato soup. For whatever reason, Doug's captors were determined to keep him alive, however close to death he might fall. But the improved care didn't last long, and the winter grew steadily colder. If the bonds stayed off now, it was only because they knew how little resistance Doug could muster.

One of the paramount tools in the breaking process was taking away the captive's hope. Julio had done that with a cold malice that was as effective as it was thorough. With evident pleasure, he had detailed the steps they had taken to ensure that Doug would never be found. Until that point, Doug had held out stubbornly, gritting his teeth against the broken ribs and other injuries, unshaken in the knowledge that if he could just hang on long enough, some-one would come to bring him out. After all, the DEA field office—and Ramon— still had his coordinates. When he failed to return, a search and rescue team would come after him. But either Doug had underestimated the mercenary drug-dealer, or the plan wasn't his. Either way, even in his stunned disbelief Doug could recognize its brilliance. There would be no rescue mission. These people had erased him as thoroughly as any ex-narco Doug had enrolled in the witness protection program. To his family, friends, colleagues, he was al-ready dead.

Which meant the only way he would ever get out of this place was a miracle. And that made his prospects very dim.

I'm going to die here.

With that dawning realization, all the fight went out of Doug. All the struggle, the planning, the sifting through every detail for evidence, even when he was passing out from pain, dissipated in the jungle air.

I'm going to die here.

No matter how he reworked the equation, he couldn't make it add up to any other outcome. He couldn't get away on his own. No one was going to come for him. His captors would never release him. They'd continue their torment until his weakening body succumbed to injury or disease—or until they grew bored with their game and ended it by executing him.

I'm going to die here.

The stunned disbelief of that first admission passed through fear to cer-tainty to resignation—and then to yearning. Death itself had never held terror for Doug. He knew what lay beyond. But what purpose was there in prolong-ing the pain and discomfort, the hunger and thirst, if the end was inevitable?

As many other prisoners in impossible situations, Doug discovered the body's mechanism for dealing with despair and physical agony. He learned how to detach his mind from his body even while lying bound and immobile on a cold, hard floor. Sometimes he retreated into past happier places and times until he could truly reexperience their sights, sounds, smells, and feel. He felt again the fierce hug of small arms and saw the beaming smile of a willful little face ringed with dark curls. A long-legged, lithe figure laughed and splashed toward him through a sun-dappled surf. Outside of time, he envisioned long-lashed amber eyes and a courageously tilted chin. A man could bury his face in that long, shining curtain of silky hair. He had struggled to avoid these trips along Memory Lane. Now they were a refuge from which one could refuse to emerge while waiting for final release.

And yet there was still an obstinate corner of Doug's mind and will that would not allow him to stay in that refuge.

This is dangerous! You can't just give up! No! No matter how easy it would be to simply sink into a stupor and wait for it to be over, it went against every bit of training—and every instinct—that Doug Bradford had. To give up while breath still whistled in and out of his laboring lungs was out of the question. Somewhere, in the midst of his weakness and pain, Doug made a decision. He would hold on, and he would do whatever he could—no matter how small—to come back from the brink.

Even after his arms and ankles were no longer lashed behind him, his range of movement was limited. Illness and injury, as much as lack of exercise, had dangerously drained his strength. But there were muscle flexing routines he had learned in martial arts training. Though tedious and repetitive, they helped to pass the hours, and in time he felt some energy returning to his body.

Exercising his mind was more difficult. With nothing to read and nothing to do during the long hours of confinement, his only sensory input was the gloomy shifting of shadows on the adobe walls, the sounds of wind and rain and occasional voices, and the changing faces of the guards. Especially once his deteriorating health diminished his captors' zeal for tormenting him, long periods went by when Doug didn't leave the cell at all except to use the latrine.

One task to which he set himself was memorizing every detail of his guards—every hand gesture, tilt of eyebrow, shape of ear, scar or mole. He knew the color of their eyes, and hair. He studied each man's build until he was certain he could describe the entire contingent to a sketch artist or pick any one of them out of a photo lineup, whatever use that might ever be. He did the same with the camp itself during his brief periods outdoors, cataloging every new weapon he saw lying on a table, every evidence of training, every person he saw, including the two older Latinos who reminded him more of the paid mercenaries Vargas usually dealt with than the lean, hungry, almost frighteningly well-disciplined young soldiers who were his guards.

None of these exercises occupied more than a fraction of Doug's mental faculties. If he would not allow himself to retreat into the refuge of the past, he would have to focus his thoughts on the present and the future.

What was happening in the outside world? In Miami? At Doug's last interrogation session, Vargas had with malicious satisfaction updated Doug on their own intel reports. Namely, that the Americans had mounted no search for Doug in Ciudad del Este or its environs. Were they still searching for him along that red-herring trail that Vargas had planted? Or had they just given up? Maybe there'd even been a memorial service by now.

His mother—what must she be going through? Doug knew Cynthia as well as he loved her. She would be grieving, yes. But she would also be raging bitterly, as angry with Doug for dying as with the DEA and his presumed killers.

There were others who cared enough to grieve—colleagues, friends. Ramon and Kyle in Bolivia. Even his crusty GS, Norm Kublin, who'd be furious with himself for ever approving that "sick leave."

And Sara.

Exhausted from coughing, Doug struggled up once more against the hard support of the adobe wall, closing his eyes against the glitter of the Coleman lamp, which seemed brighter than usual, bright enough to burn at the back of his eyes.

He'd tried not to think about Sara during these last weeks. It hurt too much. He didn't want to see her face, alight with hope and longing, as he'd seen it when she'd turned back toward him before leaving the restaurant. Neither did he want to remember the joy and love he'd heard in her voice when he'd called that last time from Ciudad del Este.

It had cut deep when Sara had walked out of his hospital room—and his life. Yet she'd been right in this as she was in so much else. If she'd have stayed, she'd have lost him, just as she feared.

Doug had been the one who hadn't seen clearly. And now both of them were paying the price. He'd been so sure it was some sign from God himself when she'd walked into that restaurant and back into his life. He'd been so confident that the future stretched out ahead of the two of them . . . together.

So wrong.

And now there was another person he'd hurt.

However he might try to convince himself that their last meeting didn't mean so much, Doug knew Sara cared about him. He had heard in that "yes" on the phone that she was ready to love him. And for that, Doug felt deep, painful regret. How much better it would have been if he had never walked back in—no, forced his way back in—to Sara's life.

Or walked into her life at all.

What difference might it have made if Doug had steeled himself to say good-bye back there in Bolivia, allowed her to make a new life somewhere safe like Seattle, where it seemed she had family who could offer care and a home?

Instead, he had followed his emotions and lured her into his own unpredictable lifestyle.

He had been witness to her pain the last time she'd lost a man she loved. That Doug should be responsible for inflicting such pain and loss again was as much an anguish as any of his own bodily hurts. He could only hope she'd forget quickly—that there was a future and a hope for her somewhere ahead, beyond what he'd managed to mess up. Maybe there would be someone else, someone decent and good and stable with whom she could make a home. Someone like Larry Thomas.

No!

The turbulence of emotion shook Doug. He could no longer deceive himself. He didn't want Sara to have a future with Larry Thomas—or anyone but himself! What was he doing in this jungle hell? He should be back in Miami now, brushing that decent but boring school counselor aside and sweeping Sara into his arms. Starting their own future. Starting a family. Growing older together for as many years as God gave the two of them.

Oh, God, what have I done to the people I love? To Mom? To Sara? How could I do this to them?

That was the blunder for which Doug couldn't forgive himself. He'd walked right into this one. How had it gone so wrong? Had it been arrogance? Foolhardiness? Or just plain stupidity?

Chapter Fifty-five

There had been an interrogation, at a point when Doug was still holding to consciousness, when he'd asked for reading material to pass the time, specifically a Bible. He hadn't made the request with any real expectation, so it was a surprise when one of his tormentors immediately assented.

"After all," he'd told his companions, "Even the infidel Americans allow their unjustly held prisoners the Qur'an to read and opportunity to make their prayers. One does not stand between a man and his God, however mistaken his worship."

It was Saleh, however, who countermanded the interrogator's assent even before Julio Vargas could comment.

"No," he'd said flatly, "it is a man's faith that gives him the strength to resist. You do not feed that faith if you wish to destroy the will and resistance of your enemy. Another weakness of the Americans."

A chillingly accurate analysis.

Without a Bible, Doug had turned instead to the passages of Scripture he'd committed to memory, only now regretting that he'd never taken the time or effort to learn more. It was surprising, though, how many bits and pieces resurfaced in his memory during the long, solitary hours, and the reciting of them became another mental exercise he used to keep his sanity.

The psalms that Doug had turned to after the loss of his family, and which he had given to Sara in her time of grief, were the most familiar. Doug repeated the ones he knew over and over, clinging to them as prayers when his own words seemed hollow and unheard.

Psalm 3 . . . "O Lord, how many are my foes! How many rise up against me! Many are saying of me, 'God will not deliver him.'"

Psalm 17 . . . "Hide me in the shadow of your wings from the wicked who assail me."

Psalm 18 . . . "The Lord is my rock, my fortress and my deliverer. . . . The cords of death entangled me; the torrents of destruction overwhelmed me. . . . In my distress I called to the Lord."

Psalm 23 . . . "Even though I walk through the valley of the shadow of death, I will fear no evil, for you are with me."

One triumphant response of David seemed especially appropriate for the dank mud pit of a prison in which Doug was confined.

Psalm 40 . . . "I waited patiently for the Lord; he turned to me and heard my cry. He lifted me out of the slimy pit, out of the mud and mire.'"

Inevitably, Doug went back to the one psalm he knew best. Even Saleh could not snatch away from him the promises of God, not even when Doug was marched into the room that had once been a place of worship, but was now only a place of beatings and pain.

> He who dwells in the shelter of the Most High
> will rest in the shadow of the Almighty.
> I will say of the Lord, "He is my refuge and my
>   fortress,
> my God, in whom I trust."
> Surely he will save you from the fowler's snare
> and from the deadly pestilence.
> He will cover you with his feathers, and under
>   his wings you will find refuge;
> his faithfulness will be your shield and
>   rampart.
> You will not fear the terror of night,
> nor the arrow that flies by day,
> Nor the pestilence that stalks in the darkness,
> nor the plague that destroys at midday.
> A thousand may fall at your side, ten thou-
>   sand at your right hand,
> but it will not come near you.
> You will only observe with your eyes
> and see the punishment of the wicked.
> If you make the Most High your dwelling—
>   even the Lord, who is my refuge—
> then no harm will befall you, no disaster will
>   come near your tent.
> For he will command his angels concerning you
> to guard you in all your ways;

> *they will lift you up in their hands,*
> *so that you will not strike your foot against a*
> *stone . . . .*
> *"Because he loves me," says the Lord, "I will*
> *rescue him; . . . I will be with him in*
> *trouble, I will deliver him."*

Maybe it was his imagination, but even though the mud brick at Doug's back was still icy to the touch, the wind whistling through the open door brought the gentle warmth of a Miami spring day.

Or a loving touch.

God, I told Sara I wasn't afraid on the job because I've always believed you were there, my refuge and my fortress. I've counted on those angel wings more times that I can remember, and I swear I've heard the rustle of their wings more than once.

But now it's so dark, and I can't see you anywhere. I've fallen flat into that fowler's snare. I feel the terror of night around me. And I don't see the wicked being punished. I see them getting away with murder.

I've tried to prove to these creeps that they can't break me, to show them I've got an ounce of courage in me. But I hurt in every inch of my body. I'm freezing and I'm sick, and I'm not so sure the next time they touch me I won't break down screaming for them to end all this, and disgrace my profession, my country, and you.

So where are these promises of yours? You said you'd rescue me, that when I called on you, you'd answer me. You said that you'd be with me in trouble and deliver me. So where's your hostage rescue team to snatch me out of here?

Or are those just pretty words?

Or maybe it's me! Am I just paying the price of my own stupidity?

The guard leaning forward with his eyes intent on Doug no longer seemed in such sharp focus against the glare of the Coleman lamp. His shape blurred like double images imposed one upon the other. The rain was coming harder now, its cadence on the clay tiles like that of a full set of steel drums—or the voice of God himself thundering something incomprehensible from heaven.

But it was not the crashing thunder that penetrated the haze through which Doug was seeing the guard. It was the mounting heat that spread through him, so that his breathing grew shallow and he slid further down against the mud bricks, not even noticing that the spreading puddle had now soaked him through.

Rescue.

The Bible was full of such ops, and though Doug did not have a Bible to refer to, he knew the stories well enough.

God had rescued Daniel from the lions' den, sending an angel to shut the mouths of those wild beasts.

Another angel had walked among Daniel's three friends in the fiery furnace.

Rescue had come to Jeremiah in the mud pit through a compassionate enemy soldier, and to Jonah through the gullet of a big fish.

But Stephen, the first Christian martyr recorded in the book of Acts, had not, despite his friends' prayers, been snatched from the stone-throwing mob and delivered back to his home and family. Instead, angels had lifted him up. They had carried him from that fallen, battered shell of his earthly body directly into the presence of God.

And the apostle Paul, who'd once stood cheering Stephen's death, had written to his young protégé Timothy of just such a rescue before his own martyrdom. *The Lord will rescue me and bring me safely to his heavenly kingdom.*

The Son of God himself had hung dying on a cross while ten legions of angels stood helpless to intervene until the time came to lift the Lord of the universe and Savior of the world in eager arms and wings and carry him, not to a Jerusalem throne, but home to his Father.

Safely . . . home.

How limited was human comprehension of either word.

How mysterious were God's ways.

Doug was no longer just warm, but burning hot. The steaming heat of a sauna, which belied the actual temperature of the water, now crept across most of the dirt floor so that the guard himself had risen to his feet.

God, I don't know what you're doing—or why. Whether I'm here because of my own stupidity or some bigger plan of yours. All I know is that I trust you. You are my refuge and my fortress. I've come too far with you to let go of that now. Your angels are here, whether I can see them or not. And you will lift me up and rescue me in your time and your way. And if it is into your presence instead of back to Miami, as seems pretty certain right now, then I choose to believe that your plans encompass Sara and Mother, too, and that the future you have for them is better than anything I could wish.

I just . . . it would have been nice to say good-bye.

There were definitely two guards now, the wavering twin forms no longer standing by the door, but beginning to move, their twin mouths open but inaudible against the clamor of the storm. And they were not alone. Sara was there, just behind the right guard's shoulder, her lips curved joyously, her eyes warm. And Cynthia too, angry and worried all at once. Ramon was floating near the ceiling, his expressive mouth in its usual sardonic twist, as if he were incredulous at the mess Doug had made of things. Norm Kublin's grim visage was somewhere behind him. And though it was not possible, there was Julie, tall and striding forward, with their tiny daughter clasped laughing in her arms.

The cell was crowded now, and this time human voices were piercing the thunderous staccato of the rain on the roof.

"He is burning up with fever. How could you not notice until now?"

"If you want a dead prisoner, you will soon have one."

Then Saleh's peremptory voice. "Get him out of this mud and give him some of your medicine. And you had better hope it is enough. When he dies, it will be of our choosing, not because of carelessness and stupidity."

The fire was giving way to ice again. But this time as Doug began to shake, something warm and heavy settled around him, the rough homespun fabric of a Guarani blanket. To Doug it held the softness of feathers.

He no longer heard the splash of boots in water nor felt the canvas of a stretcher beneath his battered body. He was somewhere warm and dark and cocooned from the noise and rough treatment.

And somewhere in that darkness, it seemed he could hear the whispering rustle of angels' wings.

Chapter Fifty-six

Though it was the middle of the night, it was all Sara could do not drive over to Doug's neighborhood and start pounding on doors. Instead, she spent the next hours planning and thinking, waiting only as long as decency demanded on a weekend morning before putting her plan into action.

Sara wasn't interested in Doug's apartment. She'd been there through the entire CSI process. It was the neighbors she wanted to talk to—the ones who'd said they saw Doug return that day. A list of who the DEA had questioned would be helpful, but Sara didn't bother calling the DO. She simply started with the apartment below Doug's.

"I work nights," the man said when Sara's insistent knock finally brought him to the door. "I was asleep—like I was just now—and didn't see anything." He slammed the door, leaving Sara standing chastised on the stoop.

A young mother in the next apartment was more helpful. Yes, she'd seen the shuttle pull up, as she'd told the police. She'd hoped it was a FedEx delivery she was waiting for, so she'd glanced out long enough to see her neighbor retrieving his backpack from the shuttle and heading up to his apartment.

"You got a good look at his face?" Sara asked tensely. This was the question she'd been bracing for. "You're sure it was him?"

"Who else could it be?" A baby in a playpen started fussing, and the woman turned to lift it to her shoulder. "He headed straight up the walk to that apartment, and he must've had a key because he went right in. He looked like the right guy. I didn't even think about it. Blond hair, great build. He had a big sombrero on, so I didn't really see much of his face. I remember thinking he must have gone to Cancun or some place like that. But the walk was right— quick, like a cop or soldier, you know. Besides, I've seen him leaving with that backpack before."

"So you didn't actually see his face," Sara persisted.

"I guess not, now that you put it that way. If you really want to know, I'd talk to old Mrs. Fougere four doors down. She's a bit of a snoop, and if anyone sees everything, it's her. I saw her out on the sidewalk when I was checking for the FedEx truck."

Mrs. Fougere turned out to be an elderly Haitian immigrant whose poor English made it hard for Sara to get clear details.

"He nice man. Always stops to say hello." The old woman's dark face wrinkled into a scowl. "Not like most people here. Carries out my garbage too when it is too big for me."

"Did he stop to say hello that day?" Sara asked.

"He is in hurry, but he wave. He wear big hat—like Indiana Jones, but bigger. It is him. I know his travel bag. My husband when he is young is in American army. He has bag like that."

Sara was getting the hang of the old woman's conversation, mentally translating her present tenses to past. "So you were standing on the sidewalk in front of your house. You didn't go over to talk to him. And he was wearing a hat so you didn't really see his face. Just a man with a sombrero and backpack who waved at you."

Mrs. Fougere was shaking her head. "Oh, no, he takes off his hat when he opens his door. His hair—it is yellow like yours."

Sara eyed the thick lenses the old woman wore, then glanced down the block. At least a hundred feet to the stairs leading up to Doug's apartment.

"So he took off his hat, and you saw blond hair. But if he was opening the door, then his back was to you. So you still didn't see his face, right?"

The old Haitian woman hunched her thin shoulders. "Maybe." Her black eyes narrowed shrewdly behind the thick lenses. "You think it is not really him? That someone tries to fool us, a *malvant,* a criminal who wishes to steal his belongings or documents? Or government spy? It is true he does not come to say hello as he does always."

Funny how this old woman from a poverty-stricken nation plagued by violence and corruption so easily made the leap to Sara's own suspicions while Americans found the possibility so incredible.

"I don't know," Sara admitted. "But Doug Bradford was my friend, and I sure am going to find out."

"Good! You do this. You can never believe what police say or do," the old Haitian nodded. "Or so it is in my country."

A dozen more doors turned up the neighbor who'd reported seeing Doug drive away. Barring the backpack, left behind in Doug's apartment, her story was the same. A man of Doug's general height and build, sombrero obscuring his face, hurrying down the walk to Doug's car and driving away.

I'm right! I know I'm right! So why hadn't the police or the DEA brought this out of these witnesses?

Because they started their questioning with a foregone assumption. They asked the neighbors if they'd seen Doug without ever pinning down exactly what illusion these people had really seen.

Sara unearthed her cell phone as she drove. The DO's public switchboard might be shut down outside of office hours, but there were always agents working. She made a sour face when Peggy Browning's cool tones came on the line.

"Look, Sara. I'm in the middle of a mission planning right now. This better be something that can't wait."

"It can't!" Sara could already feel her blood pressure rising at the female agent's dismissive tone. "Did you know that no one actually saw Doug come back to his apartment?"

"What are you talking about? The neighbors—"

"The neighbors saw what they were meant to see. Someone Doug's size and build with a hat conveniently tipped over his face, hurrying in and out of Doug's apartment. I talked to them all myself."

"You talked to them yourself." The female agent's tone grew icy. "Ms. Connor, you are a civilian. You've no business interfering in a DEA investigation."

"I don't see a lot of investigating going on," Sara returned just as icily. "You've got all your pieces put together just like someone intended, so you'd tuck Doug into some file, forget him, and go on to something else. Except you've got no body, and no proof that Doug ever walked through immigration at MIA or came anywhere near his apartment. You don't even know if he was the one who called your office."

Sara softened her tone to a plea. "Can't you guys even admit you might be wrong and check it out? I know Doug, and until I see some convincing proof that he ever came back to Miami, I'm not going to buy it—or that he's dead."

"Then where is he?" The patience in Peggy's voice showed she was trying to be reasonable. "Because that's the question. If we're so far off in our investigation, why hasn't he turned up somewhere else—dead or alive? That's the big hole in your theory, Ms. Connor. We don't shove missing agents into a file and forget them. This investigation is still very much open and will be until we know exactly what happened and the ones responsible are behind bars.

"As for no body, let me tell you how many scenarios could account for that. Do you know how many ways bad guys have of making people disappear without a trace? Bradford could be at the bottom of the ocean with a concrete anchor chained to his ankles. Or shark bait. Or both. Excuse the plain speaking, but it seems to me the only reason you've got for concluding this office hasn't done its job properly is because Bradford didn't take time out of his op to call you and confirm a dinner date."

Her voice turned several degrees colder. "Of course we only have your word for that. Maybe he did call you, and you just didn't bother telling us. Did he want to break the date? And you wanted to hang on to the relationship? Maybe you aren't telling the truth when you say you never saw him after his return. Maybe you've got your own reasons for not coming clean."

It was the same kind of badgering the DEA interrogator had turned on Cynthia after Doug's disappearance. Sara's back stiffened, her own tone turning coldly furious. "Are you accusing *me* of having something to do with Doug being missing? You really think I'd do anything, hold back anything, that might find Doug? Why would I come to you in the first place if I wasn't telling the truth? For that matter, if you suspect me, why don't you check me out for yourself? Check the telephone records and see if I'm telling the truth!"

"We did." The flat answer stunned Sara. "Did you think we'd overlook something so obvious?"

Sara recovered her equilibrium. "Then you know what you're saying is nonsense," she said angrily. "Not that I care what you think. You can waste your time investigating me or Doug or Cynthia all you want. Meantime Doug could still be out there, and I'm not going to stop pushing until I find out what happened to him. Civilian or not, if you're not going to do this job, I will!"

The pause at the other end might have held incredulity. Then the agent drawled sardonically, "Well! Getting a little pushier than that sweet little girl Doug used to bring around. Okay, so you're not a serious suspect in this investigation. Just remember we're all on the same team here. You think I don't want to be wrong? That I wouldn't jump in a heartbeat if someone came across one shred of real evidence that we were barking up the wrong tree? But sometimes you've got to face reality too.

"Sure, I'll pass what you've got to the proper channels. Not that you've got any evidence that it *wasn't* Bradford the neighbors IDed. And we do have other corroboration. Meanwhile, keep in mind you're a civilian and stay out of this investigation from here on out."

Sara had no intention of answering that, but heartened by a tempering in Peggy's tone, she pressed, "Thank you. And is there any chance I could take a look at the case file, just to see exactly what corroboration you do have?"

At that, the female agent exploded. "No, of course you can't look at the file. Didn't you hear a thing I said? You are *not* an agent. You're a *civilian*. So act like one. Go home, get on with your life, and let us do our job. We'll find out what happened to Bradford, let me assure you, if it takes the next ten years. But you're not going to help us by getting in the way."

Ten years!

There was other information that Sara wanted, but she didn't bother asking. Going through official channels was not going to get her any cooperation. But maybe if she called Ramon.

It had been weeks since she'd spoken to Doug's former partner, and on this Saturday morning, he wasn't in the new Santa Cruz DEA compound. But Kyle Martin, the pony-tailed intel analyst, was there.

"Kyle, this is Sara Connor. What are you doing in the office on a Saturday?"

"Checking out the capacity of our new data system," he replied. "You should see the new satellite dish SouthCom's set up out back since the move."

Playing around with his new computer banks! Does he even have a life? Not that Sara cared, so long as Kyle kept his promise to pass along her message. He must have pulled away from his data banks long enough to make a call, because a half hour later Sara's phone rang. It was Ramon.

He was silent for a moment after Sara explained what she wanted. Then he said slowly, "Sara, are you thinking what this sounds like?"

"I just want to know if anyone in Ciudad del Este actually saw Doug face-to-face that last day."

"I thought that had already been checked out and confirmed."

"Sure, that's what they said here too, but nobody actually saw him." Sara explained how she'd passed her morning. "Ramon, you've got to help me, because no one else will listen to a civilian like me. If I'm wrong, I'm wrong. But I have to know."

"Sara—" Ramon began. His quick intelligence hadn't missed the appalling implications of Sara's request. "Odds are, you're way off base. But if you're right . . . after all this time—"

"Then there's no time to sit around chatting on the phone," Sara finished tonelessly.

As Sara hung up, it occurred to her that Ramon wasn't her only back-channel possibility. She hadn't seen Mike and Debby Garcia since the first days of the search when the tall, lanky agent and his wife had driven over to express their condolences. She looked up the number Mike had given her and dialed.

"Oh, hi, Sara." Debby answered the phone. "Sure, Mike's here. Playing with Junior, in fact."

Debby's warm contralto held supreme contentment, and in the background Sara could hear a baby's irresistible giggle and a deeper masculine chuckle. So at least one agent was home with his family on a Saturday morning. Listening to those homey sounds, Sara felt such a wave of envy sweep over her that she had to clamp her lip before she could say evenly, "May I speak to him? I'm sorry to bother him on a weekend, but it's—it's kind of important."

"Oh course, he won't mind."

Mike didn't sound bothered as he came to the phone. "Hello, Sara. How's everything? I'm . . . I heard about the "presumed dead" ruling. I'm so sorry. If there's anything I can do, just name it. I owe Doug big time."

"There is," Sara said. "I need some information. Did Doug ever tell you about the Cortéz case? Luis and Nicolás Cortéz?"

"Not really." Mike's tone was suddenly cautious. "But I know the case. I heard that's how the two of you met."

I'll bet you did! I think the whole DO's gossiped about it often enough. "Then maybe you know that part of the Cortéz clan moved here to Miami, and Doug was checking them out. I . . . it was kind of my fault. I got spooked when they came around. That was what he was investigating when he went to Paraguay."

"Yes?" Even more caution entered the agent's voice. "And just what is it you want?"

"I need to know what he found out. What he was working on in the investigation. Especially from the time I went to Seattle until he left for Paraguay."

"Sara, you know I can't do that. Besides, why should it matter now? It's a dead case. There was nothing there, that much I know."

"Please! If there was nothing there, why should it hurt if I take a look? But—well, I know the Cortéz, and I know the man Doug was looking for when he went to Paraguay. I might be able to see something they didn't."

"Regulations, Sara. You want me to get canned?"

Sara wanted to scream. "Can't you just forget that DEA handbook for one minute, Mike? Do you think I don't know you guys do things like this all the time for each other? You think Doug wouldn't do it for you no matter what some stupid rule in a book says?"

She finished in despair, sure she'd lost. But after a pause, Mike said slowly,

"You know, Doug told me once I'd be a good agent once some of the Quantico spit-and-polish wore off. Of course, he was a bit of a cowboy like all those overseas agents, and I didn't appreciate his crack at the time. But I guess what he was really trying to say was that sometimes you've got to put the mission above a list of paper do's and don'ts. And, yeah, Doug would do it for me in a heartbeat."

There was another pause except for the nearby burble of a baby. "Okay, I can't promise anything, but I'll see what I can do."

"Thanks. That's all I'm asking."

Chapter Fifty-seven

IGUAZÚ RAIN FOREST

The *throp-throp-throp* of rotors alerted Saleh before the Huey came into view directly overhead, hovering slowly downward into the deep, green well formed by the break in the jungle canopy. Saleh waited until the rotors quit tossing up a whirlwind of dirt and leaves before hurrying to the aircraft. The team climbing wearily out began peeling off fire helmets and heavy yellow rubber coats. The acrid smell of smoke and chemicals mixed with the petroleum fumes of the helicopter and wafted across the clearing.

"You're late. What took so long?" Saleh demanded.

"It got out of control." One of the team members removed his helmet to reveal a long, angry burn slashed across his chin.

Julio Vargas strode around the side of the helicopter. "They were playing around with the chemical starter fluid, thinking the vegetation was too damp to be hazardous. They have learned their lesson. A number received minor burns, and one was knocked out by a falling branch." He gestured toward the open side of the Huey where the Palestinian doctor was helping a trainee with bandages around his head and arm climb down from the helicopter. "The medic says he won't be able to travel for at least a week."

"The entire exercise was a waste of time," one of the force members said as he tossed his sooty coat and helmet to the ground. "If our purpose is to start a fire, why should we risk our lives working to put them out?"

"Because on this mission you must be able to fight a fire in order to infiltrate the attack zone," snapped Saleh. "At least now you look the part." He uttered an oath as he surveyed the injured man. Accidents were an inevitable part of training, but this one raised the number of casualties unfit to travel to six, three from this team alone. Were the seven remaining team members adequate for their part of the mission? Only if no one else moved to the injured list.

"Sir!" The salutation diverted Saleh from his calculations. The man limping across the clearing was Team Three's communications specialist, his sprained ankle the result of a zip-line accident. He handed Saleh a computer printout. "You asked to be informed if a message arrived from Team One."

The message had been routed via separate e-mail accounts in two European countries before being downloaded at the training site by sat-phone modem. Even so, its contents were deliberately innocuous.

Hey, bro! It's good to be home. The luggage all made it for a change! The new driver's license came through, no problem, though the pictures are ugly as sin, as usual. I'll get back to you in more detail tonight.

"So they had no problem with their documents," Julio said, scanning the e-mail over Saleh's shoulder. "Did I not tell you the Americans are easy to fool? The equipment arrived safely, and they will be ready to move tonight. Excellent!"

Tonight.

Saleh glanced around the clearing as the members of Team Three began carting away their firefighting gear. The injured man leaned heavily on two teammates as he hobbled toward the main building. The camp was quiet, almost deserted. The thatched shelters were almost empty of work projects. It had been ten days since Team One began trickling across the U.S. border. Those with European passports had taken connecting flights through their "home" countries, and those holding American identification had crossed "home" from Canada.

Team Two had left a few days after Team One and by now should be approaching their target zone. Tonight's mission was the final stage of preparation for Team Three.

As Saleh strode across the clearing to the old church, the smallest ripple of concern tempered his elation. After months of practice raids, tonight would be the inauguration of the new jihad he had envisioned. His sweeping survey of the camp took in the neat clearing, the thatched shelters, climbing course, and firing range, the solidity of adobe walls that had endured centuries of rain and plant growth.

What will happen to this place once we're gone? Will we be back?

If they were successful, if they struck their targets with precision, they would begin again soon with a new group of warriors.

If they failed—

But we will not fail. We have trained too well. We have planned for every possible contingency.

A bitter gust took advantage of the break in the jungle canopy to blow its icy breath across the clearing, a reminder that in these parts winter was still advancing.

But up north, in the land of their enemies, it was summer.

And what a summer, if the weather reports Saleh had been following were accurate.

A summer the Great Satan would never forget.

The summer of Allah.

Chapter Fifty-eight

JUNE 13
FRONT RANGE OF THE ROCKY MOUNTAINS

They'd been warned.

The big, blond Chechen trained his binoculars on the ice field flowing down the side of the mountain. The blinding whiteness arrowed downward between two ridges to a scattering of dark splotches just above the tree line. The newly inaugurated ski resort.

It was still early, the snow pack just lightening to gray, the resort's morning crew only now rolling out of bed to start breakfast. Above the ridge where the Chechen watched, the ancient glaciers slumbered. Hundreds of feet thick, they had lain undisturbed for eons, pushing southward into the tree line in cold years, shrinking back during hot summers.

Then had come the invasion: tourists searching for the perfect winter playground; developers anxious to build their fortune. With the human invasion came digging and blasting, the stripping away of vegetation that anchored the fragile topsoil to the mountain slopes.

During the 1950s, long enough ago to be forgotten by this generation, a piece of the glacier, disturbed by the blasting of a road bed, had detached itself from the peak the Chechen now studied. The avalanche had swept away a logging operation that the road was intended to service. It could happen again, environmental groups had warned when plans were drawn up for the ski resort.

Their warnings had been ignored. To civic leaders and the local voters, an influx of tourism dollars to shore up the area's foundering economy well outweighed any tree huggers' bleatings about impending catastrophe. So the ski resort was built, the mountainside blasted away for a road, the ice pack drilled through to install ski lifts and comfort stations.

To date, the gainsayers had been proved wrong. The ice pack lay as quiescent as it had for thousands of years. If the threat remained, if an unusually hot summer might someday loosen the glacier's grip on the mountain, just let it be far enough in the future for a good investment return.

A cold smile curved the Chechen's mouth below the binoculars. The future had just arrived for those developers. Speeding down the ice field above the ski resort, flashing into view only because of the momentary contrast of a patch of blue spruce, four white dots appeared right on schedule. Four skiers clad head to toe in white, invisible against the snow.

Storing away the binoculars, the Chechen walked briskly back to the SUV parked under the overhang of a stand of fir trees and started down the road. The icy gravel track was a far cry from his last assignment—driving through Miami's disorderly traffic. If the demolitions experts had done their job right—and their quick return indicated they had—the environmental groups need no longer speculate as to when gravity and weather would complete the destruction that human greed had begun.

Ten minutes later, the Chechen braked cautiously against the slickness of the track before pulling over to the shoulder. He had not yet grown impatient when the first white figure emerged from the tree line up the bank. The skier slid to a halt with a spray of snow as he caught sight of the SUV. The other three soon followed, piling their packs and skis into the rear of the SUV.

As soon as the last door slammed shut, the Chechen gunned the SUV back onto the roadway and headed down the mountain. Beside him in the front seat, the lead demolitions specialist flipped open a cell phone. He waited until the vehicle had left the mountain track and was speeding up the on-ramp to the highway before punching a series of numbers on the cell phone.

High up on the mountainside, muffled by the cover of ice and snow, the sharp cracks of explosives detonating might have been the snap of a chunk of ice breaking off the glacier wall or the crash of a dead fir losing its battle with gravity. Below, a number of guests rolled over in their beds. A resort employee hauling in logs for the lodge's fireplace glanced up the mountainside. Then he dropped the logs and began to run.

Even at a distance, the five force members could hear the growing rumble as the glacier broke free from its moorings. As the avalanche swept down toward the sleeping holiday playground, millions of tons of snow and ice carried with them all evidence of human tampering.

The Chechen smiled and stepped on the accelerator.

Chapter Fifty-nine

MIAMI, FLORIDA

Sunday was the longest day Sara could remember. She went to church with Cynthia but cringed at every understanding glance and murmured expression of sympathy. When one of the deacon's wives pressed her hand and asked if it was true that there would be a memorial service, Sara mumbled an incoherent reply and escaped to the parking lot. Back at Cynthia's house, she excused herself before lunch and drove out to the Everglades. There, she sat on the same observation platform as before, cell phone in hand in case Ramon or Mike should call back with any information. She ignored the tourists and the mosquitoes until it was time for the park to close.

Monday was the start of teacher evaluation week. Calculating grades and entering them into the computer required enough concentration to keep her mind occupied. She was on her way home, listening to a news update about an avalanche in Colorado over the weekend, the worst in that state's history, when Ramon called. She turned off the radio in order to hear him clearly. The frustration in his voice was not promising.

"I've spent the whole weekend trying to get a hold of those dudes down there. Sure, the locals in the office all tell me Doug came by and dropped off some equipment, but I can't nail down one person who actually talked to him. The SAC is out of town on R and R, and I've left messages for the intel analyst, but nothing so far. For all I know, the Paraguayans haven't even passed them on. That's why I don't like these field offices with so few American personnel."

So Sara was back where she'd started. It might have been Doug, or it might not. No one could say for sure.

"I'd fly down myself and choke it out of someone," Ramon went on, "but we're in the middle of a biggie right now. But don't you worry. I'm not letting it go. It just might take a few more days."

A few more days. And with the passing of each one—

"Sara, I wish I could do more." The urgency in Ramon's voice echoed her own feelings. "I'll tell you this: If things go down here as expected, and we don't hear back in the next couple days, I'll get down there and check it out personally. Even if I have to call in some sick leave myself. I won't let the ball drop—that you can take to the bank."

"Thank you, Ramon." Here at least was one friend of Doug's that Sara could count on.

She had less confidence about Mike Garcia, but she had barely walked in the door at Cynthia's when Debby called. "Mike's on his way home. He told me to call and have you come by. He's got something for you."

Mike's Firebird pulled up right behind Sara as she turned into the Garcia's driveway. Debby opened the door, her small son in her arms and a distressed look on her face as Sara climbed out of the Neon. "Oh, Sara, I'm so sorry! I wasn't even thinking when you called the other day. Mike told me afterward about the 'presumed dead' finding. This is so terrible for you! I . . . I am so sorry."

Debby shifted the baby to reach up for a hug, and Sara was touched to see tears in her eyes. Sara shook her head as she hugged Debby back. "Don't be. I haven't given up yet. If the DEA wants to bury Doug, they can, but I won't until I know he's gone."

"But—" Debby shot Mike a troubled look as he entered the house behind Sara, but he made no comment. Stepping past the two women, he tossed a folder down onto the dining table.

"There's what you asked for. I didn't see anything there remotely useful. But you can see for yourself. Just don't mention this to Kublin or anyone else in the office—" he affixed both women with a sharp look "—or it'll be my neck."

Sitting down at the table, Sara opened the slender file and began leafing through its contents. A report on the drive-bys at the Cortéz residence that Doug had already told Sara about at the restaurant. A background check on each one of the Cortezes' immigration status and Diego and Raymundo's employment at Tropical Imports & Exports.

So those two were actually holding real jobs for a change? Sara's eyes opened wide at their listed salaries. *No wonder they were living in Coral Gables!*

She picked up the trash run report and flipped through the garbage-spotted receipts and photocopies still stapled to the form. As she reached the bottom of the report, she grew still.

This is it! The connection that had prompted Doug's sudden departure to Paraguay while Sara was in Seattle.

Sara read quickly through the rest of the file. The investigation of TI&E had turned up nothing. The DEA-6 of the freighter raid projected Doug's own fury through every line of the report. Sara wrinkled her forehead over the shipping list her former brothers-in-law had sent to Julio Vargas. Survival gear for a tourist agency called Jungle Tours? *How unimaginative.* That didn't sound like the Julio Vargas she knew. Which would have been all the more reason for Doug to check him out.

What had Doug told her when he'd called from Ciudad del Este? Not much. He'd been in his usual tight-lipped DEA persona. Just that he'd found Julio Vargas. That the former Cortéz security chief was up to his old tricks again. That Doug had come up dry in Ciudad del Este as to what Julio was doing, and that he was hoping to find out with this trip out of town he was taking.

That had been the end.

Sara leafed through the file again. If Doug hadn't been able to make anything out of these bits and pieces, how could she expect to? Tropical Imports & Exports. Jungle Tours. The *Buena Vista* shipping tourist gear between the two. Legitimate commercial ventures, all three, and seemingly honest business transactions—except for the integration into the mix of the Cortezes and Julio Vargas, who wouldn't know "legitimate" or "honest" if they were served on a legal summons.

Sara looked up from the file to see Mike Garcia watching her closely. "So what has the DEA done to follow this up? Did they talk to Diego and Raymundo after Doug disappeared? Or check out the phone records for when this shipping list was called in?"

"We've checked out every case and every person that Doug dealt with over the last several months," Mike said bluntly. "These Cortéz people haven't left the city since they moved here. An agent talked to your brothers-in-law, yes. They were filing a complaint for harassment over that freighter incident. Their lawyer withdrew the complaint when they found out Doug was missing and wouldn't be available for court dates. There's no indication they knew he was missing before then.

"As for their phone records, there were a number of calls to and from Paraguay in the last several months—all to a number registered to this Jungle Tours. Makes sense if they were the purchasing agents in this country. By their account, they've had no other contact with Bradford except in Bolivia, where they claim he was also accused of harassing them."

"Harassing them!" Sara choked off her indignation. She wasn't even going to get into that. "What about this Ciudad del Este connection? Did anyone ever fly down to check it out?"

Sara saw the answer in Mike's face. "They didn't, did they? They just shoved it under the carpet because it didn't agree with their theory of how—and where—Doug disappeared."

"Now, whoa!" Pulling out a chair, Mike sat down across from Sara and looked her square in the eyes. "That isn't fair, Sara. Look, I know what you want to believe. And believe me, I understand why you're doing this. I'd give anything if the data added up different than it does. But you need to keep some things in mind, too. Doug had at least a dozen investigations going when he disappeared, all of them current and some of them dealing with some pretty bad guys. Every one of those cases has a potential of dozens of informants and narcos we've had to track down and check out. Do you have any idea how many people we've had on this for weeks now? Enough that Washington's been screaming down our backs about the man-hours involved.

"This one—" Mike slammed a hand on the folder "—is the *only* file with a cold trail. The field office down there in Paraguay did everything they were supposed to do. Another dead end. Sure, we can run all over the world chasing down every cold trail, but there's only so many agents and so many bucks, and at some point, the brass in D.C. start making noise about the drug agency we're supposed to be running here. And that's when guys like Norm Kublin have to make choices as to which fish are hot enough for casting bait. Do you understand what I'm trying to say?"

Sara swallowed hard, but her face was mutinous as she stared back at him. "Sure, I get it. Norm Kublin and Peggy Browning and the others think this whole Cortéz investigation is a waste of time . . . that Doug was just doing it in the first place as a favor to me, and that there was nothing in it. So they haven't bothered following it up the way they have Doug's other cases."

Mike didn't have to answer because just then his pager went off. Glancing at the number, he flipped open his cell phone. "Yeah, I can come in. Give me half an hour."

Without looking again at Sara, he rose to his lanky height and scooped the folder off the table. "Something's breaking. Kublin needs me. Sara, I hope this helped settle things for you. Now, if you'll excuse me, I'll return this while I'm down there. Debby, hon, I'll call when I know what's going down."

Then he was striding toward the door. Sara blinked back tears as the door slammed behind him. Pushing back her chair, she stood up unsteadily, glancing over to meet Debby's carefully blank expression with a wry twist of her mouth. "Sorry to get in a squabble with your husband. Another crazy, hysterical female, right? No—" Sara stopped Debby's denial "—I know how they think. Don't worry about it. But—"

Sara walked around the table to study a cross-stitch hanging on the wall. In meticulously even stitches, it read, "For He will command His angels concerning you to guard you in all your ways."

"I remember when you gave me that psalm," she said over her shoulder. "You told me you had it posted all over your house to remind you every time Mike walked out. I guess you weren't kidding. I've never forgotten it."

Sara leaned forward to examine the hanging more closely. Cross-stitched in a border around the words was a narrow, stony path in browns and blacks and grays. Hovering above the path in each corner of the hanging was the outline of an angel. Sara swallowed again before she could ask shakily, "Debby, do you really believe, wherever Doug is right now, that there are angels around him, watching him? That he isn't alone?"

Debby took the time to place her small son in a nearby playpen before crossing to Sara's side. Her voice trembled as she answered, "Yes, of course I do, with all my heart. There are angels all around, wherever Doug is."

Sara caught the pained inflection in Debby's last phrase and turned swiftly to her. "You don't believe he might still be alive, do you? You think I'm as crazy as Mike does. I'm just making up reasons to keep hoping so I don't have to admit he's dead. No, Debby, you're a sweetheart, but I know what the evidence looks like as well as you do. It's just—"

Swinging around again to the cross-stitch, Sara traced the delicate handiwork of one of the angels with a wavering forefinger. "It's just . . . I remember what else you told me. That I couldn't live with Doug until I learned to live without him. I did that. And these last weeks . . . I've come to terms with the possibility that he's—gone. Really, I have. I know I'll survive. I'll go on with my life. It isn't Doug's death I can't accept. I know God loves him more than I ever could and that Doug would be . . . better off in heaven than wherever he's been.

"No, it's the thought that he might still be alive out there, alone, hurting, wondering when anyone is going to bother looking for him, that hurts. I just can't sit still waiting for someone to come up with answers if there's anything I can do. Doug wouldn't be sitting here. He'd be out there hammering on walls until he *knew.* I know, because he did it for me. And I can't rest either until I know he's okay—one way or the other."

"Oh, Sara!" Debby gave Sara another hard hug. "Of course you're not crazy. Maybe . . . maybe mistaken. I know what Mike thinks and what the DEA findings say, and I wish I could say I believe there's any hope. But if you're crazy," Debby added fiercely, "then I'm crazy too. Because, all I can see is that if it were Mike out there, I'd be doing exactly the same thing. So you just go ahead and do what you have to do—no matter what they say!"

The baby's wail added emphasis to Debby's speech, and as she hurried to the playpen, she said over her shoulder, "The only thing is, Sara, I don't see what you're going to do next. Not unless you saw something in those reports Mike didn't."

Sara didn't answer, her expression closed and her thoughts turned inward as Debby swung her son into her arms.

"Sara? What are you thinking? What are you going to do? Sara?"

Sara looked up as Debby anxiously repeated her name. Then she walked over to gather up her purse from where she had set it. "Oh, I know exactly what I'm going to do next." She gave Debby a hug good-bye, kissed the baby, and started for the door. "Tell Mike thanks for me. He was a big help."

"*How* was he a help?" Debby called after her. "Sara, what *are* you going to do?"

Sara was already at the door. She glanced back as she opened it, her smile unrevealing. "I'm sorry, Debby, but you don't really want to know."

Chapter Sixty

"These at least were not illiterate peasants!" Saleh made no effort to downplay his jubilation as he tossed the computer printouts in front of Julio. The news coverage had reached the Internet almost as soon as Team One's triumphant e-mail. The JPEG photos Saleh had downloaded offered a spectacular panorama of the avalanche's destruction.

Saleh dropped a second e-mail printout on top of the photos. "Team Two is in position now as well. Tonight they strike. Then it will be our turn. But we must move. If the boat does not cast off soon, they will not clear the worst of the channel before dark."

Saleh and Julio would be flying the Huey out to Ciudad del Este, but the rest of Team Three was already aboard the riverboat, waiting for the go-ahead from Saleh.

"Manuel and Eduardo insist on coming with us," Julio told Saleh, pushing aside the photos. Manuel and Eduardo were the two mercenary instructors he'd hired. "They say they have been here long enough without women or diversion and that if there are no teams left to train, there is no reason why they should be stuck out here any longer. If you have further need of instructors, they are willing to negotiate a new contract. But first they wish to enjoy what they have earned."

Saleh was silent for a moment, then shrugged. "It is a reasonable request. They can accompany us to Ciudad del Este. There I will speak to my father. He will arrange for the reimbursement of their services. They have served us well, and we are grateful."

That would leave the camp almost empty except the Guarani caretakers and the six men still on the injured list.

And the prisoner.

Saleh looked over at Julio.

"What about the American? To keep him until our return is one more arrangement to be made—and a pointless one. Would it not be easiest to dispose of him now?"

"Bradford is still alive?" Julio's eyebrows shot skyward. "I would not have thought so. Your Palestinian doctor is skilled."

He pushed back his chair. "You are right. He has outlived his usefulness for training, and it is an unnecessary chore for those who remain behind. It will be my pleasure to deal with him. Would you care to come along?"

Saleh had to stoop his tall frame to step through the low doorway behind Julio. The American agent was curled up on his side in the corner, his breathing so quiet that only a close look confirmed he was indeed still alive. A thick bamboo mat had been slipped beneath him since the two men had last been to see him, and there was a blanket around his shoulders. Whether asleep or unconscious, he did not stir as Julio snatched the blanket away. Despite the improved care he had received of late, the prisoner did not look much improved, his over-long hair and beard matted and filthy, the closed eyes sunken into dark pits.

Julio nudged the still form with his boot. A lifetime would not be enough to punish the arrogance of this man, or the self-righteous indifference with which he'd reduced Colonel Julio Vargas, of a proud military lineage, to the status of a common criminal. To see that tall, strong body weak and helpless, the once confident lift of the head now bowed, was a source of great pleasure to Julio.

"Wake up, Bradford. I know you can hear me."

Julio tugged the Uzi SMG clear of his shoulder holster as he leaned over to grasp the prisoner's shirt. Yanking him to a sitting position, he ground the end of the gun barrel hard against his jaw. Julio Vargas had killed dozens of men before, for the most part with the cold detachment of a job to be done. But this one was to be savored. He wanted the man's eyes open, to see the terror and subjection in them before they glazed into death.

"Look at me, Bradford," he grated. "Open your eyes. You thought to destroy me, but now I have won, and you know it. And you have lost! You are going to die, do you understand that?"

The prisoner's body remained slumped against his grip, so that Julio began to believe the man was indeed unconscious. Then, for one brief instant, the American's eyelids lifted and his gray eyes met Julio's flat black gaze, not glazed with abject terror, but cool and watchful.

The eyelids dropped immediately and the prisoner relaxed against the weapon, his gaunt features smoothed to a peace that fueled Julio's fury. How dared his victim look like this? Did he not recognize that the last lingering seconds of his life were in Julio's hands?

Julio's finger tightened on the trigger, the muzzle grinding against Bradford's jaw with a violence that should have generated a sound of pain. But there was none. With a muttered curse, Julio snatched the Uzi away and rose to his feet.

"Look at him! He is not afraid to die. He expects to find himself in Paradise."

At the sneer in Julio's tone, Saleh shrugged. "Perhaps he will. He is a warrior, a man of faith and follower of the Commandments, if not the Qur'an. Who can understand Allah's will?"

"I wouldn't know," Julio growled. "But if there is a Paradise, I will not so easily release him to find it. If he expects to escape, he will not find it so easy. He will remain here. Watching him will occupy those who remain so they do not become lazy. And since it would seem that even now he possesses the will to resist . . . Ariel, Reuben!"

Julio snapped his fingers for the two guards presently on shift. One had a strapped ankle, the other a wrist splint, though it did not affect his preferred shooting hand. "Remove the mat and blanket and give orders that the prisoner be returned to his former diet."

Allowing the prisoner to fall back to the mat, Julio glared down at his slumped form. "And bind him too—tightly! Arms and feet." Julio returned the Uzi to its holster, a thin smile spreading as the two guards hurried forward.

"If there is no hell for this man, then I will create one for him myself."

Chapter Sixty-one

Why am I alive?

Doug kept his eyes shut, his body limp, as rough hands yanked his ankles up behind him and lashed them to his arms. That one glare of defiance had been a mistake. Or had it? He was still alive. The pain of the cords biting into his flesh assured him of that.

But why am I still alive?

It wasn't so difficult—it was even restful, Doug had discovered—to resign oneself totally and absolutely to the inevitability of death.

It was the rousing again of hope that was painful and unsettling. The antibiotic injections, the warmth, and the food had proved more effective than he'd allowed anyone to suspect. Whatever his appearance might be, Doug was feeling stronger than he had in weeks. And with returning strength had come the slow recognition that the background noise of human occupation in the camp had sharply diminished, the rotation of his guards reduced, then reduced again.

Not that the remaining wardens had in any way diminished their vigilance. Neither could Doug fool himself into thinking that his returning strength would carry him far. But even a shift from impossible to improbable revived hope, and with it came the tension—and yes, the fear—of renewed responsibility.

It would be so restful to lie back and let go. But if there was the smallest chance of making it out of here, of getting what intel he'd gathered of this bizarre place out to the right ears, he had to take it. If he were given the time to continue gathering his strength. If his remaining guards lost their focus for even an instant.

Then had come that Uzi SMG pistol barrel against his teeth and the absolute certainty that in the next instant he'd at last meet the Creator of the universe. And with that certainty had come a depth of peace he'd never anticipated.

Had he heard a rustle of angel wings?

Only—he was still alive!

And with that unanticipated reprieve had come the reversal of all the meager advances that had been the basis of his revived hope. He was back where he'd started. Already, the tightness of the bonds cut deep into his wrists and ankles, and the winter chill and dampness of the dirt floor sapped away any lingering warmth of the Guarani blanket.

God, what are you doing to me?

Chapter Sixty-two

MIAMI, FLORIDA

I should have done this before. Except the Cortéz turned up clean, even under Doug's meticulous scrutiny. And the DEA was so sure they knew the direction of this investigation—and that it didn't include the Cortéz.

It was Doug's DEA-6 on the *Buena Vista* raid that sent Sara speeding up the Palmetto Expressway, knuckles white on the wheel, as she watched for the exit to Coral Gables. Like Doug, she had recognized the pattern of that raid. In Doug's terse reporting, she could see every smug play of expression, the penguin-chested strutting, as Diego and Raymundo congratulated themselves on making a fool of the American agent one more time. Every line Doug had written brought back another terrible scene when she'd watched those two lackeys pin down a helpless boy whose bravado couldn't conceal his terror, indifferent to anything but saving their own skins while the man she'd once loved and trusted pulled out his gun.

Maybe they really had turned over a new leaf. Maybe they were genuinely ignorant of Julio Vargas's doings. But if they had any scrap of information, Sara would know the instant she looked them in the eye. They might fool the police, might get away with lying to the DEA, but they couldn't hide their guilt from her.

Turning off the Palmetto, Sara headed east down Bird Road until she caught a glimpse of the landmark Biltmore Hotel. Two blocks later, she turned into the upscale neighborhood surrounding the historic hotel zone. She slowed the Neon to a crawl until she pinpointed the opulent colonial-style residence that corresponded to the address Reina had given, then continued down the street and back around the block.

This time she pulled up half a block before the Cortéz residence. Some kind of teen party was going on, and cars were parked everywhere on the grass and along the verge of the sidewalk. Latin hip-hop blasted from the open door of a garage, whose interior had been remodeled into a rec room. *Celebrating the end of school.*

The festivities allowed Sara to blend in as she nosed the car up against the low-hanging branches of a mango. She didn't get out but set herself to watching the Cortéz house. There was still plenty of daylight on this early summer evening, and she took note of the empty driveway less than fifty yards up the street, a heartening indication that Diego and Raymundo were not home yet from work or wherever they spent their days. Sooner or later they'd be here, and this time they would not find Sara without defenses.

She had been sitting for more than an hour, and was wondering if she dared take time to look for a restroom, when a car passed her parking spot and turned into the Cortéz driveway. A silver Porsche.

Snatching up her purse, Sara slid out of the car, stretching her legs into a rapid enough stride to reach the Cortéz driveway before the driver of the Porsche had opened the car door. Sara braced herself with a deep breath as the door swung open. The moment of truth!

But neither Diego nor Raymundo emerged. This possibility had not entered into her calculation. She stood stock-still as Reina planted daisy-yellow spike heels on the asphalt, gracefully unfolded her elegant body from the driver's seat, and reached in to drag out a pile of shopping bags. Straightening up, Reina turned lazily, slamming the car door shut with a kick that couldn't be too healthy for the Porsche's paint job. She was fumbling for her house key when her languid glance landed on Sara, who was watching her from only a few feet away. Reina's eyes went wide with shock, then in the next instant narrowed into a blaze of triumph that snatched Sara's breath from her lungs.

She knows!

With a long step forward, Sara blocked Reina from moving away from the Porsche. "Where's Doug? What have you done with him?"

But Reina was now recovered from her shock. Drawn up to her full height on those ridiculous heels, she towered at least six inches above Sara, and she used every bit of her superior stature and practiced arrogance as she elbowed Sara from her path, her beautiful mouth twisted into a sneer. "I don't know what you're talking about. You are a crazy woman."

Sara shocked even herself with the sheer intensity of the cold rage sweeping over her. Gone was the collected, sensible, unruffled school teacher her friends knew. She reached into her purse and drew out the backup she'd brought with her to face down Diego and Raymundo. The .22 caliber pistol was as steady in her hand as on the firing range at her self-defense class. The look of triumph vanished from Reina's lovely features as she stared incredulously from the polished metal of the gun barrel to the stony set of Sara's expression. The long sweep of her false lashes narrowed speculatively. "You wouldn't dare. You are such a good girl."

Then into the silence dropped the audible snick of the pistol's safety being snapped off. For the first time, Reina's arrogant composure cracked, and fear crept into her eyes as she looked away from Sara's unwavering gaze. "What do you think you're doing? I don't know where your Doug is. I don't know, I swear! I just know . . . he isn't a problem anymore."

"And who told you that?" Sara demanded. The truth was there in the expression flitting across Reina's face. "It was Julio Vargas, wasn't it? Doug never left Paraguay, did he?"

Sara took a step closer, her grip tightening on the gun so that Reina took a hasty step backward against the side of the Porsche. "Where is he? Is he still alive? Tell me!"

Reina's glance went from Sara's whitened knuckles to her face, and her mouth twisted again in a sneer, as if she caught some of the desperation behind Sara's resolute expression. "How should I know? We were told nothing—only that he would not bother us anymore."

She was telling the truth. Sara knew Reina well enough to be certain. Blinking back disappointment, Sara took a step back, lowering the pistol fractionally. Catching her withdrawal, Reina's sneer deepened to belligerence.

"We have done nothing. You have no right here. After all, we have broken no law. It is you who have broken the law, coming here and threatening us with a gun. I could call the police. They will arrest you for this."

"Go ahead." Sara glanced up from her introspection and smiled thinly. Lowering the .22, she shook out its chamber, showing that it wasn't loaded. Reina looked chagrined as Sara snapped the chamber shut.

"Why don't we call the police?" Sara went on as she shoved the pistol back into her purse. "And the news cameras too. I think our past relationship would make a great ten o'clock news story, don't you? I'm sure Diego and Raymundo—and Mimi too—would just love the P.R. Oh, and by the way, I do have a permit to carry this. A lot of bad guys, you see, in this city for a single woman on her own . . ."

A snarl of fury exploded from Reina's lips. Snatching up her shopping bags, she stormed up the driveway to the house, her high heels clicking loudly on the asphalt. Sara lengthened her own strides to a trot as she hurried back to her car. She no longer had the stomach for encountering her former brothers-in-law or any of the rest of the clan.

Besides, she had what she'd come for. Whether it would do any good was another matter. How did you explain to pragmatic, down-to-earth agent types like Norm Kublin or Mike Garcia that an expression on the face of a dead husband's jealous ex-girlfriend was incontrovertible evidence?

No, it would be dismissed as one more crazy assertion of a hysterical, desperate woman.

Which makes my next step very clear.

Chapter Sixty-three

IGUAZÚ RAIN FOREST

From his seat at the controls of the helicopter, Saleh glanced back with contempt at the former Venezuelan commando and Colombian army colonel who were squatting among the luggage they'd brought with them to the jungle camp. The two men were laughing and talking as boisterously as children released from school, shouting above the roar of the engines what they planned to do with their freedom and money. The finest hotel in the city. A bottle of Puerto Rican rum. And women.

"So tell us, Julio, where we can find them beautiful and quick?" the Venezuelan called out.

"Especially quick!" the Colombian added. The crude joke that followed elicited such a gale of laughter that Saleh might have suspected they'd already been sampling that Puerto Rican rum if he hadn't known it was not available.

Saleh's lip curled as he skimmed across the Paraná and began his approach to Ciudad del Este. So these infidels looked for prostitutes and drink. Though they'd taught Saleh and his comrades many valuable fighting secrets, they had not in turn learned anything about holy living.

He lowered the helicopter onto the gravel landing pad with an expertise that earned an approving nod from Julio Vargas. The two mercenaries lifted out their luggage.

"We are ready to leave, Julio," the Venezuelan said bluntly. "Just as soon as you can settle our accounts."

"A hotel tonight and some fiesta," added the Colombian. "Then for me a ticket to my country and my family, who will be wondering if the guerrillas have kidnapped me. I will let you know where I am, Julio, if you should have need of me for another job such as this. If the entertainment has been poor, please understand we are not ungrateful for the employment."

"Yes, a little less isolated next time, and we might stay longer," the Venezuelan joked. "I might not have accepted your proposition had I known you expected me to live like a priest. Though for the terms you offered, perhaps I would say yes again. That is, if I see the money soon in my hand."

"You will see the money," Saleh cut in curtly. "If you will come with me. Julio, if you will go to the hotel to make arrangements for the team's arrival, I will ensure that your colleagues receive what is owed them."

The two men looked questioningly at Julio. Under the black silk jacket he had donned for the trip into town, Julio's narrow shoulders rose and fell. "Sebastian's father holds the purse. He will make the arrangements. I will let you know how soon your return will be required."

With a shrug of their own, the two mercenaries climbed into the cab Saleh waved down.

"Wait here," Saleh snapped when the cab had deposited the three men at the curb outside Mozer Jebai's office building. Leaving the two soldiers standing in the foyer, Saleh rode the elevator up to his father's office. The mullah rose to kiss his son on both cheeks, then stepped back to survey his appearance. Saleh had changed into civilian attire for the trip, but to an experienced eye there was no hiding what he'd become: the tautness of discipline and muscle; the air of command and decision; the blaze of purpose in his eyes. These past months had changed his son even more than the years overseas. If the rest of the team was as ready as this, the jihad had acquired a force to be reckoned with.

"The disbursements have been finalized for the equipment," the mullah said simply. "I am informed it is all in place, awaiting only your arrival. Khalil complains that the cost has been excessive, but if it succeeds, no one will object to the price."

"It will not succeed if we cut corners," Saleh said shortly. "Fortunately, Uncle Khalil does not make command decisions."

"No, I do," his father agreed. "But in this I have supported you—not because you are my son, but because you are right. It is foolishness to practice economy at the risk of the mission. And your men?"

"They are ready," Saleh said. "But . . .we have a complication."

"Speak."

Saleh explained about the men waiting down in the foyer. "We have sufficient funds to pay the agreed-upon fee. But I do not like it that they have left the camp, especially now with so much at stake."

Mozer Jebai ran a hand over his long beard. "What do they know of your plans?"

"Only what they have seen and heard. And that is not so much. They do not even know about our raids across the border, only that we conducted training missions. From what they say, they believe we are involved in narcotics trafficking. Perhaps one of the Colombian cartels that keeps an army of its own. But they are only hirelings. They do as they are paid and know not to ask questions. Still, they know enough. And they are immoral, looking for prostitutes and alcohol. A dangerous mixture."

The mullah stroked his beard again, his face contemplative. "So what are your thoughts?"

"They are a liability," Saleh answered flatly. "And they are not useful to us anymore. We have learned all they can teach us. We can train the new recruits ourselves."

"And you propose—?"

"To deal with them—tonight, before they begin searching for their sinful diversions."

Mozer Jebai did not need a blueprint of what his son had in mind. He considered the matter, then nodded. "A sound command decision. But not alone. There are two of them, and they are soldiers."

As Saleh opened his mouth, the mullah raised a hand. "No, son. Do you think you are the only warrior in this family? I was killing my enemies long before you were born. We will attend to this together. And another matter— what of Vargas? He too is an infidel whose knowledge may prove dangerous now that you are ready to move. And will he not inquire about his friends?"

Saleh's thoughtful expression was the mirror of his father's. Then he shook his head. "No, not yet. We need a second helicopter pilot. Besides, his hatred for the Americans will keep his mouth shut. As for his hirelings, if they do not return, he will simply believe they have tired of the job and taken their pay to go play where they cannot be made to return."

* * *

The street lights had already blinked on to banish the dark when Mozer Jebai and Saleh descended to the foyer. The two mercenary training officers were pacing impatiently.

The mullah greeted them graciously. "I am told you wish to return to your own countries and families for a time. That is reasonable. My travel agency will arrange your flight for tomorrow. Now, about your compensation, do you prefer a direct deposit or cash?

"Cash!" the two men chorused.

"American dollars," added the Venezuelan.

"Unfortunately, it will take until morning to arrange for your compensation as well. The banks are now closed. If I had known you wished to leave so soon . . . but no matter! It will be simple in the morning. I will make arrangements with the bank before you leave for the airport. Meanwhile, we are happy to offer our hospitality for the night."

"It is not necessary to trouble yourself," began the Venezuelan. "A hotel—"

"No, no!" Mozer Jebai raised a hand. "We cannot treat you so poorly when you have done us such a service. No, I insist."

The two men exchanged dismayed glances. But it would be rudeness to protest further, and they had not yet been paid.

"Thank you. We are honored."

The chauffeur brought the black Mercedes up to the curb, but Saleh dismissed him and took over the wheel. The mullah took his place beside him, leaving the spacious rear of the vehicle to their guests. Bored, the two men stretched out on the luxurious upholstery as the noisy city streets flowed past them. A turn onto a main traffic artery allowed the Mercedes to gather speed.

Chapter Sixty-four

Sara made one stop on the way to Doug's mother's. Cynthia hadn't yet returned from her current remodeling contract when Sara entered the house. She headed straight for the second floor bedroom where football pennants were still tacked to the walls and sports trophies sat on shelves. Doug's room before he'd left home. On Doug's old school desk, Cynthia had dumped his mail after the investigating agents were done with it, pulling out only the necessary utility bills in the defiant hope that Doug wouldn't come home to find electricity and other essential services shut off.

Digging through the pile, Sara unearthed a bill Cynthia had already paid—the prior month's credit card charges. The card had been among those that turned up with Doug's wallet. The billing had come through several weeks later. Most of the charges were related to his Paraguay trip. An airline ticket. An exorbitant number of cash withdrawals.

And a hotel bill. Hotel Las Americas in Ciudad del Este, Paraguay. Sara copied names and phone numbers from the bill into her date book. She had her cell phone open before she reached the guest room, punching in the numbers even as she began to turn out the contents of her drawers. It seemed she'd spent an inordinate amount of her life adhered to a phone lately, but that was about to change.

The travel agency that had billed Doug's ticket was her first call. The first available flight to Ciudad del Este was not until tomorrow evening, and that was on a Central American airline that changed planes in Costa Rica, Ecuador, and Peru, along with Asunción, before making the final leg to Ciudad del Este. Technically speaking, Sara and the other teachers at Juan Rivera Elementary School weren't done for the year until the end of the week, but she'd already turned in her grades, and her aide could handle the rest, even if it meant a black mark on Sara's performance evaluation.

She grimaced when she realized that her savings wouldn't cover the cost of the airline ticket, but she had a new credit card. As she read out the account number, she dug out a knapsack she'd left tucked into a back corner of the closet when she'd moved to her own apartment. It was not a large backpack, the size college students used to carry books, and the memories it triggered were not ones she cared to explore. Doug had given it to her, rigged at that time with a GPS tracking unit, to take into the Bolivian jungle almost a year ago now.

Though travel-stained and well-worn, the knapsack was still in good shape and would allow her to carry with her everything she needed. That same jungle sojourn had taught Sara just how little that really was. While she called the hotel in Ciudad del Este, using Cynthia's cordless phone for the international call, she thrust two pairs of jeans, four T-shirts, and a sweatshirt for winter weather into the knapsack, then added underwear, toiletries, insect repellent, and sunscreen.

Hiking boots—those she'd wear. Setting them out with a pair of khaki slacks and shirt that would do for the plane ride, she went into the bathroom and filled a plastic sandwich bag with common remedies. Tylenol. Cold capsules. Some bandages. It was incredible to Sara that modern communications allowed making a hotel reservation in a Third World country halfway around the world. But by the time she'd finished with the knapsack, it was done. The Hotel Las Américas receptionist rattled off a list of acceptable credit cards, including Visa, which Sara had.

I'll need cash too—and plenty of it. Sara counted through the small amount in her pocketbook. In Bolivia, she had learned its usefulness for obtaining information. She'd stop at an ATM on her way to the airport tomorrow.

Sara removed the pocketbook from her larger handbag, stripping it of every piece of identifying material except her driver's license and the one credit card. Only these, along with her passport, would go with her. Even her cell phone would stay behind, because her service didn't include overseas. Instead she retrieved Doug's cell phone, which had been returned by the investigators. He'd used it to call Sara from Ciudad del Este, so it must have international service, and Cynthia had paid the bill. The only other item she transferred from her handbag to the knapsack was her date book.

There! She hadn't even packed this light for her Bolivian jungle sojourn. She zipped the backpack shut as she reluctantly dialed another number. Although she knew what their reaction would be, Sara couldn't very well just disappear without at least making an attempt to pass on her findings to Doug's colleagues. She was almost relieved when her call was routed to Mike Garcia's voicemail.

"Mike, this is Sara Connor. The Cortéz know something about Doug. Don't ask me how I know, but just—*please*—have your people go back and lean on them a little. I'm traveling for a while, so you won't hear from me, but . . . just please do that much, okay?"

Sara rang off and dropped the phone back in her purse. After a moment's thought, she fished it out again and dialed Joe and Denise's number in Washington. The anticipation of traveling alone had roused in her a sudden longing for contact with family. This time she would not leave without saying good-bye.

With the three-hour time differential on the West Coast it was still within work hours, but it must have been one of Joe's off-duty days because he, rather than Denise, answered the phone.

"Hey, Sara! Great to hear from you. When are you heading back this way? The boys keep asking for Auntie Sara."

Despite her preoccupation, the genuine pleasure in her cousin's voice warmed Sara through. "When you get some decent summer weather, give me a call."

"Hey, I'll bet we're warmer than Miami right now—running over a hundred in the shade. And dry!" Joe's voice turned serious. "It's bad enough my department has placed me on loan to the Forest Service indefinitely—or at least until we get some rain. I've been out to half-a-dozen wildfires this month already. But, hey—!" Joe lightened his voice "—don't let that discourage you from taking a trip west. School's out soon, right? Why don't you come on out and spend the summer? We'll put you to work on one of the fire crews."

Something in Sara's lack of response cut through her cousin's joviality. "What is it, Sara? I guess you didn't call to hear about the fire season—or schedule a visit. What's up?"

"I—I just wanted to give you and Denise a call," Sara said. "I'm heading to Paraguay, and I wanted to say good-bye before I left the country. And to leave my info in case anyone needs to get a hold of me. Do you have a pen?"

"I can get one. Just a minute."

When Joe came back on the line, Sara read out the hotel data in Ciudad del Este and Doug's cell phone number as well. "Oh, and if I don't come back, just—please let someone know to come looking for me."

Joe heard right through her attempt at lightness. "You're serious!" he said incredulously. "Sara, what are you up to? And don't give me any hogwash about a sightseeing trip to South America. What's wrong?"

"Nothing," Sara said quickly. "I'm . . . just going to look for a friend."

"A friend? All the way to Paraguay? Sara, is this the guy who called you while you were here? The guy who went MIA a few weeks ago?"

Sara might have known that Aunt Jan would pass along her occasional updates. Sara had told her as little as possible, and only because Aunt Jan had pressed for an update on her "friend." Unfortunately, her cousin was not only shrewder but also better acquainted with Sara than her aunt would ever be.

"Are you nuts, Sara? What in the world does Paraguay have to do with this? And what can you do that the authorities can't?"

"Look, Joe, I don't want to talk about it. I . . . it's just something I have to do. I just wanted to let you know I was traveling. Give my love to Denise and the boys. I'll call you when I get back."

"Sara—"

I never should have called. Now he's going to worry about me. But it was too late to change that now.

She dialed the last call on her list. At least there was one person who would take her seriously, who knew the Cortéz well and despised them accordingly, who would understand what she was doing and why.

Come on, Ramon. Answer the phone.

When Ramon didn't pick up his cell phone, Sara tried the Santa Cruz DEA office, even though it was after hours. *I can reimburse Cynthia for the international charges when I get back.* Instead of Ramon, she got Ellen Stevens. Sara had not spoken to the warm-hearted, outspoken DEA administrative officer since she'd left Santa Cruz, and she jumped in quickly to avoid any of the condolences she had come to expect these days. "Is Ramon available? Or would it be possible to get a message through to him?"

"Neither, I'm afraid, Sara. He's at work at the moment, and I can't say when he'll be back in contact. Is there any way I can help you myself?"

At this hour, with Ellen Stevens still in the office, that could only mean a raid. The "biggie" Ramon had mentioned?

"No, don't worry about it, Ellen. I'll just leave a message. If you could just give him this name and phone number. It's a hotel in Ciudad del Este. I'm flying down there tomorrow night. If he's available before then, I'd like to talk to him. Otherwise, he can call me at this number—" She read off Doug's cell phone number "—or I'll call him back when I get a chance."

The DEA administrative officer read back the digits slowly, and from her tone, Sara knew she had recognized the number. "I'll pass it on as soon as possible." Then, in a rush, came the words Sara had dreaded. "Sara . . . I'm so sorry about Doug. How are you doing, honey? If . . . if there is anything I can do . . ."

"I'm fine." Sara didn't have time to be sidetracked, though she felt her throat tighten at the choked-back tears in Ellen's voice. It was a reminder that Ellen, like Ramon and Kyle, had not only been a colleague of Doug's but a good friend.

As far as I know, that was the last arrangement to make before I go.

But there was one more detail—one more lesson she had learned during her time as a fugitive in Bolivia. Retrieving a pair of scissors from the Wal-Mart bag she had tossed on the bed, Sara walked over to the dresser. She'd been putting this off, but now was the time. Even as she stood with scissors in hand, she hesitated, the bedroom light glinting on the shining fall of flaxen hair that spilled over her shoulders to below her waist.

Pursing her lips, she cut through the fine, straight length with quick, decisive snips, leaving a rather jagged line just below her shoulders. Reaching once again into the Wal-Mart bag, she opened the box of Clairol and began to work.

When Sara was done and her hair blown dry, she stared at her reflection with incredulity. Even though she'd planned it, she had not expected the difference to be quite so striking. The hair coloring she'd chosen was the same dark brown as her eyelashes and brows, and with her amber eyes and the deep tan she'd picked up during her months in Miami, she could pass for a *latina*— or at least not stand out as much as she had as a blonde. Now if she could just even out those ragged ends.

"Excuse me, but what are you doing in here?"

Sara whirled around at the frosty interrogative. She'd missed the sound of the van pulling in. Cynthia's eyes went wide with shock. "Sara—what on earth! You looked like . . . I thought you were someone else!"

As Cynthia stepped into the bedroom, her glance fell on the knapsack, and the look of shock grew greater. "What is this, Sara? Why are you packing up? Are you leaving?"

Sara crossed the room as the older woman's voice rose with bewildered disbelief. "I'm going to Paraguay, Cynthia. Not tonight—after school tomorrow. I was going to tell you. This—this is just preparation."

"Preparation for what? What's going on here? Why have you made yourself up to look like someone else? Is this one of Norm Kublin's ideas? Are they trying to drag you into their games now?"

"No, this has nothing to do with the DEA. In fact, I'm sure they wouldn't appreciate it at all." Sara gentled her voice. "Cynthia, I haven't said anything to you before because . . . well, I didn't really know, and I didn't want to get up any false hopes. But—I think Doug may still be alive, and I'm going to Paraguay to look for him."

If Cynthia had looked stunned when she first saw Sara, she looked even more so now. Slowly, she sank down onto the side of the bed. "Sara, how can you say such a thing? What possible proof could you have to come up with something like this?"

How did she explain a gut feeling? The look in Reina's eyes? The growing conviction that this was what she was called to do? Instead, she sat down on the side of the bed beside Cynthia. "Cynthia, don't you think it's odd that Doug would come back to Miami and never contact you before taking off somewhere else?"

"Not if he were called out on a case," Cynthia answered bitterly. "He'd always figure he could call when he got back. No, Sara, if you're still harping on that phone call for proof, you need to face the facts. I know what you're going through, honey. I know how much you're grieving for Doug. Do you think I want to admit my son is—gone? But Norm Kublin is right."

Cynthia took one of Sara's hands into hers, shock and bewilderment giving way to concern. "Honey, I've come to terms with what's happened, and you need to accept it too . . . that something happened when he met that Colombian, and that maybe we'll never find out just what."

Sara shook her head, the shortened length of her hair feeling odd against her shoulders. "I'm sorry, Cynthia, but I can't do that. Maybe Doug is dead, I don't know. But I do know he never left Paraguay, though I can't tell you how I know, and the DEA won't believe me. You'll just have to trust me when I say I have to go down there myself and find out what's happened. And to do that, well—I'm a little too recognizable with blonde hair, that's all. This way I'll blend into the crowd a little easier."

"Blend into the crowd? Now you sound like an agent . . . like Doug. Sara, can't you see how dangerous this is? You can't do it. It isn't safe. If you do have something, why can't you just turn it over to Kublin and the others? Why do you need to go off somewhere yourself instead of staying here safe while the authorities take care of it? I mean, if Doug could get himself into trouble down there, what do you think you're going to do?"

"Maybe nothing. But I can at least try. Which is more than the authorities are willing to do."

Getting back to her feet, Sara snatched up a hair band from the dresser, wrapping it swiftly around her remaining length of hair to sweep it back into a ponytail. Grabbing up the knapsack, she swung it to her back.

"As for safety, you can't always choose *safe*, Cynthia, don't you see that? I never really understood that when Doug told me why he does what he does. But I do now. Sometimes there are things that need doing. Hard things—and dangerous and unpleasant things. But someone has to do them, or there'll be no safety for anyone. Doug was one of the people who did those things. And now he needs help. And, okay, so I'm far from the most qualified person to go after him, but it seems I'm the only one who is willing. So I'm going to go, and nothing you say is going to make me change my mind. I am not leaving Doug down there. He'd come after me in a minute, you know that, if he thought there was a chance in a million. And now, safe or not, I'm going after him."

Cynthia stared at her house guest. Maybe it was the shorter, darker sweep of hair pulled sharply back that accounted for the unfamiliar steeliness in Sara's jaw, the unyielding obstinacy in the uptilted chin, the amber eyes under their long lashes no longer desolate but unwavering with a resolution that sent a chill up Cynthia's spine.

"You know, you've really changed," she said slowly.

"Yes, well." Sara wriggled her shoulders to settle the knapsack into a position comfortable enough for the longest hike. "Maybe I've finally just realized it's time to grow up."

Cynthia made no answer but rose from the bed with a swift movement. A pang twisted in Sara as the older woman hurried out of the room. *So not even Doug's mother understands. It doesn't matter! All that matters is Doug—and what I have to do.*

Then Cynthia was back, a pocketbook in one hand and a pen in the other. "You're going to need plenty of cash. Doug taught me that." Ripping out the small rectangle, she pushed it into Sara's hand. Sara looked at it in disbelief. A check for five thousand dollars.

"Then—you believe me?" she said slowly.

"I don't know what I believe. But if this matters to you so much you're willing to run yourself into debt—no, Sara, I know what your bank account looks like—and risk your neck looking for Doug down there in some back-woods corner of the jungle, well—he's my son. If there's any chance in the world he's alive, I'd spend every cent I have to get him back. And if he's . . . gone—" for an instant Cynthia's face twisted with the grief and anguish she'd held in check, then it hardened into a determination that matched Sara's own "—then I don't know any better way to invest that insurance policy the DEA tells me they've got on him than finding out just what happened. So, honey, you just go on and do what you have to do. And if you need more, just give me a call."

Even as she spoke, Cynthia was reaching for the scissors Sara had dropped onto the dresser. "Meanwhile, let's do something about that hair, shall we?"

Chapter Sixty-five

CIUDAD DEL ESTE, PARAGUAY

The drive was longer than either man had expected. After a long day, and with their hosts not extending themselves in conversation, both men had relaxed into a doze when the jolt of springs jolted them awake. It was a jolt well known to any Third World traveler, the bump of a car leaving pavement for the ruts of a dirt road. Sitting up, the two men realized that the lights of the city were only a yellow stain against the night behind them while to either side and ahead stretched only scrub jungle intermixed with cleared pasture. The only illumination came from the headlights of the Mercedes and the stars overhead.

From the front seat, the elder host glanced back. "We have a country hacienda not far ahead now with excellent accommodations. You will be comfortable there tonight."

The mullah grabbed for the back of the seat as the Mercedes gave a sudden jerk. The car swerved violently, hitting the bank, then bouncing back down into the ruts. It jerked again, then began to slow. Saleh gunned the engine with no result. Mozer Jebai, glancing over at the dashboard, took in the gear indicator set in neutral without comment. Then the Mercedes braked so suddenly that the two backseat passengers were thrown forward by the force of it. The headlights showed only an empty dirt lane ahead.

Saleh looked over at his father. "A difficulty with the engine, I'm afraid. It is probably only bad gas, but it will take time to check." He glanced back at their two guests. "I'm sorry about this. If you wish to get out and stretch your legs, you are welcome to do so."

Climbing out with an annoyed mutter, the two men wandered over to the side of road to urinate. When they returned, the hood was up, Saleh bent over behind it. They had just reached the car when the hood slammed down. Both men's faces went blank with shock as the glare of the headlights outlined unmistakably the Uzi SMG in Saleh's steady grip. That he could use it effectively was a question that did not cross their minds. They'd taught him.

The two men swung around, only to see Mozer Jebai step around the rear of the vehicle with a duplicate weapon in his hands. The shots rang so close together they sounded as one, their only audience a flock of macaws that fluttered up in protest from their night's perch.

Searching the bodies, Saleh pulled out their wallets, but neither he nor his father made any effort to haul the bodies off the road into the concealment of the brush. The vultures would give them away as quickly as a passing donkey cart or farm truck, and when they were found, they would simply be two more undocumented dead men, shot for money, revenge, a fight, or a falling out of criminals—the list of possibilities was long—in one of the planet's most lawless cities. With less than ten percent of the local crimes solved or even reported, the police would waste little time on two unidentified strangers without families to demand justice.

Saleh listened to the engine purr back to life, then jolted up onto the edge of the bank to turn around, swerving to avoid an arm dangling into his path before pointing the nose of the Mercedes back toward the city.

* * *

It felt good to be home. To take a hot shower and turn the cable to ESPN. To sink his teeth into battered catfish and deep-fried chicken and biscuits drowned in sausage gravy. To toss a rod into the bass-filled waters of the lake behind the causeway on which he stood.

It felt so good that the man identified on his new driver's license as James Baker, formerly Mohammed Usaabi, born William Jefferson, had to remind himself sharply of the holy duty that had brought him back.

His companion, a Palestinian demolitions specialist, exhibited no such nostalgia for his present surroundings as he raised binoculars to study the demonstrators picketing the riverbank below the dam. To any media helicopters circling overhead, the Palestinian was interested only in the protesters and news crews with their mikes and cameras. But James was well aware that his companion was studying angles and water currents and structural strength.

The reason for the bedlam below was the same one that had drawn Team Two to the site—the dam's deteriorating condition, a consequence of monies designated for upkeep that over the years had been funneled into politicians' pet projects. If the widening cracks in its foundation were not immediately repaired, according to the voice blaring over the bullhorn down below, the next flood or tectonic shift could collapse the entire structure. The marching civic groups had vowed not to leave the riverbank until something was done about this disgrace.

Having seen all they needed, the members of Team Two made their way down from the dam. The next step had to wait until nightfall, which promised to be dark and rainy.

By midnight, the conditions were even better than mission planning had projected. Hovering clouds had opened up into a steady, chilling rain, which had accomplished the added benefit of driving all but the most fanatic protesters from the riverbank. It also ensured that no late-night fishermen were out on the water or wandering the beachfront, and any nighttime security personnel of the River Reach Energy Company had long since retreated to shelter on top of the dam.

By 2 A.M., the only movement on the lake was on the deck of a rented pleasure boat tied up at a dock several hundred yards from the dam. James Baker adjusted his black wetsuit, pulled diver's goggles over his eyes, and lifted his air tanks into place before slipping noiselessly over the side of the boat.

The diving skills for which he'd been assigned to this piece of the mission had been acquired during a stint in the U.S. Navy before an attempt at "economic betterment"—selling off military equipment—landed him behind bars, where he'd been introduced to the True Faith by a Muslim chaplain. James had supervised the demolition specialist's diving training himself and, as the black lake waters closed over their heads, he kept a watchful eye on the phosphorescence of the diver's watch that marked his companion.

Three other Team Two members remained on the boat, a selection of handguns discreetly out of sight but within easy reach if anything went wrong. The backup half of Team Two was divided between two area motels, waiting for the phone call that would alert them to the success or failure of the mission.

It took a slow, cautious half-hour of swimming to reach the dam. But the slapping of charges against a visible crack in the concrete foundation took seconds, the Palestinian only a ripple of black on black as he worked. The phosphorescent glow of the diver's watch stretched toward James, a gloved hand gripping his wrist to signal the job was done.

The two men started back, a GPS signal in their wristwatches retracing their course. The beauty of this mission was that the very force of the dam's collapse would erase all signs of their tampering, and the civic groups would be too busy screaming "I told you so" to offer any suggestion of foul play. Too bad the ensuing deluge wouldn't touch the luxury homes situated around the lakefront. But a high death count was not necessary to this mission. The inundation would wipe out extensive farmland downstream, and with the destruction of the area's main power source, and the lake itself with its bonus of tourism, the economic damage would be enormous.

Back at the boat, the two black figures slipped aboard as noiselessly as they'd entered the water. Stripping off scuba gear and wetsuits, they left the equipment on the boat. Only the handguns went with the five men as they made their way ashore. In whatever heap of rubble the rented boat ended up, the equipment left aboard would attract no attention.

When the team reached their hotel, they made their way to the twentieth floor where the team leader's room was booked. The balcony would have offered a glorious view of the lake, were it not for the continuing rain.

The team leader pulled out a second cell phone and without fanfare punched in a number. The depth of the lake water prevented any sound from making its way to the surface, and over the next moments, James Baker became increasingly certain the Palestinian's explosive device had somehow failed.

But though he could not see it, far below the lake's surface, pressure from the dammed-back waters had begun forcing its way into the newly amplified seam at the dam's base. Slowly at first, it began to widen, the crack running up the concrete wall like a run in a woman's nylons, until with a rumble that could be felt even on the twentieth floor of the nearby hotel, the concrete gave way.

The placid surface of the lake began to move, imperceptibly at first to the watching team members on the balcony, then growing to a maelstrom. Despite his callous indifference to death and destruction, James Baker gawked with open-mouthed awe as the liberated waters of the lake roared through the gap in the dam wall to sweep away everything in its path downstream.

Chapter Sixty-six

Sara might have gotten away cleanly if not for Linda, her aide. Sara had checked books and supplies back into inventory, cleaned out her desk, and was digging through the knapsack to ensure that both her passport and plane ticket were where she'd put them, when Larry Thomas walked into the classroom.

"Excuse me, have you seen—?"

He stopped in midstride as Sara looked up from her desk. If she'd needed further assurance her alteration was effective, Larry's expression as he recognized her behind the spill of dark hair was confirmation enough.

"Sara—I didn't recognize you." Larry advanced further into the room. "You—you cut your hair," he added unnecessarily. His glance fell on the passport in her hand, and his startled expression hardened. "Then it's true what Linda told me. I didn't believe her, but you really are leaving, and without even bothering to tell your friends."

Sara sighed. The last thing she wanted was another long explanation, but Larry was too good a friend to just brush off. "It's just for a few days, Larry, down to Paraguay. At the most, maybe a week or two."

"Paraguay?" Larry's mouth opened, then snapped shut before he said flatly, "You've got to be joking. That's the other end of the world—and a pretty unpleasant end too, from what I've heard. Hardly the kind of place for a young woman wandering around alone."

He took another step forward. "What is this, Sara? Why have you changed your appearance? And don't tell me you just decided to go for the brunette look. You think I don't know that Paraguay is where Bradford was when all this blew up? What kind of crazy scheme have you cooked up? Or has the DEA somehow dragged you into one of their messes?"

"No, they haven't dragged me into a mess!" Sara dropped the passport and ticket back into the knapsack. "Now, if you'll excuse me, I don't have time to talk, Larry, I need to get to the airport."

"Not if I have anything to say about it." As Sara started to swing the knapsack over her shoulder, Larry's hand shot out and grasped her wrist, his voice rising in unaccustomed anger. "Sara, do you know how dangerous those places are down there? What could happen to a woman on her own? Haven't you had enough . . . adventure for one person?"

Sara stood still, not trying to tug her wrist away, but her tightly controlled tension flared up into annoyance. *Why does everyone I know have to treat me like some half-wit, incapable of being let out on her own?*

"Then come with me," she said quietly. "The flight doesn't leave for another three hours. It isn't full. We could call in a reservation, swing by your apartment and pick up some luggage. You have a passport . . . you told me you went to Germany for that ESL counseling conference last year."

"Just like that?" Larry demanded incredulously. "With student evaluations and parent meetings scheduled up to my ears? And I can't just leave my apartment. My roommate's leaving right after the last day, which would mean finding someone to watch the place. Besides, I don't have the proper vaccinations for a jungle climate."

Dropping Sara's wrist as if it were suddenly scalding hot, he lapsed to silence, his fair skin flushing bright red. "You think I'm some kind of wimp, don't you?" he said with a tinge of bitterness. "I suppose Bradford would have jumped at going in a minute. Well, I'm sorry, Sara. I love you, and I'd do anything to help you. But I guess I'm not the kind of guy to jump on a plane and fly halfway around the world on a whim without even taking the time to think things out."

He looked more tired and stressed than Sara had ever seen him. As she rubbed the red mark his fingers had left on her wrist, she felt more pity than irritation. An admirable man, kind and gentle, Larry had never been outside of Florida, except for that one trip to Germany. It wasn't his fault he was more at home with troubled elementary students than bad guys or tropical hot spots.

That the same might be said about Sara didn't even cross her mind.

"It's okay, Larry," she said gently. "I was just joking. I don't need any company."

"But you're still going," Larry said harshly.

"I'm still going."

Larry was silent, then straightened up and tried a twisted smile. "Okay, if you're so determined to go, I suppose I could shuffle around those evaluations . . . ask Melanie to check in on my plants and fish tank."

"No, Larry, don't," Sara cut in. "I don't want company. I mean it." Shouldering her knapsack, she stood on tiptoe and brushed her lips against his rigid cheek. "I do love you, Larry—you've been a good friend. And I'll be back . . . before you've had time to worry about me. You'll see."

She left him standing at her desk, his face haggard and miserable as he watched her go.

Chapter Sixty-seven

JUNE 17
CIUDAD DEL ESTE, PARAGUAY

Sara ached with exhaustion by the time she lifted her knapsack out of the overhead bin and made her way up the aisle of the thirty-passenger prop plane and down the stairs onto the tarmac of Ciudad del Este's Garcia Airport. The nature of her schedule—a series of commuter flights—had meant exiting one plane for another all night long. She had slept only in short naps, with an early-morning three-hour stopover in Asunción, before the final hop to Ciudad del Este.

Sara's first glimpse of her destination was depressingly similar to her arrival in Santa Cruz, Bolivia, a year ago. A stiff winter wind bent the tops of the palm trees dotting the far side of the runway, cutting icily through her sweatshirt. Patches of scrub jungle mingled with dirt alleys of shabby cinderblock houses and thatched huts and even shabbier storefronts. Here and there, and rising in the distance above the city center, were the glass, chrome, and fresh paint of new construction.

The terminal itself was small and shabby and depressing, a single waiting area crowded with native businessmen, Guarani Indians with their broad-rimmed hats, and the occasional tourist in Bermuda shorts and bright shirt, busily filming.

At least there was no customs to clear. She had gone through Immigration in Asunción. A yawn brought longing thoughts of her hotel reservation. A few hours stretched out flat would improve her outlook.

She settled instead for a cup of coffee from a food counter placed strategically near the exit. The coffee was served so black and sweet that only its high caffeine value made it drinkable. But Sara had barely taken the first swallow when a surge of adrenaline made the coffee superfluous. She carefully set the cup back down on the counter, but she couldn't control the shaking of her hand. Grabbing a handful of napkins, she wiped up the spill, keeping her head bent forward so that her dark hair shielded her features while out of the corner of her eye she frantically scanned the busy terminal.

No, that single, appalling glance had not deceived her. Not in a thousand years would she forget the man who had taken her captive, threatened her death with cold satisfaction, and hunted her through the jungle night with as little pity as a hound pursuing a rabbit. The black clothing head to toe, the flash of gold at his throat and ears, those cold, high-cheeked features and the flat black gaze now sweeping the terminal were seared into Sara's memory.

Julio Vargas.

The shock jolted Sara past wide-awake to panic. Had Julio recognized her? Or the knapsack he'd once searched himself? Why hadn't she considered this possibility?

But there was no break in Julio's stride as he swept past the food counter and the dark-haired young woman bent over a coffee spill. Sara let her breath out as her father-in-law's former security chief melted into the throng of departures and arrivals.

With an apologetic smile at the waitress, Sara abandoned the rest of the coffee and the mess of stained napkins. Her instinct screamed to throw herself at those exit doors and beg the first taxi driver she saw to rush her away. But how could she run away from the one person who beyond any doubt knew exactly where Doug was and what had happened to him? So she didn't move until she could stop trembling.

After all, if he does see you, what can he do but run himself?

Thrusting down the several possibilities that came to mind, Sara pulled a T-shirt out of her knapsack and draped it over the top, a feeble camouflage but enough she hoped that her well-worn pack would blend with those of other tourists. Then, with a deep breath to steady herself, she drifted back into the terminal until she spotted the telltale black silk jacket.

Julio was standing in line for a boarding pass, his dark features tight with impatience. The flight posted above the ticket counter was scheduled to leave in forty minutes for Mexico City. And he wasn't alone. He was talking in low, annoyed tones to a tall young man with proud, olive-skinned features and an athletic build.

Julio's impatience was understandable. The line was long and moving at a crawl, winding though the plastic chairs provided for waiting passengers. Threading her way around the crowd, Sara settled herself into a chair further along their route. From an empty seat, she picked up an abandoned newspaper, taking advantage of two noisy German tourists beside her to distract attention from her bowed head behind the spread pages. That she did not understand German helped her to focus on the low Spanish of the former Cortéz security chief and his companion as they inched closer.

"The boat should have been in twelve hours ago." The irritated comment was from Julio Vargas.

Julio's companion lifted his shoulders. "Humberto says there were engine problems. What matters is that they are here now and should have no difficulty making their flights. Those with connections from Buenos Aires through London and Frankfurt must be here by noon to make their flight. The others not until this afternoon."

"And those who will meet us in Mexico City?"

"They too connect in Buenos Aires but north to Manaus and Panama."

All of which told Sara nothing except that Julio was on his way out of Paraguay. Then, without a single glance in her direction, the two men were past Sara. She waited until they'd reached the ticket counter, obtained their boarding passes, and walked through the far doors to board their flight before she rose to her feet. She'd give almost anything to push after Julio, grab that black silk collar, and choke out of him what he'd done with Doug. It was perhaps just as well that a guard with an assault rifle stood at the boarding gate to keep her from making such a strategic error.

Sara swung her knapsack to her shoulder. Was it a plus or minus that Julio Vargas was on his way out of the country just as she arrived? His appearance at the airport put to rest any lingering notion that Doug had found this place a dead end and tamely headed home.

But Julio's departure also placed beyond Sara's reach the most likely trail she had to follow. And what did his leaving mean to Doug and his status? If he was not personally holding Doug prisoner—

No, don't go there! Sara drew in deep, quick breaths as her head began to swim. *Just focus on what comes next! Don't think, just do!*

At least Julio's departure removed Sara's greatest concern—that she'd be spotted and recognized. The only attention she attracted now as she exited the sliding glass doors was the whistles and suggestive leers of a group of teen boys loitering outside. She hurried to the first taxi in line, her fluent Spanish as she negotiated the fare disabusing the driver of his hopes for a gullible foreigner.

Sara had printed out the Web-site data for her hotel reservation, but for the first destination she'd chosen, she had no street address. She'd just have to hope that here, as in Bolivia, the average taxi driver was more savvy than the U.S. State Department liked to admit.

"Please, can you take me to the American DEA?" she answered the driver's questioning glance in the rearview mirror.

In the mirror, the driver's eyebrows shot up. "La DEA? Los antinarcóticos americanos?" he repeated, and Sara knew she'd struck water when he pronounced the initials as "day-ah" with unhesitating familiarity. Truth told, the average citizen of drug-producing and smuggling nations were far more conversant with and interested in the activities of the U.S. Drug Enforcement Administration than their American counterparts, their overseas programs providing a regular soap opera on the local news.

"Do you have an address?" When Sara shook her head, the taxi driver picked up the mike of his CB radio. "*Despache, despache.* This is number twenty-one. I need directions to the *oficina* of the americano 'day-ah.'"

Sara couldn't decipher the static that crackled back, but the driver apparently could because he moved off into traffic. The trip into the city took less time than the crowded roads would seem to allow, and if the adrenaline rush of her encounter with Julio Vargas hadn't left Sara wide awake, the swerving in and out of lanes, zipping just behind the wheels of cargo trucks and tour buses, missing a donkey cart with inches to spare, would have done it. Ciudad del Este's commercial nature was advertised everywhere in billboards and signs on buildings and buses and even the sides of donkey carts. Coca-Cola. Sony. Chanel. Adidas.

An entire series of billboards boasted the enigmatic smile of Leonardo da Vinci's masterpiece. "Come visit the Mona Lisa. She is waiting to welcome you" seemed to be the gist of the ads. If Sara had cared, it would have been a letdown when she reached the city center and discovered that the mysterious smile was simply advertising a modern and large department store called Mona Lisa.

"You can buy the same merchandise much cheaper on the street," the taxi driver offered over his shoulder. "They say it is less genuine, but if it looks the same, why should it matter?"

The city itself had the same mix of crass commercialism and squalor Sara remembered from Santa Cruz. The pavement was crowded with vendors and strewn with garbage, the storefronts dirty and graffiti-marked even though their windows were filled with luxury items few Paraguayans would ever be able to afford. Elderly cars and jeeps so dilapidated they had to be held together with baling wire jostled along next to brand-new Mercedes and Mitsubishi Monteros, while ragged, filthy children dashed into traffic, eager to earn a few cents polishing shoes or carrying bags—or lifting wallets if employment were not forthcoming.

The taxi broke free of the city center and entered the wide avenues of an upper class neighborhood with spacious homes. Turning a corner onto a quiet tree-lined street, the taxi drew up in front of a guard shack. The high, white wall and two-story home behind it didn't stand out from its neighbors except that the two guards wore combat fatigues and carried M-16s along with the usual hip holster.

"Do you want me to wait for you?" the taxi driver asked as Sara counted out the fare. "Or—if you like, I am available by the day. One hundred dollars U.S. But for you we can make a special price."

"No, I'm sorry. I don't know my plans right now." But Sara took the card he offered. "If I do need a taxi, I'll definitely ask for you. You've been very kind."

As the taxi drove away, Sara stopped on the curb long enough to dig out of her knapsack the one extra item she'd brought with her on the trip. It was a photo Cynthia had allowed her to choose from among the dozens around her home. It had been a favorite of Sara's—a close-up of Doug glancing up from something he'd been working on, his head lifted with an alertness that said he was searching for what had caught his attention, his gray eyes narrowed in the watchful gaze that Sara knew so well.

It was so . . . Doug, Sara had not looked at it as she packed. She couldn't afford tears. Neither did she look now as she advanced toward the two guards. One of them immediately stepped forward, his M-16 sliding from his shoulder into his hands.

"*Señorita,* you will step back, please, and place your bag on the ground."

Paraguay or Bolivia, embassy routines were the same. Sliding her knapsack to the ground, Sara unzipped the top and let the guard peer into its depths. When he gave a satisfied nod, she held out the photo. "I'm looking for this man. An agent of the DEA. Could you please take a look and tell me if you've seen him?"

The guard stepped forward, but the second guard, who had stayed two steps back, assault rifle ready in a clearly choreographed procedure, spoke up. "I am sorry, but we are not allowed to give out such information. You will have to speak to the Americans inside."

Sara grimaced inwardly as the first guard retreated. She should have expected this. "I understand." Sliding out her passport, she handed it over instead. "I'm an American. May I speak to the agent in charge?"

The U.S. passport must have been the proper password because the assault rifles immediately eased and the second guard raised a hand radio to his mouth. "Señor, there is a gringa here who says she wishes to speak to *el jefe americano*."

Sara didn't have to wait long before an electronic buzz unlocked the pedestrian door beside the guard shack. "*El agente* is waiting for you inside," the guard told Sara, pushing the door open for her.

Stepping through, Sara blinked with surprise when she had to drop her eyes to see the agent who'd come to meet her. The powerfully built black man wheeling a motorized chair toward her gave a wry smile that said he was used to her reaction.

"Andy Williams," he introduced. "The intel analyst here. I understand you're asking for an American agent? May I ask who's calling and why?"

The question was cool and uncompromising, and even from his wheelchair, the intel analyst projected a daunting presence, the muscled brawn of his upper body compensating easily for the immobility of his lower limbs. He'd been an agent, Sara would bet. And he knew well how to conduct an interrogation.

But Sara had not come this far to be intimidated, nor was she a criminal suspect. Lifting her chin higher, she reached to meet his strong grip. "My name is Sara Connor. I'm here from Miami to talk to you, if you can give me a few minutes, about Doug Bradford."

"Bradford?" The intel analyst's sharp gaze narrowed. "And your connection is—?"

"I'm—" Glancing away from his astute scrutiny, Sara voiced aloud for the first time what she knew now to be the truth. "Doug was the man I was going to marry."

"I'm sorry." There was patent sincerity in the intel analyst's abrupt pronouncement. "Bradford was a good agent. I was sorry to hear what went down with him up there in Miami. So what can I do for you?"

"I just . . . I want to talk to you about Doug—and to anyone else who actually saw him and spoke to him while he was here."

"Sure. Don't know what all I can tell you, but come on in." Expertly reversing the wheelchair, the intel analyst led the way across the patio. "As long as it doesn't take too long. We're kind of busy right now."

That they were, Sara saw, as she followed the wheelchair indoors, a busyness she'd been around the DEA long enough to recognize. The open down-stairs area was crowded with men in camouflage fatigues milling around or bent over tables piled high with equipment or spread out with maps and docu-ments. There were maps on the walls as well and assault rifles and backpacks and other gear piled in corners. She'd interrupted a raid in progress.

Andy Williams led Sara past the confusion, wheeling through an open door into an office filled with computer equipment and communication gear. "Okay, what is it you want to know? I have to say I didn't really know Bradford . . . never met him until he came down here. But he'd got quite a rep as an agent, and he seemed like a nice guy, even if he did get me into hot water with that GPS system stunt."

Sara's ears pricked up immediately. "What do you mean? What GPS system?"

"Well, if you follow technology, you know GPS is a tracking system." As Williams described Doug's "borrowing" of his equipment, Sara marked the date down in her planner. Friday afternoon. It had been the next day that Doug called Sara for the last time. Sara stared at the entry with dawning excitement as she processed what the intel analyst was saying.

"Mr. Williams . . . uh, sir. This GPS tracking system. If Doug used it to fol-low this guy he was after, wouldn't the system have the coordinates where he went? Couldn't you track just where he'd been by the course he followed on the unit?"

"Call me Andy. Mr. Williams is my father," the intel analyst said with a faint smile, but he went on to shake his head. "Sure, you could follow the coordinates, except that when Bradford returned the unit, he'd wiped it clean—inside and out, if you know what I mean. Carrying case dusted off, every piece wiped down, and, unfortunately, the memory erased. I know because I checked it over good. It's one expensive piece of equipment, and Patterson was practically foaming at the mouth over it. Just as well Doug didn't show up in person, or Patterson might have punched him out."

Andy shot a rueful grin at Sara. "Wipe that off your memory chips, if you don't mind. Patterson wasn't too happy with Bradford, with reason enough, and he has a thing about handing out intel to civilians—any intel, restricted or otherwise. But it's no secret Bradford was here, and I figure if anyone's got a right to know, it's family."

"Of course . . . thank you." But Sara's attention was several sentences back. "What did you mean, it's lucky Doug didn't show back up in person. I thought you said—well, the Miami DEA office said . . ." Sara's breath was growing tight.

"The report said Doug came here to return equipment after he got back to Ciudad del Este from a trip and just before he flew out to Miami. That's how they confirmed he'd gone back to the U.S."

"And I'm sure he did. He must have, since the equipment was returned, all right. He just didn't show up in the office here itself as far as I know. At least I didn't catch him personally."

"Then who did catch him? Who actually saw him after he borrowed that stuff? Or after he got back from that trip out of town Saturday afternoon?"

The intel analyst's massive shoulders rose and fell. "I've no idea. But here's the guy who does. He's the acting SAC here. Actually, the only other agent in the place, since we've only got two Americans here. Chris—we've got a guest."

Sara had seldom experienced such an immediate negative reaction to a new acquaintance. But her hackles rose the moment she turned around to set eyes on the man who was striding into the RAC's office. He was about Doug's age and as ash-blonde as Sara's cousin Joe, but there all resemblance ended. His mouth was compressed into what looked like a permanent angry line, his angular features supercilious, and the pale blue eyes cold as they landed on Sara.

"The guard said we had guests," he said curtly. "What seems to be the problem? This is hardly a good time for social visits. We've got a mission ready to head out."

Andy Williams waved a hand toward Sara. "Sara Connor, Chris Patterson. Sara is Bradford's fiancée. She's got some questions for us."

Catching the change in the other agent's expression, Sara realized with a chill: *He doesn't like Doug.* But there was something more urgent she'd caught in Andy Williams's introduction.

"You are the SAC here, Andy says," Sara began. "Then I have some intel— that's what you call it, right?—you might need right away. That man Doug was here looking for, Julio Vargas, did he tell you about him?"

"I know who he is," the SAC answered impatiently. "I checked his file when Doug requested info on him. Why?"

"Well, I saw him today at the airport when I flew in. He was getting on a flight to Mexico with another man. I overheard him say he was meeting some people in Mexico City."

"Really." The DEA agent did not display the slightest interest in her news. "Well, if you give me that in writing, I'll certainly let the Mexico office know that this Vargas has moved into their territory."

"That's all?" Sara demanded incredulously. Were fugitive drug dealers so common down here, they didn't raise a flicker of interest, much less action? Was this the kind of cooperation Doug had gotten, the reason he'd been alone on that trip? "But . . . don't you want to arrest him or something? Stop him at the other end of the flight? He's a drug dealer . . . that should be in your file. That's why Doug was down here looking for him."

"A drug dealer." The impatience was back in the SAC's tone, and Sara did not like the way he leaned his superior height forward above her as if to use his body language to intimidate. "Look, lady, I know this guy's a big deal to you—oh, sure, I read the file—and I'm really sorry to disappoint you. I have no doubt you're right and this guy belongs behind the bars. But let me enlighten you a bit on how things work down here. Do you know how many thousands of these guys—just the known ones in our files, like this Vargas of yours—move back and forth across the borders down here at any given time? We don't have the manpower or time to run around trying to pick them up, even if we had the jurisdiction. Which we don't. It's up to the locals if they want to take issue with a slime like Vargas flying in and out of their country. And they won't, let me assure you, not unless you've got a reliable tip he's carrying a suitcase of coke on board—and he's forgotten to pay off the right guys at the other end. If this Julio Vargas is heading to Mexico, then he falls under their federales.

"Like I said, I'll get it into the system that there's a potential perp moving into their area. That doesn't mean the intel's no use. If something comes down the line, that piece of the puzzle might even be just what they need. We always appreciate concerned citizens. Now—what is this about Bradford?"

"This whole thing is about Bradford!" Sara cried. "Don't you see? If Julio was here all this time, then that means Doug wouldn't have given up and gone home like the report says. Which means he couldn't have disappeared in Miami, but here in Paraguay."

She hadn't expressed her hypothesis as tactfully as she'd intended, because the SAC's pale complexion flushed into anger. "Ms. Connor, I don't know what you're trying to imply. I understand how hard it is for families to accept these things and let go. But if you are insinuating that this office filed a false report—lady, we've got things to do here."

In a moment he'd be walking out.

"Please, I'm sorry," Sara said hastily. "I didn't mean to imply any negligence here." Holding out her day planner, she indicated the entry she'd just made for Andy Williams. "I'm just trying to track down Doug's movements during his last days here in Paraguay—where he went, who he saw, who saw him, who spoke to him."

"Before or after he returned our borrowed equipment is what she's trying to nail down," Andy Williams spoke up lazily.

Chris Patterson shot him a hard look, and Sara had no doubt that the intel analyst's presence was the only reason the SAC would even answer her. Patterson paused to glance at the planner Sara had opened on the nearest counter surface. "Well, he got in here sometime Sunday night. I know because he left a voice message. He came by Monday morning, didn't you say, Williams?"

As the intel analyst nodded, Sara marked the date in her planner. Doug had called her in Seattle on Saturday night to say he was flying to Paraguay, making his arrival from Asunción to Ciudad del Este sometime Sunday. The first weekend was now accounted for.

"He came back in here on Friday, saying he'd seen this Vargas and demanding we go after him," the SAC went on. "I told him categorically we couldn't get involved. We had reasons you don't need to know. For one, Bradford was poking around across the border in Brazil. That's Brasilia's responsibility, not ours, and so I told him here, on Saturday—" he tapped the planner again "—when he called. He said then he'd be leaving town . . . in his own sweet time. I told him to return the equipment he'd stolen—pardon me, Ms. Connor—from our office, and he hung up on me."

"Then neither of you actually spoke to Doug that Monday when he was supposed to have flown out."

"Of course I did," the SAC snapped. "It was in my report. He told me he'd come to a dead end and was heading back to Miami. And that he'd drop off his stolen equipment—all without an apology, at that."

"But none of you actually saw him that day," Sara persisted. "Face to face so that you could identify one hundred percent that it was really him."

There was a pause, and she saw red flush all the way up the SAC's neck under his pale skin. Again, she was certain that only the intel analyst's lazy gaze finally elicited a response. "Well, no, he called from his hotel. But if you're implying—"

"I'm not trying to imply anything," Sara cried as he stopped again, "But if none of you saw Doug yourselves, who did he give that GPS thing to? And how could you put in your report that you were so certain he flew home from here?"

"Americans aren't the only ones with eyes," Chris Patterson said coldly. "If you'll look around this place, you'll see a whole lot more than three people. Yes, it's true my own last exchange with Bradford was over the phone. But let me assure you we didn't simply file an unconfirmed report. Doug was here. The guards will vouch for that. I am sorry about your loss, Ms. Connor—" his clipped tones held no emotion at all "—but I'm not going to stand here and let you imply I fell down in some way on the job. If you'll excuse me, I have an op to kick off and no more time to waste."

"Wait. What about a report? Didn't Doug leave anything with you or make any report that said where he was going, maybe gave the coordinates on that GPS tracker?"

"If he did, that information would certainly not be available to the public. Good-bye, Ms. Connor."

He was gone. Swallowing back her frustration, Sara gathered her belongings. "May I at least talk to the guards?" she asked the intel analyst. "They wouldn't talk to me without permission."

Andy Williams spread his hand. "Good for them. At least they're following regs, for a change. But . . . I don't know. Patterson's pretty—"

Sara'd had enough. "I don't care what Patterson says," she said flatly. "I'm not leaving here—not Paraguay, not this office—until I get the answers I came for. If you want to get rid of me, the easiest way is to let me finish. Otherwise, believe me, I'm going to be out front making such a nuisance of myself you'll have to call the police or the embassy to drag me away. And if it makes CNN, so much the better!"

"Wow!" The intel analyst let out a soft whistle. "I'm beginning to see how you and Bradford would make a pair. Okay, come along. I'll see what I can do."

The main work area was even busier when Sara followed the wheelchair back out. The Paraguayan counternarcotics troops were shouldering packs and slinging assault rifles into place. At one table, his back turned to them, Chris Patterson bent over a spread-out map, a Paraguayan military officer beside him.

The two guards at the front gate lost their wariness when they saw Andy Williams escorting Sara. The first guard took the photo from Sara, then passed it to the other guard. "Yes, I remember him well. *El agente americano.* We do not get many gringos, and he came more than once."

"Can you show me when?" Sara drew out her planner. "I know he was here on this Monday because he spoke to Señor Williams here when he came."

Glancing at the calendar date, the guard shrugged. "If Señor Williams says he was here that day, then he was. I could not say. All days are alike out here, and it was many weeks ago. I do remember that the gringo came more than once, and Señor Patterson—"

He stopped, throwing a cautious glance at the intel analyst. Andy offered Sara a crooked grin. "I think you'll get more out of them if I'm not here," he said in English. "They're afraid they'll get in trouble if they talk around me. And since guard duty here pays several times what they can make in the regular army—or anywhere else—they don't want to say anything that's going to get back to Patterson and maybe get them fired."

In Spanish, he added, "Santos, I need to get back to work. But any help you can offer this lady will be well compensated."

The intel analyst didn't wait for the electric buzzer but pulled out his own keys and let himself in. As the gate shut behind him, Sara turned pleading eyes on the guard. "Please! Señor Bradford is my *novio*—my fiancé. I'm trying to find out what happened to him. Anything you can tell me will help."

The guard looked sympathetic. "Yes, of course. We heard that the *agente americano* disappeared in America. I am truly sorry. He was a good man and respectful—not like some of the gringos." He shot a baleful eye toward the door behind him. "I remember when the *agente* came. He was smiling. He showed me his '*day-ah*' identification. Patterson came to take him inside. He was not there long. He came out carrying a black case."

"You're talking about Friday, then," Sara said. "That's when he talked to Señor Patterson. And that's when he borrowed the GPS unit from Señor Williams."

Sara made a mark on the calendar as the guard went on, "When Señor Bradford came back the next time, he did not stop to speak to any of the *agentes americanos*. He seemed very much in a hurry. He simply told me to give a package to Señor Patterson and left. But—"

He hesitated, looking cautious, then went on, "Well, the truth is that it was a busy day with many people coming and going. I did not remember the package until the night. Señor Patterson was very angry that it had been left all those hours in the guardhouse, even though there was a guard on duty all the time."

"But you're sure it was Señor Bradford. Couldn't you have mistaken another gringo for him? They are often similar."

The guard shook his head. "No, I am sorry, but there could be no mistake because he smiled and was very respectful and took time to speak to me before giving me the package. And he asked that I make certain it went to Señor Patterson and no one else. Which I did—just not immediately. Then Señor Bradford got back into the taxi and drove away. I did not see him again."

Sara felt physically ill, her stomach squeezing acid up into her throat, her breath coming hard. Had she come all this way for nothing, deluded herself all this time? She could hardly get her next words out through dry lips. "Then you were the one who returned the GPS unit—the black case Señor Bradford borrowed—to Señor Patterson. And you are absolutely certain it was Señor Bradford who gave it to you."

But rather than confirming those cruel, hopeless statements, the guard was looking astonished. "But, señorita, it was not the case Señor Bradford took from here that he asked me to give to Señor Patterson. It was an envelope. A big yellow one—*maneela,* they call it. Of the return of this case, I know nothing."

Sara's knees went so weak she would have groped for a chair, had there been one. It must have showed in her face because the guard reached out a hand to steady her.

"You're saying that when Señor Bradford came by that Monday morning on the way to the airport, it was *not* to return his equipment, but to leave an envelope? Then—who brought back the GPS?"

"Ah!" The guard raised a hand now. "There is your problem. I did not see the *agente americano* on a Monday. The day Bradford gave me the envelope was a Saturday, the very next day after I saw him first. How can I be so certain? It is simple. I do not work Mondays. My days are Wednesday through Sunday. My *compañero* here works Saturday through Wednesday. There is another *guardia* who takes our place during our days of liberty. José!"

Sara tried to tamp down the hope that insisted on surging through her as the other guard ambled over, still with Doug's photo in hand. "Yes, of course, I was here with Ruben, the other guard, the first time Señor Bradford came. Señor Patterson was not here, so I took the *agente* in to speak to Señor Williams. I would have to look at the visitors' logs, but it must have been a Monday or Tuesday if Santos was not here. And, yes, it was I who returned the case Señor Bradford borrowed, to Señor Patterson."

Sara could not breathe as she asked sharply, "And you're certain it was the man in this photo who handed you the case? Did he show his ID?"

The guard pushed back the strap of his M-16, rubbing a forefinger along the bridge of his nose as he considered the question, until Sara was dizzy from lack of air. Finally, he said, "No, I remember. It was the taxi driver who brought me the case and said it belonged to the *agentes americanos*. Señor Bradford did not leave the taxi this time. But I did not take the case before ascertaining that it was the *americano*. Bombs, you know. It was the gringo in the taxi. He wore a sombrero, but he was big and blond—*americano*—and he held up his passport and '*day-ah*' identification when I looked into the taxi to see. So I knew it was not a bomb. Still, we did not take the case inside until Señor Patterson had checked it himself."

Bingo!" Sara's breath left her in a whoosh. The same technique used on Doug's neighbors. And she'd bet the person making that phone call to Chris Patterson had been suffering a bad cold.

He's here. He never came back. Someone came back, but it wasn't Doug. Sara's speculation went to the young man with Julio at the airport. He'd been the right size—maybe even taller. But no one could mistake those aquiline, olive-skinned features for Doug.

Sara looked down at her day planner. Doug had been here on Monday—the day he'd arrived in Ciudad del Este. Friday he'd come back to borrow the GPS tracker. In that intervening time, then, he'd come across Julio Vargas and concluded it would be necessary to track him outside the city. Saturday he had stopped by, but not to talk to the DEA agents. Which made perfect sense to Sara if Doug had "borrowed" that GPS tracker without Chris Patterson's permission and was trying to avoid the guy. By the time frame, it couldn't have been long before he'd called Sara and left on his trip. *So why take the time to swing by here on his way out of town?*

His report! Doug never worked without a backup plan. Murphy's Law. If you can't avoid it, you prepare for it. The thought brought Doug's tone of voice to her mind.

A bedlam of voices and other noise broke into Sara's deliberations. Down the perimeter wall from the guardhouse, a rusty screeching denoted the main gate sliding back. A Landrover rolled out onto the street. Behind the double-paned windshield, Sara spotted Chris Patterson at the wheel and beside him the Paraguayan officer. Behind the Landrover came an army truck, the back packed with Paraguayan counternarcotics troops. The SAC didn't acknowledge Sara with so much as a flicker of his eyes as the convoy went by, though she was certain her continued presence had not escaped his notice. She turned back to the first guard, Santos.

"This envelope. You say Señor Patterson has it now?"

The guard shrugged. A car was coming slowly down the street, and he was beginning to look edgy, his M-16 sliding off his shoulders into his hands. "I took it inside for Señor Patterson, yes. Who has it now, I would not know."

Sara had lost them. The guards were stepping away to confront this new challenge, the second guard falling back two paces in their practiced choreography.

But the car was only a taxi cruising for a fare. "*La señorita* needs a ride?" the driver called out, rolling down his window. Sara gathered up her knapsack and retrieved the photo from the second guard. She'd gotten what she could, and pressing the two guards further would only turn their cooperation into annoyance.

"Thank you so much. You've been of great help." Pressing a ten dollar bill into each guard's hands, Sara waved the cab to a stop.

Where next? Exhaustion pressed down on Sara as the driver glanced back at her. But it was still short of noon, and according to the Hotel Las Américas Web site, Sara couldn't check into her hotel until at least 2 P.M. Refolding the computer printout, Sara unfolded another sheet of paper she'd tucked into her planner.

The local DEA agents had been as singularly unhelpful as their Miami counterparts, barricaded from intrusive civilians like her behind their wall of bureaucracy and handbook regulations. But she'd found out what both this field office and Miami had failed to verify, thanks to Chris Patterson's arrogance in dealing with the locals, and perhaps his dislike for his fellow agent, Doug, which had caused him to neglect information that was right before his eyes—and ears.

So, as in Miami, Sara would do what Chris Patterson had not, following in Doug's footsteps and asking questions herself until she knew exactly what he had done down here and where he'd gone.

Passing the computer printout over the seat to the driver, Sara said crisply, "To this place right here, please. Jungle Tours."

Chapter Sixty-Eight

Jungle Tours was less impressive than its Web page, a single shopfront in the crowded shopping bazaar that anchored the center of the city. The street in front was crammed with market stands, vendors, and tourists, and beyond a large parking area, Sara caught a glimpse of brown water and the arch of a bridge.

The inside of the agency was more luxurious, and she was greeted by two receptionists in tight red minis. They were as cordial and accommodating as the DEA guards had been—and of as little help. "Yes, he was here. So good looking!" the one behind the desk sighed over Doug's photo. *"Muy americano."*

Very American. An attribute that makes up for any other as long as its possessor is competent to sign an immigrant application.

"He was showing a photo, just as you are," said the second. "That is why I remember him. Many gringos come in here for tours, but he was looking for his friend, because he wished to take a tour with him into the jungle."

"And did he find his friend?" Sara caught the curious gleam in their eyes and knew she'd made the question too urgent. Quickly, she added, "The man is an acquaintance of mine, too. I haven't seen either of them for a long time, and I'd hoped to see them again while we're all here in your city. But I don't have the directions to where they're staying—only that they were interested in your tours. I'd really like to catch up with both of them if I can."

Every word the literal truth and—judging by their nods—acceptable enough.

"No, your *americano* friend did not find the other—not here at least. And it was not one of our tours," the receptionist from behind the desk put in. "The tour he wished to take was the one next door. Rain Forest Survival Treks. We told him they were full. He chose to take our tour instead—much more comfortable. Would you be interested in the same tour?"

Sara didn't respond to the offer of brochures, but went instead to the door to glance down the street. She'd noticed activity next door when she descended from the taxi, and took notice of the RST over the window because it too appeared on the Jungle Tours Web site.

Now, taking a longer look, Sara separated the activity next door into its components. A black Mercedes was pulled up to the curb. Beside it stood two men in sober business suits, both with thick black beards, one a head taller than the other and leaner.

Drawn up behind the Mercedes was a white pickup, its passengers occupied with unloading packs and burlap bags from the bed of the pickup into the open door of the RST agency. The half-dozen men moving back and forth were as varied in ethnicity as any group of tourists, but all were young, male, and dressed in the khaki outfits typical to jungle tours.

"One of the survival treks returning." Lacking other customers, the two receptionists had crowded with Sara at the door. "They do not return often. They are long treks. They have a boat down on the river that takes them back and forth." The one who'd spoken shuddered. "Why anyone would wish to crawl around in the jungle when they can live in comfort makes no sense."

"And the men with the Mercedes—who are they?" Sara asked.

"That is Señor Mozer Jebai, the owner now of Jungle Tours. He is a very important man in Ciudad del Este. He bought this business from our former employers some months ago and opened up the place next door soon after. The other is one of his relatives. They do not often involve themselves with the running of this place. They have many businesses, you understand. But they come sometimes to see if it is running well. Now—"

The receptionist who had been seated behind the desk interrupted. "So, would you like us to book you a tour? Perhaps the same one your friend found of interest? Most of the package tours left this morning, but we have a few afternoon excursions."

The brochures were coming back out. Sara shook her head apologetically. "Perhaps later. What I'm really interested in is the same survival trek that interested my friend. Now that they're back, maybe they have an opening for me. If they don't, I'll be back, I promise." Offering an apologetic smile to their hand-waving protests, Sara stepped out of the tour office. The unloading crew next door had just finished and one of the men was lowering the metal shutters of the storefront. A young, olive-skinned woman in a demure blouse and skirt lifted a metal grating over the door and began snapping a padlock in place.

The trekkers were already climbing back into the pickup, and as Sara walked toward them, the vehicle pulled away from the curb, leaving only the two Mercedes passengers and the woman for Sara to approach.

"Excuse me, but I'm looking for this tour—a rain forest survival trek. Do you know where I can sign up for it?" Sara held out the Web site printout in the general direction of all three. The woman stepped forward with the accustomed bearing of a secretary, but it was the taller of the two Mercedes passengers, the one the Jungle Tours receptionists had called Mozer Jebai, who spoke up, in accented Spanish, "We are no longer accepting applications for these tours. This office will be shut until further notice."

Here was the place to bring in Doug's photo, and there was no reason to hesitate . . . except for something in the cold dismissal of the two men's glances and the avaricious curiosity in the woman's large, dark eyes. With reluctance Sara held the photo out to the two men. "Then . . . could you tell me if you've seen this man? He came here some time ago to apply for one of your survival treks."

There was no recognition in the cold eyes. Waving Sara off with an impatient gesture, Mozer Jebai turned toward the Mercedes. The chauffeur was already striding around the car to open the door. Sara pulled the photo back as the stockier of the two men began climbing into the Mercedes. But as she did, the secretary's eyes widened in unmistakable recognition. It was not a look of pleasant recollection.

The woman turned in a swift flow of speech to the two men, her language unintelligible, but not her low, urgent tone. Then Sara caught a word she did understand, and her blood turned cold.

Vargas.

The agency owner swung around. "Señorita, perhaps we have been hasty. It is possible we may still find an opening for you on our latest tour. If you would care to come with us, we will speak about it."

But Sara was already stepping backward off the curb, melting into the crowd of people, her heart pounding so hard it had to be audible to the jostling throng around her. She stepped behind a large, ambling man with a sombrero, then heard a car door slam as she ducked behind a young couple speaking French.

The Mercedes was moving away from the curb into the congested street, the tinted windows rolled down so that the occupants could survey the crowd. But Sara had already threaded her way between two market stands. Stooping down behind the hood of a cargo truck, she watched, heartbeat gradually slowing to normal, as the Mercedes moved slowly down the street.

* * *

"Vargas!" Khalil spat out, signaling to the chauffeur to give up the search. "Always Vargas! You should have disposed of him when you took care of the others."

As the chauffeur stepped on the accelerator, Khalil glanced across the plush leather interior of the Mercedes. "Could it be the Americans have learned something of our project?"

Mozer Jebai made a negative gesture. "And send a single agent and a woman? No, it is Vargas's past life, not his present, that brought the agent here and now this woman. A complication we did not consider when we took him from the prison."

"He said the American agent was taken care of. That all was arranged so no one would come looking for him. Even Saleh agreed that the plan was foolproof. Now what are we to do?"

Khalil's plump features looked as worried as any financial advisor contemplating the ruin of a considerable investment. "When I think of the great wealth we have poured into this venture. If we must now call all this off . . . curse that mongrel to the fires of hell! We should have left him to rot in prison."

"All things cannot be anticipated," Sheik Jebai answered calmly. "We needed Vargas. And be assured, when he is no longer needed, he will be dealt with."

Khalil nodded. "All things cannot be anticipated."

"No," the mullah continued, "we have come too far to panic this easily. The mission has already begun. Saleh is on his way. And until he reaches his destination, we cannot even alert him. Besides, the Americans know nothing. It has been two months, and no authority has even come to ask questions. This is but a woman looking for her lover, unsatisfied with the official report. Still—" he steepled his long fingers and brought them to his lips "—thanks to Vargas, the agent did find his way to our camp. That we have remained undisturbed all these weeks makes it unlikely he left a record behind. But here at least we will err on the side of caution. Rashima—"

The Lebanese woman in the front seat turned her head.

"—as of today, Rain Forest Survival Treks will cease to exist. You will take care of it. And the camp must be shut down. Khalil and I will deal with that ourselves."

* * *

When the Mercedes had turned a corner and was out of sight, Sara continued walking across the parking area, threading through buses toward the glimpse of river ahead. She passed near a helicopter on a gravel landing pad, its looming bulk a bleak reminder of Julio Vargas and the combat helicopter in which he'd taken Sara hostage.

A chill winter gust tugged at Sara's sweatshirt as she pushed her way through packing crates, strewn garbage, and what had to be fish parts down to the water. On a direct line from the Jungle Tours office, a riverboat rocked lazily to the slow current. The boat looked empty of life, but a rubber inflatable boat, only half-deflated, lay at the far end of the deck. Sara eyed the *RST* stenciled on its side.

This must be the boat those receptionists referred to. But does it have anything to do with Doug?

However abandoned the boat might appear, Sara kept out of sight behind a stack of lumber. She was still shaken by her last encounter. That she hadn't considered this possibility simply underscored her own inexperience as an investigative agent. An inexperience that could prove more hazardous than she'd allowed for. The Jungle Tours receptionists had told her that Doug was interested in this Rain Forest Survival Treks. The equipment Julio Vargas had ordered from Diego and Raymundo might even be in those packs she'd seen carried into the trekking agency.

Which means I might be asking questions of the very people Doug was after— the very people involved in his disappearance. Were those two men and the woman in the Mercedes among them? What about the men in the pickup? How am I supposed to know? I could be walking into the same trap as Doug. What do I do?

Her gaze didn't shift from the riverboat's gentle rocking, though a mounting headache had begun pressing at the back of her eyes. Those men—and that woman—had frightened her even more than seeing Julio Vargas in the airport. Would they have snatched her into that car, had she not run? Would she too have simply disappeared? Every step she took was fraught now with possible disaster. And yet if she didn't continue to probe, how could she find out the truth? She might as well give up in defeat and go home.

God, I have no idea what I'm doing, and I'm so scared! Where do I go next? Back to Doug's next step, that's where!

Sara straightened her shoulders under the knapsack. *Why be so apprehensive? After all, Julio Vargas is out of the country now. The RST people are gone. Don't wimp out now, Sara.*

Still, threading back through the parking lot was one of the more difficult tasks she had ever forced herself to, her heart beating too fast, her eyes roving constantly for a glimpse of a black Mercedes or a white pickup.

But the coast was clear, and when she slipped back into the Jungle Tours office. the two receptionists displayed only the professional pleasure of seeing a returning customer. When Sara walked in, they were dealing with a group who'd overslept and missed their departure, and she had to wait until they rebooked for the next day before the receptionists could turn their attention to her.

"So . . . you were not able to book your tour after all?" the receptionist behind the desk beamed.

"No, they're still full up." Sara drew her pocketbook out of her knapsack. "You said my friend took one of your tours instead. Any chance I could follow the same tour? Maybe one of his guides might know something that would help me locate my friend or our mutual acquaintance."

Sara ignored the knowing exchange of glances. If they thought she was chasing a couple of male tourists, so much the better.

The receptionist behind the desk shrugged. "He took the same tour they all do . . . to the Falls of Iguazú. It is why the tourists come."

"On a tour bus? Do you have records of which one?"

Sara misinterpreted the undecided look that went between the two receptionists, so when the second woman spoke, her words were totally unanticipated. "He didn't go by land."

"Then how did he go?"

Again, the hesitant glances. By now, Sara was well-versed in local custom. Peeling off a fifty-dollar bill from Cynthia's largesse, she laid it on the counter. "It is very important to me to track down my friend."

Now the glances were directed at the U.S. currency. The desk receptionist answered. "He flew out in the Jungle Tours helicopter."

When Sara's hand did not leave the bill, further grudging admissions disclosed that Jungle Tours ran helicopter flights over the Brazilian side of Iguazú Falls, and if it wasn't quite regulation for the pilot to take passengers on his border hop—a wink here—arrangements could always be made, one understood, of course.

It was Sara's first concrete piece of data, and her spirits rose. Here at last was someone with whom Doug had spent time. The helicopter wouldn't be back until dark, but Sara refused to consider that an obstacle. She'd just have to hope that a helicopter ride over the falls wouldn't be too noisy for conversation.

"When does your afternoon excursion leave?"

Sara made no attempt to dicker over the price, leaving the two women smiling as she threaded her way across the parking lot toward a man dressed in a bright red Jungle Tours uniform. Only then did Sara learn that her late arrival had cost her a trip on one of the red tour buses featured in the brochures. Instead, she was ushered to an ancient city bus that apparently handled overflow tourists.

"If you are ready to return by 6 P.M.," the Jungle Tours guide assured Sara, "you will be able to return on one of *our* buses. You have only to show this ticket."

Sara clambered up the steps with reluctance. This was no well-appointed tour bus. The seats were hard vinyl benches, and the air-conditioning consisted of jamming the windows half-open to let in the breeze and dust. Brazilian samba blasting from the radio drowned out the engine's noisy rumble, but not the diesel fumes.

Settling herself gingerly in an aisle seat, Sara watched the bus fill up. A heavily built peasant woman with sombrero and heavy pack tucked her burden behind the driver's seat before moving to the back of the bus. An Asian man handed the driver a food container redolent of garlic and onion, reminding Sara she'd eaten neither breakfast nor lunch. As the driver began eating, the Asian passenger stowed packages under seats and between the driver's seat and outer wall of the bus.

Everyone climbing on seemed just as loaded with baggage, but only when a well-dressed woman with a Portuguese accent asked Sara to hold a carton of cigarettes did it dawn on her that the other passengers were preparing for the customs inspection coming at the border just ahead.

Sara turned down the offer of cigarettes, but a Guarani woman with a baby suckling at her breast, who was just now squeezing into the seat beside Sara, accepted two boxes before thrusting a large blanket-wrapped bundle between the seats so that Sara had to move her feet into the aisle.

The bus had barely begun to roll when the Cigarette Lady, as Sara mentally dubbed her, pulled out an *empanada,* one of the cheese-filled fried turnovers that were as popular here as an order of French fries back home. Polishing it off with a few quick bites, she wadded up the greasy paper sack that came with it and tossed it out the window. Sara's American-bred impulse to protest was curbed as the driver finished his own lunch and tossed out the Styrofoam container.

All around, the other passengers were breaking out their lunches. Out the windows went orange and banana peels. Chicken bones. Bags and containers. It seemed no one had heard of a trash can. No wonder the streets were so thick with garbage.

The last of the trash was hastily tossed out as the bus neared the arch identified in the brochures as the Bridge of Friendship connecting Paraguay with Brazil. Both sides of the street were jammed solid with market stands and ambulatory vendors catering to the creeping lines of buses, trucks, cars, and horse carts crossing the bridge. Pedestrians streamed on by, but as the bus inched up to the bridge, it stopped. Just ahead was a barrier and guard booth that had to be the border crossing, though the official who ambled forward to board the bus wore an extraordinary uniform of blue jeans and pocket-studded cloth vest.

Sara had her passport out for the expected tourist stamp, but the customs officer didn't ask for identification documents. Instead, he walked down the aisle, glancing casually into the seats. Out of sheer annoyance over the littering, Sara was tempted to disclose the cigarettes and other contraband, but then she caught on to the game that was being played. As the customs officer made his way toward the back of the bus, a hand went up and tucked a package of cigarettes into one of the vest pockets. The Asian man slipped a folded bill into another. Sara had read about the *intermediación* or black market traffic for which Ciudad del Este was best known, but she'd never expected to have a front-row seat.

Once across the bridge, Cigarette Lady left her seat to gather up her scattered possessions. Except for a package of cigarettes left with the driver, Sara saw no recompense exchanged. It would seem this was a courtesy people here extended to each other, like giving directions back home, because you never knew when you might need such a service yourself.

The bus was now driving through Foz de Iguazú, the Brazilian counterpart of Ciudad del Este. After more bumper-to-bumper traffic, the bus pulled up at a curb, and the driver turned off the engine. At least half the passengers—and their contraband—disembarked. The driver stepped down to a curbside food stand to stretch his legs, and Sara shortly spotted him with a bulbous gourd in his hand, from which he was sipping through a long metal straw. *Mate* was not as common in Bolivia as in this region, but Sara recognized the *poro*, with its foaming mixture of silage and hot water.

This is—pun or no—the last straw! Snatching up her knapsack, Sara disentangled herself from her Guarani seatmate's belongings and climbed down from the bus. It wasn't just the illicit activity, or the diesel fumes and loud music, or the queasiness in her empty stomach. It was the passing of time. At this rate, the Jungle Tours buses would be returning from the Falls before she ever reached them!

Chapter Sixty-nine

It had to be the knapsack that identified her as a tourist, Sara concluded, because her modified coloring didn't stand out among many of the locals. This time she didn't have the language to argue with the taxi driver. But the gringo rate was worth it when the driver dropped her off only a half-hour later well inside the entrance to Iguazú National Park. The pink walls of the Hotel Das Cataratas rose beyond a fleet of green park shuttles.

Sara located the helicopter tours by their noisy drone, a rather irritating counterpoint to the musical roar of the falls. The now-familiar red of the Jungle Tours franchise was easy to spot, one helicopter hovering like a winged cherry out above the gorge, another resting with stilled rotors on the asphalt helipad.

That there was more than one Jungle Tours helicopter was a complication the two receptionists hadn't mentioned. At least two other helicopters with different markings were hovering above the falls as well. Sara made her way to the landing pad where a line of tourists waited their turn, camcorders ready. Several were draped in plastic rain ponchos.

The pilot of the Jungle Tours helicopter on the landing pad, a thin, middle-aged mestizo, was taking tickets as the next tour group scrambled into the helicopter behind him. Pulling Doug's photo from her knapsack, Sara took a deep breath and went forward. Here at least with all these tourists as witnesses, it would be safe enough to ask questions.

"Hey, get in the back of the line!" The angry shout was in English.

"You can't cut through here! You've got to buy a ticket. Over there!"

"¿Qué haces, idiota?" This one was in Spanish. "What do you think you're doing?"

Maybe not so safe! Sara grimaced as the hostile babble swept down the waiting line. She held up her photo as armor. "I'm not cutting line. I just need to ask the pilot a question. If you'll excuse me, please."

The pilot looked as annoyed as his clients as Sara jostled her way to the front. Slamming the helicopter door, he waved Sara back with an irritated shake of his head.

"Please, if you can just look at this picture before you take off," Sara pleaded, thrusting the photo out where the pilot couldn't avoid it as he rounded the helicopter to his own seat. "Have you seen this man before?"

The pilot barely glanced at the photo before shaking his head and pushing past Sara. Moments later, the dust and wind of the rotors forced Sara, along with the others waiting, back to the edge of the helipad. Disappointed, Sara gave in to the glares and distanced herself from the line. *No one said this was going to be easy.*

By now, the other Jungle Tours helicopter was coming in, the wind of its touchdown whipping the air and flapping at rain ponchos. The pilot who jumped down was much younger than the other and as blond as any northern European. The line surged forward as he hurried around the side to open the door for his passengers. When Sara once again stepped forward, she attracted another barrage of dirty looks and comments.

"Please, I don't want a ride, really. See—no ticket." Sara held up the photo. "I just need to speak to this man for a moment." Sara repeated herself in Spanish, attracting the attention of the pilot, who was already collecting the next set of tickets. His expression changed to pleased approval as his measuring blue eyes assessed Sara's slim form.

"*Si, señorita,* may I help you?" Despite his European fairness, there was something very Latino in his mannerisms and body language.

Once again, wearily, Sara held out Doug's picture. "Have you seen this man? The receptionists at Jungle Tours told me he'd flown on one of your helicopters here."

Sara's weariness evaporated as the pilot's face lit up. "But of course, Señor Bradford! Are you a friend of his? Did he recommend my services to you? I served him well, did he tell you? I can fly you too as I did him, anywhere you wish to go."

To her relief, Sara detected nothing but friendliness—and avarice—in his cordiality. "Yes, Señor Bradford is a very good friend. You said that you flew him around? Would you have a few minutes to talk?"

"Of course!" The passengers were still threading past onto the helicopter. "Come, if you have a ticket. You may sit up here beside me, and we will talk."

Sara was already shaking her head in dismay. This wasn't going to work. Even if she wanted to discuss Doug shouting over the roar of an engine with a chopper-load of tourists listening in, she'd be lucky to avoid lynching if she snatched the prime, front-row co-pilot's seat from one of these legitimate ticket holders.

"No . . . wait! I don't have a ticket. But—" Cynthia's $5000 wasn't going to last long at this rate, but there wasn't much help for it "—I'd like to hire you to fly for me like you did for my friend, Señor Bradford. Perhaps when you return from this tour? I'll be happy to compensate your time for the rest of the afternoon."

Sara could read the pilot's calculations as he glanced from Sara to the long line of paying customers.

"Certainly, I will be happy to fly you. Señor Bradford was a most generous employer, and I am happy to serve any of his friends. But I would not wish to disappoint these visitors who have waited so long to see the beautiful sights of our cascades. I will be most happy to take you up—" he calculated mentally "—in two hours?"

In other words, you're going to have your cake and eat it too! Still, the guy had to make a living, and why shouldn't he try to maximize profits from the occasional "rich" American who came into his orbit?

It just left Sara at loose ends for two whole hours, which should have been easy enough to fill. She was, after all, in one of the most beautiful spots on the planet. Countless visitors spent small fortunes traveling across the globe for a glimpse of the falls. Under any normal circumstances, Sara would have happily joined the throngs wandering down the trails to the lookouts or feeding the raccoon-like coatimundis.

But though she did wander over to the precipice, it was with a restlessness that didn't allow her any delight in the awesome panorama. According to the brochure, this time of year boasted the highest flow of water, and Sara could believe it. Dozens of cascades joined into one massive flow that was the churning, roiling color of whipped hot chocolate. Down below, in the famed Devil's Throat, the boiling brown waters were so high they lapped over one of the observation lookouts. Pulled high onto the bank, the motor launches sat empty, as the current was far too strong for safe passage.

Sara's thoughts churned as chaotically as the raging torrent of water. Ever since she had spotted Julio Vargas, the feeling had been growing that, despite her efforts, time was running out.

Straight across the gorge, above the thundering crash of measureless tons of water pouring over the plateau's edge, the green jungle canopy stretched as far out to the horizon as Sara could see. Was Doug out there somewhere in all that? Was he hungry? Cold? In pain? What terrible things could be happening to him right now while Sara sat here idly taking in a tourist scene? Or had the sick twisting of her heart when she'd seen Julio Vargas been a premonition that it was even now too late?

She could go mad thinking these thoughts, watching the hypnotic, endless flow of water. Especially when there was nothing she could do to change things—except whatever slow, small steps she was taking. *That's why it's better to keep busy.*

Sara straightened up from the railing. A parrot flew past her in a jeweled flash of green, red, and blue, disappearing into the spreading branches of an avocado tree. A coatimundi chittered at Sara from a few paces down the trail.

It really would be astonishingly beautiful, if only her heart did not ache so. Turning her back on the incredible panorama of thundering cascades, lush rain forest, and arching blue sky, she walked away. But in her heart, she made a silent promise.

Someday—God, I'm just going to believe it, however impossible it seems— someday, I'm coming back here with Doug.

* * *

Wandering back to the busy tourist center with its bustle of arriving and departing shuttles, Sara was reminded again by her rumbling stomach that she hadn't yet eaten. Finding a sidewalk café willing to take American dollars, Sara ordered the lunch special: vegetable soup, followed by rice and beans and a grilled chop, and the day's dessert of avocado ice cream. Sara took her time over the meal, pushing away the ice cream after one taste of its oily texture, and finished with a cup of coffee black enough to banish any longing thoughts of the siesta hour.

Precisely two hours had passed when Sara walked back to the landing pad. The blond pilot was there unloading passengers, but with a wink and conciliatory grin, he waved one more batch of tourists aboard, leaving Sara to wait through the arrival and departure of three other tours before the bright red helicopter returned.

Sara didn't wait for the dust to settle this time before cutting through the dismounting passengers to the pilot's side. This time he simply waved Sara toward the copilot's seat.

"Señorita, I am so happy you waited. Now I am ready to fly you to any sight you wish to see. The *cascadas*, the Itaipú dam, the rain forest . . . they are all very beautiful." His beaming approval as he gave Sara a hand up might be interpreted as admiration or downright leering. Sara chose to interpret it as the former. "Please, make yourself comfortable," he said.

The line of tourists hadn't diminished at all during the last two hours, though surely they must be different customers by now, and a rumble of protest rose as the pilot started to shut the helicopter door.

"Please, there will be another helicopter," the pilot called out. "This one is no longer in service." As he climbed into the pilot's seat and pulled the door closed, the decibel level of the falls dropped immediately. He turned another beaming smile on Sara.

"There, now we can speak of business. If your friend did not tell you so, my name is Alberto Stroessner." To Sara's uncomprehending expression, he added, "Like our so-famous *dictador* who has now left us, may he rot in hell."

Despite the irrelevance, Sara asked curiously, "You mean, he died?"

"No, alas. If he had, perhaps our country would not be so destitute. He has simply retired, along with much of our nation's wealth, in Brasilia, leaving our country now to the mercies of his friends and relations. But I myself am not one of them." He grinned at Sara. "So I fly helicopters instead. Now, you say you are a friend of Señor Bradford. Has he too returned to Iguazú? Do you wish to hire me as he did? I can take you on beautiful tours, or if you require discretion, anywhere else too. The price—" he spread his hands "—that we can negotiate. Señor Bradford was a very generous man."

And you'd better be too, lady, Sara concluded as he added another suggestive wink. She was in a quandary. She couldn't forget the hair-raising sensation of danger when she'd shown Doug's photo to the Jungle Tours owner and his companions. She had no reason to trust this man, either. If she was wrong—

And yet the very openness of Alberto Stroessner's cupidity was in some odd way reassuring. And his apparent familiarity with Doug led her to believe that Doug had at least employed—if not trusted—him.

Besides, if this man couldn't help, it was probably the end of the trail. Sara had no idea where to start next. This blond Paraguayan, named for a dictator and—not unlike his namesake, perhaps—only too willing to seize an opportunity to profit, was more than a straw she was grasping at. He was the only straw she had left.

Sara spoke quickly before she could change her mind. "Señor Stroessner, I have to tell you that I haven't been completely honest with you, and to plead for your help. I am not just a friend of Señor Bradford. I am his *novia*. We had hoped to—to make plans after he returned from your city. But he never returned. And now they say he may be dead. So I am here to look for him and to talk to anyone who might have spoken to him."

Sara couldn't keep her voice from quivering as she finished, and it drew an immediate sympathetic response. "Señorita, I am so sorry. Señor Bradford has truly disappeared? But this is terrible news!" The pilot seemed genuinely shocked. "But of course I will help you. Anything I can tell you . . . any place I can fly you . . ."

Doug's disappearance itself did not elicit the surprise it might have back home. There were so many ways for people to disappear down here. The crossing of a political adversary. Choosing the wrong underworld partners—or enemies. Flashing too much cash as a foreigner. Or just one more random victim of countless unsolved crimes.

"Have you received a request for ransom? Is there a police report?" The pilot shook his head regretfully. "Truly the criminals and kidnappers grow more bold every day. But perhaps there is something that can be done." He waved a hand around the interior of his aircraft. "Of course, there are expenses."

Of course. "I would be grateful if you'd allow me to hire you at your usual rates plus a commission for your goodness of heart," Sara said. "Would $500 in American traveler's checks be enough for a beginning?"

The pilot's sympathy broadened into a smile that signaled his acceptance. Sara pulled out her planner. "But first, could you tell me everything you remember about Señor Bradford—everything he said to you, every place you took him?"

"There is no time." Stroessner nodded in the direction of an approaching helicopter. "I must make room. But we can speak in the air, see?"

Handing Sara a flight helmet, he helped her adjust it. "It is brand new," he said proudly. "Purchased with the commission of your Señor Bradford. The tourists pay extra to hear in comfort." Adjusting his own helmet, he started the rotors. His voice came in clearly though the earphones. "You see, we can speak. Now let me tell you how I met Señor Bradford."

Sara soon recognized that she had grasped the right straw. Somewhat dazed, she focused on jotting swift shorthand notes in her planner. This was more than she'd ever hoped to find out. According to Stroessner, he had flown Doug out to Iguazú Falls the Monday of his arrival and back again that evening. Doug had shown him a photo of Julio Vargas, and Stroessner had recognized Julio as the pilot of the huge red-and-white SAR helicopter parked at Jungle Tours. He'd promised to keep a lookout and call Señor Bradford if he spotted the man.

On Thursday—Sara noted down the date—Stroessner had seen the man in the photo descending from the SAR helicopter and called Señor Bradford. Doug had paid him for the information, then hired Stroessner to fly him out into the Iguazú rain forest reserve.

"The way he asked me to fly made no sense for a tourist. Back and forth, back and forth, like a dog searching to pick up a scent. He had a device he was using, some type of GPS unit, I think." The pilot met Sara's surprised glance. "I have wished to add such a system to this aircraft so that if I should ever have engine trouble in this jungle, they would be able to come and find me."

So even Paraguay was becoming high-tech.

"Though the unit your Señor Bradford carried was very new," the pilot went on, "such as I have never seen for sale. Then he must have found what he sought, because he no longer wished me to fly back and forth, but directed me to follow a course on his machine. I knew when he arrived at the coordinates he sought because he asked me to take him back to Ciudad del Este."

"So this was Friday," Sara verified.

"Oh, no. It was Friday evening when Señor Bradford asked me to fly for him. By then it was dark. It was the next morning that we flew out. It was perhaps two in the afternoon when we returned to the city."

Sara stared down at the planner. Doug's movements were at last beginning to fall into a timetable she could trace. He'd arrived Sunday night. Monday he'd met with Andy Williams, shown Julio Vargas's picture around Jungle Tours, and flown out to Iguazú Falls and back with this pilot. The next four days must have been occupied with watching and searching for Julio Vargas, but he'd had no results until Stroessner called him Thursday night to say he'd seen Julio dismounting from the helicopter.

Friday morning he'd spotted Julio, because he'd gone then to the DEA for that abortive meeting with Chris Patterson. He'd left with the GPS tracking unit. Saturday morning, he was up in the air putting the GPS unit to use.

"Could you see what Señor Bradford was following?" Sara asked.

The pilot's flight helmet moved from side to side. "No, the jungle was too thick and tall. Men moving though the jungle, perhaps. Or a canoe or boat. Me, I think it was a boat. The course moved too fast to be a canoe or men on foot, and it was too winding for a road. Besides, there are few roads in this territory. Most travel is on the rivers."

A boat. Could it be the riverboat I saw down at the docks? Maybe Doug also spotted that RST equipment on board. But what was Julio Vargas's connection with that equipment?

That was something Sara might never find out. But then, she didn't care any more about the former security chief or Nicky's family and what they chose to do with the rest of their miserable lives. All that mattered now was Doug.

During their conversation, Stroessner had automatically banked out over the falls on his usual tour itinerary. The view was spectacular, but Sara spared it hardly a glance. Her attention was drawn instead to the wide, placid river above the falls, where the thickly wooded hillocks and islands merged in the distance into the Iguazú rain forest. How easy it would be to lose a boat—and its passengers—up one of the tributaries and into the cover of that trackless jungle.

"Could you fly me out to where Señor Bradford ended his search?" Sara asked.

With a crisp nod, Stroessner banked the helicopter. Within a few minutes, the Iguazú River was behind them, and below stretched only the arching crowns of the jungle hardwoods. The pilot was right. If there were waterways down there, the tangle of vegetation was too dense to see them.

As the helicopter flew on, Sara's mind continued to trace Doug's timetable. Stroessner had flown Doug back to Ciudad del Este Saturday afternoon, arriving back about 2 P.M. Sometime later that afternoon, Doug had stopped by the DEA office, not to talk to any of the agents but to leave that manila envelope with the guards. Still later, he'd called Ramon in Santa Cruz and Sara herself to say he was going out of town after Julio Vargas.

How had he gone? Not by helicopter, barring the unlikelihood that he'd scraped up another available pilot. Maybe he'd rented a boat and planned to use the GPS system to trace the course he'd followed with Stroessner.

Sara rubbed at an ache behind her eyes. If only she had the envelope Doug had dropped off at the DEA. There had to be more information in it than she'd found out for herself. What was for sure was that, as far as she could determine, no one had actually seen Doug face-to-face since he'd phoned Sara late Saturday afternoon. Except, perhaps, the quarry he'd been seeking.

They'd been flying another half hour when Stroessner banked the helicopter again, tracing a lazy circle above the jungle canopy. "We were somewhere in here when Señor Bradford told me we could return to the city."

"Somewhere in that? You mean . . . I was hoping . . ." Sara stared down at the tossing green sea of treetops, looking for *anything* that would distinguish this spot from every other stretch of treetops they had flown across in the last half hour. "You didn't mark down the coordinates of where you were flying?"

The pilot shrugged. "It was not my affair. It is better not to know these things . . . and to be able to swear truthfully that one does not know, if need be. And now, if Señor Bradford has truly disappeared, it seems I was right to mind my own business."

"What do you mean?" Sara demanded incredulously. "Just what do you think Doug was looking for down there?"

Stroessner shrugged again. "A drug cargo. A lab. An enemy. It is none of my concern. I fly as directed, and I was paid well. But I am truly sorry it proved dangerous for Señor Bradford. It is healthier only to fly and not to ask questions."

"Well, I'll have you know it was nothing like that. Doug is—"

Sara broke off her indignant protest. If Doug had chosen not to tell this man that he was a DEA agent, perhaps it would be wiser if she didn't offer that information either. After all, this helicopter did belong to a business owned by those men in the black Mercedes.

"Señor Bradford is my fiancée and would never do anything questionable," she finished lamely. Her heart sank as she looked down again at the endless sea of green. She now had a good grasp of how Doug had spent his last week here, and she was as certain as she could be without actual photo proof that Doug had gone out into that wilderness. She was equally certain, despite all the carefully laid trail of evidence, that it had not been Doug who emerged out of it that Monday.

But it hadn't been Julio Vargas either. The description given by all those witnesses was clear enough. Maybe someone working for him? Someone who could pass for Doug at a distance with a sombrero tipped down over his head. Sara's mind leaped to the pickup load of young men she'd seen at the RST agency. There'd been one or two Caucasians in that group.

Still, now that she knew—or thought she knew, what was she to do with the information? However much they had narrowed the search grid, the stretch of jungle down below was still a vast untracked piece of rain forest. Sara had been in a similar jungle in Bolivia. She knew the long catalog of dangers for the unwary, and the everlasting sameness that could lead a person to stumble around in circles forever. Even Doug had ventured in only with a GPS. Whatever Sara's impulse, to go bumbling into that maze down there on her own would not only be suicide, but it would do absolutely nothing toward finding Doug.

On my own—

"Thank you, Alberto. You've been of great service. Now, if you could please take me back to the city, I think I am finished here."

At the Jungle Tours helipad, Sara counted out the promised $500 in traveler's checks and added another $100. The pilot riffled through them, then stored the checks in a pocket. "You are as generous as your friend, señorita. I hope you will find Señor Bradford. And if you—or any of your friends—need me again, I am always available."

"I just might, at that." Waving down a taxi, Sara wearily gave the address of her hotel. As the taxi maneuvered through the pedestrian crowd onto a main avenue, Sara unearthed Doug's cell phone from her knapsack. Once again, it was Ellen Stevens who picked up the phone at the Santa Cruz field office.

Sara identified herself, then asked urgently, "Is Ramon back?"

"Ramon? Oh, didn't he get back to you, Sara?" Ellen said apologetically. "Yes, the guys got back from their op this morning, but Ramon left again right away. After the zoo this place has been the last couple weeks, he put in for some R and R."

Sara couldn't believe what she was hearing. "And Kyle? May I speak to him, then?"

There was the muffling of a hand going over the phone and a murmur of voices in the background before Ellen came back on. "Grant says Kyle went with Ramon. He says they mentioned something about going on safari. They were getting their gear together here earlier. I'm really sorry, Sara. I did give Ramon your message. It was a big op yesterday, and things were pretty chaotic. He must have just forgotten. If he calls in, I'll remind him."

Sara made it to the hotel and through the check-in process. As soon as the door closed behind the bellhop, she threw herself face down on the bed, no longer bothering to fight back tears. She'd done what she'd set out to do, shown more courage than she'd ever dreamed was in her, knocked on every door of opportunity and even kicked in a few stubborn ones. And in so doing, she'd determined to her own absolute certainty what had happened to the man she loved.

But none of that had accomplished what mattered—finding Doug.

And now, with the horrible feeling that time was running out weighing even more heavily down on her, Sara had come up against a brick wall far too thick and solid to be smashed in. She could go no further . . . not on her own. And no one who might have been able to help her had proved willing to do so.

Oh, God what am I supposed to do now? I'm so afraid! Not for me, for Doug! He's out there, I just know it, waiting for someone to believe he's alive and care enough to come looking for him. And I'm going to let him down—because I don't know what to do next!

The sleepless night, the tension and worry and frantic rush of the last days, the utter helplessness she was feeling had at last caught up with her, and with no need anymore to show either courage or decision, Sara let the overwhelming despair have its way.

But just as the burning behind her eyes began to spill over onto the bedspread, a knock sounded at the door. Sara remained silent and unmoving. The last thing she wanted right now was room service or anyone else. If she made no noise, maybe they'd go away.

But the knock came again, louder, imperative. "Sara? Sara Connor?"

Sara rolled to a sitting position, brushing a quick hand across her eyelashes. The voice sounded American. Who would be looking for her here? Then she relaxed and got to her feet. Of course. The local DEA office—they knew where she was staying. Had they found something? Maybe even decided to help her?

Unless it's a trap. Sara halted her eager rush toward the door. It would be foolish to forget the black Mercedes and the swift, cold look in Mozer Jebai's eyes. Noiselessly, Sara covered the distance to the door. A peephole allowed room guests to examine their visitors before choosing whether to admit them. Sara stretched up onto her toes to peer through it. Then she stared, frozen in disbelief, as she saw who was raising a fist for another knock.

Recovering her senses, Sara wrenched open the door before the knock could land. "Ramon . . . Kyle . . . Rocky!" she stammered. "What . . . what are you doing here? Ellen told me you'd gone on safari!"

Stepping past Sara into the hotel room, Doug's former partner and his two colleagues lowered bulging field packs onto the carpet. "Hello, Sara. I hope you don't mind us barging in like this. But we thought maybe you could use some help."

Chapter Seventy

If the three men were taken aback by the sudden flood of tears, they didn't say so. Rocky Harrell, married and father of three small girls, sat down beside Sara on the bed, offering both a handkerchief and an expert arm around the shoulders, while Ramon and Kyle hunkered down in front of Sara with murmurs of comfort and occasional pats on the knee.

Mopping her face with the handkerchief, Sara blew her nose. "I'm sorry. It was just the surprise. I . . . I was feeling so helpless. I had no idea what to do next. Then you guys walked in like—like angels." She mopped again at her eyes, then managed a slight smile. "If you could just see your faces! Don't worry, I'm done." Pushing her hair away from her face, she straightened her back. "But . . . you don't know how good it is to see someone who doesn't think I'm crazy."

"You're not crazy," Ramon stood up abruptly, his narrow, dark features tight. "Not unless we're nuts, too. I wish HQ had your guts. You should have never had to come down here alone. If we hadn't been smack in the middle of taking down the Salviettis—"

"Salviettis?" The name was familiar. "You don't mean the family with the handicrafts exports?" Sara's memory flashed back to the genial Italian-Bolivian couple who'd shared her table last Fourth of July. They'd been the trigger for her first quarrel with Nicolás—and of so much more. It all seemed a lifetime ago now, not simply a year.

"That's them. We've been after that bunch for a long time, but they were good. Customs never turned up coke in any of their shipments. Their Indian weavings turned out to be saturated with it instead. We'd never have caught it if we hadn't seen the same method used by the Cortéz. We raided their warehouse last night and caught them red-handed with a load ready to ship."

Ramon's mouth curved ruefully. "I got your message right when we were taking off for the place, or I'd have gotten back to you sooner. Let me tell you, the ink wasn't dry on the Salvietti indictment before I was packing to come here. I told Kyle and Rocky where I was headed, and they insisted on coming along. I hope you don't mind."

"Mind?" Sara's exclamation choked in her throat. She had no words for what she was feeling right now. Her acquaintance with these three men had actually been quite brief, though the circumstances of that acquaintance created a bond stronger than many a lengthy friendship. These three had been among the first to put their careers and even lives on the line—for a woman they didn't even know. And all because a friend they trusted told them she was in trouble. Being who and what they were, they hadn't even hesitated to respond.

To be sure, when Sara had encountered them in the shambles of the Cortezes' jungle hacienda, they'd been more alarming than reassuring with their battle gear, cradled weapons, and green and brown camouflage paint. But she would never forget the gentleness and courtesy they'd shown when it was over, never dropping a suggestion of blame for Sara's stupidity in getting herself into a situation from which they'd had to risk life and limb to rescue her.

Now again they'd responded, not to Sara's pleading—she had no illusion—but for Doug's sake, coming to the call of a friend in need without hesitation or calculation of their own personal cost. What bred men like this . . . friends like this? Did it come out of a crucible of combat together until they didn't even glance back to question whether their comrades would be there as they plunged into harm's way?

Regardless, now with their arrival, Sara could lay down the burden she'd carried alone and that had grown too impossibly heavy. If she didn't know what to do next, they would.

"No, I don't mind," she finished inadequately. "I'm so glad to see you all."

"Good." Snaking a chair from the room's one table, Ramon straddled it backward, resting his forearms on the back. "So—tell us what you've got."

Sara dug out her planner. Step by step, she outlined where she'd been since she arrived in Ciudad del Este and what she'd uncovered. She couldn't read the silence as she finished.

"Is it . . . did I do it right?" she asked hesitantly.

Ramon cleared his throat. "I think I can say for all of us that what you've done is—impressive. You've saved us a lot of time. Now, if you'll lend us this—" he picked up the planner "—we've booked into the hotel. You get some sleep. You've earned it. Meanwhile, we're going to have a bit of a pow-wow. In the morning, we'll make our next move."

* * *

Sara wouldn't have believed she could sleep, but whether from exhaustion or relief, she didn't stir or dream the whole night. Only the shrilling of the bedside phone finally roused her.

"Sara?" At Ramon's crisp tones, Sara scrambled up. "We're ready to roll. We'll meet you downstairs in fifteen."

Sara made it in ten, hair brushed, face and teeth freshly scrubbed, knapsack on her shoulder. Makeup was not one of the essentials she'd packed for the trip.

"Hey, that was quick!" Kyle handed Sara a cheese empanada and foam cup with coffee. "I told Ramon it'd be at least thirty."

The intel analyst ran an eye over Sara, lingering quizzically on her hair. "I've got to say I wouldn't have recognized you. I can't think of you as anything but a blonde."

Sara touched her short, dark hair self-consciously. "I guess you're wondering why I changed it—"

"No, we know why you did it," Ramon cut in. "A good move. I'd have suggested it myself if you hadn't thought of it. It's bad enough to have these two gringos sticking out like a pair of giraffes." He jerked a thumb toward Kyle and Rocky, who towered well above everyone else in the lobby. "Now let's get a move on. We don't have time for chit-chat."

"So where are we headed?" Sara asked. The three men were carrying the field packs she'd seen last night, but were dressed for business in slacks and button-up shirts.

"The DEA." Rocky grinned at Sara. "Gotta touch base with the locals."

"The DEA?" Sara repeated doubtfully. "I don't think . . . well, I'm afraid you'll find it a waste of time. They haven't exactly been much help. In fact, they'd hardly even talk to me."

"They'll talk to us," Ramon said with a curtness not directed at Sara. "They've got some explaining to do, big time."

The guards outside the DEA compound were the same as yesterday. They acknowledged Sara with a nod but stepped apart into ready position at the sight of the three men with her. They relaxed their weapons when Ramon flashed his DEA identification. "I'd like to speak with Special Agent Patterson, please."

"*El señor Patterson?*" The guard's sudden lack of expression was as revealing as open distaste. "He is not yet in this morning, señor."

"Then who is?"

"*Bueno, el coronel Andrade . . . Capitan Benitez.*"

"No, of the Americans."

"*Bueno, el cojo.*" The lame one.

"Then call Señor Williams. Inform him there are *agentes americanos* here to see him."

Ramon was pacing back and forth, his fingers drumming impatiently against his thigh, when the electronic buzz signaled the unlocking of the gate. When Andy Williams met them inside the gate, Ramon held out his hand. "Ramon Gutierrez, Santa Cruz office. I came through a few months back on the Oviedo case."

"Sure, I remember," Williams said. "They were shipping the stuff down the Paraná River by paddleboat, then sending it out with Iguazú tourists. Thanks to your intel, we nailed 'em good."

His glance went to Ramon's companions. "And you're Rocky Harrell, chemical seizures, and Kyle Martin, the intel analyst up in Santa Cruz. You were at the seminar in La Paz last year. New developments in chemical precursors and detection. So what are you doing in these parts? Business or pleasure?" His eye fell on Sara, who had stepped in the gate behind the agents. "Or maybe I can guess."

"No pleasure, that's for sure." Ramon nodded toward his companions. "And you've met Ms. Connor."

"Yes, I have. Good morning, Ms. Connor. I really am sorry we weren't able to be of more help yesterday."

"Well, maybe today you can," Ramon said curtly. "I understand a colleague of ours, Special Agent Doug Bradford, left a package here some weeks ago with instructions that its contents were to be sent immediately on to me. Since I never received that material, I'd like to collect it now."

"Did he?" Williams looked genuinely puzzled. "Patterson never mentioned it. I have to say it doesn't ring a bell."

"A yellow manila envelope dropped off with the guard," Ramon prompted. "The day after Bradford borrowed a certain piece of equipment from you, if that rings a bell. The envelope was addressed to Patterson and should have contained Bradford's latest report, and a copy to be forwarded to me. Your guard remembers it well enough, because when he forgot to turn it over immediately, your SAC chewed him out enough that he's still shaking in his boots. Well deserved, I'm sure."

"Sure, of course!" The baffled look dissolved from the intel analyst's face. "I don't remember Bradford filing a report—and I would have, since I'd be the one forwarding it on to you. But I remember that manila envelope. The guard was begging me to keep *el jefe* from firing him. It stuck in my mind because I was thinking Bradford was a smart one, leaving it with the guards instead of letting Patterson catch sight of his ugly mug again."

The grin accompanying his last sentence evaporated, and he added quickly, "Of course, that was weeks ago. For anything more, you'll have to ask him."

Sara spun around in the direction of the intel analyst's gesture. She grimaced inwardly as she saw Chris Patterson coming through the gate, his pale features tight with annoyance.

"What is going on here?" His expression soured further as his glare fell on Sara. "So you're back, Ms. Connor. José informed me you'd showed up with your own DEA detail." The SAC's pale-blue eyes swept over Sara's three companions. "I apologize for this waste of your time, gentlemen. What's she been feeding you?"

Rocky and Kyle were staring down at the slighter SAC with the bemused interest of two zoologists who'd just encountered an interesting, if repellent, specimen of biological life. But Andy Williams took one glance at Ramon's darkening expression and intervened hastily. "Chris, this is Special Agent Ramon Gutierrez from the Santa Cruz office. The Oviedo affair, remember? And . . . uh, Rocky and Kyle, right? They're looking for a package Doug Bradford dropped off to be forwarded their way while he was here. That manila envelope you had to reprimand José over for tardy delivery? That was, uh . . . during all the other fuss, if you remember."

The SAC's pale-blue glare took in the entire circle but landed with particular abhorrence on Sara. "Frankly, I don't. I've chewed José out more than once for holding mail in the guardhouse or screwing up messages. And, frankly, I don't keep track of every bit of mail that moves in and out of here. If it contained anything of urgency, I'm sure I'd remember. And since, frankly, it doesn't ring a bell, I'm sure it didn't."

"Why don't you let us be the judge of that?" Ramon said with deceptive mildness. Sara caught the expressive exchange of glances between Rocky and Kyle as Ramon added gently, "Shall we go have a look for it?"

Ramon's wiry frame barely topped the SAC's shoulder, but despite the heavy field pack he was carrying, he strode briskly across the patio toward the building, forcing Patterson to stretch his legs to catch up. Here, too, the door had been converted to an electronic security lock. Grudgingly, the SAC stepped in front of the surveillance camera. At his signal, the door buzzed open. Inside, the scene was much quieter than the day before, with only a few uniformed Paraguayans working in the room.

"Yes, and how can we be sure you are telling the truth?" Sara heard a man in an officer's uniform demand into a phone as they went by. As the group reached the middle of the big work space, Ramon paused, his black eyes sweeping the room. His cool gaze settled on a table toward the rear of the room, piled high with mail and stacked documents. He walked swiftly in that direction.

"Hey, what do you think you're doing?" Chris Patterson followed him angrily. "I don't know what you call manners in Santa Cruz, but this is my territory, not yours! You can't just walk in here and start prying through our op."

Ignoring him, Ramon began rifling through the table's contents. Kyle joined him. Rocky angled over to a pair of file cabinets and began sorting through the paper material piled high on top. Tossing aside a stack of Motorola user manuals, Ramon unearthed a manila envelope, pulled out its contents, then shoved them back inside with irritation.

"Now look here," Patterson barked. "You're way out of line, Gutierrez. I don't know what this woman's been telling you, or what you think you're going to find in here—"

Ramon abandoned the table, its neat piles now in total disarray. "Hey, Williams, is there any other place you've got back-files?"

With a sardonic grin, the intel analyst powered his wheelchair away from the wall where he'd been watching the invasion. "Sure, just about any place you look," he said dryly. "But if it was earmarked for us and not our local colleagues, you're going to find it in Patterson's office, not out here. I sort the office mail from that mess over there myself, and I would've dumped that manila envelope in with the rest of Patterson's stack."

"And which office is that?"

The intel analyst didn't have to answer because Patterson was already striding angrily over to block an ornate wooden door. When he turned and saw the look on Ramon's face, he hastily stepped aside. Sara trailed the five men into the room.

Across the room from the SAC's office, a door led into the comm center, allowing for easy communication between the two American agents. Inside, a small group of Paraguayans were listening with headsets to communications intercepts and poring over printouts of radio transmissions. They glanced up, startled, as Ramon kicked the door shut.

Tidiness was not one of Chris Patterson's signature traits. Piles of reports, opened mail, and newspapers were strewn across the desk. Another stack of newspapers, a Kevlar vest, night vision goggles, and a pile of banana clips for the M-16 occupied the office's two guest chairs. An array of crumpled fast food wrappers scattered near the wastebasket bore mute testimony to the SAC's abilities as a basketball player. Sara retreated to a corner out of the way, watching with stunned amusement as files were yanked out of drawers, stacks of reports and magazines were shuffled aside, a box heaped with opened mail was dumped out. This was *not* the first time her three companions had trashed an office.

Chris Patterson stood in the middle of the room, his pale skin red with fury. "You're nuts! You're all nuts! Do you know what kind of report I'm going to be filing on this? I'm calling Santa Cruz immediately. No, not Santa Cruz. Between you and Bradford, it's clear your field office fosters insubordinate behavior. I'm calling Washington. Williams, you're my witness."

"You do that." With a savage thrust of his arm, Ramon swept one of the chairs clean of a stack of newspapers that included both the *New York Times* and *Miami Herald.* "I'm looking forward to having a chat with your superiors myself. I'd like to know just what kind of arm-twisting went on up there to put a whining desk weenie in charge of a field office, even a two-bit one like this."

"Maybe some people appreciate the value of going by the rules and following regulations, something too many of you cowboys seem to have forgotten."

Kyle's triumphant whoop cut through Chris Patterson's indignation as the lanky intel analyst scooped up a manila envelope tucked in among the scattered newspapers. As he turned it over, Sara could see that it was unopened. She felt her heart squeeze as she recognized Doug's bold, untidy scrawl.

"Now just a minute. That's addressed to me," Patterson protested stiffly.

Ignoring the SAC, Ramon took the envelope from Kyle and ripped it open. The room grew still as he scanned the sheets of paper inside.

"Look, you're making a big deal over nothing," Patterson blustered. "I was on my way out when José brought that up here. The envelope must have got piled in with those newspapers. I was out of the office for the rest of the weekend, then took some R and R. By that time, the amount of mail we get around here, I never got around to reading those newspapers and, frankly, until now it totally slipped my mind."

Ramon spun around on his heel, the sheets crumpling in his hand. "Slipped your mind?" he demanded harshly. "It never occurred to you that when you've got intel coming in from an agent on the ground, it might be urgent enough to glance through *before* taking off for the weekend?"

"Frankly, no. I knew what was in it—Bradford's report he insisted on filing on his mucking around our territory. I got an earful over the phone. And, frankly, since he'd agreed to wrap up his games and was leaving Paraguay, the whole report became irrelevant anyway."

"Irrelevant?" This time it was Rocky who spoke up, straightening up and staring incredulously at the SAC as if he'd never before encountered such a specimen of idiocy. "Even after the guy went MIA?"

"That was in Miami, not here," Chris Patterson replied lamely. "I saw no connection between his poking around on some personal vendetta against a two-bit fugitive and whatever hornet's nest he stirred up with the Colombians. I made that very clear in my report. And, frankly, I don't care for your implications that I did less than carry out my duty."

If he says frankly *one more time,* Sara gritted her teeth, *I'm frankly going to scream!*

"Frankly—" Rocky started to reply, but stopped abruptly when Ramon slammed the sheets of paper down on the desk.

"Duty! Do you know what is in this report that you didn't figure was worth reading, Patterson? A detailed explanation of Bradford's final objective *before* leaving Paraguay, including the GPS coordinates. And a note requesting a copy be faxed to me so that if he did not return within a reasonable time schedule, a search could be made using those coordinates. His backup, that's what it was!"

"Bradford *always* planned for a backup," Rocky interjected bitingly. "Only this time he didn't count on a knife in the back from his own side."

The SAC drew himself up to his full height. "Irrelevant and unreasonable. Keep in mind, Bradford did, in fact, return, and he went missing—may I remind you—in Miami, not here."

"So we've been led to believe," Ramon snapped. "The assumption was based in part on your own testimony, which now turns out to be somewhat less than exact. Enough!" Recovering Doug's report from the desk, he spun around to Andy Williams. "The GPS tracker Doug used . . . I'd like to see it."

"What for?" Chris Patterson took an angry step forward. "Now don't *you* start! If you think you can walk in here and start misappropriating equipment like Bradford did, think again. What are you up to?"

"What I'm up to is what you should have done two months ago—to check out these coordinates and find out just what it was Bradford was looking for out there."

"You can't do that! You know the rules. Any ops mounted on foreign soil have to be sanctioned and conducted by local troops and authorities. As for those coordinates, you're talking Brazil, because Bradford admitted he'd crossed over the line there. As I told him, the only legal recourse is to contact Brasilia and see if they can get the local park rangers or police to go out there and take a look."

"You want the locals out there bumbling around? Don't be stupid, Patterson," Ramon retorted. "Why not just fly overhead instead and announce we're coming. That is, if they aren't on the bad guy's payroll already. This isn't a drug op we can afford to have blown. It's a DEA agent's life. Williams, if you don't mind, that GPS unit."

As the intel analyst began rolling toward the comm center door, Chris Patterson exploded. "You do this, Gutierrez, and you're finished! Don't think I won't be making a formal complaint here, because I will. As for you, Williams, I am still in charge of this field office. You make one move to cooperate with these nuts, and I'll see you're busted to fixing parking meters. Besides—" he added nastily "—it's been two months. Even if there were anything to your allegations, which I categorically deny, what difference is dredging all this up now going to make?"

Ramon stopped dead in his tracks, and Sara's heart skipped a beat as she caught sight of his expression. Doug had told her once that Ramon was considered—by other agents and bad guys alike—to be the most dangerous man in the Santa Cruz field office. Considering Ramon's slight frame and friendly grin, Sara had taken the information with a large grain of salt. But now, as she saw the taut readiness of his frame, the stone cold expression on his face, and the deadly intensity in his piercing black eyes, all bets were off. Maybe all the stories she'd heard about the street fighter turned Ranger and DEA agent were true.

When he spoke, his understated tone nevertheless had the SAC stumbling a pace backward. "Just try to stop me, Patterson. And you'd better start praying you're right and we're wrong. Because if you're lucky, your next duty posting will be so far behind a desk somewhere that you'll never get the chance to hold another human being's life in your hands. But if this intel proves to have any bearing on this case, you've got my word: You're going to wish you'd never been born."

In the absolute silence that followed, the wiry Latino agent gave Andy Williams a nod. The wheelchair started for the door. Then, as if the office were his own, Ramon turned to the desk and picked up the phone. There was a stunned look in Chris Patterson's pale-blue eyes as Ramon dialed.

"Hello, Norm Kublin, Miami? This is Ramon Gutierrez, Santa Cruz field office. I'm in Ciudad del Este at the moment, standing in the local SAC's office with a mutual acquaintance, Sara Connor."

A stab of his finger put the call on speaker so that Sara could hear Norm Kublin's gruff response. "Oh, are you? What's she doing down there? I thought I told her to stay put."

"Yes, you did," Sara spoke up evenly. "I guess I don't listen too well."

"Lucky for us, she didn't," Ramon broke in. "Ms. Connor is responsible for turning up Doug Bradford's last filed report, misplaced down here for the last two months."

"Misplaced—!"

"That's right. If you'll give me your fax number, I'll send it to you right now."

Jotting down the number, Ramon began feeding the report into a fax machine beside the phone. Andy Williams was back with a black case by the time he finished. There was silence in the office as Norm Kublin scanned through the sheets at the other end. If Chris Patterson was incapable of grasping their significance, Doug's GS was not, because his voice came sharp over the speaker.

"Is this for real? You're saying this was buried down there for two months? Just let me get my hands on the—! No, we'll take that up later. First things first. Do you have any reason to believe this information has present pertinence?"

"I believe so," Ramon answered evenly. "Had this report surfaced at the time, the intel in it would at least have received some notice. Doug Bradford was a good agent and a good friend to a lot of people down here."

"Then . . . you realize what you're saying here, Gutierrez. We have conducted a very thorough and lengthy investigation here, based on ample and unambiguous intelligence. Do you have any serious reason to question the record? I mean, besides any bee in Ms. Connor's bonnet, I wasn't aware any investigation was being reopened on your end."

Under Chris Patterson's bristling glare, Ramon answered coolly, "Let's just say that the same deficiencies that buried this report have cast some doubts on the intel provided to your office for positive identification—something else that Ms. Connor is responsible for turning up."

Now the silence was on the Miami end, and when Norm Kublin spoke again, the pain in his voice came clearly through the speaker. "This . . . is truly a distressing development. Sara, maybe we owe you an apology."

The clearing of his throat rattled the speaker. "This is going to be complicated," the GS went on gruffly. "The last thing we want is the Paraguayans or Brazilians rushing in announcing our intentions to the world—or to the bad guys." This drew another bristling glare from Chris Patterson. "Anything we do at this date has to be discreet. I will immediately call the embassy in Asunción and touch base with Brasilia. But it's going to take some time to get wheels moving. I'm going to pass this on up through my own RAC, to start with. Can you expect any assistance from the local field op?"

Ramon glanced icily at Chris Patterson. In response, the SAC turned on his heel and shoved past his visitors, almost knocking Sara over as he stormed out of the office, slamming the door behind him. Ramon turned back to the speaker. "I think we can work something out. Problem is, no personnel."

"And it'll take at least a day or two to move any in . . . even if we get the FBI and CIA on this too. But if you'll sit tight, I'll be pushing as hard and fast as I can."

"Yeah, well," Ramon said, "You do what you have to do. But my friends and I aren't the sitting-tight type. We came here with vacation plans for a bit of safari, and if we've got time on our hands, that's just what we'll do."

"Safari." The GS's grunt came over the speaker. Then he said slowly, "Well, *you* do what *you* have to do. This time just make sure you leave those vacation plans with us just in case you—uh, get lost."

"It's all in the report. Talk to you later."

Chapter Seventy-one

"I don't understand you guys!" Sara shook her head, perplexed, as Ramon rang off. "It's like you're talking in code or a whole other language."

Rocky grinned down at Sara. "We understand each other; that's all that counts."

Ramon had taken the black case from Andy Williams and lifted it onto the desk. "Williams understands," he said briefly as he opened the case to reveal the pieces of the GPS unit tucked into their foam niches.

"It's simple." The intel analyst didn't look at all disturbed by his superior's exit. "We don't have the jurisdiction to cross over into Brazil or mount a DEA op without authorization—and if we tried, it would be the responsibility of your SAC up there to stop it. And mine too, probably," he added thoughtfully. "Now—there's no law about heading out into the jungle for a few days of vacation on safari."

"Like Doug did." Sara said. She'd picked up Doug's DEA-6 report and was speed-reading through it, stunned at how close she'd actually come to piecing it all together. "Then . . . you all could get in trouble for this. Are you sure—?"

Ramon was busy with the GPS tracker, but he looked up as he plucked Doug's report from Sara's hands to begin programming in the coordinates. "Don't you worry about us, Sara. There's an old saying in the Special Forces—and the DEA. 'Better to ask forgiveness than permission.'"

"Yeah, kinda hard to say no once you've gone and done it." Kyle's eyes were bright with excitement as he grinned down at Sara. "And once you've got a successful op, there's not much they can do but forgive you. If it flops—well, that's when you'd better start counting how much you've got in your retirement account."

"I see where Bradford gets his 'borrow first, ask later' philosophy," Andy Williams spoke up dryly. "But you can count me in—and any equipment I've got in my inventory. I'm not much of an asset on safari anymore, but anything else I can do, you've only got to ask."

Ramon glanced up from the GPS tracker, which he was restoring to its case.

"What you can do is maintain a comm link for us—not just out in the field, but to Miami and Asunción. I'm going to touch base with Santa Cruz and see what they can do for us—unofficially, of course. It's a lot to be asking, but we're going to need you here twenty-four seven until we get some back-up on the way. Is that doable?"

"It'll have to be," the intel analyst said calmly. "If something did fall through the cracks on our watch, I'd like to make sure it's put right. Though, don't be too hard on Patterson. He's not a bad guy—just a little stiff in the neck. If it isn't in the handbook, it isn't in his vocabulary, period."

No one else in the room offered to affirm his exoneration. But then, to the others, Doug Bradford was not just a passing colleague, but a personal friend.

Sara, for her part, would not so easily forgive the SAC's pig-headed obstruction. She might acquit Chris Patterson of any deliberate design to harm Doug or impede the investigation of his disappearance. But his personal dislike and prejudice against Doug had swayed him in his less-than-meticulous undertaking of those precious handbook procedures of his. Now two valuable months were gone because a moment's irritation had tossed urgent intelligence aside, a loss that made Sara so angry she had to clench her hands to keep them from shaking.

How many other failures in the agencies responsible for her nation's security had been the result of petty human bickering or in-house politics, rather than a critical lack of intelligence or an invincible enemy?

Like Doug always said, in the end it was all personal. It was a sobering realization that America's very survival depended on human beings who were all too faulty and motivated by personal ambition and emotions. She glanced around at her companions, who were already moving into high gear. Thank God that for every Chris Patterson, there were also guys like Ramon and Rocky and Kyle.

And Doug.

While Ramon was working with the GPS system, Rocky and Kyle had opened their field packs. Sara watched with disbelief the assorted inventory that was emerging. Collapsible assault rifles with scopes and laser designators, which Sara identified only because Doug had shown her the same weapon in the Miami DO arsenal. Grenades. Bars of C-4 explosive.

And more innocuous supplies. MRE. Canteens. A first aid kit. Radio headsets. A sat-phone hardly larger than a laptop. Her companions had definitely not cleared the same Customs checkpoint that Sara had.

Andy Williams didn't seem to find anything out of the ordinary in the assortment of weapons and supplies. He looked it over with a professional eye. "Looks like you've got what you need. I'd recommend a backup UHF radio, in case the sat-phone goes down. We've got a new stripped-down version. Only fifteen pounds, including batteries."

Ramon nodded. "Thanks, we'll take it." He glanced up with a glint of malicious humor at Rocky's tall frame. "Rocky can carry it. Now, what about transport? If Doug followed up these coordinates on his own, he probably got himself a boat. We don't have time for that. You got a Huey on hand—a pilot you can trust to keep his mouth shut?"

The intel analyst was already shaking his head. "Hey, this is a two-man post, remember? Asunción has an arrangement with the locals for ops transport. After all, we donated their Hueys. But that would take some time—and it sure wouldn't be what I'd call discreet."

Ramon let out a Spanish curse, then slanted an apologetic glance toward Sara. "Excuse the language. What about your pilot pal, Sara? Think he'd do the job and keep his mouth shut?"

"I don't think there's much Alberto wouldn't do for the right price," Sara said dryly. "But he'd be out at the falls at this hour."

"Then we'll track him down. We don't have time for alternatives. Williams, you got a vehicle we can borrow? Sara, you come with me. You know the guy so you can do the talking. Rocky . . . Kyle." Ramon threw a withering glance over the chaos on the floor. "If you can have everything loaded and ready to roll when we get back . . . oh, and, Rocky, you might want to touch base with the local FBI and CIA guys and see if you can stir up some discreet action on this Mozer Jebai. Kyle, fax Grant Major a copy of Doug's report and let him know what's going down here. If he hits the roof, we can count on some action." Ramon slid a final item out of the manila envelope—a laptop DVD disk. "Williams, from Bradford's report, this has photos you might want to run through your database—see if anyone turns up there. Sara? Let's go."

Tracking Alberto Stroessner down was simple. Ramon appropriated the Landrover in which a local counternarcotics sergeant chauffeured Andy Williams. This was clearly not his first visit to the region, because he threaded through the city center to the Paraná River without directions or a map. There, his diplomatic passport proved a magic card to speed them across the Bridge of Friendship in record time.

At Iguazú, they had to park outside the entrance and take one of the green shuttles down to the falls. Both Jungle Tours helicopters were in the air when they reached the helipad, but they had to wait through only one landing and takeoff before the blond pilot touched down.

But negotiating a deal didn't prove as easy. The pilot beamed at the sight of Sara, but he wouldn't stop collecting tickets long enough to talk.

"But I have a proposition for you," Sara called out above the thunder of the falls. "A friend—" she indicated Ramon behind her "—wishes to hire you for a very generous compensation."

The pilot shook his head even as he reached for the next ticket. "I have a lunch break in one hour. Four more trips. We can speak then. Now I must go."

Since he was already slamming doors and climbing back into his seat, there was nothing Sara could do to argue. Ramon, his dark features tight with annoyance, walked away to spend the intervening time on his cell phone. Sara found a bench near the landing pad and filled the time counting the landings and takeoffs.

Predictably, the Jungle Tours aircraft made six roundtrips before Stroessner left the helipad and strode toward Sara. His hints made it evident he expected his visitors to shell out for a "business lunch," and if Ramon was in a hurry, long experience with informants and officials in these regions had taught him to curb his impatience. The DEA agent led the way to the exclusive restaurant inside the Hotel Das Cataratas, and if Ramon and Sara both ate sparingly, the pilot took full advantage of the lavish buffet, then lingered over the dessert tray, before allowing his hosts to turn the talk to business.

But after all the lavish preliminaries, Alberto's answer was blunt and disappointing. "No, I cannot leave my post again. Already yesterday the other pilot spoke to Jungle Tours because I left early. They threatened to fire me."

"But we can pay well," Sara pleaded. "We've made it worth your while until now."

"That is true. I have profited well. But a few good commissions are of no advantage if one must then lose his job. After all, you will not always be around to pay me."

And from that the pilot would not budge. "If it is after the tours are over. Or you must wait for my day off, which is still two days away. Then it is possible to negotiate."

Sara had to bite back her frustration. For all Stroessner's talk, they could have flown just about anywhere and back in the time they'd wasted over this very expensive lunch. But Ramon kept his dark features impassive and his tone even and calm. "What about sunrise? We'll pay well if you'll fly us to certain coordinates and leave us there. That leaves plenty of time to get to work. Then if we need a pick-up, we'll radio you to make arrangements."

Stroessner's sudden thoughtfulness told them they'd won. But now a new complication arose.

"You want to climb down on ropes?" the Paraguayan pilot demanded incredulously. "Yes, of course I know of what you speak. I served my time in the military. That is where I learned to fly. But not from my aircraft. There is no place to attach ropes. Nor is there room for these packs of which you speak. Tell him, Señorita Connor. You have been inside. It is a small aircraft for a few tourists to ride—four or five, no more, without luggage."

Sara threw a troubled look at Ramon. What now? If they only had an aircraft like—

She sat up suddenly. "Alberto, what about the search-and-rescue helicopter? That's big enough, isn't it?" She turned to Ramon. "Julio's—the one Doug mentioned in his report. It's a Huey, just like Bolivia. And it's sitting outside Jungle Tours right now. I saw it there yesterday."

"Oh, no!" Stroessner's hands were already in the air. "No, that is *loco*. Do you know how much trouble that could bring? If this Vargas found out . . ."

"But that's the point," Sara argued. "Julio Vargas left the country yesterday. And you said yourself: Sometimes it sits there for days without being used. If we went out early enough—I mean, you're a Jungle Tours pilot. If you had the helicopter back before it was missed, who'd know it wasn't authorized? The question is, can you fly it? Can you—I don't know—hotwire it or whatever you'd have to do if you don't have the keys?"

For the first time the pilot actually looked amused. "Oh, yes, I can get into the machine and fly it. But it is not worth the risk."

"Not even for—" Sara tried to calculate how much of those traveler's checks she had left "—three thousand American dollars?"

The acquisitive gleam in the pilot's eyes told her she'd won. But she should have remembered that in this culture you didn't begin with your final bid. In the end it took four thousand dollars, the remainder chipped in by Ramon, with half laid out in advance and another thousand dollars if Stroessner had to make a pickup. Even then the pilot insisted on takeoff while it was still dark. They agreed on a 5 A.M. liftoff. "Then I will have the aircraft back before any of the guides arrive."

The pilot looked immensely pleased with himself as he stowed the traveler's checks. "Thanks to you and Señor Bradford, perhaps I may now buy my own aircraft and fly where I want. And for you—" Stroessner bowed gallantly toward Sara "—there will always be a discount.

At least they'd positively affected the economy for one local citizen!

"He could have flown us all out there and back by now," Sara fumed as Ramon headed the Landrover back toward Ciudad del Este. "Now we've lost another day. If Doug—"

"No!" Ramon's quick head shake cut Sara off abruptly. "Don't get caught in that trap. You've got to focus on the mission, not on what's going on outside of your control. You start stressing yourself over what might be happening because you aren't moving fast enough—that's when you make mistakes. We're moving as fast as we can, but doing it right is more crucial than rushing out there unprepared. Now, where is this Jungle Tours? I want to see that chopper."

The SAR helicopter was still sitting alone on its gravel pad. From behind the tinted glass of the Landrover, Ramon studied the Huey through a pair of palm-sized binoculars.

"It'll do," he said briefly, then looked over at Sara as he started the Landrover. "Now you. I'd appreciate it if you'd back Williams while we're out there. We'll get news to you there as soon as we know anything."

"What?" Sara bolted upright. "Oh, no!" she said vehemently as the DEA agent's expression began to close over. "No way! You don't think I found you that helicopter so you could dump me behind to be Andy Williams's secretary. I'm going with you!"

"It isn't safe. Look, you've got to understand." Ramon ran an expressive hand through his hair before explaining with commendable patience, "This isn't a stroll through the woods we're talking here! We're going in on the ground into hostile territory. We've no idea how much country we'll have to cover or what we're going to walk into. We can't have—"

"No, *you've* got to understand," Sara interrupted. "If I wanted to be safe, I'd be back in Miami." It had been an enormous relief to have Doug's friends lift the burden of decision-making from her. But since their arrival, she'd begun to feel, as she had back in Miami, that after all she'd done, she was being shunted aside out of the action. *Go sit in the corner out of the way, little girl, so the big boys can go out and do their job.* "And if Andy Williams needs someone to hold his hand, he can talk to Chris Patterson. I'm going with you."

"No, please!" Sara pleaded as Ramon's dark features grew even more adamant. "I know . . . okay, so the last time you saw me, I . . . I wasn't exactly at my best." *Just dripping wet and covered with swamp slime and in enough shock that I can't remember what I did or said.* "But I'm not the same person you knew then. I've taken self-defense. I . . . I've even learned to shoot a gun."

Sara's amber eyes were dark with emotion. "I won't hold you back, I promise. But you've got to let me go. I didn't come this far—and by myself—to sit around behind again waiting for bad news. Whatever . . . whatever happens, I need to be there."

When Ramon's expression didn't relax, Sara tried a different tack. "Besides, Kyle isn't an agent either, and you're letting him go. I'll bet I keep up as well as he can."

"Can you zip-line out of a helicopter?" Ramon demanded. "Because Kyle can. There aren't any airfields out there, you know."

"If I have to, I will," Sara answered stubbornly. "And I'll tell you this. If I tell Alberto not to fly you out there without me, he'd do it. Especially since those traveler's checks are mine, and I can still cancel them. I will, too, so you might as well—"

"Okay, okay!" Ramon cut her off with a raised hand. "You've made your point." He turned his head to look Sara over, appraising not only the altered hairstyle and battered knapsack but also the tanned litheness from months of training, and the steady amber eyes that met his without flinching. His mouth twisted into a crooked grin.

"No, maybe you aren't the same person we pulled out of that hacienda. Or maybe we didn't really see you the way Doug did. You didn't give up on Doug when the rest of us did. You went after that intel and pieced it together like a pro. I guess if you've come this far on your own, you've earned the right to go the rest of the way."

He glanced at Sara again, then shifted his attention to the manic traffic he was navigating, his dark eyes brooding. "Doug would be proud of you."

"Doug would be—" Sara broke off, then said forcefully, "Why do you say it like that?"

Ramon's eyebrow went up. "What do you mean?"

"You know—in past tense, like . . . like . . ."

As Sara's voice faded, Ramon reached over to touch her arm briefly. "I'm sorry, Sara. I just—I wish I had better vibes about this. But—I don't like Vargas taking off like this, and Patterson's right about one thing. It's been two months."

He slammed a fist against the steering wheel, his mobile features savage. "Two unnecessary months, *por Dios!* I know that scumbag, and I just can't figure him keeping a prisoner around one minute longer than is useful to him. Especially one he hated as much as he hated Doug. Not unless he figured he could hurt Doug more by keeping him alive than—"

He didn't finish the sentence, but Sara could do so easily enough. It was everything Sara herself had feared, but hearing it spoken aloud hit her like a blow.

"Then—why are we doing this?" she cried out. "Why are we even bothering if you think it's hopeless?"

"To get answers," Ramon answered grimly. "And because someone's got to pay. And because—" he paused "—until you've seen the body, there's always hope."

Chapter Seventy-two

The riverboat rocked under Team Two's demolition specialist as he ignored a healing wrist fracture to dump an armload of M-16s onto the deck. On the bank, Sheik Mozer Jebai and his brother-in-law, Khalil Mehri, turned to make a survey of the encampment. Already it was looking abandoned, the thatched shelters empty except for the makeshift tables, the sanctuary portals standing open where two more of the injured were carrying out the last of the communications gear. It had taken little more than twenty-four hours since the American woman's appearance to move the boat upriver and strip the Jesuit mission of all that marked it as a training camp.

Khalil bent to scratch behind the ear of the German shepherd that had served as camp watchdog, then nodded toward the rope course strung among the branches at the river's edge. "What about that? None of the men are in condition to climb that high. We would have to remove it ourselves."

"Not necessary," the mullah said decisively. "We are not trying to hide that a camp was here, only its purpose. For a survival camp, such an obstacle course will raise no questions. Nor will it be possible to cover up all signs of gunfire." He nodded toward the firing range across the river. "But teaching adventurers how to handle weapons is also expected of such a wilderness safari. As for anything else, how could we know the survival instructor we hired was actually a fugitive with narcotics charges against him? Or that he had chosen to take our clients over the border into restricted territory."

The mullah stroked his beard as he watched the cleanup efforts continue. This place had served their purpose ideally, and it was a pity to have to abandon it. But perhaps in time, when this had all blown over, there was no reason the place could not be returned to use. So long as no one could be found to dispute their version of what had gone on here.

At the edge of the clearing, a spattering of gunfire broke out and just as instantly died away. From behind a thatched shelter, one of the injured train-ees strolled into the open, a MAC-10 submachine gun in his left hand, his right arm still in a sling. At the mullah's imperious gesture, the man approached. Lifting the MAC-10 from his grasp, Mozer Jebai glanced across at Khalil.

"Now—to deal with the American."

The two men turned and walked rapidly toward the far wing of the old Jesuit mission.

Chapter Seventy-three

JUNE 19
RIO GRANDE, USA

The sky had paled just enough to allow visibility without using lights. The local residents were still sleeping or too groggy to notice anything out of the ordinary in their surroundings.

Such as two Huey helicopters flying low over the desert.

The terrain was not flat, as it appeared from a higher altitude. The desolate landscape was broken up with irregular ridges and gullies that reminded Saleh of the surface of the moon in the predawn grayness. If anything was stirring besides rattlesnakes and scorpions, it would be a smuggler of drugs—or humans—heading for the dark, irregular slash in the landscape that was the Rio Grande.

Or a member of the border patrol detailed to intercept the smuggler.

Saleh knew how many—or, rather, how few—border patrol officers were spread along the narrow line dividing Mexico from the United States. As for the radar stations intended to compensate for the lack of personnel on the ground, they wouldn't register two helicopters skimming this low over the border. Anyone else who was awake enough at this hour to spot them would take the gray-green machines as either Mexican or American law enforcement.

Still, his stomach muscles tightened as the Huey skimmed over the muddy ribbon of water separating the two countries. His companion in the copilot's seat looked even more anxious than Saleh felt. The Yemeni-American gripping the handheld mike would be their radio voice, if necessary. One of the African-American Muslims would perform the same responsibilities for Julio Vargas in the other Huey.

The Hueys were the only mission equipment they'd chosen to acquire outside the United States. The purchase of the surplus military helicopters had raised fewer eyebrows in Mexico, where any number of aircraft donated by their northern neighbor had ended up on the black market. Their Mexican broker had arranged for delivery at a hacienda not far from the border. The rest of Team Three and their equipment would be waiting at their final destination.

If all went well.

The aging radio system remained silent as the Hueys flew unchallenged into American airspace. Saleh followed the preprogrammed course until the sun began to clear a series of mesas to his right. The landscape below was showing the first hints of irrigated green when he spotted the outbuildings of their preliminary destination.

Minutes later, the main ranch buildings came into sight. Saleh set the Huey down next to a civilian helicopter, of the type used by ranchers for herding cattle as well as for transport. As Saleh killed the engine, the second Huey touched down. A tall man with a full beard emerged from the main house as the four visitors climbed down from the Hueys.

"Welcome. We have been watching for you." He gripped Saleh's shoulders and kissed him soundly on both cheeks. "I am Abdul al Rasheem—Abe, here in the U.S. Did you have a good flight?"

It was the name he'd been told to expect. Saleh relaxed. "Yes, all went well. I am—"

The man raised a hand. "No, no introductions are necessary. I was told you will be here for a day. Let us remove your aircraft out of the sun. Then I will show you the accommodations."

The ranch was owned by a conglomerate of Saudi horse-breeders who raised thoroughbreds for racing and export. This was the type of thing that made Saleh realize just how far-reaching his father's network was, even in this alien and infidel territory. It was not, as so many American analysts seemed to think, a master conspiracy of tightly knit militant organizations. It was more the bond and courtesy attendant to a common faith and purpose, so that any true member of the cause could call for help and expect to receive it.

Not having to establish an independent local support base had certainly simplified Saleh's mission planning. He'd just have to trust his father that these people, and others positioned to help him along the way, were as reliable as he'd been assured.

Repositioning the two Hueys inside a large, corrugated metal Quonset hut didn't take long. The remainder of the day was spent resting, when Saleh was not on his cell phone. The other Team Three members had made it to their final destination, and preparations were on schedule.

The guest quarters were furnished with cable television. Turning to the news,

Saleh saw for the first time the full havoc rendered by the first two teams' successful missions. At the avalanche site, a lugubrious newscaster was announcing the suspension of rescue efforts, all hope for further survivors gone. Aerial shots of the burst dam showed wreckage of crops and farm houses as far as the Skycam telephoto lens could see. A teary woman was being interviewed in the rubble of her home, three forlorn-looking children picking through the debris behind her.

Annoyed by a twinge of pity, Saleh switched channels. His mouth tightened with disgust as a woman disrobing for a room of men replaced the news. It tightened further as he flipped through the other channel selections. A cartoon of a vicious young boy named Bart speaking rudely to his parents. A group of drunken teenagers. Two male lovers kissing to the applause of a live studio audience.

All impulse to pity gone, Saleh switched back to the news channel. *No,* he thought coldly, listening to an avalanche survivor whine about his ordeal, *the mullahs are right. This nation, with its moral decay and licentious corruption, deserves destruction.* Let them moan, as the commentator was doing now, over the great cost of human life and rebuilding. These two disasters were only a taste of the punishment Allah, through Saleh and his companions, were about to unleash.

Chapter Seventy-four

CIUDAD DEL ESTE, PARAGUAY

Hope! That night, Sara didn't sleep well, and she was awake well before their planned 4 A.M. departure. It took only a minute to dress and she was ready to go when Ramon rapped sharply on her door.

The streets were empty at this hour, and as the Landrover rounded the corner of the Jungle Tours parking lot, Sara saw that the dock where she'd seen the riverboat yesterday was empty too, a single street lamp reflecting off the brown water.

Despite his demands, the Paraguayan pilot was nowhere in sight when Ramon pulled the Landrover to the curb not far from the gravel helicopter landing pad. The parking lot was full of tour buses and shuttles stationed for the night, and a guard was making his rounds. As Ramon killed the engine, they could see the guard turn to stare.

"Better stay here until Stroessner shows," Ramon suggested. "Last thing we need is to have this guy calling the local cops."

"You sure he'll show?" demanded Rocky.

"More important, are you so sure he won't run to his boss—this Jebai character—and tell him what's going down?" added Kyle.

Ramon shook his head in the darkness of the car's interior. "No, Stroessner isn't a player. He's out for the bucks—wouldn't you agree, Sara? Oh, I wouldn't put it past him for a minute to cut a double deal . . . if he had any idea Jebai would be interested. But if he had any clue what his boss is up to, he'd have shown it by now. My guess is, he thinks we've got some kind of drug deal going on out there. Which he couldn't care less, as long so he gets paid."

Grunts of agreement were drowned out by the sound of an approaching car's engine. Sara's companions straightened to attention as a pair of headlights turned into the street. By the time Stroessner's Volkswagen Beetle pulled up in front of the Landrover and the pilot emerged, the three agents were out of the car.

Stroessner wasted no time in taking care of business. The guard was still watching from the edge of the parking lot, but as the pilot crossed over to him, it was clear the guard recognized the Jungle Tours employee. Sara, clambering out of the Landrover behind Rocky Harrell, saw something exchanged from one man's hand to the other. The guard drifted away and Stroessner headed straight on to the helipad.

Sara's companions had already unloaded their packs from the back of the Landrover. Andy William would be sending one of his men by to pick up the car later in the morning. By the time Sara shouldered her knapsack, and the four crossed the parking lot, Stroessner had the side panel of the SAR helicopter open. He riffled through the envelope Ramon handed him, then jerked his head toward the interior of the helicopter. "We are late. Let's go."

Sara climbed in while the three men tossed up their packs and vaulted in after her. For a search-and-rescue aircraft, the interior of the chopper was unexpectedly bare. The only seats were those for the pilot and copilot; fittings on the cabin floor showed where the field guns had been mounted during the Huey's military career. Rocky slammed the door panel shut as the rotors sprang to life. Ramon, GPS unit in hand, climbed into the copilot's seat. Sara swallowed hard against the pressure change as the helicopter rose and banked sharply. There were no flight helmets or ear pads here, and Sara wished too late she'd thought to ask if the first aid kit carried Dramamine.

The noise, vibration, and pitch didn't seem to bother Sara's companions. With the economy of practiced teamwork, Rocky and Kyle were digging into packs for ropes, running them through a series of metal loops above the Huey's side panels before digging into the packs for rappelling harnesses.

It's showtime, Sara thought hollowly, swallowing hard as the aircraft lurched. Had she made a mistake? Even Kyle was sliding harness straps between his legs and around his waist with an expertise that said he hadn't been totally wedded to his computers during his stint in Bolivia. Maybe Ramon was right—she was in well over her head.

A tap came on her shoulder. Wordlessly, Kyle handed her a juice pouch and granola bar—along with a Dramamine tablet in its blister pack. Acknowledging her grateful smile with a grin, he popped a tablet into his own mouth.

A half hour later, Sara felt at ease enough to rise from her hunkered-down crouch and make her way forward.

It had still been dark when they left the lights of Ciudad del Este and Foz de Iguazú behind, but now, beyond the windshield, dawn was approaching, a thin shiver of light above the vast blackness of the Iguazú rain forest reserve. As the helicopter flew steadily east, the band of light gradually broadened, transmuting the blackness below into green. Then, with a suddenness seen only in tropical latitudes, the sun sprang over the horizon, rising from the jungle canopy so rapidly that Sara could see its movement. Pinks and oranges evaporated into deep, unblemished blue. They were being offered a glorious day.

Ramon showed no awareness of the dawn's beauty. He was concentrating on the GPS, using hand signals to communicate course corrections to the pilot. The helicopter was following the course of one of the many jungle rivers, this one wide enough to create a break in the canopy so Sara could see the brown twistings and turnings of the waterway below.

She leaned forward suddenly to tap Ramon's shoulder. He nodded acknowledgment. A riverboat was moving below them, its white foam trail giving it away as it headed west out of the nature reserve. Sara leaned further over Ramon's shoulder for a closer look. It could have been the riverboat she'd seen tied up at the Ciudad del Este docks—or any of thousands like it that plied these waterways. Though it was much farther into the undeveloped wilderness than regulations allowed.

The pilot noted her interest. "Good fishing here . . . no competition," he called out above the roar of the helicopter.

A possible explanation. Native fishermen cared little about borders or environmental treaties—if they were even aware of them. Another correction banked the helicopter away from the open river over the thick green carpet of jungle. They hadn't seen a single opening in the canopy in some time when Ramon nodded for the pilot to bank into a slow circle. Stroessner dropped his airspeed to a hover.

Sara swung around in response a tap on her shoulder. Rocky, stooped low to avoid the ceiling, held out a rappelling harness. His own gear was in place, heavy gloves over his hands, his pack set by the door. With hand signals, he helped Sara step into the harness and tighten the straps. Threading a nylon rope through the safety loop at the front, the tall DEA agent tied it off. Sara wouldn't be zip-lining down; she would be lowered like the packs.

Wind whipped through the helicopter as the side door slid open. For all Sara's brave words to Ramon, the dizziness of vertigo made her head swim as she looked down. The highest branches of the massive jungle hardwoods were almost close enough to brush the skids, and the ground was at least 150 feet below that.

Ramon left the copilot's seat and tucked the GPS unit into his pack. Fastening his own harness as nonchalantly as if he were standing on solid ground, not by an open door above empty space, he tested his weight against the rope by lifting his body completely off the ground before leaning out to study the ground below. With a tap on the shoulder, he gave Stroessner a signal. Accordingly, the pilot maneuvered the helicopter a few hundred meters forward.

Peering out gingerly, Sara saw what Ramon was aiming for. A storm or disease had toppled one of the great hardwoods. Its crown had stretched for more than an acre, and the hole it left was wide enough to allow safe maneuvering through the leaves and branches of the canopy.

Kicking their ropes over the edge, Rocky and Kyle slid backward from the helicopter, boots reaching for the skids beneath. Sara watched incredulously as they leaned back against their ropes, allowing their body weight to pull them into a sitting position, right hands holding the rope out to the side to control its feed through the safety loop, left hands at the small of their backs to curb the swiftness of the descent. She'd seen this done on television often enough, but it was far different in real life. Especially with that sheer drop if they should slip.

The helicopter hovered into its new position. Then Ramon was shouting "Go! Go! Go!" next to her ear, and Sara discovered the purpose for those gloves as the two men kicked off backward, dropping down the ropes at a speed that would have ripped through bare hands. The two men hit a patch of elephant ears that buried them momentarily under the huge leaves. With a quick roll, both men were on their feet and waving a hand up at the helicopter.

Ramon kicked the first of the packs over the edge, controlling its fall so that it caught up before hitting the ground. As Rocky and Kyle loosened the knots and lifted it aside, Ramon followed with the next one. In a combat situation, where speed was essential, they'd have zip-lined down with packs in place. But because they weren't racing the clock, there was no reason to assume the unnecessary risk of rappelling with the added weight.

When the last pack was lifted aside on the ground, it was Sara's turn. Stroessner turned his head and gave Sara a smile and wave while Ramon steered her to the open door, his gloved hand gripping her bare fingers tightly as she crouched down obediently, back to the door.

She made no attempt to emulate the agents' fancy rope work, simply clutching tightly to her lifeline as she slid her legs over the edge. The wind whipped through her hair as her boots felt out the metal of the skid, and when she spared a glance below, the green sea of the treetops began to spin crazily, and she could feel icy perspiration in her palms. *You're crazy to do this, Sara!*

Then Ramon's hard grip turned her chin upward, and though she couldn't hear his words, she could see their shape. "Don't—look—down." Loosening his grip to wrap Sara's fingers tightly around her rope, he ran a hand over her eyes, closing them. Then, with a gentle push, she was dangling free.

It might have been cowardly, but it was certainly easier with her eyes shut. Sara didn't open them again, even when she felt herself spinning in thin air, until hard hands grabbed her, and her boots touched solid ground.

By the time Rocky and Kyle had Sara detached from the rope, Ramon was down, his harness unhooked. As one, they all looked up to watch the Huey bank away. From ground level with the rain forest closing in around, it was like looking up a long, green shaft, the helicopter hovering like an ungainly dragonfly against the blue of the open sky, its side door still open and ropes dangling.

"There's no one left to pull up the ropes," Sara suddenly realized. "How's he going to get them up and the door shut?"

"That's his problem," Ramon shrugged. "For what we paid him, he'll figure it out—or fly back to town that way."

"He'd better watch he doesn't drop too low and hook those on a branch," Rocky offered his professional judgment.

Catching Sara's expression, Kyle grinned down at her. "Hey, don't mind these guys. If your pal can't put that machine on auto long enough to shut the door, he's not much of a pilot."

He swung around to Ramon. "I'll tell you, though; I've got my questions on that chopper. Except for the paint job, I'd swear I was back in Santa Cruz doing that zip-line training Grant let me do with the locals."

"Yeah, I was thinking the same thing," Ramon shielded his eyes with one hand as he watched the helicopter bank out of sight. "I'd say that machine's seen more military use than search-and-rescue. If that's Vargas's personal transport, my call is that the whole SAR thing is for show."

Ramon shed his pack and dug out the GPS system. "Question is, who's he transporting and where? And who's the banker? Like Doug said, you don't waltz out of prison and buy yourself the odd chopper with pocket change."

"And I'm betting your answer's in that." Rocky nodded to the GPS system.

Ramon looked grim as he lifted out an M-4, clicking its collapsible stock into place with an audible snap. "Just so we don't come up with more answers than we can handle."

Sara, what have you gotten yourself into? Her DEA companions were already shedding the civilian personas they'd maintained for Alberto Stroessner, digging green and brown jungle fatigues out of their packs, along with weapons, ammunition, and radio headsets. Sara stepped to the other side of a tree as the men stripped down, and though she knew what to expect, when a soft whistle signaled for her to return, her eyes opened wide.

If Sara hadn't known her three companions, she'd have never recognized them—with their fatigues blending into the jungle background, caps low over their eyes, assault rifles slung over shoulders, and the green and brown and black camouflage paint making their faces and hands as indistinct as the rest of their outfits. Even Kyle, the laid-back intel analyst, looked so much more competent than Sara could ever hope to. What arrogance or foolishness had ever made her think she could keep pace with these men?

Ramon simply nodded to a pile of camouflage next to his pack. "Here, try these on for size. Williams swears they'll fit. Some of the recruits here are pretty small." He looked approvingly at Sara's hiking boots as he scooped up the clothing and handed it to her. "Those boots should do. Just as well, since Requisitions didn't have any women's size six."

The outfit he'd given Sara included shirt, pants, and cap. She stepped back around her tree to change, stuffing her own clothing in her knapsack. The fatigues were big, but not by much. When she emerged, Rocky was ready with the sticks of camouflage paint. A grin split his painted mask as he finished. "Got a mirror to see this? You look like Che Guevara's girlfriend."

"No thanks," Sara grimaced. "What I can imagine is bad enough."

Ramon showed Sara how to settle a headset in place with the mike at her mouth and earpiece in her right ear. "Only for emergencies," he warned. "We leave here, it's no chit-chat, got it?"

The GPS unit was activated, its liquid crystal screen looking to Sara more like a child's video game than a piece of high-tech military hardware. "I'll take point," Ramon said. "Kyle, left. Rocky, right. Sara, all we need from you is to stay on Rocky's heels just as close and quiet as you can. Step where he steps, stop where he stops, crawl if he crawls. Can you handle that? I've dropped us further back than I'd like. The sound of a helicopter engine carries a long way out here. Figuring a couple clicks an hour, I'm allowing four to five hours to arrive on target. Eating and drinking will be on the move. If opportunity allows, we'll break for a short rest before hitting the red zone. Any other bodily needs . . . just let your neighbor know before dropping out of sight."

None of this was news to the other men. They'd gone over mission planning in detail last night. Ramon was repeating it, Sara was aware, for her benefit—and perhaps Kyle's as well. The formation was a much-abbreviated version of the arrow shape the DEA agents used with local counternarcotic units for moving through this kind of terrain. Kyle a dozen paces back to Ramon's left. Rocky and Sara to the right. Comm sets allowed them to fan out beyond line of sight, giving Ramon, as point man, a warning interval without his companions on his heels.

"Ramon," Kyle said, handing the sat-phone receiver to him. "Williams says he's had calls screaming up the line from Miami, Santa Cruz, and Asunción over that misplaced report. They're not convinced it changes anything. The powers-that-be still figure the odds are on Doug going AWOL in Miami. But they're not too happy with Patterson."

Ramon took the receiver. "Yeah, we're in on the ground, about to move out. Just keep that sat-link locked on the GPS. It stops moving and we don't check in within the hour, you break out the cavalry, you hear? No screw-ups this time. We're counting on you. Oh, and just for insurance, have someone stake out this Stroessner for the next couple days until we're back. No need for a reason. Just make it a surveillance exercise for one of the new units."

When Ramon rang off, Kyle stored the sat-phone and swung the pack to his back. The two agents followed suit. Even with their weapons and added canteens hooked to utility belts, the men carried their heavy loads more easily than Sara could her knapsack.

Tucking the GPS by its handle into a canvas loop, Ramon walked over to hand Sara a canteen. As she hooked it onto the utility belt that went with her fatigues, he added abruptly, "You said you were firearm-qualified. Can you handle this?"

"This" was a 9-millimeter Beretta and magazine. Wordlessly, Sara took the weapon from Ramon. With a fluid motion, she slammed the mag into place, clicked off the safety, and sighted in on a rotting limb thrusting up at the far end of the fallen hardwood, using both hands to steady her aim. Ramon stopped her with a hand on the barrel before she could fire. "Okay, you've got it. Keep that with you. Don't fire unless you have to. But if you do, make the shot count."

Just what her firearms instructor had always told the class. Snapping the safety back into place, Sara shoved the pistol into her utility belt. It was a sobering reminder of what the flurry of preparations and travel had pushed to the back of her mind. This was no excursion or training exercise. What would they find at the other end?

Don't think of it! Don't hope! Don't give up! Just take the next step.

"Okay, it's showtime," Ramon echoed Sara's fierce reminder. "Let's move out."

Before taking the first step, he looked over at Sara, his painted face sober. "We're going to do everything humanly possible out there, you know that. But sometimes that's just not good enough. Maybe—well, since Doug's not here to do it, maybe you could do the praying . . . you know, for out there."

"I never stop," Sara said simply.

Ramon's somber expression lightened to a glimmer of a smile. With a nod, he was gone, noiselessly, without so much as a flutter of the elephant ears into which he'd stepped. After an endless wait—that was actually only two minutes by Sara's watch—she heard a soft "go" in her earphones. Nodding at Sara to follow him, Rocky stepped into the underbrush.

The last time Sara had been in a jungle, it was night, pitch-black, and she was running for her life. It was far different by day, the enormous hardwood trunks stretching their crowns far overhead, and the wind in the leaves like a distant sighing of the sea. The rain forest around them was unnaturally still, the usual chattering and screeching falling warily silent as the band of intruders passed by. The quietness offered at least an illusion of peace and serenity.

Underfoot, the ground was spongy with decaying plant matter, but the height and density of the rain forest canopy filtered the light to a dim, cool green, keeping undergrowth to a minimum. At this winter season, even with blue skies above the canopy, it was not unpleasantly warm. More like a late spring day back in Seattle.

But Sara was too keyed up to appreciate her surroundings. The feeling of urgency was strong again now that they were on the ground. Left to herself, Sara would have raced forward through the jungle at all possible speed. She'd wondered at Ramon's estimate of several hours to cover the few kilometers separating the drop site from their objective. She soon learned why. Her companions might move with a noiselessness and invisibility she couldn't hope to match. But they also moved with excruciating slowness.

Sara, at Rocky's heels, concentrated on placing her boots precisely in his footsteps, which was not an easy task given that his strides were far longer than hers. Her head turned when his did to search the jungle before advancing another stride. At intervals, they didn't move at all until Ramon's soft "go" came into their earphones. By the end of the first hour, Sara's muscles ached more than if she'd been running. By the end of the second hour, she was gritting her teeth. Despite the coolness of the day, she could feel sweat tracing paths through her camouflage paint.

But she was rewarded by Rocky's approving grin and a thumbs-up the next time they waited for Ramon's "all clear." From a compartment of his pack, the tall agent pulled out an energy bar, noiselessly peeled off the wrapper, and handed it to Sara before repeating the maneuver with another bar for himself. They ate in silence, washing down the high-calorie food ration with water from their canteens. Then Rocky tucked the wrappers into a zip-pocket and stepped away from the protruding tree root against which they'd found cover. Sara followed.

In all that time Sara hadn't once caught a glimpse of Ramon or Kyle or any other living creature. Once, they came across a game trail wide enough for a wild pig, jaguar, or even a heifer-sized tapir to pass, but the trailblazer didn't bother showing itself to these invaders. For the short distance they followed the track, walking was easier.

"For He will command his angels concerning you to guard you in all your ways; they will lift you up in their hands so that you will not strike your foot against a stone."

There were no stones here. But were angels hovering above the trail somewhere beyond her perception?

At the end of the third hour, Ramon called a halt. This time he waited for the others to catch up to him, though it was only when he stood up and waved that Sara spotted him in the fern patch where he'd taken cover.

The resting place he'd chosen was beneath one of the openings in the canopy that dotted the jungle, allowing for an explosion of plant life where the sun's rays reached the earth. This one appeared to be the result of a forest fire or perhaps a slash-and-burn operation by a jungle Indian tribe, though not recently. Burn scars still charred the surrounding trees, and the clearing was a tangle of saplings, dwarf palms, elephant ears, and other jungle plants.

"It's the best spot I see for an FOB," Ramon commented laconically to Rocky. Catching Sara's questioning eye, he added. "Forward Operating Base. We'll leave our packs here."

They took time as well for a real meal, hunkered down under a fern patch so thick that someone walking by even a few feet away wouldn't have seen them. They didn't risk heating the MREs, but hunger made even the cold beans palatable. Sara was just feeling the stiffness beginning to leave her muscles when Ramon rose to his feet.

"Okay, let's roll out." He studied the liquid crystal screen of the GPS. "Our objective is just over nine hundred meters ahead. So far so good. But the easy part's behind us. Whatever is waiting out there, it's up ahead. We take it careful from now on—no sight, no sound." His stern look was for Kyle and Sara. "And don't get any ideas about blazing in on any kind of a cowboy rescue op. This is a reconnaissance mission. We go in there quiet, see what's there."

"Then what?" Kyle demanded. "We didn't come this far just to take a look around."

"We can't say at this point," Ramon answered just as bluntly. "Best case scenario, we find a processing site and Doug tied up with a couple of guards. We take out the guards and call in our ride. Worse case . . . well, we won't talk about the options. If we walk into any kind of hostile situation, we back right out and wait for the cavalry."

"If those coordinates mean anything to start with." Kyle sounded unusually dispirited. "How do we know we'll find any sign of Bradford . . . that this whole thing isn't just a wild goose chase? I mean, he took those coordinates from the air. We don't know he actually followed them up himself."

It was a thought Sara hadn't even allowed herself to consider. The parallels to her own experience in Bolivia were so strong, she'd taken for granted that finding these coordinates meant finding Doug—one way or another. But what if he'd never even reached them? There were so many ways for peril to strike in this wilderness besides human ones. Drowning. A caiman attack. A poisonous snake or angry jaguar. If Doug had come to harm in this vast wilderness area, she'd never know.

But Ramon was already shaking his head. "No way. Let's not forget—his stuff came home. Either Doug carried it himself and we're barking up a tree way out in left field. Or someone went to a lot of trouble to get it there. And I don't think it was some good samaritan who found it all washed ashore. Someone didn't want anyone poking around where Doug was last supposed to be. No, if he came out here at all, this *X*—" he tapped the GPS screen "—marks the spot."

Rocky, shooting a glance at Sara, spoke up quickly, "It really is a very positive indication. If they just wanted to get rid of Doug, all they'd have to do is dump the—"

He broke off into a cough at Ramon's poisonous glare, then finished lamely, "Anyway, it's all we've got."

"That's right! It's all we've got, and we're not getting there by sitting around."

The men had already shed their packs and Sara her knapsack, shoving them deep under the cover of the ferns. Now they gathered every remaining trace of the MREs and stowed them. Each retained a single canteen hooked to their utility belts, and Rocky deftly showed Sara how to duct tape an MRE to the side of her canteen. Whatever lay ahead, they would have food and water.

Ramon programmed the coordinates for their belongings into the GPS, his fingers flying over the minute keyboard. The tracking unit was now the only load he carried, other than his assault rifle, and the other two men also had their weapons unslung and in their hands. Sara fingered the butt of the Beretta thrust into her belt, tension knotting her stomach. Ramon had already melted into the ferns up ahead. Kyle took up his position off to her left. As Rocky moved out, she followed in his steps.

If she thought they'd moved slowly before, now Sara could have crawled faster. Rocky stepped deftly from the cover of one patch of underbrush to another, with Sara close on his heels. There was a lot more cover now, because they'd come upon the twisting of another river and were moving parallel to its banks. After several hundred meters, Rocky dropped to his belly, and Sara followed. The ground was soggy under her body as she inched forward on elbows and knees, the vegetation closing above her head so that her only point of reference was Rocky's boots ahead of her.

Then, for a long time, the DEA agent didn't move at all. Ramon and Kyle were silent and invisible somewhere up ahead. Sara cautiously moved her watch so that she could see the hands.

Ten minutes. Twenty.

The earth under her face smelled rich and musty with decay, the broad fronds over her head muting the soft sigh of the treetops, the man lying in front of her so still. Only an occasional twitch of his heel told Sara he was still alive and not, as she'd considered for one wild moment, lying there dead of a snakebite or something else, with Sara stuck there unsuspecting at his heels. With the stillness and passing minutes, Sara moved from impatience to worry to—incredibly, despite the tension—drowsiness.

Twenty-five minutes. Thirty.

The second hand had just swung past the half hour mark, and Sara was debating reaching forward to nudge Rocky's heels, when the silence in her earphone ended.

"Guys, you'd better get up here. And fast. The chickens have flown the coop. Repeat, there are no chickens in the coop. Come on in."

The dizziness sweeping through Sara was an indication of how much she'd let her hopes rise. Rocky was already on his feet as Sara scrambled to hers. He gripped her shoulder hard in a gesture meant to be comforting before he strode off, no longer making any attempt at stealth. Sara broke into a trot to keep up.

They located Ramon by simply following the river. The explosion of vegetation along the bank ended with an abruptness that stopped Sara in her tracks. The scene in front of her was so fantastic that she blinked before she was sure it was really there.

Chapter Seventy-five

She might have been looking at an abandoned set from the Robert De Niro classic movie *The Mission*. The ruins of the old mission, the swathe of open ground with its scattered fruit trees sweeping down to the river, the thatched *pahuichis* the Guarani had used as residences for centuries.

But what was this place doing in the middle of the wilderness?

And not so abandoned, at second glance. This clearing was freshly reclaimed from the jungle. The brighter orange of new roofing glinted among the centuries-old tiles. Those shelters should have long since rotted back into the jungle.

Still, if there'd been people occupying those shelters, there was no sign of them now. Under the sunlight burning through an opening in the jungle canopy, the place stretched silent and empty.

"A Jesuit *recolecta*," Rocky exclaimed incredulously. "I didn't think there'd ever been any out this far. How is it no one knew this was here?"

"Someone did." Ramon was standing at the edge of the clearing where Ramon and Sara had caught up with him, binoculars to his eyes. "But there's no one here now. I did a recon of the entire perimeter. The place is empty."

He glanced down at Sara. "I'm sorry."

Disappointment and pain welled up so sharply in Sara that she wanted to strike out at something—anything.

"And Doug?" She was suddenly, furiously angry. "This is what you were expecting, wasn't it? You didn't really believe he'd be here! I wondered why you let me come. Is this it? Because you knew it'd be safe enough, that there'd be nothing here?"

"Now, just hold it," Ramon answered sharply. "You know better than that, Sara. I let you come, if you remember, because you insisted. But you're right about one thing. I wouldn't have let you, or anyone else here—" his glance went to Kyle, who'd just stepped out of the vegetation to join them "—walk into anything that might be problems. If I'd caught a whiff of trouble here, I'd be back there, turning this party around right now. That's why we've got a point man. But I had no more idea what we'd find here than you. Just—hope."

His voice was grim, and with the last word, he looked more tired than Sara had ever seen him. Her shoulders slumped.

"I'm sorry, I shouldn't have said that. I just—" Sara turned away as tears stung her eyes. Her companions pretended not to notice. Ramon went on swiftly with his report.

"If the place is empty, it hasn't been for long. Maybe less than twenty-four hours. The ashes are fresh. This vegetation has been trimmed back within the last week at least. There's enough junk left scattered around for a small army to have been living here."

Sara could see at least some of what Ramon meant. There were tables and benches under the thatched shelters, rudely built but serviceable and, like the shelters themselves, of recent construction. Under a shelter on the far side of the clearing, she could see an outdoor cooking pit with the huge aluminum pots still sitting on the ground.

"An army. That isn't so far-fetched," Rocky's eyes were narrowed to squint through his own binoculars as he trained them on a grove of mango trees bordering the river. "You see that ropes course?" Sara had to look hard to spot what he was referring to. The maze of cable-like ropes stretched among the huge limbs looked like something built for a child's playground, but it clearly held significance to her companions. "What were these guys? What were they up to out here? You see any evidence of drugs?"

Ramon shook his head. "Not a sign. Not a whiff of chemical precursors. No maceration pits or signs of mixing, no waste dumped on the ground."

Who cares! What about Doug?

Sara didn't have to speak up because Kyle did it for her. "More importantly, what about Bradford? Is there any sign of him? Was he ever here?"

Ramon looked tired and grim again as he glanced at Sara, then looked quickly away. "I think so. It looks to me like you called it right, Sara. At least they were holding *someone* prisoner. Over here."

Ramon led the way toward the closest of the two adobe wings stretching out on either side of what had been the old mission sanctuary. Numbly, Sara trailed behind the three men. She would take it all in later. Now she did not want to—could not allow herself to. Doug wasn't here. She was too late. Her quest, after all it had cost her, was futile. Everything else was only details.

But that detachment did not last past the threshold of a low doorway through which Ramon stepped at the far end of this wing. The smell was what hit Sara first as she stepped across after Ramon. The rank, musky scent of an animal's den. A very sick animal. The stench of it was so overpowering it drove the breath from Sara's lungs, and Ramon, thrusting out an arm to block her entrance, said sharply, "Maybe you'd better not come in here."

But Sara was already pushing past him. The room, if it could be called such, was more akin to a dark, dank cave, its only opening the rotted doorframe. The walls were clammy and slick with mildew and pallid plant growth and dripping water. Even on this dry day, the dirt floor remained damp enough to cling to Sara's boots. Any number of spiders dropped down from a timbered roof that had definitely seen no recent repairs. Surely no animal could ever be housed in these conditions, much less a human being!

But as Sara stepped farther away from the scant rectangle of light, she saw—incredibly, horribly—that she was wrong. In the far corner, where crumbling tiles overhead gave evidence of rainwater leaking in and the earth floor was worn away like an animal wallow, an enamel cup and plate sat on the ground. They were empty, but Sara could see as she picked them up that they'd held food and water. A thin reed mat such as the poorest peasants used for sleeping was rolled up against another wall, as filthy and mildewed as the rest of the room.

And beside the enamel dishes was something that stopped Sara's heart for a full beat. A wad of cloth strips that still showed in spots the original white of the material. But when Sara picked it up, the stiffness told her the splotches of brown were not mud from the floor.

They were bandages. Bloodied bandages.

And there by the door was a chair, neatly set for maximum light and fresher air, where someone had sat watching, guarding the person who'd worn these bandages and eaten the scant rations in those dishes.

Sara spun away from Ramon as he touched her arm. "I . . . I have to get out of here, Ramon. Excuse me."

She was hyperventilating as she stumbled out into the open, the fresh air of the clearing blowing the stench from her nostrils. She had no doubt that it had been Doug who'd been held in that vile place. What other terrible things that horrible cell represented was more than she could bear to consider.

Oh, God! Oh, God!

Sara began to walk swiftly. There had to be more here, some sign of what had gone on in this place, what it all meant. And why!

The rest of the rooms along the wing were just empty, dirty holes, their doors rotted away. But through the open portals of the old church, Sara could see more of the rough tables and chairs, even a blackboard leaning against a whitewashed wall. Beyond, a huge fallen timber and pile of rubble blocked what had been the rest of the original mission sanctuary.

There were more rooms in the next wing, but these were cleaned out and whitewashed with patches of fresh roofing overhead to keep the interior dry. In the first rooms, Sara found only a few empty burlap sacks and makeshift shelves. There were several that had been fitted with new solid-wood doors that did not respond to Sara's push. Then came two long rooms whose entire length was strung with hammocks tiered three high. Here there were windows, the shutters opened wide to let in light and a cool breeze, the adobe walls whitewashed, the earth floor swept clean. Rough shelving around the walls was empty. But a few scattered belongings were still strewn around—items of clothing, a notebook—as if the occupants had cleared out hastily.

Sara's heart grew hotter, tighter, as she looked around. *Were these Doug's jailers, living in this airy place while he was left in—that—that—?*

Back outside, Sara headed toward the thatched shelter where she'd seen signs of food preparation. The three DEA agents had also abandoned the prison cell and were doing as Sara was, making a more leisurely and thorough search of the premises. They broke in the locked doors, and Ramon and Rocky disappeared inside while Kyle stood guard. But they emerged so quickly that Sara knew they'd found no more than she had.

The cooking *pahuichi* showed the same signs of hasty departure as the dormitory. As Ramon had said, the ashes in the cooking pit were fresh, the fire cold but not yet blown over with dust or rain. There were still a few bags of rice and dried beans stacked under a table.

On top of the table, a tin pail had been knocked over, its contents spilled onto the rough planks. Scattered about were the cheap cooking utensils of country peasants. Hand-carved wooden spoons and ladles. Hollowed-out gourds used as scoops and water containers. Hammered aluminum grilling forks and tongs. The pots had been pulled off the fire, but they were still more than half-full of food—rice in the first pot, some sort of lentil stew in the other. Both had been left long enough to begin spoiling, small bubbles rising to the top in the center.

Oh, God—I told you I'd accept whatever you sent. But I guess I didn't really mean it, because I can't bear this. And if Doug was here, then where is he now? I just want to take him home. I won't leave him in this horrible place.

The spilled pail of utensils caught at Sara's eye again, and she walked back to the table. Pushing away an aluminum ladle, she lifted the pail to one side, spilling out the rest of its contents as she did so. She saw the source of the glint that had captured her attention, and she reached out her hand, slowly, as if in a dream.

It was a knife. A large, well-sharpened kitchen knife.

A very bloody knife.

And unlike the scraps of bandage in the prison cell, the blood here was not rusty brown but a rich, bright red. Sara, still entranced, closed her fingers on the handle. As she picked up the knife, a drop of vibrant, living red fell onto the wooden plank of the table below.

Blood so fresh it hadn't yet coagulated. And in an empty camp.

Sara raised disbelieving eyes, and as she did, she saw what had escaped her notice until now. Beyond the cooking shelter, under the spreading branches of a mango tree was freshly turned earth. In a rectangular patch.

She couldn't help it. The scream ripped through her, splitting the silence of the clearing. Her companions scrambled out into the open, weapons at the ready. They were racing toward Sara even as she scrambled across the shelter toward the patch of dug-up earth. Rocky caught her back as she reached it.

"No, Sara—you don't want to do this."

With a strength she'd never have believed she possessed, Sara twisted from his grip, flinging herself down beside the mound of earth. With no tools but her hands, she dug at the fresh dirt, acid rising to her throat as her hands felt cloth beneath them, then something soft and yielding. And above that, matted with dirt, the unmistakable feel of hair.

Then she stopped, her scrabbling paused, her eyes wide and unbelieving, though tears still poured down her cheeks. The dirt she had shoveled aside revealed enough for her to realize that the hank of hair beneath her hands was not sandy blond, but black. The black of a crow's wing. And it was braided. A long, black braid of hair belonging to whoever lay face down in that shallow grave.

Sara didn't resist this time as Ramon lifted her aside. It was Rocky and Kyle who turned over the body, who shoveled aside more dirt to unearth a second body lying beneath the first. Two women. Middle-aged. Guaraní, by their features.

"Dead less than twenty-four hours," Ramon judged. "Not that I'm a doctor."

"But—I don't understand!" Sara cried out dazedly. "Who are they? Where . . . where is Doug?" Brushing off helping hands, she staggered to her feet and walked unsteadily back to the *pahuichi*.

The knife was as red as she remembered it. However limited her expertise, it could not have been there twenty-four hours. She raised her eyes from the table. She did not want to search further, could not bear to uncover more. But if there was another mound such as she'd walked away from, she had to know! Sara took a step away from the *pahuichi* toward the line of trees that formed the clearing's perimeter.

It was then that she spotted the intruder.

He stood in the shifting shadows that filtered through the thick foliage of a mango tree, a gaunt scarecrow, eyes deep-set in their sockets above sharp cheekbones and a heavy beard. His hair was shoulder length and matted with filth. His clothes hung loosely on his bony frame, his chest rising and falling under the ragged clothing as if he'd just run a mile.

Sara took a shaky step forward from the shade of the *pahuichi*. In a moment she would do the prudent thing and call for her companions. But at this instant only one thought was in her mind. Answers!

She dragged the Beretta from her belt even as she wiped a hand across the tears that blurred her focus. Her hands shook as she clicked back the safety. She took a deep breath to steady herself as she raised the pistol.

"Where is he?" she cried out. "What have you done with him?"

At her sharp demand, the intruder turned his head, the dappled shadows of the branches above his head obscuring his face but not so much that Sara couldn't feel the hooded gaze of those sunken eyes on her, blank of recognition, dark with astonishment.

"Tell me what you did, or . . . or I'll shoot!"

The gun trembled dangerously as Sara took another step forward.

Then the intruder, too, was moving forward—one step, then another until he was fully out of the shadows into the sunlight falling between the *pahuichi* and the tree line. He did not answer but only blinked at the sudden brilliance of light. Instead of tightening her grip on the Beretta, Sara lowered it uncertainly, incredulously, one hand coming up to brush away the tears that obscured her vision.

Then, in a voice unsteady and rough, as if it had not been used in a long time, the intruder spoke one soft word.

"Sara?"

Chapter Seventy-six

Sara tried to move, to speak. But her feet were cemented into place. Was it possible that this gaunt scarecrow—with nothing familiar about it—was the man she'd crossed the world to find? The man's sunken eyes swept over Sara's dark, shoulder-length hair to the combat fatigues and the weapon in her hand. He took one more step forward, into full sunlight. Above the matted tangle of beard Sara looked full into the bruised sockets of his eyes. They were gray—wounded and darkened with pain and weariness. But so familiar!

With recognition came the freeing of her limbs. She covered the intervening distance without quite knowing that she'd moved. Then she was against the sharp angles of his body, her arms closing convulsively around him, her face buried against his chest. He smelled horribly reminiscent of the terrible prison cell and was so thin that every bone of his rib cage was starkly defined under her arms. The tears came again.

It was Doug and he was—incredibly—alive and breathing. His hands brushed across her hair and down her back, wonderingly, as if he too could not quite believe it. Then he drew his arms so tightly around Sara that she had to draw away to speak. "Doug, where did you come from? We searched the camp. It was empty. How did you get here?"

His chest rose and fell quickly under the rags. "I heard you scream."

"I thought you were dead!" The horror was back in Sara's voice.

"I thought I was too." His voice was rough and uneven.

"Doug?"

"Bradford!"

Sara lifted her head, reluctantly loosening her grip to turn around. One more eternal, frozen moment passed before the three DEA agents were skidding to a stop next to Doug and Sara, their hands still caked with red earth, gripping their M-4s.

"Bradford, you're . . . you're alive." The obvious observation came from Kyle.

"Doug, man! What did they do to you?" Sara read the cold rage on Ramon's dark features and knew it was just as well Doug's captors were not within range of his M-4. "Oh, man, Doug!"

"Bradford, man, where did you walk out of? We thought you were—" Rocky's eyes were suspiciously bright as he lowered his own weapon.

"Well, as you can see, I'm not." Doug swayed on his feet, and it was only Sara's grip that kept him from falling. Ramon quickly caught him and eased him down next to the solid support of a mango trunk. His dry, cracked lips twisted apologetically. "Sorry about that. Guess I'm not as steady as I thought. I don't suppose you guys are packing any MREs. I haven't eaten since they left."

"Left?" Ramon was already back on his feet, weapon up again, his black eyes making one more sweep of the tree line. "How many? Who? No—never mind," he retracted as Doug started to speak. Kyle was already slicing through the duct tape to yank away the MRE bound to his canteen. Grabbing the first food item that appeared—the bread loaf each meal ration held—Ramon shoved it into his friend's hand. "Eat now. Just tell me—is the perimeter secure?"

The shaggy head nodded as Doug crammed the food into his mouth. Sara could feel in her own stomach the twisting of hunger with which he bit and swallowed. Around the food, he got out, "If there was anyone still around, you'd know it by now, let me tell you."

It was Sara who took the juice packet while Kyle unwrapped meatloaf, mixed it with water in the cap of her canteen, and handed it to Doug. Now that the first shock was over, she could take in more of the details—details that made her shake with as much fury as she'd seen in Ramon's face.

There were burn marks on the bony arms thrusting out of the tattered and filthy shirt, burns whose perfect circumference left no doubt as to their source. An ugly, partially healed scar ran from one cheekbone down into the beard that masked his jaw.

And his wrists. The lacerations were new, the bright-red blood still seeping through clumsily wrapped strips of cloth. *How much more can't we see under those rags? What terrible things have been done to him?*

"Sara."

At the quiet repetition of her name, she raised her eyes, but the face in front of her was a blur of moisture. Setting down the canteen cap, Doug reached for her hand, and with a grip stronger than Sara would have thought possible, he tugged her down in front of him. Ramon noticed Doug reaching reflexively for a handkerchief that wasn't there, and he quickly pulled out his own and handed it to Sara. As she wiped the square of cloth across her eyes, Doug's face swam back into focus and Sara caught a glimmer of a smile.

"I'm okay, Sara," Doug said gently. "I'm all in one piece. I'm going to be fine."

"But—" she wiped her eyes again, then blew her nose "—they hurt you. You . . . you're still bleeding."

Doug glanced down at the makeshift bandages. "That, I'm afraid, I can't blame on anyone but myself. I got clumsy."

"I take it you sawed through the cuffs with that knife," Ramon summarized, squatting down again beside his friend. As if synchronized, Rocky rose to take his place on alert, M-4 up as he turned slowly to make a thorough scan of the clearing. "You up to talking, man?" Ramon said. "I don't want to push you, but I'd like to get Kyle on line with the cavalry as soon as possible. It would be helpful to know what kind of set-up we can tell them to be expecting."

"Sure, I can talk." Leaning back against the mango trunk, Doug peeled open the chocolate chip cookie that was the MRE's dessert, finishing it in two bites. "Funny, I don't remember these tasting that good. All I need now is a cup of coffee. Haven't had a whiff of that since—I've lost track of the weeks."

His nostrils flared above the beard as he glanced down at his filthy clothing. "And a shower. Haven't had one of those since I had that coffee."

Doug brushed the crumbs from his hands as Ramon pulled a notepad from his pack. Doug's shaggy head moved wonderingly back and forth as he looked around at the four expectant faces, lingering again with disbelief on Sara. This time when he reached for her hand, he did not let go.

"Then you're going to have to tell me how the four of you managed to show up in the middle of the jungle right in the nick of time. I figured I'd been given up for dead a long time ago."

All of Sara's resolve was not enough to keep tears from spilling over again as Doug told what had happened since the last time she'd spoken to him. He dwelt only briefly on the interrogation sessions and the injuries that had kept him from attempting escape, but the cold savageness on the faces of his DEA colleagues indicated they knew even more than Sara could guess. Doug's matter-of-fact retelling of events could not mitigate the image of the dark, foul cell, and the thought that he'd been there bound and alone and in pain all those long weeks.

"I knew when they started to leave, because the rotation of the guards was dwindling to fewer and fewer of them. Then Vargas and his sidekick, Jebai's son Saleh, took off with just about everyone who was left. I still have no idea why Vargas didn't shoot me right then and there. Maybe God's own hand just came down between me and that Uzi. What he *said* was that he wasn't about to let me out of my misery that easy. At the time, I wasn't that far from begging him to go ahead and do it."

Shifting his long legs to a more comfortable position, Doug went on, "Still, their lowlife cretin of a medic knew his stuff, and I was feeling a whole lot more alive than I was letting on. When I saw they'd trimmed their people down to a minimum, I began to think maybe there was a chance after all—so long as I was still free to move. But whether he figured I was dying or not, Vargas wasn't going to miss a chance to make me suffer. It was back to ropes and dog food—and minus the mat and blanket. That's when I knew it was just a matter of time . . . and not for a rescue op to drop in."

Doug's grip tightened on Sara's as her fingers moved convulsively in his. "I kind of lost track of time after that, but it wasn't more than a few days, because I'm still alive. They'd reduced the guard to one man . . . guess they figured I wasn't much of a flight risk anymore. It was easy to figure out why these ones had stayed behind. They were all sporting some kind of training injury. Then, it must have been just yesterday, though my stomach's been telling me it was a week, take a guess who showed up here."

Doug's glance around his audience was rhetorical, but Sara spoke up flatly, "I think I know. Mozer Jebai, right?"

Doug's eyes flashed with amazement above the tangle of beard. "How did you possibly figure out that one?"

"Because it was my fault. I spooked him. I showed him your picture. . . . I knew I shouldn't have done it, that he was going to do something . . ." Sara shook her head at the memory. "Anyway, go on."

"I see we've got more than one story to tell here." There was something of the old Doug in his dry tone. "Well, you hit it. Jungle Tours' big honcho himself. If there was any doubt he's in this up to his ears, that ended it. Not that I could see much, but I heard the boat come in. Next I knew, there was all kind of commotion outside. I heard shots and thought maybe they were under attack. I was wrong. It was an evacuation. Then in comes Mozer Jebai and his brother-in-law, Khalil. I'd IDed both of them back in Ciudad del Este. I'd gotten pretty good at playing possum, and even the guard—some Asian type, Indonesian or Malaysian—told him I wasn't going to last much longer. I caught that, because they were speaking Spanish, the only language I'm guessing they had in common. Because when the other two started chattering in Arabic, it was clear the guard didn't have a clue what was going on. I just kept on playing possum, but when Jebai leveled a MAC-10 at my face, I didn't have a shadow of a doubt I was going to meet my Maker."

Doug's fingers tightened again at Sara's jerk.

"I was more stunned than anything when the old man put the gun away and told the guard to move out. Said I couldn't move and wouldn't get anywhere in my condition if I could. If the Americans did track down the place, it would be better for them find the body without a bullet hole. They knew our rep, that we'd hunt an agent-killer to the ends of the earth. So they figured if I was found dead of natural causes, even if in captivity, the brass would write it off as a personal vendetta between myself and Vargas and close the file. And since Vargas had left the country, from what they said, all Jebai had to do was disavow any knowledge of Vargas's activities and apologize for being suckered into hiring a former dealer. He's got the pull to carry it off, that's for sure. That he was condemning me instead to a slow, nasty death was irrelevant. Next I knew, he and Khalil and the guard—and everyone else—were gone."

"But what about those other bodies? If everyone left, who were they?" Sara couldn't keep her voice from trembling as she added, "We . . . we thought for sure it was you when we found the grave."

"Grave?" Doug glanced questioningly over at Ramon, and the other agent filled him in quickly about the two Indian women they'd found.

"The Guarani cooks." Doug looked sober as Ramon finished. "That must have been the shots I heard. I had a feeling those two would never walk away from here alive. I wish I'd been wrong. Anyway, once I heard that boat engine heading downstream, I knew I was alone. But it didn't make my position any better, not with my hands tied behind my back and lashed to my ankles so tight I couldn't even roll over."

Sara looked aghast at the long stretch of open ground between the distant doorway and the thatched *pahuichi* behind her. "Then how did you possibly reach that knife?"

"It took a while," Doug answered simply. "All night, anyway. But like I said, I wasn't as close to death's door as they thought, or they'd have gone for that bullet after all. If I couldn't roll, I could hump myself along—barely. It must have taken an hour or more just to pull myself up over that threshold. After that I kind of lost track. I think I lost a few hours when passed out along the way. I could see the place was emptied out. My only chance before

I starved to death or some animal claimed an easy fast food meal was fire or something sharp.

"The worst was when I finally made it to the cook hut and saw that knife standing up in a pail of utensils—so far out of reach it might as well have been the moon. It took longer than I care to think about to kick that table hard enough to knock the pail over and jolt the knife to the ground. By that time I was worn out enough I was thinking Jebai was right about how far I'd get. To add to it, the dumb thing landed on the other side of the table in the ashes. But I got there and—" Doug held up his wrists "—as you can see, I was a little clumsy."

Sara was crying again, soundlessly, as the images of that slow, painful, dogged crawl that Doug had related so matter-of-factly ripped at her heart. Doug reached to hand her the handkerchief wadded in her lap.

"Hey, it wasn't so bad," he said gently as she blew her nose again. "I'm here. . . . It's done. In any case, by the time I got the ropes off, it couldn't have been too long before you all showed up. I'd gone through the place looking for anything to eat. I was hungry enough to start thinking that didn't look so bad." A nod toward the vats of spoiled food. "Then I realized my only chance was going to be to make it back to the canoe and hope the supplies I'd left behind were still there. But I wasn't quite as up to speed as I'd hoped. I'd made it only a few hundred meters when—well, that's when I heard Sara scream. You know the rest."

Yes, Sara knew. The mad race back through the jungle in his weakened condition that had brought him here, lungs heaving for breath, so exhausted with hunger and thirst and pain that only adrenaline could have kept him on his feet—all because he'd heard Sara's voice raised in horror and fear.

But none of that was evident in the grin he now slanted down at her. "So, are you going to tell me how you guys managed to show up out here like a bunch of genies—or angels? I still can't believe I'm not dreaming you all. Ramon, I figured you guys had written me off a long time ago, especially after Vargas rubbed it in how he'd gone about erasing me. What made you come after me now? And, Sara, how did you ever talk these hardnoses into letting you come along? And with a—was that really a Beretta you gave her, Ramon?"

Ramon raised his hands in mock protest. "Hey, I didn't bring her along! You've got it turned around, Doug. It was Sara who brought us into this. Tell him, Sara."

Sara shook her head, embarrassed at the four pairs of eyes suddenly trained on her. "It wasn't much."

"It wasn't much!" Ramon let out a whistle. "Doug, you're not going to believe what this girl of yours has been up to. If you're not going to tell him, Sara, I will."

Sara turned slowly red as Ramon began with her first frantic phone call after Doug's disappearance, outlining her dogged investigation with a startling accuracy and detail that showed he'd listened more closely than she'd thought that first night. Ramon was relating their tracking down of Alberto Stroessner when Doug leaned his head back against the tree trunk to close his eyes, and Sara might have thought he'd fallen asleep except that his grip didn't relax on her hand.

When Ramon finished with the morning's jungle trek, Doug opened his eyes and looked at Sara. She was seated on the ground facing him, arms wrapped around her hunched-up knees, so close that had the length of her ash-blonde hair not been chopped off, it would have spilled across his outstretched legs, her cheekbones flaming red but her eyes never leaving Doug as if he might vanish again should she look away.

"Nothing much?" Doug repeated flatly. "Sara—I don't know what to say. I thought I knew you . . . knew what you were capable of when you wouldn't believe it of yourself. But this! All these weeks I'd given up because I knew everyone had given up on me. And all that time you were out there."

Doug straightened up from the support of the mango as he spoke, his gaunt frame leaning forward slightly, his eyes looking deep into Sara's so that the two of them might have been alone in this wilderness instead of with three onlookers. Sara saw his Adam's apple, far more prominent below the beard than two months ago, move convulsively before she got in quickly, "I . . . guess it wasn't really necessary after all. In the end you rescued yourself."

"Not necessary! Don't ever say that, Sara. It was your showing up in Jebai's back yard that sent him up here to pull off those guards. For the rest . . . I hadn't covered the first hundred meters before I knew I wasn't going to make it out of this place alive, not in this condition. If you hadn't shown up when you did—"

Doug paused, then went on quietly, "Just tell me, Sara, what made you so sure I might be out here when everyone else bought Vargas's game? Enough for . . . all this?" Doug scanned Sara's slight figure in the too-big camouflage fatigues, the Beretta now on the ground beside her where it could be snatched up at moment's notice. "What you did—what you pieced together—was incredible. And coming down here alone . . . you took your life in your hands. Don't tell me otherwise. I know."

Because it mattered more to me than to those others . . . more than anything else in the world. Because God really did speak. Because I love you. Aloud Sara said simply, "I don't know. I just knew. Not that you were still alive, only that you'd never left Paraguay. And . . . well, I knew if it was me down here, even if there was only one chance in a million, you'd come. So—I just asked myself what you'd do, and . . . here I am." Sara had to swallow before she could go on. "Maybe . . . maybe it really was those angels watching your back."

"Sara—" Sara's fingers were almost crushed under Doug's tightened grip, his eyes no longer dulled with the wounded *oldness* that had so frightened and hurt her, but blazing now with a flame that carried her back to that Italian restaurant where she'd so heedlessly said good-bye without ever dreaming what it meant. But what Doug might have said next was interrupted by a noisy clearing of the throat.

"Uh . . . guys."

Snatching her hands away from Doug, Sara sat back hastily to catch three pairs of eyes watching with unabashed relish.

"Sorry to butt in," Ramon said apologetically. "But we need to make some decisions here."

"Yes, we do." Doug rose slowly to his feet, wincing as he straightened up but moving with new energy. His gray gaze narrowed with some of its old alertness as it swept around the clearing. "Kyle, you go ahead and call in our ride. Ramon, I wasn't on the lookout for more than food and survival items when I got out of here. I'm assuming you did a better sweep of the place. What did you find?"

Ramon shook his head. "No sign of drugs—production or transport. It would have made sense if we'd found something, but without it—well, what do we got?"

He began ticking off points on his fingers. "Sheik Mozer Jebai, the local guiding light for Hezbollah, in it up to his ears. The cleanup didn't leave much, but we did find a copy of the Qur'an someone missed in the sleeping quarters, and—guess what—a Special Forces training manual. The kind wannabes buy off the Internet. None of the arms you described, but plenty of spent ammo on the firing range. Still can't figure out what any of this would have to do with a druggie like Vargas."

"That's because you don't have his file memorized," Doug said matter-of-factly. "Vargas was one of Bolivia's first candidates at the School of the Americas. One of the best too, believe it or not. Only reason he didn't graduate was because they found something funny in his psych profile."

"School of the Americas." Ramon stopped short, then said slowly, "You thinking what I'm thinking?"

"I'm thinking we've had this all wrong," Doug said flatly. "Vargas never was back into the drug business. He's hired out his other assets—the best Special Ops training on the planet."

"To whom?" Ramon demanded, then stopped again. "Of course. The Qur'an—and Sheik Mozer Jebai and his son, who dropped out of this country a few years ago. Okay, I may be a DEA agent with drugs on the brain, but I can spot a terrorism connection when it slaps me in the face. Forget Bin Laden-style training camps with every satellite camera on the planet snapping pictures. Just take a chosen handful of their 'best of the best' and give them the same training we get. Set up shop clear across the world from where anyone's looking for them, and throw in a jungle canopy that the sat-cams can't penetrate anyway. It's a brilliant concept—bound to happen sooner or later, unfortunately."

"Makes sense," Rocky spoke up laconically. He was still tacitly on sentry duty and had made a quick tour around the *pahuichi* area before returning to the others. "Except those drug raids. Assuming these are the same guys, the general consensus is they're some kind of personal army to one of the cartels. If they're not, why would they be bumping off drug dealers in Bolivia?"

Ramon and Doug looked at each other. Ramon spoke first. "Robin Sage."

From the bleakness of her companions' expressions, Sara knew she was the only one not immediately illuminated. "Robin Sage? Is that a name?"

Ramon turned to look at Sara. "It's a test. The final graduation exercise of what they called the 'Q' course when I took Special Forces training. First phase is basic training. Combat arts. Navigation. Weapons training. Missions planning, etc. Like the army, only a whole lot tougher. Then you train for your different specialties. Mine happened to be weapons officer. The final phase of the 'Q' course is called 'Robin Sage.' It's a large-scale war-games exercise that basically takes everything you've learned and tests it in worst-case scenarios designed to be as tough as anything you'll ever encounter in actual combat. Only in Robin Sage, no one's meant to actually die."

"You mean—" Sara felt nauseous as she processed the implication "—those raids were training exercises?"

"It's the perfect set-up—if human life isn't your priority. Give your recruits a live-fire field exercise the Americans couldn't hope to match and pick off some of your old competitors at the same time. That hit on the DEA compound was Vargas all the way. He's hated us ever since we rolled up his op and stashed him in Palmasola."

"Assuming we're reading this right," Doug cautioned.

"And if we are," Rocky added gloomily, "with as little as they left behind here, are we going to get any more cooperation than we've managed to scare up to date?"

"Uh, I don't think that's going to be much of a problem anymore."

The other four swung around as Kyle spoke up from where he'd been setting up the sat-phone equipment. He handed the receiver to Ramon. "Ciudad del Este on the phone. Looks like you—or rather Doug here—finally stirred up that hornet's nest you were after."

Ramon took the phone. "Uh-huh . . . Yep . . . I get it." Ramon nodded his head quickly while he listened. "Yeah, I'll let him know . . . that's not such great news. Sure, we'll be waiting."

He handed the sat-phone back to Kyle. "That was Andy Williams. Seems that film of yours, Doug, has finally instigated some action. They haven't identified them all, beyond Jebai's son and Vargas. But a certain Palestinian explosives expert wanted for a series of car bombings in Israel popped up in Technicolor when they ran your pictures through the mainframe, and they're investigating several other possibilities in your group photos. So now the powers-that-be have decided that six report of yours is a Level One priority and so are these coordinates. They've already scrambled a team from the nearest U.S. FOB in Brazil and another from Asunción. They were tickled pink, to put it mildly, to find out you'd survived, and they're planning to haul us back for debrief on the first inbound chopper."

His mobile mouth twisted into a sardonic grin. "Oh, and one other thing. The FBI and CIA are both screaming that they didn't have that report and your photos weeks ago. Seems Patterson's already on his way to Washington to do some explaining. Somehow I doubt he's going to be back."

Chapter Seventy-seven

ASUNCIÓN, PARAGUAY

Tom Sandoval, the FBI liaison officer to the U.S. embassy in Asunción, Paraguay, swept a glance around the long oval table, ending with the five newcomers clustered at the far end. "Okay, say our guests here are right. Say this is some kind of super terrorist training camp. Having our Palestinian friend, Abbas, show up there makes it more than an even bet. But that doesn't necessarily constitute a clear and present danger to the U.S. This isn't the first instance we've had of militant recruitment down here. The Lebanese community has always been a hotbed of Hezbollah and Hamas activism. But their quarrel has been with Israel, not us."

The FBI liaison officer settled his gaze on Sara. "Ms. Connor, you said these men were catching a flight to Mexico. If they've put together some kind of special fighting force—and to be honest, I'm only surprised it's taken them this long—there's every reason to assume they're on their way to the Palestinian territories to join the conflict there. Or somewhere else in the Middle East."

"You don't hope for the best," snapped Stan Weaver, the Asunción CIA station chief. "You assume the worst possible scenario. And worst case is that they weren't on their way to the Middle East but heading north across the border to the U.S."

"So you want to issue another terror alert?" Tom Sandoval fired back. "With no further evidence than possibilities? The American public is tired of alerts. It has become counterproductive."

Sara stifled a yawn. It was close to midnight, and these men had been arguing for hours. She looked across the end of the long oval table to where Doug was sitting, flanked by Rocky and Kyle.

Rocky had volunteered to switch seats, but Sara was happy to be where she could see Doug. At least they'd allowed him time to shower and shave and come up with clean clothes before calling this meeting in the U.S. embassy's conference room. His gauntness still twisted at Sara's heart. Lines of weariness grooved his cheeks and stained the hollows under his eyes. But without the beard and with his hair clean and slicked back into reasonable tidiness, he was Doug again and not the terrible stranger who'd staggered out of the jungle. He was looking, in fact, a lot more alert than Sara herself felt at the moment.

Catching her eye on him, Doug curved his mouth into a rueful grin as he cocked an eyebrow at the men arguing further down the table. Sara blinked back the sudden dampness stinging her eyes. Yes, if he was not yet completely the old Doug again, he was going to be all right. And for that Sara could bear anything now, including the excruciating boredom of this meeting.

She hadn't been alone with Doug for even a moment since they had found him. The rescue helicopters had arrived at the old Jesuit mission right on the heels of the sat-phone conversation. The five of them had been bundled into a Blackhawk for transport to the embassy in Asunción, the nearest U.S.-controlled location.

Doug had slept the deep sleep of utter exhaustion on the way in. Not even the roar of the Blackhawk's engine had been able to disturb him. When they'd touched down on the embassy lawn, Ramon's pithy commentary on the joys of the flight resulted in Doug's shower and change before the five of them were herded into this room. The embassy's medical officer had also taken advantage of the intermission for a quick preliminary physical on Doug, and the grimness of his expression when he emerged from the embassy infirmary told Sara more than she wanted to know.

The medical officer's insistence that Doug belonged in a hospital and not a meeting had been ignored as much by Doug and his DEA companions as by the embassy personnel anxious to debrief him. Instead he'd strapped up Doug's ribs, injected him with tetanus and antibiotic shots, and ordered him brusquely not to move from his present seat except to bed.

They'd been stuck in this room ever since, the debriefing session broken only by sandwiches and coffee partway through the evening. At least Sara hadn't been barred from the meeting, though it was clear that both the FBI and CIA station chiefs did not really want her there. But their oblique suggestions that Sara acquaint herself with the embassy's accommodations had fallen on deaf ears.

"It isn't necessary to alert the public," the CIA station chief was saying. "But the relevant agencies need to be put on alert. We've already begun a discreet circulation of Bradford's photos. And we'll have to hope our teams come up with more than our DEA colleagues—" he nodded toward the end of the table "—were able to uncover in their short time there."

His discourse was interrupted as the conference door opened and an embassy staffer walked over to set a file in front of Ambassador John Greenley and murmur briefly in his ear. The ambassador's change of expression as he flipped through the file ended the bickering between FBI and CIA. Shaking the file's contents onto the table, the ambassador glanced around grimly.

"It seems this discussion has become irrelevant," he announced bleakly. "Two more of the subjects in Bradford's photos have just surfaced . . . in the U.S. And from the circumstances of their surfacing, we have a problem. A very serious problem."

From the pile he'd shaken out, Ambassador Greenley withdrew a number of photos which the FBI and CIA station chiefs immediately seized for examination as he went on, "A few days ago, in Kentucky, a dam collapsed, wiping out an entire farming community downstream as well as interrupting electrical service for a municipal area of several million people. Estimates are several billion in economic damages, beyond the loss of life. The president has just declared the area a disaster zone. Until today, it was assumed to be a natural disaster. The dam was poorly constructed, and a number of civic groups have been prophesying the potential of such a collapse for years. Except that now—" Ambassador Greenley nodded toward the photos that Tom Sandoval and Stan Weaver were studying "—some security camera coverage taken before the disaster, has cross-referenced with two of the men featured in your photos, Bradford. If you could just pass him those—"

Reluctantly, the station chiefs released the photos to be passed down the table to Doug, who glanced at them before passing them on to his companions. When they reached Sara, she examined them closely. The shots were of a flock of tourists, crowded up to the railing on the walkway of a hydroelectric dam. Two faces had been singled out of the crowd for blow-ups, one a light-skinned black, the other of some Mediterranean background, Italian or Greek or even Middle Eastern. In one set of close-ups, both men had binoculars raised to their eyes. In the next shot, the binoculars were lowered, allowing for a clear view of their features.

"We wouldn't have these," the ambassador explained, "except that a standard investigation of a disaster of this magnitude includes running any photo evidence through the data banks, even when it's been presumed an accident. Especially with these protestors involved."

"May I see the pictures I took?" Doug asked. As the photos were pushed his direction down the table, he studied them closely. Then his own mouth straightened into a grim line.

"Team Two," he said, tapping one of the pictures. The men around the table looked at him questioningly. "Those two at the dam. They were both among the men playing boat crew when I took these pictures. Every one in that group was among the second bunch to disappear from the camp."

Stan Weaver frowned. "How can you be so certain?"

Doug's mouth straightened further. "Let me assure you, I had plenty of time to memorize their faces," he said grimly. "And to note who disappeared and when. These two men—" he tapped the dam surveillance photos "—left the camp at the same time as the rest of the men dressed as boat crew in those pictures. There were maybe ten of them altogether, about a third of the men in the camp. My judgment is that they all form part of one team. An A-team, the Special Forces would call it."

"Then . . . you're saying that dam break wasn't a natural disaster." The appalled outburst came from a man who had spoken little until now, Ambassador Greenley's immediate subordinate, Andrew Stobbe, the embassy's deputy chief of mission. "It was terrorism."

"There's more than that, I'm afraid," Doug answered bleakly. "These guys were the second bunch to disappear from guard duty at the camp. Like I said, Team Two. Unfortunately, the photos I took at the camp itself were confiscated. But there were three groups altogether. The other team left a week or so before Team Two."

He looked down the length of the table at Ambassador Greenley. "Can you tell me, have there been any other notable disasters in the news within that time frame? Particularly any involving major loss of human life?"

The embassy personnel glanced around the table at each other, looking startled. It was the FBI liaison officer who spoke up. "Well, of course there's been the usual. A twenty-car pileup on I-75 down in Florida. A chemical explosion at a factory in New Jersey. A number of wildfires out west. But as a matter of fact, the news anchors have been commenting that last week was a bad one for America. Until that dam break swept it off the front page, the biggest story of the week was an avalanche up in Colorado. Totally wiped out a ski resort and left a town below the resort buried, though most people made it out of there alive at least. Of course, that wasn't totally out of the blue either. Environmental groups have been warning for years that if developers didn't stop blasting and drilling at those glaciers, something like this was bound to happen."

Sara didn't understand the bleak glance Doug and Ramon exchanged until Ramon spoke aloud, "That's it, then. Their MO. An impending natural disaster."

The other State Department personnel around the table looked as puzzled as Sara, but Tom Sandoval gave Ramon a thoughtful look. "You could be right. It's a brilliant concept—if you're a terrorist. Look for some potential natural disaster that's got the local protesters up in arms—the Internet must be full of them—and help nature along a bit. All you'd have to do is check out the Web sites of some of these protest groups for ideas. Do it right, and who's going to suspect a terror attack? They could go on indefinitely, do incalculable damage before they got caught."

"Except for these photos. They must have assumed they had them all when they seized what Bradford took at the camp." The CIA station chief glanced toward the opposite end of the table. "But that's what it always takes. Just one miscalculation from the bad guys."

"But—that's monstrous!" Andrew Stobbe sounded even more appalled. "All the loss of life in that avalanche and dam collapse alone . . . surely no one could be so callous as to deliberately—"

"I don't think these people are too concerned with loss of life," Ramon cut in dryly. "And if they've gotten away with it twice—"

There was silence as the significance of Ramon's remark sank into every mind. This time it was Sara who connected the dots aloud. She'd sat silent, content to be forgotten in this room of professionals. Now the horror burst forth in a torrent of words.

"Then Julio Vargas and this Saleh and . . . and those men I saw come in on the barge, they're the third team, aren't they? And they weren't going to Mexico. They were heading to the U.S. to carry out a mission." Her amber eyes were wide and dark with the calculations going through her mind. "It's been almost three days! They could be in the States by now! Ready to strike!"

The grim, tired lines of Doug's face settled even deeper into the grooves of his cheeks. "I wish I could say you were wrong, Sara, but I don't think you are. And I don't mind telling you that's what scares me to death right now. Vargas and Saleh Jebai and every other able-bodied man at camp left together. Like you said, Team Three. And I can assure all of you that whatever mission Julio and Saleh have reserved for themselves, it won't be an afterthought to these others. Saleh Jebai is the leader of whatever this group wants to call itself. And what he's got cooked up for his own team is bound to make these first two incidents look like a Sunday school picnic. Or a practice run, which is precisely what I'm betting they're meant to be."

"But what? And where?" Stan Weaver slammed his fist down on the table. "We can scream red alert up the channels. But without some clue of the target, we don't have a chance of finding it in time. An impending natural disaster. That's an MO we can work with. But the possibilities are endless. A nuclear plant going ballistic. A subway collapsing. Where do we start? Oh, we'll put our analysts on this immediately. But Ms. Connor is right. They have three days start on us. For all we know, they could be in strike position right now."

"What about the senior Jebai?" the ambassador asked somberly. "Isn't there something you can get out of him?"

Tom Sandoval spoke up. "Thanks to Bradford's statement, we've finally been able to put enough pressure on the Paraguayans that they've brought him in for questioning—something we've been after since early in the war on terror. We've picked up his brother-in-law, Khalil, too, and the secretary who ran this trekking office. They, of course, are screaming innocence, throwing Vargas to the wolves. They had no idea he had a criminal past. They are horrified he used his position in their employ to mistreat an American agent. It had to be quite a shock that Bradford survived, but they're not cracking.

"Unfortunately, Jebai is a powerful man in this community. The Paraguayans have agreed to keep him and the others incommunicado for the time being, so they can't tip off their accomplices. But they won't turn them over for interrogation. We've made a search—with the locals, of course—of Jebai's home, business offices, and the tour agency. But all that turned up was, predictably, some black market merchandise, plus a few recruiting videos for Islamic extremist groups. None of the weapons Bradford described. Not one bit of incriminating correspondence or computer files. No equipment that gives any hint that his businesses—and this RST agency in particular—are anything but what they're purported to be. Which means nothing. If they're as smart as they've shown, those goods are sitting right now on the bottom of one of those jungle rivers. We'll keep digging. But we won't be able to hold these guys much longer on what we've got. And once they're loose, you can be sure any advantage we've gained will be gone."

The men around the table were professionals, experienced enough to have reached their present prestigious positions. But all their training couldn't keep the palpable fear in the room from showing in their expressions. Fear not for themselves, but for their country, for the people under their charge.

And with fear came anger. It was the embassy's deputy chief of mission who burst out furiously, "And what about you, Bradford? Are you telling me you spent two months with these goons without finding out one doggone thing?"

The slumped shoulders and sudden, deep weariness of Doug's expression made Sara ache to throw the cup of coffee in front of her at the State Department diplomat. But Doug answered in measured tones, "Do you think I haven't asked myself the same thing? All I can say is, these guys are good. They've read the book, and they followed it—not a wrong word dropped, no eavesdropped confessions, no slips in the interrogations, not a single break in field discipline . . . other than leaving me alive."

Beside Sara, Ramon stirred angrily as Doug finished. But unlike Sara, he made no effort to restrain himself. "Yeah, and you can count yourself lucky they did leave Doug alive. For you to even ask a question like that just shows your ignorance! It's a miracle Doug survived to give us what we've got. And if you think you could do better—" leaning forward in his chair in a manner that managed to project an astonishing level of aggression for his slight build, he added coldly "—then maybe we can arrange to let you try!"

Ambassador Greenley raised a hand before his DCM's angry glare became words. "Enough! We're all well aware of the miracle of Doug Bradford's survival, and of the debt we owe him. If it wasn't for his testimony and the photos he had the foresight to provide for us—" no mention of the two-month delay "—we'd have no warning at all. It's not as hopeless as we're making it sound. From Doug's testimony, both of the other incidents took place a week or more after they left Paraguay. Makes sense. No matter how well they've prepared, they'd have to get into position, scope the place out. We will have every resource our country has to offer applied to this crisis. Now that we know what to look for, we'll have teams at both disaster sites. There may be a trail, more photo matches. And we'll continue to lean on Mozer Jebai and the Paraguayans. If we can just get one break, one single thread to give us a starting point for unraveling what they're after, I'm still optimistic enough to think we've got a chance of stopping this thing.

"Problem is—" the ambassador's face turned suddenly weary as he added heavily, "—all of this takes time. And I'm very much afraid—"

That we're running out of time. The unspoken words hung in the air. The wave of frustration and helplessness and despair sweeping over Sara in her exhaustion made her dizzy. It was all so familiar. Evil men getting away with murder because their power and wealth put them above the law and gave them the delusion that other human beings were simply pawns to their own ambitions, and that they had a right to do as they would to others' lives to achieve their own ends.

Like her former in-laws.

Her in-laws.

Sara stopped breathing. Maybe . . . just maybe there really was that thread.

Excitement shot her upright in her chair just as Doug suddenly straightened his own slumped frame across from her. Judging by the blaze in his eyes, Sara knew the same thought had come to them both. Impulsively, she reached her hand across the table. Doug's long fingers folded around hers before their heads turned to face the rest of the table. Their blunt statements emerged as one.

"The Cortéz."

Chapter Seventy-eight

JUNE 20
WESTERN UNITED STATES

The White House.

Capitol Hill.

And, of course, the Pentagon.

These were targets that would bring glory. But the very obvious and spectacular nature of these targets ensured the probable failure of even a suicide mission. After months of training, and the satisfaction of repeated successful missions, Saleh was beginning to understand the Americans' reluctance to risk unnecessary personnel losses. Especially when it cost so much to train and prepare them.

It was sheer chance—or perhaps Fate, as the mullahs taught—that Saleh stumbled over the perfect plan.

Impending natural disasters.

The brainstorm had struck Saleh like a bolt from heaven during his Internet probing. A ski resort under construction near a fragile glacier. A major dam in desperate need of repair. Either of them an environmentally sensitive issue and a magnet for protestors. How easy it might be to transform the protesters' fears into reality was at first only an idle thought. But as Saleh turned the ideas over in his mind, the sheer economy of effort blossomed into inspiration. Why wrack his brain to ferret out the weaknesses of his enemy when they were so willing to do it for him? And there were so many possibilities! These Americans were always protesting one impending disaster or another.

And like so many other things, the Americans did it so well. Surveys. Maps. Diagrams. Detailed analysis of every flaw and potential danger. The dam picketers' Web site even included a blueprint with the stress cracks marked on it. As much as Saleh had studied this American freedom of expression, it still astounded him. *Do they not care how they aid their enemies?*

It made Saleh's task that much easier. How long would it be before anyone suspected human intervention in this unusual spate of natural disasters? Inevitably, it would happen. The Americans were not stupid, even if they insisted on allowing their freedoms to expose them to their enemies. But no matter. When they finally figured it out, Saleh's force would simply fade back across the border to regroup and develop a new strategy. Just so long as that didn't happen before Saleh's own mission was completed.

The two Hueys flew northward over rugged and barren wilderness terrain. Though both helicopters now displayed a small American flag and had a registration number painted on the tail, Saleh felt naked and exposed in the open sky. He'd just have to trust that his father's network of contacts had done its job, and if the regional Department of Forestry and Fire Protection didn't know they owned two more Hueys for wildfire duty, their computer system did.

The Hueys dropped in altitude as the GPS unit indicated their destination lay just ahead. Like the day before, the terrain below was barren and brown, broken with rises and shallow ravines. But unlike yesterday's desert, the landscape today was a thick carpet of sagebrush, prairie grass, and stunted, windgnarled trees barely taller than the sagebrush.

The scattered buildings that Saleh had been told to expect were now coming into view. As the Huey dropped lower, he made out running figures and waving arms. A cold smile curved his lips as the runners touched down. The last phase of all their planning and training was about to begin. If his mission went as planned, it no longer mattered whether his jihad should be exposed. The damage would already be done, and not even a country as rich and powerful and arrogant as the United States of America would easily recover.

Chapter Seventy-nine

MIAMI, FLORIDA

Sara stirred. The pillow beneath her head was uncomfortably hard. She shifted her position and emerged from her slumber enough to recognize that her pillow was actually a shoulder.

Doug's shoulder.

The astonishing wonder of that realization warmed Sara through as she eased herself upright in the plush, reclining seat of the small aircraft. *Thank you! Thank you! Thank you!*

Then the reality of why she was speeding northward in a twenty-passenger Gulfstream intruded, and her joy dimmed. Things had moved faster than she'd expected once Doug had completed his debriefing at the embassy. After two hours of phone calls, dragging embassy staff out of bed, and a flurry of last-minute preparations, Sara, Doug and the other three DEA agents, along with an embassy party that included the CIA station chief and the embassy's deputy chief of mission, had boarded the Gulfstream, a favor called in from someone in the Paraguayan oligarchy wealthy enough to own such a toy.

Pushing back tousled hair, Sara rubbed her stiff neck as she glanced around the cabin. The other passengers were still sleeping, Rocky's and Kyle's lanky frames looking uncomfortably cramped, even in these luxury-class seats.

Sara turned her eyes to the seat beside her. Dawn had come and gone during their flight northward, and even with the window shade drawn, the light was enough for Sara to study the man stretched out in the seat beside her, his head tilted awkwardly against the cabin wall. The emaciated frame, and the prominence of his jawbone thrusting against the skin now that the beard was gone, still twisted at Sara's heart, but at least in sleep the lines of pain and weariness were smoothed into relaxation.

And your neck's going to be stiffer than mine when you wake up. Somehow, in all her hopes and prayers for finding Doug alive, she'd never envisioned a scenario in which, hours later, they still would not have had any time alone together, not even a single moment to say the things that pulsed unspoken between them.

But that hardly mattered now. There were issues far bigger than either of them at stake here. Doug was—incredibly, miraculously—alive. But how many others had died? And how many more might die—today or tomorrow or the next?

"What is it, Sara?"

Sara suddenly realized that Doug's eyes were open, not sleepily but with the quick transition to alertness that came with his profession. "Are you okay?"

Sara's mouth twisted into a grin. "Shouldn't I be asking you that?" She reached past him to push the window shade up. The Gulfstream was dropping now as they approached land, and a white line of surf edging a stretch of sandy beach was now visible up ahead, bounded by a string of luxury hotels and condominiums. Keeping her voice low so as not to awake the other passengers, Sara said, "I was just thinking about that avalanche and the dam . . . all those people dead! More are going to die if we can't stop Julio and his people, aren't they?"

Doug didn't answer immediately, straightening up in his seat to rub at the back of his neck before he admitted, "You might have been safer staying in Paraguay." His eyes dropped to hers. "I'm beginning to kick myself for not leaving you there."

"You know I wouldn't have stayed," Sara answered quickly. "And I'm not worried about what might happen to me. I'm just—" As her voice quivered, Sara dropped her eyes to her lap. "I'm so angry at what they've done. At the way they—hurt you. And now they're wanting to hurt a lot more people, and they've already gotten away with it twice, so why not again? It just seems so—unfair."

Sara was clenching her fists, she discovered, and relaxed them enough to busy her hands fastening her seat belt instead. "I guess I thought that when we found you, it was finally all over. We could go home, and I could stop trying to be brave and . . . and strong, and just let go. But instead of ending, it's just beginning. Like . . . like making it all the way to the top of a mountain and then finding out it's just the first foothill of a whole range."

Her voice dropped even lower as she added, "I'm just not sure I have your faith or strength to climb that next mountain."

Doug's hand shot out and grasped Sara's wrist, stopping her fiddling with her seat belt as he said incredulously, "Do you think I'm not afraid too, Sara? I've never been so afraid—and felt so unprepared. I can't help feeling if I do the wrong thing—overlook something or make the wrong call—I might be responsible for more people dying. And though I keep telling myself that God can reach down and stop this in a heartbeat, I look at that avalanche and that dam, and I'm not so sure he will. Who am I to think I know what God has in mind for the world?"

Doug shifted his long legs so that his body was turned to face Sara, and his hand rose from her wrist to her chin, tilting it upward so that Sara couldn't avoid his eyes, dark and intent now on her face.

"Sara, if there's anything I learned in that terrible place, all those weeks when I had no hope I'd ever leave there alive, it's that real faith isn't believing that God's going to make everything turn out with a fairy-tale ending. It's believing in God's goodness and love, even if it means going through the valley of death all the way to the bitter end and out the other side. I learned out there what it means to be standing in the middle of the storm with nothing to hold onto, and maybe God didn't send in a SWAT team the moment I prayed, but I can tell you there wasn't a minute I didn't know he was right there with me in that storm."

Sara's throat tightened at the rough intensity of his tone. Though Doug had seemed to snap back with amazing resilience in the past twenty-four hours, she'd been even more anxious over the spiritual and mental effects of the hell-on-earth he'd endured than the physical damage inflicted. But the conviction and quiet passion that shook his deep voice were the signs of a man whose faith had not been devastated by the horror of his experiences but stripped down instead to the unshakable bedrock of its foundation.

Whatever happens from here on out, I love you, Doug Bradford.

"I know," she said shakily. "I've learned something like that too these last weeks. It's just—" She tried to curve her mouth into a smile. "It would be nice to be able to say at some point that the storm's finally over. You know, like the end of a book where you get to shut the last page and say, okay, now they all get to live happily ever after, ride off into the sunset, all that."

"Sara—" Doug's hand rose from her chin and brushed across her wet eyelashes, then rested against her cheek with a tenderness that made her swallow hard. "All those weeks out there, I tried not to think about you . . . because there was no point . . . because it only meant more hurt. But now—"

"Ladies and gentlemen, forgive me for awakening you, but we will be landing in Miami in just a few minutes. If you will, please return your seats to their upright position and fasten your seat belts."

Around the cabin, groggy travelers began to stir and shuffle to upright positions. The embassy DCM, seated behind Doug and Sara, stumbled to his feet and staggered down the aisle toward the restroom. Across the aisle, Rocky and Kyle came to life with noisy groans. Doug dropped his hand with a grimace. "There seems to be a conspiracy against personal conversation around here."

His gaze did not release Sara immediately. "Sara, I'm afraid things are about to get pretty crazy around here, and I don't know when we can come back to this—to us." The tenderness of his touch was translated into his voice, his eyes, his wry smile. "But, I promise this *will* be over sooner or later, and then there'll be time for that last page, that ride into the sunset." Doug paused for an instant before finishing, "One way or another."

"One way or another," Sara echoed bleakly.

Kyle cleared his throat loudly from across the aisle.

"Yes, Kyle!" Sara raised her voice in resignation.

Leaning his lanky body across the aisle, Kyle glanced from Doug to Sara. "Hope I'm not interrupting anything. Just thought Doug would want to see the cable traffic that came in while you guys were snoring." He held up the satphone he'd kept on his lap during the flight. "Got some info about an hour ago," he grinned sheepishly. "I told them I'd let you know right away, but I must have fallen back asleep."

Doug brought his seat upright with a thunk. "You're not interrupting. What do you have?"

Flickering an apologetic glance at Sara, Kyle went on, "They've got the warrants you requested for the Cortéz residence and should be moving in right now. It'll be all over by the time we land. They're going to have a helicopter waiting at Tamiami to get us out there as soon as we touch down."

Sara was up to speed, because the details had been hammered out while they were waiting for their flight arrangements. Unfortunately, grabbing up Sara's former in-laws and squeezing information out of them was not simply a matter of a phone call. Doug's and Sara's statements had to be passed up the ladder to the higher-ups of the federal agencies represented at the embassy's conference table. Numerous cable transmissions and phone calls had flown back and forth across the two continents, complicated by the fact that it was middle of the night in Washington, D.C., Miami, and Paraguay.

That the arrangements had come together so quickly was further proof of just how seriously the potential threat was being taken. So was the helicopter waiting with its rotors already turning when the Gulfstream touched down at

Tamiami, a small private airport not normally open to international traffic. Someone had been calling in chips big-time.

The thirtysomething redhead who met them as they emerged from the airplane wasn't wearing the stereotypical dark suit, tie, and sunglasses of an FBI agent. Instead, he was clad in blue jeans and a T-shirt, though his black windbreaker with the bright yellow letters betrayed his Bureau affiliation. He flipped open his badge. "Keith Donovan, Special Agent in Charge for the Miami DO counterterrorism group. We've got the subjects in custody, but they're not talking. Are these the two that know them?" His glance toward Doug and Sara revealed no particular genius, since Sara was the only woman.

Moments later, the two of them had been bundled aboard the helicopter, while the rest of the Gulfstream's passenger list left to follow by car.

Despite the urgency of the situation, Sara found an acute satisfaction in swooping down into the pandemonium that now engulfed the upscale neighborhood where her former in-laws had sought refuge. The task force had scrambled every available resource, judging by the throng of Miami-Dade police cruisers and nondescript sedans that must be FBI or DEA. Up and down the street swarmed a host of brown-uniformed police officers and black-windbreakered federal agents. Along the perimeter, black-clad SWAT team members hunkered down behind their assault-rifle scopes.

That's right, let the neighborhood see just what kind of people their new neighbors really are!

A section of the Cortezes' front lawn had been cordoned off for the helicopter to touch down. Special Agent Donovan was out and waving for Sara and Doug to follow while the rotors were still turning. The front door of the house opened swiftly before they even reached the steps.

The scene inside was just as satisfying for Sara. The large residence teemed with federal agents, poking into drawers and cupboards, dumping out the contents of closets, hurrying in and out of doors. Sara spotted her former in-laws herded together into the huge living area, right down to the children and nanny. The raid had apparently caught them in bed, because Diego and Raymundo were in their bathrobes, and the children were still in their pajamas. The women had been allowed to dress, but no time was spared for grooming or makeup.

They were also unmistakably afraid, Sara saw at once, though Diego and Raymundo, fatter than she remembered, were defending themselves with irate hand gestures to a circle of agents.

"I don't know what you're talking about!" Diego repeated several times angrily. "We have done nothing wrong here. We are in this country legally. We know our rights." But sweat dotted both men's faces despite the air-conditioning, and their bloodshot eyes darted nervously around the room.

"We know you've had business dealings with this Julio Vargas," a Hispanic agent answered patiently in Spanish. "We've checked your phone records. You've had several long-distance phone calls from Paraguay."

"That was a business venture," Diego retorted. "Much of our import/export business is conducted with South America. It is all totally legal. If you think we are dealing in drugs, then prove it."

Raymundo cut through his brother-in-law's bluster. "No more! We want to speak to our lawyer. We know the law here. We will not say another word until he arrives."

Sara could see the frustration on the agents' faces, the clenching and unclenching of fists as they restrained themselves from choking information out of the two men. The women had huddled together in the farthest group-ing of sofas and armchairs, Janeth and Delores puffy-eyed with tears, their children close around them, frightened and uncomprehending. By contrast, Sara's former mother-in-law and Reina sat rigidly upright, their beautiful fea-tures stony with contempt, their dark eyes blazing hate, so that Reina—rather than Janeth and Delores—might have been Mimi's daughter.

Now you know what it feels like, Sara thought without sympathy. This moment was for every tear she had shed over Nicky's betrayal, every heart-sickening jolt of terror, every humiliation at the hands of a twisted law system controlled by people like the ones now cowering in this room, every terrible, stumbling step of that long, unrelenting flight into the jungle. What they were now enduring was the smallest part of what they deserved.

Then Sara caught Janeth's pale, frightened face as she pulled a wailing toddler onto her lap, and fierce satisfaction shifted unexpectedly to pity. Whatever these women had done—what they had condoned, if not actively participated in—their present distress was very real.

The flash of sympathy lasted as long as it took for the Cortéz clan to notice Sara's entrance into the room. A moment of stunned recognition was followed by a chorus of incredulous gasps. Reina was the first out of her seat, lunging toward Sara.

"So it is you who has done this," she spat out. "We should have known."

Her hand would have connected with Sara's face if a female agent hadn't caught her back. Then Reina's eyes, looking oddly naked without her false eyelashes, widened as they shifted to Doug, and she fell silent.

"Yes, he's still alive," Sara responded flatly. Around her, the initial astonishment was breaking into a babble of angry protests.

"What did she tell you?" Diego snarled. "This woman is a liar and a criminal. You have only to ask the authorities in our country."

"This *agente* has been reprimanded before for harassing our family," Raymundo added.

"We will sue every one of you for this! We have high friends in Miami. We will have your jobs!"

Mimi's aristocratic tone rose icily above the rest. "The girl is a tramp. She has brought nothing but shame and trouble on our family."

"We demand to speak to our lawyer!" Diego and Raymundo shouted in unison.

Ignoring the insults as well as the venomous glares, Sara walked straight over to her former sisters-in-law. A pang again twisted her heart as stony anger replaced their earlier fear. These women had once been as close to friends as Sara had known in that alien country she'd tried to make her home. But she met their eyes without flinching as she said flatly, "Don't be fools, Janeth . . . Delores. Right now, as far as we know, you've broken no laws except for not reporting information on a kidnapping." She gestured toward Doug. "If you cooperate, you might even walk away from this."

"Sure!" Reina spat out angrily, making a futile effort to pull away from the female agent. "And be once again without money, without income?"

Sara rounded on her so quickly that Reina stepped back, wide-eyed. "At least you'll be alive, which is more than you planned for Doug!"

As Reina quieted down, Sara swung around again to her former sisters-in-law. "Janeth, Delores, you have to listen to me! Did the police tell you that Julio Vargas has been training terrorists? That's what the equipment Diego and Raymundo have been shipping was for—to help in their training. Now those terrorists are attacking this country. The avalanche and dam break you've seen on the news . . . all those dead people? . . . That was Vargas's doing. Now he's planning an even bigger attack—unless you can convince Diego and Raymundo to help stop him. Is that what you want on your conscience?"

Reina and Mimi looked scornful, but Janeth and Delores absorbed Sara's resolute expression and exchanged alarmed glances.

"Do you mean—like the World Trade Center?" Janeth asked fearfully, clutching at the toddler on her lap.

"Maybe," Sara shrugged. "Maybe even worse."

Her two sisters-in-law let out a gasp. "You mean—like a nuclear bomb? I have heard such warnings on the news." Delores was now trembling.

That particular thought hadn't crossed Sara's mind, but she pressed home her advantage. "It's possible. We don't know. That's the problem. We need anything you can tell us to try and figure out what Julio and his men have planned."

They're buying it, Sara thought with satisfaction as the two paling women looked from her to their children. "But—he can't do such a thing." Janeth's clasp tightened on her youngest until the toddler struggled to get free. "This is our home now too. This is our children's home."

"Somehow I don't think Julio cares about the consequences for you and your family," Sara answered deliberately. "So I suggest you cooperate and help us to find him."

"Raymundo! Diego!" The two women were on their feet now, setting aside their children to hurry across to their husbands. "Whatever these people need to know, you must tell them. For the sake of our children. Whatever that madman has promised you, it is not worth our children's future."

Sara's move to follow them was stopped by Doug's hand on her arm. He arched his eyebrows in mock disbelief as he looked down at her, but his eyes held bright approval. "Quite the job there. Not an agent in this room could have done that better—or half as well. Maybe you should consider changing professions."

"Yeah, well . . ." Sara dismissed the praise with a shrug and a half-smile, though her cheeks reddened. "We'll see if we get any more out of them."

"Oh, we will." Doug's voice was matter-of-fact. "Now, if you'll excuse me, it's my turn to do a little work."

* * *

"But we don't know anything!" Raymundo and Diego were protesting as Doug ambled over to the sofa where they were seated. "If we knew, we would tell you. Yes, we bought equipment for Julio Vargas. But he did not tell us what it was for. We believed it to be for this agency of his. This Jungle Tours. And why not? It was all legal and legally purchased."

"And the salaries you were being paid?" Doug's scathing comment cut into their protests. "Are you telling me you never wondered why Vargas would bother paying you two a fortune to middleman purchases he could have accomplished at half the price on the open market? Or did you think he just wanted to do you a favor?"

The two men glared resentfully at Doug as he leaned forward to loom above them. Despite the weakened condition of his emaciated frame, there was menace in his posture. They shrank back immediately against the leather upholstery.

"He owed us a favor . . . our family gave him one in turn. . . . We had no reason to ask questions as long as he paid."

"Quiet." The soft steel of Doug's voice cut through their stammering. "You two are a pair of spineless cowards, unlike Vargas. You won't dirty your hands with blood. . . . You're too gutless to pull a trigger yourselves, but you've got no problem letting someone else do the dirty work to preserve your own skin or pad your bank account." Both men stirred uncomfortably under the contemptuous tone of his voice.

"Now, I'm a really forgiving man. I'm even willing to forget the last two months—and your part in it—if you can come up with some answers I like. If you don't—" Doug's voice dropped another few decibels, but the two men shrank back further "—I will make it my personal mission to ensure that you never spend another night outside prison for the rest of your filthy, little lives. Do I make myself clear?"

Total silence descended on the living area. Even the children broke off their whimpering to watch with wide eyes. Sara had never seen Doug in his official capacity, and though she swallowed back a nervous laugh, she felt only slightly less stunned than the expressions on her former brothers-in-law's faces. Their Adam's apples bobbed in unison as they tried to speak. They nodded instead.

"Good, that wasn't so hard, was it? Now—" Doug went on briskly "—when was the last time you spoke to Julio Vargas?"

The two men looked at each other. At Raymundo's nod, Diego said sulkily, "More than a week ago. Maybe ten days. He was still in Paraguay, because the connection is always very poor. But he said nothing of what he was doing. He wished only to be sure we had completed his last orders of equipment. And the new shipping directions."

"New shipping directions." Doug straightened up, the gray eyes narrowing. "Then your last order didn't go to Paraguay like the others?"

Diego's shoulders rose and fell. "No, of course not. That is why he called. This time the shipments were within this country. And it was very complicated to follow all the instructions. Some things are difficult to ship."

"And the shipping address . . . ?"

As the two men looked at each other again, Doug added impatiently, "Come on, we don't have all day. Where did you ship the order to? And exactly what was on that shipping manifest?"

Their attention swiveled back to Doug.

"He told us to destroy the orders and shipping addresses," Raymundo said.

All over the room shoulders sagged. Then Raymundo went on sullenly, "But how are we to remember so much by memory as he expects? What if something goes wrong with the shipping? We had to pay ourselves in advance. It did not go by the boat."

Raymundo lumbered awkwardly to his feet, a process that allowed a view of far more pale flesh under the bathrobe than Sara would have preferred. Crossing the living area to the phone on the wall, he pulled out a folded slip of paper. Doug was removing it from his hand before Raymundo could even turn around.

They'd hit pay dirt, Sara knew by Doug's expression as he spread out the paper on the nearest table. The other agents crowded around, and at some point, Sara noted with surprise, her fellow Gulfstream passengers must have arrived, because Ramon and Kyle were among them.

"Look at that," Keith Donovan, said incredulously. "Scuba diving gear. Skis and winter survival clothing. Hand radios. Commercial blasting materials. Cell phones. That would match up with the two attacks we already know about. But what's all this? Flame-retardant clothing and fire-fighting gear? And used, at that? Trying to save a buck, are they?"

"More to the point," Doug added grimly, "Take a look at these shipping addresses."

"There are three separate destinations here," Stan Weaver, the CIA station chief spoke up. "The first two correspond with the avalanche and dam incidents. The ski gear went to the first location, scuba equipment to the second. A demolitions expert would have an easy enough time building an explosive device from some of the other materials listed here."

"Then the last address must be the FOB for the third team. Richland, Washington," Doug read aloud. "Why does that ring a bell?"

"What matters is that we've got the thread we needed," Stan Weaver stated definitively. "We'll get the word out right away. Maybe we can head this one off. Though what they plan to do with fire-fighting gear . . . I hope someone's got some ideas, because I haven't got a clue on this one."

Sara wasn't listening to him. Her face went pale as she grabbed Doug by the arm.

"Doug, Richland—that's where my family is! Where I was staying when I was up in Washington. My cousin's out there now fighting wildfires. That means whatever Julio and Saleh have planned, it's in my family's backyard!"

Chapter Eighty

RICHLAND, WASHINGTON

"What do you mean the equipment is not yet delivered? Did you not receive my orders?"

Saleh's cold glance swept across the open yard to where a canvas pavilion was being assembled to protect the Hueys from blowing dust and prying eyes. There was no building here big enough to serve as a hangar amid the low bunkhouses, horse stables, and barns arrayed near the huge log construction of the main lodge.

Above the lodge doors hung the same sign that was at the property gate. New Hope Boys Camp. The graceful flow of Arabic lettering repeated the name below the English words. The Team Three members dispatched ahead of the Hueys were gathered under the sign, along with the camp director to whom Saleh had addressed his complaint.

"Yes, I received your *request*," the camp director responded with emphasis. A short stocky Jordanian, who unlike his visitors wore turban and full beard along with the sweeping robes of his birthplace, the director showed no signs of being intimidated by the imperious Team Three leader.

"You are our brother in the Faith, and we have been requested to assist you in any manner possible. It will be our honor to do so. But the orders given here are mine." The director's curtness grew a shade more placating as he went on, "You have not been here to understand the changes in this country. There are suspicious eyes everywhere now on those of our Faith. And we have our own project to consider. To move such quantities of equipment now where a careless eye not committed to our cause may see is a foolish risk. Once your mission is set in motion and our own part begins to play out, there will be ample time to transfer your shipment here. Then who will notice it among all the rest?"

Our own project! As if a camp to introduce the American underprivileged to the Faith compared to Saleh's own mission. Little did this supercilious fool realize how little worth this place would hold by the time Saleh was finished. Still—

Saleh tamped down his anger to consider his host's words objectively. The Jordanian had a point. The shipment was safe enough where it was. Once the invasion of personnel and equipment began inundating this property within the next twenty-four hours, their own gear would pass unremarked.

An assenting nod was as far as Saleh went in apology. "What about the other arrangements? The vehicles? The identification and maps? Above all, the driver?"

"The 'driver,' as you say, is in the dormitories. A homeless drifter from Portland who will not be missed. The rest is ready when you need it." The director's stiff gesture indicated an open garage with a variety of cars, vans, and pickups.

"That will be at once," Saleh responded curtly.

But his first move was not toward the garage. Instead, he walked swiftly around the lodge to where he could see beyond a playing field to the triple strand of barbed wire that marked the camp's perimeter. Julio Vargas tagged along, a mechanical reflex that was beginning to annoy Saleh. He walked on, seething, ignoring Vargas behind him. The truth was, every mishap in this operation could be traced to the personal failings of the mercenary at his heels. Outside of Julio's blunders, the execution of this operation, from conception in the icy mountains of Afghanistan to this moment, had been flawless. It was only luck—or Fate or the hand of Allah—that had kept any one of Vargas's slip-ups from seriously jeopardizing their mission.

Well, no more. Saleh had made his decision on the helicopter flight north. Within another day—two at most—Julio Vargas will have played his final role in this venture. If all goes well, Saleh's next mission will be to send the Bolivian military colonel to join his companions. The return of his Panamanian bank account will compensate for some of the losses the man had caused.

The playing field bordering the perimeter fence was identified by a soccer net at each end. Running outward from the fence, the gray-brown sagebrush, prairie grass, and tumbleweed stretched to the flanks of a distant mesa. The vegetation was dry, even for this arid region, the sagebrush brittle under Saleh's boots, the ground parched and cracking. A stiff wind brought no cooling, only a blast of grit in the face, piling up the tumbleweed snarls against the perimeter fence. Smoke rising beyond the mesa identified a wildfire somewhere in the distance.

"It is perfect," Julio Vargas commented complacently, strolling up to the fence beside Saleh. "Just as you said. It will work."

Saleh didn't grace the intrusion with a response, but inwardly he had to agree. Weather . . . terrain . . . the local conditions he'd researched on the Internet—all were even more perfect than he'd visualized.

As perfect as if Saleh had personally ordered it, as he had the rest of the elements for this mission.

The summer of Allah.

* * *

MIAMI, FLORIDA

Kyle poked his head into the Cortéz dining area, now a chaotic jumble of laptops, maps, and computer printouts. "Okay, guys, we've got good news and bad news here."

The intel analyst strolled over to the table to set down the sat-phone he'd been using. "First the good news. Those addresses checked out. All three correspond to rented storage units. And guess what! It looks like the equipment is pretty well all there. Scuba gear, skis, your fire-fighting stuff."

Doug straightened up from his perusal of a map of the North American continent. "A storage unit—that makes good sense. Anonymous, and what better way to dispose of your equipment? Have it shipped to a storage unit with your advance detachment sent ahead to receive it. You show up clean, collect your gear, do the job, then drop the stuff back in storage and walk away. As long as the rent's paid, the stuff could sit there indefinitely without anyone being the wiser. These guys don't miss a trick."

"Except hiring idiots like the Cortéz," the CIA station chief put in. "Not that I'm complaining. If they hadn't slipped, we wouldn't have a hope."

"That's the way it always is," Ramon said philosophically. "You gotta pray they make just one mistake. So, Kyle, what's the bad news?"

"The bad news—there's no way to ID who rented the units. They're both 'take cash and ask no questions' types of places. The FBI units who've moved in will keep the landlords quarantined just in case they have some connection with our perps. But at the moment we've got zilch."

"Not zilch," Doug said firmly. "The first two teams may have returned their gear and split, but there hasn't been another attack. So if that third storage unit still has its contents, then Team Three hasn't picked it up yet. Whatever they're up to, at least we know we've got a few hours."

Keith Donovan snapped his fingers at one of his aides. "Archer, get on the horn with Richland. We want that team pulled back to surveillance immediately—nothing touched in the unit. If so much as a mouse gets near, I want to know. And make sure the local guys know enough to be really invisible on this one. These people are pros. A couple of suits in a dark sedan on the corner is not going to slide by them."

Running a hand through his red crew cut, the FBI SAC straightened up. "Good job, everyone. For once we're ahead of these guys. Now, if we can just catch them in the act, we've got a real chance of taking them out before anyone else gets hurt."

"Great! So if we've got a few hours, I want to call my family while they can still get their kids out of town." Sara had been arguing the point for the past two hours, but the agency heads had repeatedly and flatly denied her request. As urgent communications flew across the continent setting in motion the unwieldy apparatus of America's Homeland Security system, Sara had been patient. But she was also acutely aware that every hour diminished the chances of getting Joe and Denise and the boys, and Aunt Jan beyond range of what-ever Julio Vargas and Saleh Jebai had planned.

I should have just phoned them instead of being the good citizen and asking permission. What was it Ramon said—better to ask forgiveness than permission? Now it's too late. They've got every phone line in the house under surveillance so the Cortez don't sneak off and try to sound the alarm.

Sara's chin rose mutinously at the negative response she could already see forming on Stan Weaver's lips. "It's absolutely out of the question," he declared. "This is a matter of national security. The smallest leak, and we may end up losing our one chance of cutting this off at the source. Not to mention the panic that would break out the minute your relatives started calling their friends. How long do you think it'd take before it was all over the news?"

His glance swept censoriously over the dining area, lingering on Doug and his DEA companions. "As it is, there are far too many extraneous personnel here with intelligence they have no business being in possession of. This whole thing has been badly managed."

"My cousin is a captain in the fire department there. He's no more of a risk than you are," Sara replied heatedly. "Don't tell me you wouldn't be on the phone right now if your wife and family were out there. You wouldn't even have this 'intelligence' if it wasn't for 'extraneous personnel' like me and . . . and Doug and the others. You owe us—you owe *me*—this much at least."

Sara met the CIA station chief's glare with flint in her eyes, even though she couldn't quite believe her own temerity. *You're standing here arguing with the CIA!*

But this was her family she was arguing for. Sara glanced around for Doug. She'd already determined not to put him on the spot by appealing to him. That wouldn't be fair. But to see him huddled in conversation with the local FBI SAC as if he hadn't even noted her predicament—! Sara's chin rose further as Stan Weaver shook his head. "Young lady. You need to be aware—"

"Okay, just a minute, Weaver." Keith Donovan looked away from his conversation with Doug to intervene. "Ms. Connor, you say your cousin is a captain in the Richland Fire Department." He looked over at the CIA station chief. "Seems to me this family member of Ms. Connor's might be just the person we should be talking to right now. Who better to take a look at this shopping list of ours—maybe give us some idea how this particular collection of firefighting gear might fit into a terrorist scenario. As it is, we'd have to call in a consultant to do that anyway, and who knows how long that'll take. And ten to one he'd have no better feedback than this guy. Less if he's never been on the ground out there. Bradford here guarantees the guy's legit." Stan Weaver looked sour. "I don't think—"

"No, this one's my call," Keith Donovan cut in. "Terrorism on U.S. soil is an FBI jurisdiction, not CIA. Ms. Connor, you make your phone call. Then I want to talk to this cousin of yours."

Sara's gratitude and relief lit up her tired face and amber eyes so that the FBI chief blinked, sharpening his gaze on her as if seeing her for the first time. Doug's expression was impassive, but he dropped one eyelid in a wink as Sara took the sat-phone passed to her.

Please, be there.

"Yes? Connor residence."

"Joe?" Sara's voice wobbled with relief.

"Sara—you're back?" Her cousin quickly noted the tone of her voice and added, "It's bad news, isn't it? You didn't find him."

"No, I did find him. He—" Her voice wavered again. "He's alive, Joe!"

Sara heard the exhaling of breath on the other end of the line. "Thank God, Sara! We've been praying for this. I guess God does work miracles. Or—" the apprehension returned to his voice "—he is okay, isn't he? You don't sound so sure."

"Yes, Doug's fine. He's right here with me. And you're right, Joe. It was a miracle. But—it's not over yet. I don't have time to tell you about it right now, because there's a lot more critical things going on right now—things that concern you too. I just need you to let me do the talking. I'll be as fast as I can."

Sara took a deep breath. "First, you need to get Aunt Jan and Denise and the boys and drive to Seattle or Portland. Today. As soon as you're off the phone."

"Sara, what in the name of—?"

"What Ms. Connor is trying to tell you is that in the process of finding Bradford alive, she has also been responsible for uncovering a possible terrorist attack on this country." Keith Donovan's voice cut smoothly into Sara's jumbled explanation. While Sara had been talking, he had set up a second line. "And there is credible intelligence that this threat may be directed at the Richland area."

"And just who are you?" Joe demanded.

"He's FBI," Sara broke in. "They're all here, Joe—CIA, DEA, police. It's all for real. And they think maybe you can help them. But you've got to get Denise and the kids and Aunt Jan out of town right away."

Keith Donovan cut Sara off again. "Mr. Thornton, Ms. Connor here tells us you're a captain in the local fire department there. We are hoping you might be willing to be of assistance to us. First, do you have video conferencing capacity?"

"Sure." There was a note of incredulity in Joe's firm voice. "My computer has digital imaging."

"Good. Let's get you hooked up to our system so we can see who we're dealing with. If you call this number back—"

"You want to see who you're dealing with!" Joe laughed. "Sara, you swear you're not pulling my leg?"

"I wish I was," Sara said soberly. "Please, Joe, if you can just do what they ask. I guess they want to make sure you're not some big plot of mine." She shot a withering look toward the FBI agents who were scurrying around to set up a laptop, video camera, and sat-phone lines. "They can't help being paranoid. They're bred that way. And this time they really are trying to save the world."

"Thank you, Ms. Connor for that endorsement," Keith Donovan said dryly, but there was a hint of a twinkle in his eyes. "Now we'll be getting off line. Anderson, if you can switch over."

Joe's half-disbelieving expression was reproduced in startling fidelity on the laptop's display. Sara, reseated within range of the camera angle, waved at the image.

"I see you, Sara." The image bounced slightly with Joe's nod. "Where's Doug Bradford?"

Leaning forward to enter camera range, Doug raised a hand. Joe studied the gaunt, tired features closely, and his expression relaxed. "Glad to see you made it back, Doug. Sara's been worried."

"Okay, let's cut the chit-chat!" the CIA station chief cut in.

The image on the screen jumped again as Joe turned his head. "We're getting there. I take it the rest of you are the world-savers. Okay, shoot."

Stan Weaver did not look at all pleased with Joe's casual address. But Keith Donovan studied the strong, tanned features under the military haircut and gave an approving nod. Then, in phrases far more succinct than Sara could have mustered, he explained the situation.

"Here's the Richland shipping manifest."

Doug silently pushed over Raymundo's scribbled shopping list as the FBI agent groped for it, then read it off slowly. By the time he'd finished, Joe's demeanor was all business.

"And what do you want of me?"

Sara was proud of her cousin's even tone when she knew the fear that had to be gripping him for his young family.

"We just want you to think from your perspective as a firefighter. What possible use could equipment like this have for the perpetuation of a terrorist act? The scuba and ski gear we understand. On a ski slope or recreational lake, who's going to take a second look? But dressing up like firemen in big hats and yellow rubber would seem to draw more attention, not less. Everyone stops to watch a fire engine go by."

"Is that so?" Joe said dryly. "I take it you're all from back east?"

As the agents exchanged uncomfortable glances and shrugs, Doug leaned into the camera frame again. "I grew up in Arizona. What's your point, Joe?"

"We're in the driest summer in two decades. We've got firefighters mobilized clear over to North Dakota and down to California, New Mexico, and Arizona, plus everything in between. I just got back myself from the Idaho border. A small incident—just a few thousand acres and two homes. Whatever these terrorists are planning, they did their homework, because no one's going to get in the way of a firefighter around here except to say, "God bless you.""

"So they won't stand out." Keith Donovan was thinking aloud. "Still, a guy in a T-shirt and jeans would stand out a lot less. You pick an undercover persona because you're looking to go somewhere regular civilians can't. But where? You think these people are planning to dress up like firefighters to bluff their way into some government building or military installation?"

"Good thought," the CIA station chief interjected. "We'd have to check out what security's like out there."

"And what kind of installations are around this Richland."

"Uh, excuse me, gentlemen." Joe cleared his throat. "But you're thinking like Easterners again."

Every head swiveled to the computer screen.

"Go on," Keith Donovan said briefly.

"You asked me what use a terrorist would make of your shopping list. But you're overlooking the strategy you just described with the first two incidents."

"What are you trying to say?" the FBI SAC demanded.

Joe's face on the screen was looking grim. "One of our worst nightmares in this business is a firefighter deciding to help a fire along instead of putting it out. It's happened more often than we'd like to admit. Just last year a firefighter decided he needed summer work, and since wildfires were scarce, he started one of his own. It got away to become the biggest fire of the season, taking out several hundred thousand acres and a bunch of homes. The point is, one box of matches could set half the West on fire, and out in wilderness areas, where civilians might be restricted during a high wildfire alert, any guy in fire gear is going to be assumed to be on the job. Like I said, whoever these people are, they did their homework."

Sara suppressed a smile as she saw expressions change around the table.

"That's an excellent analysis, Mr.—uh, Captain Thornton," Stan Weaver said with a note of genuine respect. "I think you might have hit the nail on the head. You start multiplying the billions of dollars we already spend fighting wildfires by deliberate, systematic arson and not even a bomb blast could do as much damage. Nothing short of a nuclear blast, in fact. It's only a wonder no one's thought of it earlier."

"Thank God there aren't that many out there who are that twisted," Doug commented dryly.

"But why Richland?" the CIA station chief went on. "I don't get it. Why not Idaho or Montana or Colorado? Surely they'd be more suitable for arson . . . with all those forests. No—wait! Why does the name Richland ring a bell? Donovan, maybe one of your men can call the place up on that DSL hookup over there."

"Don't bother." Even through the digitalized pixels of the computer image, the bleakness of Joe's expression stood out. "I can answer your question. It's funny you mentioned a nuclear blast."

Sara's breath caught in horror. "Of course! The Hanford Reach. Oh, Joe."

"The Hanford Reach." Stan Weaver sank back heavily into his chair. "Oh, my—"

"That's right," Joe said grimly. "Eighty percent of all the nuclear waste material in this country conveniently buried under five hundred square miles of government reserve land not a stone's throw away from here. It was just a few years ago that a wildfire swept through here so fast that in twenty-four hours two-thirds of the reserve was on fire. It came dangerously close to a number of nuclear waste disposal sites before we got it contained. We've always known next time we might not be so lucky."

"And how much you want to bet every detail of that fire is posted all over the Internet," Ramon spoke up with disgust. "There's our MO again. What are we doing handing the gun to our enemies to shoot us in the back?"

"Now, let's not be alarmed here." Stan Weaver had recovered his composure. "Assuming Captain Thornton is right—and it's a plausible enough scenario— we're well ahead of the game. A wildfire is one thing we're equipped to handle once we're mobilized. Actually, I'm feeling very optimistic. We've got the Bureau now on that storage unit. The moment these birds move someone in to pick up that equipment, we'll be on their tail. Meanwhile, we don't want to be starting a general panic. But a discreet alert to your agency heads—uh, chiefs or marshals, whatever you call them—down there, Captain Thornton, would be in order. Who better to pick out these guys if they do give us the slip? Any strangers move in around your crews, your people can let us know. Then we move in, pick them up and run their ID."

"Except that the photos Bradford supplied only included the team leader, this Saleh, and Vargas himself of the third team," Keith Donovan reminded him.

"Then we JPEG their mugs back here to Bradford and let him ID them."

"Uh . . . sir?"

At the lack of enthusiasm in Joe's interruption, the CIA station chief had the grace to grimace. "Another East-Coast city slicker mistake?"

"I don't think you understand the number of personnel we're talking about," Joe said carefully. "A Type 1 Incident like we're likely to have can involve upward of a thousand firefighting personnel moving in and out of one base camp. At any given time there may be a number of wildfires around the area. We're talking thousands of hand-crew personnel airlifted in from all over North America. And from every conceivable ethnic background. Sure, there's check-in procedures. But so long as they show up with the proper ID card, no one on the fire line is going to run a background check. They'll just hand them a shovel or a rake and their next assignment."

"Well, if that doesn't take the cake." Stan Weaver slammed his hand down on the table.

"Maybe if we—" the DCM started.

"Excuse me, but it's clear there's only one logical course of action here." Doug's quiet interjection commanded everyone's attention. Heads swiveled. "The only way we're going to find these guys, is if I go in on the ground and eyeball them for myself. I don't care what they're wearing or how big the crowd, I'll know any of them the instant I see them."

"And me," Ramon spoke up quickly. "I can ID Vargas, at least. I've spent too many hours staring at his ugly mug on surveillance not to pick him out anywhere."

"So can I," chorused Rocky and Kyle together. "The more of us to spread out on the ground, the more chance we have of finding these guys," Rocky added.

"Count me in," Sara said quietly. As heads turned to stare at her, she reminded, "I'm the only other person who's seen this Saleh guy with Julio and the other team members too."

Doug shot Sara a sharp glance, and for a moment she thought he would countermand her offer, but he kept silent. Keith Donovan and Stan Weaver considered the matter only briefly before nodding. It was Andrew Stobbe, the State Department DCM, who protested, "This is highly irregular. Ms. Connor is a civilian, and Bradford is clearly unfit. The medical officer was definite that he should stay off his feet, even be in a hospital bed, not running around crowds looking for terrorists."

Doug looked at him impassively. "Ever play a championship with a bum ankle and handful of Tylenol?"

"No. Wait, what do you mean?"

"I didn't think so. You do what you have to do when the stakes are high enough. I'll be fine." Doug turned to Keith Donovan. "How soon can you get us some air transport?"

"Donovan—" Andrew Stobbe began.

"I'm sorry," the FBI SAC cut him off brusquely. "When you're in a tight corner with only a handful of chips, you play what you've got. And right now these people are the only chips I've got." He looked over at Doug. "You'll get your air transport as fast as we can arrange it."

He turned back to the computer screen. "And Captain Thornton, I hope we can count on your assistance on the ground out there. I'll be calling your department to have you released for the duration."

"Now wait a minute." Sara half-rose from her seat in protest. "You can't ask that of him. What about getting his family out? They could still be at risk if you can't stop Julio and Saleh in time."

"And if that doesn't sound funny after what I just heard from you, Sara," her cousin responded dryly from the computer screen.

"That's different. I don't have a family to worry about," Sara began, but Joe cut her off with a sharp negative jerk of his head.

"I'll send Denise and the boys to Seattle." His glance shifted to the rest of his audience. "Without details and without causing a panic. But I can't leave. I'm a firefighter. If all hell breaks loose here, this is where I belong."

The quiet resolution and determined set of his jaw tightened Sara's throat. It hurt to care. And yet she'd never been more proud to acknowledge her kinship to a family.

"So it's settled," Keith Donovan said before any more objections could be raised. "Captain Thornton, we'll be back in touch as soon as possible."

The computer screen went dead. "Give me the phone," Donovan snapped to one of his agents. "Rodriguez, get me the Forest Service on line—now! Kyle, dig up anything you can find on this Hanford Reach and what kind of worst-case scenario we could be looking at there. Weaver, call SouthCom."

The room erupted into activity, and for a few moments Sara and Doug were the only ones left in their seats. Sara looked over at him.

"Thank you," she said quietly.

Doug's mouth curved into a quizzical grin. "For what, exactly?"

"You know. You think I didn't see who put that bug about Joe in Donovan's ear? And . . . well, thanks for not telling me I should stay here . . . out of trouble."

"Would you have listened if I had?" Doug said dryly. He shifted his long legs, crossing one ankle over the other, and gave her a keen look. "Don't think I didn't want to. But . . . well, you told me once—and I've never forgotten it— that I treated you like a piece of porcelain. Trying to keep you safe and protected, I wasn't letting you stand up and grow strong on your own. And you were right. Much as I'd like to keep you out of the line of fire, if I were you, looking at the same set of facts, I'd make the same decision to go. I've no right to ask you not to do what I'd do myself . . . what I *am* doing myself. Besides, you *are* the only other person who's gotten a good look at Team Three. For all

I know, your being there just may tip the scale to stopping these guys. It's not easy to set aside my natural protective instincts, but I guess if you can come clear across a hemisphere to find me, you can handle this."

It was not at all what Sara had expected him to say. As she blinked at him in surprise, his mouth tilted in a crooked smile. "Besides, from a purely selfish standpoint, after these last two months I don't want to let you out of my sight." The line of his mouth straightened to seriousness. "Guess those angel wings are just going to have to stretch out wide enough for both of us."

"Doug—" Sara's hand went out to him, but right on cue, Ramon thrust his head around the dining room divider arch. "Hey, you two still sitting there? They've got a limo waiting outside for us. Donovan says by the time we get to Tamiami, our ride will be standing by."

Doug stood up with a sigh. Gripping Sara's hand, he pulled her to her feet. "Come on, Sara, let's finish this."

It wasn't quite a limousine, but the late model Cadillac DeVille in the anonymous dark shade of a government car was definitely the most luxurious Sara had ever ridden in.

"Our State Department johnny called this one in," Ramon nodded toward the DCM, who was looking morose on the steps below them. "It was supposed to be his ride. Must be what they use for picking up African dictators."

In the doorway, the CIA station chief thrust out a hand. "This is as far as I'm going with you all, so I'll say good-bye. Donovan will be coordinating our assets on the ground out there." His twisted smile was probably the closest he'd ever come to an apology, "I am not unmindful of what you have done for our country. Thank you."

"You're welcome," Doug answered with a note of irony. He jerked a thumb toward the inside of the house. "Just keep an eye on our pals in there and make sure they don't get access to a phone. They're acting pretty repentant at the moment, but don't think they wouldn't tip off Vargas if they get a chance. They're well experienced in playing two sides against the middle."

"Oh, we will," Weaver assured him. "I don't think there's much of a criminal case we can build against them at the moment. But we do have that little loophole called 'material witness.' Possibly the witness protection program, if there's any chance this group might come after them. We've got plenty of other fine citizens stashed away in that. Either way, we'll have this crowd out of circulation as long as there's anything they can do to hurt us."

Sara turned on the threshold to look back. Catching Reina's eye earned her one more sullen glare. Strange to think that their chance meeting at the mall and Sara's loathing of her former in-law's intrusion into her new life had precipitated all this. But they didn't seem threatening anymore, only pathetic.

I'm free! I will never be afraid of them again. They're part of the past, and I can let the past go now.

Swinging around, Sara walked without further hesitation out the wide double doors and down the steps. This time she did not look back.

Chapter Eighty-one

RICHLAND, WASHINGTON

It was at once astonishingly like what his Internet research had led him to expect—yet very different.

Pulling the rented Ford Explorer over to the shoulder of the road, Saleh climbed out. Julio Vargas and Team Three's demolition specialist clambered out after him. The spot he'd chosen to stop was where Highway 240, the principal route heading north through the Hanford Reserve from Richland, intersected the Columbia River. Just ahead, the Vernita Bridge spanned the river gorge, connecting the nuclear reservation to the outside world.

Saleh walked to the canyon edge, surveyed the sheer drop to the river below, and made a slow turn. There was a certain eeriness in matching what he was seeing so exactly to the map he'd memorized. 'U.S. Department of Energy Hanford Site,' as the road signs had euphemistically identified it. Was it possible that travelers driving up this highway did not know they were transversing the largest nuclear experiment on the planet? Or that the 586 square miles of government-owned land around them contained the greatest concentration of lethal substances ever amassed in history buried under its placid surface?

A sharp bend in the Columbia River Gorge as it turned north from Oregon into Washington meant that the river here ran both east-west through the northern part of the Hanford reserve and north-south along its eastern perimeter. Southwest of the bridge, the landscape looked innocent enough, a desolate plateau without a hint of green, marked on the map as Arid Lands Ecology Preserve.

But to the east, Saleh could see the tall stacks and concrete buildings his map identified as one of nine mothballed plutonium production reactors lining the banks of the river. Beyond those stacks, along the river's edge, lay the K East and West areas, where according to Saleh's research more than four million pounds of spent uranium rods were kept stored in corroding concrete pools of water.

Southeast of the highway, the landscape looked no different from the ecology preserve, but Saleh's mental blueprint pinpointed exactly where, over that horizon, the nuclear reserve's infamous 200 East and West areas were located. Fifty-five million gallons of high-level liquid radioactive waste stored in their underground tanks was only a beginning. There were the long, low mounds of underground rail-line tunnels, where items too large and radioactive to be handled had been driven inside and abandoned. Hundreds of buried disposal cribs were packed with radioactive waste, toxic chemicals, and contaminated material, even sections of nuclear reactors and submarines.

And billions more gallons of radioactive waste liquids were vented over the decades directly into the soil, until the ground was so "hot" that not even protective clothing and breathing apparatus could protect anyone who dared enter those areas.

Frustrated by the impracticality of attacking a nuclear power plant, or a government or military installation—any of which would have made a more glorious target, Saleh's interest had been piqued immediately by the Internet accounts of the 2000 wildfire season that threatened three separate nuclear facilities, sweeping over two-thirds of the Hanford site alone to come within a few thousand meters of those tank farms over the horizon.

He turned again to study the landscape. What his research had not prepared him for was the emptiness of the countryside. Considering the lethal nature of what was collected here, Saleh had expected far more visible security. A military base. Checkpoints. Roadblocks. Though the highway was marked on his map, he hadn't expected unchecked access to it. Yet here they were driving unhindered through the middle of the reserve, and so far, Saleh had not seen a single military vehicle or uniform. There were chain-link fences around the actual reactor and waste disposal sites, and Saleh was under no illusion that the site was completely unguarded—electronic surveillance would set off at least an alarm if an intruder approached. But he'd spotted no human sentries, and there was nothing to keep explorers from wandering around the rest of the plateau. There were even walking paths along the top of the river gorge and a picnic area in the ecological reserve. It was as if these people had sat so long on top of their volatile mountain of waste that they did not see its menace anymore.

The landscape, at first glance, was a disappointment. For the first time, Saleh felt some misgivings. *Is there enough combustible material in this brown and gray wasteland for what we have planned?*

A closer examination was more reassuring. The barrenness was only apparent; in fact, a thick carpet of sagebrush and waist-high prairie grass stretched out across the plateau. There would be plenty of fuel.

And plenty of wind. It whipped at Saleh's clothing, far more powerfully than down on the ranch, bending the prairie grass in gusty waves. Not since Afghanistan had Saleh seen such a wind, though this one was scorching instead of icy, carrying with it a whiff of smoke from beyond the mountain ridge. He could not have asked for better.

* * *

As the 707 settled into its approach to the Richland airport, Sara shifted restlessly in her seat and gazed out the window at the barren terrain and smoke-tinged sky. Although there was ample room on the customized jet, normally reserved for ferrying SouthCom VIPs, she was beginning to feel she'd spent a lifetime cooped up in the cramped confines of an airplane. Around her, the jet's only other passengers, Doug, his three DEA companions, and FBI Special Agent in Charge, Keith Donovan, were stowing laptop computers and packing up a stack of photos and computer files they had been poring over during the flight.

Sara had positively identified photos of Sheik Mozer Jebai and Khalil Mehri as the men who had tried to pick her up in the black Mercedes, and the sheik's son, Saleh, as the young man who had boarded the plane with Julio Vargas. But none of the other photos had included any of the young men she'd seen unloading gear outside Jungle Tours. Doug had made a tentative identification of a notorious Chechen militant, once a bit of computer magic removed the beard and turban, as one of his former guards. But careful scrutiny of the dam security footage turned up only the Palestinian and Nation of Islam convert who'd already been identified.

The acrid smell of smoke greeted them as the 707's steward cracked open the door. Joe was waiting on the tarmac, along with two noticeably nondescript civilians that Sara pegged as FBI, even though Keith Donovan didn't introduce them. Her cousin looked tired and grim, but his expression lightened when he saw her hurrying down the roll-away stairs. She leaned gratefully into his hug.

"The smoke, is that—?"

Joe shook his head. "No, that's drifting in from the Saddle Mountains, north of here. A lightning storm started half a dozen fires out there last week, but it looks like we've got it contained now."

He released Sara to turn his attention to the group of men who'd accompanied her off the plane. Twenty-four hours of freedom had made a world of difference in Doug's appearance, but the lingering stiffness from his strapped ribs, the looseness of his borrowed clothing, and bandaged wrists made identification easy. Joe held out a hand. "You must be Doug Bradford. Glad to finally meet you."

The two men were much the same height, and Joe met Doug's steady gaze with a long, considering look of his own. Then a genuine smile banished his tiredness as he repeated more definitely, "I'm *really* glad you guys are here. I hope you can make some sense out of all this."

As he looked back over to Sara, she asked anxiously, "What about Denise and the boys? Are they gone?" She faltered as the grimness returned to her cousin's face. "Oh, Joe, you did believe us. You did send them away."

"Yes, of course I believed you," Joe said heavily. "But what I didn't get a chance to tell you this morning was that I'd pulled myself off the Idaho fire because Joshua's been sick. All this smoke has really played havoc with his asthma. We thought he was doing better, but after you called this morning, he woke up a lot worse. Mom took Jonathan over to Portland to visit John and Alyssa, no questions asked. I told her I wanted him out of the smoke. But Josh's in the hospital right now under an oxygen mask. There's no chance of moving him—or Denise, of course." His mouth twisted painfully. "So I guess we'll just have to depend on your friends here to stop anything before it happens."

"Oh, Joe," Sara cried. "I'm so sorry. And then we dragged you into this." Sara swung around to Keith Donovan. "At least we can do something about that."

"No, Sara." Joe touched a hand to Sara's shoulder. "If there's anything I can do, I want to be in on it. There's nothing I can do right now for Josh. The doctor's say he'll be fine, and he's got Denise with him. But if there's any part I can play to stop these crazies from hurting my family or anyone else, that's where I need to be, not sitting around hoping someone else gets it right."

Sara knew the set of her cousin's jaw too well to try arguing with him. It was just what Doug would do. Besides, nothing had happened yet. And now that they were here, maybe nothing would.

"So what's the local situation?" Keith Donovan looked from Joe to the two

FBI agents with him. "I understand an orange alert has been issued to all law enforcement agencies in the area."

"Let's get you to the van, and then we'll fill you in." The two agents were so similar that Sara mentally dubbed them Tweedledum and Tweedledee. They steered the group toward a white van that had pulled onto the runway to eliminate the need to enter the terminal. When their guests were all inside, Tweedledum took the wheel, while Tweedledee turned in his seat to address Donovan. He was all business.

"Now we can talk without being overheard. After we picked up Captain Thornton here—" he nodded toward Joe "—we established surveillance at the storage site. No one's shown up yet, but even a mouse couldn't slip through our team."

"It's not a mouse slipping through we need to worry about," Donovan said dryly. "It's the mouse spotting the cat."

"We've taken care of that," Tweedledee answered stiffly. "They're under strict orders to lay low and stay invisible. We're working with cameras from a distance as much as possible. In any case, they haven't made a move yet, we're sure of that. Not only are the goods still in place, but there's been no suspicious activity, fire or otherwise, in the Richland area. I must say that with as many alerts as we've seen issued in the last couple years, we're in the unenviable position of Peter crying wolf. Without some clear indication of what this threat consists of and where, we won't get a lot of buy-in from local law enforcement. However, it is our assessment that we've gotten a jump on these people. I think we can sit back, relax, and let them come to us."

Keith Donovan was nodding, but Sara didn't see similar agreement on the faces of her DEA companions. Ramon was looking openly disgusted.

"With all due respect, gentlemen, don't underestimate these guys," he said flatly. "How can you be so sure these guys didn't have that storage unit under their own surveillance and spot your boys poking through it? It would be inconvenient but not impossible to replace that gear if they had to. And just what kind of relaxation did you have in mind for us? Strolling through the streets on the off-chance we might spot Vargas or one of his pals buying lighter fluid and matches at the 7-Eleven?"

"We consider the likelihood minimal that our operation has been compromised," Tweedledum answered even more stiffly. "We were extremely cautious in approaching the storage site and we're satisfied there was no countersurveillance in place. That there has been no terrorist attack would seem to support our conclusions. However, we have considered the possibility that some of this group may already be moving into place. Captain Thornton here has made certain suggestions on how we might profit from your service."

At the mention of his name, Sara's cousin turned to look at the FBI SAC. "Well, I wish I could say I was as optimistic as your men here about having a jump on these guys. But one thing did slap me in the face going through that shipping manifest. Except for the blasting materials, which we would use for clearing a firebreak, everything on that list—hard hats, clothing, boots, gloves, goggles, smoke masks, walkie-talkies, canteens, axes, shovels,—is the kind of stuff a guy would be packing on a line crew. Or a group masquerading as a line crew. So I figure the most logical place to look for these guys would be in one of our base camps. There's no better place to hide an ethnically diverse group of young men. Whether they've already filtered in to a base, or plan to after they pick up their gear, it seems like looking around the camps would be a start."

Joe looked straight at Doug. "If you can look over the on-site personnel for anyone you've seen before, maybe these guys—" he jerked his thumb at the FBI agents "—can post some people to film anyone who comes in new after that. And if you do see someone you recognize—" he shrugged "—I guess you'll know better than I would where to go from there. Either way, it may be a long shot, but it sure beats sitting around waiting for these guys to walk up to that storage unit—or start a fire."

"Now you're talking," Ramon said. "How many camps are we looking at? And how do you propose getting us out there?"

"With the Saddle Mountain fires now, there's maybe half-a-dozen," Joe said. "I'm looking only at those within a reasonable radius of the Richland area. If they were farther away, they'd have ordered that equipment into Spokane or Seattle. As to getting out to the camps, I've already made arrangements for a chopper, one I've flown before, part of our Search and Rescue fleet. It's still early afternoon—"

Surprised, Sara glanced at her watch. Just past 2 P.M. Once again, she'd forgotten the time change.

"We can hit two or three of the camps before dark, then pick up again in the morning," Joe said. "Unless other circumstances develop by then, of course."

Chapter Eighty-two

JUNE 21

The helicopter Joe had commandeered was a bright-yellow Bell 407 Search and Rescue aircraft belonging to the Washington Department of Forestry and Fires. It was much like Julio Vargas's Huey, except that it had seats. As Joe hovered in for a landing, Sara saw flames rising from the Saddle Mountain ridge above the base camp. Overhead, air tankers and helicopters dangling water buckets traced a counter-clockwise pattern to dump water and red flame retardant on the fire.

The base camp itself, in what was usually a wide-open pasture, was hot and dusty and as busy as any self-respecting beehive. Sara now understood her cousin's dry remarks to those East Coast federal agents. The camp was larger than a good many towns, with the equivalent of an entire trailer court holding the offices of a dozen different coordinating agencies. Other tractor-trailer rigs contained a first aid station and various supply depots.

One end of the pasture mushroomed with sleeping tents. Nearby was a line of porta-potties and mobile showers. A water truck was in the process of filling large rubber bladders with potable water. Out on a recently bulldozed dirt road, a pair of deeply tanned young women in orange safety vests directed a cavalcade of trucks and heavy equipment.

"We've got more than a thousand firefighters deployed on this one," Joe told the group as he led them toward a Quonset hut allocated for their control center. "Maybe 150 overhead staff. Fifty-plus hand crews. We bring in everything from food and supplies to our own electricity, water, and phones. The night shift will be sleeping right now, but they'll be emerging for supper in another hour or so before moving out to relieve the day shift."

He paused as they entered the Quonset hut, then went on, "My thought was that you could look around here, check out the base personnel, until the night shift makes its appearance. Gives you a chance to look them over while they're eating. Then we'd fly out to the next base camp. That's about a half-hour air time. Do the same thing there while people are up and eating, then stay till the day shift arrives off the lines. Then back here where you can take a look at the incoming day shift before they turn in to the sack. It's a little more running and gas, but it'll let you check out pretty close to a hundred percent for both camps. Those badges the IC gave us will let you poke your nose any place you want."

The Incident Commander in charge of the Saddle Mountain operation was the only person in camp who knew why they were there. He'd also arranged for the proper attire—green pants and yellow T-shirts with Washington Department of Forestry and Fires lettered on front and back, along with the green caps worn in camp in place of hard hats, also marked WDFF. All of which had the effect of making the group immediately anonymous in the scurrying knots of yellow and green, especially once the supply unit leader handed out polarized sunglasses that were as much a relief from the sun, dust, and smoke as they were a disguise.

Doug considered Joe's suggestion and gave an approving nod. "That's first-rate thinking, Captain. Unless someone has a better idea, let's do it. We'll need to split up, though. We can cover more ground, and our present group is a little on the conspicuous side."

His ironic glance took in the two FBI escorts that with Keith Donovan brought the group up to nine people. "Sara and I are the only two with a good idea what we're looking for. Ramon, you take Sara with you. I'll take Captain Thornton with me. Kyle and Rocky, you know Vargas, and you've seen the surveillance photos of Saleh Jebai. You can at least be on the lookout for them and anything else that looks off in any way. Everyone's got walkie-talkies. If you've got something to communicate, clue in Donovan here first. If we do spot any of our targets, he'll be the one to call in support."

Doug looked straight over at the FBI SAC with a raised eyebrow. "Assuming that sounds good to you, of course. Or did you want to send any of your people with us? I figure two people walking around together is about all that's practical."

"No, it sounds like you've got things well under control," Keith Donovan replied. He glanced around the Quonset hut, which held only a lone dusty table and a trio of folding chairs. "You do your thing. I'll talk to the base commander about requisitioning a corner and a few extension cords to set up our communications gear and computer uplink. We'll assemble back here when Bradford and Captain Thornton decide it's time to head out."

If Sara suspected that Doug had assigned Ramon to her more as a protective measure than as an extra pair of eyes, she didn't mind. She was glad for his company. And if having her under the watchful eye of a trusted friend was one less distraction for Doug, that was what counted. She had no illusions about how much she, with her brief glimpses of Julio and Saleh's team, could contribute to this search. In the end, it would boil down to Doug, exhausted and injured as he was, and the catalog of faces he had branded painfully into his memory. Anything the rest of them could do to ease the weight of that burden would be a welcome contribution.

Sara studied every face she passed, drawing an angry glare from one young firefighter whose dark curls reminded her of Saleh's. As Joe had warned them, the fire crews were ethnically diverse, which didn't help. By the time she and Ramon had prowled their way through camp and stationed themselves near the sleeping tents to watch the night shift stagger out of their sleeping bags and head for the dining area, Sara had picked out at least a dozen faces that looked vaguely familiar.

But only vaguely.

"I wasn't around them long enough. That's the problem," Sara told Ramon despairingly. "Half these guys could be one of the men I saw in Paraguay."

Ramon discreetly aimed his digital camera at an olive-skinned man that Sara had pointed out. "Never mind. Just keep pointing out the likely ones and we'll see if Doug can ID any of these photos." He pocketed the camera to answer the radio at his belt. "Donovan's calling us in. Maybe Doug's had better luck than us."

But Donovan's terse report dispelled that hope. "Let's pull back to the command center and regroup."

The bleak weariness on Doug's face when Sara and Ramon entered the Quonset hut was further discouragement. He shook his head as one of the agents uploaded the digital images from Ramon's camera—and several that Kyle and Rocky had shot— onto a computer screen. "No, I don't recognize any of these guys. And I didn't spot anyone myself. They just aren't here—at least not now. Can we head over to the other camp now Joe?"

* * *

Vargas and Saleh and their team weren't at the other camp either, the searchers had to concede, by the time the last outlying hand crew had checked in for the night. Back in the first camp, only a skeleton night crew was still on duty when Doug finally called a halt.

"I can't even see straight anymore," he said wearily, rubbing at his eyes before peering at the latest batch of digital photos they'd brought back from the second camp. "Any longer, and I'll be blipping over something important. We'll just have to pick up in the morning and pray the bad guys take the night off as well."

The sleeping quarters they'd been assigned were not in the tent city where most of the crews were bedded down, but in one of the coveted sleeping trailers. Bunk beds, stacked three high, lined both sides of the fifty-foot length, and air-conditioning and soundproofing allowing shifts to sleep in comfort around the clock. Set into each bunk was an individually controlled air vent and reading light.

Like her companions, Sara did no more than peel off her boots and cap before crawling under the blanket and adjusting the air vent to blow onto her hot face. Doug, predictably, was still out taking care of details with Keith Donovan. Across the trailer, Joe had turned on his reading light and was talking in a low voice into his cell phone. In the busyness of the past hours, Sara had almost forgotten about little Joshua gasping for breath under an oxygen mask. Her cousin snapped the cell phone shut, and she saw his head bow and knew he was praying.

Sara closed her own eyes. *Oh, God, watch over Josh and Denise, and please get them out of there to safety.*

Then she stopped. There were other small boys and girls out there, besides the one she loved, and even if she didn't know them, they were no less precious to someone.

In the next set of bunks, Sara caught Kyle's low comment to Rocky. "This is like looking for a needle in a haystack. You really think we're doing any good here?"

"It's going to take a miracle," Rocky responded somberly. "We'll just have to hope someone out there's having better luck than we are."

A miracle.

God, are you listening?

Chapter Eighty-three

Darkness took longer to fall than Saleh had expected. Though he'd read about the phenomenon of northern summer twilight, there still seemed something unnatural about being able to see clearly at an hour when many people would be in bed or at least indoors. Instead, even children were outside riding bikes and kicking soccer balls until long after Saleh had planned to move. On the river, dozens of people were still indulging in water sports or casting fishing lines.

It was well after midnight before the Ford Explorer left the campground and turned onto Highway 240, headed north toward the Hanford reserve. With no need for Julio Vargas's piloting skills, Saleh had gladly left him behind to sleep. Instead, the passenger seat was occupied by the American-raised Yemeni who had been Saleh's copilot on the flight north. Stretched out on the seat behind them was the third participant in this phase of the mission.

The moon rising over the nuclear reserve was only a sliver of a crescent, and once the last lights of the metropolitan faded in the rearview mirror, the only illumination beyond the cold glitter of the night sky was a distant yellow gleam marking the 200 Area far off to Saleh's right. To the left, the ecological preserve stretched black and endless, giving an illusion of flatness against the night. Saleh slowed to watch for the landmarks he had chosen.

Starting a fire would not be difficult. The wind had slacked with the fall of night, but occasional gusts were strong enough to buffet the SUV, and even as little as a cigarette butt tossed out the window had a even chance of igniting the tinder-dry grass.

Increasing the odds of a surefire blaze while maintaining the appearance of an accident was somewhat more complex. The Americans were the best in the world at tracing the cause of a fire, and for the success of the mission, it was essential that no suspicion of arson be raised, at least until they had finished what they had come to do. Even longer, if possible. To date, the news coverage of Team One and Two's missions had dismissed those catastrophes as accidental. If Saleh's team could pull off the same feat here, there might still be opportunity for a fourth mission. Even a fifth and sixth. Possibly even to repeat this same scenario. There were other nuclear waste sites vulnerable to wildfire.

The Internet news reports had given Saleh the blueprint for what came next. The last near-disaster had occurred when an automobile crashed into a semi-trailer at a highway junction not far from here. The ensuing sparks had been whipped into a wildfire that had consumed more than 192,000 acres in less than three days. In the end, only a change in wind direction that blew the fire back on itself had stopped the inferno.

This time, it wouldn't matter which way the wind blew.

The yellow glow of the 200 Area floodlights, now falling behind the SUV, alerted Saleh that their destination was now close ahead. Saleh reached for his cell phone and punched in a number. The Ford Explorer had advanced another hundred meters down the highway before he got a response.

"Is it done?" he demanded.

"It is done," came the flat answer. "All has gone as planned. We are just leaving now."

Saleh envisioned the other half of the operation—two force members paddling a canoe up the Columbia River along the uninhabited stretch of the Hanford Reach. If anyone was out on the water at this hour to see them glide past, they would appear to be sport fishermen making their way upriver after a long summer day. And if they were seen resting on the bank, that too was unlikely to arouse suspicion.

The onshore location had been carefully chosen. Beer cans. Cigarette butts. And broken shards of glass from a bottle of vodka dropped against a stone. Clear, thick glass, capable of focusing the burning temperatures of the day on the tinder-dry grass beneath.

No arson investigator would question that a spark smoldering during the day had finally burst into flames. The single match had been carefully retrieved and the two force members were now drifting downstream to the opposite shore to meet the pick-up team, who were waiting in a rented van with a roof rack for tying the canoe on top.

Now that the river team had completed its mission, it was Saleh's turn to set the stage. The highway was empty at this hour, except for the SUV. Slowing the vehicle, Saleh consulted a handheld GPS unit and made a right turn onto a rough, rutted dirt track. The Explorer jounced another hundred meters before the track made a sharp bend leading to the edge of a ravine. Pulling up, Saleh glanced over at the passenger seat. There was no need for conversation as both men climbed out, leaving the engine running. Walking around to the rear of the vehicle, Saleh opened the back hatch. Together the two men maneuvered a Honda dirt bike down to the ground and over to the edge of the track. The two men returned to the SUV and dragged the third passenger out of the back seat. He was a slightly built man, underfed, dirty—and unconscious.

Saleh and the Yemeni hoisted the limp form into the driver's seat of the SUV. The man was an infidel and a parasite, one of many worthless drifters who roamed the streets of American cities, preferring to beg or steal the money needed for drugs or alcohol than work. It had been an easy matter for the advance team to pick the man up and lure him out to the camp with a promise of a meal and a bottle of vodka. A dose of sedatives in his last drink had ensured he would remain unconscious until his part in the plan was done. As a bonus, the man's driver's license had been used to rent the SUV.

Saleh's nostrils flared at the stench of liquor as he leaned in to fasten the shoulder strap across the drifter's chest and wedge the man's foot onto the gas pedal. When everything was set, he climbed down, moved to a position about ten meters in front of the vehicle, and gave his partner the go-ahead signal. The Yemeni stepped onto the running board of the SUV and stretched his leg into the car to press down on the brake. Shifting the car into gear, he eased off the brake pedal and jumped clear of the vehicle as it started to roll. Saleh held his breath as the vehicle picked up speed. Had they allowed enough distance to achieve the necessary velocity? As the SUV passed him, he reached out and slammed the driver's door shut.

The front wheels struck the bank where the track made its sharp turn and lumbered up onto the grass. The impact slowed the SUV visibly, but the remaining distance was now less than two meters. The vehicle wobbled briefly at the edge, then tipped forward into the ravine. The two men were racing for the edge of the cliff even before a crunch of metal signaled impact.

The one question mark in Saleh's planning had been whether the force of the crash would be enough to ignite a fire. If not, his companion would have to climb down and do the job, risking the possibility of a belated explosion that could jeopardize his life. Martyrdom came in all forms.

A glance below proved that such a venture would not be necessary. Already, flames licked at the steep slope of the ravine, catching at the dry grass and sagebrush. The two men sprinted toward the dirt bike.

Grabbing the handlebars, the Yemeni climbed aboard and kick-started the engine while Saleh swung himself onto the back. Bumping over the rough prairie, the dirt bike jolted back onto the blacktop and roared down the high-way toward the Columbia River Gorge. The Yemeni did not slow down until they were across the bridge. From the back of the bike, Saleh consulted the GPS unit and signaled his companion to pull over. Minutes later, a van with a canoe tied on top pulled up beside them. As the side door slid open, two pairs of hands reached out to help lift the dirt bike inside.

The van had just pulled back onto the highway when a pair of headlights pierced the darkness up ahead. Clambering around the dirt bike to peer out the windows in the back door panels, Saleh saw a pickup speed by them. It had reached the bridge when it pulled abruptly over to the shoulder. Saleh spotted the first red-yellow glow of fire against the night as the driver of the pickup, silhouetted in the distance, scrambled out onto the roadway. The alarm was about to be sounded.

Saleh put out a hand to keep his balance as a gust of wind shook the van. With that kind of wind, the fires would take hold long before the fire depart-ment could begin mobilizing its resources. And with a blaze racing across both ends of the reserve, it would not matter which way the wind turned.

Would the American firefighters have enough time to stop the conflagra-tion before it reached the hazardous sites on the Hanford reserve?

That, too, no longer mattered.

Chapter Eighty-four

If there was ever a night when Sara might have expected to be troubled with nightmares, it was this one. Instead, she slept dreamlessly and with such exhaustion that it seemed she had only just shut her eyes when a firm hand on her shoulder shook her awake. Reaching up to flick on the reading light, she blinked bleary eyes to focus on the freckled features of FBI SAC Keith Donovan.

"Sorry to wake you this early, Ms. Connor," he said quietly, "but Captain Thornton says we need to be in the air shortly if we're to reach our next target in time for the morning changeover of shifts."

Stifling a yawn, Sara fumbled on the floor for her boots and cap. Kyle, Ramon, and Rocky were already sliding noiselessly out of their own bunks, so as not to wake the sleeping firefighters around them. Doug and Joe were nowhere to be seen.

As Sara stepped outside and eased the door of the trailer shut behind her, something in Keith Donovan's expression caught her attention in the dim predawn light. Hurrying over to his side, she caught his arm and demanded tensely, "Something's happened, hasn't it?"

"Yes, but I'd just as soon not discuss it here in public." He looked around at the rows of tents and blank, dark trailers. "Let's get inside."

He led the way briskly to the Quonset hut command center. It was barely 4:30 A.M. by Sara's watch—no wonder it felt as if she'd just crawled into bed when they woke her up—but Tweedledum and Tweedledee already had the computer equipment booted up. Donovan swung around to address Sara just as Ramon, Rocky, and Kyle entered on her heels. "As you were asking, Ms. Connor, there's been an incident. No, not a terrorist attack. But a fire did break out during the night—" he paused, giving his next words added punch "—on the Hanford reserve."

"Then it *is* a terrorist attack," Ramon said sharply. "Isn't this what we've been waiting for? But—what about your watch on that warehouse? I thought you said not even a mouse could get by your men. Are you telling me that after all our running around, they did it right under our noses?"

"The storage unit has not been approached," Donovan replied curtly. "I assure you, not a fly could get near without setting off our alarms. As for this fire—oh, there you are, Captain Thornton."

Sara spun around as Joe entered the Quonset hut, followed by Doug. Both men had clearly been awake for a while.

"What did you find out?" Donovan inquired.

Joe glanced down at a notepad. "Here's the latest. The fire started some time within the last six hours. More likely after midnight than before. We were fortunate it was spotted early on by a swing-shift security guard driving home. But with these dry conditions and a wind that's upwards of thirty miles an hour right now up on the reserve, the blaze is already out of control. Because of the sensitive nature of its location, the speed of spread, and the alert that you people were responsible for putting out, it's already been upgraded to a Type 1 incident. But it will take time to move resources into place. The bad news is there's two ignition points, but so far the fire line is nowhere near any restricted zones. In fact—" Joe's brow wrinkled as he looked back at his notes "—there's nothing in the initial reports to arouse any speculation of arson. Having two fire heads will complicate the situation, but with 580 square miles of territory in question here, there's no reason to believe having two fires break out at once is more than an unfortunate coincidence. Especially since the environmentalist watchdogs have been warning Hanford for years of the dangers of another fire on the reserve."

Joe tapped a sketch he'd drawn on the notepad. "The principal flashpoint seems to have been a car crash, some drunk driver taking a wrong turn in the dark and running his vehicle over an embankment. The exhaustion of fuel in the immediate vicinity has allowed investigators to confirm that the driver was still in the vehicle at the time of impact. The other fire seems to have originated from boaters picnicking up on the riverbank. They found broken glass and cigarette butts at the fire head."

Joe looked around at the group of agents. "Any chance this is coincidence and we've been barking up the wrong tree the whole time?"

Doug and Ramon looked at each other.

"It fits their MO," Ramon said. "Just like the dam and the avalanche. Make it look like an accident so the authorities concentrate on the clean-up, not the perps."

"Leaving them free to move on to their next mission without having to look over their shoulder," Doug said.

"Yeah, and I'll bet whoever was behind the wheel of that vehicle didn't volunteer for duty," Rocky added.

"No, this was our Team Three, all right," Doug said definitely. "Though if they did their job right, your investigators may never prove it, and you have only our word."

"Yes, your word," Tweedledum said flatly. He turned to address Donovan. "Sir, is it possible we're staking out an empty mouse hole?"

"Are you insinuating we invented all this?" Ramon began heatedly, but Keith Donovan raised a pacifying hand and gestured toward Doug. "I saw footage of the jungle pit this man came out of. What they did to him there was real, believe me. So if he says we've got a threat here, I believe it."

Tweedledee spoke up. "Maybe they never came back to the storage unit because they ended up getting what they needed out of one of these camps and decided to ditch the rest."

"Maybes don't help," Donovan said. "Only what we know to be fact. And the fact is we've got a Type 1 wildfire sweeping across a nuclear reserve." He glanced over at Sara's cousin. "How high would you assess the threat level, Captain Thornton?"

Joe had slept less than any of them—except maybe Doug. But his expression was more relaxed than the night before and he sloped Sara a half-smile as he answered, "Well, we're going to lose a lot of terrain, of course—probably most of the ecological preserve. With this kind of fast-burning vegetation and the winds, we'll have to drop our fire lines as far back as possible to protect our people. But the truth is, I feel pretty good about this one. We caught 'em both in time. Sure, we're going to lose a lot of sagebrush and prairie grass, but there's no homes or businesses out there, and that fire isn't going to reach anywhere near the waste sites. Those are our first priority, and we'll have the lines dug long before the fire head can reach them."

Joe looked directly at Doug. "I'm just a firefighter, not a federal agent. But as far as I can see, we beat them on this one. Your terrorists might have got away with murder on that dam and avalanche. But they won't on this one. We mobilized in time. It's over."

He studied Doug's face and looked suddenly less certain. "Right, Bradford?"

"I hope so," Doug answered slowly. "But this won't be over until we catch these guys. I know them too well to sit back and relax. They're good, and they're deadly. And if we really have managed to thwart this one op, they'll just move elsewhere and strike again. And next time we won't have any advance warning."

"Great motivational speech," Ramon said sourly. "But how do we find them now? They're probably long gone to earth. I agree with the feds—they've most likely decided to junk the stuff in that locker. They may have even moved out of the area by now."

"Not in my book . . . not this fast . . . not without waiting to get a look at their handiwork." Doug dropped into a chair and Sara looked at him worriedly. However much he chose to ignore his injuries, they had to be hurting. Was he pushing himself beyond his capacity?

Not that he would ever admit it. His voice was strong and definite as he answered Ramon. "Either way, it looks to me like we're down to two choices. We can throw in the towel, pat ourselves on the back that this incident isn't going to be a deadly as the others, file those photos of Vargas and Saleh and those few recruits we caught on film and hope that someone somewhere down the line—maybe after another attack—gets the chance to cross-reference them."

"Not a very attractive choice," Ramon interjected wryly. "*Or*—?"

"Or—" Doug ran a weary hand over his face before he went on "—much as I'd like to crawl back into that sleeping trailer, we can push on exactly as we'd planned for this morning. If they're still in the area, there's still no better place for them to fade back into the woodwork than at one of these base camps. And let's not rule out that they may have a backup plan if they see the first one has misfired." No one smiled at the pun. "It's just—I know these guys, and I still have a bad feeling. I can't just sit back and do nothing. Okay, so maybe the odds are poor, and at the end of the day we may still have nothing. But if we drop out now, that's definitely what we'll have."

Joe nodded a slow agreement. "Hope for the best, but prepare for the worst— that's what my mother used to say. Doug's right—we can't get complacent here. I hope and pray we've dodged the worst. But I'd rather be wrong than sorry, and as long as Bradford here is willing to keep searching, I'm willing to play chauffeur."

"That settles it, then." Keith Donovan gestured to his two subordinates, who immediately began disassembling their communications gear. "We keep to the game plan until we're out of options—or something breaks open."

* * *

Sara caught up to her cousin as he and Doug headed for the helipad at the far end of camp. "Joe, I've been wanting to ask you. How's Josh doing—and Denise?"

Joe's sloping smile lit up his tired face as he slowed his pace and glanced down at Sara. "Much better. They've taken him off the oxygen. They'd send him home today if it wasn't for the smoke levels."

He stopped abruptly to catch Sara's arm, and his smile vanished. "Sara, your friend Bradford, I can tell he thinks there's still a threat to Richland, even if we stop this fire. Do you think he's right?"

Sara shook her head. "He doesn't know for sure. But I'll tell you this. I've learned to trust his instincts."

Joe released her arm. "Then let's get this bird in the air."

They had no better results at the next three camps. By well past the lunch hour, when Doug finally called a halt to the search, the faces were beginning to blur to the point that if Julio Vargas himself had walked by, Sara wasn't sure she'd notice him. When she and Ramon joined the others in the Quonset hut, they were happy to see that someone had delivered a box of brown bag lunches.

Doug was already seated at a computer, munching on a sandwich and poring over the latest surveillance images forwarded from their earlier inspection sites.

He looked up as Sara and Ramon sat down next to him with their lunches. "I don't see anything in these. And this camp was the last one on our list. That leaves us at a stalemate until evening when we can go back and take a look at the incoming shifts. I'd say we've got a few hours for siesta. Unless one of you guys has another bright idea."

"Actually—" Joe Thornton walked across the room, unwrapping a cookie "—that wasn't the last camp. Not anymore. The base camp for the Hanford fire is now up and running. I just got off the radio with the Incident Commander and got clearance to head over there. But if you're tired—"

"Hanford camp," Doug repeated slowly. He straightened up so suddenly that every eye in the room was immediately on him. "Of course! That's it!"

He glanced impatiently at the baffled faces staring at him. "What do you get when you start a big enough fire? A base camp. We've been looking at this the wrong way around. They weren't trying to sneak into a base camp as an FOB to start this fire. They started the fire so they could sneak into a base camp. The *Hanford* base camp in particular. Looking at it that way, it makes perfect sense why they haven't picked up their gear yet. They didn't need it. Not until your people—" he nodded at Joe "—started setting up their camp."

Keith Donovan's cell phone shrilled, interrupting Doug. The trailer fell into silence as the SAC listened. "What do you mean, you lost them? . . . No, I'm not interested in excuses . . . just get the surveillance photos uploaded to our com-link here immediately."

The FBI agent slapped the cell phone shut and cursed. Looking over at Doug, he shook his head. "I don't know how you do it, Bradford. That was our surveillance team. Four subjects, all male, just moved in with a pickup and cleaned out the storage unit."

"And they got away." Doug's flat response was a statement, not a question.

Tweedledee spoke up defensively. "Our units had first priority on making sure that the surveillance would not be detected. We had to keep our pursuit vehicles out on the perimeter."

"The surveillance was within acceptable parameters," Donovan interjected. "I approved the layout myself." He looked apologetically at Doug. "You said these guys were good, and they were—peeled out of there like bats out of a cave. Whether they suspected a tail or were just taking precautions, they did everything right, even changed vehicles. We've already located the pickup, which they abandoned in a mall parking lot. It was a rental. We did get surveillance photos though."

Moments later, the images began scrolling onto the computer screen. Sara gasped as a photo of two men lifting a crate into the back of the pickup sharp-ened into focus.

"I recognize those two. They were unloading the white pickup in Paraguay."

"They were among the last group to leave the camp," Doug affirmed. "Team Three. And so were those two," he added as the image shifted to two other young men emerging from the storage unit with another load.

He watched until the last of a dozen images finished flipping through. "I don't see either Vargas or Saleh in there. But then I can't see them acting as errand boys, either. But I'd bet my badge that your units will pick up the lost trail out there at that Hanford base camp."

"But why? It doesn't make sense," Kyle said. "So they start a fire to get a base camp going nearby and then ship all their gear out here to get onto the base as firefighters. Then what? Blow up a fuel tanker? Sabotage the entire air fleet? What possible damage could they do in camp compared to the fire itself? Es-pecially if that alarm hadn't come in as early as it did."

"I can't even begin to guess," Doug said grimly. "But if we don't find them soon, my gut tells me we're gonna have front row seats."

Chapter Eighty-five

As Joe Thornton dropped the Bell 407 down for a landing, Sara could see that the Hanford base camp—more like a mini-city—was still under construction. Tractor rigs were pulling lines of trailers into place to form streets. The porta-potties were already situated, but the sleeping area was still a heap of rolled-up tents. From the air, the camp appeared to be situated on some sort of vacation ranch with a large central lodge. Beyond a surrounding cluster of buildings and corrals, Sara noticed what appeared to be playing fields and the aquamarine glimmer of a swimming pool. From her vantage point, Sara could see a van pulling into a multi-vehicle garage next to the main lodge. Beyond the lodge was a huge canvas pavilion, much like ones Sara had seen erected at the other base camps.

A steady stream of supply trucks and other vehicles moved up the gravel drive from the entrance, but instead of following the road to where it ended at the ranch buildings, they were turning off onto the dusty open grazing land that had been appropriated for the base camp.

"A local boys ranch volunteered their facilities to the fire department," Joe enlightened his passengers as he set the helicopter down in an open field. "A real community service, because there's not a lot of open space big enough to house a base this size. Except on the reserve, of course."

"That perimeter fence is a plus." Doug was the first to unfasten his seat belt. "Means that anyone coming in or out of the property will have to have come through that gate."

Rocky pulled open the side panel a bit too soon, and dust stirred up by the rotors billowed into the cabin as the group began climbing out. Doug tipped his cap down over his face as he stepped down from the helicopter, an automatic gesture designed as much to hide his face as to shield it from the sun. Narrowing his eyes against the swirling dust cloud, he focused on the line of vehicles bumping slowly across the grazing land. "I'll take the gate. Ramon, can you track down security—make sure they know just what we're after here? The rest of you know what to do. Everyone got photos?"

Sara glanced down at the color composite photo the FBI agents had run off for each member of the group. The four faces were clear enough that Sara was sure she'd recognize them even in a crowd. At least now there would be more eyes searching for them than just her and Doug.

"We'll need to get a few more run off for any local security." Keith Donovan moved up beside Doug and scanned the distant perimeter. "My guys and I will head over to base command and get our gear set up. I'd like to make sure our rapid response team is ready and close enough to make a move when we find these guys. The last thing we need is a shooting situation with this many civilians."

"*If* we find them," murmured Tweedledee or Tweedledum.

Doug spun around on his heel. "We'll find them. Count on it!"

But the FBI agents were already striding away. Joe Thornton cleared his throat. "Doug, if you'll excuse me. I need to talk to the helispot manager. I'd like to fuel up before we use this bird again."

"Of course," Doug nodded. "I'll catch up to you later."

"We're heading out too, then," said Rocky. "Time to start showing pictures around." With a thumbs-up, he headed after the FBI agents with Kyle at his heels.

Moving reluctantly out of the shade of the helicopter, Sara tried to muster up the enthusiasm for another search. But in the long hours of tramping around, thrusting photos under noses, and searching faces, the original urgency that had driven her had dissipated, and all that was left was exhaustion. As she moved out into the sunlight, the heat hit like the blast of an oven, and the air was acrid with smoke. A light ash sifting through the dust formed tiny snowflake patterns on her clothing and sunburned flesh.

She wiped a hand across the sweat that trickled down her face, looked at the grime on her fingers, and gave up. It would just add to the camouflage.

She looked at Doug. Though he had given direction to others, he had not yet moved himself. Instead, he was pivoting slowly, making the same careful scan of the area that he always used to evaluate new surroundings. Under the tilted cap, his gaunt features were preoccupied, the gray eyes distant. Sara knew that his mind was sifting through his next moves as his narrowed gaze catalogued every detail around him. Unlike Sara, he looked as tense as a runner in the starting blocks.

"Uh, Doug?" Ramon tapped his friend on the shoulder as the others disappeared into the chaos of the camp. "Why don't you let Sara and me do the stakeout down there at the gate? Don't forget—if you know their faces, they know yours too; they had long enough to memorize it. If they happen to come through while you're parading down there—"

"What's that?" Doug's gaze shifted from the horizon to look at Ramon and Sara, but it was no less remote. Sara was quite sure she had not crossed his mind in hours, except as a useful pair of eyes. Not long ago, that would have bothered her, but now she felt only a slight pang as she studied his frowning, abstracted features.

Oh, God, will this ever end? Will we ever get to just—live?

Finally, Doug nodded. "You're right, Ramon. The two of you would be a lot less noticeable. See if the traffic controllers remember seeing any of these guys pass through. If not, stay down there and stake out the gate until they do. Just be careful, Ramon. The rest of that crowd may not know your ugly mug, but Vargas does, and unlike Sara here, you haven't changed any since you helped throw him into Palmasola."

A ghost of a smile banished Doug's preoccupied expression as he reached to pluck away a dyed strand of hair that had plastered itself to the dampness of Sara's cheek. At the same time, his eyes focused on Sara—the sweat-streaked face, the dark shadows under her eyes, the uncertainty with which she met his intent gaze. Doug's smile softened to rueful tenderness as he shook his head.

"What has this guy been doing to you, Sara? You look all done in. Don't let Ramon push you around—he's got a rep as a slave-driver. If you need a break, feel free to take one."

Then he was off, his long strides just short of a jog. Sara watched him dodge into a traffic snarl of tanker trucks bringing fuel in for the aircraft until a helicopter settling in for a landing stirred up a cloud of dust that hid him from view.

"You coming, Sara?" Ramon demanded. He turned a sharp eye on Sara as she swung around. "Doug's right—you do look all done in. This doesn't have to be more than a one-person job if you'd like to head in to camp for a rest."

Sara shook her head. "No way! I've seen these other guys, and you haven't."

But she suppressed a sigh as she began trudging after Ramon toward the gravel drive. It was going to be a long walk to that distant gate.

The blare of a horn cut into her tired thoughts. A tractor rig that had shed its trailer was pulling up beside them, the driver leaning out of the cab. "Looking for a ride?"

The cab was air-conditioned, and Sara gratefully accepted a box of Handiwipes to clean the ash and dust from her face and arms. It would be her last moment of comfort for the afternoon. There was no shade out by the gate, and she had no idea how the traffic controllers could stand it for an entire shift. Between the dust clouds stirred up by the traffic and drifting ash from the fire, she was soon as dirt-streaked as ever. One of the orange-vested traffic controllers was not at all pleased by the interruption, but when Ramon finally pulled out his DEA badge, she stopped her hectic activity long enough to look at the photos.

"Undercover, eh?" she sniffed, eyeing Ramon's firefighter clothing with disapproval. Yes, she was sure she'd seen any number of the men in the photos. But as to when and where and which ones, she was less certain. Vargas, she was positive, had been among a pickup-load of Mexicans who had been among the first arrivals to man the fire lines. Two others she was equally sure were with a batch of prison conscripts bused in by the Department of Corrections to do heavy labor.

The other two other traffic controllers had only come on shift within the last hour. But they, too, were sure the men in the photos looked familiar. *The problem is*, Sara thought despairingly, *with this large a movement of people, everyone looks like someone*. Finally, Ramon yanked his radio from his belt with disgust.

"They may have come through, and they may not have," he told Keith Donovan tersely. "These people don't know nothin'!"

"We'll proceed accordingly," Donovan replied laconically. "I'll pass this on to Bradford. Just stay in position until you're relieved. If we spot them up our way, we'll send someone down to pull you out."

Not a vehicle passed through the gate in the next few hours that didn't earn sharp scrutiny from Ramon and Sara. Ramon had managed to come up with a pair of orange vests that at least allowed them to blend in, and at one point one of the controllers walked over to offer them bottles of cold water.

By now, Sara was convinced they would not see anyone who matched the crumpled digital images in her hand. Silence from the command center indicated that the other teams weren't having any better luck. Rocky showed up just as the blood-red circle of the sun dropped out of sight, marking the beginning of the long summer twilight.

"Not a peep of 'em all day. Doug's still holding out for the incoming shift." Rocky nodded toward a late-arriving pickup filled with soot-covered firefighters. "But that's only last-ditch hoping. If we haven't seen them by now, I doubt we will. But I'll hang around here for a while," he said, gloomily accepting the orange vest Ramon was peeling off. "They've started the supper shift. You two go on up and grab some chow before it's all gone."

"Thanks, we'll do that. Sara here at least has earned a break." Ramon's black eyes were approving as he flicked Sara lightly on the nose. "I can't tell if that's sunburn or heatstroke that's responsible for the Rudolph look, but I've seen strong men keel over with what you've put up with today."

The command center of the camp was in a large army tent, and with the fire still less than twenty-four hours old, a scene of quiet chaos reigned with whiteboards propped against walls, aerial maps spread on folding tables, and incident management team personnel rushing in and out and congregating in huddles for consultation. Somehow, the FBI agents had managed to appropriate an entire trailer next door for their own operation. As Rocky had promised, it was air-conditioned. But the cool flow of air was not the only chill in the atmosphere.

". . . not a sign," Keith Donovan was saying as Sara and Ramon walked in. "I can't keep this many assets on standby indefinitely."

Doug's face was closed and grim, and only a flicker of his eyes acknowledged Sara and Ramon's entrance. "They're here, I know it." He shoved a food container away with enough force that it went skittering off the end of the table. "Somehow we've overlooked them. They didn't come as far as they have just to leave it at this. There was a reason they went by that storage unit this morning, and every gut feeling I've got tells me it has to do with this place."

"We've done everything we can," Keith Donovan said reasonably. "We've fine-tooth-combed the whole camp, shown these photos to everyone we could get to look. We passed out copies to local law enforcement doing crowd control. They've had their eyes peeled. And nothing! Of course, we could still plaster flyers to every building or try a lineup of the entire camp."

"That's out of the question," Joe said flatly from across the table. "The fire is burning hotter and faster than we projected. We're barely holding the line out there, and the next few hours are going to make or break us. You disrupt the smooth operation of this camp or pull personnel off duty, and you might as well wave good-bye to that fire while it sweeps across every waste dump in that reserve."

"Don't worry, he wasn't serious," Doug said wearily. "We'd do just as well announcing over the PA system that we're on to them. Which would lead to just the kind of suicidal standoff we're trying to avoid."

"Then we may just have to accept that for here and now, at least, we've done all we can," Donovan concluded. "Those photos are popping up in every law enforcement database in the country, and at least now we have four members of this last team as well as the leaders and your original photos." The look the FBI chief turned on Doug was both understanding and sympathetic. "We'll get 'em, Bradford, however long it takes."

"Not before more people die." Doug's fists clenched on the table. "If not here today, then somewhere else. What are we missing? If only every government agency in the area wasn't tied up with this fire, maybe we could get enough personnel on this to come up with some answers."

His clenched fists went flat on the table. "Or is that it?" he said slowly. "Why today? Why here? This whole thing—the fire, the camp, the whole town set upside-down—what if it's not an end in itself? What if it's a diversion? A misdirection to allow them to do something they couldn't get away with under normal conditions. But what?"

"Maybe they're trying to get into one of the Hanford buildings, a nuclear reactor or something," Kyle suggested, "using their firefighter gear to bluff their way past security in all the confusion."

"Wouldn't work," Joe shook his head. "I know. I was part of the fire readiness inspection team out there. The buildings are battened down tight with this fire. Confusion or not, there are any number of check-points, X-ray machines, body and bag searches. Even if they could bluff their way through security as firefighters, they couldn't smuggle anything in with them—that I can assure you."

"Well, there's got to be something," Rocky said. "What about this place we're sitting on? You said the camp owners here volunteered the land. What do you know about them? When did they volunteer?"

"That at least we can find out." Kyle's fingers were already flying over the keyboard of a laptop. Doug reached for a stack of folders, his frustrated expression giving way to intense concentration as he began to flip through them.

Keith Donovan waved a hand at Sara and Ramon, hooking a thumb toward two food containers. "You two better grab a bite while you've got the chance. Looks like we're going to be here a while."

Ramon grabbed a meal container and a stack of data files. But though Sara had not eaten since lunch, food was not the most urgent need on her mind at the moment. There had been no restroom facilities down at the gate, and she was only now realizing how many hours she had spent down there.

"Uh . . . I think I'll wash my hands first," she said. "If you'll excuse me."

Kyle raised his head from the keyboard. "There's a sink setup over there," he announced, gesturing to the trailer's tiny kitchen area.

Sara escaped before she had to answer. The row of porta-potties formed the outside perimeter line of the camp, which suddenly seemed a lot farther away than it had before. She picked her way through the bubble-shaped sleeping tents, now ready for occupants, their hodgepodge of colors and patterns swaying in the stiff wind like a field of moored hot-air balloons. Her steps quickened as she approached one of the green plastic boxes. But her urgency evaporated as soon as she opened the door. The portable toilets had been in use for a long day, and though surely some kind of disposal unit would soon be dealing with them, their present condition—

I can't use that! I just can't!

Her eyes were burning with more than smoke and ash as she tried one door after another. *What I wouldn't give for a real bathroom about now.*

Backing away, she glanced through the line of porta-potties to the dusty field behind them, this one bordered by a corral-style fence and packed-earth track that looked like a training area for horses. Beyond the track was the collection of ranch buildings and corrals she'd seen from the air. A boys ranch, Joe had said. *Which means sleeping quarters. And restrooms. Real ones.*

The walk took longer than Sara had calculated, and by the time she had passed the riding field and a series of empty corrals, and reached the first outbuilding of the ranch, she was regretting her decision.

Idiot! Why do you think they put the base camp so far away? So a few thousand firefighters wouldn't be tramping through their buildings. What were you thinking? No real firefighter would have thought of coming over here.

Still, the long trudge back was a daunting proposition. Now that she was here, she might as well do what she'd come for.

The first outbuilding beyond the corrals was a large barn. From the soft whinnies and whuffling snorts Sara caught as she passed the open doors, the ranch's livestock had taken refuge from the smoke and ash indoors.

Several long, low buildings with rows of doors leading onto a paved area looked like typical camp bunkhouses. A much larger building with a wide veranda and tall glass windows looked to be a dining hall or meeting area. Just beyond was the two-story lodge and an assortment of sheds and smaller barns.

But Sara had no interest in them. She had just spied a smaller, square, concrete edifice between two bunkhouses. No matter that the familiar symbols on the doors were only male cutouts. This was, after all, a boys camp. So far, Sara had not seen a single living soul. Surely, under the circumstances, no one would mind a girl using the boys' restroom.

She quickened her pace toward the nearest door, only to find it was locked. If her situation had not been so dire, she might have laughed. But at the moment there was nothing funny about her situation.

"Miss?"

Sara whirled around, her hand flying to her throat with surprise. A man was walking toward her around the side of one of the sheds, a wide-brimmed hat shielding his face and a mechanic's toolbox in one hand. Red flamed right through Sara's sunburn as she dropped her other hand from the restroom door. She hadn't felt this mortified since she'd accidentally walked into the boys' locker room her first week of middle school in Seattle. She stammered the only explanation her rattled brain could produce on such short notice.

"I'm looking for a restroom. Is there a ladies' room around here somewhere?"

The man's uncomprehending stare might have meant he didn't buy her story or that he didn't understand her at all. The sombrero shadowed his face so that all she could make out was a deep tan—or naturally dark complexion. But he was too old to be one of the men she was looking for. What hair she could see was iron gray.

"A bathroom?" Sara repeated, knocking hopefully on the door. Maybe he'd at least unlock the restroom. "I'm really sorry for the bother, but it's a bit of an emergency."

The man had to understand her pantomime. But with an angry shake of his head, he gestured toward the distant base camp. It immediately became apparent that he had no intention of unlocking the door, nor was he going to walk away and let her make her attempt at lock-picking. The firmly planted spread of his boots between Sara and the rest of the ranch buildings was as definite a boundary line as a wall. Stepping reluctantly away from the restroom door, Sara began the long trudge back toward the base camp.

But she had barely rounded the corner of the bunkhouse out of the ranch worker's sight when rebellion boiled up inside her.

Okay, so I shouldn't have intruded here. But would it have hurt to let me use the restroom before booting me out? What ever happened to common courtesy?

She looked across the corrals at the long distance that separated her from the green line of teeming porta-potties. Plain and simple, there was no way she was going to make it back there.

Which made her decision a no-brainer. However ill-mannered and intrusive it might be, she was going to find the nearest restroom. This now constituted a real emergency.

After all, what's the worst they can do? Throw me out on my ear? Arrest me for being in the wrong place? I'd settle for either if I can use their bathroom first.

The determined lift of her chin didn't keep Sara from feeling vaguely criminal as she slipped from under the bunkhouse eaves and cut over to the back of the locked restroom. Around the corner she could see a straight shot across a grassy lawn and gravel driveway to the wide, one-story veranda that edged the front of the lodge.

She took a swift look around. The ranch worker had drifted away, and there was no one else in sight. The dashes had never been her sport in school, but ten seconds later, she was under cover of the veranda roof and knocking urgently at the front door.

If I can get inside before that guy comes back—

Her hand was raised for a third knock when the door swung open with a soft creak. Sara blinked as she took an instinctive step backward. The person who had opened the door was a young woman, certainly no older than Sara, with a toddler clinging to the hem of her garment. There was no mistaking her ethnicity. The shapeless, enveloping robe and head cover that concealed all but a few tendrils of her dark hair and most of her face were that of a very conservative Middle Eastern Muslim.

As the young woman leaned down to lift the toddler into her arms, Sara caught the look of apprehension in her eyes and felt instantly ashamed. How often had this girl—for she was little more—been faced with that same automatic response since the tragic events of 9/11 had launched America's war on terror? It wasn't her fault that evil people in the name of her faith were choosing to do unspeakable things. And if this was the young woman's home, she had certainly been here long before Julio Vargas and Saleh and his company had moved northward.

Down a long hall that ran the length of the house, Sara caught a flicker of distinctive yellow and green as someone alerted by Sara's knocking glanced out a door and then disappeared back inside. So there were other firefighters who had found hospitality in this house. The prospect encouraged Sara to step forward.

"Please, I am so sorry to bother you, but I've got a bit of an emergency. I really need to use a restroom. It would only be a minute, I promise."

At first Sara was afraid the young woman didn't understand English. But after a thoughtful contemplation, she opened the door wider.

"Of course, please come in. We are happy to assist the firefighters." Her English was melodic and soft. As Sara stepped eagerly into the hall, the young woman moved ahead of her, the toddler in her arms.

The bathroom was just beyond and across the hall from the doorway where Sara had seen the firefighter. As she passed, she could hear the murmur of voices through the closed door. The young woman reached past Sara to flick on the bathroom light.

As Sara stepped gratefully inside, an infant's wail from somewhere upstairs drowned out the murmuring across the hall. The harassed expression on the young woman's face was identifiable the world over.

"If you'll please excuse me, my daughter—" With a bashful apology, the young woman disappeared down the hall. Sara quickly shut the bathroom door.

She didn't dawdle, but she did take time to wash her hands and face and the exposed parts of her arms, luxuriating in the coolness of the water before reluctantly drying herself with a hand towel and stepping back outside.

She would have liked to express her gratitude, but the young woman hadn't returned, and Sara could still hear the baby crying. Better to let herself out than to bother the woman again. Switching off the light, she took a single step down the hall before she heard the creak of the door across the hall beginning to open. Her retreat into the bathroom was as instinctive as her recoiling response had been on the porch, but for different reasons. Doug and the others had to be wondering where she'd disappeared to by now. The last thing she wanted was the delay of explaining once again who she was and what she was doing over here out of bounds. With the woman of the house still upstairs with her children, the visiting firefighter who had glanced out the door would never know Sara had entered the house. If she kept out of sight, she could simply slip out the front door once the firefighter was gone.

The heavy thud of boots indicated that more than one person was emerging. There were voices as well. The language Sara heard was neither English nor Spanish. And they were heading her way toward the back door instead of the front. Hastily, Sara slipped further back into the darkness of the bathroom, edging cautiously, with as little noise as possible, behind the shelter of the door. She stiffened as two of the voices began speaking Spanish.

"I do not like making last minute changes in our plans. It leads to hastiness and error. Our timetable was for dawn. Now we will have to install the explosives while there is still light outside."

"Then we will simply have to set a close guard. We cannot wait. The fire is moving faster than we allowed for. Another twelve hours, and it will have swept past the zone or burned out. Our only window is now."

Sara's breath was coming shallow and fast, her fingers stiff on the doorknob. Those cold, flat tones—was she dreaming, or was that the same voice that had echoed too often through her nightmares?

The rumble of heavy footsteps moved past the bathroom door. There were at least half-a-dozen in the group, but they were moving too fast for Sara to catch more than a quick impression of yellow and green firefighters' clothing.

But she had no difficulty identifying the last two who clumped by the door more slowly.

The man Sara feared and hated above any living being in the world—Julio Vargas.

And the young Islamic militant Doug had identified as leader of this terrorist group—Saleh Jebai.

Chapter Eighty-six

Sara did not move until she heard the outside door slam at the end of the hall. Easing the bathroom door shut, she locked it and sank down weakly on the woolly softness of the toilet lid cover.

Pull yourself together! she told herself sternly. *Isn't this is what we've been praying for?*

Yes, but not with me trapped in a house with the terrorists!

Her fingers fumbled uselessly at her handheld radio. Not only were her hands shaking, but she could not remember how to use the unfamiliar instrument. Then something she pushed produced a crackle so loud she panicked and turned the unit off, grabbing instead for her cell phone. *Please, let me have enough battery.*

The number was still in her quick-dial, and she breathed again as it rang through. "Yes?"

"Doug . . . they're here!"

Her relief came through as a ragged sob barely above a whisper, but there was no hesitation in Doug's response.

"Sara—where are you? I've been worried. And who's there? I can hardly hear you."

Sara steadied her whisper. "I can't talk any louder. I'm at the lodge."

"The lodge!" Doug's disbelief echoed in her ear. "What are you doing up there?"

Sara hesitated for only a moment. "I . . . I came up to use the restroom."

"You shouldn't be there." Doug's voice was sharp. "We just finished a background check on this place. New Hope Boys Camp is sponsored by an Islamic charity. The owner is a Lebanese Muslim—immigrated from the same city as Mozer Jebai. They volunteered their property to the fire department, if it should be needed, six weeks ago. Donovan is already applying for a warrant to search the place."

"I know," Sara answered. "They're the ones who Julio and Saleh and the others have been staying with. They're all right here in the house."

"Sara—you're telling me you're in that house with Vargas and the others? Have they seen you? Can you get out? Are they armed?"

Sara had never heard fear in Doug's voice. Determination, command, irritation, weariness, pain, tenderness—but never fear. But she heard it now, sharp and edged with anguish. If in his abstraction and total absorption in the mission at hand she had doubted her place in his heart and thoughts, that doubt was gone.

Oddly, his fear lightened Sara's own terror. "I'm fine," she whispered firmly. "I'm locked in the bathroom. They haven't seen me—only the woman who let me in. She's upstairs, and they all went out back. I can walk right out the front door. As for weapons, I didn't see any, but I didn't really get a good look."

"Then get out of there—now! And call me again as soon as you're clear."

"No, wait—let me finish while I'm sure I can. They're all dressed as firefighters. And they're planning something right away. It was supposed to happen at dawn, but they said the fire was moving too fast, and they had to do it now. They said something about explosives, that they'd have to install them while it was still light instead of waiting till dark."

"I've got it. Now go! We're on our way. We'll move in as soon as you're clear."

The phone went dead. Sliding it back into her pocket, Sara slipped to the door and unlocked it, peering into the hall. It was empty. Sara glanced at her watch and was astonished to see that she'd been in the house for no more than five minutes. It had seemed an eternity. Despite her wariness as she slipped quietly out of the bathroom, the adrenaline knot in her stomach had eased. She had passed on the important information, and as she'd told Doug, she was less than ten seconds from walking out the front door. Even if the woman reappeared, she could not know what Sara had heard or seen.

Did that young mother have any idea her house was being used as a haven for terrorists? Could any mother be party to evil that could harm her own small children as much as the "infidels" who lived around her? Sara hoped not. The woman had been kind and gracious. Like millions of her faith, she was as much a victim as Sara of extremists like Saleh Jebai.

I can at least put in a good word for her when they move in and arrest them. It occurred to her as she cautiously moved down the hall that maybe there was a purpose behind this humiliating experience. Had it been God's purpose, after all, to answer their prayers and uncover the lair of these evil men?

The buoyant relief of that thought lasted only until she came abreast of the doorway from which Julio and his men had emerged. The door stood open, and Sara could not stifle an audible gasp as she saw the scene inside. In the center of the room, the lodge's recreation center, a billiard table had been covered over and was being used as a work space. Spread out across the top, as well as on a built-in wet bar, were maps and blueprints and hand-drawn diagrams.

Sara could not take another step. Beyond a shadow of a doubt, she knew she was looking at the mission plans for whatever evil Julio and Saleh had planned. She also knew that if she delayed her exit, she had no guarantee that Julio and his men wouldn't be back before she could get away.

From somewhere, Sara heard the creak of a floorboard, and the terror she had been holding at bay since she'd laid eyes on Julio Vargas swept over her like a flood. It carried her back to a black jungle night where—in an endless nightmare—she had desperately fled from gunfire, searchlights, and relentless, slobbering bloodhounds that would not release her trail.

I can't go through that again! I can't let him catch me!

She'd done her part. She'd found the terrorist cell when no one else had. Doug had told her to get out now. He'd be the first to tell her not to stop for anything.

Only because he cares enough to put your safety first! But what if those papers might make the difference between people dying or not? By the time the authorities arrive, this might all be cleared away, even destroyed, and precious time lost when every minute counts.

Sara reached into her pocket and fingered the digital camera she hadn't needed when she was with Ramon. It wouldn't take long to snap a record of those documents. As long as she was gone before anyone returned, they wouldn't even know.

An enormously risky "if."

Oh, God, I'm so afraid! It was one thing to flee from pursuit. It was another thing altogether to walk deliberately into a very real and imminent danger. Sara had no illusions about the viciousness of Julio Vargas and the delight he would take in exacting vengeance on the woman who'd brought down his corrupt little empire if he ever had her in his power again. Not after the sadistic and drawn-out punishment he had taken pleasure in inflicting on Doug. The terror again washed over her in a wave that left her dizzy. But some dogged wellspring of stubbornness kept her feet where they were.

Oh, God, I know what I have to do. I'm just not brave enough.

The eternity of that inner battle could have been measured in a few pounding heartbeats, and it did not end with the dissipation of her fear. But somehow, when Sara's feet finally came unglued from the wooden floorboards, they carried her steadily through the open door.

Safety is not in the absence of danger—or fear—but in the presence of God.

It's not about being safe, it's about standing strong in the middle of the storm.

Doug had said both of those things to her—and had lived them out.

What was the Bible story he'd brought up in the hospital about Daniel's three friends?

"If we are thrown into the blazing furnace, the God we serve is able to save us from it. But even if he does not . . ."

Oh, God, I know your power is enough to save me! And I know that if you choose not to, it isn't because you don't love me but only because you have something better in mind for me and this situation. But I'm still so afraid. I can't feel your angels around me, but I know you're there. Just . . . just give me the courage to do the part that you've given me.

Her tension and lack of practice with the camera made the process take longer than it should have, and more than once a nervous twitch necessitated repeating a shot. But Sara didn't stop until she had photographed every piece of paper on display in the room, though she understood little of what she was recording and didn't waste the time studying it.

She slid the camera back into her pocket and was stepping back through the door when she heard rapid footsteps entering the hall. Her heart stopped. She had gambled—and lost.

But it wasn't Julio Vargas or any of his associates. It was her young hostess, and the woman looked both surprised and relieved to see Sara.

"I am so sorry to take so long!" she apologized in her soft, melodic English. The total lack of interest with which she glanced past Sara into the cluttered recreation room convinced Sara once and for all the woman had no part in what was going on. "My daughter—she was very upset. Did you find everything you needed?"

"Yes, it was wonderful!" Sara answered with genuine fervor. "I just wanted to say thank you in person before I left. Really, thank you so much!"

Sara gabbled her appreciation all the way to the front door. She was just stepping out onto the veranda when she caught the unmistakable click of the back hall door closing. With a final quick thank you, she hurried off the veranda and across the gravel yard.

Ten paces. Twenty.

Emerging from the barn, a blue-jeaned figure in wide hat, but now minus the tool kit, stared across the corral in her direction.

Don't run. He's too far away to intercept you.

Other men now appeared, three that she could see loitering with seeming aimlessness between the ranch house and the corrals. They didn't look like the terrorists she'd seen indoors, their blue jeans and wide hats the attire of ranch hands, not firefighters. It was obvious from the watchful lift of their heads that they'd seen Sara.

Are those the guards Julio was talking about?

Whatever Julio and Saleh were up to, it had to be back behind the ranch house where Sara had seen the canvas pavilion. But this time she felt no compulsion to investigate.

Don't run!

Against every instinct, Sara slowed her pace instead of speeding up. Glancing back toward the house, she saw the front door swing open in the deep shadows of the veranda. Two people stepped out. She dared not look long enough to identify the figure in yellow and green firefighting clothes, but there was no mistaking the long robes and head covering of the young woman. On seeing the two at the door, the man near the barn turned and walked toward the house.

Don't run!

Sara was among the corrals now and could no longer see the other men, but she could still feel the prickle of their watching eyes between her shoulder blades. Head high, steps even, she turned a corner. With the turn, the wall of an outlying shed blocked her view—and theirs. Straight ahead across the fields now was the base camp, a twinkle of lights in the fading twilight.

Between Sara and the sanctuary of the camp, an SUV was speeding straight toward her, the dust cloud billowing around it indicating how fast the driver was pushing it across the open grazing land.

Enemy or friend?

There was no time to make a judgment. The vehicle jounced down off the prairie onto the gravel of the driveway, its brakes squealing as it skidded to a stop near Sara. Just as she caught sight of Ramon's dark, angry features behind the wheel, Doug hopped down from the front passenger seat.

"Sara!" His grip on her upper arms was tight enough to be painful, and the expression on his face might have been anger, if not for the lingering fear in his tone. "I was beginning to think—are you okay?"

Then he was pulling her tight against him, and the strength of his grip was infinitely comforting. Now that she no longer had to be brave, Sara buried her face against his chest and burst into tears.

Chapter Eighty-seven

"My wife erred. She should not have invited the woman into the house. Still, there was no harm done."

Saleh nodded curtly at his host. Despite his anger at the breach in security, it might have seemed suspicious, as well as churlish, to deny such a simple and ordinary request. What was done was done, and there was no time now to concern himself with a stray female firefighter.

"We are finished here," he announced. "Get this cleared out."

Two team members began gathering the evidence of their planning session, wadding it up into a trash bag for disposal. Saleh took possession of the maps and blueprints that he and Julio would need to guide their flight.

Team Three's demolition sergeant entered the room. "It is done," he told Saleh.

"Good. It is time." Saleh took the cell phone the demolition sergeant handed him and tucked it into the breast pocket of his yellow shirt. "Let us leave this place before it is too dark to fly without lights."

Outside, in the clearing behind the lodge, the canvas pavilion had been taken down, revealing the two Hueys. Team Three split into two groups and headed to their assigned aircraft, lifting in their gear before climbing aboard. Julio had already turned on his Huey's engine, the throp-throp-throp of the rotors gradually picking up speed as the engine warmed up.

Climbing into the pilot's seat of his own aircraft, Saleh reached for his flight helmet. The gray-haired camp director stood in the back door, watching them leave. But Saleh did not bother with a backward glance. They would not be seeing this place or these people again.

Chapter Eighty-eight

"Sara, are you all right? Did they hurt you?"

The controlled fury in Doug's tone straightened Sara up from the comfort of his embrace. Others were crowding around them now. Kyle and Rocky and Ramon, his dark face still tight with anger. And her cousin, looking worried at her tears. A second vehicle, a white van, had pulled up behind the SUV, and Keith Donovan was stepping out.

Accepting a handkerchief from someone, Sara mopped at her face. "I'm sorry, I'm fine, really. I was just—I didn't think I was going to make it out."

Stepping away from Doug, Sara dug into her pocket for the digital camera. "Whatever they're planning, it's all in here. I managed to get pictures of all their diagrams and maps before I got out. That's what took so long."

As incredulous comprehension flared in Doug's eyes, Sara managed a shaky smile. "You were right, Doug. Doing something brave doesn't mean you're not afraid. I was so scared while I was taking those, I thought I was going to throw up."

Doug reached for the camera and tossed it to Kyle. "Get this uploaded stat! We need them yesterday."

As Kyle took off at a run toward the base camp, Doug spun back to Sara. "We started to move a response team into place as soon as you called, but we were beginning to think they'd grabbed you in there. We're assuming they've got weapons stashed somewhere, so we can't just roar in for an open assault. But we have forces moving in on foot."

Sara saw no sign of movement in the sagebrush and prairie grass, but she knew better than to question his statement.

"And we've got Blackhawks on their way with a couple of SWAT teams. Another fifteen minutes, and we'll be in position to move in. Donovan's team will be ready for a takedown when the time comes. Now that you're out, Joe and the rest of us need to get that bird in the air for surveillance. Which leaves you."

Doug's mouth crooked as he turned his attention back to Sara. "Can you make your own way back to base, or do we need to turn a car around to take you?"

"But—" Sara's glance toward the SUV was only the smallest flicker of her eyes, but Doug caught it. His fingers tightened again on her arms.

"Sara, I know now how you've felt every time you've had to see me walk out the door on a mission. I lived a lifetime knowing you were in there and that there was nothing I could do to help. But now I have a job here that has to be done, and I need you to let me go do it."

Sara could feel his impatience to be moving, but he stood still, waiting. He was right. She had made what she knew was a valuable, even pivotal, contribution, and the best help she could offer now was to get out of the way, and let these men do what they were trained to do.

And pray.

"*He who dwells in the shelter of the Most High . . . he will cover you with his feathers, and under his wings you will find refuge.*"

"Of course I can get back on my own. You . . . you go on and do what you have to do."

Sara's step back was meant to release Doug, but now she felt herself swept up against him. For just an instant, his lips came down firmly on hers.

Then he was gone, climbing into the front seat of the SUV. Before the door had even closed, Ramon roared into reverse to make a sharp U-turn toward the helicopter landing field. Sara watched them go, the dust cloud rising against the darkening sky as Ramon floored the SUV over the rough terrain.

"*You will not fear the terror of night nor the arrow that flies by day, nor the pestilence that stalks in the dark . . . for He will command His angels concerning you to guard you in all your ways.*"

The familiar phrases of Psalm 91 brought comfort as the taillights of the SUV dwindled in the distance and the man she loved raced headlong into duty and danger.

Oh, God, let your angels be there around Doug and all the others involved in stopping this evil. Be with the team breaking into that house. You know how dangerous Julio and Saleh are!

But that prayer was already too late. Sara was turning to start back toward camp when she heard the rhythmic throp-throp-throp of rotor blades. Her first thought was that it came from the distant shape of a helicopter that was hovering over the helipad. Then came the realization that the sound was closer at hand. Spinning around, she watched with horror and dismay as the long, sleek shape of a Huey lifted slowly above the peaked roof of the lodge. Though the long summer twilight was at last giving way to darkness, the helicopter was not using running lights, making the gray-green of the military aircraft little more than a blurred shadow against the sky. But it could have been a twin to the one that had taken Sara captive almost a year ago in Bolivia, and she had no doubt that Julio Vargas was at the controls.

A second thropping shadow rose from behind the lodge. For a heartbeat and then another, the two aircraft hovered against the night. Then, turning leisurely, they banked away from the ranch buildings, the steady roar of the engines and beat of the rotors diminishing as they picked up speed, until the two shadows disappeared into the night over the Hanford nuclear reserve.

* * *

The occupants of the SUV had seen those rising shadows too. Ramon and Doug looked at each other in grim recognition. "Julio Vargas!"

Ramon's foot rammed the accelerator. Doug grabbed his hand radio. "Donovan, the chickens have flown the coop! The chickens have flown the coop!"

The FBI SAC crackled back. "We saw it. But it's going to be another ten before those Blackhawks get here. And that much to get an alert out."

A sick feeling twisted at Doug's gut. How much of that nuclear reserve could be reached within ten minutes' flight time? "Got it! We're going after them."

He swung around to face Joe in the back seat. "How fast can you get your bird in the air?"

"As fast as you can climb aboard." The fire captain looked stunned, but his answer was immediate. "But—this is unbelievable! These helicopters . . . is that what you were expecting?"

"We wouldn't have been caught flat-footed if we had. Vargas *is* a helicopter pilot. But here in the U.S. . . . with two military surplus aircraft? There wasn't a hint . . . not on that shopping list or anywhere else." Doug thumbed the hand radio again. "Kyle! You got those images of Sara's uploaded?"

"I just got here. I'm working on it," Kyle's voice came back.

"Well, work faster! Julio and a second pilot just lifted off in a pair of Hueys, heading over the reserve. I'm guessing Saleh's the second pilot. He was training with Julio down in Paraguay. We're going after them, but we need directions."

"Are you kidding?" Kyle demanded. "Okay, you got it! I'm working faster."

Ramon ignored all the directional signs, gunning the SUV right up onto the helicopter field, barely dodging a mechanic's truck that was making its way toward a parked Sikorsky as he skidded to a stop beside the Search and Rescue helicopter.

The helipad manager was trotting toward them as they piled out of the SUV. "Hey, you see those two Hueys? I didn't clear them! You know who's driving?"

"Call Command Central," Doug tossed over his shoulder as he scrambled into the cabin of the Bell with Ramon and Rocky right behind him. Joe was already in the pilot's seat. "They'll fill you in."

"Hey!" the helipad manager called as Ramon reached for the side door. "I didn't clear you either! And you can't leave that vehicle here!"

"No time!" Ramon called as the door slammed shut. The engine screamed as Joe pushed it to the limit. As the helicopter shuddered off the ground, Doug reached for the Glock he'd tucked into the back of his pants when they'd scrambled to answer Sara's frantic call.

Beside him, Ramon had already pulled out his own Glock, and in the co-pilot's seat, Rocky was double-checking his Beretta. They were the only arms the agents were carrying. Not much to go up against a trained band of terrorists.

Doug glanced up as the Bell banked away from the helipad. "Uh, Joe . . . no running lights."

Joe glance back, startled. "Oh—of course." He reached across to the control panel, and the cabin grew immediately darker. "So what are these Hueys going to do? Drop a bomb? And where am I heading? What's their target?"

Despite the steadiness of his voice, the fire captain's face was tight with worry in the dim glow of the instrument panel. Doug knew he had to be thinking of his young family down there on the ground. Doug did not allow himself to think of Sara or even of how Donovan and the others might be frantically working against the clock. He could do nothing to change the situation anywhere but in the cabin of this aircraft, and he needed every ounce of energy and focus for the situation at hand.

"Not a bomb," he said tensely. "Sara heard them say something about installing explosives. Which says to me they've designed the helicopter itself as their weapon—one up on their typical car bomb. As to target, I'm hoping *you* can tell us. You know this area. You ran an inspection team through here. If they want to hurt us bad, where would they be heading?"

It was an urgent question because in the time it had taken them to get off the ground, the Hueys had vanished completely into the smoke and haze and night. The SAR helicopter had a radar system, but the screen showed dozens of dots—not only helicopters but fixed-wing aircraft making their runs to dump water and retardant on the fire. With some time and the coordination of air control and the helipad manager, they could eliminate those who legitimately belonged in this airspace.

But time was something they didn't have.

Doug rose to a half-crouch to peer through the windshield. At the moment, they were flying straight out over the reserve. The terrain below was as black as the deepening night, the blaze having already exhausted the available fuel in its race before the wind. Scattered here and there were patches of flickering red where hot spots still smoldered. Running as they were, without lights, the pockets of fire offered a welcome orientation in the darkness.

The main body of the fire was dead ahead, an ominous, red-orange streak stretching from one end of the horizon to the other. Beyond the red glow were the fire lines, where a division of hand crews and heavy machinery teams were frantically scraping out a barrier between the advancing inferno and the operational sectors of the reserve. Doug knew they had only until they reached the flames to make their decision. There simply wasn't time to zero in on more than one destination before the terrorists reached their target.

"Talk to me, Joe," Doug repeated urgently. "Which way do we go? Where can they hurt us the most?"

"I'm trying to think!" The fire captain's hands were steady on the controls, but his voice reflected Doug's desperation. "The nuclear plants—I don't think so. You could run a helicopter straight into the walls, and even if you blew through the concrete, you wouldn't do more than kill yourself. The solid waste sites might throw some radiation into the air, ignite a few barrels of uranium chips—but the fire may do that much! No, there's only two sites where they could count on catastrophic results. One, the K basins. If they blow a hole in one of those so that uranium is exposed to the air for any time—" Joe shook his head "—well, the atom bomb wouldn't have a patch on it."

Doug's hand radio crackled. "Bradford? Donovan here. We've redirected those Blackhawks your way. They'll be right behind you. But they've got to know where to go. Have you spotted Vargas and his boys?"

"That's a negative. Kyle, you got anything yet?"

"Just getting them uploaded," Kyle came back. "I've got a map of the Tri-Cities and a diagram here of explosives packed into the belly of a Huey. I got to tell you—by these specs, it'll pack quite a punch."

"Then get us a line on where they're heading, will you?"

"It'll go a lot faster if no one hassles me." Kyle sounded enviously unperturbed by the urgency of the situation. "Like they say, don't call us; we'll call you."

They had now halved the distance between base camp and the red streak on the horizon. Signing off, Doug swung back to Joe. "And choice number two?"

A shudder went through the fire captain's body before he responded. "The tank farms. If they've found a way to blast a hole down into one of those tanks and spark off a chain reaction . . . well, no one seems to agree on just how bad it will be. It may just blow a few billion gallons of toxic goo straight up into the air and back to earth. Or it may contaminate a major portion of the continental U.S. But one thing's for sure: The Tri-Cities won't be habitable for a few thousand years, and anyone in the area at the time won't be around long enough to sue for compensation."

"So—which?" Doug would not let himself dwell on the horror of either prospect, only the calculation of probabilities. The line of flames ahead had grown to a leaping, red-orange wall, and the smoke was beginning to make breathing difficult, even at this altitude. Several helicopters circled above the wall of fire, but the smoke was too thick to determine their make, and all were running with lights. "We've got a crossroads coming up here, folks. We've got to make a decision."

"Does it really matter?" Rocky demanded suddenly. "I mean, I'm on board here, Doug, but let's get real. If they choose to run those choppers into the ground either place, what do you expect us to do except watch the fireworks while we make our last confession?"

Doug was momentarily silent. Then he said soberly, "You're right. If Saleh chooses to do a 9/11, we're all lost. I guess I choose to believe that isn't what he has in mind. Not out of wishful thinking, but reasonable analysis. This group hasn't pulled a suicide mission yet. Their methods have been textbook Special Forces, and the last two missions included an evac plan—we know that because they returned to dump their stuff back in those storage units. Besides, even if Saleh Jebai and the others are in a hurry for Paradise and their seventy virgins, I can assure you that Julio Vargas is looking for nothing more than a long, well-paid vacation right here in this life. My bet is that they've got one chopper rigged as a bomb. The other is their evac."

Still nothing from Kyle. Doug debated reaching again for his hand-radio. But if the intel analyst had found anything, they would already know. Doug looked instead at Sara's cousin. "Either way makes no difference to our mission. Captain Thornton . . . Joe . . . I guess the call is yours. You know the area better than anyone else. What's it gonna be—one or two?"

But the fire captain was shaking his head, his features pale and distressed in the control panel lighting. "I don't know. I can't make a decision like that. I've got a family down there. If I choose wrong—don't ask me to take that responsibility!"

"You have no choice." Doug gentled the sharpness of his tone as he laid a hand on the other man's shoulder. He'd been forgetting that Sara's cousin wasn't a trained agent like the rest of the helicopter's contingent. "Any one of us could make the wrong call here. But you're the best qualified here to make that judgment. Right or wrong, the decision has to be made, and made now! And you're the only one who can do it."

Chapter Eighty-nine

The apocalypse might have already started.

The Hueys had left the burnt-out region of the reserve behind and were now flying directly above the blaze. Saleh found himself gaping like a tourist at the flames leaping a hundred feet or more into the air.

More incredible was the smoke. Black and thick and noxious, even inside the helicopter, so that all the Huey's occupants had pulled the large handkerchiefs that were part of their firefighting gear up over their noses, goggles pulled down to protect their eyes. The heavy pall not only billowed high above the flames, but spread in an acrid, dark cloud clear across the reserve. The haze was dense enough that Saleh could only barely make out the frantic line of men and equipment bulldozing a firebreak between the flames and a suspiciously regular stretch of rolling mounds.

Between the smoke and the darkness, their unlit aircraft would be no more than a blip on a radar screen until they were on top of their target.

Originally, the inferno below was all Saleh had planned. In keeping with the objectives of their first two missions, even if the flames threatened only a few of the numerous dump sites, the panic and public outcry, and the added billions in clean-up costs would strike another blow to an already hurting nation and its economy.

But that was before he'd grasped the sheer magnitude of toxic waste that was stored here and the vulnerability of its storage. It was a sign from Allah, a judgment, that these people should create the very weapon of their own destruction. And it was Saleh who had been chosen by Allah to light the fuse.

The means to do so had come to him so simply that it too must've been a sign from Allah. With personnel and equipment and aircraft swarming everywhere, who would question a pair of Forest Service helicopters filled with firefighters blundering slightly off-course in the middle of all the confusion? Especially with the added advantage of the smokescreen.

All they needed was a few minutes—and a target that would deliver the maximum punishment.

Saleh's first impulse had been to strike the K-East or K-West basins on the bank of the Columbia River. With their more than four million pounds of spent uranium rods protected from interacting with the atmosphere only by a covering of water, a crack that would drain just one of the pools long enough for the exposed uranium to reach spontaneous fusion would eliminate the need to smuggle a nuclear bomb into the country. The 1986 Chernobyl disaster would be a blip on the screen compared to the scale of death and destruction that would follow here.

But could he be certain that workers would not somehow repair the breach and restore the water covering the uranium before fusion was reached? It was too risky.

The nuclear reactors themselves and the buried solid waste were too well-protected by their physical infrastructure, if nothing else, for a blitzkrieg assault whose timetable would have to be measured in minutes, or even seconds.

Instead, Saleh had been drawn back to the horror of the tank farms. A photo on one of the Internet sites showed the inside of one of the tanks, where a lethal, bubbling stew ate away at the steel sides. Bubbles originating from hot thermal gases generated by the toxic mixture necessitated a regular stirring to keep the whole thing from exploding. The concern of the nuclear watchdogs was that if so much as a single spark were somehow introduced into that volatile atmosphere, the resulting explosion would release nearly two tons of radioactive waste into the environment.

And there were 177 such tanks, millions of gallons of radioactive material, all interconnected by a half-century-old system of pipes used to shift the waste from one tank to another.

To give the Americans credit, the possibility of such an intrusion had been reduced as far as possible. A full six feet of concrete protected the surface of the tanks, and regular inspections monitored the thermal gas buildups against a spontaneous explosion.

But they had prepared for an accidental calamity, not a deliberate assault.

Saleh's mouth thinned with satisfaction under the handkerchief. His first impulse to simply crash a helicopter into one of the tanks had been swiftly rejected. With the heavy reinforcement of the tops of the tanks, the chance of success was too iffy. And this was a mission that could not be repeated.

Dropping a bomb had been considered and rejected as well. Too much of the explosive force would be expended upward. Besides, there was still the hope that the destruction would be ruled accidental.

The helicopter just ahead, with Julio Vargas at the controls, did not look like the weapon it had been fashioned into. It had been the Palestinian demolitions expert, author of dozens of Israeli-aimed car bombs, who had modified the helicopter body itself into a weapon. Centered in the belly of the helicopter, an explosive device had been fashioned to blast downward through far more than six feet of concrete. Furthermore, the tanks had inspection hatches, openings for surveillance cameras, and the mixing units. The explosion need only create a single breach to touch off the chain reaction.

The most difficult part of the planning had been the evacuation plan for the other helicopter's personnel, a contingency so alien to the usual mission plan of any Islamic militant group that they'd had to brainstorm entirely new concepts. It was for more than Vargas's piloting skills that Saleh had chosen him to fly the lead aircraft.

Saleh fingered the cell phone rigged as the detonator. If anything went wrong, he would use it, even at the cost of sacrificing the task force members on board the other Huey. But the bomb would only serve its intended purpose if Vargas had touched down on one of the tanks.

They were beyond the fires now, if not the acrid cloud of smoke, and approaching the area identified on Saleh's aerial map as 200 West. Both Hueys were running with lights now, just two more aircraft in the night sky above the reserve. Ahead, dimmed by the smoke, stadium-style lights illuminated a huge, vaguely L-shaped stretch of pavement, far larger than Saleh had envisioned. A profusion of small, rectangular structures and a maze of pipes dotted the surface.

It was easy enough to pick out where the waste tanks had been buried under the pavement. They were marked by roughly circular clusters of round and oval-shaped access hatches that stood out as pale blotches against the darker pavement. A number of vehicles, including at least one fire rescue truck, were situated in a parking area beyond the tank farm. The heavy blanket of smoke had been exacerbated by a fire break and back burn not far beyond the chain-link fence marking the west boundary of the 200 Area site. Through the haze, Saleh could see several people walking around on the paved surface of the tank farm, where they could keep an eye on the progress of the fire.

He coughed as, even with the handkerchief over his face, the density of the smoke caught at his throat.

It was time.

Right on schedule, Saleh heard a faltering in the rhythmic throb of the other Huey's engine above the roar of his own aircraft. The engine evened out, then faltered again under its pilot's expert hand. This time the Huey dropped in altitude and slipped sideways before it picked up a smooth beat again.

Saleh was beginning to think their actions would go unchallenged, making the next part of their careful rehearsal unnecessary, when the radio crackled.

"To the unidentified aircraft approaching the 200 West, you are entering a restricted airspace. Please identify yourself and redirect your course."

From the other Huey, the communications specialist, a Chicago-born Muslim convert, responded on Julio's behalf, his voice sharp with panic and unmistakably African-American as he recited the registration number painted on the Huey's tail. "We've got a load of firefighters here—and some engine trouble. Looks like ash or something in the intake valve. I'm afraid I'm going to have to put this baby down."

Another slip sideways and the Huey was inside the perimeter line of 200 West. The response from the ground was immediate and curt.

"You can't put down here. Can't you read? This is a restricted zone. If you've got a problem, put down west of here, and we'll scramble some help your way."

"You think I'm not trying?" The Huey dropped another twenty meters inside the perimeter as Julio's expert hand played with the controls again. "I'm doing my best here, but right now I've got a choice of setting this thing down or crashing it into the ground."

The Huey was now no more than a hundred meters above the paving of the tank farm, and through its open side panel the Team Three members aboard in their firefighting gear had to be visible to the observers below, despite the smoke. Saleh knew what had to be racing through the mind of the ground controller. To allow the Huey to set down within the perimeter of the waste site was a serious breach of security protocol. But the impact of a crash against the tank farm surface could precipitate a far worse catastrophe.

The Huey dropped further in altitude as the radio remained silent. They would be running the Huey's registration number through the computer. Would it check out? Or were they already calling in an air strike?

"I can't wait any longer! Unless you want a bunch of dead firefighters on your hands, I've got to set this down *now*!"

That did it.

"Okay, your registration checks out." The controller sounded thoroughly unhappy, but he continued, "You can set down. But you will evacuate your aircraft immediately and move toward the personnel you will see coming toward you, hands out where we can see them."

He added more apologetically, "No offense intended, of course. We appreciate what you're doing out there. But we've got a procedure to follow."

With another hiccup of its engine, the Huey began to hover down to a landing. It was Saleh's cue. He signaled to the Yemeni-American who was manning the radio.

The Yemeni reeled off the registration number and said, "Hey, Sammy, man, is that you down there? We caught your problem. We're running practically empty up here. We can retrieve your passenger load, if you like."

Saleh fingered the cell phone detonator again as the Yemeni spoke. If all went as planned, in a few minutes the crew of the other helicopter would be aboard his craft, and the team would be on its way at full throttle out of the danger zone before the bomb detonated.

If not—

Julio's engine cut out completely a few feet above the ground, landing hard enough to convince any onlookers of trouble. He'd managed to drop the helicopter near one of the tank lid clusters, over several manhole covers and pipes that led down into the tank interior. A white, table-shaped protrusion had made it impossible to land dead-center, but he was close enough to achieve the objective. Already, several figures in white coveralls could be seen racing toward the aircraft, waving furiously.

Saleh's fingers tightened on the detonator. It was done. The next moments would tell whether he would trigger the speed dial or set down his own aircraft. At worst, the tank under the first Huey would blow, taking his comrades with it but creating the most disastrous nuclear incident ever on American soil. At best, the expected chain reaction from the blast would set off the rest of the tanks, discharging into the atmosphere enough lethal waste to contaminate at least a third of the continental U.S. for the next few thousand years. Meanwhile, Saleh and his team would slip away to safety and continue the jihad.

Either way, Saleh and his comrades had earned their place in Paradise. Perhaps even Julio Vargas, infidel that he was, would be granted mercy.

The radio crackled and the ground controller repeated back the ID number the Yemeni had read off. "Your ID has been verified. You may proceed with retrieval. Please do *not*—I repeat, do *not*—set down on any of the light-colored hatches where your friend parked. We cannot guarantee they will hold the weight of your craft. Your best bet would be the parking lot."

Rejecting the almost-empty parking lot as too far away from the other Huey,

Saleh dropped down instead over the nearest patch of open pavement. Through the windshield, he could see his team members, dressed in fire gear, climbing down out of the grounded helicopter.

"That's not what I meant!" The ground control's protest was sharp with exasperation. "The parking lot is to the west of the restricted zone."

Saleh felt his runners touch solid ground.

He was down.

Chapter Ninety

Doug waited with a patience he was not feeling. The flames were beneath them now, and it was decision time. He understood Joe's agony. The wrong call could mean the death of everyone here and for a considerable distance beyond.

Including Sara.

Ramon cleared his throat. "Uh—Doug? We've got to call it!"

Doug leaned forward to search the horizon for the smallest flicker of a gray shadow against the night, his ears straining for the drone of an engine above their own. *Oh, God, people's lives are depending on how I call this! Give me wisdom—or a sign!*

What his choice would have been, he couldn't have said, because Joe spoke suddenly, his eyes unwavering on the horizon, his hands white-knuckled on the controls, but his tone definite.

"The tanks. My boss told me once that with government types, if you want to know where there's a problem, you look where they're spending the money. And if they're willing to spend a million bucks a pop to stir that molasses down there, they're scared to death what could happen."

Just then Doug's hand-radio crackled. "Doug, I think I've got it. Do a couple rectangles the size of a football field, polka-dotted with circles mean anything to you?"

"A tank farm," Joe said definitely. "Two hundred West." Already the helicopter was banking right.

Thank you, God! Doug breathed before raising his Motorola to his mouth. "Kyle, you've got a tank farm there. Area 200 West. We're heading in. You call Donovan and get those Blackhawks out here."

They were over the back burn now, rapidly approaching the chain-link perimeter fence of 200 West. Beyond, lit up like a stadium, was the enormous rectangular expanse of the tank farm.

"There!" Ramon gripped Doug's shoulder hard as he pointed groundward. At the nearest end of the tank farm, landed almost squarely in the center of one of the circles, was a Huey, its rotors already still. Several yellow and green figures in hard hats and fire coats were climbing out. Sprinting toward them across the pavement were a number of other figures in white and beige. And not far away, on a stretch of black pavement, was a second Huey, its rotors still making a slow rotation.

"That Huey on the tank lid's got to be the bomb," Ramon said urgently.

"And you were right about an evac plan, Doug," Rocky added. "Looks like the first bunch is heading to the second chopper. They're going to lift off and then blow the place."

"We've got a loudspeaker." Joe's voice was calm, now that the indecision was over, and his gaze as he studied the ground ahead was the steady one of a firefighter who'd had to assess his own share of hazardous situations. "If you want to warn security down there."

"No." Doug vetoed the idea immediately. "We can't risk doing anything that would provoke these guys into going suicidal."

His mind raced as he appraised their options. The side door of the second Huey was now open, and its occupants were climbing down. Nine in all, he counted, between the two aircraft. Though it was not possible to tell whether they possessed weapons, at least the ground security had taken the precaution of ordering their hands held out where they could see them.

"We'll just take a page out of their own book," Doug said aloud. "Joe, hit your lights."

The fire captain threw him a questioning glance, but reached for the control panel. As the red and green and white of the helicopter's running lights flashed on, Doug reached for the mike of the helicopter's radio system. "Area 200, this is Search and Rescue." Doug looked at the control panel and read off the registration number. "We've seen your situation on the ground there and we're on our way."

During the pause, in which Doug knew the number he'd reeled off was being run through a computer database, the helicopter reached the perimeter fence. Doug's muscles tensed, but not with any serious misgivings. The SAR markings on their aircraft had to be obvious from the ground. And it seemed the security forces were not in a "shoot first, ask later" mood tonight.

A resigned voice filled the cabin. "Roger, we've got you. You here to join the party?"

"That we are. We're coming down. We'll have these guys out of your hair in no time." Doug clapped a hand on Joe's shoulder. "Set her down right there between the two Hueys, if you can. And don't think they won't push the button if they get cornered. First priority is that detonator. Saleh or Julio will be holding it, though we can't rule out a backup. My bet's on Saleh. He wouldn't trust Julio to push the trigger if it went suicidal. Rule of thumb: If it wiggles a finger, shoot it!"

All three agents now had weapons in hand. They grinned wolfishly at each other as they moved into position and the tamped-down excitement that invariably went with the kick-off of a mission began to build. As perilous as the situation was, they were all three warriors by nature and superbly good at what they did. And this was just the kind of action they'd signed on for.

As the Bell dropped in over the perimeter fence, Rocky slid out of the co-pilot's seat, joining Doug and Ramon braced in a half-crouch at the side door. Startled faces below looked up as the Search and Rescue aircraft swooped down over them.

"Showtime!" The declaration came out as a chorus. As Ramon reached for the door release, he added, "Let's roll!"

* * *

So, the Americans are not totally foolish, Saleh admitted as he climbed down out of the Huey, both hands in clear view, palms outward. At least half the security detail running toward them had dropped to cover behind control boxes and other protuberances, with only their assault rifles left in view as an obvious and unmistakable warning. Saleh was glad that his team had not tried to emerge carrying weapons, though both aircraft held well-concealed arsenals. He had learned that simplicity and boldness often worked better than a blaze of gunfire. A valuable lesson the jihad could take to heart.

Saleh could see that his men were obeying instructions. The other three from his helicopter had stepped out into the open, hands held high and inoffensively away from their bodies. Julio and his crew were already striding toward them, hands similarly held wide. Two of the security detail, assault rifles at the ready, sprinted toward the "disabled" aircraft, their heads and shoulders disappearing into the open door as they made a swift inspection of the interior.

A second pair hurried up to Saleh's aircraft. Saleh kept his face deadpan as they glanced inside. Security was not as loose, then, as he'd come to believe, despite the lack of an overt military presence on the reserve. Had he made any miscalculation in the casting of their role here? Would this inspection be thorough enough to uncover the stash of weapons? The explosives?

He dared not shift his hands, but his mind moved to the thin oblong slipped into his breast pocket under the fire retardant rubber of his coat.

A simple "1" on the speed-dial.

But the investigative detail was already stepping back from the Hueys, giving the thumbs-up. One of the security force stepped into the open close enough to call out to Julio and his men. "Go on, then, and good luck. We'll have our mechanics take a look at your bird and get it moved out of here. We'll give your base a holler to let them know where you can pick it up."

That they might have expected the pilot to remain with his aircraft had been a calculated risk—and doubly so, given that Vargas was an unlikely martyr. But it seemed the security detail had no interest in keeping any unauthorized personnel on their turf any longer than they had to.

The roar and flashing lights of an approaching aircraft were an infuriating disruption. Saleh cursed inwardly as he glanced skyward at the Search and Rescue helicopter now hovering down over them. The do-gooders must have seen the phony emergency landing from the fire lines and felt compelled to offer their services.

No matter. Julio and his men were more than halfway to their escape transport. By the time the newcomers could get involved, Saleh's force would be loaded and in the air.

Saleh lowered his hands fractionally, his foot tapping impatiently as the SAR aircraft settled to the ground, their choice of landing site forming the third point of a triangle with the other two helicopters, the side door facing toward both halves of the assault team. They had set down irresponsibly close, Saleh noted angrily, so that Julio and his companions actually had to scatter backwards against the wind blast of the rotors.

Well they'll find themselves paying for that!

As Saleh eased his hands further down, he caught the eye of one of the security guards, who had not yet lowered his assault rifle. He decided to leave his hands where they were. The door of the SAR helicopter slid open and Saleh caught a glimpse of the yellow-and-green clad rescue team.

His complacence lasted only the split second it took to register the weapons in the hands of the three men jumping lightly to the ground from the open side door. As the newcomers' faces were illumined by the full beam of a floodlight, Saleh's deadpan expression melted into disbelieving astonishment.

It can't be!

But it was. Gaunt features scored deep with tiredness, but very much alive, the cool gray eyes disturbingly alert as they riveted immediately on Saleh.

A dozen paces away, Julio Vargas had seen him too. The prisoner he'd left to die half a world away. His bewilderment came out in a scream of rage. "Bradford!"

The DEA agents had the advantage of not being caught by surprise. They scattered with an efficiency born of their long experience working together. Ducking behind a control box, Rocky covered Julio's group with his Beretta. Ramon went left to cover the second contingent. Doug leveled his Glock—not on his old enemy, but dead-center on Saleh Jebai.

"Don't move any further and keep your hands in the air. You're all under arrest!" he called loud enough for site security as well as the phony firefighters to hear him clearly.

With the fiasco of his last Miami mission in mind, Doug had already pulled out his DEA badge and tossed it to the closest member of the security detail. He had no desire to end up at the wrong end of one of those assault rifles.

"DEA!" he announced tersely. "These men are terrorists. That chopper's a bomb."

The site security personnel didn't need anything else. They knew what they were sitting on far better than any of these intruders. The assault rifles shifted to cover the two Huey contingents.

Caught flat-footed and unarmed, Julio and his companions froze, their hands shooting skyward, the fury of defeat twisting at their features.

Rocky and Ramon, without relaxing their stance, exchanged a peripheral glance of muted triumph.

* * *

Saleh knew he'd lost the instant he identified Bradford and heard Julio Vargas's scream of rage.

I should have killed both of them!

Fury, disappointment, and disbelief ran together in his mind, fusing at once into a murderous rage and ice-cold determination. Why Allah had fated this ill-fortune, he was not permitted to question. But if this was the end, he would not spend the rest of his life rotting in an infidel prison. Not when the pathway to Paradise and revenge lay within his grasp. It would take only a fraction of a second to press the speed-dial.

* * *

Ironically, it was Julio Vargas who first comprehended the movement of Saleh's hand. He was as angry as anyone at the turn of events, and if he could have gotten his hands on one of the weapons stored under the floor of his aircraft, he would have used it with great pleasure on the American agent standing across from him.

But he did not have a death wish.

Where there was life, there was always hope. It was the only lesson of value he'd brought out of Palmasola.

"Bradford!" he screamed. "Saleh—the cell phone!"

* * * * *

Doug had been carrying a weapon like the one in his hand for almost a decade. And though he'd had reason to use it from time to time, it had never been with the intention of taking a human life. Like any good agent, he'd questioned his ability to make that decision if the time ever came. But in the end it was easy.

Pop. Pop. Pop.

Three shots ripped between the assault leader's eyes as neatly as on a paper target. Ramon was there to scoop up the cell phone before it hit the ground.

A moment later, the shouts and pounding boots of the security detail were drowned out by the approaching scream of a combat helicopter overhead. Donovan's Blackhawks had finally arrived. As the first black shapes began ziplining to the ground, Doug lowered the Glock.

This time it really was over.

Chapter Ninety-one

JUNE 22

In the end, it really was all personal.

Doug lengthened his stride through the maze of colorful sleeping tents toward the base camp's main street of command trailers. He'd meant to close his eyes for only a brief catnap, but from the angle of the sun overhead, he'd slept half the day away.

As personal, it would seem, in hunting down terrorists as it was with the drug dealers who were Doug's usual quarry. With all the efforts of Homeland Security—the thousands of agents, military, and law enforcement personnel—when it came down to it, it was the personal vendetta of one sleazy criminal against the agent who'd brought him down, and the agent's personal crusade to put a piece of scum back behind bars that had gotten in the way of the most brilliantly conceived and potentially catastrophic assault yet launched against American soil.

Not to mention the personal determination of one young woman who had refused to give up hope, without which all the rest would not have mattered.

Passing the base camp command center, Doug took the steps to the FBI trailer two at a time. The interior was virtually empty, the agents having packed up the computers and communications equipment after a long night of filing reports and writing cables.

"Hey, Bradford! What are you doing up and around?" Keith Donovan looked up from the room's lone remaining table where he was hammering away at a laptop computer. "Pull up a chair and I'll bring you up to speed."

As Doug walked across the room, the FBI SAC pushed a box of Dunkin' Donuts and a sheaf of digital photos across the table. "Those guys you bagged last night were a tight-lipped bunch, but thanks to your pal Vargas, we hit the safe houses for both of the other teams before they had a chance to wiggle. Just in time. They were just waiting for the go-ahead from Jebai to hit another nuclear waste site and a water purification plant. We just got these photos. You want to make some IDs?"

Doug lifted a maple bar from the donut box, but shook his head. "Later. Right now there's something else I've got to do. That SUV Ramon was driving last night—mind if I borrow it?"

"Not at all." Without comment, Donovan reached behind himself to a key rack and tossed Doug a set of keys. "Just make sure you gas it up before you bring it back," he added with a smile.

* * *

"I hope you don't mind my calling, Sara, but I thought you'd want to know. Cynthia gave me your family's number out there."

"Of course I'd want to know, Melanie. I just can't believe it, that's all. Larry Thomas had a heart attack? He's only thirty-two years old—well, you know that."

"They're not sure yet how bad it is, but he did make it through the night and I was able to talk to him this morning. If you get the chance, I know he'd want to hear from you."

"Thanks for letting me know, Mel. I will—I'll give him a call as soon as I can."

Sara replaced the phone in its cradle. *If it doesn't rain, it pours!*

Despite her concern for Larry, the situation in Miami didn't seem quite real in light of yesterday's events at Hanford. After hearing Doug's voice crackle over the command center radio, announcing the completion of the mission with only one casualty—the assault leader, Saleh Jebai—Sara had waited at the base camp for him to return. But the DEA guys had been swept into a debriefing session as soon as they touched down at the camp, and only her cousin Joe had shown up at the FBI trailer.

Instead, she had gone out into the night to shed a few tears of relief and thanksgiving before riding with Joe to the hospital, where she'd spent the rest of the night on a recliner next to Joshua's bed. After some protest, Denise had gone home with Joe for their first decent night's sleep since the beginning of their family crisis.

Joe and Denise had been back at the hospital before 6 A.M., and Sara had managed a few hours sleep before Aunt Jan, driving in from Portland to go to work, had stopped by to drop Jonathan off.

"Sara, when are my mom and dad coming? I thought they'd be here."

Sara turned at the plaintive demand behind her. Jonathan had laid down his markers, the straightening of his small shoulders and the brave set of his jaw reminding Sara of his father. Walking over to the table, Sara pulled him into a hug.

"They'll be here soon, honey. They called from the hospital. The doctor is going to let Joshua come home this morning. But they have to sign some papers."

Sara sighed as she saw the sheen of tears being valiantly blinked back. How do you explain bureaucracy to a five-year-old?

"Why don't you come outside and play for a while?" she said gently. "Jack has been missing you."

Jonathan followed Sara halfheartedly out the French doors onto the deck. But within moments he was racing down the steps to roll on the grass with the family's black Lab. Under the awning that gave some respite from the sun, Sara paced from one end of the deck to the other as she kept an eye on them. But her restlessness did not run deep. Everyone she loved was alive this morning to greet a new day. She would never take that for granted again.

Oh, God, I don't know just how you brought this miracle about! But we're still here, and if we are, it's because you still have a purpose for us in this life.

The hot, dry outdoor air still held the tang of burning sagebrush and grass, but the smoke and ash had greatly diminished, and for the first time in two days Sara saw blue sky overhead. The two blazes were at last contained, Joe had told her when he called from the hospital, the back burn merging into the main body of flames so that, barring some unexpected jump of the fire lines, the fires should burn themselves out once their present fuel was exhausted.

And although the flames had overrun one field of buried solid nuclear waste and come perilously close to some barrels of uranium chips that were inexplicably stored above ground, the only consequences were likely to be a negligible rise in radiation from dust and ash blown into the atmosphere.

From somewhere in front of the house, Sara heard the sound of an engine turning into the drive. A car door slammed shut.

Is that Joe and Denise? Maybe they managed to escape the hospital sooner than Joe thought they would.

Sara didn't leave the deck immediately. Down below, Jonathan was squealing and laughing with the dog. There'd be time enough to call him up once his parents were in the house.

But only one pair of swift footsteps was crossing the tile floor of the kitchen toward the French doors. Sara's heart began pounding before she slowly turned around.

"Good morning, Sara," Doug said quietly as he stepped onto the deck. His mouth quirked as he glanced skyward. "Or I guess that's afternoon now. I took a chance I'd find you here."

He made no immediate move to cover the remaining distance between them, instead leaning up against the siding of the deck wall. Like Sara, he had shed the firefighter clothing he'd lived in the last two days, but with no other alternative, he was back in the borrowed clothing he'd been given at the Paraguay embassy. But not even the baggy Dockers and XXL polo shirt could detract from the lean grace and assured body movements that were a trademark of his profession. If only she could see his eyes behind those sunglasses.

Was he feeling any of the sudden uncertainty that was gripping her? How long had it been since they'd actually been alone together like this? Not since that restaurant dinner when Doug had warned her he was through being patient. Was that image as clear in his mind right now as it was in hers?

"Joe told me what happened," she said before the silence could grow awkward. "Are you . . . can you talk about it?"

As if the question ended his uncertainty, Doug peeled himself away from the siding, and crossed over to Sara's side. Leaning his forearms on the wooden railing and gazing across the windswept landscape, he told Sara everything that had happened since he'd left her standing in the dust of the SUV the night before.

"Are you—okay with it?" Sara asked quietly when he'd finished. "Saleh, I mean."

Doug's sleeve brushed against her arm as he turned to look at her. "I think so. . . . It's funny. In the end, the easiest part about it was knowing when to shoot. If I hadn't, he'd have pressed that detonator and killed countless people. I guess that's why they train you so hard. The training just took over, and I didn't even have to think. I just knew I had to take him out, and I did it. Taking someone's life isn't a pleasant experience, and maybe I'll take time to talk to the shrink like the department always wants. But I'm not expecting any regrets on this one."

He turned again toward the horizon. Resting her forearms on the railing beside his, Sara turned her head to see what Doug was looking at. A glint of sunlight on water in the distance marked the curve of the Columbia River. A flock of Canada geese soared upward in their familiar arrowhead formation, honking encouragement to one another.

With the sky arching blue overhead and only a tint of red still marring the perfect gold of the sun, the scene held a peace and beauty that left no place for destructive fires and evil terrorist plots.

Doug nodded toward a deer that was grazing on the far side of the gully that ran behind the back fence. "Wonder if she's got any idea how close she came to losing her home."

"I know," Sara said softly. "It was all so close. I still can't believe it's really over, and we're all alive. I feel a little like Abraham must have felt after God stopped him from killing Isaac and gave him the ram to sacrifice instead. I had completely surrendered to whatever God chose to do—even if it meant taking us all home. And for a while I really thought that's what it would be."

"If it weren't for you, we wouldn't be here alive." The sunglasses finally came off as Doug turned sideways to look at Sara. "If you hadn't come after me, if you hadn't gone into that house and taken those pictures—"

"It was—I just did what I had to do." Sara was having a hard time breathing. Doug's turn had brought him disturbingly close, and she could feel the heat of his body. His gray eyes seemed to darken as they bored into hers. Searching frantically for conversation, she asked, "And what about Julio—what's going to happen to him?"

"Rot in jail—does it matter?" Doug's answer was terse, but she was drowning in the intensity of his gaze. Gathering up her hands in his, Doug placed them palms flat against his chest so that Sara could feel the bandages wrapping his rib cage. Focusing on the buttons of his shirt, Sara moved her palm against the coarse feel of the material. "This must hurt. All that running and jumping out of helicopters—you should have a doctor check you out."

"Sara . . . shh!" Doug tightened his grip on her hands, but there was a hint of a laugh in his voice above her head. "Just let me say what I need to say, okay? Here, look at me."

It would have been fruitless to try to tug her hands free, so Sara raised her eyes instead. Spreading one of his large hands to keep both of hers where they were, Doug reached with his other hand to lift a strand of dark hair spilling over Sara's shoulders. "I could get used to this, though I miss the towhead look."

The laughter left his tone. "Sara, you told me once that I needed to find someone independent and strong and competent at life—like Peggy Browning.

Someone who could stand by my side and be a partner instead of being a burden. Well, I've found that person. Do you think, if I asked her to marry me, she might say yes?"

The confident lift of his head was there, the controlled ease of his body as he waited. But under her open palms Sara felt a rhythm as rapid as her own.

"She just might," Sara said demurely, "if you asked her."

"Sara Connor, will you marry me?"

Any answer Sara made was inaudible as she found her slim form crushed against the warm strength of his body, his hands tightening in her hair, his lips hard on hers. Giving up speech, Sara made use instead of the sudden freedom of her hands and raised her arms to wrap them around his neck.

* * *

"There's still no guarantees," Doug said sometime later. "My job hasn't changed. There will still be times I'll be walking out that door and neither of us will know when I'll be walking in."

"Somehow, that doesn't seem too important anymore." Sara's fingers tightened in his as she looked up into his eyes. "Besides, I guess there's really no guarantee in anyone's life."

Sara told Doug about Melanie's phone call. "Here we were running around with terrorists and a doomsday scenario, and it's Larry who's in the hospital, not knowing whether he'll live or die. If there's anything I've learned in these past few months, it's that only God knows the hours of our lives, and those hours won't run out one second earlier than he plans—or one second later. So you've got to hold the people you love in an open hand. You can't just stop loving and enjoying them today just because someday God's time may come to take them away."

Sara's eyes were pools of amber flame as she looked straight at Doug. "I lived with losing you once, Doug, and though it hurt—horribly—it didn't destroy me. Now . . . I love you, and all I want is to be with you today and maybe tomorrow and for as long as God chooses to give us to each other."

Doug's reply was not in words.

Chapter Ninety-two

Sara had never thought of herself as anything but ordinary. But today, even her self-critical eye could see nothing but beauty reflected in the tall mirror of the church's bridal room—the same room from which she'd once stormed away from a certain Doug Bradford. The silken spill of her hair had been restored to its natural ash-blonde shade, if not its usual length. The lovely curve of her smile and the glow of her amber eyes lit up her features as she smoothed the cream lace dress that fell in an exquisite swirl around her slim figure.

The fire that leapt to Doug's eyes when Sara stepped through the sanctuary doors told her he at least was in agreement. Three weeks were not really enough to organize a wedding, but Doug and Sara saw no reason for further delay, and neither was concerned about an elaborate ceremony. Once Cynthia had weathered the emotional storm of welcoming her son back from the dead, she had thrown herself into the planning with her usual whirlwind of energy. With the hospitality committee turning the sanctuary into a bower of flowers, and the women's society organizing a reception, the short-notice plans had not been difficult. Behind Sara in the bridal room, their suitcases were packed to leave directly from the reception. Doug was carrying their passports and tickets for Iguazú Falls. The Argentine side.

As the familiar music began, Norm Kublin offered Sara his arm. Without a father on either side, Doug's GS had almost begged to do the honors, his pain and regret at the reality of Doug's captivity evident. Sara's smile as she slipped her hand into the crook of his arm reaffirmed her wholehearted forgiveness.

At the front of the church, Sara's maid of honor, Denise, glided into place across from Joe, whom Doug had asked to be his best man. Aunt Jan was seated across the aisle from Cynthia, and beside her were both of Joe's brothers and their families.

Her family.

They were not the only guests. Despite the short notice, the pews were filled, not only with church members but also DEA agents and dozens of Doug's friends from other government agencies. Rocky was back in Santa Cruz with his wife and three small daughters, but Ramon and Kyle were both there, as was Keith Donovan of the FBI. Mike and Debby Garcia were seated next to Peggy Browning—it was the first time Sara had seen the female agent in a dress. As Sara moved past her down the aisle, Peggy caught her eye with a nod of approval.

Larry Thomas was there too, still pale but recovering from his heart attack. Melanie sat beside him, and as Sara passed, she noted with pleasure that Melanie's fingers were intertwined in his.

There were other guests too.

Shadows.

Memories.

But today they had no power to hurt.

Norm Kublin released Sara and stepped back to sit beside Cynthia. Doug's strong hand closed around Sara's as he led her up the steps toward the minister. In the past three weeks, he had gained back some of the weight he'd lost, and the bandages had come off his ribs a week ago. The only remaining outward marks of his ordeal were the deepened grooves around his mouth and on his forehead that vanished when he smiled. He looked so handsome in the perfect fit of his tuxedo that Sara's heart constricted as her smile met his.

The scars hidden by that tuxedo were another story. The reminders of his captor's brutality would never totally fade. Neither Doug nor Sara would ever be totally without the inner scars that pain and loss and the bitter turns of life had left on them.

But then, was any human being?

Safety is not the absence of danger—not even for those you love—but the presence of God.

It's not about being safe, but standing strong in the middle of the storm.

"I now pronounce you man and wife."

Doug looked down into Sara's upturned face, the feel of the gold ring he'd just slid onto her finger cool and smooth beneath his grip. Her long lashes fluttered as her amber eyes rose to meet his, and for the first time since he had first set eyes on her in the co-op school courtyard in Santa Cruz, there was no hint of shadow in her gaze. In its place was such a blaze of love and trust and sheer joy that his long fingers tightened too hard over hers. The understanding

curve of Sara's mouth as he hastily relaxed his grip was impish and fleeting—
for him alone. She was his, the end of one long road and the beginning of
another, as long as they both shall live.

"I love you, Mrs. Sara Bradford."

As Doug pulled Sara close, the gray flame of his joy blazing into hers, his
firm mouth coming down hard, for just an instant both of them were sure
they heard it, as clearly as the music swelling loud in triumph around them.

A rustle of angels' wings.

Epilogue

CIUDAD DEL ESTE, PARAGUAY

So it hadn't worked.

In the end, Saleh's new war had come to nothing.

Sheik Mozer Jebai took the briefcase from his Paraguayan lawyer.

"You are free to go," the lawyer said. "The necessary paperwork has been purchased. But you cannot stay here. The Americans are pressing hard this time. By tomorrow another judge will issue the papers to have you picked up again."

The threads of the terrorist attacks on the United States had led too clearly back to Ciudad del Este for the Paraguayan authorities to brush them aside—no matter how big a bribe the mullah might offer. With the eyes of the world on them, the Paraguayans would have to cooperate with the Americans, at least for now.

So he would do as others had. Across the river, the Brazilians continued to stand firm against American pressure. More than one of the sheik's country-men on the Americans' wanted list had slipped across the Bridge of Friend-ship and taken up open residence in Foz de Iguazú. Mozer Jebai had offices there, as well.

A glance at the security cameras showed that the military police stationed outside his home had indeed vanished. He would bother with only a single small suitcase. His servants would pack up the rest of his possessions later.

Until his lawyer arrived, Mozer Jebai hadn't known the details of his son's final mission. The Paraguayan intelligence unit responsible for his three-week-long house arrest had kept him isolated from his associates. But he'd known something had gone wrong. Even in Ciudad del Este, the cable news covered the dam collapse and avalanche disasters. When no report came of a third disaster, he'd known his son had failed.

And knowing his son, he would not have allowed himself to survive that failure.

Now it was confirmed.

His only son was dead.

And for nothing.

That was the irony. Had Saleh kept to the old way of martyrdom by ramming the helicopter bomb into the ground, his mission would have succeeded, and his death would have at least held purpose. Following the infidels' style of warfare, which valued the lives of men above the success of the mission, had led only to destruction.

But there'd been successes, as well.

Perhaps it would be possible to take the old way and the new and create a third, more deadly than either. Khalil was already across the border in Foz de Iguazú, the movement's funds safe in numbered accounts the Americans did not have the power to seize. Though the old Jesuit mission was forever closed to them, Brazil had plenty of jungle. If it occupied every breath he had left in this life, the Americans would pay.

But it was not revenge or the future of the holy war that gripped the mullah's thoughts as the black Mercedes pulled out of the drive and headed toward the distant arch of the Bridge of Friendship. Behind the mask of impassivity, Sheik Mozer Jebai's mind was screaming out a cry of anguish as old as human history.

Oh, my son! Saleh, my son, my son! If only I had died instead of you!

* * *

Other books by Jeanette Windle

CrossFire
Where all Sarah's troubles began—

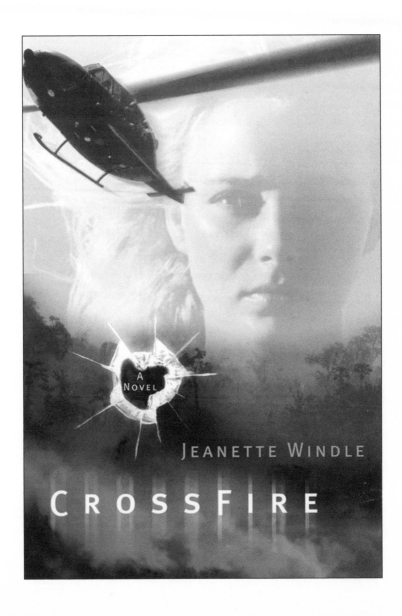

Other books by Jeanette Windle

The DMZ

*The ultimate weapon of revenge against
the U.S. lurks in the Colombian jungle.*

"Come on," she said impatiently, turning swiftly as Tim emerged to shove the doors shut behind them. "Let's get you back before someone squeals to the guerrillas that their corralled sheep are going astray."

Her answer came as the soft clop of a hoof on the cobblestones. Then—from a different angle—she heard the gentle whoosh of a horse's breath being released. Slowly, reluctantly, Julie turned around. The circle of riders, their faces hard, shadowed silhouettes under the moon, carried her horribly, terrifyingly back seven years.

"I think it's a little late for that," came Tim McAdam's American drawl from beside her, and for once there was no joviality in his tone.